STEPHE. ...

'This is the book Step. ... was born to write. It brings together a lifetime's love and appreciation of horror films in a novel which is sure to entertain and intrigue a generation of fans . . . Laws is a master craftsman and this novel takes him into new and uncharted territory . . . *Daemonic* is a hugely satisfying and entertaining read'

David Howe in *Shivers*

'Mainstream horror writing very well done. One of the most inventive young writers on the British horror scene'

The Times

'Riotous gory fun – should have British horror fans hooting with delight'

Chris Fowler in *Time Out*

'It's nice to find a fresh, chilling voice among the multitudes of authors feverishly clawing to be the best imitation of Stephen King or Peter Straub. Stephen Laws is no imitator'

Knoxville News Sentinel

'Laws' work typifies a new generation of horror writing: [it] inhabits the world as we know it, and is all the scarier for it . . . this acknowledges its debts to Roger Corman but moves triumphantly beyond them'

Maxim

'Great contemporary British horror writers are few and far between . . . Stephen Laws is in the first division of doom merchants'

Alex Gordon in the *Peterborough Evening Telegraph*

'Direct, punchy, action-packed horror . . . Fans of the genre will enjoy picking up the movie references, while anyone at all who enjoys a thumping good chase through a murky architectural nightmare with murderous security guards and/or pit-bull daemonic entities from the nether regions in hot pursuit, is guaranteed an enthralling read'

Samhain magazine

*Also by the same author
and available from New English Library:*

Ghost Train
Spectre
The Wyrm
The Frighteners
Darkfall
Gideon
Macabre

About the Author

Stephen Laws was born in Newcastle-Upon-Tyne, where he lives and works as a full-time writer.

Time Out's admonition, that 'Nobody sleeps while Stephen Laws writes,' has never been more true. With his eighth and most ambitious novel he is set to establish himself as the future of British horror.

Daemonic

Stephen Laws

NEW ENGLISH LIBRARY
Hodder and Stoughton

First published in Great Britain in 1995
by Hodder & Stoughton
A division of Hodder Headline PLC

A New English Library paperback edition 1996

10 9 8 7 6 5 4 3 2 1

British Library Cataloguing in Publication Data

Laws, Stephen
Daemonic
I. Title
823.914 [F]

ISBN 0 340 66673 0

Printed and bound in Great Britain by
Cox & Wyman Ltd, Reading, Berkshire

Hodder and Stoughton
A division of Hodder Headline PLC
338 Euston Road
London NW1 3BH

Dedicated to Ray, Alison and Andrea

Acknowledgments

I would like to thank the following for their very kind assistance during research for *Daemonic*:

Harry James of James Associates, Mike Hunter of Scotdem Ltd, Alison Steel of Bradley Hall Ltd, David Milne, Lecturer at the University of Northumbria, Julie Lamb, Harry Nadler, Gil Lane-Young, Keith Durham (for the usual), and Alan Crawford of Cussins Construction.

In a more general way, of course, it's unlikely that *Daemonic* would ever have come to be if not for the influence of the following, to whom I'm greatly indebted for a misspent youth: Leslie Stevens, Joseph Stefano, Richard Matheson, Jacques Tourneur, Jack Arnold, Henri Georges Clouzot, Robert Wise, William Castle, Val Lewton, Don Siegel, Larry Cohen, Don Sharp, Brian Clemens, Alfred Hitchcock, George Romero, Terence Fisher, Gordon Douglas, Ray Harryhausen, Howard Hawks, James Bernard, Bernard Herrman, Nigel Kneale, Edward L. Cahn, Richard Fleischer, Nathan Juran, Fred F. Sears, Mario Bava, Les Bowie, Daniel Haller, Don Banks . . .
And, of course, Roger Corman.

PART ONE

MR DRAEGERMAN REQUESTS

News Item from *The Independent Daily* February 23rd.

The controversy concerning the archaeological site at Tempra Abruzza was further complicated today when claims were made that Draegerman Enterprises had secured the destruction and removal of the recently discovered Sabbarite temple by outright bribery.

The claims have infuriated archaeologists and preservation societies worldwide since a major campaign was organised to prevent the authorities from complying with the Drageman request. Although the area is known to be potentially rich in natural oil resources, the site was regarded to be of international importance and previous geological surveys had suggested that the likely yield from the site would prove minimal.

A spokesman for Drageman Enterprises would only say today that: 'This is a business matter between Mr Draegerman and the civil authorities.' He would not confirm rumours, however, that in addition to the monies required to secure and demolish the site, an undisclosed cash donation had been made available for the country's 'social development reforms'.

In responding to Draegerman Enterprises' refusal to allow experts access to the ruins either before, during or after the demolition, Professor Robson Rothwell of the Primavera Institute stated that: 'This is an act of outright desecration. Just another example of business interests taking precedence over a country's rich national heritage.' The Sabbarite temple is thought to have been the site of a ritual massacre in 1264, in which an estimated three thousand were put to death. A Draegerman Enterprises' press statement responding to the initial complaints caused further furore when it questioned whether such mass murder could be equated with any aspect of a 'rich, national heritage'. Further approaches are to be made, but it is felt unlikely that the site can be saved ...

ONE

Just before everything turned really bad, Frank Wells said: 'Nice day . . .' and lifted a coffee cup to his lips.

'How the hell would you know?' Roy Jensen smiled wryly, cleaning a beer glass on the other side of the bar.

Frank looked over the top of his cup, raising his eyebrows in that familiar way; a gesture that could mean anything at all.

'Could be raining gallstones and scorpions out there,' continued Roy. 'And we would never know.'

The Wayside had been described variously over the years as a bar, a diner, a restaurant, a cafeteria, and a dump. With a long, low ceiling and its one window at the entrance providing the only light during the day, it was hardly possible when you were in the depths of the place, standing beside the bar, to tell what it was really like out there, or indeed what time of day it could be. The faint light from the window illuminated the tables beside the main door, but deep down here at the bar, situated at the furthermost end from the entrance, everything during the day seemed to be in perpetual gloom. The owners of the place had a rule about saving on electricity: no lights on during the day, the first light switch to be flicked at 5 p.m. prompt. There also seemed to be a mistaken belief that having the place in semi-darkness might convince people that it was cooler in here than outside. The air-conditioning had never functioned during the eighteen months that Roy had been working here.

'Might be a good idea to clean the window,' said Frank, sipping from his cup again.

'Not in my contract,' replied Roy. 'And they're getting more than their money's worth out of me as it is.'

'The service in here stinks,' said Frank, straight-faced.

'I like to be at one with the customers,' replied Roy. This time, Frank laughed; a wry cough that cleared his damaged lungs.

There were only four or five customers in the bar, which was usual for this time of day. Two or three locals, like Frank, might call in for a beer or a coffee. The main trade came in the evenings, but during the day the best that *The Wayside* could expect might be someone stopping for

3

coffee, or a family stopping for a bite to eat, as they passed through. For most people, it seemed, Pawlington was a place to pass through. Very few seemed inclined to stay, particularly since the steel mill had closed and the job prospects were virtually zero. Roy had 'won' his barman's job against stiff competition, and he gritted his teeth and put up with the owners' little peccadillos, since he had bills to pay like everyone else. There was a family here now. Surprise, surprise – they were just passing through. A mother, father and seven-year-old son; the latter sniffing suspiciously at the sandwiches that Roy had made to order.

'Not keen on the sandwich filling,' said Frank absently, observing the customers and then returning to his coffee.

'Don't know why,' said Roy quietly, replacing the glass behind the counter. 'Had a hell of a job taking it off the dog in the kitchen. He obviously liked it.'

Frank gave his cough-laugh again and held out his cup. 'Fill me up . . . nah, second thoughts I'll have a beer.'

'What kind?'

'Newcastle Brown Ale.'

Roy looked impressed. 'Exotic.'

'Drinking man's drink,' replied Frank, and watched Roy take a bottle from the cold cabinet.

From somewhere outside there came the sound of distant, growling engines.

Roy Jensen was twenty-five years old, slim and athletic, taller than average with brown shoulder-length hair. The latter feature provided a source of light-hearted banter when Frank became bored. Roy's faded blue jeans looked threadbare, and Frank often tipped him before leaving on condition that he save up the money to buy a new pair.

The sound of engines had grown louder. Motorcycles, perhaps. Not passing by, but revving up somewhere close. Frank turned to look out of the front window, waiting to see if anything would eventually pass. But nothing did, and when the sounds of revving ceased, he turned back to see Roy expertly flip the bottle top six feet down the bar and into the bin.

'Shot,' said Frank, taking the bottle. Roy never missed that bin.

And the clatter of the bottle top in the bin seemed somehow to match a clattering sound down at the front of the diner. The clatter was followed by an angry curse, as if someone had barked their shin, and in the next moment the main door burst open. The family sitting at the window table shrank back in alarm as three men blundered into the diner; one still cursing, the others laughing. The men were well-built and leather-clad. Matted hair hung down over the cursing man's shoulders and back, and he was wiping at something on the front of his leather jacket.

'Shit!'

The other two laughed, and walked on past him, heading towards the

4

bar but still looking back, as if they had pulled the greatest practical joke in the world. The cursing man looked at the family and then moved towards their table. Roy saw the mother clutch the kid tighter as the man seized a paper cloth from their table and began wiping at the black mess on his jacket.

'That's our . . .' began the father. The long-haired man just looked at him and kept wiping. Wisely, the father said nothing and returned to his coffee in misery. The man nodded and then slowly followed the others, just as another biker entered behind him. The newcomer flipped a finger at the cursing man, laughed and headed for the fruit machine.

'Beer,' said one of the laughing men, taking off a muddied sweatband and wiping his face. He swung on to a stool next to Frank and the other joined him. Frank slowly sipped at his Newcastle Brown but did not look at the newcomers. The sweatband man turned to look at him, as if expecting some kind of comment.

'What kind?' asked Roy.

'Any fucking kind. Just so long as it's cold.'

Roy nodded and looked at the other man. Could a pig squeeze into biker's leathers and stand upright? If it could, then this was it. The man's nose seemed positively porcine, not so much turned up as turned into a snout. Suddenly, there was a strong smell of sweat.

'What about us, Harwood?' asked the pig-man.

'You already owe me three beers,' said the man with the sweatband. 'Get your own.'

'Tight bastard,' said the pig-man, turning to Roy. 'Give me the same. And the same for my friend with the split tank.' The man with the messed-up jacket joined them at the bar. Up close, Roy could see that he was a lot older than the other two, perhaps in his fifties. His face was weatherbeaten, heavily lined and creased. Clearly, he was not a happy man.

'Big joke,' he said. 'That job needs tools, and I haven't got any. Hey, you . . .'

Roy looked back as he pulled three bottles of beer out of the cold cabinet.

'You got a garage near here? Somewhere I can fix a Harley?'

'Henderson's place,' replied Roy, flipping off the tops and planting the beer on the bar. 'About a mile and half south on the main road.'

'Fucking oil,' said the older man, screwing up the paper cloth and discarding it on the floor. The other biker at the fruit machine had begun feeding it with coins and jabbing at the selector buttons.

'Another beer?' asked Roy, nodding to the man at the fruit machine.

'What am I?' said the older man. 'A mind-reader? Let him get his own.'

Fishing loose change out of his pocket, the sweatband man called Harwood slammed the coins down on the bar and took his bottle.

'That pays for them all. See? I'm not so tight.'

Roy swiped the coins off the inner edge into his palm, exchanging a non-committal look with Frank. Both of them knew there wasn't enough money for the beers. Roy rang up the cash in the register, noticing from the corner of his eye that the family near the murky front window were hastily packing up and heading for the front door. The long-haired biker turned to look, swallowing half his beer in one enormous mouthful.

'Hey!' he called.

The family did not look back as they exited.

'Don't forget to leave a tip.'

The others laughed. At the fruit machine, the biker was losing his temper at the lack of winnings. He kicked the machine, force-feeding more coins into the slot.

'What?' asked the pig-man, very quietly.

Roy looked over at him, expecting another beer order, but the pig-man was rising from his seat; even now was walking around behind Frank. The other two bikers at the bar laughed softly and sipped at their beers, shaking their heads. Slowly and deliberately, the pig-man sat on Frank's right, keeping one bar stool between them. His face was set on Frank.

'What was that you said, old man?'

Frank continued to look ahead, sipping at his beer and with a deliberately blank expression on his face.

'Look,' said Roy. 'No trouble . . .'

'If I want a beer, then I'll talk to you,' said the pig-man. 'In the meantime, shut it. I'm talking to this prick here.'

Frank did not reply. From somewhere outside came the sound of the family's car revving up and taking off fast down the main road.

'What did you say to me just now?' asked the pig-man, eyes like slits, face pushed forward towards Frank.

Frank still did not reply.

'He didn't say anything . . .' said Roy. 'Now, come on. He's just sitting there enjoying his drink. Why don't you have a drink on the house and just take it easy.'

'Keep *out* of it,' said the older biker, now taking a delighted interest in the proceedings.

'What did you call me?' asked the pig-man. 'What did you *call* me, old man?'

Frank lowered the bottle, turned slowly and looked him full in the face. He seemed about to speak.

'He didn't call you anything,' interrupted Roy. 'It was me.'

The pig-man continued to hold Frank's blank stare, then turned slowly to look at Roy behind the bar.

'Yeah?' The look of malice was now firmly fixed on Roy.

'Yeah,' replied Roy, still cleaning a glass with the cloth.

'Roy,' began Frank. 'This is my . . .'

'It's all right, Frank,' continued Roy. 'Our friend here is just a little hard of hearing.'

'So?' continued the pig-man. 'What did you call me?'

Roy continued cleaning the glass.

'I said you've got a face like a pig, you smell like a pig, and it's the first time I've ever seen a pig put biker's gear on and walk around on two legs.'

The pig-man looked – and goggled. This was not what he had learned to expect.

Then the older biker with the long hair began to laugh.

'Only two ways to go,' said Frank quietly.

And then with one swift sideways motion, he swung the Brown Ale bottle away from his lips, smashing it directly across the bridge of the pig-man's nose. At the same moment, Roy swung a left hook over Frank's shoulder and the long-haired biker fell backwards from his stool. Frank followed his bottle with a bony elbow in the pig-man's solar plexus. Still clutching his face, the pig-man *whumped* and followed his friend backwards off the bar stool.

Only two ways to go. Be intimidated and beaten to a pulp. Or step in fast before it got to that stage. Something Frank had told Roy many times over the bar, neither one believing that they would ever have to resort to such red-neck methods.

And then their upper hand was lost.

The pig-man lashed out at Frank's bar stool as he fell, using both feet to tip it over. Frank was not fast enough to come around, and fell heavily to the floor. The pig-man groped for him, out of Roy's sight – and then Harwood lunged across the bar, grabbing Roy by the collar and delivering a jab-punch to the side of his head. Bright white light exploded behind his eyes, and the next thing he knew, Roy was on the floor behind the bar looking up, just as the biker from the fruit machine came hurtling over the bar, landing beside him. Roy struggled to rise, hearing Frank grappling on the other side. Then the biker was kicking at Roy as he struggled, trying to stamp on his head. He lashed out defensively, trying to tangle the biker's own legs. But he could not get sufficient leverage, and when the biker kicked him hard in the ribs, it knocked the breath from his body. He fell again, sobbing for air. The biker was standing astride him now, and from somewhere above, Roy heard a voice say:

'Cut him, Frosty. Go on, cut the bastard . . .'

Roy struggled around again, to see the biker standing above him pull out something from the waistband at the small of his back. He brought it around, slowly and deliberately. Something *clicked* and light glinted on the blade. Roy saw that same glint of light reflected in the man's face. He was smiling; a broad smile, with lots of pearly white, shining teeth. One of those teeth was gold.

Then someone else, from the other side of the bar, began to scream in a high falsetto.

The man looked back over the bar in alarm – and Roy pulled both feet up to his chest, in a foetal position. Uncoiling, he kicked a leg up hard and straight. His heel hit the man in the crotch. The man made no sound, did not scream. One moment he was looking over the bar, the next he was bent double, holding his crotch and with his contorted, silently screaming face only inches from Roy's own. Roy seized his ears, and head-butted him on the bridge of the nose. This time the man collapsed backwards like a dishevelled scarecrow across Roy's legs. And from behind the bar, the falsetto screaming was continuing.

'Oh God, *Frank* . . .' Roy scrabbled to his feet, wincing at the pain in his ribs, using the edge of the bar to pull himself erect. What in God's name where they doing to make him sound like that?

The two other bikers were standing close together, with their backs to Roy, looking down. But Roy could not see Frank or the pig-man. Both men were struggling on the floor beyond and the bikers' attention was focused there. Harwood noticed Roy and moved around to keep him in sight, unsure now whether to launch at him or keep his attention directed at what was happening on the floor. Roy seized a bottle, smashing it on the bar with as much savage emphasis as he could, leaving a jagged dagger of glass in his hand. The other bikers heard the crash and began to weave from side to side, looking back at Roy and now unsure of what the hell to do.

'Leave him!' snapped Roy – and then saw at last what was happening on the floor.

Frank was not in trouble, was not the one who had been making the screaming sounds. Those sounds had been coming from the pig-man, who seemed to be in very big trouble indeed.

Frank and the biker were lying together on the floor, in the ruins of an overturned table. Frank's wiry arm was locked around the pig-man's throat from behind, so that he was clutching his head to his chest. With his other hand, he had managed to get out his penknife. Roy recognised the stubby old blade that he used to clean his pipe; the worn-out old thing that had been in his jeans pocket for God knew how many years, and which he had complained about so often of being worse than bloody useless. It seemed that he had found another use for it today. Because the point of the penknife was being held against the pig-man's throat as they lay there. A bead of blood quivered around the tip, where it had just pierced the flesh. Incredibly, Frank's expression was just as blank as usual; there were no signs of exertion or anxiety or terror. Just the same kind of resolve that Roy had observed when he cleaned his pipe with it. Each time a biker jerked or shuffled or tried to get a better position, Frank twisted and countered, keeping them in view and eliciting another shrill cry from the man he was holding.

8

'Are you okay, Roy?' he asked calmly from the floor.

'I suppose so,' said Roy, trying to keep his voice even. 'One behind the bar here needs a balls transplant, though.'

'And this one here's going to need a head transplant in a minute. Because if anyone tries anything else, I'm going to cut his ugly head right off.'

'Okay,' said the older biker. 'So what happens now?'

'What happens,' said Harwood, 'is this.' Standing to one side, he moved to show Roy what he had taken out of his jacket.

It was a gun. Grinning, Harwood wagged the barrel at him.

Roy felt cold fear in his stomach and throat. 'There's a hundred, maybe a hundred and twenty in the register. Just take it and get out of here.'

'We were going to take it anyway,' said Harwood. 'But it seems to me that Frosty and Joe might want to give you something to remember us by when we've gone. Drop the glass.'

Dust began to swirl at the front window, great billowing clouds of it whipping against the glass.

'I'll cut his throat,' said Frank from the floor. 'I mean it.'

In response, Harwood swung the gun up towards Roy – and fired. Roy flinched, and the shelves behind him exploded, showering him with glass. Instantly, Roy dropped his improvised weapon to join the spray of glass on the floor behind the bar. The biker lying down there was covered in it, still motionless.

As the echoes of the shattering glass tinkled into silence, another sound seemed to fill the bar. It was coming from outside, beyond the glass – and it had clearly begun to unsettle the bikers. Roy was barely aware of it, still in shock from the shot, expecting the bullet to have blown a gaping hole in his chest and not understanding why he had not been slammed back against the shelves. Harwood was hopping nervously from foot to foot now, casting anxious glances back at the window, and trying to see the source of the noise beyond. It was impossible to tell what was out there. The window-glass was completely obscured by dust and the sound was growing louder.

At last, it began to register with Roy. It was the sound of some kind of motor; a chopping, engine sound.

'Harwood,' said the older biker. 'What the hell *is* it?'

'The money,' demanded Harwood. 'Give me the money.'

Roy moved to the register, feet crunching on broken glass. From the floor beyond, the pig-man squawled: 'Get this old bastard *off* me . . .'

Frank twisted his arm tighter, and the pig-man's voice squawked into silence.

Beyond the window, the sounds of the clattering engine seemed to fill *The Wayside*.

'Come on,' said the older biker. 'Leave it and let's split!'

'The *money!*' shouted Harwood, waving the gun at Roy again but still keeping his eyes on the cloud of dust beyond the glass.

Roy grabbed a handful of notes out of the register and slammed them down on the bar. Harwood moved towards them . . . and then the engine noise changed. It was slowing down; slowly but gradually losing its impetus. And the dust beyond the window was beginning to gust and drift away from the glass. Harwood edged uneasily towards the bar, still watching.

The dust swirled and parted. Faint light seeped into the bar.

The older biker began to edge in the direction of the window.

Harwood closed on the money.

'Christ!' exclaimed the older biker. 'It's a damned *helicopter*.'

'What?'

'It's landed out there, on the other side of the road.'

That engine noise had resolved itself into a lazy *chop-chop-chop*.

Harwood screwed up the bunch of notes in his hand.

And Roy seized the hand, dragging the man hard against the bar edge, simultaneously grabbing the gun in his other hand. Something cracked in Harwood's side and he shrieked, but would not let go of the gun. Roy pulled back hard, now clutching both of the biker's hands in his own. On the floor, the pig-man squawked and thrashed again as Frank held tight.

'You're fucking *dead!*' snapped Harwood, his face twisted in a paroxysm of fury. Roy let go of Harwood's free hand then grabbed at the gun-hand with both of his own, trying to tear the weapon free. If only he could get hold of it . . .

But the older biker had lunged back to the bar as Harwood lashed out at Roy's head with the fisted hand that had been released. In an amazing display of vitality for his size, weight and age, he vaulted on to the bar and pulled back a leg to kick Roy in the face.

And then there was another gunshot, but this time from the main entrance to the bar.

The biker on the bar stumbled and fell to one knee as Roy recoiled, still clinging to Harwood's gun-hand. For a gut-wrenching moment, Roy thought that someone else had shot him. Harwood still struggled viciously to be free, still tried to wrest the gun back, even though everyone else had frozen and turned their attention to something that was happening at the entrance. Even the pig-man had ceased to thrash in Frank's grip on the floor.

Three men had entered the bar, and were standing calmly watching them. All three were wearing black business suits and black ties; all seemed to have the same short black hairstyle and were wearing sunglasses. They looked like boxers at a funeral.

And one of them was calmly holding an automatic pistol, pointed at the ceiling. Flakes of plaster were floating in the air above the three men's heads, where the bullet from the automatic had punched through the roof.

'Let's be nice,' said the black-suited man with the gun. As he spoke, two others entered behind him, calmly and casually dusting themselves down. Five men, all in the same business suits, all with the same utterly impassive expressions on their faces. Beyond the main window that framed these new arrivals, a sixth man, also in black suit and shades, was sitting behind the controls of a helicopter on the roadway, its rotor blades still turning slowly and quietly.

'Down from the bar, please,' said the man with the gun. His voice was so casual that he almost seemed bored.

The older biker remained kneeling on the bar, unsure and astonished.

'*Please,*' said the black-suited man. Now the threat in his voice was unmistakable.

Slowly, the biker climbed down. Slowly, the men in the black suits began to walk towards them. The pig-man remained silent on the floor in Frank's grip. But Harwood was still thrashing with Roy at the bar, still trying to retrieve the gun. It seemed that the biker's rage had completely taken over, the threat of these sudden and strange visitors not serving to quiet him. The Black Suits seemed unperturbed that this single struggle should continue, and just ignored it, as the Black Suit leader with the gun spoke again.

'Jensen?'

At the bar, Harwood twisted around again and tried to land a blow on Roy's face with his free hand. Roy ducked, grabbed the free hand, and they were face to face over the bar again, hands locked.

'We're looking for someone called Jensen,' continued the Black Suit leader. 'Does he work here?'

'He's at the bar,' said Frank in his matter-of-fact manner. 'Having a small difference of opinion with a customer.'

The Black Suit turned his head slowly to watch the struggle, as if assessing it. Then he nodded his head. At the signal, two of his companions walked casually forward. The older biker backed off, out of the way. For a moment, they stood beside the two struggling figures, as if – like their leader – they needed to assess the situation. One of them stood to one side, still examining them. He scratched his nose, as if weighing up some difficult shot at the ninth hole. Then, face utterly impassive, he suddenly delivered a short, sharp jab under Harwood's ribs.

Harwood made a sound like he was swallowing his tongue.

One moment he was struggling with Roy at the bar. The next, he was lying on the floor. Unconscious.

Roy barely had time to register just what the hell had happened. The Black Suit stood back, gave a casual shrug to adjust his jacket collar and tie. Then he stood aside as his companion retrieved the gun from where it had fallen. They both stood back, hands clasped formally in

11

front of them as if expecting further instructions. Roy just looked in astonishment.

The Black Suit leader with the gun walked calmly forward.

'You're Mr Jensen?'

Flushed, pulling at his collar, Roy said: 'That's right.'

'Good. Then you other gentlemen can leave.' The Black Suit waved the gun at the bikers in a casual, dismissive manner.

The older biker shuffled uneasily. 'What about ...?' He pointed to Harwood on the floor. The Black Suit nodded, and the biker moved forward, hauling Harwood aloft and flinging one arm over his shoulder.

'There's one behind the bar,' said Roy. The Black Suit nodded again, and this time the two Black Suits who had dealt with Roy's difficult customer moved behind the bar and dragged the unconscious biker out.

'What about me?' squawled the pig-man from the floor.

'You too.'

Frank released his grip, pulled the penknife away, and kicked at the man with both feet. The bulky figure rolled away anxiously and gratefully, clutching his neck. He staggered to his feet as Frank nimbly jumped up and away. As the pig-man backed away to join his companions it looked as if he was about to say something.

'No empty threats, please,' said the Black Suit leader. 'Or you'll force me not to be nice any more.'

The pig-man hawked and spat on the floor. In the next moment, he clattered out through the main door after the others. Two Black Suits followed him, then stood outside the building with their backs to the window, watching as the sounds of motorcycle engines filled the air again.

The Black Suit leader put his gun away, shoving it into the holster under his armpit. Turning to Frank, he said: 'Our business is with Mr Jensen.'

Frank snapped his penknife shut and shoved it into his jeans. Calmly, he asked: 'That what you want, Roy?'

'Yeah ... yeah, everything's okay. I think.' Roy turned to the Black Suit. 'But listen, I don't want Frank going out there if those bastards are still around.'

'My associates are supervising their departure,' said the Black Suit. 'Believe me, they won't be back. And my colleague here ...' The Black Suit leader nodded at the one remaining Black Suit. '... can escort the gentleman home.'

'I'm not in the habit of having men walk me home,' said Frank. 'Thanks, but no thanks.' He took off his cap and ran a hand through his thinning hair. 'As long as everything's okay with you, Roy.'

'It'll be fine.'

12

'Thanks for an interesting afternoon.'

'Thanks, Frank. I won't forget what you did.'

'You remember that tomorrow afternoon, when I come in for my beer.'

'They're on the house.'

The older man grunted and pulled on his cap, casting an eye over both of the remaining Black Suits. These people had the unmistakable mark of government about them. He grunted again and moved off. With a last wave of the hand, he left the bar just as the two Black Suits who had disposed of Harwood returned.

When Frank had gone, Roy took a bottle from the cold shelf, flipped the top and drank deeply. He flushed a mouthful around his teeth and spat into the sink. There was blood mingled with the beer. He rubbed his jaw and grimaced sourly. The Black Suits waited for him to finish. Then the leader stepped forward and placed a small attaché case on the bar in front of him.

'Have you heard of Jack Draegerman?' asked the Black Suit.

At first, Roy was too puzzled to react.

'Draegerman,' repeated the Black Suit softly, as if he was talking to a child. 'Have you heard of him?'

'Of course I've heard of him. Who hasn't? Who the hell *are* you people . . . ?'

The Black Suit flicked open the attaché case, and swivelled it around on the bar so that Roy could see what was inside.

It was filled with cash. Crisp, brand-new notes, bundled together with elastic bands.

'There's fifty thousand in here,' continued the Black Suit. 'Cash. You get it if you come with us.'

Roy cleared his throat, unnerved at the sight of so much money. 'Where?'

'To see Mr Draegerman.'

'Why?'

'Mr Draegerman requests the pleasure of your company.'

Roy still did not reply.

'He wants to see you,' continued the Black Suit. 'That's all we're allowed to say. If you come with us, this fifty thousand is yours. You get another two hundred thousand when you get there.'

'Is this a put-on?'

The Black Suit produced an identification card and handed it to him. *Aiken, Todd: Chief Security Officer: Draegerman Enterprises.*

As Roy studied the ID, the Black Suit flicked the attaché case shut. 'You come, you get the money. You don't come . . . you don't get it. Simple as that.'

Roy took another deep draught of the ice-cold beer. Then he wiped his face and cleared his throat.

'You sure you've got the right Jensen?' he asked, handing the ID back.

'What's your answer?'

Roy took another swig at the beer, looked again at the attaché case, and wiped his hands on the cloth behind the counter. He thought about the back money owed on the rent on the crappy little place on the other side of this 'just passing through' town. He thought about the nights spent lying on his bed, looking at the ceiling, and praying that something might come along to get him out of this hell-hole. He thought about all the wasted opportunities, all the blasted hopes and the hopeless optimisms. Now, in the space of ten brief minutes, in a sudden outburst of horrifying violence and sudden, mysterious appearances by faceless men in black suits making incredibly unreal offers, it looked as if everything might change. Part of him, even now, was telling him that people did not just arrive out of the blue like this and make such offers. What the hell did he know of Draegerman other than what he'd read in the papers and seen on the television? What possible reason could this incredibly rich, world-famous figure have to want to see him? Wasn't there something wrong with this offer? What were the snags? Maybe he should ask more questions. But . . . the man had said he wasn't allowed to say more.

So, in that one moment, even as the alarm bells were ringing in his head, Roy thought of another thousand nights lying on that same mattress, looking up at that same ceiling and watching his ambitions drifting and dispersing like the cigarette smoke he blew up there.

'So what the hell have I got to lose?' he said. 'Let's go.'

The Black Suit nodded, lifting the attaché case from the bar.

'I'll need to lock up and . . .'

'No you don't,' said the Black Suit, without turning to look at him. 'We'll take care of everything. The important thing is that you come with us now.'

Roy shrugged and followed the Black Suits out of *The Wayside*, into the hot afternoon sun.

Frank had been right.

It *was* a nice day.

They began to walk towards the helicopter.

TWO

The office was a mess.

Although it was mid-afternoon outside, the blinds were drawn against the day and the outside world. The silent, dark figure of a man sat behind the desk with his head in his hands, staring at the empty vodka bottle on the desk blotter in front of him. He had been sitting that way for a long time.

There was an air of desperation here. Too much paperwork waiting to be filed, a general air of tattiness about the office, about the business. Most desperate of all was the demeanour of the man who sat in darkness with his head in his hands.

When there was a knock on the door, the man didn't look up or respond. The empty vodka bottle seemed to be the only thing in the world to him at the moment. Somewhere beyond the drawn window blinds, a taxi horn blared – as if trying to tell him that someone had just knocked on the door.

Another knock, but still no response.

When the door handle began to turn, the unoiled spindle screeching, the man looked up from the bottle. But his face remained as blank as before. The door was locked. This time, the handle rattled and from somewhere beyond a man's voice said:

'Mr Boone? Are you in there?'

The man reached for the bottle, perhaps forgetting momentarily that it was empty. It rolled from his grasp, off the table, and clattered on the floor. The person beyond the door heard the noise.

'Mr Boone?'

The man watched the vodka bottle roll lazily across the darkened floor, but still did not respond.

Now someone was putting pressure against the door. It was light-weight, would not take a great deal of effort to break down. Something cracked in the frame, and now it began to shudder open, casting shafts of light into the darkness and spilling over the desk.

Three figures stood silhouetted in the doorway, looking directly at him. The man called Boone seemed uninterested in them; more interested in the progress of the empty bottle as the edge of the door span it back into the centre of the room. Only when the bottle stopped spinning, the neck pointing back at the intruders, did the man look up at them.

The three men were wearing dark suits, and designer sunglasses. The black lenses glinted, like insects' eyes. For a while, they stood silently evaluating him. Then, on what seemed an invisible signal, they stood to one side, and a fourth Black Suit walked into the office from behind. A long dark overcoat was draped around his shoulders, the arms hanging empty – what was once fashionable in the Seventies, now decidedly old-fashioned. But there seemed nothing self-conscious about this man as he moved past the others into the darkened office. He was carrying an attaché case. Without speaking and without any change on his expressionless face, the man walked straight up to the desk and placed the attaché case in front of him.

'Mr Boone, I presume?'

The man looked up.

This time, light spilled directly from the landing outside across his face. There was a burn scar on his left cheek stretching from eyebrow to neck, and the burn had pulled the corner of his eye down slightly, adding to what was already a melancholy expression. Clearly, there had been attempts at plastic surgery here, but the skin remained shining, almost plastic. The sight of that burn was no surprise to the Black Suit.

'Yes ...' When the man with the scar spoke, the word was harsh and guttural, as if speaking was a great effort.

The Black Suit looked momentarily at the empty vodka bottle on the floor. Turning back to the man, he flipped the clasps on the attaché case, but did not open it.

'Edward Boone. Twenty-four years old. Import and export. Always on the eye for a quick killing. Until you underwrote an import of stolen computer equipment, and it was seized by the Customs people. Busted, at one stroke.'

The man called Boone made a grunting sound that could have been a laugh.

'So, you torched your office. Tampered with the electricals to make it look like a short in the main fuse box. Used petrol to keep the fire going. But some of it splashed back in your face. Result? Third-degree burns to the face, business burned to the ground – and an insurance company that won't cough up the money, because their investigation found an attempt at deliberate fraud. Not only that, but they're going to prosecute you for it. Pretty messy, Mr Boone.'

'Messy,' laughed the man, fingering the burn scar on his cheek.

'Have you heard of Jack Draegerman?'

'Messy,' laughed the man again.

16

'Mr Draegerman?'

The man looked up at the Black Suit as if really seeing him for the first time, and attempting to sober up. 'Millionaire – engineering, aviation, oil, stock markets . . . used to make movies.'

'Good,' said the Black Suit indulgently, as if responding to a child who had just answered a question correctly. He spun the attaché case around to face Boone, and opened it. Boone's eyes were instantly drawn to the bundles of cash inside.

'There's fifty thousand in here. And it's all yours if you agree to meet with him.'

When Boone looked up again, his mouth was open, his eyes even more glazed than before.

'All you have to do is come with us now. To see Mr Draegerman.'

'Why . . . ?'

'And when you arrive, there'll be a further two hundred thousand. Guaranteed.'

'But I don't understand . . . why does he want to see me?'

'That's Mr Draegerman's business, Mr Boone. All we're instructed to say is that Mr Draegerman requests the pleasure of your company. When you arrive, all will be made clear.'

'But I . . .'

'Yes or no, Mr Boone. It's as simple as that.'

'But there must be something . . .'

The Black Suit spun the attaché case away from him again, slamming it shut and lifting it from the table.

'No, no!' exclaimed Boone, lurching up from his seat. It fell backwards to the floor, and he clutched at the desk for support. 'I mean . . . yes, of course I'll come.'

'Good,' said the Black Suit, smiling for the first time. His teeth were perfectly even and whiter than a toothpaste commercial. The faint light in here seemed to spark on them. He held out a hand to Boone as the man shambled around the desk, now looking around him as if he needed to pack.

'You won't need anything,' said the Black Suit. 'We have everything you need. And there's transport waiting for us downstairs.'

'Where are we going?'

'I told you, to see Mr Draegerman.'

'No, I mean, where is he?'

'Where he always is. At The Rock.'

'Oh.' Boone's expression was one of genuine awe. 'Oh. Right. Yes. Of course.'

'Shall we go?' asked the Black Suit, gesturing towards the open door.

The Black Suits standing in the doorway stood aside as their leader escorted Boone out of the darkness and into the light.

The last Black Suit looked back, smirking into the shambles of the office. He pulled the door shut, consigning it to darkness once more.

THREE

Only darkness.

And the sound of gently hissing steam. Beneath that hissing was a barely audible humming sound; like some kind of machinery far below ground.

A thin sliver of parallel light split the darkness in two. And gradually, slowly, the thin wedge of light widened in the centre of the darkness. Hinges creaked in protest – and suddenly there was a woman's silhouette standing in that door. The bright light and the silhouette were blurred by a gently wafting cloud of steam, and the silhouetted figure waved it away from her face as she continued to open the door and peer into the darkness.

Clearly, the woman was terrified.

Her hand moved to her throat. And now, she looked behind into the source of the light, as if afraid of being followed. Not only was she reluctant to step through into the strange room and its hissing steam, but the prospect of turning back seemed equally daunting. This time, when she turned back to the room, she pushed at the door. It swung open slowly to bang against the far wall, and the light from outside spilled jaggedly across the floor and the strange, chaotic jumble of glass and machinery inside. Still standing in the doorway, still reluctant to step across the threshold, she fumbled at the wall for a light switch.

With a buzzing stutter of noise, the faded overhead strip-light reluctantly fizzed into life. But the light was still dim in here. The woman was in her late forties, but seemed to be dressed not only to look too young for her age, but also in a manner more reminiscent of the 1950s. Her hair was blonde and tightly curled. She was wearing a pastel-pink sweater à la Marilyn Monroe and her heavily made-up lips were the colour of blood against her pale, classical face. The skirt hugged her hips and thighs right down to her knees without a split. The woman could see that she was standing on the threshold of what seemed to be a greenhouse laboratory. The hissing sound came from heated pipes that ran across the floor and along the walls, apparently providing heat and nutrients for the bizarre and exotic flora on display in glass cabinets standing against the walls. Some of those cases were filled with clouds of gushing steam, making the tendrils and leaves of the verdant South American plants writhe and twist as if they were alive.

'Dr Chaney . . . ?'

The woman's hand went to her throat again as she searched for any sign of the man she was looking for. When there was no response, she walked slowly and nervously into the centre of the greenhouse, casting anxious glances back at the door as if afraid that it would suddenly slam shut behind her. As she walked, she passed close to one of the glass cabinets against the wall, perhaps the tallest of them all. Within, the clouds of steam wreathed and curled – and could it be that the tangle of vines, shrubbery and gnarled foliage inside the case seemed to unfurl even more hungrily than before?

'Dr Chaney . . . ?'

The woman paused, turning her back to the glass case. Had she heard a noise?

'Please, Dr Chaney. I have to speak to you.'

The foliage in the cabinet seemed to press up against the glass, as if straining to reach her. The woman began to turn.

And suddenly the case exploded in glittering shards. With a fierce and sibilant rattling, the tangled mass of foliage lunged out of the exploding cabinet towards the woman. Her hands flew to her face as she whirled, screaming – and two wizened roots emerged from the hideous mass like a parody of arms, ready to seize her in an embrace as she stood there, frozen in terror . . .

And then the mass of foliage tripped up and fell clumsily to the floor.

From within the seething mass, something yelled: '*Shit!*'

No longer terrified, the woman turned from the thrashing figure with a look of quiet and resigned contempt on her face.

'Amateurs!' she said through gritted teeth. 'For God's sake, someone give me a cigarette.'

'Cut! For Christ's sake, Jerry!' snapped another voice from somewhere else 'What's the matter with you?'

'I can't see where the hell I'm *going!*' yelled a muffled voice from inside the wriggling mass.

Instantly, the laboratory was brightly lit. The clouds of steam from the pipes in the floor were snuffed out. Two men in overalls rushed past the woman, grabbing the struggling mass of foliage and trying to haul it upright. From above, a camera boom swung low. Cursing again, casting a venomous look at the boom operator, the woman ducked below it, swatting upwards with one hand before striding away from the set. As she passed, a young woman with a clipboard proffered a cigarette. The woman took it without acknowledging the girl's presence and waited while she struggled to produce a cigarette lighter from her coat pocket.

Impatiently again, the woman snatched it from her, lit up, and stalked away across the studio floor.

'Ten minutes,' said the same, amplified young man's voice. 'Then we'll go again. Gloria, love . . .'

'Go to hell!' snapped the woman without turning back.

'Gloria, look . . .' And then: 'Will you get him off the bloody *floor*, Jerry!'

'I told you to cut some eyeholes in there, Dave!' snapped another disembodied voice.

The woman reached what her employers called her dressing-room, but which she called with derision a wendy house. She slapped open the door, stalked inside, and slammed it shut again with the heel of her foot without turning around. Moving quickly to what was supposed to pass as a make-up mirror, she furiously ground out the cigarette for no other purpose than to focus her anger, and then reached for the Pernod bottle.

'Not even any *ice*, for Christ's sake!' she snapped. Sitting, she poured out a half-glass, slumped back in her seat and drank deeply. She sat back, looking up. The so-called dressing-room had no roof, giving her a clear view of the studio ceiling overhead, with its catwalks and power cables. Drinking again, trying to shut out the nerve-jarring and echoing clashes of equipment being moved and gantries shunting across the studio, she examined her surroundings. Four hastily constructed chipboard walls. Maybe as a bad joke to remind her of better-furnished days, someone had put wallpaper on the walls, for crying out loud. All of which only seemed to make things worse, highlighting everything that depressed her so much. There was a sofa in the corner; probably a discarded prop from one of the soap operas that were filming in the aircraft-hangar-that-was-supposed-to-be-a-studio next door. Her bureau, her dressing-table and mirror, and her chair.

And the dozen or so black-and-white photographs that had been stuck up on the cardboard walls to remind her of previous days. She gained no solace from looking at the studio portraits and stills from the 1970s. Sometimes, when there was enough Pernod inside her, and the right kind of people were around, she could even convince herself that she was still who she was twenty-five years ago. Gloria Pernell, sex goddess, hanging on the arms of men from the dream factory. Envied and loved by her public. And not Gloria Pernell who had emerged from self-imposed retirement to find that, despite her hard work, the parts were smaller and fewer as the years progressed; now working on a low-budget horror movie for a crew that couldn't shovel shit, and with a second-time director who was supposed to be the new 'cult *auteur*'.

Gloria scanned the images on the walls, catching sight of the one particular photograph that caused her so much pain, but which she was unable to take down and put in the bureau drawer. It was a picture of

21

her son, Bobby. In the photograph, he looked bright-eyed and cheerful, leaning casually forward in a studio portrait from the third movie he'd made as a teenager: *Hot Rod Hell*, another deliberate 1950s spoof. Now Bobby was a semi-derelict drug addict. His life had crashed, and he had simply walked away from his career and from Gloria. Despite hiring professionals to trace him, she had never seen him since. He could be dead, and she would never know. The sight of that photograph brought a familiar crashing wave of pain. Instinctively, she drained the glass and reached for the Pernod bottle again. The alcohol was an anaesthetic. Two more glasses, and she would not be working any more today. She looked back at the chipboard door. Any second now, there would be a knock – and the director would be there, apologising profusely and trying to coax her back on to the set.

How much more of this could she take?

'You'll take it,' Gloria told herself. 'You need the money, you silly cow.' She drank again. 'Just finish this piece of crap and take your cheque.'

Sure enough, there was a tap on the door.

Gloria angrily finished her drink against her better judgment – then poured another. 'You said ten minutes!' she snapped, without turning around. When the door opened, she banged the glass down hard on the dressing-table shelf and turned in her seat, ready to deliver her objections when the director stepped inside.

But it was not the director.

'Who the hell . . . ?'

A man in a black suit, wearing jet-black sunglasses, was stepping into her dressing-room. He had short-cropped, blond hair – and his expression was just as impassive as that of the two similarly dressed men who were entering behind him. Panic suddenly overcame Gloria. Something about the demeanour of these men reminded her of times long gone and 'business associates' in the seventies' film world whom it would have been better never to have met. The alarm must have registered on her face, because now the first Black Suit was holding up a friendly hand towards her, and was smiling. But there was something about the smile that precluded the sense of ease that it was trying to convey; something too glacial to register any real emotion.

'Miss Pernell? Please excuse us.'

'Like I said . . .' continued Gloria, but this time her voice did not sound as confident as she would have liked. '. . . who the hell are you?'

'We've been sent to see you. By a friend.'

One of the last men to enter closed the door behind him.

Gloria's hand moved involuntarily to her throat, just as that of her character had done when she had first been forced to step into the fake, hissing laboratory set.

'A friend?'

22

'Mr Draegerman.'

Gloria cleared her throat, involuntarily reaching for the Pernod bottle. For a while, she was unable to speak as she poured herself another drink. All the time, the leader of the Black Suits was smiling his glacial smile; the men behind him displaying no emotion whatsoever. The alcohol lubricated a throat that had become instantly dry.

'Jack Draegerman?'

'One and the same.'

Gloria laughed as she drank again. 'Do you mind if I ask you gentlemen for . . . ?'

'Identity cards? Certainly, Miss Pernell.'

The Black Suit stepped smartly forward, taking a black leather wallet out of his inside jacket pocket. Gloria took it from him and examined the photograph. His eyes seemed somehow too small without his sunglasses. But this was unmistakably the same man who stood before her, and he was listed as *Travis, James: Assistant Chief Security Officer: Draegerman Enterprises*. Gloria nodded and handed it back.

'So what brings Jack Draegerman back into my life after twenty-five years?'

'Can't say, Miss Pernell. We've just been given instructions to come and see you – and to give you this.' Travis nodded over his shoulder at one of the others, who stepped forward with an attaché case. He took it from him and flicked open the catches, nodding towards the dressing-table shelf. 'May I?'

Gloria waved her hand, and Travis put the attaché case on the table, flipping open the lid.

'What the hell is this?' asked Gloria, looking at the contents.

'It's fifty thousand,' said Travis. 'Mr Draegerman requests the pleasure of your company. He told us to say that it's yours if you'll agree to come and see him. There's another two hundred thousand waiting for you when you arrive at The Rock.'

'*The* Rock?' said Gloria incredulously. 'The place where nobody goes?'

'One and the same.'

'He wants me to make another movie for him? After twenty-five years?'

'Perhaps. But I really couldn't say, Miss Pernell. Our instructions are just as I've described.'

'Not another *Swamp Water Woman* or *Spider Venom*— I hope?'

'Like I say, we've no idea.'

'So I don't hear from him in all this time, and now he wants to make movies again. I thought he'd given all of that stuff up. Made his millions and done his Howard Hughes bit.'

'Really, Miss Pernell. We've no idea.'

'He should go through my agent.'

'Miss Pernell. The offer only stands if you come with us . . . now.'

Gloria drank again, casting an anxious glance at the photograph of Bobby on the chipboard wall.

Maybe the bastard wants something else.

She finished her drink. 'Do I get time to change?'

'Not really. He wants you to come as you are.'

'What? In *this*?'

'As you are.'

'That's Jack. Always impulsive.'

Gloria paused then, as if weighing up some inner argument. Finally, she swivelled in her seat and slapped the case shut. Standing again and smoothing down her skirt, she said: 'Okay, let's go Rock.'

Travis flicked the locks shut and slid the case from the table. The two others opened the door and stood aside as Gloria passed them.

'Thank you, gentlemen.'

Back in the studio, the man-eating plant had been raised to its "legs" again and a new fake-glass sheet had been fitted into the case. Two labourers were sweeping up the shards while a further two assistants attempted to push the plant back into the case. As Gloria and her escort moved towards them, the director turned and saw them all for the first time. He was perhaps the same age as Gloria's son, with dyed-blond hair and wearing the same style of black polo-neck sweatshirt that had so impressed him when he had seen Martin Scorsese wearing one on a television interview.

'Who are these people?' he demanded, running his hands through his hair in irritation. The knees of his Levi jeans were torn for purposes of fashion, and he had not liked Gloria's earlier suggestion that they had got that way by constant grovelling in front of the studio chief for his second directorial assignment. He turned away from the 'clearing and resetting' activity and moved towards them, head down. 'This is supposed to be a closed set, Gloria. You know that.'

'I've finished for the day, Drew. If you're lucky, you might see me tomorrow.'

'If you're lucky you might be asked back, darling.'

'Be polite,' said Travis, grinning his glacial grin as they finally drew level.

'I'm telling you, Gloria. You'd better be ready for filming in five minutes. I want this sequence wrapped.'

'Wrap your head, Drew.'

'You're fired, Gloria. Who the hell needs . . . ?'

'*Not* polite!' said Travis, and the director's face registered very real fear as the big man leaned forward and seized his face in one huge hand. He shoved hard. Somewhere on set, the script girl screamed – and Drew The Cult Figure pinwheeled backwards on to the set. The two labourers sweeping up dived aside, and Drew's body crashed into

24

the ambulant plant and its minders. The replacement fake-glass sheet in the cage disintegrated, and everyone went down in a thrashing tangle of limbs.

'You don't hire and fire, Drew,' said Gloria quietly, enjoying the moment. 'The producer does that.'

'Get the hell *off* me!' yelled the plant, thrashing at Drew.

'And, in any event,' continued Gloria. 'You can tell him from me that I've just quit.'

'You'll never, *ever* . . .' came the muffled cries of the director.

'Never work for you again?' asked Gloria. 'Sorry, Drew. That's just as corny as all the other lines you've written and asked me to say. Get a life rewrite, you worm.'

Smiling, Gloria allowed herself to be escorted from the studio and to the black sedan waiting outside.

FOUR

Farrow was a very angry man.

Hands thrust into the side pockets of his dirty leather jacket, he kept on walking. He had already been down this same dirty street three times today and it looked as if his luck was never going to change. Four weeks back rent to pay, and no prospect of getting the money. The landlord had told him not to bother coming back unless he had the cash. No cash, and the locks were going to be changed – but not before that same landlord had arranged with his friends to have Farrow's legs broken. He had not eaten since yesterday afternoon, and his stomach had begun to growl.

Farrow's hair was thick, curled and jet black. It hid from sight the fact that his left lobe had been bitten off by someone in a street fight three years ago. He had one jacket, one shirt, one pair of jeans and a pair of shoes – and he was wearing them.

His options were worse than they had ever been. Today, he was only walking up and down this bloody street because sitting still somewhere, without the price of a cup of coffee to buy him ten minutes in a café or bar, would freeze the balls off him.

If nothing presented itself shortly, he was going to have to go back to the 'old reliable' again. Find someone alone, ask for a light or street directions – and then take the fucking money off them. He looked at himself in a store window as he walked. Hell, with a nose like his, curved like a beak, someone was bound to be able to give a good description. It had happened before. He passed a side alley, and kept walking.

Then he stopped.

There had been a pair of crooked legs sticking out from behind a refuse skip back there. In the split second as he passed he had seen those legs almost subliminally, lying amidst the garbage and the stained cardboard boxes. It was 9.30 in the evening, just about the time the first of the street people would be bedding down for the night. There were lots of them around, no reason why he should pay particular attention to this person. Farrow walked on. But a dozen or

26

so steps further on past that back alley, he stopped again, head bowed and thinking.

His 'street sense' was tingling.

He had tried to explain what that feeling was like to a probation officer once. But the more he tried to explain, the more elusive it became. It was like ... instinct, he supposed. But much, much more than that. It was what had kept him alive on these dirty damned streets for the past ten years, ever since he had run away from that bitch who called herself mother and he had been forced to live rough. From every early mistake he had made on these streets, he had learned a valuable lesson. It had all been registered, catalogued and indexed – and he never made the same mistake twice. That 'instinct' had begun tingling the moment he had seen and walked past those legs. Trusting it, he turned back and looked around the corner of the alley.

The legs were still there, still lying awkwardly in the same position.

But there was something wrong.

The owner of those legs had made no attempt to cover him or herself over with the cardboard – and it was freezing tonight, with a frost expected in the early hours. Maybe the owner was smashed out on crack, or pissed out of his or her head. Or maybe ... ?

Farrow moved cautiously down the alley, picking his way through the litter and looking back at the main street. There was no one around, no one to pass and notice him, and no one else down here lying in the garbage.

When Farrow rounded the skip and finally saw the owner of the legs, he realised what it was that had so alerted his sense. The legs were lying awkwardly and unmoving for a very good reason. Because the owner of the legs was dead.

It was a young guy, maybe Farrow's own age. Perhaps twenty-three, twenty-four. And it looked as if someone had smashed his head against the wall of the alley. There was a round bloody patch on the wall about four feet or so above the place where the man lay with his back to that wall, and his head was twisted to one side. There was a thin smear of blood from the patch on the wall, all the way down the brickwork to where he lay. There was blood on his mouth.

'Well, well, well,' said Farrow – and kicked at one of the legs.

The figure did not move.

Quickly, he stooped down, looking back at the main street only once to make sure that no one could see him. Rummaging through the jacket pockets, he could find no wallet.

'Bastards. Must have took it when they brained him ...'

He rummaged in the corpse's jeans pocket, watching the dead and bloodied face intently all the time, just in case it came to life and frightened the hell out of him. There was an overlooked packet of

27

some kind in there. He yanked it out – a see-through plastic packet, with white powder inside.

Singing 'Happy Birthday to Me', Farrow fumbled at the sachet, opened it and dipped his finger in. He smacked his lips in delight and blew a kiss at the dead face. It was good stuff too, by the taste of it – even if his taste buds were a great deal less efficient these days than they used to be. Shoving the packet into his pocket, he stood quickly back, checked all around and headed back to the main street. Briefly, he felt a spasm of fear in his gut. Wouldn't it be just his luck if there was a cruising police patrol car up there on the main street, seeing him emerge and deciding to roll him? Wouldn't that be fucking ace? Arrested for murder, just because he found what the bastards who had really done the job had missed? But no, his 'street sense' told him to keep his cool, just turn smartly on to the main street and keep walking. Tonight was a real gift. He could use some, and sell some.

Head down, hands in pockets, he turned onto the main street.

And stopped abruptly when the black sedan screeched to a halt on the other side of the street.

Farrow barely had time to register the two faces in the front seats; short dark hair, sunglasses and dark suits. He saw the driver mouth *'There he is!'* and point directly at him. And then Farrow was off, running back along that street as fast as he could move. He could smell police a mile away. The others in the back of the sedan – three of them – had begun to open their doors. But the sight of Farrow running hard in the opposite direction made them slam the doors shut again. The sedan screeched after him.

There was another alley off to his left. Veering wildly, arms pinwheeling, Farrow spun around the corner and almost collided with a rubbish bin. Flinging it aside with a curse and an explosion of rotted vegetables, he kept his head down and ran hard. What the hell had happened to his 'street sense' now? Frantically scrabbling in his jeans pocket, Farrow pulled out the plastic envelope and threw it away as he ran. Why the hell was he running? He should have kept his cool. Now he knew, knew for *sure* that they were going to take him in for what had happened to that bastard back there. He heard another screech of tyres, and the slamming of doors. Looking back, he saw that the sedan had stopped at the entrance to the alley and that black-suited figures were piling out of the car even now, hurtling down the rubbish-strewn alley after him.

'Farrow!' one of the men shouted.

He kept running, not knowing this alley at all, and not knowing where in hell it led. There was another rubbish skip ahead. He ducked around it.

'Shit!'

There was a fence here, about ten feet high with barbed wire laid raggedly along the top.

'Shit, shit, shit!'

Farrow yanked at a rubbish bin, pulling it to the fence, hearing the curse of one of his pursuers as he slipped on rotting vegetables and fell. Leaping up on to the bin, Farrow grabbed for the rim of the fence. His hand caught the barbed wire and closed around it. A barbed metal thorn scored across his palm, making him cry out aloud as he swung one leg up to find a ridge for his foot. Cursing, he managed to haul himself up to the edge of the fence.

And then a hand closed around his ankle.

Farrow kicked back, yelling obscentities. But the grip held fast, and now his other foot was seized.

'Let go,' commanded a voice from behind.

'Get the hell off me! It wasn't me . . .'

'Please, Mr Farrow. Just let go.'

Oh, *Mister* Farrow, is it . . . ?

This time his legs were yanked hard and the barbed wire raked his hand again. He yelled and fell away from the fence behind the bin. A mass of garbage broke his fall. He struggled and twisted to rise, then slipped and fell back into a crouching position against the fence.

There were four of them, all dressed alike in dark suits and sunglasses.

'So . . .' Farrow struggled to get his breath, hugging his hand. 'So, what's the fucking charge?'

'No charge.'

'What do you mean "no charge"?' Farrow held up his injured hand. 'See that? That's a sueable offence. Wrongful arrest, police brutality.'

Now the four men were standing aside as a fifth man – dressed identically – walked calmly down the alley to join them. Had he been the one sitting next to the driver of the car, the one who had identified him? Farrow had never seen him before. He was carrying an attaché case, and as he drew level, he stooped down to where Farrow crouched, placed it on the ground and opened it.

'You're not police?' said Farrow, eyes boggling at the display of cash inside.

The man with the attaché case was still crouched down, looking directly into Farrow's face. Farrow could not see his eyes, but could not help feeling that those eyes were somehow not sharing the smile that came over the man's face when he shook his head.

'Then what the hell do you want?' asked Farrow.

'Mr Draegerman requests . . .' began the black-suited man.

FIVE

Jessica Morell was aware of the fact that her colleagues on *The Independent Daily*, both male and female, were fiercely competitive. Her recent successes had led to snide comments about power dressing, but she had long ago learned that to *be* the part, you had to *look* the part. She had a clear idea of where she was going, and what she was after. If it gave anyone a problem, then that was their look-out. She was variously described as young, vital, highly intelligent and obsessed with her job; some of her colleagues had taken to calling her Lois Lane. Always behind her back, of course. Once, she had caught a snatch of conversation from two of her female colleagues in the ladies' room, alluding to the nickname. Rather than being irritated, she was secretly pleased by it. But if anyone used it when she was in earshot, she would take the opportunity to set matters straight.

'I *need* to see him,' she said into the telephone, balanced in the crook of her neck and shoulder as she worked on the word processor. 'And you owe me at least three favours by my last count, George.' She enunciated the last words slowly and meaningfully. 'Don't get shitty with me! If I don't get into that meeting, then that's the last favour you'll get from me, George. I'm warning you.'

Peterson, working at his console on the desk opposite her, was looking at her legs again. He caught sight of her icy glare, and returned to the screen, trying to pretend that he had just been staring off into space while he thought about the article he was working on. Somewhere else in what the editor always liked to call 'our frantic hive of activity,' someone dropped a lever-arch file on the floor, spilling its contents and drawing a round of sarcastic applause from the dozen or so other reporters working in the main office.

'Thank you, George,' continued Jessica. 'That's better. And can I ... can I what? Okay, you smooth bastard. I've got two press tickets to the concert. You can have one now, the other when I get into the meeting. What do you mean, "hard bargain"?' Jessica quickly put the telephone down and returned to the screen, suddenly seeing in her mind's eye the turn of phrase that she had been searching for to make sense of the report she was working on.

There was always noise in the main office, always a constant ringing of telephones, murmurings of conversation, chatter and outright arguments. So much so that Jessica actually found it more difficult to work from home than she did in the office. She needed that continuous drone in the background; had actually incorporated its familiarity into her working style. In perfect silence, she felt uneasy. It was a wall of white noise that she had screened off so well that she actually needed it to perform efficiently.

So when the main office doors banged open and three men in black suits, wearing sunglasses, strode into the office and headed in her direction, she neither saw nor heard a thing as she continued to work at the console.

'Can I help?' asked someone, suddenly looking up as the three men walked past.

They ignored the enquiry. Their attention remained fixed on the dark-haired woman in the smart business suit working at her console.

'Excuse me,' began Petersen, turning once more from Jessica's legs to the strange new arrivals. 'But should you be in here . . . ?' Something about the demeanour of the three men was slightly alarming. Petersen reached for his telephone.

'Miss Morell?' asked the Black Suit with the attaché case.

Jessica looked up in surprise, seeing them for the first time.

'Yes . . .' She pushed her seat back, now aware that the normal bustle in the office was beginning to subside as others caught sight of the strangers in black standing in front of her desk. She cleared her throat. 'If you're from the taxman, I'm all paid up. I promise.'

'Can we speak?' asked the Black Suit. 'Privately.'

Rallying quickly to this strange situation, Jessica exchanged a look with Petersen, who still had the telephone raised to his ear.

'Is everything okay?' he asked.

'Yeah, it's okay.' Jessica feigned nonchalance as she rose from her chair. 'Is this business, gentlemen? Or maybe I'm under arrest or something?'

'We haven't come to read you your rights, if that's what you're thinking,' said the Black Suit, and tried to smile at her. Somehow, the smile did not seem to work, and the expressions on the faces of the other two remained unchanged.

'Okay, there's an office just over there we can use.' Jessica pointed behind her and moved off. The Black Suits followed, with all eyes in the office on this strange group. The assistant editor had been in a meeting all morning elsewhere in the building. It was possible to see through the wall-to-ceiling glass partitions of his office. No one in the office was sure whether those glass walls were there to enable him to keep an eye

31

on everybody working in the main office, or vice versa. But to Jessica, it seemed the ideal location. She was uncomfortable about being alone in a screened-off room with these three. Quickly, she opened the door and walked in, moving straight across to Harrison's swivel seat, and planting herself in it. The Black Suits followed, closing the door. Two remained standing by the door, the third – presumably the head man – walked calmly to stand before her, in front of the desk. Before she could open a conversation, the leader said:

'Have you heard of Jack Draegerman?'

Jessica looked at him for several seconds.

'Well, that's like saying have you heard of the Pope.'

'But *do* you know who he is?'

'Jack Draegerman: industrialist, architect, aviator, film-maker.'

'The same.'

'So?'

'He has a proposition to make. According to our records, your newspaper has made twelve specific attempts to interview Mr Draegerman over the last two years on various matters. Four of those requests were made personally by you.'

'He wasn't polite. Not even a "Sorry, I'm too busy" card.'

'Well, today's your lucky day, Miss Morell. Because Mr Draegerman requests the pleasure of your company. He wants to see you.'

'Why?'

'Because he's decided that it's time to tell the world his story. He's seen and read your work. He likes your style. So he wants to give you an exclusive interview. Nothing held back. The truth and nothing but.'

Jessica paused, rocking from side to side in her swivel chair. 'Do you mind if I ask you for credentials?'

Silently, the man took out an identity card and handed it to her.

'Pearson, Eric,' she read aloud. 'Assistant Chief Security Officer. Draegerman Enterprises.'

The leader nodded.

'This is all a little sudden. Why has he *really* had such a change of heart?'

'That's all we've been allowed to say, Miss Morell. Other than if you're not interested, if you're not prepared to come with us – here and now – then we've been authorised to go to another reporter, another journalist.'

'Who?'

'Bernie McMasters at *The Big Voice*.'

Jessica flinched visibly. Pearson had mentioned her most hated rival. Then she began to nod thoughtfully as she worked hastily on her options. Finally, she said:

'Okay, let's go. Where is he?'

'We're taking you to The Rock.'

32

'The Rock!' Normally, Jessica was able to handle most professional situations without appearing flustered, but this invitation really had come out of the blue. Getting to meet and interview Jack Draegerman had been one of her greatest dreams in the past few years. She had first been drawn to the idea of getting his side of the story about the numerous archaeological sites that he had acquired and apparently destroyed in his quest for minerals or oil worldwide. It had caused a storm in academic circles with Draegerman cited as a typical example of material greed overcoming national heritage. She felt sure that he would be only too willing to set the record straight from his own point of view. But she had been wrong, and her inability to get through the inpenetrable barrier of security surrounding him had sorely frustrated her. She had realised, in retrospect, that she had been less interested in the so-called 'industrial desecration' of the sites, but had been using this journalistic approach simply as a means to meet this fascinating man with his equally fascinating and mysterious past. Now, to have received such a direct invitation when she had given up hope of ever getting through, and to be told that the interview would take place in The Rock, was genuinely breathtaking.

Draegerman's Rock – known as 'The Rock' to everyone – was a massive, fiercely protected and heavily guarded edifice which Draegerman had designed and built himself in the middle of the city, like some dark Xanadu. No one, apart from the security force that Draegerman employed, had been in there to her knowledge since the opening festivities when building work had finally been completed.

The door shuddered open behind the two Black Suits standing guard. Harrison pushed his way in, carrying a pile of paperwork, his face almost purple with rage.

'What the hell are you doing in *my* office?'

Composure regained, Jessica said: 'These gentlemen have come from Jack Draegerman. I've checked their credentials. And they've been sent to take me to The Rock for an exclusive interview with the man himself. Naturally, I knew you would want me to accept.'

Dumbfounded, Harrison simply looked and nodded.

'Good,' said Jessica, swinging out of Harrison's seat. 'Gentlemen, shall we go?'

It was the best moment of her day when Jessica left the office with her Black-Suited escort. She basked in the looks of bewilderment and bafflement on the faces of her colleagues as they passed. She knew that she was heading for the biggest story of her career.

Just how big she could never have dreamed.

SIX

This is a dangerous part of the city, and these are streets it's better to avoid. Only the utterly hopeless can expect to find a night's sleep down here, in this rat-run of alleyways and abandoned warehouses. Only the utterly hopeless have nothing to lose if someone should slit their throats in the night; only those who have nothing left to steal, nothing worth rummaging through pockets for.

But the two men in black suits who stride purposefully down this alley seem unconcerned by their surroundings. They are watched from the shadows as they move; watched by those who assess whether there is anything here worth acting on, whether by handout request or taking money by force. But no one approaches them as they continue on their way, and the watching figures remain in the shadows as the two men pick their way over the muddy and littered ground, heading for the source of guttering light at the bottom of the alley. Their faces betray no emotion, do not even show disgust at what they find down here.

This is where the hopeless are sleeping tonight. In an alley at the side of an abandoned haulage firm, its steel shutter doors still locked and rusted after nine years. Sometimes, when the wind gusts, the steel shutters make a rumbling sound, like distant thunder. Lying under cardboard sheets on tattered mattresses dragged up against the walls, or under mounds of refuse and ragged linen, twenty or thirty individuals huddle for warmth. Someone has started two fires in oil drums to try to keep the deadening chill at bay.

Some of the figures look up as the men in black suits pick their way through the mounds of garbage and filth. Some even think about asking for a handout, but a closer inspection of the men precludes the possibility of charity. The Black Suits continue to move, stepping over figures huddled under cardboard, lifting soiled blankets and remaining impassive as the figures beneath curse them and turn over in their delirious slumber. They ignore the figures who are shooting up, the rambling arguments, the young man giving a blow-job for half of what his partner is drinking from a greasy bottle.

Half an hour later, they have found who they were sent to find.

34

He is sitting with his back against a crumbling wall, staring vacantly ahead. His eyes seemed filled with awe, as if those gusting sparks are miniature universes of stars, flaring up and fading; and with each new flaring of light, he seems to be searching for the answers to his lost life. His face is dirty, but his features are handsome.

Two looming shadows fall over him. Slowly, he looks at the newcomers. But there is no recognition in his eyes, no real interest in why they are here as one of the Black Suits kneels directly in front of him and takes a photograph from inside his pocket. He looks at it, then turns it around to show the young man.

It is the face of Bobby Pernell, the same studio portrait that adorns the dressing-room wall of Gloria Pernell's 'trailer'.

'Is it him?' asks the man behind.

The kneeling man nods, but as the man behind moves to open the attaché case he is carrying he says: 'No need. He's completely spaced out.'

Bobby smiles at some inner memory, but has heard not one word.

Suddenly, he is being lifted by the two men. He offers no resistance, and simply smiles again. They have been sent by the clouds behind his eyes to provide all the answers he needs. He need take no active part in the proceedings, just allow himself to be taken where those answers are.

Without speaking, the two black-suited men carry him away, an arm over each of their shoulders. No one in the alley says a word, or asks a question.

The night swallows them up.

SEVEN

'I can't get Carl's shoes on,' said Bennet from the living-room. 'Anyway, he should be able to put them on himself. He's supposed to be old enough.'

Susan DePaolo gripped the plunger again and leaned into the sink.

'It's not my fault,' complained the invisible Carl. 'It's the shoe.'

'Just ...' began Susan, then yanked hard at the plunger. 'Just ... *put the shoe on, Bennet!*' She yanked hard again, to no effect, knowing that she was in danger of losing her temper. Getting her seven-year-old twin sons ready in the morning was always a complicated series of manoeuvres at the best of times, but this morning had been a particularly bad one. The sink was blocked, and the sodden remnants of cornflakes and other breakfast cereal swirled around her elbows as she tugged at the plunger, trying to clear it. She blew at a renegade strand of hair that had come loose from her headband. With irritating persistence, it refused to stay out of her eyes. Susan stood back, wiping her hands on her coverall, looking long and hard at the plunger as if it was somehow sentient and engaged in a battle of wits with her.

'The other shoe's coming off ...' began Carl.

'Right, *right!*' Head down, Susan marched back into the living-room. But her need to sort her sons out had been headed off at the pass. The apartment door was opening, and a familiar figure was peeking around the corner.

'Grandma!' Miraculously, both of Carl's shoes were on his feet now, as both kids ran to greet their grandmother. Susan pulled off her rubber gloves, smiling, pulling her hair back under the headband and moving to join them.

'You kids not ready yet?' admonished Susan's mother.

'Hiya.' Susan planted a smacking kiss on her mother's forehead as the older woman put down a carrier bag full of shopping. 'Didn't expect you this morning, Ma.'

'No ... here's some groceries I got on the way up here ...'

'Oh, *Ma!*'

'It's nothing, nothing. I had to see Mrs Frazier, and it was on the way.

36

So I thought, you know, why not?' Sara DePaolo yanked two comics out of the carrier and shoved them at the boys. Carl and Bennet took them gratefully, jostling away from her and fighting over ownership. 'Power Men – Carl! Junior Jeff – Bennet!' snapped Sara, sorting out potential difficulties. Susan kissed her mother again and moved back to the kitchen. Sara followed.

'You can't afford to be buying me stuff, Ma. Not on your pension.'

'I enjoy being destitute,' said Sara, and now they were both laughing hard at this catchphrase of the late Joseph DePaolo, father and grandfather. Susan thanked God for the sound of her mother's laughter. Sara was first-generation Afro-Caribbean. Even after all these years, she had maintained the wonderful accent, refusing to relinquish it as a statement of her individuality. Joe had been third-generation Irish-Italian: a construction worker. A fall from scaffolding had paralysed him from the waist down when he was forty-seven. There had been insurance, but not nearly enough.

'I can take the kids to school for you this morning, if you like,' said Sara. 'You got any coffee going?'

'How many kisses do you want in one morning? And it's over there. Hot and ready.'

'One coffee will do. But kisses? I'll take as many as I can get.'

Susan unhooked a mug from the wall-rack and moved to the percolator as Sara unpacked the groceries on the kitchen bench. The kids were silent in the living-room, as if by a miracle, each one absorbed in their comic for the ten minutes or so it would take to read them.

'I'm paying you for this stuff,' said Susan.

'No you're not. This makes up for buying my lunch last week. Money you can't afford with two kids.'

Susan made an exasperated sound, but felt good inside. That stupid bloody blocked sink had been working on her this morning, testing her reserves. If nothing else, the DePaolos had seen hard times through, had learned to stand and take it – and give it back. She should not allow herself to be strained by something so trivial when they had weathered so much together. Things like the racial abuse, for instance. The kids were two tones lighter even than Susan, but had still suffered a hard time at the local school, having been bullied by both black and white kids – the standard lot of mixed-parentage kids around here, it seemed. But even they had stood up to it. They were survivors. They would come through. So to hell with blocked sinks.

'Now what's this?' enquired Sara, drifting to the sink and to the plunger sticking out of it.

'Oh, damn thing's . . .' And before Susan could say blocked, Sara had lunged into the sink, both meaty arms working on the plunger. In the next instant, it came out of the morass with a wet *thwock*, followed by a loud sucking sound as the drain cleared.

'You two kissing in there again?' said Bennet from the living-room, his laughter combining with Carl's. Susan and Sara joined in.

'Less of the lip,' rejoined Sara, wiping her hands. 'Or I'll be coming in there to put the lip on *you*!'

Bennet and Carl made sounds as if they were drowning and returned to their comics. When Susan had finished laughing, Sara said: 'When it came to the kissing department, let me tell you – your father was a happy man.'

'I know it,' said Susan.

'Well?'

'Well what?'

'You given any more thought to what Den asked you?'

'Oh *Ma*. I wish I hadn't said anything to you now.'

'Don't give me that. There's no secrets in this family, and you know it.'

'I know, but . . .'

'Look, that boy's been practically living with you here for two years now. The kids think he's the best. You keep him hanging on a thread for too long and he might go looking somewhere else.'

'I don't want to spoil it, Ma. Things are great as they are. I'm not sure I'm ready for a second marriage.'

'That bastard . . .' began Sara, and quickly covered her mouth, guiltily looking back towards the living-room.

'Yeah, right. That's just what he was. And I thought I'd got it right then, Ma. Just like you. Remember what you said to me about your first husband? How right it was, and how wrong it turned out to be? How the only thing good you got out of it was . . .'

'You. That's right, Susan. And don't ever forget it.'

'Well, that goes double for me. Double with Bennet and Carl.'

'But the point is . . . the right man *did* come along for me, eventually. Just like Dennis has come along for you.'

'You're forgetting about your *third* marriage after Joe died, Ma.'

'Never mind that. That was something else altogether. You love each other. I can see it every day.'

'I know. But maybe I need more time?'

'What's the matter? You waiting for a nice *white* boy to come along?'

Susan slapped her mother on the shoulder, eyes flaring.

'Okay.' Sara began to back away from the conversation, worrying that maybe it had gone too far again. 'What time's Den finish his shift?'

Susan turned to finish packing the perishables into the refrigerator as Sara returned to the sink, turning on the tap and flushing the detritus away, wiping the drainer with a cloth.

'Not till late all this week.' Susan laughed, and the tension was swept away, just like the water down the sink. 'Says he sees more of his forklift than he does of me. Even started talking to the damn thing recently.'

'Ah, first signs of a weakening brain. Marry him quick and get his money.'

Ten minutes later, the comics were finished, shoes were firmly anchored on feet and the sink was cleaned. At lunchtime, the kids would be making their way to Grandma's house – it was nearer to the school. And Susan would join them there as usual, after she had straightened the apartment, made the beds and finished the ironing.

Ironing was a good time for thinking.

She had never known her real father, had been unaware that Joe DePaolo was not her real father until she herself had married and had kids. Unable to keep the truth from her any longer, and feeling that she had the right to know since she had started a family of her own, Sara had told Susan the truth.

'*The man was bad – and dangerous. I can't tell you any more.*'

She had been desperately worried about Susan's reaction, but it had made no difference to the way Susan felt. The only real father she had known was Joe, a good and loving man. It was all the father she needed. And she had never felt the urge to follow up and try to find out more about her real father. Her own marriage had started to go bad almost immediately. Her husband Tommy had made it plain that he wanted her to have an abortion when she found out she was pregnant. Clearly, fatherhood was going to interfere with his ability to live life just the way he wanted it – which involved never being questioned about why he came in drunk every other day at three in the morning. When the hospital scan had revealed that Susan was carrying twins, Tommy had shown a clean pair of heels. Seven years later and she had received not one penny in maintenance money. Then Dennis had come along – and Sara was proved right. Not all men were bastards after all. Now, after two years – a proposal of marriage. It came come right out of the blue.

'What's this?'

'It's a ring.'

'What for?'

'For you.'

'You trying to make a decent woman out of me?'

'I prefer you the way you are – indecent.'

'You're not joking, are you?'

'Do you see me smiling?'

'Den . . . I . . . just . . . Aren't things okay the way they are?'

'*They're more than okay. I've never been happier. That's why I'm asking you to marry me.*'

That had been two days ago, and Susan had asked for time to think.

39

She was still thinking, still absorbed in her thoughts as she ironed one of Den's work-shirts, when there was a knock on the apartment door.

She unplugged the iron, stood it on the kitchen bench to cool and moved across the room to the door.

'Who is it?'

'Miss DePaolo?'

'You selling something?'

'This is an official visit, Miss DePaolo.'

She opened the door warily on the chain. This was a rough neighbourhood. Just last week someone had been mugged in the apartment block frontage.

A man in a black suit, wearing black sunglasses, smiled at her from the other side of the door.

'Who are you?'

In answer, the man took a wallet out of his pocket and flashed a badge at her. Susan did not have a chance to see the ID, but gave vent to a deep sigh.

'So what's Bennet done this time?' Two weeks ago, he had been caught by a shop detective, shoplifting from a newsagent. He had protested his innocence, saying it had been the other two who had been with him. He had been cautioned, and Susan had chased him around the apartment with a rolled-up newspaper, making him promise he would never get involved in anything like that again.

'If we could just have a word,' continued the black-suited man.

There were two other characters standing behind him, both dressed in the same manner and both with the same 'official' bearing. Sighing, Susan began to unlatch the chain – then changed her mind.

'I'm sorry. I didn't see that identification.'

Still smiling, the man took it out again and this time held it up close so that she could read.

'Kennedy,' read Susan. 'Security Unit "C": Draegerman Enterprises.'

'Can we have a word . . . ?'

'What the hell do I want with Draegerman Enterprises?'

'Please, if we could speak inside. We've got a proposal for you which may be to your advantage.'

'So you *are* selling something?'

'Please . . . ?'

'Not today, thank you,' said Susan. She zipped the chain shut, pushing the door closed.

And then the door burst open as the Black Suit put his shoulder to it. The impact sent Susan reeling back into the apartment. Before she could regain her balance, the other two had followed the man in, the last to enter quickly pushing the door shut again. The Black Suit leader was holding his hands out to her, as if trying to placate her rising anger at their sudden and brutal entrance.

40

'Get the hell *out of my house*!' Susan looked quickly around for a weapon, saw the iron on the kitchen bench and lunged towards it.

The Black Suit moved faster, catching Susan by the arm and propelling her on to the sofa. His face still bore the same indulgent smile that she had first seen when she opened the door. The two other Black Suits quickly joined him.

'Now if you'll just . . .' began the leader.

Susan opened her mouth and gave vent to the loudest scream she could muster.

One of the other Black Suits lunged at her, seized an arm and clapped a meaty fist over her mouth, silencing the scream. Susan thrashed and clawed at the man, but now the other one had joined him, had seized her other arm. She was pinned on the sofa and could only twist her head from side to side as the Black Suit leader, still smiling, sat on the coffee table in front of her. An attaché case seemed to have appeared from nowhere in his hands. Now he was opening it, turning it around to face her and showing her the wads of cash inside.

'Mr Jack Draegerman requests the pleasure of your company. Now I've no doubt you've heard of Mr Draegerman. Let's face it, who hasn't? Well, we're his employees – and he's asked us to come here and make you an offer. There's fifty thousand in here, and it's yours – all of it – if you just agree to come and see him at his place of residence. That's the place the press like to call "The Rock". That's all you have to do. Agree to come and see him, and this cash is yours. When you get there, there'll be a further two hundred thousand for you. I know you're going to ask *why* Mr Draegerman wants to see you. But a condition of the offer is that you have to come with us now, if you want this money. Now. At once. So – what do you say?'

The hand was withdrawn from her face.

At once, Susan began to scream again, thrashing and kicking all the more violently. Instantly, the hand was clamped back over her mouth.

'Oh dear,' said the Black Suit, closing the case. He placed it on the coffee table and reached into his coat pocket. When Susan saw him withdraw a small bottle and begin to screw off the top, she began to struggle as hard as she could. But the grip of the two men was unbreakable. She could only watch in horror as the Black Suit took a wad of cotton from another pocket and carefully wrapped the wad over the bottle top. Then he carefully upended the bottle, so that some of the liquid inside splashed on to the cotton.

Chloroform! Oh my God, it's chloroform!

'Hold her still,' said the Black Suit as he moved calmly back to the sofa. Susan tried to twist her head, but was held fast.

'I'm sorry, Ms DePaolo. Our instructions are specific. If you won't

41

take the offer, we're authorised to bring you to Mr Draegerman by any means at our disposal.'

Suddenly, the hand was taken away from her mouth.

Susan drew breath to scream.

And then there was only darkness.

EIGHT

Roy Jensen squeezed back into his seat as if he wanted to merge with the fabric and hide from sight. He had travelled on aeroplanes before, but this helicopter ride was a first – and not a pleasant first. At least with an aeroplane, you had a feeling of distance between yourself and the empty air outside if you kept away from the window seat. (He considered himself a non-travel-sick kind of person, definitely not someone with a flying phobia – but he never, ever took a window seat. Just in case.) But in a helicopter? The damn passenger compartment had a large viewing window on both sides. There was no feeling of sitting next to a 'wall'; no comfort sitting next to what seemed to be such thin glass. And even though he was strapped in, every time the helicopter swooped and dived, he found himself being drawn towards that glass. There seemed to be nothing preventing him from hurtling out into the darkening sky beyond – and the glittering city below. He had checked his seat-belt at least two dozen times since the 'copter had lifted off in a cloud of dust, leaving *The Wayside* far below and behind.

And Roy was deeply unappreciative of the aerial view of the city. There was no sense of wonder for him as the helicopter swooped and clattered and dived between skyscrapers and office blocks. Each time they passed close to a towering concrete mountain, he could not bring himself to examine it. The sight only served to reinforce the immensity of the drop below and heightened the nauseating drop-away into these concrete canyons.

The city below was a hostile and alien place. Roy had little call to travel there for business or pleasure, preferring the arid countryside surrounding it. The feeling of alienation he always got from the city, of downright hostility, seemed even more accentuated up here in the sky. He tried to look at the horizon, tried to concentrate on the thin red ribbons of cloud that smeared the face of the sinking sun, tried not to look at the glittering bustle of ant-like activity down below on the streets and the highways that honeycombed the city. It was a losing battle.

'How long?' he shouted over the sound of the rotor blades. 'How long before we get there?'

'We're there,' said the Black Suit sitting next to him, impassively. He raised a hand and pointed out of the passenger window on the far side of the cabin. And this time Roy forced himself to look. Night would be on the city very soon now, and there were gigantic shadows in the concrete valleys of the city. The passing shadow of the helicopter flitted dark and bizarrely elongated along the façade of a glittering tower block as they passed, like some skimming, night-time bird. His stomach lurched again at the sight. But then the tower was gone and the Black Suit's finger was still pointing as the helicopter took a tight right turn, swooping down and round. Roy clung to his seat-belt. He could not understand why he had not seen it before, even when the 'copter had been skimming the suburbs of this huge, decaying city. He had seen photographs before, seen film footage on the television news, although he had never seen it in real life. But nothing could have prepared him for the sight of this incredible grey-black monolith. Feelings of giddiness temporarily abating, Roy looked in true awe at Draegerman's Rock.

The damn thing was gigantic. It stood alone, and Roy guessed that there was no comparable skyscraper or multi-storey building within a five-mile radius. Perhaps that was why it seemed to dominate the skyline as they sped towards it; perhaps that was why it seemed to dwarf all the other buildings, standing like a mountain of stone dead centre in the middle of the city.

There were four towers on the top of the edifice, at either corner; from this distance looking like some parody of a crown. And it seemed to Roy that there was something else about the massive structure which made it even more incongruous in this highly urban, densely populated area. He struggled to find the right kind of word to describe it, and the only word he could find was – archaic. Despite the obvious technology that had gone into the creation of this gigantic needle, something about its shape and form had more to do with prehistoric monuments to dead gods and ancient civilisations than modern-day pantheons to the gods of concrete, glass and steel. As the helicopter headed towards the tower and began to ascend, it seemed as if The Rock was set right in the middle of the worst, most dilapidated and rundown slum area of the city. Huge tracts of blighted apartment blocks, furrowed roads and closely crowded buildings engrimed with dirty-black soot seemed to huddle up close to the foot of the structure, until it was almost impossible to see anything moving on the streets down there. It was like trying to look down through the impenetrable and chaotic canopy of some blighted urban jungle. The fact that all these surrounding buildings were less than a couple of storeys high made The Rock all the more imposing.

As the helicopter drew closer, Roy could at last see what it was about this building which seemed so different and so ancient.

There was hardly any reflection from the face of The Rock; no level upon level of glass windows showing a glittering kaleidoscope of office strip-lights, no dying sun reflected and sparkling there. Whereas most of the city's office blocks and skyscrapers seemed to consist mostly of glass, Roy had to struggle to see if there were windows in this towering edifice. And now, as the helicopter continued its climb and The Rock seemed to fill everyone's line of vision, Roy could see that there *were* windows after all. But only at every third or fourth level, it seemed, although it was impossible to assess 'levels' in the bizarre architecture of The Rock. Something about the glass in the windows seemed strange. Because they did not reflect the dying light in the way that the rest of the glass structures in the city did, The Rock's walls appeared mostly blank; towering walls of grey concrete with strange and apparently meaningless contours in the mainly sheer planes. Did Draegerman value his privacy so much that all the glass in the building was 'smoked'?

As they drew nearer and higher, Roy could see what seemed to be rococo buttresses and intricate parapets emerging from the sides of the building to support swooping Gothic arches; vertical shafts of stone mullions for vast cathedral windows where there were *no* windows. The designs on these sheer walls seemed to serve little architectural purpose; just a chaotic mixture of architectural styles, a puzzling jigsaw of concrete and steel which had been both admired for its audacity and reviled for its excesses in professional construction magazines for many years. Roy knew nothing of architecture, but seemed to recall hearing or reading something about Draegerman's reputation as an eccentric; a multi-millionaire able to indulge his wildest fantasies. Maybe this chaotic design meant nothing to anyone but himself.

Suddenly, the helicopter had cleared the roof and the feeling of giddiness and nausea swamped Roy again. He closed his eyes, took a few deep breaths and tried to lose the impression that the floor beneath him was only inches thick. When he opened them again, it seemed as if the Black Suit sitting next to him was smirking, although it was impossible to work out his real expression because of his sunglasses. The sight of the towers at each corner of the roof drew Roy's attention. There was a suddenly overpowering impression of immensity. But there was also something else. Looking at those strange rococo designs on the sheer walls of The Rock, and then seeing the towers and their strange, almost Arabic, twisting design, had struck some kind of chord deep inside Roy. It was as if he had recognised or seen something here from a distantly remembered dream. But it was impossible to grasp or analyse the feeling – and now the helicopter was swooping low over the roof of the building and the pilot was speaking into his mouthpiece, to be answered by a crackling, static-filled response making no sense to Roy at all.

The helicopter began to circle the roof.

Despite himself, Roy could not help but look. His feelings of giddiness were intense, but the spectacle below was something from which he could not avert his eyes.

He could see that Draegerman's Rock was sitting in what seemed to be a huge shaft in the ground, far, far below. It was as if someone had excavated a gigantic borehole in the middle of this decayed neighbourhood, and then planted the building in the centre of the yawning aperture to separate it from the rest of the city. The Rock appeared to be 'anchored' to the walls of the gigantic shaft by four reinforced concrete driveways or walkways like the huge spokes of a wheel. Roy could see high-tension cables above the walkways, making each one look like a miniature suspension bridge. A reinforced concrete platform on the 'neighbourhood side' provided security and presumably stopped anyone on that side from climbing over and falling into what seemed to be a bottomless 'moat' all around the building. The effect only added to the impression that Draegerman had constructed some kind of mediaeval castle in the centre of the modern city. Roy had a dizzying eagle's-eye view of security vehicles patrolling each of the walkways and of the ant-like security men on the neighbourhood side. He seemed to remember hearing that the guards down there were heavily armed.

Now he could see that they were not alone in the sky. Another helicopter had appeared and had begun to circle as their own 'copter stabilised over the roof of the building. He could see that it was the same make and design: an Augusta 109. Was this helicopter also intending to land? When he looked down again, he saw that they were hovering above the roof.

There was a landing pad down there, centred in the roof between the four towers.

There was more crackling, static-filled conversation.

The tone of the helicopter engine changed.

They were going down.

And Roy had to look away. Now he knew that he was flight-sick after all at the sight of the roof coming up to meet them, and the huge void on either side of the four gigantically towering walls. Christ, what if the wind blew them a little off course? What if the rotor blade should just nick one of the towers, and send them crashing over the side? Roy saw the 'copter disintegrating and erupting into flame as it fell into the bottomless moat that surrounded the man-made fortress. As they descended, it seemed as if the roof and its landing pad were getting smaller and smaller, not larger and larger as they should be.

He looked up at the helicopter roof, and wished with all his heart that the four strange men in their black suits and black shades with their strange offer had arrived in a black limousine. Why the *hell* couldn't it have been a car, rather than a helicopter? Why the *hell* was he putting

46

himself through this? The sound of the rotors and the engine seemed louder than ever before, and Roy clenched his teeth, waiting for the sudden rending clatter of a broken prop, and the horrific tilting motion that would precede their plunging disastrously over the edge. Was this *really* worth fifty thousand now and two hundred thousand later?

The chassis of the helicopter bumped. Roy got ready to yell his lungs out.

And then the rotor blades started to slow, the engine noise fading from a full-throated roar to a slowly descending whine. Roy opened his eyes, and could barely believe it.

They were down.

Down at last on the roof of Draegerman's Rock.

He suddenly realised that his fingers were hurting. He had been clenching them tight in his lap. When he raised his head again, the Black Suit was not looking at him any more. He had turned away, but he still had that bloody smirk on his face. For the very first time, Roy suddenly became truly aware of what a preposterous situation he was in. He was stranded. He had taken their offer of cash without asking any questions and now he was utterly stranded a hundred storeys or more high on top of this gigantic monument to a stranger's monstrous ego.

'Okay,' said the pilot, looking back. 'Time to go.'

The Black Suit, still smiling, unfastened his seat-belt and moved across the cabin to open the glass door at Roy's side. It seemed as if the entire side of the 'copter had suddenly swung open. Roy tried not to think about what might have happened had he leaned on that handle while in flight. Angry at the Black Suit's smile, angry at the fears that had risen within him when he had been well aware of the risks of this strange offer from the very beginning, Roy tugged at the seat-belt and pushed aside the harness. Now the shadows of the rotor blades were visible as they slowed. The Black Suits scrambled out of the machine, the one Roy recognised as the leader, who had been sitting up front, taking him by the arm and guiding him across the landing pad towards one of the towers. The ground felt strange beneath Roy's feet. There was a weird tingling in his toes, as if the roof was only pretending to be solid and would collapse underneath them at any moment. He could feel the vibrations of the helicopter, which served only to reinforce this weird, unsettling feeling. Now the shadows of the rotors had disappeared again as the pilot revved his engine after they were clear and the whine returned to the full-throated roar. Wind gusted at Roy and the Black Suits as they sought shelter around the corner of one of the ornamental grey towers.

The helicopter lifted again, the pilot giving one brief wave of acknowledgment as the machine seemed to leap from the pad into the air. It steadied itself, like some great glass bird waiting for just the right air stream; and then it veered away to their right, roaring overhead and up into the sky. Shading his eyes from the grit that was thrown up from the roof by its passage, Roy looked back to see that the second helicopter was veering towards them.

He watched with the others as the second helicopter steadied its position directly over the landing pad, and then began slowly to descend. As it came down, the feeling of giddiness returned and Roy forced himself to look away. He shaded his eyes, pretending that he was protecting himself from more wind-stirred dust and grit. But the Black Suits' attention was fixed on the machine as it finally came to rest, rotors slowing.

The second batch of Black Suits – three of them – emerged crouching from the helicopter, one hand clenched to their ever-present sunglasses. Now Roy could see that this 'copter also had a passenger. His shoulder-length hair was whipping around his head like a nest of snakes, his face contorted against the blast of wind. He was wearing a dark knee-length coat of some kind. Unbuttoned, it flapped and wrapped itself around his body, as if it wanted to tear itself free and take flight. One of the Black Suits took his arm as they hurried in a crouch away from the landing pad. Even before they had reached them, the second helicopter had also lifted from the pad and whirled away, clattering into the sky. Roy could see that the first machine was barely a glinting dot on the city skyline, a small spark of orange caught in the rays of the descending sun.

He turned back to the others. The Black Suits were still watching the helicopters – all except the one who had taken the newcomer's arm. A small personal radio had materialised in his hand and he was holding it close to his ear, now speaking into the mouthpiece. The newcomer adjusted his windswept coat and looked directly across to Roy, then to the others, clearly waiting for some kind of introduction. Roy noted that one of the new Black Suits was holding an attaché case identical to the one that had been opened in front of him back at *The Wayside* and which, he was pleased to see, was still being carried by one of his own escorts. Obviously, the offer of cash in return for coming to The Rock had not been given to him alone. So who the hell was the new man?

'Jensen . . .' he began, extending his hand to the newcomer.

But before the newcomer could take it, the Black Suit with the radio stepped between them, saying into his mouthpiece: 'Area Code 365783. Security 1A Max 4.'

And Roy turned in surprise at the whirring sound behind him. The noise had come from the tower behind which they had taken shelter, and as Roy watched, a door slithered open in what he had first presumed to be a blank grey concrete wall at the base of the tower. Beyond, he could see a brightly lit interior and a mirrored wall reflecting their figures, with a handrail at waist height all around. This was obviously an elevator cabin.

'After you,' said the Black Suit with the radio, extending a hand. Roy could not suppress the mental image of himself stepping in there, the ribbed metal floor beneath his feet suddenly caving in – and his screaming body dropping a hundred or more storeys below. But his anxiety at the helicopter flight and landing had also angered him. He did not want to see that smirking grin again. Quickly, he stepped in. The others followed and Roy found himself standing next to the stranger again.

'Jensen,' said the stranger. His breath was heavy with the scent of garlic. 'Right?'

'Right,' replied Roy.

'Area Code Max A4,' said the Black Suit with the handset. 'Going down.'

'Not on me you're not,' grinned the newcomer as the invisible door slid shut again. His smile did not waver when no one laughed or commented.

'You're not *with* these guys, are you?' he continued.

Suddenly, Roy instinctively did not want to get too close to this character, regardless of whether they were in the same boat or not. He shook his head and looked at his feet. The feeling in his stomach told him that they were descending. Even so, this must be the smoothest elevator he had ever been in.

'Strong silent types,' smiled the stranger again. 'Couldn't get a laugh out of one of 'em coming over. First they give me a ride in a sedan, then they transfer me to a helicopter for a sightseeing tour of the city. Not a whisper out of one of them. Name's Farrow.' The stranger held out his hand. Roy took it, uncomfortably. The palm was wet. Clearly, Farrow was not as cool or as unflustered by his present situation as he was making himself out to be.

Farrow was nodding his head enthusiastically now, as if this simple act of shaking hands had given him all the answers he needed. He breathed out heavily, filling the air with garlic, then crossed his arms and looked around.

'No lights,' he said at last.

'Pardon me?' asked Roy.

'No lights on the wall up there. Like a department store. You notice that? Every time people are in an elevator, and they get to feeling uncomfortable – they look up at the lights. See, up there? We could be on the lingerie floor, or the hardware floor, or the toy department. And we'd never know.' He laughed again.

Roy checked his watch. It had been a minute and a half since they had started their descent. Just how far down into The Rock were they going? As if on cue, the Black Suit with the radio said: 'We're here, gentlemen.'

The elevator door slid open. The sound seemed more like a human sigh than the pneumatic hiss Roy had heard up on the roof.

The Black Suit with the radio stepped out first and the others stood aside in a gesture that signalled Roy and Farrow should follow. Farrow brushed imaginary dust from his jacket and straightened a tie that was not there. He stepped smartly out and Roy followed, glancing back nervously as the other Black Suits filed out after them.

They were in a corridor of sorts.

About three or four feet above their heads there was a row of dimly lit lanterns set into the walls on either side. They were curiously old fashioned and would have seemed more appropriate in Victorian London, where hansom cabs clattered down foggy, cobblestoned streets. They gave off an orange light and were spaced perhaps six or seven feet apart. By following their curving line it was easy to see that the corridor curved away to the right, but the lamps seemed oddly placed, giving poor illumination down here on the ground. And it seemed to Roy that the walls were somehow wet, like the stone walls of an underground vault. Surely that couldn't be right?

The Black Suit called Aiken moved forward, indicating that they should follow. Farrow shrugged and walked ahead. Roy set off after him, hearing the others come up behind. The ground beneath his feet seemed oddly uneven, and when Roy did look down he could see to his astonishment that the corridor floor *was* cobbled, reinforcing his first image of the lanterns and Victorian London.

Farrow waited for him to draw level and said: 'How the hell can these guys see where they're walking? They still haven't taken their shades off.'

Roy gave a non-committal half-laugh.

They continued in silence, following the curve of the lanterns in the walls.

After what seemed a long time, Roy pointed to the wet stone walls and said: 'Seems to me he must have enough money to afford a plumber.' It was merely a remark to break the silence, but he wished he had said nothing when Farrow broke into guffawing, braying laughter. The sound seemed to bounce and echo. When he had finally finished, he slapped Roy on the shoulder.

'Not sure if you're here for the same reason. But I think me and you are going to really hit it off together.'

He turned and looked back at the Black Suits following.

'Don't you drop my case, pal.' The man's face remained blank and Farrow laughed again. There was no comment from those who followed. Roy just wished that Farrow would shut the hell up.

There was a brighter light ahead, emanating from below. Somehow this light was much cleaner, reflecting in even greater detail the gleaming wetness of the stone on all sides. It threw the figure of Aiken into sharp

50

relief as he suddenly stopped dead ahead. As Roy came up behind him with Farrow, he could see that the man had paused at the top of a flight of stairs, almost impossibly steep. In the ceiling, curving away down what Roy could now see was a circular stone staircase, were what could only be described as office strip-lights, set into carved, ornate stone surroundings. Stone gargoyles' faces grinned at them. This bizarre mélange of modern and ancient was at once fascinating – and disturbing. These lights were obviously more highly powered than the dull orange lights back in the corridor, presumably to aid vision because of the steepness of the flight of stairs. But why have dull lights back there anyway? Someone could still slip on one of the cobbles and break their leg.

Aiken turned back and smiled. 'May I suggest that you use the handrail set into the wall? The steps here are stone, and a little slippery.'

'Gross,' said Farrow.

The Black Suit's smile did not waver as he turned and grabbed the iron handrail, starting down. Roy followed. There were narrow vertical slits set into the wall all the way down, about thirty or forty feet apart. Each of the slits was about eight feet high, but only a foot and a half wide, with strange orange windows set into that. There was light beyond the glass, but it was impossible to see any details of what might lie beyond. As they descended, Roy suddenly remembered what they looked like – arrow-slits in ancient castle walls. But arrow-slits? Here, in what was supposed to be the biggest office-block-cum-tower in one of the biggest cities?

They continued to descend.

'Shit!'

Something slithered behind Roy, and he looked back quickly to see that Farrow was clutching at the iron handrail with both hands. His foot had slipped.

'What the hell is going on here?' he snapped. 'I'm going to break my neck . . .'

'Not far to go now, Mr Farrow,' said Aiken without looking back.

'Cash is cash, and fun is fun,' continued Farrow. 'But my sense of humour is beginning to wear thin.'

'One more turn . . .' continued Aiken. Suddenly light flooded over them as the staircase ended. Aiken walked ahead on to a concrete platform. '. . . and we're here.'

Wincing at the light, Roy followed him and saw that its source was a spotlight set high up on the wall directly ahead, its beam trained down to where they stood. Aiken halted and turned to face them, extending a hand to his left.

Roy moved to join him, saw a black iron rail in front of him – and then recoiled. His vertigo suddenly overwhelmed him again when he realised where they had emerged.

The staircase had given access to a stone platform and balcony at least a hundred feet from the ground below, overlooking what seemed to be some ancient, gigantic cathedral. There was nothing between Roy and the hundred-foot drop except the thin iron handrail, and although the Black Suit appeared utterly unperturbed by his proximity to the edge, Roy felt his own legs losing their strength.

'Bloody hell ...' murmured Farrow in awe as the other Black Suits drew level. He stepped forward to clutch the rail, still keeping a respectful and sensible arm's length from the immensity of the drop. Roy did not want anyone behind him on this platform. He edged slowly back until he could feel the stone cold wall against his back.

As they looked out over this vast, cavernous space it seemed that they had suddenly emerged into something even more like a mediaeval castle than the exterior of the building had led Roy to believe. There was a gigantic black-stoned roof, covering an area bigger than a cathedral. Huge, carved pillars of black stone stretched upwards like petrified prehistoric trees until they reached the huge bat-wing arches in the cathedral roof. There seemed to be walkways up in the reaches of the massively intricate roof, although it was impossible to be certain from this distance. Were they gangways and trellises on which people could scurry, or were they merely distant and elaborate stone carvings?

A black stone staircase in the wall to their right wound away down to this bizarre chamber, the same thin handrail being the only protection from a sickening fall. And as their eyes followed the staircase down, Roy and Farrow could see that far below, in the shadows and apparently all over this enormous chamber, were what seemed to be dozens and dozens of small glass screens set into the stone walls and pillars at varying heights, most of them just above head height. They were all emitting a blue-white flickering light, making shadows dance on the vast flagged floor. Were they television screens? Could they really be looking at dozens and dozens of television screens, set into the black brickwork of this strange place?

Down in the centre of the gigantic black chamber, in the middle of a vast, stone-flagged floor, they could see a long dining-table, apparently designed to serve a battalion of men. And in front of the table was a gigantic fireplace containing what looked like a blazing log fire. The fireplace could surely not have been designed by men for men. It was much too large. Maybe this entire cavernous chamber had been built for giants in a time long forgotten? The logs were thicker than a man's leg. And the flames curled and danced in great orange tongues, casting more light and shadow to join the chaotic blue-white flickering of the irregularly placed television screens.

There was a figure standing far below in front of the fire, his silhouette sharply etched by the flames. His wavering shadow stretched way out in front of him to twenty feet or so, the angles of the shadow sharp and menacing.

Roy felt an arm on his sleeve and looked up at Aiken.

'Gentlemen?' said the Black Suit, now carrying both attaché cases and pointing with one of them to the stone staircase that wound down away from the platform.

Roy tried to clear his throat, but found it too dry. This poor excuse for a stair-rail was not comforting. Moving quickly past Aiken and keeping close to the damp stone wall, Roy headed down. There was a Gothic arch on the platform to their immediate right, with a black stone corridor beyond. Farrow moved quickly to join him, still grinning and with one hand on the rail, awed but unconcerned about the drop on the other side. Glancing into the dark corridor to the right and finding it empty, he too started down.

'Not good,' he tutted.

'What isn't?' Roy was not in the mood any more for Farrow's one-liners, but found himself asking anyway.

'Fella down there by the fireplace, waiting for us. All that money. And he can't afford a damp-proof course.'

The echoes of their footsteps seemed somehow amplified in this cavernous place, but as they descended Roy became aware for the first time of a tinny, distant conversation and a snatch of music that he seemed to recognise. All of it sounding thin and far away, in the ether. Farrow had noticed it too.

'Man likes his television,' he said as they continued down. 'That's what you can hear. Different channels, different movies on all those screens. Turned way down low.' Now Roy could see that his first impression had been right. These really *were* television screens, showing dozens of different movies – all apparently in black and white.

The man in front of the log fire remained unmoved, watching them approach.

Behind Roy and Farrow, the Black Suits descended in silence.

When they at last reached the stone-flagged floor, Roy became suddenly aware that his shirt was sticking to his back under his jacket. But the temperature down here seemed all wrong. It was as comfortable as a five-star hotel lounge. But with all that stone, and the water running on the walls, the place should surely feel as cold as a tomb. The Black Suits walked on past Roy and Farrow, moving towards the figure.

At last, the figure moved forward – now hurrying towards them, his footsteps ringing on the stone flags. At first the silhouette had seemed menacing and stark as it stood silently watching them descend. Now it seemed eager; almost apprehensive of their arrival.

'Mr Draegerman, I presume,' said Farrow, his humour sounding more forced than ever.

The figure suddenly emerged from the darkness of its own shadow and they saw his face for the first time.

At the sound of Farrow's voice, the figure halted.

Roy saw an expression of confusion and doubt on its face. As it turned to look from Farrow to himself, he could see that the man was perhaps his own age, maybe a little older – but he had suffered some terrible accident in the past. The left side of his face looked as if it had been burned. The skin was stretched from the corner of his eye to his mouth, the eyebrow missing. When he opened his mouth to speak, he no longer appeared menacing or spectral at all.

'Draegerman? My name is Boone. I thought that *you* were ...'

'Mr Boone is another guest,' said Aiken, moving past them and placing the briefcases on the banqueting table in front of the log fire.

'Wait a minute,' said Farrow, holding his arms wide, all the humour draining out of him. 'This is taking the mystery bit a little far, isn't it? I mean – how many more ... ?'

Everyone moved back to the banqueting table.

'Well ...' Boone coughed nervously, a hand moving to his face as if he had suddenly decided to try to hide the scar. 'There's someone else ... in the ...' He gestured weakly to an ornate, high-backed chair, facing away from them towards the fire. Roy looked over and could just make out a hand on the armrest. Farrow moved quickly to the chair, moving around to stand in front of it.

'Draegerman?' he demanded.

The unseen figure in the chair did not move.

'No ... no ...' continued Boone. 'I'm afraid not.'

A head appeared around the side of the armchair. It was a young man's face, with bright red curling hair. He raised a wine goblet in their direction and toasted them, without saying a word. From the look on his face, he was clearly very drunk. Still smiling, the face vanished back around the edge of the chair again.

'Then who the *hell* is *he*?' demanded Farrow.

'The gentleman's name is Bobby Pernell,' said Aiken.

'He doesn't ...' Boone coughed nervously. '... doesn't say very much, I'm afraid. We've been here for an hour or so, and he's never said a word to me. At first, I thought ... thought that *he* might be Mr ...'

'All right!' snapped Farrow. 'How many more people are in on this? I thought it was just *me*!'

'There are others,' said Aiken calmly. 'But they're not all here yet.' He then gestured to his black-suited colleagues, and they silently began to file away into the darkness, some of them heading back up the staircase, others simply melting into the darkness of the strange banqueting hall or cathedral, or whatever in hell it was

54

supposed to be. Roy watched them go, listened to the footsteps fading away into the darkness – and felt that sick feeling in his gut again.

'So what happens ...' He cleared his throat again, forced his words to sound calmer and stronger than he felt. 'What happens if one of us says we've suddenly changed our minds? What if someone says they're not interested in the offer any more?'

'You mean you've changed your mind, Mr Jensen?' asked Aiken.

'No, I'm just asking.'

'Well, if you wish to leave, there's nothing to stop you doing so. I'll just call one of my men back and you'll be escorted from the premises. No harm done.'

'How much did he offer you?' Farrow asked Roy, moving to the banqueting table and eyeing the various liquor bottles on display. He looked back, and when Aiken nodded assent, quickly scooped up a crystal decanter, unstopped it and sniffed. Giving a grimace of pleasure, he poured himself a large measure of brandy.

'The same as you, I expect,' replied Roy non-committally.

'And you?' asked Farrow, turning to the man with the scar.

Boone fidgeted nervously. 'Well, I'd rather not ... that is, until Mr Draegerman ...'

'I'm willing to bet it's the same for us all. What's the old bastard up to, Aiken?'

'Help yourself to refreshment,' said Aiken, ignoring the question. 'I promise you won't have long to wait for the others. Once they're here, all assembled, Mr Draegerman will talk to you all about his proposal.'

From the darkness came a distant scream.

Startled, they turned to look anxiously around in the gloom.

Aiken, unmoved, was smiling. 'One of the movies on the television screens. That's all. Most of the movies you'll see on the screens were made by Mr Draegerman himself. The others are films which have a special meaning to him. Please ... feel free to look around. Maybe watch a movie – have something to eat and drink.'

Roy scanned the hall and its glittering screens, then moved to the table and poured himself what seemed to be a whisky. He turned to Boone, holding up the bottle.

'Yes ... yes please.' Boone moved nervously to join him.

'So how long is *long*?' asked Farrow. 'I mean how long before ... ?'

Farrow's words faded when he looked up. Roy and Boone turned back in Aiken's direction.

Aiken had vanished into the darkness.

Somewhere on one of the television screens there was a distant gun battle taking place.

Farrow made an impatient sound, lifted his glass and drank again.

'Well, at least he didn't take the briefcases with the money,' he said, toasting Roy and still smiling.

Roy poured Boone a drink.

Their eyes were on the four cases on the banqueting table.

How many more would be there before Draegerman turned up?

NINE

When the Black Suit opened the back door of the black sedan for Jessica, she was slightly taken aback by the sight of the other woman already in there.

'You didn't say I should expect guests,' said the woman inside. 'But then again, you don't say much anyway.' The woman shifted over to her side a little more – a useless but polite gesture given the size of the seats in the back of the car. 'Please,' she said by way of invitation, and Jessica climbed in.

As the door closed and the sedan slid smoothly away, Jessica realised that she knew this woman from somewhere, and wondered whether it was all part of the gimmick; all part of the theatrical invite to attend Draegerman's Rock and interview the great man himself. Her professional cool had been severely shaken by the visit of the Black Suits and their offer, more so than she cared to admit to herself. This was, after all, a one-in-a-million chance for her. Struggling to regain her cool and professional exterior, Jessica examined the woman next to her. She was straightening her dress and looking across as if expecting an introduction from their escorts. She looked to be in her mid-fifties, but had obviously worked hard to retain her figure. Her clothes were too young for her, as if someone has told her that it was chic to wear mid-sixties gear again. What Jessica had assumed to be a blonde curled wig now looked up close as if it was real after all. She decided to break the silence.

'I'm sorry, my name's Jessica Morell.'

'Don't be sorry. It's a nice name.'

There was a pause then. The woman was still looking at Jessica and smiling, as if she *must* recognise her eventually.

'And you are . . . ?'

This surely must be a mistake, some sort of social gaffe she had committed, and of which she was unaware. Why else should the woman turn away like that to look out of the window? In the reflection of the window, Jessica could see that the woman's face seemed to have turned to stone. But now, as she turned back to her again, the expression had changed magically. The smile seemed unforced, but had replaced the stony expression seamlessly in a single turn of the head.

'I'm Gloria Pernell.'

The name. Where the hell had Jessica heard that name before? There was an association with Draegerman there somehow, she knew it. But for the life of her she couldn't remember just what it was . . .

And then she had it.

'Of course, Gloria Pernell. I'm sorry . . .'

'There you go again. Don't be sorry.'

'You used to make movies for Mr Draegerman.'

'I made seven altogether. But I didn't make them *for* him. Not in the strictest sense.'

'Oh, you collaborated? I seem to remember that you were one of his . . .' Jessica bit her tongue on the word "starlets". '. . . leading actresses. But I didn't know you'd written anything for . . .'

'Did you ever read any of the scripts for those things?'

'No. Can't say I did, I'm afraid.'

Gloria lit a cigarette, offering one to Jessica. Jessica declined.

'You're not a film fan,' said Gloria at last, a statement more than a question.

'I guess I am. But – no disrespect – I just never got into that kind of film when I was a kid.'

'What, you mean horror movies?'

'As I said, no disrespect intended. Some of those old films are very well regarded.'

'They're becoming fashionable again. Big cult hits, some of them. Not so much for the scripts, let's face it, but for the way they were filmed, the style. *Gothique-noir* is what the "cineastes" call them. I didn't "collaborate", but some of the scripts were pretty bad, so I changed some of the dialogue. Not so much the ones that Jack wrote himself. The others that he farmed out to other writers were churned out pretty quickly. Sometimes the dialogue and the characterisation were pretty . . . am I boring you?'

Jessica had turned and was looking out of the window. Night was falling on the city, creeping in down the alleyways that flashed by as they drove. Already, they seemed to be on the other side of the city, driving through streets that Jessica found unfamiliar. Something seemed to move in one of the alleys, as if something had leaped from a third storey window into the alley below, catching Jessica's eye.

'No,' she said, looking back. 'I just thought I saw something strange out there. Please, carry on. You were saying?'

Gloria drew on her cigarette. 'Well, the characterisations were – let's say, a little on the "shallow" side. Jack allowed me to develop some of my roles, allowed me to rework some of the tin-ear dialogue . . .'

And now Gloria's voice was drifting away from Jessica. She continued to look at her face, instinctively nodding when Gloria made a point, but not listening to anything else she was saying. She needed a little time to think, a little time to put everything together and work out just what she was going to say when they finally arrived at The Rock and she was ushered into the "presence". Quite what a faded starlet was doing here too was another matter, something she would no doubt get around to discovering eventually. Obviously anything relating to Draegerman was going to be a source of interest, but right now she had to work on her first approach, on her opening lines. There had been no chance to prepare. Her request to return to the offices and at least dig out the file that had been prepared on the great man had been denied. The request had been specific. Come now. Straight away. Or don't come at all. Professionally, all she had was a dictating machine, three tapes and a pen and paper in her personal bag to support her. She hoped to God that she could borrow the other materials she required when they finally got around to the interview.

She had no idea how much time had passed when she suddenly became aware that Gloria Pernell seemed to be waiting for an answer to something. She tried to cover up for her blank-out.

'I saw you in one once,' she said quickly. 'What was it . . . swamp something, I think.'

'*Swamp Water Woman,*' replied Gloria with a blank face. She lit another cigarette. 'Yeah, that was me. A cult favourite, I'm told. Draegerman's sexiest monster. Can you imagine? In the movie I'm bumped off by my lover, dumped in the swamps – and come back "regenerated by the Dark Side of Mother Nature" into a cross between a woman, a snake and the bloody Gorgon. Try being sexy in *that* make-up!'

'And something else, I think,' said Jessica, still trying to make up for her lapses in attention. 'About a ship that gets wrecked on an island, and these bizarre . . .'

'*Cape Sinistre.* They say it's one of Jack's best. My best-ever death scene in that shipwreck.' Gloria drew on her cigarette and looked back at Jessica. She seemed to melt a little then. 'Look, I'm sorry. I don't think we're getting off to the best start here. I'm going through my fantasy film convention routine, and I don't know who you are. These days it seems as if people are only interested in my old "cult" movies, not what I'm doing now. It's no excuse for bad manners. Please forgive me.'

'Nothing to forgive.'

'Am I being too personal if I ask whether you're on your way to The Rock for business or pleasure?'

'Business. I work for *The Independent Daily*. Mr Draegerman wants me to interview him.'

Gloria made an approving noise. 'You're honoured. I'm sure I don't know what's happening to Jack after all this time. Seems he's tired of being one of the most famous hermits in the world.'

'And you?'

'I think – I suppose I *hope* – that he wants to get back into the movie business again, after all these years. Our friends up front there were sent to collect me.' Gloria strained forward, addressing her next remarks to the Black Suits.

'He must be getting bored, eh, boys?'

The Black Suits did not respond.

'But still tight with his money, I see. Getting the girls to share a taxi.' She laughed, but the Black Suits still did not respond.

'What's the film?'

'No idea. No details. Just come as you are. Hence this ridiculous get-up.' Gloria indicated her early-sixties clothes with a dismissive wave of the hand. 'Didn't have a chance to get out of wardrobe. Hope you don't think I look like this all the time.'

'It's . . .' began Jessica, embarrassed by her first assumptions about this woman and now struggling to find a description.

'Fab? No – it's *blah*! Mutton dressed as lamb, my dear.'

Something seemed to catch Gloria's eye through Jessica's window. Jessica turned to look. The street down which the sedan was travelling looked somehow more than just decrepit; it looked like something out of a war zone. Most of the windows were boarded over or broken. It seemed impossible to find a blank wall; every inch of brickwork appeared to be covered in obscene, multi-coloured graffiti. Every one of the streetlights was broken, and there were no lights in the few windows that weren't boarded up. Gloria gave a low whistle.

'Are you boys giving us the scenic route, or what? Surely there's a more direct way to get to The Rock?'

She was right, and Jessica knew it. Just why the hell were they taking this route? If the sedan had stuck to the motorway and taken the third exit past the city centre, the side route would have brought them to The Rock without having to approach it through one of the most rundown and potentially dangerous parts of the city. As the sedan glided down these streets, making apparently meaningless twists and turns, Jessica began to feel uneasy. Why did it seem that the further they travelled and the nearer they came to Draegerman's Rock, the more decayed and threatening the streets became? And why the hell wasn't there one single soul out there as the darkness settled? Surely someone must need to go to the store? Come to think of it, why the hell couldn't she see any sign of a convenience store, or any *other* kind of take-away restaurant or garage or bar? Surely there must be *something* down here to suggest that people lived and worked on these streets? Jessica had never been in this part of the city before, she realised. Maybe there was something in her uneasy observations for a story? Suddenly, she became aware that she was drumming her fingers on the armrest: a sure sign that her professional cool and resolve were slipping. Angry with herself, she clenched her hand – and smiled at Gloria.

'Didn't you have a son?' she asked, looking for something to say that would take her mind off these dilapidated streets. 'In the movie business as well, I mean.'

'*Used* to have a son,' replied Gloria.

Jessica searched for any sign of bitterness, but Gloria's professional blank face told her nothing.

'He made a few films, but then he . . . what's the word? In my day, the phrase was "dropped out". I'm not sure what the right phrase is now. But that's what he did. He made his decisions, quit the business, went his own way. I don't like to talk about him any more.'

Jessica nearly said: 'I'm sorry,' but remembered that she had already been told twice not to be. Instead, she nodded and turned her attention to the three Black Suits sitting up front. 'I don't suppose you're able to tell me . . .' she began.

And then something hit the car.

Both Gloria and Jessica recoiled in their seats as something crashed on the roof, rolled off and bounced away, clattering into the darkness

'Shit,' said one of the Black Suits. It was somehow not an exclamation of surprise. The man's 'cool' was still completely in evidence, as if this sudden impact was to be expected.

'What was it?' asked the driver, also ridiculously calm.

'A litter bin,' replied the third. 'Looks like it was torn off a street light.'

There was no sign of anyone on the streets, no sign of their attacker.

'Just what the *hell* is going on . . . ?' began Gloria again, her words stabbing colder than an icepick.

'Sorry, ladies,' said the first Black Suit. 'We're only minutes away from The Rock. You can't see it from here because the area's so built up, but in just a few moments we'll be . . .'

'. . . in big trouble,' finished the driver, slamming on the brakes.

Jessica clutched at the head-rest in front of her as the car screeched to a halt. She looked back through the tinted windows and saw the litter bin still rolling in the middle of an empty street. Then she turned to look ahead, and saw what the driver was talking about.

Her alarm began to turn into something rapidly approaching outright fear when she saw that the road ahead was suddenly blocked by a barricade of debris – planks, old pushchairs, bins and bent fencing. Fires had been lit in oil drums, since even the electricity for street lamps seemed to have failed down here.

'Is this *real?*' asked Gloria.

Even as she spoke, figures began to emerge from the smoke and

61

the darkness beyond the barrier. Ragged silhouettes, calmly picking their way through the tangle of urban refuse. Their very calm approach suggested an unspeakably horrible confidence in their intent. As if by magic, figures were now also appearing on the sidewalk on either side of the car; dark shapes emerging from doors that had been boarded over, climbing through broken window frames, all with that same ugly confidence.

'There are people behind us,' said Jessica, trying to keep calm. 'Coming down the street.' As she watched, one of them took a swing at the rolling litter bin with what seemed to be a baseball bat. Most of the figures approaching the car were carrying something – lengths of rusted pipe, chains, guttering. Could she even see one youth with a machete?

The deserted, blighted streets had suddenly become a truly hellish urban jungle.

'For God's sake, *do* something!' screamed Gloria, and Jessica twisted around to see that a face had suddenly squashed itself up against the car window next to her. She recoiled in alarm as the face began to lick the window glass in an obscene gesture, grinning manically.

'Gonna *rape* youuuu . . .' said the shaven-headed face.

Both women screamed as something impacted on the windscreen, cobwebbing the glass in a six-inch fracture. The black-suited driver, still impossibly impassive, said: 'Shit. That was a bullet.'

'For God's SAKE!' yelled Jessica.

'Reinforced glass,' said the Black Suit sitting next to him, half turning to look at them. 'No problem.'

'Seat-belts please, ladies,' said the driver.

'What . . . ?' goggled Gloria.

'Could you make sure your seat-belts are fastened.' The Black Suit sounded as straightforward and polite as some airline steward doing the rounds of the jet before take-off. Automatically, both women scrabbled at the clasps, just as the approaching crowd outside made a communal whooping noise and rushed the car. The leering face next to Gloria was trying to jump up on the roof of the car now, the flies of his ragged trousers unbuttoned.

And then the driver put his foot down hard on the accelerator.

The sedan roared straight ahead, directly towards the man-made barrier in the middle of the littered street, and the shapes that were heading their way from it.

Jessica and Gloria both clutched the seats in front of them, too shocked to protest or question or say anything other than a joint . . .

'OH . . . MY . . . GOD!'

. . . as the sedan crashed straight into the tangled barrier ahead with a screeching roar, scattering debris everywhere. Tyres shrieked as torn mattresses, bent scaffolding poles and wrecked furniture flew past the car windows on all sides. Something screeched across the roof, something that must surely gouge a hole right through the metalwork to find them. Up front, the driver twisted at the wheel and gunned the engine.

Impossibly, the sedan exploded through to the other side. A cloud of feathers filled the windscreen – a bizarre and surreal sight – and then was gone. Jessica thought that she saw the shape of a man go whirling away over the roof, but could not bring herself to look back. Even above the sounds of the shrieking tyres and the grinding crash of metal and broken wood, the screams of rage and frustration of the mob behind were still horrifyingly close.

The car swerved and straightened – and now the sedan was in a clear street.

Directly ahead at the end of the street was a driveway leading to a concrete structure that looked like some kind of gate, the stonework covered in graffiti. From behind came the sound of gunfire, making Jessica and Gloria shrink down in their seats, not daring to look back even if there *was* reinforced glass in the rear window.

The sedan seemed miraculously undamaged. The driver put his foot to the floor and the vehicle hurtled down the street towards the strange concrete gateway as it began to open. Beyond the opening, there seemed to be nothing but a black void. In panic, but still unable to speak, Jessica had the horrifying thought that the Black Suit driver was going to take the car straight over the edge of some precipice ahead. Why couldn't she *see* anything beyond that strange gateway?

'This can't be happening to me,' said Gloria breathlessly. 'Things like this don't happen. I know there've been riots, that things on the streets are bad, but this just doesn't *happen* . . . Oh, GOD!!!'

An unmistakably armed man in a uniform had suddenly appeared in the gateway, already lining the sights of his automatic weapon on the sedan.

The driver kept his foot down, heading straight for him.

Gloria covered her eyes. Jessica could only watch open-mouthed in horror as the guard suddenly lowered his weapon and gave a hugely exaggerated nod of the head which indicated that he was somehow expecting this car. Suddenly he ducked from sight behind one of the gate walls.

Something made that familiar *spang!* sound on the rear windscreen, just as the sedan roared through the stone arch and into the darkness. Jessica wanted to yell, but somehow her voice had gone. Involuntarily, she was looking back through the cobwebbed rear window as the guard suddenly stepped into the gateway entrance behind them again, and opened fire with his automatic weapon on whoever or whatever had been following them. Quickly, he was joined by another guard . . . and then another . . . all levelling their weapons back into the darkness.

And despite the fear, despite the racing heartbeat and the shaking of her hands, all Jessica could think was: *'This is going to make one HELL of a story!'*

She turned to face the front, no longer able to tell what was happening back there, but feeling utterly exhilarated. That exhilaration swelled to awe and amazement when she saw at last where they were headed. The gateway had been an entrance – one of four at ground level – to Draegerman's Rock.

They were on a narrow driveway, like a miniature bridge, heading out across empty space over the 'moat' that surrounded the gigantic edifice ahead. This was one of four such Walkways connecting Draegerman's Rock to the surrounding neighbourhood, and Jessica was uncomfortably aware of the yawning chasm beneath them as the sedan raced ahead. And although Jessica had studied this building, had flown over it, had researched its construction, had indeed *watched* parts of the construction on television when she was a girl, nothing could have prepared her for the sight of this massive, dark palace filling her line of vision, rearing impossibly high into the night sky.

From behind, she could hear the sounds of gunfire again. Didn't the police have *any* jurisdiction in the decayed slums surrounding Draegerman's Rock?

'Oh my God . . .' said Gloria, in a quiet voice filled with something like dread.

When Jessica turned back, she could see that some kind of gigantic door was opening in the wall of The Rock, at the end of the driveway. The sheer face of the cold grey, blank wall was sliding up into darkness, revealing a black maw beyond. Despite the massive construction of this fortress door, there was somehow no sound. Both women had the same thought as the sedan roared towards the black aperture. The sight of the opening door, and the silence, reminded them both of some giant ogre's mouth – slowly opening, ready to swallow them.

Jessica fought to regain her composure, focused her attention on the Black Suit driver. He remained as imperturbable as ever as the car sped on. Surely he must know what he was doing? Surely he wasn't about to drive straight into some yawning chasm? Once more, she found herself clenching the upholstered arm of the seat as the gaping blackness rushed to meet them.

'Isn't life fun?' said Gloria.

In the next instant, the sedan was swallowed by the darkness and the sounds of distant gunfire were instantly snuffed out.

TEN

Sara DePaolo was at her wit's end.

Susan had not showed up for lunch with the kids as planned. After a while, Sara had telephoned Susan's apartment, just to check and make sure that something hadn't happened to prevent Susan from turning up as usual. Punctuality was always one of her personal 'musts'. Even if there was a possibility that she might be ten minutes late for an appointment with her mother, she always telephoned to let her know.

There was no answer.

Trying to control her nervousness, trying not to overreact, Sara had continued serving up lunch for the kids. They seemed unperturbed that their mother hadn't shown up. Why should they be bothered, when it was more important to discuss the chances of their school football team kicking the hell out of a rival school team that afternoon? Today there was nothing else on their minds but a football match to cheer on, a trophy to be won, and no boring classes to attend.

But Sara's uneasiness continued to grow. She tried telephoning again three times. Still no response. Telling herself that she was just a fussy, over-protective mother hen, she prepared the kids, made sure they were wrapped up warm for an afternoon to be spent on the sideline cheering their team, and bustled them off to school again.

By the time she was waving them goodbye at the school gate, Sara was feeling sick to her stomach with worry. She had left Susan finishing the ironing. What if the fuse had blown in the iron and she had been electrocuted or something? She might be lying there now, on the kitchen floor calling her name. The image in her mind was too disturbing; she could not wait for the local bus to take her to Susan's apartment block. Hailing a taxi, she was there in ten minutes flat.

And there was no answer when Sara rang the front door bell. She tried again, trying to look through the fluted glass panes at the side of the door to see if there was any movement. When there was none, she took the spare key out of her purse to let herself in. Something was wrong. No matter how much she twisted the key, the door would not open. She took it out and tried again. Then, on instinct, she simply pushed the door.

It swung open.

The door had not even been locked in the first place. That first turn of her key had locked it.

Now Sara was really worried. Susan always locked the door when she went out, as a matter of course. And if the door was unlocked now, then it meant she was at home. And if she was still at home, why on earth hadn't she answered the telephone . . .?

There was a chair in the middle of the living-room carpet, knocked over on to its back as if there had been a struggle.

'*Susan!*'

Sara rushed to the kitchen where she had last seen Susan doing the ironing. The ironing board was still standing, the iron left unplugged on the kitchen bench to cool. But no sign of Susan.

Sara checked every other room. But clearly, Susan was not in the apartment.

A note? Had she left a note for her mother somewhere?

Again, Sara searched the apartment. Again, she found nothing. There was only one other thing she could do. Sara rushed to the telephone, found the address book and the number she wanted. Her fingers would not stop trembling as she dialled.

'Fanright Industries? I'd like to speak to Den Lucas please. *Lucas!* Den Lucas. He's working shiftwork there today, on the forklift. What . . .? I don't care if it's not convenient to get to the shop floor, this is an emergency!'

Is it an emergency, Sara? Or are you just being a stupid, over-protective cow? Are you going to make yourself look a proper fool when the door opens now and Susan calmly walks in with a shopping bag in her hand?

'An emergency, yes. A family emergency. Yes. Thank you.'

It took ten minutes before another voice came on the line. The familiarity of that voice served marginally to take the edge off the creeping sickness of horror inside.

'Den Lucas here. Who's speaking?'

He sounded on edge, as if using the telephone like this was a major breach of company rules and regulations which might just get him fired.

'Den! It's me, Sara. Now, nothing bad's happened, so don't get upset. It's just that . . . just that . . . oh, I feel such a fool.'

'Okay, take it easy. Just tell me what's wrong.'

'Susan was due to meet me and the kids at my place, for lunch as usual. And she didn't show. She didn't answer the telephone so I came back to your place. The door wasn't locked, and she's not here and . . .'

'Where are the kids?'

'I've taken them back to school. They're okay . . .'

'All right. I'll be straight over.'

'I'm sorry to ring you at work, Den. It's just that it's not like Susan to . . .'

'I know. That's okay. Really. Just stay there, and I'll be straight over.'

As Sara was hanging up the telephone, her feelings still balanced between sick concern and the fear that she was overreacting, she saw the plastic wallet sticking out from under the sofa.

She walked over to it, pushed the sofa gently aside, stooped and picked it up. There was a photograph inside: a man in his late twenties, perhaps. Black hair. Blank face, big eyes. Shirt and dark tie. Beneath the photograph, the words: *Fenriss, Andrew: Security Unit 'C': Draegerman Enterprises*.

Sara looked around the flat again, as if the owner of this identification wallet might be hiding in one of the cupboards, ready to spring out. Then she reached for the telephone, ready to dial the police.

'No,' she said, withdrawing her hand, and weighing the wallet in the other. 'I'll wait for Den.' She looked at the face in the photograph.

It looked back at her with that blank expression, betraying nothing.

Sara screwed it up in her hand.

'I'll wait for Den . . .'

ELEVEN

A surging feeling of nausea brought Susan DePaolo up from the dank and troubled depths of her sleep. In that one moment when the bile rose within, it was as if she was fifteen years old again, had been out 'on the town' with girlfriends and had danced until closing time at the local nightclub. With four or five too many Bacardi and Cokes inside, she had staggered home singing with her friends, stumbled through the front door and gone straight to bed. As always, that drink-induced slumber had lasted until the early hours of the morning, when the dreaded 'whirling pit' which always caught up with her had forced her to the surface again. First, the feeling that the bed was spinning around, and then the instinctive knowledge that she must get out of bed at once and stagger to the bathroom before the pit exploded and the excess drink was forced out.

In a blur, Susan pulled herself to the edge of the bed, groping at the counterpane.

Instantly, it seemed, the familiar whirling pit from her teenage years dissipated and vanished. She was dizzy now, but there was no fear of being forced to vomit.

The floor felt cold beneath her feet.

This was not the familiar deep pile of her bedroom carpet.

And she was not fifteen years old, home in bed after a night out with the girls.

She rubbed a hand over her face and looked again. She was in a strange room, well furnished with a dressing table she had never seen in her life before. Two chairs, ridiculously ornate to be dressing-table chairs. A wardrobe, perhaps made from teak with handles that looked like gargoyle door-knockers. A full-length mirror, which reflected her bewildered figure sitting on the edge of a large, four-poster double bed with drapes. There was no carpet, and when she looked down she could see that the floor was made of flagged stone. Strangely, the walls seem comprised of rough stone blocks, almost like the walls of a castle dungeon. This didn't make sense.

She must surely still be dreaming. She rubbed her eyes again, but when she looked once more, the strange bedroom was just as she had previously seen it.

Then her memory returned.

The men in black suits, who had forced their way into the apartment.

Had someone used *chloroform* on her?

'Oh my God. The kids!'

Susan hurled herself at the only door in the room, an intricately carved wooden door with strangely interlocked forms cavorting and dancing and leering at each other. The doorknob was the same design as the wardrobe door handles, a three-pronged downward-curving claw. Susan twisted and tugged at the handle, but the door remained resolutely locked.

'Let me out of here, you bastards! *Let me out!*'

She pulled her leg back to kick the bizarre door, but remembered that she was not wearing shoes. Instead, she whirled around, looking for something – anything – she could use on the door handle. She would batter the bloody thing down if necessary. But there appeared to be nothing in the room she could use. She looked at the full-length mirror, considered smashing it and pulling off one of the wooden supports. But the wood seemed too flimsy. She flung open the wardrobe. It was full of women's clothes, none of them hers. Dresses, smocks, satin off-the-shoulder numbers. She dragged them out one by one, hurling them on the floor in her search for some kind of weapon.

Nothing.

'You *bastards*! What have you done with my kids?' The children had been taken to school by Sara, would have been taken home for lunch and then returned to school again. The chances that the Black Suits had taken them also seemed remote, but it was Susan's overriding concern, so much so that it swamped any fears for her personal safety. She ran back to the door, smashing the flat of her hands against the woodwork. The bloody thing must be inches thick. It seemed as if it was swallowing the impact of her blows, which made hardly any sound at all.

No one beyond the door seemed to be listening or to care even if they could hear her.

The window!

Susan whirled again, scanning the room.

The room had no windows, nothing through which she could smash the full-length mirror, screaming down to the street below that a bunch of black-suited bastards had forced their way into her home and kidnapped her.

Fear swamped her then.

She swallowed hard, refused to allow it to make her give in. And with that resolve came an overwhelming wave of anger.

In a fit of powerless fury, Susan set about smashing everything that was breakable in her prison cell of a bedroom.

TWELVE

The sedan hurtled into the gaping black throat that had opened up in the side of The Rock and was instantly engulfed in darkness. The only light emanated from the driver's dashboard.

Both women passengers had the same sickening feeling in the pit of their stomachs; as if they were in an elevator and it had started to drop into the shaft, out of control. Were they falling into some black and fathomless pit? Had the sedan driven off the edge of the Walkway? It was impossible to tell their direction in this Stygian darkness, but their stomachs were trying to convince them that it was *down*.

'How the hell can you guys *see?*' Gloria broke the deeply unsettling silence within the car, a quaver in her voice. Jessica realised that she had broken a fingernail clutching the armrest.

'Don't worry,' said the driver, still in his imperturbable and matter-of-fact voice. 'You're quite safe. When the exterior door closes, the lights will come on. We're in a narrow, channelled road here. We can't drive off it.'

'So why the hell can't we have *lights?*' demanded Gloria. 'You mean Jack is cutting corners on the electricity bill?'

'You saw what happened back there,' said the Black Suit sitting next to the driver. 'We've had trouble with snipers in the past, taking pot-shots at The Rock from some of the abandoned buildings on the edge of the Moat. If there are visible lights inside when the door goes up, it serves as a focus. Makes for easy targets.'

And as soon as the Black Suit had finished talking there was a shuddering, grating sound from behind as the massive sliding door on to the driveway finally closed. Now that they were inside, they could hear the mechanisms. In that instant, as predicted, the lights came on.

They were travelling down a floodlit tunnel, apparently built of black stone. There was water running down the walls and the orange floodlights in the ceiling and set high on the gleaming walls gave the impression of some labyrinthine passageway under a river. Before either passenger could really take it in, the tunnel had ended and the sedan

71

slid, swerving, into a vast and cavernous space. The black stone ceiling was at least two hundred feet above their heads, the walls constructed from the same black stone. The orange floodlights in here seemed to be arranged in a bizarre and random manner, casting gigantic shadows that only served to accentuate the unnecessary size of what they could now make out to be some sort of surreal garage. The sedan was easing into a parking bay. There were twelve such bays. Quickly, Jessica counted seven other black sedans, parked side by side in the bays. The other spaces were empty.

'*This* is a car park?' asked Gloria. 'You could park the *Queen Mary* in here.'

The sedan slid to a smooth halt in the bay and the three Black Suits climbed out of the front, opening the back doors for both passengers. Jessica had supposed, given the look of this cavernous, almost mediaeval setting, that the air would be cold and stale. On the contrary, the air was fresh and the temperature comfortable. Without speaking, one of the Black Suits walked off into the darkness. They watched him go, Gloria suddenly seeming enraged at his silent departure.

'Right,' she said, taking a deep breath.

Jessica watched her fellow passenger close her eyes as if gathering her thoughts, and realised that she was really reasserting the confidence within after their ordeal back there on the streets.

'Right! I have just been shot at back there, gentlemen. *Shot at!* The car driving me here was used as a battering ram, and a little shit back there threatened to rape me. So let me tell *you*, my silent black-suited friends. Whatever Jack has in mind had *better be fucking GOOD!*' Gloria finished by dusting imaginary fluff from her skirt, now in control.

'Snap,' said Jessica, taking strength from Gloria's demeanour.

The Black Suits remained unmoved.

'I'm deeply sorry for the inconvenience,' said the driver, in an unconvincing monotone. 'But now that we've arrived, I've been asked to escort Miss Pernell to the Screening Room. My name is Payne. My colleague Mr Lamb has been asked to escort Miss Morell to the Banqueting Hall.'

'So now we get the introductions,' said Gloria sarcastically. 'How come you wouldn't give me a name before?'

'Mr Draegerman's instructions were very specific, Miss Pernell. We follow them to the letter.'

'And what the hell is the Screening Room?' asked Gloria. 'I suppose I'll get to see the man *himself* eventually?'

'Yes, of course,' replied Lamb. 'I can tell you that there are other guests here waiting in the Banqueting Hall. Mr Draegerman will arrive after Miss Pernell has seen the movie in the Screening Room, when she'll be brought to join everyone else.'

'Shot at, threatened with rape, used as a battering ram – and now

I'm being taken to the movies. At least it's been an eventful evening. Lead on, Mr Lamb.'

'Other guests?' queried Jessica.

'That's all I can say at present,' said Payne, and he gestured towards a ramp leading up from the bay to a steel door, overhung by another orange strip-light.

'And we go this way,' he said, pointing to what looked like elevator doors on the other side of the bay.

Gloria shrugged at Jessica. 'Heigh-ho. See you later, newspaper lady.'

Jessica allowed herself to be led away up the ramp.

'Enjoy the film. Whatever it is.'

'Do you think I should ask for popcorn?'

The exchange between the two women failed to conceal the underlying tension that they were both feeling.

'This way, please,' said Lamb, and Gloria followed him across the bay to the elevator, the sounds of her high-heeled shoes echoing up into the gigantic reaches of the chamber. The sound only served to accentuate her anxiety, as if something crouching up there in the rafted girders of the ceiling might hear and swoop down to snatch her away.

Just what the hell are you doing here, Pernell? she asked herself.

The elevator itself seemed incongruous in this setting; as if a department store elevator had been installed in a mediaeval castle. The doors were already open.

Gloria looked back – but Jessica and her escort were gone.

Shrugging, Gloria stepped inside the elevator, Lamb following to position himself beside a panel in the elevator wall. There were no numbers on display above the door. How the hell did he know where to get off?

'Level nineteen,' said Lamb, and Gloria turned to see that her escort was speaking into a handset radio. As he placed it back in his inside pocket, the doors slid closed. Gloria felt a nervous flutter in her stomach as the elevator began to rise. She watched Lamb as they ascended. His face remained expressionless. She began to whistle, drumming her fingers on the handrail.

'How much longer before ... ?'

And then the doors slid open.

The sight ahead was equally incongruous: a black stone corridor, again with water glistening on the walls, and again with the only light being provided by orange lanterns set high up near the ceiling, casting long and angular shadows. It was as if the doors had opened on to the dungeon corridor of a twelfth-century castle.

'This is bloody ridiculous,' said Gloria, following close behind Lamb as he moved ahead.

'It's to Mr Draegerman's taste,' replied Lamb in his usual taciturn manner.

There was a door set in the left-hand wall; indeterminate wood almost the same colour as the surrounding stone. Gloria would have walked past without noticing it if it had not been for Lamb. The wood seemed to have been hand-carved into a twisting myriad of shapes, some of them human – but there was something about the configurations, something about what these figures were doing to each other, which made Gloria even more uneasy. But before she could begin to look closer and unravel the intricate design, work out just *why* it was so disturbing, Lamb swung the door wide into the room beyond. Remarkably, the room was brightly lit – and the sudden glare of it made Gloria wince.

'The Screening Room,' said Lamb, and held the door for her.

The Screening Room appeared to be, in fact, a cinema. Just like one of the old-style movie houses that Gloria remembered from her youth, albeit on a miniature scale. There were perhaps twelve rows, twenty seats in each, 1950s style, all facing down a gentle slope in the floor to a cinema screen flanked by plush, red velvet ceiling-to-floor curtains. The floor was carpeted; deep red pile. At the back, a projection booth, with projectionist's slit looking out over the seats.

'Any seat in the house, I take it?' asked Gloria.

Lamb assented with an open-handed gesture and turned from her towards the projection booth.

'So do I get any clues about what I'm going to watch?' She made her way to the mid-section, choosing a seat.

'Mr Draegerman wants you to have another look at a movie you made for him,' said Lamb from the small flight of stairs leading to the booth. In the next moment, he had vanished inside. Gloria shrugged again, facing front and sitting down.

'Do I get to sit through fifty minutes of advertisements and trailers first?'

There was no answer from behind. Instead, the lights began to dim.

'I hope this cinema has a ladies' room, Mr Lamb. That was a long drive.'

From behind, the familiar whirring of an outdated movie projector.

Now the Screening Room was in complete darkness apart from the light on the cinema screen. A sequence of scrawling numbers, '... 4 ... 3 ... 2 ... 1 ...', and then the familiar logo of Jack Draegerman's distribution company and the trumpet fanfare that always accompanied it.

Gloria settled down to watch as the main title credits appeared in black and white on the screen.

THIRTEEN

Confused and disorientated, Jessica followed her escort through the stone archway.

The Black Suit, Payne, led her down corridors and tunnels that seemed to be part of some mediaeval film set; twisting and winding, sometimes apparently changing direction for no reason at all. And always the same black stone walls and ceilings, the gleaming wetness on the stone. There were no archways, doors, or openings as they walked. At times, she felt sure that they were heading downhill, at other times ascending. Occasionally, she was convinced that the corridor had turned in the opposite direction from which they had just come. And Payne, like his companion, had been equally terse and monosyllabic in response to her queries or attempts to lighten the tone. Despite everything, despite this once-and-for-all chance to interview the great Jack Draegerman, the terrible feeling of anxiety that had been growing inside Jessica since their encounter with the street gang remained lodged inside her; a constant apprehension that felt physically real, under her breastbone.

Now that sense of dislocation was further compounded as they turned another corner and stepped through an ornate stone arch.

They had emerged into a gigantic chamber, with vast swooping arches and gigantic columns of stone that stretched hundreds of feet into the air and seemed to be holding the fantastically complicated structure in place. She had seen something like this before, in her youth – but could not recall its dark grandeur. Some childhood image of the Great Feasting Hall in Valhalla, perhaps?

'The Banqueting Hall,' said Payne, walking calmly ahead.

Jessica followed him across the vast, flagged floor.

'All those screens set into the walls . . . all over the place . . . they're showing . . .'

'Some are showing Mr Draegerman's movies,' replied Payne without turning around. 'Others are showing movies from other studios – Mr Draegerman's favourites.'

At last, as they came round a massive and ornate buttress serving no apparent architectural purpose, Jessica saw the long banqueting table set before the open log fire. There were three figures standing there, silhouetted against the leaping yellow flames; two standing and one sitting on the edge of the table, sipping from a goblet. No, there were four – she saw at last the figure sitting in the high-backed chair. Could one of these men be Draegerman?

'Your fellow Guests,' announced Payne as they neared the table.

The silhouettes looked up, but the indistinct figure in the chair remained unmoved. Surely this seated figure *was* Draegerman?

As they finally drew level, Jessica could see their faces. If the young man with the shoulder-length hair and the denim jeans was obviously sharing Jessica's own anxieties, by the look on his face, then the man standing next to him looked to be on the verge of hysteria. What she had at first taken to be a shadow on the man's face in the half-light was obviously some awful scar. The man sitting on the edge of the banqueting table with the goblet had a smile that was perhaps too easy. His eyes did not share the friendliness that his smile was trying to convey. Already, he was weighing her up from a sexual angle; an expression with which she was very familiar from the newspaper office.

'Mr Draegerman?' Jessica addressed her query to the shadowy form in the chair.

'Not unless he's had a lobotomy,' said Farrow, draining the last of the wine from his goblet.

'So where *is* he?' Boone's question was addressed to Payne, his hand straying to his face as if Jessica's first sight of it was deeply embarrassing to him. 'How long has this to go on? I've been here for an awfully long . . .'

'Mr Draegerman will be here shortly,' said Payne.

'Yeah, we keep hearing that,' said Farrow, swinging from the table. 'But *when*?'

Payne did not reply. Instead, he turned and began to walk back the way he had brought Jessica.

'Look!' snapped Roy, stepping forward. 'We were told that if any one of us wanted out, we just had to say so. Isn't that right?'

Payne stopped and turned back. 'That was our instruction from Mr Draegerman.'

'Well, that's it. I've had enough. I'm not sure any of this mystery crap is going to be worth fifty thousand now and two hundred thousand later.'

'Are you crazy?' Farrow laughed, the sound of his laughter echoing and bouncing back from the lofted arches above them. 'Listen, I don't care what the hell he wants me to do. For two hundred and fifty thousand I can't think of *anything* I wouldn't do.'

'Wait a minute,' said Jessica. 'What's going on here? You mean you've all been offered money for some reason?'

'That's the thing with people getting here late for the party when there's a story to tell. You end up telling the whole thing over and over.' Farrow moved back to the banqueting table and filled his glass.

'Are you saying you *haven't* been offered any cash just to come here?' asked Boone.

'My name is Jessica Morell. I'm a reporter from *The Independent Daily*. Mr Draegerman invited me here to interview him. That's all. Would you mind telling me what you're . . . ?'

'Fifty thousand to come,' said Roy. 'And two hundred thousand when we meet. No questions asked. All the answers when we get here. Except we're still waiting, and that means . . .' Roy turned back to Payne.

He had gone.

'Hey!'

Roy hurried around the edge of the banqueting table, to the spot where Payne had been.

'*Hey!*'

There was no sign of the Black Suit anywhere. Even though this great vaulted chamber was poorly lit, surely there could be no way that he could vanish like that? It was a good fifty feet to the nearest wall, and there had been no sound of footsteps. Roy swivelled around, trying to look for a swiftly moving shadow. There was nothing.

'Great . . .'

'What about *him*?' asked Jessica, pointing to the high-backed chair.

Farrow smiled his non-smile, put down his goblet, and moved to it. Grabbing the top and one armrest, he turned it towards Jessica so that the light from the fire fell over the figure sitting in it. The grating of the chair legs on the flagged stone was worse than fingernails on a blackboard, making her wince.

'This is Bobby Pernell,' said Boone, still fingering his scar. 'At least, that's what I think the man said . . .'

'Pernell?' Jessica moved forward to get a better look at his face. 'Yes, of course.'

'What do you mean "of course"?' asked Roy, rejoining them.

'He used to be an actor. His mother is here, too. Gloria. We came in together.'

'So where is she?' asked Farrow.

'One of Draegerman's men – Lamb – took her to a Screening Room somewhere. To watch one of her old movies. He said she'd be here soon.'

'So has she had the same offer as us?' asked Boone.

'I don't know about money offers. She just told me that she thought Draegerman was wanting to make movies again, wanted her for a part. That's why she's here.'

'So you're a movie *star*?' Farrow crouched down in front of Bobby. '*Ooooh*, Bobby! Can I have your autograph, pretty please?' Bobby made no reply, still sitting with a wine glass in one hand and the same half-amused look on his face, staring into the middle distance.

'Is he all right?' asked Jessica.

'Spaced out,' replied Roy. 'Hasn't said a lot since we got here.'

'Wish I had some of what he's on,' said Farrow. 'This place doesn't exactly give out good vibes.' He sauntered away from the others, studying the arches overhead and the giant columns of stone.

'Listen,' said Jessica, addressing them all. 'While we're waiting, I was wondering if I could – you know – just have a brief chat with each of you. Like I said, I'm here to interview Jack Draegerman, and I'm sure that for whatever reason you're here, it's bound to have a bearing on what I'm writing about. So, would you mind? You know, just a brief chat about who you are, what you do for a living, why you think you're here.' She began to fumble in her bag for the dictating machine.

'Yes, I do mind,' said Farrow, walking past her towards one of the first television screens set irregularly into the nearest wall. There appeared to be a western gunfight taking place on it, the black and white jumble of light flickering and dancing. 'So don't take offence if I say – "No fucking chance". Tell you what. I'll just go have a look at the old television screens. Let's see what Big Jack likes to watch when he's eating his TV dinner.'

'I don't mind,' said Roy. 'Ask away. Maybe it'll help pass the time. The name's Roy Jensen.'

Fifty thousand now, thought Jessica. *And two hundred thousand later. Now why the hell couldn't he have offered me THAT to come here? I reckon I'm worth it just for what happened in that bloody car.* And then another thought from the professional inner voice, a thought that cheered her considerably: *Just think about the possibilities of syndicating your story about Draegerman. Just think about that, and the two hundred and fifty thousand seems like a drop in the newsprint ocean.*

Roy told his story, quite openly. And after a while, Jessica realised that he was doing it to take his mind away from the very real anxieties beneath the surface. She recognised and empathised with that inner disquiet. She had shared it with Gloria Pernell not so long ago. Jensen was open. He'd lived most of his life in the same town, drifting from one casual job to the other. After a broken romance, he'd taken a job in a local bar, was on the verge of moving on and seeking pastures new. Maybe Draegerman's money would allow him to do just that.

'But you don't know what he wants from you in return,' said Jessica, by way of winding up their preliminary chat. 'Ever thought that it might be something you don't want to give him?'

'Well, let's wait and see. If what he wants is unacceptable, then he won't get it. And like our black-suited friends told me: I get to keep the fifty thousand no matter what happens.'

Boone had been nervously pacing in front of the fireplace throughout. When Jessica turned from Roy towards him, he held out both hands.

'Look, I got the same offer as him. I don't know why. I'm just as much in the dark as anyone else. Further than that, I don't want to say.'

'But just a little background . . .'

'No, I don't want to talk about my personal details.'

'That's because you're just as crooked as I am, Mr Boone,' said Farrow, returning from his stroll through the shadowed arches. 'And the less said the better, eh?'

Boone seemed to flush, his fists bunching together. For a moment, it seemed that he was about to fly into a rage. Farrow stood square, smiling at him. Boone lowered his eyes, and turned back to the fire, pretending to warm his hands. Farrow laughed again and turned to the others. 'Not such a good success rate, Lois Lane.'

Jessica flinched inwardly at this use of her in-house nickname which Farrow had plucked out of thin air.

'Only one interview from four. Take it from me, you'll get nothing out of good old Bobby. He's not even on the same planet as we are. So the two crooks and the junkie are staying quiet – and only the boy scout is opening his heart.'

'I am *not* a crook!' said Boone angrily, turning from the fireplace. 'I am a businessman, a legitimate businessman responding to a . . . business venture.'

'Business venture!' laughed Farrow. 'Fifty grand just for turning up, and two hundred for who knows what. Listen, Boone. I can smell something crooked a mile away, and I've been smelling you ever since I walked into this place. Never seen such a jumpy Adam's apple before.'

Still in a rage, Boone said: 'My company specialises in electronic components, computer hardware and software. Not that it's anyone's business but mine. I put a lot of money into an import package that had been misappropriated abroad . . .'

'I knew it!' laughed Farrow. 'You tried to smuggle in a crooked shipment, and you've gone bust.'

'. . . and Mr Draegerman's offer has come at a very opportune time,' continued Boone, still struggling to control his anger and now desperately uncomfortable that he had given away more than he had wanted. 'Whatever he wants from me, whatever I may have to offer – I'm sure that we can come to some arrangement.'

'There you are, Lois,' said Farrow. 'Half a story from Mr Boone. Maybe you'll get more out of these people than I thought. Hey, Bobby! Bobby baby! You want to tell a story? No? I seen you on one of those screens back there, you little devil. In one of those movies. There's a little electronic sign under each screen, saying what the movies are – and there you are, in a shitty little thing I've seen on late-night television.

Had a lot to say for yourself there, didn't you? *Ten Little Mannikins*, it says. And there you are, sitting at the piano, playing away. And then you fall backwards off the piano stool. Poisoned. What about that, then, eh? The stuff you're taking now takes a lot longer to poison you than the stuff in that movie. But it'll get you in the end, just the same.'

The fixed half-smile on Pernell's face remained unchanged, even when Farrow leaned down and pinched one cheek between his thumb and forefinger, like a father playing with a child.

'Don't do that,' said Roy.

'Or what?' said Farrow, turning back to him.

'Just don't do it.'

'Yeah . . . ?' Farrow stepped forward.

'For God's sake!' Jessica shoved the dictating machine back into her bag. 'Let's not get macho, boys.'

Farrow laughed again. 'Plenty of old-time movies back there for any film fan. You a film fan, Jessica? They're all there, playing away to themselves. Thing is, you'd have to be twenty feet tall to reach some of those screens and see what's on 'em. Crazy. Maybe they're for the movie fans who bring their own step-ladders. Let's see, there's *Swamp Water Woman*, *Speed Demon*, *Spider Venom*. Regular film festival.'

'Is there a connection between you?' asked Jessica, ignoring Farrow. 'Since Mr Jensen here's the only one willing to co-operate, maybe you've already found out for yourselves if there's any connection between each of you.'

'None that I know of,' said Roy. 'Seems to me we're all from completely different backgrounds.'

'Vive la fucking difference,' said Farrow, suddenly striding away from the table and out into an open space. Holding his hands wide he yelled: '*Hey, Draegerman!*' The sound of his voice bounced and echoed around the great Banqueting Hall. 'How long are you going to keep us all waiting?'

He returned to the table.

'Maybe that got him out of bed,' he said, smiling his no-smile, reaching for the goblet.

'I was a star once,' said Bobby Pernell, and then was silent again.

'Yeah?' said Farrow. 'Well, you talk too much.'

Silence descended on the great hall again, apart from the crackling hiss of the flames in the fireplace. For what seemed a long time, Jessica was unable to think of anything else to say.

FOURTEEN

Gloria shuffled in her seat.

Jack's attention to detail was perfect; this cinema seat was just as uncomfortable as the ones she remembered from her childhood. In those days, her infatuation with the movie screen had sown the seeds for what would eventually become a career, despite the whole catalogue of obstacles in her way. She remembered that she had only been aware of discomfort if the film unreeling before her was not generating that special kind of magic. If she was engrossed, something like an uncomfortable seat never mattered.

For this movie, she was less than engrossed.

Cape Sinistre, written and directed by Jack Draegerman himself. Starring Gloria Pernell, and an actor who had been called on to portray a rough, no-nonsense sea captain on a dangerous voyage, but who had spent more time crying in his dressing-room that his make-up was never *right*. Not that she wasn't proud of the film, despite the poor reception on its release. Time had been more than kind, and it was now admired as one of the classic *Gothique-noir* movies, whatever in hell that was supposed to mean. It was just that she had seen the damn thing at least twenty times over the last two years, while attending the fantasy film festival retrospectives.

She shifted in her seat to get a better position.

The SS *Gotham* was sailing through oily waters into a black-and-white sunset. For all the film's strong points and faults, no one had ever seemed to notice that the ship was a miniature. It was one of those behind-the-scene stories that she had told at festivals so many times. She remembered the day when she had stood on the sidelines in the studio and watched Jack yelling at the effects men with the smoke pellets who were trying to get a realistic fog barrier for the ship to sail through. The movie had some style despite its cheap budget, but as she watched the ship heading for its lost island of horrors, she realised that almost everyone she had known who had been involved with the movie was dead. It was a sudden and deeply unsettling thought. All the actors, and the actresses – and although she didn't know all the technicians involved on this film, the ones she did remember had long since passed away. Perhaps only Jack Draegerman and herself remained. The sight of that ship and its lost souls was now a deeply melancholy one. She found herself thinking about her own career; about the lost opportunities and the happiness she had sought but which had proved so elusive. How much of that had been brought on by herself?

Bobby ... The thought of her son brought back crowding fears. She refused to let them focus. Clearing her throat, she shifted position again and looked back at the flickering aperture behind.

'So where's the ice-cream girl?'

There was no reply, only the soft whirring of the projector in the booth.

Gloria turned back to the screen.

Something seemed to be wrong with the movie.

Surely this was a scene that didn't belong? At this stage, there was a cut to a discussion between Gloria's character and the captain, up on deck. They were supposed to be speculating on what they could expect to find on the island, and the chances of her uncle being found alive (having been missing for over two years). Instead, the screen was dark, apart from the occasional puff of hissing steam, and the vague reflections of light on pipes and machinery. Was this a scene from the ship's boiler room, perhaps? Maybe it was one that had been filmed and edited out at a later stage, something she had never seen before.

A door opened in the darkness, spreading bright light and silhouetting a female form.

Fearfully, the figure asked: *'Dr Chaney ... ?'*

'What the hell is *this* ... ?' said Gloria, shifting uncomfortably in her seat.

It was the last scene she had been shooting on that crappy horror movie today just before the Black Suits came to give her Draegerman's invitation. But this rough cut was in black and white, not colour.

She watched herself enter the room, the camera turning with her to reveal that she was in a laboratory filled with machinery, throbbing pipes, hissing steam and glass cases filled with exotic shrubbery and plant life.

She turned back to the projection booth: 'Okay, so what's the joke?'

Again, no reply.

Why had this been cut into the movie, why in black and white? Gloria's mind began to race. How on earth could they have got this rough cut over here so fast?

'Wait a minute. Are you telling me that I've been working for Jack *already*, and I didn't know anything about it?'

Gloria saw herself pass the glass case containing the hammy carnivorous plant.

'Dr Chaney? I have to speak to you ...'

She turned again, this time leaning over the back of the seat.

'I don't like being made a fool of, Mr Lamb. So you just get yourself out of there and go get Jack.'

No answer.

Gloria pulled herself out of the seat and stormed along the row to the aisle. Swinging around the last seat, she headed for the projection booth.

'Enough is enough! I want some answers . . .'

She reached the small flight of stairs, stamped up them, and pulled open the door.

The projection booth was empty.

There were no other doors in here, no other way that Lamb could have left the booth. But the place was empty and the projector whirred on, unspooling the movie. Angrily, Gloria slammed the door and clattered back down into the Screening Room.

'Dr Chaney . . . ?'

She looked back at the screen just as the man-eating plant in the glass case behind her came alive, its fronds and tendrils twisting and groping. The glass case exploded, the thing writhing free with its vegetable tentacles lashing the air. Gloria's character screamed and backed quickly away as a glittering rain of glass fell around her.

'I know just how you feel,' said Gloria, hands on hips, now furious.

And then something burst through the movie screen itself, ripping and thrashing through the canvas, tearing the movie-screen image apart. Something that twisted and thrashed and groped and emitted a shrieking, hideous gobbling sound. The Shape blundered through into the Screening Room in a blind, shambling frenzy, the fractured images of Gloria the actress's screaming face and the thrashing plant-thing still projecting over the chaotic form. Indeterminate, a dishevelled mass of movement, flailing wildly – it was now completely through the disintegrating screen, turning something that could not possibly be a head to look in her direction.

And then, whirling down from the raised stage area, it plunged into the first row of seats, in her direction.

Suddenly, the lights went out.

And this time, Gloria was screaming for real.

FIFTEEN

Den Lucas almost slammed the telephone down, but then remembered that Sara was putting the boys to bed. It had taken a long time to allay their instinctive fears about Susan's absence, and finally, Den had been forced to lie – no matter how much he had promised Susan and himself that they would never lie to the kids. He had told them that Susan had gone for a job interview on the other side of the country. They knew that she had been looking for a job, and the prospect of extra pocket money as a result seemed to do the trick. Den hated himself for this, but had discussed it with Sara. Maybe they had done the wrong thing, but at the moment, thinking straight was at a premium.

First, on arrival at Susan's apartment, he had insisted on hearing the story from Sara at least a dozen times. Then he had telephoned the police, holding the ID pass from Draegerman Enterprises all the while. They had promised to send someone around straight away, but that had been two hours ago – and still no one had arrived. Now, after the seventh telephone call and the seventh promise that someone would be there 'at any moment', Den's patience had finally snapped. There was a bad feeling deep down inside; something that he couldn't afford to let Sara and the kids see when they were depending on him. He refused to let it surface, this premonition that everything was about to turn out for the worst.

And then someone knocked on the apartment door.

In three quick strides, he was there. Two uniformed policemen stood outside in the night.

'Mr Lucas?'

'Quick, come on in. Sara's trying to quiet the kids down. If they see you, everything's blown.'

Den ushered them into the living-room, quietly closing the door, waving for them to follow him into the kitchen. Anxiously then, he scanned their faces for any sign of developments.

'Have you heard anything? Have you found her?'

'No, we don't have information about Ms DePaolo,' said the older policeman, a sergeant. The other, younger man was a constable and seemed to be more interested in the décor of the kitchen and the cupboards; as if there might be a Grade A 'classified substance' hidden somewhere in there, maybe in the sugar bag. Den slumped back against the kitchen bench, head lowered. He took a deep breath.

'This just isn't like Susan. Not like her at all. She's so careful. And there's absolutely *no way* she would have just gone and not left any kind of message.'

'You sure there hasn't been a message or a note?' asked the sergeant.

'We've turned the place upside down. The only thing we found was that ID card.'

'Yes, the ID card . . .'

'Well, what about it? We don't have any connection with that guy's company, don't know who the fella on the ID is. So how come we found it in here?'

The sergeant shuffled uneasily, but his face was a blank. The younger man looked as if he wasn't interested in the situation at all. He opened one of the kitchen cabinet drawers.

'Never mind the fucking cabinet!' snapped Den. 'What about the ID pass?'

'We've checked it out with Draegerman Enterprises,' continued the sergeant. 'The man on the ID pass doesn't exist. No such person.'

'No such *person*? But there's a photograph on it. Who the hell is *that*?'

'We've run a trace through the Police National Computer. He doesn't match with anyone we know. But we'll be putting out bulletins. The thing is, Mr Lucas – a batch of ID cards was stolen from the Draegerman Corporation not so long ago, and it's assumed that someone has been using them without authorisation.'

'You're telling me that Susan has been kidnapped by some maniac posing as a Draegerman employee?'

'We're not jumping to conclusions, Mr Lucas. But it looks as if . . .'

'*Not* jumping to conclusions? Well, by Christ, you'd better jump to something! I come home from work to find someone's broken in and kidnapped Sue, and all you can tell me is "we're not jumping to . . ."'

Words failed Den at that point. He turned and gripped the bench. Turning back to them, he asked: 'So what are you going to do?'

'Everything we can, Mr Lucas. Believe me. It's no consolation, I know. But Mr Draegerman himself is deeply unhappy that the theft of his organisation's ID has been used in this way, and if Susan has been kidnapped he'll do everything he can to assist us. But we still mustn't rule out the possibility, despite what you've found, that she's simply decided to leave of her own accord, or decided to take a break away from the kids without telling anyone.'

The sergeant could hear Den gritting his teeth.

'Nevertheless,' he continued, 'Mr Draegerman will be assisting the police with his own resources to find out what's happened to Susan. He's personally putting up a reward for information.'

'So what the hell can I do?' asked Den. 'What do I tell the kids?'

The younger policeman was examining the ceiling. Blank-faced, the sergeant shuffled again.

When Den looked up, Sara was standing in the doorway. She had obviously been there for some time listening to their conversation. She was looking thoughtful, as if weighing up her own course of action.

When the police left, and Den turned to look at her again, she had the same expression on her face.

'What?' asked Den at last.

'I've got an idea,' she said hesitantly. 'About what we should do . . .'

SIXTEEN

'Why so thoughtful?' asked Roy at last, to break the silence.

Jessica was sipping at mineral water, taken from a bottle on the overly extravagant banqueting table. For a long while, she had been sitting there, thinking things over. Farrow had retreated into a sullen gloom, still drinking red wine from his goblet and staring into the flames of the log fire. Bobby Pernell had fallen asleep in his chair, and Boone had taken to walking around the chamber, looking at the television screens, returning to the fire at last with the usual look of confusion on his face.

Tinny soundtrack music, gunfights and dialogue, floated in the ether.

'I've been thinking about our other guest,' replied Jessica. 'The one I told you about.'

'Oh yeah, Gloria Pernell. Watching a movie somewhere in here.'

'Yes. I'm thinking about something she said to me while we were travelling here.'

'Which was?'

'She said her son Bobby had made some films, like the one Farrow was talking about a while ago. And that he'd "dropped out", that she didn't see him any more. When I asked about him, she said that she didn't want to talk about it.'

'So, it's a sore point.'

'But the point is – I got the distinct impression that she wasn't expecting him to be *here*. I can't be sure about it. Maybe she *was*. But I just felt . . . oh, I don't know.'

'Maybe Draegerman's organising a family reunion for them?'

'This doesn't tie up. Any of it. Whatever's going on, Draegerman won't be here until Gloria's finished in the Screening Room. With all of us here waiting, he must have something in mind that affects all of us. Don't you think?'

'I think that if our black-suited friend hadn't suddenly done a disappearing act, I would have asked to be out of this godforsaken place. Enough is enough.'

'You don't mean that.'

'Oh no? Listen, I'd still be fifty grand better off . . .'

Farrow snorted in disdain, taking another swallow from the goblet.

'Listen, Farrow,' said Roy in a calm, matter-of-fact voice. 'I've decided that you and I just don't get along. In future, I'd prefer it if you just didn't say anything to me, okay?'

'Oh-*ho*, who's the touchy one, then?' said Farrow.

'I'm warning you.'

'*Please!*' implored Boone, stepping between them. 'Don't you think it's better that we . . . you know . . . stick together? I mean, we don't . . . don't know quite what Mr Draegerman has in mind . . . and if we just quarrel . . .' His words dried up and he moved back to the banqueting table, pouring himself some wine with shaking hands.

'That's it, Boone,' laughed Farrow. 'Get some of the red stuff inside you. You'll feel better. That's what our friend here needs. A bit of Dutch courage.'

Roy stepped forward, gritting his teeth.

And then a voice from the shadows said:

'Good evening, everyone. Please excuse the delay.'

Boone fumbled with his drink in alarm. The goblet tipped on to the banqueting table, spreading a gleaming red pool. Farrow cursed, pushing himself from the edge of the table, before the wine could reach him. Roy whirled around. But the suddenness and nearness of the voice had frozen Jessica to the spot. Bobby slept on.

A tall silhouette emerged from the darkness, standing perhaps twenty feet from where they were grouped around the table. Just as Lamb had vanished without a sound, this new figure seemed to have appeared soundlessly, out of nowhere.

The figure took a step forward, out of the darkness.

And light fell over it for the first time.

At last, they were face to face with their host.

'My name is Draegerman,' said the figure, smiling. 'Jack Draegerman.'

PART TWO

THE HOUSE THAT JACK BUILT

**Extract from *Cinema Today* by Ken Nordman:
'The Draegerman Effect'**

*What was at first declared by the producer and director himself to
be merely a rich man's conceit now seems to be regarded as the work
of a committed auteur. That such a film-maker can have succeeded in
producing and directing over twelve movies which were ignored, reviled
and forgotten on their initial release is nothing short of astonishing
given that the same movies have now been declared largely responsible
for a complete rejuvenation of a genre falling prey to its own excesses.*

*In very basic terms, it is possible to claim without too much argument
from committed cineastes that Tod Browning and James Whale
(directors of* Dracula *and* Frankenstein *respectively) were masters of
the genre in the 1930s. Although Universal Studios dominated the
1940s with their* Dracula, Frankenstein, Mummy *and* Wolfman *series,
employing such workmanlike directors as Earle C. Kenton and Reginald
LeBorg, it is the movies produced by Val Lewton (such as* Cat People, I
Walked with a Zombie *and* The Body Snatcher*) for which the critical
accolades are reserved. The 'threat of the atom', Cold War anxieties
and potential threats from outer space dominated the greater part of the
1950s in which science fiction and horror became closely allied, but the
later half of the decade gave way to the Technicolor Gothic 'opulence'
of Hammer Films and the Poe series by Roger Corman which continued
into the 1960s. Hitchcock's* Psycho *(1960), Romero's* Night of the
Living Dead *(1968), and Polanski's* Rosemary's Baby *(1968) were the
key works from that decade, whose imitators can be seen right through
to the present day. In the seventies, Hooper's* Texas Chainsaw Massacre
and Friedkin's The Exorcist *(both 1973) instituted a cycle of rural
Gothic and 'demonic possession' movies which needs little analysis here.*

*But our first clues to the Draegerman phenomenon might seem
to find a reflection in the success of Ridley Scott's* Alien *(1979)
which went on to pave the way for an explosion of techno-horror
movies throughout the next decade and beyond, both up-market and
down-market. (Even though Draegerman's first movie,* Swamp Water
Woman, *pre-dated Scott's movie by ten years.) However, if the plot-line
of the Scott movie is little more than a remake of Cahn's* It! The Terror
from Beyond Space *(1958), there the comparison ends since the entire
shooting budget of the latter would probably have not paid the cast and
crew's catering bill for the former. But the Scott movie nevertheless had
its roots in the 'B-movie' tradition even if the sensational design and
effects of the movie were beyond anything seen in the 1950s. Analysing
the subsequent work throughout the eighties and nineties of directors
such as James Cameron, John Carpenter and Art Franklyn reveals not
only a love and understanding of their craft, but importantly for the*

purposes of this essay, an appreciation of the movie traditions which influenced them in childhood. Quite often, those 'roots' can be seen in the B-movie horrors of the fifties and sixties.

And it is in the roots of the B-movie tradition that the real 'essence' of Draegerman's movies lies.

Franklyn's subsequent assertion that the movies of Jack Draegerman were a huge influence on his own work seems to be a fatuous claim given the way in which critics and exhibitors alike ignored Draegerman's output until the recent rescreening of A Multitude of Sins proved to be such a massive success. However, Franklyn's recent lecture at the NFT did successfully pinpoint the reasons why the movies are only now getting the audience they deserve, and are having such an impact on the current genre. Andrew L. Searle, fresh from his blockbusting success with Savage Saint, has already announced his intention to remake Draegerman's At Death's Door although it is uncertain whether the recluse will release the rights to his work. A term has already been coined for the Draegerman style: 'Gothique-noir'. At once pretentious and plainly false, it nevertheless is the new buzzword and will no doubt soon be entering the genre texts as 'the way forward'.

Dragerman himself has had little to say about his work in films. But a recently discovered interview in the French movie magazine L'Incroyable from 1970 proves to be most revealing. In it, Draegerman cites George Romero's Night of the Living Dead (1968) as the seminal influence behind his enthusiasm to work in the horror genre. While acknowledging that on the one hand the movie obviously had a tremendous impact on the development of horror movies from then on, he also suggests that the slew of down-market European imitations brought the genre staggering to a halt. His own preoccupation was a 'step back', not a 'step forward', as he goes on to explain:

'The Romero movie was a real eye-opener for me. After all, this was 1968 – and the movie was in black and white. By then, of course, it was fairly unusual to see a commercial movie that wasn't in colour. Black and white were reserved for art-house movies or documentaries. But the impact of the film was heightened by that grainy black-and-white approach. What had been basically a budget-orientated decision not to film in colour had resulted in a truly gruesome real-life documentary feel. The movie was also more graphic than anything I had ever seen before, and it seemed as if the black-and-white 'tone' served to heighten that sense of 'realism'. Bear in mind that the exploding blood-sacks of Peckinpah's The Wild Bunch were still a year away, and so the use of those effects in the Romero movie was very 'new' in the way that they were presented.

'By the time I came to make my first movie in 1970, I had decided on a very simple approach to what I wanted to do. My movies would be made in black and white, and would be set in the era in which I grew up – the 1950s. No period Hammer or Edgar Allan Poe pastiches. I would deal with the same 'science-horror' themes that had been covered by film-makers such as Jack Arnold, Roger Corman and others in the field. The fifties-period detail would be authentic. But the difference was this – I wanted to do within that specific milieu what Romero had done with his movie in 1968. The horror would be very real, very up-front and very graphic. I must admit, I did have a conceit in mind – I used to laugh at this image of someone perhaps sitting down to watch one of my movies, either in the cinema or on late-night television, not knowing anything about me or my work, and becoming completely convinced that what they were about to watch was a bone fide horror or science fiction movie from the 1950s. No camp, very straight. And then – when the nasty stuff began – Wham! It would knock them out of their seats! Even the trailers for my movies were made and edited in the 1950s 'style', with melodramatic voice-overs and corny tag-lines. I thought that people would get the joke. But I suppose at the end of the day, the last laugh was on me. I had a great deal of trouble with the censors, the critics hated the movies, and they made no impact at the box office. There was bad publicity too, when both Peter Cushing and Vincent Price walked off two of my movies because they considered them 'sick'. As it stands, it's rare to find one of my movies ever showing on late-night television without huge chunks cut out of it . . .'

Now that Draegerman's movies are at last being seen in a different light, these independently produced and directed features are being shown at retrospectives to great acclaim and effect; although in my own view the cineastes who have declared that Draegerman's oeuvre gives the only true reflection of 1950s Cold War paranoia and contemporary anxieties are only kidding themselves. In the days before Draegerman became the richest and most famous recluse since Howard Hughes, it's interesting to note that he never made any claim to be making works of art. Instead, he was quite open that his forays into cinema were 'a rich man's conceit, with too much money to spend and too much boredom in his life'. The fact that the movies were reviled at the time and made no box-office impact seems not to have caused one of the world's richest men to lose any sleep. Technicians and crew who worked with him back in the seventies now suddenly find themselves in great demand for their views and 'behind-the-scenes' stories. But until such time as Draegerman himself is prepared to emerge from his self-imposed exile one can only speculate on what his reaction might be to the sudden and amazing popularity of these movie 'trifles', which are now influencing some of the most important genre directors working in the field today . . .'

ONE

Jessica remembered the photographs on file of this man, taken twenty years ago.

In particular, she remembered the photographs taken on the last occasion on which he had ever been seen in public. Without a doubt, this man had weathered well. Only the grey hair around his temples showed the passing of the years. He looked fit, slim and with a healthy tan, despite the fact that he had kept himself locked up in The Rock for all that time. He was tall, perhaps six-three, and with a face that many had thought would have guaranteed him a career in front of the camera as well as behind it, had he so chosen. He was fifty years old, if the files back at *The Independent Daily* were to be believed. He was wearing a well-cut grey suit in contrast to the all-black business suits of his hired hands. About his neck was a pendant which hung down over his black polo-neck shirt. It was not possible to make it out from this distance, but it looked like a three-taloned claw, perhaps an eagle's claw. Despite herself, Jessica felt attracted.

There was amusement in his eyes now as he watched the surprise on his guests' faces.

'I apologise for the mystery. There's a reason for it, which I'll explain. You've been waiting a long time – so now it's time to tell you all why you're here.'

Flustered, Jessica reached back into her bag to retrieve the dictating machine. 'I thought Gloria had to be here before . . .' she began.

'I don't suppose that I have to give you a complete personal history,' Draegerman went on, appearing to ignore her. 'Without wishing to sound too egotistical, I'm sure that you've read about me at some time or other in the tabloids. I began to make my fortune, as I'm sure you'll know, in the aviation business. From there, I used my profits to establish my own movie company. Most of those movies you'll have seen on late-night television. Modest from a budgetary point of view by today's standards, but now held in high regard, I believe, by some critics. Shrewd investments, a certain degree of business acumen, gave me . . . wealth beyond measure, if you'll pardon the colourful phrase.'

93

Jessica had retrieved her dictating machine, and held it out towards him. Looking around, she could see that the others were clearly uncomfortable, waiting with anxious curiousity for the time when Draegerman would let them know why he had asked them all to The Rock. Bobby Pernell had awoken, and was rubbing his face.

'I spent many years building this place,' continued Draegerman, holding his hands wide. 'It has many features of a . . . curious . . . design. And at the beginning, it attracted a lot of attention. Draegerman's Folly, that's what they initially called it. To some extent, I suppose the newspapers were right. The interior design is something that has remained largely secret, apart from the limited events held in some of the galleries when building was completed, and an unfortunate leak in the early days from one of the sub-contracted construction firms, which did not please me. You see, everything around you – everything in The Rock – was built for *me*, not for the public gaze. So I took steps to ensure that, for the greater part, the interior of The Rock should remain my private abode. I value my privacy above all else. Even my security people are sworn to vows of personal secrecy.'

He looked up, smiling.

'But now, the time is right, and there is so much I want to share with *you*. For instance, I can break from my usual reticence to let you know that this Banqueting Hall, and other chambers within The Rock, are inspired by Piranesi's *Carceri d'Invenzione*. There you are, Ms Morell. I think that might qualify as a scoop.'

His eyes, thought Jessica. *What on earth is the matter with his eyes?* They seemed somehow to be reflecting light, like pieces of glass in his face.

'When The Rock was finally completed, all those years ago, I had what you might call a crisis of belief. Please, bear with me . . . I promise that I'll make everything clear . . .'

Draegerman paused then, as if gathering his thoughts. The spotlight illuminating him seemed to flicker for a moment.

'I had wealth enough, you see, to fulfil every dream and every fantasy. That's really why I started making movies, as a kind of creative outlet for the inner dissatisfaction that was becoming such a burden. I had tasted just about every sensation, indulged myself in all manner of ways. And it just wasn't *enough*. I wanted so much more, wanted to be free to experience everything life had to offer. But it seemed that everything *on* offer was limiting. I wanted *more*. That great dissatisfaction led me to what I call the first phase of my enlightenment.

'I had become, at that stage, what the tabloids liked to call a recluse – and it's true that my depression had led me to lock myself away in here. If the world couldn't provide me with what I wanted, I would retreat to my own self-created world and try to find the answers. Those answers weren't here.

94

'So one day, I left the seclusion of The Rock.

'Just for a day. On my own, wandering the streets. Pretending that I was someone else. No one on the streets noticed me, someone even tried to mug me. I found that rather amusing. He took my wallet, and it must have made him a very happy man, because there was ten thousand in new notes in that wallet. No one in the outside world, from which I had become so aloof and detached, recognised me. I realised that despite my fame and my fortune, I could still walk the streets and not be recognised. I thought about that a lot on my return to The Rock. In a way, it was the first really refreshing thing that had happened to me in many years. Difficult to make you understand that, I suppose. But it's true. Next time, I spent two days away, staying at a dreary motel, looking out through a fly-stained window at my own creation on the skyline – The Rock. And perhaps sharing the thoughts of others, lying in their beds and looking up at my monument, wishing that they could be someone else.

'My preoccupation grew, and then the next liberation occurred. My Second Phase. It was so obvious, and I was so elated at the idea. I began to assume different *guises* for myself. Began to create different characters that I could inhabit. Like an actor, even to the point of wearing different clothes, using make-up. And I began to venture out of The Rock more and more often.

'That's when I realised – I could be anyone I wanted to be, could travel where I wanted, do exactly what I wanted. And I found that in creating different characters and different personas, I could actually *be* those other people. And my intervals away from The Rock became longer and longer, with business affairs handled by my security force while I was gone.

'One day – one very important day – I met a young girl in a motorway café. She was serving there, waiting on tables. And I told her that I was a travelling salesman. I enjoyed flirting with her, enjoyed telling her all about my fabricated existence. And then, much to my surprise, after a period of time and many return visits to that café – she fell in love with me. I told her that I had to be away on business quite often, sometimes three or four days in a week, travelling. But she didn't care about that. She only cared about me.

'And so we were married. Another scoop, Ms Morell.

'Later, in a library on the other side of the country, in my guise as a long-distance lorry driver, I began a relationship with one of the librarians. That was harder, because at first she didn't like me. But I worked at it, made her feel sorry for me because I had to spend three or four days a week on the road, hauling livestock across the country. But I succeeded.

'We were married three months later.'

'Let's get this right, Mr Draegerman,' said Jessica, checking that her

95

dictating machine was still working. 'Are you telling me that you're a *bigamist?*'

'I became addicted,' continued Draegerman, ignoring Jessica once more. 'I had been feeling so empty, you see. Empty for all these years, and now I was feeling really *alive*. I could be anyone I wanted to be. And I was addicted to this ritual of courtship, to meeting new women, to flirting with them and seducing them. Once started, I found it difficult to stop.

'In the space of a year, I married six women. All unaware of the others' existence, all deeply in love with the characters I had created, and all quite happy to put up with my travelling existence. And I was addicted to balancing my life with them all. Spending one day with one wife, two days with another. Not seeing another for weeks and then coming home again *for* a week. Balancing the personas. Balancing my wives and living to the full this complicated and incredibly rewarding combination of lifestyles. I had the wealth, you see, to support my act. If my schedule was too tight, I could always have a private plane fly me between counties. I had enough money to forge identification details, always to cover my tracks. And there were times, back at The Rock, when I could sit and think of my other selves out there – all over the country – and the homes they had created. When things became too complicated, I would simply leave a wife, and never return. Allow myself a little breathing space, do you see?'

'This is a joke, right?' said Roy. 'I mean, all this stuff is a big joke?'

'It took about a year before the novelty of it all wore off,' Draegerman went on. 'A year before the pangs returned again, and the new personas became wearisome. In some cases, when the romance wore thin, some of my wives began to wish for better things. They began to grow weary of my long spells away from home. Some of them wanted me to quit my "travelling" jobs, and settle down to something in the neighbourhood. That led to friction. There were other reasons . . . but I shan't bore you with those.

'I returned to The Rock, leaving all six of my wives to mourn the disappearance of their loving husbands.

'And, very quickly, the Third Phase of my liberation began. Instead of going to the outside world, I had the outside world brought to me. I don't know what the turning point was, don't know what it was that suddenly brought me around to this new outlook. I only knew that it was time to throw away all vestiges of the old morality. I knew then that if I truly wanted to be *free*, truly wanted to experience sensation *beyond* sensation, then I had to throw away all my learned and assumed beliefs about morality. It was *morality* itself, do you see, that was holding me back and preventing me from reaching those sensations that I craved so much. Perhaps it was actually an instinctive realisation of the truth, not an intellectual arrival at all. Perhaps I'll never know. But that's when I began to invite guests to The Rock. For the parties . . .'

There was movement in the darkness now, beyond the banqueting table. Shapes were emerging from behind Draegerman, in a crescent formation around him. At last, those shapes took form, standing with hands clasped formally in front of them. The Black Suits again, still wearing their sunglasses, even in this darkness. All with those familiar impassive faces. There were fifteen in all.

'Parties?' said Boone, his voice sounding strangled with tension.

'There have been many such parties at The Rock. My security firm has arranged the invitations. And I've never yet had a turn-down, or "sorry, otherwise engaged" reponse. Also, none of the guests invited to attend has ever been heard to complain about my hospitality.'

Draegerman paused to smile then, his eyes glinting like shards of ice.

'Let me tell you about some of those Parties,' he said without humour. 'And the party games I've played with my Guests . . .'

TWO

The man in the tattered panama hat sat in his deckchair on an empty beach, looking out at a calm Mediterranean sea.

He wore a gaudy Hawaiian-style shirt, featuring dancing girls and swaying palms. His shorts had once been jeans, now cut off at the thigh and with a ragged white fringe where the scissors had done their job. His arms and legs were deeply tanned, and on examination heavily scarred. One thin white scar traced through the brown flesh of his right leg from knee to ankle. There was a large white circular scar on his left thigh, and a white vein-tracing of scar tissue on his left arm just below the sleeve of his shirt. His face seemed carved from brown sandstone as he stared out across the ocean, the sunglasses a permanent fixture. His rugged face was also scarred, but scarred in the way that a professional boxer's face might be scarred. The nose had been broken, but set properly. The jaw had also been broken, making the hinge on either side of his face apparent. The skin was lined, as if this man had spent most of his life in tropical climes, to the extent that it now it looked like quality leather. His age was almost impossible to guess; anywhere from late forties to late fifties. Beneath the ragged hat, his hair was jet black. With no change of expression and as mechanically as a machine, he lifted a tall glass to his mouth and drank deeply. The ice in the drink had melted a long time ago.

Something about the man seemed to negate the beauty of the weather, the potentially relaxing soft swell of the sea. When a gull called raucously overhead, it was as if nature itself was objecting to his presence here on this beautiful long stretch of deserted white sand. Despite his stillness, despite his lack of expression, the man seemed anything but relaxed. If anyone were actually to see him without his sunglasses on, they might marvel at the amazingly pale blue quality of his eyes, a quality that seemed to suggest coldness rather than any baby-blue warmth and kindness. The rare few who had seen those eyes had also felt something else; something other than the raw, controlled power inside the man. It seemed to suggest that behind those eyes something had burned out and died in the man's soul. Maybe he saw that himself every morning in the bathroom mirror. And maybe that was why he wore sunglasses all the time, even at night. Just in case he should catch sight of those eyes again, reflected back at him from restaurant and bar windows, where he sat at his solitary tables, eating and drinking like a man with absolutely no appetite for anything at all.

A black, white-coated waiter approached from the villa behind the man. He carried a cordless telephone on a silver tray, and the soft white sand disguised any sound of his approach.

But, without looking around, the man was aware of his presence when he was still thirty feet away.

'There's a telephone call for you, sir.'

The man barely acknowledged the waiter's presence. Face still expressionless, he handed him the flat, warm drink and the waiter placed the telephone in his hand, returning to the villa for a refill.

'Hello.' The man's voice seemed to have a hybrid accent; a mixture of American and Australian.

'Taylor,' said the voice at the other end simply. And even though it had been ten years or more, the man recognised the voice from the one word. Quickly, he swept the sunglasses from his face with his other hand, his face registering something like real emotion for the first time in many, long years.

'Sara?'

'Yes, and I'm sorry. I know I shouldn't be telephoning you out there. But something . . . something has happened.'

'What is it?'

'It's Susan. She's disappeared, and I think she's been kidnapped.'

Overhead, the gull cried again, its shadow swooping over the man.

'Taylor? Are you still there?'

'I'm always here, Sara.'

'We need you,' said the distant voice at the other end of the line. There was a muffled sound then, as if tears were being stifled. 'God help me – we *need* you.'

THREE

'It's truly amazing,' concluded Draegerman, with real enthusiasm, 'how long human skin can retain its pliability and texture after it's been removed.'

Jessica's tape had long since run out, her hand still held out towards Draegerman in the act of recording. Her face was waxen, her mouth open. Farrow sat on the edge of the banqueting table, his eyes staring, his grip fastened on the empty wine goblet. Roy had not moved since Draegerman had begun recounting the stories of his various entertainments. He looked like a statue, fists clenched at his side, a nervous tic on one cheek. Bobby Pernell's face remained as blank as ever, as he sat in his chair before the fire. Draegerman paused then, a big smile on his face. The crescent formation of Black Suits behind him hadn't moved an inch since they had first arrived.

'So you see,' he continued. 'Despite everything, despite my tag as a recluse – I'm still after all these years what you might call a party animal.'

Boone suddenly whirled away from the banqueting table and clutched at the brickwork of the fireplace, dry-heaving on to the ground right next to where Bobby sat, impassive as ever.

'You're sick ...' Jessica's voice was filled with horror. The words themselves choked in her mouth.

'But it's a sick world out there, Jessica. Surely, given your profession, you know that more than anyone. I brought you here by sedan through those streets surrounding The Rock to show you just how bad it's become. And it's going to get worse. Much, much worse.'

'Clues,' said Roy, his voice harsh and guttural. 'You've been giving us clues on those television screens, you bastard. *Ten Little Mannikins*.'

Draegerman did not respond, his face still set in a wide grin.

From behind, the Black Suit who had called himself Aiken stepped forward.

In that instant, Farrow pushed himself up from the banqueting table, seized a wine bottle by the neck and smashed it on the edge of the table, now holding out the jagged edge towards Draegerman.

Simultaneously, Roy lunged back to where Boone was still throwing up in the fireplace, seizing one of the ornate pokers from its stand. The sudden movement and the sound of breaking glass had shocked Jessica out of her immobility. She shrank quickly back behind the table to join Roy as Farrow also edged around to join them.

Draegerman held up a hand, and Aiken stopped.

'Please, you're misunderstanding my intent. Here I am, sharing my innermost secrets with you and getting carried away. I've never had a chance to explain my *transcendence* to anyone before. Aiken and my security force merely carry out my instructions, you see. They have provided me with "guests" from the very beginning. And have, shall we say, "cleared up" afterwards. They've never questioned me, because they're merely hired hands. It's impossible to share your deep and innermost secrets with servants, don't you agree?'

'Anybody takes another step forward,' said Farrow, waving his broken bottle, 'and they get *this!*'

'You still misunderstand,' continued Draegerman indulgently. 'You're not like the others. You're not here – strictly speaking – for a party. Oh no, you're much more special than that. But let me tell you first about the fourth and final phase of my transcendence. That Fourth Phase would never have developed, if it hadn't been for what I learned from the parties. You see, it was during my ... experimentation ... and my discarding of conventional morality, that I really began to understand where my basic dissatisfaction lay. It lay not in the here and now, not in the *sensation* which this physical world has to offer. I'd experienced it *all*, do you see? No – my dissatisfaction was spiritual. And I began to realise then that if I was so dissatisfied with what this life had to offer, could it be that there was a real promise of an afterlife? Most established religions make that promise. So was there any truth in it? And was *that* where I should be concentrating my efforts? My ... investigations ... took many years and many, many millions of dollars and pounds. And I could go on at length about the ways and means available to me, the resources I had access to, the methods I adopted to hunt out the truth. In the end, I'm afraid you must trust me – must take me at my word when I tell you that, in all sincerity ...' Draegerman paused again, as if for dramatic effect. 'You see, there *is* an afterlife.

'I devoted my financial resources to establishing that fact. And, finally, after a great deal of ... personal sacrifice ... I discovered it to be true. More importantly there was something else on which I had not counted. You see, we *are* first and foremost spiritual beings, you and I. The flesh is a test. Not in the fundamentalist teachings that you may have observed. Oh no, it's much more complex than that. But, when we die, there is a reckoning. And I discovered that there would be a personal reckoning for me in that afterlife, as a result of ... shall we say, my indulgences. Imagine my horror! My pursuit of knowledge had in itself weighed the odds against me! If only I had known, what a *saint* I might have become . . .'

'What the bloody *hell* are you talking about?' snapped Farrow.

Draegerman smiled his indulgent smile again, and continued: 'Put simply, I discovered that there would be a personal spiritual reckoning for me when I died. Something altogether unpleasant. That discovery in itself provided me with two very important precepts. Firstly, I must content myself with exploring what existence in the flesh can give me, after all, and forget the idea of spiritual fulfilment. Believe me, I was wrong on many counts. The parties showed me that there is a great deal *more* to be explored in my transcendence than I had originally dreamed possible. Secondly – and most important of all – I must never, *ever* die. For in never dying, I will never have to face that personal reckoning. That's the Rule of the Game, you see?'

The formless anxieties that had gripped Roy ever since boarding the helicopter had at last taken horrifying shape. Not for the the first time in his life, he inwardly cursed his inability simply to listen to his instinct. Perhaps he had always undervalued it. Now, trapped in this gigantic dungeon, he could see no prospect of escape. Unless . . . unless it was all some huge and sick joke, some kind of test before Draegerman finally decided to relent and tell them what they were *really* doing here in The Rock. Otherwise, they were in the lair of a madman. And Roy could not see how a fireplace poker and a broken bottle were going to do them any good. He clenched the poker tight to prevent his hand from trembling.

'Aiken,' said Draegerman, without turning around. 'Take two men and go fetch our other guest.'

Silently, the Black Suit leader motioned to two of the others and walked off towards the stairs. Emotionless and expressionless, the two men followed him.

'Jessica,' he continued. 'Don't disappoint me. You're the investigative journalist, after all. Tell me that you've worked it all out.'

'You stay away from me, you sick bastard!'

'Oh now, come on. I've given you all the clues, already.'

'Either you're playing word games,' said Farrow tightly, 'or you're fucking nuts. All I know is you offered me fifty grand to come and another two hundred when I got here. Now tell me what you want, and then give me the money.'

'You mean you really haven't pieced it all together from what I've told you? It's simple. Really, it is. You see, I want *you*. *All* of you . . . for a very special purpose. And that purpose relates to the means by which I intend to attain my main objective.

'In order never to die – to achieve that state of immortality which will prevent me from having to face that reckoning – I've – how shall I say it? – done a deal. I've struck a bargain, and come to an arrangement with an outside agency. In return for favours granted, the state I so desire can be granted to me.'

'Outside agency?' Jessica asked the question in spite of herself. To her own ears, the voice did not sound like her own.

'In my quest, in using what you must know to be a not inconsiderable fortune, I made contact with something really remarkable.'

Draegerman smiled his indulgent smile again.

'I made contact with ... something Daemonic.'

FOUR

Aiken led the way while the other two Black Suits – Payne and Travis – followed, ascending the staircase down which Roy and Farrow had originally been brought. Now that his back was to Draegerman, he could let the mask of non-expression slip for a moment.

Although he and the others had procured visitors for their employer over the years, visitors who had never seen the outside world again, he felt no sense of loyalty and no sense of dedication to the man. They did what Draegerman wanted because he paid them a great deal of money to do so. Problems of morality and conscience simply did not apply. Aiken himself had worked for Draegerman the longest, and personally screened any potential new recruits to the security force that protected The Rock. Only a small hardcore group actually enforced the procurement, actually knew what Draegerman got up to at his parties; the others were strictly guards and enforcers, protecting the Walkways. And it took a certain kind of person to form that hardcore group. Over the years, four such members had baulked at the task – perhaps Aiken had not researched them well enough beforehand. And the four in question had mysteriously disappeared – forever – to be replaced soon by staff who would *not* question Draegerman's requirements and who would *not* be squeamish about clearing up the mess afterwards.

Aiken despised Draegerman, and he suspected that the others did, too. But not in any moral sense. A quick scan of Draegerman's personnel files and the personality profiles, together with records of previous convictions and related professional activities, would dispel any illusion about that. Aiken despised him because, despite his wealth and despite his indulgences, he was quite clearly insane. All that bullshit about 'transcendence' and 'Daemonic forces', whatever in hell that all meant. No, this bizarre philosophy stuff was what Draegerman was all about, and it was all the product of someone on the verge of losing everything between the ears. But that was okay, because on the day-to-day stuff it seemed that Draegerman was still in charge, still sharp, even if no one saw the bastard day in, day out. Howard Hughes had a thing about personal hygiene. Maybe Draegerman was even more fastidious

– until today, he had dispensed instructions via his myriad close-circuit television monitors. No doubt he had something *really* special planned for these bastards, as he had made his first personal appearance since Aiken had started work for him. As long as Draegerman paid well, he would get what he wanted. But any sign that this 'Daemonic' stuff was taking over his mind completely, and he would soon learn that the real power in Draegerman's Rock lay with Aiken and the men he supervised, and not with the Big Man at all.

They had reached the Gothic arch at the top of the stairs and turned from the spiral staircase into the winding black stone corridor ahead. On the next left turn, at the end of the corridor, was another flight of black stone stairs and then a corridor leading to what Draegerman called with a smirk 'The Party Guest Rooms'.

Today's procurements had been no different in detail from all the others over the years. Once invited to The Rock, the guests were either entertained in private by Draegerman himself after the Black Suits had made any necessary preparations and then left the room or the chamber. Otherwise, they would do the entertaining themselves, strictly according to Draegerman's requirements, while he watched from a television screen. But today was different, and Aiken guessed that Draegerman must have something special in mind. Why else the personal appearance? Why else would he be spinning them all that stuff downstairs? Maybe he was just trying to get them more terrified than any of the others had been? Aiken remembered some of the things he had been asked to do to the guests . . . and smiled. He particularly liked what Draegerman asked some of the Black Suits to do to the women visitors while the male visitors were forced to watch. He hoped that Draegerman might have a similar idea in mind for Susan DePaolo. She was just his type. He admired her guts, having to be taken by force. He would enjoy seeing just how long it took before they could make her beg at his feet like the others.

They ascended the last staircase, orange light gleaming slick on the wet black stone.

And then heard someone screaming from up ahead.

The scream was not of someone venting their anger. Aiken knew that DePaolo had been tearing the room apart ever since she had woken up, but her room was soundproofed. And what they were hearing now were not sounds of rage. These were the sounds of utter terror. The strange acoustics of these corridors, of indeed the entire internal structure of The Rock, had masked the screams until the men had reached the top of the staircase and turned into the guest corridor. But now they were unmistakable. Muffled, but terror-stricken, and coming from behind one of the doors.

But Aiken knew that it must be DePaolo. It could not possibly be Gloria Pernell, because the faded movie star should already be dead.

Draegerman's instructions about her had been specific. She was to be taken to the Screening Room, in the same corridor in which Susan DePaolo was being held. One of Aiken's men, Lamb, was to set up and show one of her old films, saying that Draegerman wanted her to sit through it before they talked. And then she was to be left alone. Draegerman himself would come and see her – would come and see *to* her. Clearly, he had wanted time alone with the woman. And he had made it quite plain that she would not be joining the guests downstairs. That could only mean one thing. Gloria Pernell was never getting out of the Screening Room alive. As Draegerman was downstairs talking to the others, he had obviously already addressed the situation. So the sounds *must* be coming from DePaolo's room.

Draegerman wanted this girl alive, wanted her to join the others. No matter what Aiken and his men might secretly think about their employer, they always followed his instructions to the letter. And whatever was happening to the woman could not be part of the plan, so they had to stop it. *Now!*

The Black Suits dashed ahead down the corridor, their footsteps ringing on the flagged stone, heading for DePaolo's room even though, acoustically, the sounds of screaming, still muffled, could be coming from anywhere. What the hell was wrong with the soundproofing? Aiken reached the door first, remembered that he did not have the key to this great oak construction, and gestured impatiently to one of the others. In a moment, the key was in the lock – and the door thrown wide. The men burst into the room, ready to deal with the situation. In the back of his mind, Aiken believed that he had already worked out what he was going to see. Obviously, one of his men had come up here earlier and somehow let himself in, intent on starting the fun early with DePaolo.

But there was only one person standing in the centre of the demolished room: Susan DePaolo, her hair flying, her face a mask of rage. The room had been destroyed, the cabinets broken, the drawers of the wardrobes pulled out and stamped apart underfoot. The bedsheets had been torn to pieces and lay scattered all over the room. And the full-length dressing mirror had been shattered. Gleaming shards littered the floor. Although they could not see it, the interior panels of the door behind them had been scarred and slashed. The tool of Susan's rage was in her right hand. A long, glistening spear of glass taken from the mirror. She had first wrapped her hand in torn bedsheets to protect her bare flesh, and had then been trying to use it to open the door.

Now, she looked ready to use it on the first one to step forward.

'All right,' said Aiken, trying to placate her, opening his arms wide and trying to smile. 'Let's take it easy and . . .'

'One more step, you fucking bastard,' said Susan calmly, raising the spear, 'and I'll cut your balls off.'

And then the screaming began again. Muffled, and terror-stricken. The same noise they had just heard. But these sounds were not coming from Susan DePaolo.

'What the *hell* . . .?' said one of the Black Suits behind Aiken. Startled, Aiken backed off, flashing glances back into the corridor. Susan's face remained white, set and furious. 'It's not her, Aiken. It's not . . .'

'There's no one else up here, except . . .' began another.

'This isn't part of Draegerman's set-up this time, is it?' asked the first. 'I mean, he tells us *everything*.'

The screaming started again, this time even more distressed than before. Something crashed.

'The Screening Room!' snapped Aiken as he finally backed out into the corridor, joining the others. 'Payne, check it out!'

Payne rushed further down the corridor, reaching into his inside jacket pocket and taking out an automatic pistol as he moved. Three doors up, he stopped and looked back. The muffled screaming continued. Payne seemed still unsure. Checking that Susan DePaolo was not about to launch herself at him from the devastated room, Aiken shouted: 'Check it *out*!'

Payne used the master keys, fumbling at the lock. Finally turning the key, he twisted the massively ornate three-claw handle and stood back. Drawing breath then, he lunged forward, holding the weapon professionally in both hands, kicking the Screening Room door open. Despite having psyched himself up for what might lie beyond the door, Payne was still not prepared for what happened next.

The door was yanked inwards, and before Payne could lower his weapon and train it on what was beyond, a figure hurtled out of the room straight into his arms. The impetus of the frantic form sent them both reeling back against the corridor wall. Now the sounds of screaming were loud and shrill.

'What the bloody . . . ?' Aiken backed off from Susan's door, as the figure disentangled itself from Payne and blundered away from him down the corridor in Aiken's direction.

It was Gloria Pernell, somehow still alive. Mascara streaked her cheeks, her hair was flying and her face was a mask of terror. Aiken stepped forward and caught her arms, stopping her from running past; now looking back as another sound filled the corridor from the Screening Room. It was a sibilant, hissing, rattling, *gobbling* sound – unlike anything he had ever heard before. Gloria began to fight back, breath sobbing from her mouth and the force of her panic twisting Aiken away from Susan's door.

'Watch her!' snapped Aiken to the other man, Travis, jerking his head back to the doorway. Eyes wide in astonishment, Travis did as he was told, standing in the doorway as Aiken shoved Gloria hard against the corridor wall, and looked back at Payne. He was still standing with his own back to the wall, staring through the open door of the Screening Room, at something they could not see.

His eyes were wide with terror. He seemed frozen to the spot, looking at whatever was in there. Shadows fell over him, writhing, twisting shadows – as whatever it was thrashed across the room towards him.

'*Payne!*' Aiken's yell seemed to snap him out of his horrified trance.

In the next moment, Payne flung himself forward, gripping the handle and pulling the door quickly shut. Now he was fumbling with the keys to the lock, twisting hard and breathing heavily. 'What *is* it, Payne?' snapped Aiken. He had never seen him look so out of control. 'What the hell's in the room?'

Payne ran from the door, looking back.

'I don't . . . can't . . .' He seemed unable to speak.

And then Travis yelled, a cry of surprise and pain. He reeled away from the door, clutching his arm. Aiken jerked Gloria away, to see that Susan DePaolo was standing in the door frame with the glass shard held like a knife. She had stabbed him.

'*Shit!*' Aiken reacted to the sudden and apparently utter loss of control. Letting go of one of Gloria's arms, he fumbled in his inside pocket for his own weapon. Enough was enough. Whatever was happening back in the Screening Room, was *definitely* not part of the plan and it was time to disappoint Draegerman by removing two of his troublesome guests here and now.

And then something began to pound on the door of the Screening Room.

Something that sounded like a pile driver. With the first blow, slivers of wood from the great oak door flew into the corridor. Gloria began to scream again then, and Aiken struggled with her once more as Payne rushed past him. The next blow punched a hole clear through the door, sending a panel clattering to the flagged floor.

'Payne!' yelled Aiken. 'What *is* it?'

On the third blow, something momentarily twisted through a rent in the wood; something that was long, thin and ragged. Something that seemed barbed and contorted, covered in moss or vegetation, but before Aiken could focus on it, the twisting shape was pulled back inside again. Another blow, and this time the door's hinges screeched as the bottom fixture came away from the wall in a gush of plaster dust.

Payne was running away, without turning to look back. And Travis still clutching his arm, was following.

'Shit!' Aiken hurried after them, letting Gloria go, chambering his automatic as he ran; now looking back as the door screeched again. Susan DePaolo had joined Gloria in the corridor, still holding her glass dagger. She was looking up and down, from Aiken to whatever it was that was breaking down the door. Aiken thought about stopping to put a bullet in them both, but his anger at Draegerman suddenly overwhelmed him. Whatever had happened back there, whatever *was* happening back there, should not be happening at all! But he was not going to stay put and argue with something that could frighten the daylights out of Payne – one of the hardest men he knew – and smash through a three-inch oak door like that. Leave the bitches to their own fate. He had some pressing questions to put to Mr Jack Draegerman.

In the next moment, he rounded the corner and vanished from sight.

The Screening Room door exploded into the corridor in fragments.

Grabbing Gloria's sleeve, Susan dragged her in Aiken's direction, still clutching her makeshift weapon. Gloria needed no second invitation.

Behind them, something that sounded like hissing steam lurched out of the Screening Room and into the corridor. Susan did not look back as she dragged Gloria away down the corridor.

Turning, it looked in their direction.

And then followed.

FIVE

'So we exchanged promises,' continued Draegerman. 'Those others and I. They could guarantee that I would never die, never have to face that Reckoning. "Immortal" sounds such a *grandiose* word but, in essence, that's what they guaranteed me. All I had to do was provide them with certain favours . . . which is the main reason you're here.'

Despite her terror, Jessica felt apart from the others: Roy Jensen and Farrow still striking their defiant yet fearful poses, Bobby Pernell still tuned in to some other planet, and Boone now looking paralysed with terror. Jessica felt strangely detached, soaking everything up in her usual professional manner as if she might live through this to finish her report. She listened and mentally recorded, even though she did not want to do so.

'You still don't see, do you?' laughed Draegerman. 'Given what I've told you, can't you see what you all have in common?'

From somewhere above, in the lofty stone eyries of the Banqueting Hall, came a distant sound. A sound of screeching, like some huge door being pushed open, its bottom edge squealing on a stone floor. The noise was enough to distract Draegerman, who looked beyond them to the great stone staircase that Aiken and his men had ascended. Farrow and Jensen edged carefully around the table, fearing that this was just another part of Draegerman's insane plan.

Draegerman showed no sign of emotion when Aiken and his two Black Suits suddenly appeared on the platform and balcony at the top of the stairs. The Black Suits behind Draegerman seemed to have lost just a fraction of their cool. They shuffled uneasily as Aiken dashed to the handrail, and glared down at them from above. In the next moment, two women had stumbled through the Gothic arch on to the platform. One of them looked clearly distressed, having to be helped by the other, younger woman. Payne and Travis threw themselves back towards the Gothic arch, dragging shut the heavy wooden door by the extravagantly large iron ring in its centre and sliding two heavy iron bolts across the length of the frame.

They came clattering down the stone stairs, taking them two at a time. Aiken followed, each quick step downwards an angry statement. He was no longer wearing his sunglasses, but his gun was still in his hand. The women followed.

'What the hell is going on, Draegerman?' demanded Aiken as he strode across the Banqueting Hall towards his employer.

'Why, Aiken,' said Draegerman, a taunting smile on his face, 'you seem disturbed.'

'Too fucking right I'm disturbed. There's something up there that shouldn't be there.'

'Something?'

'Yeah, something that can smash its way through a three-inch door – and is up there now, coming this way.'

'What are you talking about?' Lamb moved quickly to meet Aiken as Payne and Travis hesitated at the foot of the staircase, looking up anxiously at the platform and the door they had just locked. The other Black Suits had broken formation behind Draegerman, were moving cautiously away from him and following Payne and Travis's gaze.

'There was something in the Screening Room. It got out.'

'What do you mean?'

'*I don't know!*' yelled Aiken. 'We didn't wait around to ask it. All I know is that the guest you left in there is still here. And we *know* that shouldn't be happening, don't we, Mr Draegerman? That's not part of the plan, is it?'

'Gloria?'

Jessica suddenly recognised her as the two women staggered to the banqueting table. She moved towards her, now free of her fear-induced immobility. 'Are you all right? What happened to you . . . ?'

But Gloria was still unable to speak, still clinging to the other woman. Susan was still holding her glass dagger, eyes wide with fear.

'Gloria!' said Draegerman, smiling and with arms folded. 'What a surprise. I didn't expect you to be alive. You're quite wrong, Aiken. The fact that Ms Pernell is still here isn't part of my plan at all. That, at least, is one little mistake that I won't keep from you. I'm afraid that on other counts, you're going to be a little disappointed, however.'

'What in the name of God are you *doing*, Jack?' asked Gloria, her voice returning at last.

'Mother . . . ?'

Bobby Pernell seemed to be emerging from his fantasy world, leaning forward from the chair in which he had been sitting from the very beginning. When Gloria saw him, something seemed to happen to her. She seemed unable at first to get her breath. Susan held tight with her free hand, trying to keep her from falling to the floor. Jessica could do nothing but stand and watch. And then a great choking sob of distress racked Gloria's body. She tore herself free of Susan, flung herself at the young man in the chair and enfolded him in an almost smothering embrace as he sat there. She fell to her knees, still holding tight – and now Bobby was weeping, too.

'Family reunions,' said Draegerman. 'They're so heart warming.'

'Draegerman!' shouted Aiken, and the tone of his voice made the fourteen other Black Suits turn as if it had been a rallying call. Fists clenched, faces once again impassive, they waited while the echoes of Aiken's voice died in the great hall. When he spoke again, his voice was carefully controlled, and deadly serious. 'What is that thing up there?'

'Another guest,' replied Draegerman. He checked his watch and tut-tutted at an apparent show of bad manners. 'In fact, he's a little early.'

'But what the hell *is* it?'

'It's a Daemon,' said Draegerman, matter-of-factly. 'Specifically, it's called a Berserker. Didn't I tell you that I'd made contact . . . ?'

'Okay, that's enough.' Aiken raised his automatic pistol.

'Now come on,' continued Draegerman, unconcerned, turning his attention back to the others. 'Take a guess. I've been married several times, to several wives, using different names and personas. What do most of you have in common?'

'Your children,' said Jessica in a hollow voice. 'Oh my God, they're your children.'

Again, the sound of her voice surprised her, as if she was listening to someone else.

'Jensen, Farrow, Boone. That girl over there. They're all your children.'

'And you, Jessica. Don't forget yourself.'

'Oh no, no . . .' Jessica laughed, a sound devoid of humour. 'That's not true. My father died, in a car crash when I was a year old.'

'That's what your mother told you, to hide the fact that she had been deserted.'

'I don't believe you . . .'

'It doesn't matter whether you believe me or not. The fact is that you're my very own sweet child.'

'And Bobby,' said Gloria, turning her face from Bobby's lap to glare at him, her face streaked with mascara. 'Christ, I never thought you knew. I thought I'd kept it from you. With all your money, all your power, the last thing I wanted was to lose my baby to you, Jack Draegerman. I thought you would take him away. And now . . .'

'Now you know that I knew all along.'

'Bullshit!' snapped Farrow.

'Oh no, all true. Every one of you had a father who left when you were only infants. That man was me – your father. I couldn't afford to be tied down with children at the time, of course. Think of the complications. I'm sure you understand.'

'Am I supposed to believe any of this?' asked Susan. 'I get kidnapped, drugged, wake up in this fucking mausoleum and now I'm supposed to believe that you're my long-lost daddy. Good Christ, wait until I tell Sara.'

'I don't believe any of this either,' said Jensen.

'As I've just said to Jessica, that's irrelevant.'

'What the hell do you *want* from us?' demanded Jessica.

'Just your lives. That thing up there – that Daemon – and the others that will follow it soon, have made me a promise. If I am willing to sacrifice my own seed to them – that is, all of you – then they can make me immortal. I need never die, need never face up to that Reckoning. That act of sacrifice is incredibly powerful, incredibly *magical*.'

'Will someone tell me what the HELL I'm doing here!' yelled Susan.

From above, on the stone platform, something cracked.

Something was at the great door set into the Gothic arch. Something that was putting pressure on the door from behind. The sharp noise was followed by a low groaning as the wooden boards in the door began to protest.

'It's that thing,' moaned Gloria. 'From the Screening Room. Oh God, it's behind the *door*.'

But the noise was immediately drowned by another, louder sound. It was a gigantic, slithering, sliding sound that filled the vault like a great rushing of air. The shuddering roar seemed to shake the ground beneath their feet – and was suddenly climaxed by a shivering crash, like a gigantic gate closing. The echoes of the sounds reverberated throughout the Banqueting Hall.

'Good,' said Draegerman. 'It's done.'

Aiken strode towards him, gun outstretched.

'*What's* done?'

'All the outside doors, all the windows. They've been closed. You can't get out – and no one can get in.'

Above, on the platform, something slammed hard against the Gothic arch door, sending echoes crashing and bouncing throughout the Banqueting Hall. Now it was clawing at the wood, like some ferocious wild animal.

'What do you mean *we're* locked in?'

'I mean that no one here will get out of The Rock alive. Not even you, Aiken. Your usefulness as my right-hand man is over. I'm afraid that your employment – and your life – are about to be terminated.'

'What are you playing at?'

'Cat and mouse,' laughed Draegerman. 'Let's have some fun.'

'Let's not,' replied Aiken – and shot his employer point blank.

The guests flinched, unbelieving, as the sound of the shot joined the reverberating echoes of the thing behind the door.

And, incredibly, Draegerman shattered into a thousand flashing fragments. Like a glass painting, his body fractured and collapsed in a jagged and glittering disintegration to the flagged stone floor. The shattered pieces glinted in the darkness.

Draegerman was no longer there.

SIX

'A trick!' shouted Aiken. 'One of his fucking *tricks*!'

He stalked to where Draegerman had been standing, kicking at the glass shards on the flagged floor.

'All right, all right!' said Roy tightly. 'Now let's put an end to the party games and . . .'

'He was never *here*?' demanded Lamb, joining Aiken, hands oustretched in a plea, as if Aiken could somehow provide all the answers.

'What does it look like?' snapped Aiken, kicking at the shards again, grinding them into the floor, now raising his automatic and scanning the arches and Walkways above the Banqueting Hall. Behind the table, the others flinched. Roy stepped impotently forward with the poker. Farrow looked at his broken bottle, wishing that it was full again.

'But what . . . ? I mean, how . . . ?' Lamb followed Aiken as he strode in a circle, scanning the Walkways and the staircase. 'You mean it was a mirror, or something?'

'Or something. There's glass on the floor, but it's got to be something more than that. He was moving around down here, wasn't he? We've been looking at a hologram, or something.'

'But holograms are made by lasers. Not mirrors or glass, so how did he . . . ?'

'How the hell should I know? You know Draegerman and his games. He's got enough money to do *anything* he wants. But there's got to be a . . . a projector or something. Somewhere up there.' Suddenly yelling in rage, Aiken fired a shot at one of the overhead arches. The shot ricocheted, screaming into nothingness.

And the sound of the ricochet seemed to infuriate whatever was behind the platform door. The hissing and screeching sound filled the air, and now there was a barrage of hideous blows on the door.

'Christ, Aiken!' Payne whirled round to look up the staircase. 'It's nearly through! Look, I didn't get a proper look at it, but you've seen what it can do . . .'

'Do you know what it is?' snapped Aiken. 'You! Gloria whatever the

115

fuck your name is! You must have seen it. You were in there with it. What is it?'

'It's not real,' hissed Gloria, as if afraid that it might hear her, now standing up from her son and looking fearfully back up the staircase. 'It came out of the cinema screen, and I hid from it, behind the seats. And I ran, while it *scented* me and hunted for me and ... Oh God, it *can't* be real, can it?'

The television screens, still showing Draegerman's movies, suddenly began to hiss as a static snowstorm appeared on each monitor. The hissing sound seemed to be a mocking imitation of the thing behind the platform door. There was a flickering on every screen, casting long, gigantic shadows of everyone in the chamber.

And then the face of Draegerman appeared on each screen.

'Now we're all locked in cosy for the night,' said his voice from all around the Banqueting Hall. *'And our other guests will be here soon. Remember the Pharaohs and their pyramids, Jessica? Do you remember reading when you were a little girl how, when they died, they took all their servants and wordly goods to help them on their journey to the Other Side – and sealed everything in with them?'*

'Draegerman, you're *lying* ...' Aiken spun around again and fired a shot at the nearest screen. It exploded in a shower of sparks. As the sparks scattered and faded on the flagged floor, a sound of screeching metal came from the platform above.

'Aiken!' yelled Payne as the other Black Suits milled in confusion. 'It's *getting through* ...'

'Now that's not sensible, Aiken,' continued Draegerman. *'By the time you've finished shooting out all the screens in here, our friend will be through the door. And I'm afraid he's rather impatient to get to you – having missed out on Gloria, so to speak. He's hungry, you see. No, not sensible. Far better that you listen to what I have to say since there isn't much time left. Who knows, I may give you some clues as to how to get out of here alive.'*

Aiken stalked to another screen, gun raised.

'No!' yelled Lamb. 'Listen to what he says!'

'Always the voice of reason, Mr Lamb. So – how much can I tell you in the time we have available? Let me see ...'

On the platform, a sliver of torn wood flew from the door, spinning through the air and clattering down to the flagged floor where they stood.

'Tell me I'm dreaming,' said Susan, turning white-faced to Roy. 'Please tell me this is all a joke ...' Roy put a hand on her arm but did not speak, the grim expression on his face answering her question.

'My house is very special to me,' said Draegerman calmly.

The onslaught on the door was growing ever more ferocious, and now the hideous sounds of the beast beyond echoed into the great hall.

116

'More special than you can know. There are aspects to the internal design of The Rock that not even you and your security people know about, Aiken. Features of The Rock of which only I am aware since the engineers, architects and construction experts are no longer, shall we say, in the land of the living. I arranged for that, even down to the casual labourers who were involved in the basic construction. You see, there's something about the stone from which The Rock is built, something about the origin of some of that stone. If you get out of this chamber, indeed if you want to get out of this chamber, you'll no doubt come across those features. I think you'll be surprised – and I hope I'll be entertained. Do you remember how many doors there are giving access to the Banqueting Hall, Aiken? I'm sure you remember that. Five in all. Except that I've sealed two of them, our friend is at the third – and that leaves you with an interesting choice, doesn't it? On the other hand, perhaps you prefer to stay here and welcome whatever's up there when it gets in. You'll find it a most attentive and appreciative guest. Oh dear ... so little time, and I don't seem to have helped you very much at all, do I?'

'Lamb! Payne!' snapped Aiken. 'Check out the door on the west wall, see if he's telling us the truth.' Both Black Suits hardly needed prompting. Unbidden, most of the other Black Suits joined them as they ran into the darkness.

Another torn spar of wood flew from the platform door.

'Hurry up!' yelled Aiken. This time, he moved to the bottom of the staircase.

Grim-faced, he fired a round at the door.

Fragments of black stone exploded from the Gothic arch surrounding it. Beyond, the thing screeched again.

'It's open!' Payne yelled from the darkness.

Aiken backed off from the staircase, gun still raised, eyes still fixed on the quivering platform.

'Don't forget that there's a door in the East Wall, Aiken. Remember, you've a choice of two.'

Twisting, Aiken fired another shot at the monitor nearest to the banqueting table. It too exploded in sparks and flying glass filaments. The others ducked low, Farrow almost throwing the remains of his broken bottle at the man, but then deciding against it.

'Shouldn't waste your ammunition like that,' said Draegerman's face from the dozens of other screens. 'You may well need it.'

'Go to hell!' yelled Aiken, heading towards the darkness of the west wall.

'You weren't listening. Didn't I tell you that not going there was the whole point of my exercise?'

'Wait!' Boone suddenly stepped forward, clutching at the banqueting table like a drunken man, as if by letting go he might fall to the floor. 'Take me with you! You can't leave me here!'

Aiken pointed his automatic directly at Boone as he hurried past them. Boone flinched, but maintained his grip on the table.

'Not a chance. Whatever this is about, it's you he really wants. Not us. So keep the fuck away from me.'

And then Aiken vanished into the darkness, running to join the other Black Suits.

Unable to take the tension any longer, Boone grabbed his attaché case from the table and moved to follow. Roy caught his arm, pulling him to a halt.

'Don't be a fool! He means what he says. He'll put a bullet in you.'

'Let *go* of me!' Boone dragged his arm free and staggered away from the table.

A chunk of panelling tore free from the platform door, clattering on to the stone staircase. The sound of the thing was now much louder; a stentorian, *breathing* sound that was somehow the most repulsive and the most *hungry* sound any of them had ever heard.

'*No more time, children,*' smiled Draegerman's two dozen faces from the monitors. '*Remember what I said.*'

'Two doors!' snapped Farrow. 'He said two doors.'

'Aiken's gone for the West Wall door. I'm sure he said the West Wall.' Jessica looked frantically around, trying to orientate herself. 'Draegerman said there was an East Wall door.'

'So where the hell is east?' Roy joined her, scanning the Banqueting Hall.

'Wait!' Jessica spun around. 'Aiken's gone *that* way ...' She pointed into the darkness. Boone was hovering on the fringes of the darkness, not sure now whether to run after the Black Suits or wait and see what was happening with the others. '... but I was brought in from over *there*.' She pointed across the hall, in the opposite direction.

'East is east, and west is west,' Bobby began to sing, a drunken smile on his face. 'And the wrong one I have chose ...'

Something thrust itself through one of the rents in the shattered door; something long and thin, like a whip made of seaweed. It cracked in the darkness and then slithered back again. The hinges on the door began to scream, the sound echoing like mad birds in the overhead rafters.

'Come on, then!' shouted Roy. 'Let's go for it!'

'I think I'm starting to believe all this,' said Susan, discarding her glass shard.

Farrow grabbed his attaché case from the table.

'Does the money mean that much to you now?' asked Roy.

'I'm not leaving here without it.'

'You think he'll let you get away from here with it?'

'Fuck *you*, Jensen!'

And now they were all hurrying across the hall, Jessica trying to remember just where in the darkness the door might be. Bobby was still spaced out but looking as if he might be on the verge of recovery. Gloria had rallied sufficiently to help him, dragging him with one arm over her shoulder. Roy looked back and saw that they were struggling, and moved back quickly to help. At last, Boone made his decision, and scampered over to join them.

'*Good!*' laughed Draegerman from the monitors. '*See how much more fun it is when you join in.*'

On the platform, the door finally burst under the onslaught. They heard the splintered wood raining down the staircase and clattering on the flagged floor behind them. And then a living storm erupted into the hall; a nightmare howling that sounded like the voice of a hundred storms. Roy looked back over Bobby's shoulder as they ran, but the staircase and platform were shrouded in darkness. The only illumination now as they ran beneath a gigantic arch was the light from the fireplace casting its orange glow on the flags and the flickering of the TV monitors in the walls.

'Where is it?' hissed Farrow as Jessica ran past the arch to the nearest wall, now looking back to see if she could remember the view from her first entrance. The angle seemed wrong. She moved quickly to the left – and almost ran past the door.

'It's here!' she almost sobbed. 'Here!' And a little voice inside said: *Yes, but what if it's locked?* Before the voice could immobilise her with its implications, she ran at the door with both hands and shoved hard.

It would not budge.

'Oh, Jesus . . .'

And then the newcomer, the girl called Susan, shoved past her and grabbed in the darkness for the huge iron ring in the centre of the door. She twisted it and put her hip to the door. It swung open, revealing faint illumination beyond; again the orange glow from the lamps set high in the walls, and the water running on bare, black stone walls.

Behind them the thing screeched again – a banshee sound, freezing their blood.

And Draegerman began to laugh, the sound of his laughter mingling with the unearthly screeching.

'*It won't stop coming, children. And I have to tell you – others are coming.*'

The twisting, writhing shadow of the thing that had descended the staircase and swept into the Banqueting Hall stretched out over the flagged stone floor towards them.

Farrow and Boone quickly followed Susan and Jessica. And Roy, withholding some hideous inner compulsion to turn and look at what was behind, pushed Gloria and her son through the doorway and darted after them. There was an iron ring on the other side of the door. He grabbed it and shoved hard. The door felt as if it weighed a ton – but was it as strong as the door on the platform?

119

'Help me, for God's sake!'

Farrow ran back to help, and between them they swung the door shut with a hollow boom. There were two great bolts in the door, sliding right across the frame horizontally. Farrow took one, Roy the other. They slid into place with a rattling clatter.

They backed away from the door, listening.

But now there was no sound from the Banqueting Hall beyond. Could this door have shut out even the sound of the nightmare thing?

'It's gone,' said Gloria. 'It *must* have gone.'

'Time *I* was gone,' said Farrow, and hurried off down the corridor.

'No, wait!' hissed Roy. 'Jessica, you said they brought you this way. Right?'

'Yes ...'

'Do you think you can remember your way back?'

'Of course, the parking bays down below. If we can get back there ...'

'But can you remember the way? There are two ways to go here. Left or right.'

'Right ... I'm sure of it.'

Farrow had already set off down the left-hand stone corridor.

'Are you *sure*?' he hissed.

'Yes, I'm sure.' Jessica pushed on ahead – and now the others were following, their shadows looming large ahead of them. Roy looked back at the door before they turned a corner, expecting to hear the thing throwing itself at the wood.

But there was no sound.

He caught sight of Susan as they moved. She seemed a little groggy, passing a hand in front of her face. 'Are you all right?' he asked.

'Yeah. I'm still trying to make my mind up whether I'm asleep or not. Those bastards chloroformed me when I said no to their invitation.'

'I wish to God I was asleep,' said Roy.

And then something slammed into the East Wall door behind them, sounding like a cannon fusillade in the stone corridor.

They ran on in terror as the corridor sloped and wound downwards.

It was like a descent into Hell.

Draegerman's words echoed in Jessica's mind.

Others are coming ... others are coming.

120

SEVEN

Taylor looked out of the aeroplane window at the fields of cloud beneath, and it sparked a memory; something he had not thought about in many years.

It reminded him of the first flight he had ever taken, back in his army training days when he was still full of those now redundant ideals. It had been like that then; clouds like huge white valleys, and with no sign of the earth beneath. He remembered that the sight of those white canyons had made him yearn for something he could barely understand. Those alternative fantasy landscapes seemed so much more *real* than the world below; so much more to be desired. It hadn't made a lot of sense to him then – made even less sense to him now. Twenty-five years later, this ex-soldier and ex-mercenary did not know whether he pitied that younger version of himself, yearning for cloud-worlds, or whether he envied him.

He rang the stewardess and, when she arrived, asked for more Scotch. He had already consumed the best part of a half-bottle, but it was making no appreciable difference. As time went by, it seemed to have less and less effect. Like an old friend, once so faithful, now deserting him at his time of greatest need. At times, in his luxurious exile – when it seemed that the bottle was the only answer to his pain – he found himself contemplating what it must be doing to his insides. Somehow, it never seemed to affect his kidneys or liver. The doctor who had given him the most recent not-so-startling bad news had told him after examination that they were in remarkably fine condition, and he wondered whether forty years of alcohol consumption had been good for him after all.

A year, perhaps a year and a half at most, the doctor had told him. *And then you won't feel like moving around a lot. After that, maybe six months. You asked me to be honest, paid me to be honest – and so I'm giving you the truth.*

So there's nothing you can do?

If it was up to me, I would write you a prescription for the booze. Seems to be keeping the pain at bay. I can let you have morphine when the time comes. Hell, you can have it now if you like. Just try to avoid stress.

121

The booze will do for now. A pal of mine once told me it was slow poison, but like I told him then – I'm in no hurry.

If I had to guess, I would say the whole thing's been started by the bullet you took in the left side. There's still a splinter in there.

Bullet?

Don't piss me about. I'm not about to ask what you used to do for a living, but I've seen bullet wounds before – never as many in one person, though.

So I won't be winning any bathing beauty contests. I'll try not to cry about that. Here, pass me that bottle.

Taylor threw down the first of his miniatures, hardly even tasting it – and thought of Sara. They had met at a time when he had been wounded in Angola and was convalescing at home. He had been out of the services for eight years then, had been working as a mercenary ever since. The job had not been well planned but despite his instincts and misgivings he had still gone along with it, even though he had worked with two of the men once before in the Congo, and did not rate them at all. However, he had needed the money, as always. His instincts had been proved right, and shrapnel from a mortar burst had resulted in his having to be taken off the job and sent back. There was also a chance that he might not get paid, and this was a score that he felt might have to be taken up personally with the organisers when he recovered. Convalescing, Taylor had met up with Sara DePaolo in a beach café. He had been sitting, his arm in a sling, sipping coffee and looking out at a stormy sea. She had arrived with a teenage daughter, who clearly would have preferred to be off somewhere with her friends.

He still could not understand how they got talking. Something banal and trivial, like passing the sugar. But something had happened to him then. He found himself for the first time in his life talking with a complete stranger and her daughter, in an easy, comfortable and relaxed way that he could never have dreamed possible; particularly as he'd previously been sitting there working out ways to kneecap the bastards who had set up the ill-fated venture in Angola.

He had told her nothing about being a mercenary, had stuck to his tale of being in the army; how he had fallen off the back of a supply wagon on manoeuvres and broken his arm. Despite the fact that the kid had been sullen when she arrived, she had also warmed and joined in the trivial conversation.

That first meeting had led to another – Sara on her own in a bar downtown.

And more meetings, many more. Each time, it seemed that Sara was opening him up in ways that he could not describe or believe. She told him that her first husband had deserted them when Susan was six months old. He had been a travelling salesman, away from home more often than not. It was an arrangement she had been happy with at first, but with a kid to bring up, there had been greater pressures. One day, he had gone travelling and not returned. She had never heard from the bastard since, and she had vowed never to have anything to do with men again, until she had met her second husband. That second marriage had been as happy as the first had been miserable. When her second husband died, she felt that a part of her had died with him. She was sure during the years that followed that there could never be anyone else. But then Taylor had come along and she was unable to explain why she wanted to keep on seeing him.

Taylor was able to tell her that he had not been romantically involved with a woman since his teenage years, and part of it at least was true. He felt less inclined to tell her that when the urges had been too strong, he had spent more than his share of time lying in bordello beds all over the world. But it was true, he had never had a *romantic* attachment. And he stuck to his story about the army, feeling that if she knew what he really did for a living, that special, emerging bond would be immediately severed.

Three months later, they were lovers.

And three months after that, they were married.

And two years after *that*, they were separated and divorced.

Taylor cracked open another miniature and downed it. This time, the Scotch seemed to taste bitter. He grimaced and looked out over the clouds again. Still no sign of the land below. But he knew that despite the sunshine above, rain was pissing down from the clouds on to the poor bastards on the ground. Wasn't that always the way?

Unwittingly, although perhaps it had been obvious from the start, Taylor had ended up rekindling many of the heartaches that Sara had suffered with her first husband. He had maintained the lie about still being in the army, giving military manoeuvres as reasons for his absences from home for months on end and the specialised nature of his profession. Without saying so directly, he had led her to believe that he was with the Special Air Service, part of a crack team constantly on call in trouble spots throughout the country. He had felt that, at root, this was not so far removed from the truth. But the weak points in his story had soon begun to show. Telephone calls from strange associates had not helped matters. While at home, that special feeling he had first sensed on meeting Sara in the beach café had given him an extra resolve to retire altogether from the business. But there were debts to be paid, gambling debts among other things – owed to people that Taylor wanted Sara never to know about.

One day, she had confronted him with the truth. He had no way of knowing how she had come across the information, but from that moment on, he knew that they were finished. The best part of his life was over before it had really ever had a chance to begin.

It coincided with the issue of a warrant for his arrest. During his last job, the two ex-colleagues of whom he had been so wary, had been responsible for the massacre of thirty-two villagers 'in the course of their duties'. Taylor had not been aware or involved, but the other two had implicated him out of sheer professional spite. Shortly thereafter, he had left the country. The irony was not lost on him. He had been forced not only to retire from the very profession that was causing Sara and Susan so much distress (what they had wanted all along), but now he had lost them, too. The situation was not salvageable. Setting foot back in his homeland was tantamount to risking imprisonment.

And so he had remained, these past years.

Debts unpaid, and several organisations on the lookout for him, but with enough money to keep him in this Ronnie Biggs lifestyle for the rest of his days.

But the loss of Sara and Susan had damaged him inside far more than any splintered bullet or shrapnel blast. That damage had been further exacerbated when he found out purely by accident that Susan had married, that she had given birth to twin boys – and that her husband had compounded the grief of the DePaolo family by also running away. That he found the hardest to handle of all. In his heart, he felt like a grandfather to those two boys – but knew he would never see them, and that they would never have the chance to know him.

He had not worked since his arrival on this sun-drenched prison island. He was burned out, and knew it. Even when the doctor had given him the news about his life expectancy, it all seemed to fit, all seemed to be part of the plan. He was worn out and running down. In his heart, he yearned for the unattainable. The good old, clichéd second chance.

And out of the blue, it seemed that the second chance had arrived: Sara, using the secret telephone number he had left with her all those years ago. He remembered so well telling her that if she ever needed him, for any reason, then all she had to do was dial. She knew that possession of this number was vital; that if any one of Taylor's enemies had their hands on it, then he was as good as dead. It was meant to be a gesture of his love and trust in her, but looking into her eyes on that last day he knew in his heart that she would never, ever be using it.

Until that day, on the beach.

In the course of that one telephone call, he could feel the change taking place inside. Sara and Susan had always been the only two focal points in his memory of the good things that had happened to him. In exile, he had realised that his lifetime of violence, the death and the horror, had all been taking their toll on him – turning him into the wreck he had become.

This was his chance. His chance, as a personal means of restitution, to do something *right* instead of for the money and regardless of whose side was paying. This was personal, intensely personal.

Jack Draegerman.

He knew the name, of course. Who didn't? But whereas he had never had any personal contact with his organisation, he knew inside stories about some of the man's less salubrious dealings over the years; in particular, the funding of a South American state revolution – something with which Taylor had almost become involved. By reputation, in his business dealings, the man was considered something of a monster.

Man or monster, if Draegerman had anything to do with Susan's abduction then he would be made to pay.

Taylor had deliberately been trying to keep his thoughts away from what Susan must be feeling and what she might be suffering, otherwise his rage would make him impotent and therefore unable to deal with the situation. He felt those pangs of anxiety again, but swamped them with another mouthful of whisky.

Whatever it took to get Susan back, whatever it took to right the wrongs he had done to them both in the past – he would do it.

Even if he died in the process . . .

EIGHT

'Wait!' hissed Jessica. 'This isn't the way . . .'

'*What?*' Farrow whirled round to face her when she suddenly stopped in the middle of the corridor, looking back and forth in confusion. He moved forward, as if he was going to seize and punch her. Quickly, Roy stood between them while the others clattered to a halt behind.

'We're going up again, not down,' said Jessica, running a hand through her hair. 'Can't you feel it? The way the ground's sloping?'

'In case you've forgotten,' said Farrow, glaring at Roy, 'there's a pissed-off "something" back there trying to eat its way through a door to get to us.' He swung away from Roy to the corridor wall, slamming the palms of his hands on the wet stone. 'Now you're saying you *don't know where we ARE . . .?*'

'We passed three turnings back there,' said Roy. 'Think, Jessica. Should we have turned down one of those?'

'I don't . . . KNOW!' Jessica's shout was a mixture of confusion and outright fear. She had been sure that they were headed down to the parking bays when they first scrambled through the door, but the corridors in this huge dungeon were like labyrinthine tunnels. They twisted in unexpected directions, and it was impossible to maintain a sense of direction. Having always prided herself on her ability to control any situation she might find herself in, Jessica now felt utterly out of control, knew that none of them could control the nightmare in which they found themselves. Madness and death were at their heels, and they were relying on her, *now*, to remember.

From somewhere behind, echoing out of the darkness, came the sounds of screeching and tearing. They knew that it was the door, being torn apart as the thing forced itself into the corridor after them.

'I guess we don't go back,' said Gloria, wiping mascara from her cheek.

'Okay, so let's stop talking and move it,' said Susan, pushing ahead.

Without a word, the others followed, their laboured breathing filling the corridor, their shadows frantically clambering the stone walls above them as they ran.

126

'Shit!' said Susan, stopping so suddenly that Jessica blundered into her from behind.

The corridor ended – leading out into a blank stone chamber, perhaps twenty or thirty feet high. Water had pooled on the rough, uneven floor, reflecting the ever-present orange light.

'A dead end!' stuttered Boone. 'Oh my good Christ, it's a dead end.'

'No,' said Farrow, pushing forward, splashing through the pool to the wall facing them. 'There are two doors in here. You can hardly see them, but there are two doors. Look, see the rings?'

In the distance, the sound came again: the sound of a dozen wild cats screeching in the darkness, calling after them. The sound echoed to nothingness. There were no words, but the intent was clear: '*Where are youuuuu . . . ?*'

'So *open* one of the damn things!' snapped Gloria.

Farrow struggled with the nearest, yanking at the iron ring. Roy moved to the other door and began working on that.

'Wait,' hissed Boone.

'What do you mean "wait"?' Jessica moved to assist Roy.

'I'm just thinking . . . about what Draegerman said. About the surprises. Surprises in the architecture.'

'So what?' Susan had moved towards Farrow, watching as he tugged at the iron ring.

'How do we . . . I mean . . . how do we know what's *behind* those doors? What if there's something just waiting for us to open one of them?'

'Thank you,' said Roy, tugging hard. 'Thank you very bloody much, Boone.'

'Here!' yelled Farrow, and the heavy oak door swung open. At the same time, the door that Roy was working on began grudgingly to edge inwards. Boone screwed his eyes shut.

'*Green door*,' sang Bobby, leaning against the wall while his mother went to help the others. '*What's that secret you're keeping?*'

'Shut up!' snapped Boone, eyes wide and staring as if he were suddenly ashamed of his own cowardice.

There was a corridor beyond each door, a rough stone wall separating them. Both corridors looked the same as the one down which they had come.

'So which?' said Roy.

'This one,' said Jessica, pushing past Farrow and over the threshold. 'This one leads down, the other seems to spiral up around that corner.'

'There she goes again,' snapped Farrow. 'The memory lady.'

'Fuck you, Farrow. This is the one *I'm* taking.'

'Yeah? Well, me too, only this time if you screw up I'll have to smack you in the mouth. So remember that.'

'Shut the hell up, Farrow!' Roy moved back to Bobby, taking him

127

by the arm and leading him over to the doors. He began to splash his feet in the pooled water, like a naughty child. Angrily, Roy shoved him hard at the wall. Gloria shoved past Roy, glaring at him, took Bobby's arm and dragged him after Jessica down the tunnel. Roy leaned hard against the other door, pushing it shut again.

'Mummy tell you to be a tidy boy?' asked Farrow.

'Me and you are due for a serious falling-out, Farrow,' said Roy. 'If we close both these doors behind us, and that thing finds its way down here, then it'll have to make the same choice we did. Might slow it up.'

'Okay, so you get two million brownie points, Jensen.'

As Roy passed him, Farrow stepped out into the tunnel, grabbed the ring on the inside of the door and heaved it shut again. Dusting his hands, spitting angrily at the base of the door, he turned and quickly followed the others.

The corridor seemed to spiral downwards for ever.

Soon, they had lost track of how long they had been moving.

From ahead, Jessica's breathless voice hissed back, echoing: 'This must be the way, this *must* be the way ...'

It had better *be the bloody way*, thought Farrow.

There was another sound ahead now. Something that seemed like a rushing wind. Were they getting near to an exit?

'What is it?' asked Gloria.

'Do you think it's a way out?' The desperation in Boone's voice was all too apparent.

'Just ahead,' said Jessica. 'It's coming from just ahead. And it smells like ... fresh air!'

'It *is* a way out!' exclaimed Susan. 'It *must* be a way out!'

There was a sharp bend in the corridor ahead. Jessica hurried to it, ahead of the others – and then halted, a look of crushed disappointment on her face. Now, as they joined her, they could see where the noise was coming from.

Directly ahead, the corridor took another right turn, but in the ceiling of this stretch was an aperture. They stood and looked at it, unsure whether to proceed or not. The rough gap in the ceiling was about six feet wide, and the sounds of the wind were coming through it – even though there was no evidence of wind in the corridor.

'What is it?' asked Susan.

No one answered.

Carefully then, and tentatively, they approached the gap – crouching as they moved, as if expecting that the nightmare thing which pursued them might suddenly drop through the opening upon them.

There was no light up there, no way of telling how far up it stretched – or indeed, what purpose it served.

'Come on,' said Jessica. 'It's all right. I don't think ...'

And then they heard the other sounds coming from the aperture. The distant, staccato sounds that could only be the gunfire of semi-automatic weapons, and then the sounds of shouting, of men who seemed both desperate and horribly afraid. Instructions were being yelled by someone on the verge of hysteria. The gaping hole in the ceiling was cloaked in utter darkness. There was no way that anyone could see how far up the vertical tunnel stretched, but it was obviously acting as a channel for the noises.

The screaming began then.

Intense and utterly horrifying, it was the sound of physical *and* mental pain; as if what these men were encountering was causing them to lose their minds before they lost their lives.

'Come on!' Roy hurried under the aperture and beckoned to the others, who needed no second invitation. Susan crossed under the hole with her hands over her ears, not wishing to hear any more. They continued down the corridor, and the horrifying noises behind them soon began to die away. When the corridor took another turn, the sounds ceased altogether – as if they had been swallowed up by the black stone of the walls.

Something had changed. They had been so used to the orange light reflecting down from the ever-present lanterns on to the wet, black stone all around them that the sudden splash of colour on the walls was a shock to the system. Daylight! Was that *really* daylight shining from around the next corner? Had they really reached an exit from this hellish place?

Something like a moan escaped from Boone's lips. He ran eagerly ahead of the others, anxious to enter the daylight.

'Made it!' shouted Farrow triumphantly, slapping the wall with his hand. 'Bloody made it!'

Boone reached the next bend in the corridor first, and stood apparently in awe with his arms stiff at his side. It was as if the prospect of freedom from The Rock had transfixed him. The others hurried to reach him, now turning and looking beyond with expectancy on their faces. The corridor ended here, opening out on to a gigantic open space.

Their expectancy turned to disbelief.

They had not reached an exit in the side of The Rock, after all.

The light was not sunlight. It was emanating from massive solar panels in the black stone roof of another gigantic chamber within The Rock, this one at least twice the size of the Banqueting Hall. They were standing on a platform ledge not unlike the platform that had led to the Banqueting Hall's staircase. Only this time, they were looking out over something that seemed to defy belief – and each one of them struggled to understand what they were seeing. Surely, this must be somewhere *outside* The Rock, not inside.

There was a staircase before them, just like the staircase in the Banqueting Hall. And at the foot of it, stretching impossibly before them,

129

was a tropical rain forest. The sight was at once breathtaking and deeply incongruous. As if Draegerman had arranged for a five-hundred-yard section of the Amazon to be somehow carved out of the earth, transported across the world and replanted here, tree by tree, stem by stem, leaf by leaf . . .

But this was *surely* impossible. The walls of the chamber were clearly visible on the other side, perhaps five hundred yards from where they stood. To their left and right, the towering black internal stone walls of The Rock, wet and dripping, carved with meaningless symbols, just like the external walls. A waterfall was gushing out of the very wall of the chamber to their left with a sound of soft thunder, splashing and runnelling on what seemed to be a natural outcrop of rock at the base of the wall, forming large, crystal-clear pools. In its own way, with its riot of rich colours and its verdant greenery, the beauty of this bizarre internal forest was at first sight startling enough to register even above their fear. The spell was broken instantly when Boone collapsed to his knees and began to sob.

Farrow kicked him in disgust, sending the man sprawling. Roy grabbed Boone's elbow in anger, pulling him to his feet, afraid lest his fear should be contagious and should fan his own, making him unable to think, unable to cope.

'For God's sake, Boone.'

'Draegerman . . .' Boone could only stutter the name. 'He said . . . said that all the entrances and exits were sealed. Remember that? What's the point of trying to find a way out? What's the *point* . . . ?'

'Shut up!'

'We have to go on,' said Jessica, starting down the staircase towards the bizarre, surreal tangle of undergrowth. 'We can't go back.'

'Every time I start to convince myself it's *not* a dream,' said Susan, helping Gloria with Bobby and following close behind Jessica, 'something else happens to convince me otherwise. If I pinch myself one more time, I'll start to bleed.'

'Please,' said Farrow, not an ounce of humour in him. 'Don't talk about bleeding.' He looked back the way they had come, straining to hear any sound. But there was nothing. No sounds of gunfire or hideous distant screaming. Most important of all, no sounds of the hissing, screeching thing that had come after them. 'Know what I think?' he said to Roy as they reached the bottom of the staircase and started out into the undergrowth.

'What?'

'I think that thing back there took another turning and found Aiken and his Black Suit men.'

'You may be right.'

'So maybe when it finishes with them, it might not be so hungry any more. What do you think?' This time, Farrow was grinning.

'I think the more time I spend with you, the less I like it.'

'That's no way to talk to a brother, Roy.'

'You're no brother of mine.'

'Draegerman says so. Hey – all of a sudden I've got myself three brothers and two sisters. A real family reunion. What do you think of that, Jessica?'

Jessica did not reply. She was crouching down and looking through the tangle of undergrowth. 'I think ... think I see a way. Not a path exactly, but a track maybe where people have been walking.'

'No birds,' said Bobby, rubbing a hand across his face. Was he finally coming out of his daze, or would he relapse yet again?

'What?' Gloria hung on tight to his arm. But everyone knew what he meant. One of the reasons for this mini-jungle's strangeness was the complete absence of sound, apart from the rush of water coming out of the chamber wall. There should be birdsong of some kind, but there was no sound at all. The stillness now seemed somehow alarming. Jessica looked back at the others, waiting for some kind of consensus as to what to do. Roy shrugged in a *What else can we do?* way.

'Come on, then,' said Susan. 'Always wanted to go on a safari.'

They pressed on ahead through the wet fronds and grasses, Jessica leading the way. The foliage was dank, the atmosphere humid. And as they moved the sense of unreality was stronger now than it had ever been, even when the nightmare thing had come after them. Soon, the way behind was shrouded by the greenery. But they could still see the stone chamber wall and ceiling beyond. They followed the track, looking back and listening for anything that might follow. But there was no sound other than their own laboured breathing and their passage through the forest. The implications and consequences of what was happening were bewildering. How much of this was one man's lunatic fantasy, and how much a lunatic derangement of their *own* minds?

The solar panels overhead were clearly absorbing and transmitting huge amounts of energy. In no time, their clothes were wet with perspiration, clinging to their flesh. No one had spoken since that first descent of the surreal staircase, and now that they were actually in this bizarre mini-jungle, the dense undergrowth and silence was making the atmosphere claustrophobic, despite the knowledge that they were in a vast chamber. Was the sound of their progress masking another sound behind them; perhaps the sound of the thing Draegerman had called the Berserker? Was it even now on that staircase, sniffing the air, looking down and watching their progress through the undergrowth?

'No, wait!' said Susan suddenly. The sound of her voice was shocking to the others, breaking the unnatural silence. They turned to see that she had stopped, was holding on to a tangle of vines to steady herself. Head bowed, she seemed to be struggling for breath. 'Stop ...' She sat on an overgrown log and shook her head. 'Stop ...'

131

'We can't stop,' said Roy. 'That thing might be right behind us.'

Susan continued to shake her head. 'This is like ... like some stupid kind of video game or something. Something that my kids play on their computers.'

'Listen, Susan,' said Gloria. 'You'd better get your head around how real this is, or you aren't going to make it. I didn't see it properly, but that thing nearly got me, and I can tell you – it was real enough.'

'No. It's like ... open a door, find something horrible. Go back three spaces. Open another, go forward. This is Snakes and Ladders or something ...'

Then Susan recoiled from the overgrown log when something inside the tangled vegetation hissed into life. Something bright and flickering suddenly illuminated where she had been sitting. There was something alive behind the tangle of vegetation. No, not alive ...

And as the image focused there in the undergrowth, they could see that it was clearly – impossibly – a television screen.

A television screen that had somehow been installed in the side of the log, as neatly as if it had been fitted into a cabinet designed for the purpose. Tangled threads of creeper and vegetation fell across part of the screen, but the face that now appeared was still horribly familiar.

'Snakes and Ladders, Susan,' said Draegerman from the screen. 'How quaint. But you're right in one respect – even the Garden of Eden had its snake. And there's always likely to be a worm in the nicest of apples.'

'You ...' Roy snatched up a broken branch from the ground, brandishing it and lunging towards the screen.

'You're impulsive, Roy. Just like Aiken.'

'And you're bloody insane!'

'A relative term. Smash the screen and you won't hear what I have to tell you. You never know, you might find what I have to say helpful.'

And then it was Jessica's turn to scream, making them all spin away from the screen in alarm. She was looking down at her feet, anxiously backing away and kicking at the grass. Roy grabbed at her, pulling her towards him, still brandishing the broken branch.

'What is it? What's wrong?'

Roy tried to work out what it was she could have stood on that was causing such distress, but could see nothing.

'Oh my good Christ ...' Jessica continued to make noises of disgust and horror, hands held to her face, still kicking at the grass as she allowed Roy to pull her away.

'What?' shouted Farrow, finding Jessica's horror contagious, now keeping well away from where she had been standing a moment before, trying to establish just what the hell was happening. Gloria and Boone stood stock still, staring anxiously. Boone looked as if he might faint at any moment.

'On my . . . on my foot,' said Jessica, her voice strangled. 'There was something on my foot. Oh, God.'

Now everyone had backed away from the spot where she had been standing.

'But it couldn't have been . . .' Jessica was still unable to shake off the horror that had seized her.' . . . couldn't have been. It was too big. Bigger than a kitten. It couldn't . . .'

'What the *hell* are you talking about?' snapped Farrow.

Jessica swallowed hard. 'It was a spider. It crawled over my foot.'

'*Ah, you've found one,*' said Draegerman from the screen. '*Let me introduce you. That was a* Phoneutria Draegus.' His voice remained as calm as that of the presenter of a wildlife programme. '*From Brazil. And it's the most venomous insect known to man. If it bites, there will be burning pain, blisters, dizziness, then dribbling at the mouth. Then sickness, internal bleeding, vomiting and fever. Eventually the breathing and heart stop. I've been breeding them, you see. That specimen is a new cross-breed, in fact, with* Loxosceles. *It's amazing what hobbies you can indulge in if you have the time and money. They've reproduced amazingly well down here. Shame they've finished off most of the other insect life I introduced into this little . . . back garden of mine. I haven't had a chance to restock yet. So they must be very, very hungry . . .*'

Roy saw Boone whirl away, as if to vomit over a tangled bush. Then saw him recoil from it, eyes even wider than before.

And suddenly, the grass around them was alive with rustling movement.

Was it a wind, suddenly whispering through the undergrowth, making the fronds of the exotic vegetation all around them begin to sway?

'*There's a way,*' said Draegerman, voice still calm and almost casual. '*There's always a way out.*'

'Jesus *Christ!*' yelled Farrow, lunging backwards and swiping out with his attaché case as something dark and squirming dropped out of the tangled vines above his head. It fell into the deep grass, and was gone before he could see it properly. Ineffectually, Roy swiped at the long grass all around them with his broken branch.

'Follow the path!' shouted Gloria. 'That's all we can do!'

'But the grass is *alive*, all around us.' Boone was whirling in circles now.

'The grass isn't deep ahead.' Gloria was pushing on, pulling her son with her. 'At least we can see what we might be standing on.' For the first time, it looked as if Bobby was coming back into the real world.

'Then, come ON!' Jessica forged ahead after them, and now Farrow had joined them. Roy seized Boone, shoving him after them as he swatted at the hissing long grass again with the branch.

'*Follow the Yellow Brick Road,*' smiled Draegerman from the screen.

In reply, Roy flung the branch hard across the small clearing. It

133

wheeled through the air, end over end, the thick end smacking into the glass. The monitor exploded in blue flame, coughing sparks and glass fragments into the hideously living grass.

And then he turned to follow the others, as something fell out of an overhead fern and landed on his shoulder.

NINE

When the front door bell rang, Sara did not know whether the feeling inside her was apprehension or relief. It stabbed at her heart like fear, filled her with something that seemed to be hope, but was bereft of comfort. Den came to stand in the kitchen door, drinking from his third can of beer, his expressionless face looking as if it had been carved from ebony.

Sara straightened her dress, realised that it was a ridiculous gesture, and then, almost angry with herself for it, hurried across to open the door.

'Hello,' said Taylor simply, standing on the doorstep in the pouring rain.

There was one holdall at his feet, battered and frayed. It bore no holiday stickers but had been all over the world in its time, and also on occasions to Hell itself. Water was runnelling on his black waterproof coat, his hair plastered to his head. Maybe it was the water, making his hair look just as black as ever and hiding the grey – but he looked the same as the day they had said goodbye.

Sara cleared her throat, almost straightening her dress again.

'You don't have to think of something to say, Sara.'

'Come in. You're . . . wet.'

She stood aside, holding the door as Taylor entered with his holdall. He brought the cold of the night inside with him, shaking freezing drops of rain into the air as he began to take off his coat.

He saw Den standing in the kitchen doorway, still drinking from the can and with his face still expressionless. They exchanged nods.

'Here, I'll take that.' Sara took the holdall into the room, coming back to take Taylor's coat. The atmosphere was uneasy, and showed no signs of improving.

'Are the kids here?' Taylor asked at last.

'No, they're staying with friends.' Sara gestured to the sofa and Taylor moved to it. Den simply adjusted his position in the door frame to watch as Taylor sat, making no effort to come and join them. 'We haven't been able to tell them what's really happened,'

135

continued Sara. 'We just couldn't ... but we'll have to tell them something soon.'

'What excuse have you given them?'

'An interview,' said Den, his voice flat and registering no emotion. 'For a job. She was looking for one, so it was the best thing we could think of. Even with my wages, it's hard to make ends meet. Particularly bad when someone you love runs out on you, and leaves you with nothing. Know what I mean?'

'Den!' Sara's eyes flashed with anger, but Den remained as impassive as ever, sipping his beer. She sat down on the chair opposite the sofa, turning back to Taylor. 'We've said she's away, and she'll be back soon. But they keep asking why she hasn't telephoned.'

'Have you got a towel or something?' Taylor wiped the water from his hair. Quickly, Den turned from the door. In one swift motion, he seized a towel from the kitchen and threw it hard across the room. Taylor caught it, held his gaze – and began to towel his hair.

'Have you eaten?' asked Sara, eyes flashing at Den again.

'On the plane.'

'Well ... can I get you something else?'

'Whisky, if you've got it.'

Den pushed himself away from the door frame, heading for the main cabinet in the living-room. 'I'll get it.' His eyes did not leave Taylor.

Taylor looked around the room as he towelled his hair. As if he was looking for clues – any kind of clue that might link him to this place; perhaps photographs of bygone years on the walls or mementos in the cabinets. But no, this was a stranger's home. He wondered why Sara had asked him to come here, rather than meet at her home. Was it because she did not want him relating to anything in or about their former home? Was Susan's apartment somehow meant to be neutral ground? Den brought a tumbler of whisky, and one for himself. He rapped Taylor's tumbler sharply on the glass table in front of him.

'So tell me,' said Taylor, drinking. 'Tell me everything.'

Sara took a deep breath and told him everything that had happened. Susan's failure to turn up at lunchtime. The chair lying on its back in the middle of the room. The Draegerman Enterprises identity pass. The police visit. And throughout Sara's recounting of events, Taylor weighed the identity pass in his hand.

When she finished speaking, it was as if the retelling had been a reliving of the experience for her. Her hand was at her throat, her voice trembling.

'Do you want a drink?' Taylor asked, as she slumped back into the chair trying to recompose herself. Her expression suddenly became blank, but the reprimand in her eyes was clear enough. When they were together, she had always felt his own drinking to be too heavy; was at first worried only about his health, but then as time had gone by had seen the torment behind his eyes which the drinking was meant to anaesthetise. It had been her first clue that he had not perhaps been telling her the truth about his profession, about his relationship with death. They had fought about it, and she had sworn off alcohol herself many years ago. Now, all these years later, Taylor's simple request, born from real concern, seemed to present itself as a confirmation of the bad memories that she still harboured about their relationship.

'Sorry,' he said, looking down into his own glass as he swirled the whisky at the bottom.

'So you were a mercenary?' asked Den. Still that mask on his face, still that sense of agitation.

'Is that what Sara and Susan told you?'

'No, they only told me that you'd been in the army, had seen action. That you were an expert in your field. But I put the rest of it together myself.'

'I haven't told him everything,' said Sara simply.

'That's great!' snapped Den, turning and heading back to the cabinet to fill his glass. 'So when do I finally get to be a *part* of this family, then?'

Taylor ignored his outburst. 'That's as well. The fewer people know, the better.'

'So who and *what* the hell are you, then?' Den turned back. 'James Bond?'

'What's your problem, sonny?' Taylor's eyes were cold as glass as he returned his glare.

'My problem is that Susan has been kidnapped and nobody can do anything about it. The police have been screwing everything up, and getting nowhere – and I'm not convinced about that stolen ID card business either. On top of that, instead of letting me help, Sara just ignores what I say and sends for someone I didn't even know about before. And don't call me sonny.'

'So how come you're so sure about the identification pass? How come you're convinced that the police might be wrong?'

'I can *feel* it,' said Den, draining his glass again.

'Oh, so it's instinct, then? Hell, who needs James Bond when you're around?'

'Why the hell do we need him anyway?' muttered Den, turning his back on them.

'Because he's all we've got!' snapped Sara, standing angrily. 'Don't you see that?'

'I've got contacts,' continued Taylor. 'Good contacts. Better than the police. I can check this card out.'

'So how?' asked Den, still with his back to them.

Taylor paused then, and when he continued speaking, his voice was measured, patience at a dangerously low ebb. 'Because I know the right people. Or should I say the right *wrong* people. From what I hear the Draegerman security system is the best in its field. But if the guy on this pass has ever worked for them, I'll be able to find out.'

'How . . .' Sara's voice cracked with emotion. 'How long will it take you to find out?'

'Not long. One thing's for sure, it seems highly unlikely, with Draegerman's security being the way it is, that he'd allow a batch of ID cards to be stolen so easily. And how come they weren't reported officially until *after* this pass was found? Why weren't they reported missing or stolen straight away? It doesn't scan.'

'How do you know that?' asked Den. '*Instinct?*'

'You and I are going to have to get along if we're going to make this work.'

'Please,' begged Sara, crossing to Den.

'No!' Den shrugged her hand from his arm. Turning back to Taylor, he had something like real rage on his face. 'Who the hell *are* you, anyway? You walk out on them, and then when something bad like this happens, you just walk back in like you're God almighty or something.'

'Den . . .' Sara tried to touch him again. He moved back to the drinks cabinet.

Taylor drained his glass and stood up. 'Leave this with me. I'll find out about the ID, and we'll see if we can take it from there.'

Running a hand through her hair, Sara turned away from Den, back to him. 'Where are you staying?'

'I'll get a motel room or something.'

'Well, maybe you could move in here if you think it's better?'

'Fucking great,' snapped Den. 'Why don't you give him my bed?'

'It's okay.' Taylor picked his coat up again and walked back across the room to retrieve his bag. 'I'll let you know where I am. Just give sonny-boy something to calm him down.'

'I *told* you not to call me that . . .' Den lunged as Taylor passed, grabbing him by the arm.

And in the very next moment, he was lying flat on his back, on the floor.

In one smooth, fast and professional movement, Taylor had twisted his arm and at the same time kicked his leg away. Den squirmed, trying to get up, but Taylor was still holding his arm by the wrist, keeping him pinned to the floor. Any movement was causing Den agony.

'Oh good *Christ!*' cried Sara, running to them and slapping away Taylor's arm. Taylor let go, adjusted his coat, and moved to pick up his bag. Sara helped Den to his feet.

Calmly then, but with unmistakable ice in his voice, Taylor looked Den in the eye and said: 'You get your act together, and don't get in my way. If you love Susan, and you want her safe, then just don't interfere. Okay?'

Sara began to weep when Den pulled away from her again, glaring at Taylor as he headed for the door.

'I'll be in touch,' he said without turning back to look at them.

In the next moment, he was outside in the rain again.

Fifteen minutes later, as he stood on the street, looking for a taxi, he cursed the rain, letting it run freely on his face.

'Shit. What a way to start.'

He wondered if there was rain up there *above* the clouds.

TEN

Grass thrashed beneath his feet.

Vines tangled in his hands as he tore through the undergrowth, wondering whether the vines were alive with the squirming black movement, whether another of those hideous, half-seen things might drop on him just as that first thing had dropped on his shoulder, a thing he had swept off into the grass with a cry of horror and disgust.

The others? Where were the others?

As he ran, breath sobbing in his throat, all he could see ahead was the tangle of vegetation and the bare path beneath his feet – and a sound like the hissing of wind in the trees all around him. Had they blundered off the path, straight into the deeper grasses and dense vegetation of this nightmare place? Were they even now squirming and thrashing in that green hell, while hordes of black, multi-legged monstrosities swarmed over their bodies and faces?

Christ! Was *he* still on the right path? Was *he* blundering off the path?

The vines ensnared his arms, bringing him to a stop. He thrashed and screamed, and somewhere it seemed that he could hear, even above the sound of his own hoarse cries, the sound of distant laughter.

'Draegerman, you bastard!' Roy tore free, expecting to feel the savage sting of multiple bites on his arms, through the shredded sleeves of his shirt. Swatting in horror at his hair with both hands, he raced ahead. He could see that he was still on the path.

And there, past that last multi-coloured, exotic plant or bush, he could see a small clearing, and another surreal stone staircase directly ahead, identical to the one they had first descended.

Farrow was already at the top of the staircase looking down, grabbing Boone's outstretched hand and dragging him up with contempt. Gloria and Bobby were also nearly at the top, Jessica and Susan helping each other in mid-flight. In that brief instant, Roy's terror dulled to something like relief. He continued to swat at his body, lest one of the horrifying things might be clinging to his shirt, and raced ahead to the staircase. The sound of distant laughter rang out again, and Roy heard Farrow yell back at Draegerman's invisible face.

'I'll *get* you, you bastard! Just see if I don't!'

Roy ascended the stairs, two at a time, now reaching Jessica and Susan. He stumbled, completely out of breath. Susan seized his arm by the crook of the elbow, and he staggered on the step, regaining his balance.

And then they were all at the top of the staircase, fighting to get their breath back.

'Thanks . . .' Roy took Susan's hand.

Her ashen face tried to manage something like a smile of acknowledgment.

'I . . .' Jessica was sitting on the ground, her back to the parapet. 'I . . . *hate* . . .'

'I hate spiders, too,' said Gloria. 'Had to act with a whole bunch of them once. They were rubber, on strings. But I still couldn't get close to them, know what I mean?'

'Never work with animals or children,' said Bobby, and for the very first time, he looked as if he was in their world at last. 'Or spiders.' He leaned against the parapet, and put both his hands over his face.

Roy climbed to his feet to join Farrow and Boone. They were looking out over the exotic tangle of greenery through which they had just raced, and the sense of dislocation was complete. The sight that met their eyes was exactly the same as the sight from the first staircase – the steps leading down into the greenery, and a soft hiss of thundering water to their left from a small waterfall that came out of a fissure in the wall, falling on to rocks below, a mist rising softly from the rocks. On either side of them and at the far end of the chamber that surrounded this bizarre mini-jungle rose the rock walls, just as they had first seen them. It was as if they had never descended the staircase, had never walked into the nightmare . . . and were right back where they had started.

The jungle was quiet again.

There was no hissing of grasses, no swaying of vines.

Whatever had pursued them through the greenery was coming no further.

Roy had an image of utter revulsion then, something that he could not shake off.

It was an image of eyes. Thousands of tiny black-glittering, eight-eyed faces in the long grass and the bushes and the vines; all staring out of their hiding places in their direction. All watching them there on the staircase, wondering if they would come back down again. He shook himself, saw Boone staring off into the middle distance – and then reached out to give him a small shake. Boone reacted, eyes blinking, face ashen. The sense of shock that was always so apparent on his

141

face seemed to have deepened, taking his mind elsewhere – perhaps to a safer place inside.

'Okay?' asked Roy.

'Okay . . .' replied Boone in a small voice.

'It goes down,' said Jessica, and they turned to see that she had stepped through the Gothic arch at the top of the staircase: an exact replica of the arch on the other side of the chamber, at the top of the other staircase. 'The corridor beyond leads downwards.'

'Pardon the hell out of me,' said Farrow, pushing past her and striding through the archway to examine it for himself. 'But I don't have any trust left in your Girl Guide qualities.'

'Fuck *you*, Farrow!' Jessica stepped forward, fists bunched.

Farrow turned back from the darkness, a vulpine smile on his face. 'I already owe you a smack in the mouth, Jessica. As to what you've just said, just watch out I don't return the favour.'

'So what do *you* propose?' asked Roy, stepping between them. 'Seems to me the only way to go is ahead. Unless you want to go back down there into Tarzan-land.'

Jessica seized Roy's shoulder, spinning him away.

'Don't patronise me, and don't stick up for me. I don't need your protection from that bastard.'

'Oh shut up, all of you,' said Susan, and walked past them all into the corridor.

Gloria took Bobby's hand and followed. Bobby gently took away her hand as they walked. 'I'm okay, Mother. I'm okay now.'

'You're sure?'

'Believe me, I've had some bad trips in my time. But I've never been in one as bad as this. Thing is, this time I know it's real and I'm not imagining it.'

'I wish I could say the same,' said Susan, and was gone from sight around the corner. Orange light from beyond cast her shadow large and looming on the overhead stone roof.

Silently now, they all followed.

ELEVEN

'Kendricks?'

'That's me.' And then there is a pause. 'So? Who wants to know at this time of night?'

'It's Taylor.'

'Taylor, yeah. What? Is that Mr Taylor, or Taylor somebody? I'm a busy man, in case you didn't know. So get to the point, or get off the line.'

'You're not listening, Kendricks. I said my name is Taylor. Now think about it.'

Kendricks starts to say something derogatory, then begins to hang up.

And then he remembers.

Hand shaking, he lifts the receiver to his ear again.

'Don't think about hanging up,' continues the voice at the other end. 'If you do, then I promise I'll finish what I said I was going to do last time we spoke. And this time, I won't start with a finger.'

Kendricks begins to tremble, his other hand clenched, white knuckles showing. That hand has a missing little finger. On cold nights, the joint still throbs. Now he can't understand why he didn't recognise the voice straight away, and in the next instant realises that it's because he's pushed the memory to the back of his mind, not wanting to relive the terror. So far, until this telephone call, he'd done a pretty good job of forgetting.

'What ...?' he begins, and then his voice dries up. He clears his throat and continues: 'What are you doing back in this country? I did what you said. There's been no more trouble, I haven't touched any more ...'

'Little girls? Well, I'm pleased to hear that – and one or two fathers I know will be, too. But no, that's not what I'm ringing you for, Kendricks.'

'Then what, for Christ's sake?'

'I need some information, and I need it the day before yesterday, if you get my drift.'

143

Kendricks's hand is trembling so badly now that he nearly drops the receiver. 'Information? Yes, yes. Anything . . .'

'I want to know everything about Draegerman Enterprises. In particular, I want to know who built The Rock. I want the names of the contractors and the sub-contractors. The architects, the designers, the security firm, the electrical installation firms. Everything that there is to know.'

'Draegerman Enterprises? That's one of the biggest operations in the . . .'

'Everything, Kendricks.'

'Yes, okay. Everything. I promise.'

'Good. I'll ring you again tomorrow.'

'Tomorrow! Jesus Christ, I can't possibly . . .'

'I know of at least two fathers who would rather I'd cut something else off, Kendricks.'

'Tomorrow, okay, tomorrow!'

'Good. Get working.'

The telephone line buzzes as Taylor hangs up.

And Kendricks quells the urge to weep, reaching instead for the whisky bottle in his office desk drawer.

TWELVE

They continued down the black stone corridor, wary of each new curve ahead.

Their sense of unease and anxiety was constantly fuelled by the gigantic looming shadows on the walls and ceiling; shadows that were cast by the omnipresent orange lighting. Had those lights been stage-managed when installed to achieve just that effect? Gloria felt sure they had, thinking back to her days working with Draegerman, always then in awe of his presence of mind and his creativity; never believing that over the years the man who had fathered their son could have turned into the monster he now seemed to be. She too had been suffering from the sense of unreality and inability to come to terms with their current predicament. In a way, she felt bonded with the girl called Susan, fully empathising with her frequent refusal to believe that this was all actually happening. Because Gloria had been feeling the same way since that thing had exploded through the cinema screen. At that moment, fantasy had become reality – and a living nightmare. Something else had happened to her then, something she could not understand as they hurried on down the corridor.

No matter how much she thought back to her experience in the Screening Room, she could not quite recall the proper sequence of events. Her terror had been so intense, her instinctive knowledge of imminent death so heightened, that she could only recall fragments of what had happened as that unseen 'something' had writhed and thrashed and *scented* for her in the front rows of Draegerman's make-believe cinema. Her fear had reduced her, it seemed, to something less than human for a time, something incapable of rational thought. Something about . . . *it* . . . seemed to have driven her temporarily insane. As if its existence was such an anathema to anything human that the human part of its victim would simply shrivel and wither in its very presence.

Gloria shuddered. Although she did not understand she knew that above all else she must keep Bobby safe. As they hurried on, *he* was helping her, *he* was holding her arm as they moved – and that simple act filled her with raw emotion. It had been at least two years since they had seen each other, at least eighteen months since they had spoken on the telephone. Even then, it had been to argue about his drugs habit – even though he was ringing her to say that he was safe and okay, and 'dropping out' for a while. How much she had regretted that last telephone call, wishing ever since that she had concentrated on convincing him to come home so that she could look after him. Instead, she had berated him – and he had hung up. Now, in that simple act of his touching her arm – that simple act with no hint of melodrama – she looked at his face and saw him concentrating on the route ahead; saw that his only concern at this moment was to get them both out of the nightmare as quickly as possible. How much could he have known about his arrival at The Rock? Fragments? It was only since the flight from the 'jungle', or whatever the hell it was, that he had seemed to come back to life. The others were suffering reality problems, but Bobby seemed firmly adapted to what was happening, despite the fact that he must know less about their predicament than any of the others. Had he realised that he was Draegerman's son? More clearly than anything, she remembered what Draegerman had once said to her when they were filming *Swamp Water Woman*.

'*All my movies are my children. I love them and hate them all equally.*'

'*Hate them, Jack?*'

'*I can only love them because they're "me" or a part of "me". I hate them because they insist on having a life of their own.*'

'*What the hell are you talking about? Are you giving me some kind of "auteur" lecture?*'

Draegerman's face had become horribly cold then; not at all like the face she had kissed and caressed in the darkness of her room the night before as he moved inside her, bringing her to a peak of ecstasy that her jaded senses had not known for many years.

'*I mean – that my movies are ME, and once I've created them, I don't feel like letting them have their own life. Don't want to have thousands and thousands of popcorn-guzzling, back-seat-necking, dirty-raincoat jerk-offs sitting there watching them have a LIFE OF THEIR OWN.*'

And with that last outburst, he squeezed his glass of bourbon so hard that it shattered. Gloria had watched in horror as blood oozed through his fingers on to her trailer make-up table. When he spoke again, it was in a calm and controlled voice. But the tone of that voice seemed somehow more dreadful, more threatening than before.

'*And I'll never let another woman have and keep my child. It's the same thing, don't you see?*'

His meaning had been clear. She hadn't used any protection the night before, and neither had he.

And when she had subsequently found out that she was pregnant, she was filled with fear and resolve in equal measure. He might be the

146

high-and-mighty Jack Draegerman, but she was not going to abort her child. Maybe lots of things had slipped in her life, maybe she had done some questionable things. But she was not going to get rid of that child just because Jack Draegerman did not approve. In equal measure, she feared what he might do if he found out. Even then, he was a powerful man with powerful contacts. She knew all about the mystery of Deborah Steele, Draegerman's missing mistress; knew only too well how people – and presumably children – who did not fit into his scheme of things could so easily just vanish from the scene. So, to use her own son's words in the years to come – an ironic and bitter counterpoint – she had also 'dropped out'. To have her baby. And it was this, more than anything else, which had brought her career to a full stop.

She had kidded herself that she had fooled him, made no secret of other love affairs as a cover – so that when Bobby had come along, Draegerman might assume that the child was theirs, and not his own. She remembered sleeping with one second-rate Italian spaghetti western Lothario just to fuel that lie; something she had truly hated herself for afterwards, particularly when he'd gone around on set bragging about it.

She had even been proud when her son had shown what she believed to be a natural aptitude, showing off at some of the tawdry semi-movie-world parties she had attended afterwards when her star was on the wane. She remembered how proud she had been of his acting school placement, her pride when he landed his first movie role.

And then remembered her fear when Bobby had told her about the casting call for a Jack Draegerman movie. But what could she say? Don't do it? That fear had intensified when he had been selected for the part. But nothing had happened. The movie had wrapped after a short shooting schedule, and all her fears had seemed groundless. The fear had turned to something like perverse pride when Bobby had gone on to appear in not one but three Draegerman movies. And Jack the Bastard had never known that he was directing and promoting their own son.

How wrong could she have been? He had known all along.

Now, in this House of Horrors, she watched her lost son's face as he held her hand and they ran – and was flooded with an emotion she had never felt before. The emotion was impossible to analyse. Mother love, relief, pride, concern, fear? Suddenly, she was no longer tired.

The corridor continued to spiral downwards to their left. Farrow was not so much leading the way as giving the impression that he wanted to get away from them all and out of this place at whatever cost. They had been moving for a good fifteen minutes or more without speaking, the only sounds the clattering of their feet on the flags beneath and the susurrant sound of their breathing.

And then when Farrow vanished around the next bend they suddenly heard him scuffle to a halt and curse: '*Shit!*'

When the others reached him, they too stumbled to a halt.

At this next bend, the corridor had levelled out, was no longer spiralling downwards to the left. Instead, it stretched ahead for at least fifty yards – a long stretch of dripping black stone – before veering right into darkness. But now there was a change in the lighting. The lamps were no longer casting the omnipresent orange light although the fixtures on either side were the same, ten feet from the ground. Instead, the lights were dull green, making the corridor look like a stretch of sewer. Farrow whirled round now to glare at Jessica, saying nothing but making it clear from his expression that he was holding her personally responsible for the fact that they were no longer going down.

At that moment, they heard the sounds from behind. Distant, far away and difficult to decipher, sounding at first like the grumbling thunder of an approaching storm – now more like the sound of great gates moving into position.

'Now what?' Farrow looked as if he was going to punch one of the walls. Instead, he turned and smacked one hand into the palm of the other. The sound behind was changing again; now it sounded like some kind of great, ancient machine: the noise of giant cogs, of grating, screeching metal in a foundry; now, like muffled explosions below ground, and something like the sound of ghastly, mutated locomotives travelling slowly on iron rails down into Hell.

'Well, we can't go back,' said Bobby. 'That's for sure.'

'Oh, *hello!*' snapped Farrow, whirling on him. 'Welcome back to the real world. Does this mean we don't have to carry you anymore, Bobby baby?'

'Shut your mouth, Farrow!' shouted Gloria, her voice echoing away down the corridor. 'And less of the *we*. The only one you're interested in carrying is yourself.'

'Looks like someone else wants a smack in the . . .'

'Listen,' said Boone, holding up a hand.

The sound behind them had changed again. Now, it sounded more like the muted trumpeting of wild, maddened beasts. 'It's that thing again, isn't it? Oh, Christ – it's found us and it's coming after us again . . .' He hurried on past them, away down the sick-green corridor.

The time for arguing was over again. The others followed.

Halfway down this stretch, Boone suddenly realised that he was in the lead. He turned to look pathetically back at the others, his face a green-white mask. Roy moved past him, unable to look at him this time. The sounds of deranged animals had faded; now there was only a low and distant grumbling like the thunder of invisible storms. Roy checked the walls as they moved, looking for any more doors. There were none – and now the corridor ahead was veering to the left. He began to follow it, and then saw a new source of light.

Something was flickering on the right-hand wall. A white, strobing flicker of light reflecting from some source that he could not see around the corner. He stopped, holding up a hand; heard the others come to a halt. Slowly, he began to edge around the corner, back to the stone wall. There was a sound now, something that hissed like steam.

Sweat began to bead on his face and brow.

'What is it?' hissed Boone. The unexpected sound of his voice sent a spasm of fear through Roy's gut. Impatiently, he held up his hand again for quiet and continued to edge around the corner. The light was coming from something set into the wall around which he was edging – and when Roy suddenly realised what it must be, he pushed himself into the centre of the corridor in one swift movement and whirled around to look at it.

He was right. It was another of those damned television screens, set into the wall about eight feet from the ground. There was no taunting face on it – only a hissing blur of flickering static-snow.

The others moved quickly to join him as Roy ran a hand over his sweat-beaded face. The corridor ahead continued for about twenty feet or so before making a right turn; but this time it was clear from the cant in the ground that it was heading downwards again.

'That's more like it,' said Farrow, taking the lead again. The others followed, edging past the television monitor slowly, eyes glued to the screen; always expecting Draegerman's taunting face to appear again at any moment. Farrow turned at the corner and looked back, smiling at the look of fear on the others' faces. He turned about-face again to carry on.

And yelled in fear when something lunged from around the darkness of the corner and gripped him by the shoulders.

The impetus of the lunging shape sent him whirling back against the far corridor wall with bone-jarring force. Still yelling, he hit and kicked out at the enfolding, thrashing shape. Too stunned by this sudden violent moment to react, the others could only stand and watch – and then Farrow had kicked the figure away from him. It staggered back from him, slumping against the other wall.

It was a man. And, far from attacking Farrow, he was clearly terrified.

'My God,' said Boone. 'It's Aiken.'

'What the *hell* ...?' Farrow made to lunge forward and seize him, but now the leader of Draegerman's Black Suits was cowering back against the wall, hands held out in supplication. Now they could see that his clothes were dishevelled and torn, his designer sunglasses long since lost. His face was smeared with dirt and mud, his hair dishevelled and his eyes open and staring in fear: a far cry from the super-cool and

149

ruthless figure he had presented to them not so long ago. Something had gashed his left cheek and blood from the congealed wound had splashed his shirt front.

'Please . . . please . . .'

'What happened?' Roy stepped forward, and then stopped when Aiken seemed to shrink back in terror. 'Where are the others?'

Aiken swallowed hard, staring at Roy's face as if hardly recognised him. 'There are . . .' he began, then seemed afraid at the sound of his own voice. 'There are . . . *things* in here that I didn't know about. That none of us knew about. Christ, I've been running and running. I thought I knew the layout of this place. But I've been to places, seen places that I never knew . . .' Suddenly he rummaged in his torn jacket pocket and pulled out his gun. Roy shrank back and Gloria stifled a cry somewhere behind them. But far from threatening them with it, he moved suddenly away from the wall – and thrust it into Farrow's hands.

'Here! Here! You have it!'

Farrow weighed the gun in his hand, now looking up and smiling his hungry smile as he surveyed the others. 'All-*riggght*!'

Roy looked at Farrow, and felt far from happy that he should now be empowered in this way.

'Maybe it was me,' continued Aiken in agitation. 'Maybe I wasn't shooting straight or something. It could have been that, couldn't it? Maybe *that's* why I couldn't stop it . . .'

'What the hell are you talking about?' snapped Roy.

'That thing back there, the thing that broke into the Banqueting Hall.'

'Draegerman called it a Berserker,' said Boone, looking apprehensively back down the corridor.

'Whatever.' Aiken wiped a stained and ragged sleeve over his mouth. 'All I know is that it just came after us, and killed them all. I mean killed them *all*. Christ knows how I managed to get away, but . . .'

'What do you mean, *all*?' demanded Farrow.

'*He means that everyone in The Rock, apart from yourselves, is now dead,*' said a familiar and hated face from the television they had just passed in the darkness. The snowstorm had vanished, the screen was clear and bright. Again there was that slightly bemused look on Draegerman's face. Aiken took a step forward, the familiar anger seeming to swell inside him again. For an instant, it looked as if he might launch himself at the screen – but instead, the flare of anger subsided, and he shrank back against the wall once more. Draegerman paused. Was he really looking from person to person as they stood in the corridor? As well as being seen, could he also see *them*? '*What?*' he asked at last, when no one spoke. '*No questions?*'

'Questions?' Boone's voice was strangled, his lips trembling. '*Questions?*' And then something inside him seemed to snap, as if the ongoing

150

and ever-present fear was now impossible to contain. In impotent rage, Boone flung himself at the screen – falling to his knees when he could not reach it, now leaping up again and falling heavily to the stone floor. Finally, he remained kneeling there, head in hands, and began to weep.

'*Very well,*' continued Draegerman. '*Perhaps it's time that I gave you just a little more enlightenment. Are you sitting comfortably ...?*'

'You sick, evil bastard,' said Jessica.

'*... then I'll begin. Aiken is quite right. Everyone in The Rock, present company excepted, is dead. That's what the Berserker was supposed to do, that's what it was summoned for. To hunt and kill every one of my employees in the building, which it's done admirably – with the exception of one. But it's still here looking for you, Aiken. When it does get you, it will simply go back to where it came from.*

'*You see, it isn't quite the same as the others – who are almost here, I might add. It doesn't have, shall we say, a mind of its own. As part of the ceremony, part of the summoning procedure, it was necessary to "pave the way" by an act of blooding. It just goes to show, though, that even the best-laid plans of mice and men sometimes ... require amendment. Gloria, my darling – you're not supposed to be here either, I'm afraid. Just like Aiken. Naughty, naughty. You see, you were supposed to start the ball rolling. I was advised that the best way to start would be for one of the mothers of my children to be blooded. This would have got everything off to such a good start. You were a sort of ... hors d'oeuvre, I suppose. But you managed to get away from it somehow. I must commend you on that. So I had to do a little rearranging. No matter, really. The Berserker is still here, still hunting. Aiken is the important one, since he's the last of my own people required to feed it. Once he's gone, I'm sure one of the others arriving here will see to you eventually, Gloria. Unless the Berserker gets to you first, of course. Which brings me to the really important part.*

'*There are six of you here. Six of my children. And I've summoned six Guests – six Daemons. There's one for each of you. I've promised them that. They'll take one each – and then they'll leave. Once they've feasted on your minds, bodies and souls. Afterwards, well – they'll complete their part of the bargain, and I'll have what I want.*

'*But if the Berserker takes any of you before it gets to Aiken, then my plan is ruined. The pact will be broken, since my other Guests will have been denied what they have been promised. But that's the rush that gambling gives, isn't it? The possibility of failure gives so much more pleasure in the winning.*'

'Someone will come,' moaned Boone. 'Someone *must* come. You can't just shut us all in here, kill all your own people, without someone noticing!'

'*Good point, Boone. Maybe you're not going to be the runt of the litter after all. But I've been planning for this day for a long time. All my security staff have been instructed to be ready for what I call the "Four Day Rule". It's in the security manuals. Let me see . . . "To be ready for The Rock to close down and cease contact with the outside world. To maintain that security, to ask no questions, make no attempt to contact anyone inside, and to await reopening after the fourth day of shutdown." Except, of course, that when the four-day period ends, neither you – nor I – will be here any longer. You will be dead. And I will have . . . gone on to other things.'*

'Draegerman!' yelled Aiken desperately. 'For Christ's sake, after everything I've done for you, you've *got* to let me out of here! I've kept my mouth shut before, I can still keep my mouth shut now . . .'

'So faithful, Aiken. And you never dreamed that when the Four Day Rule came into operation you'd be on the inside. *You've entertained me in life, now do so with your death.'*

'Draegerman! Please, *noooo!*'

'So there you are for now, I think. Enough to be going on with for a little while . . .'

Draegerman's face began to fade from the screen.

Aiken slumped to the ground. Susan stooped down, and took off her shoe.

'My turn, I think,' she said.

Stepping forward, face set, she threw her shoe at the screen. The glass cracked from top to bottom as Draegerman's face finally vanished, leaving only the snowscreen. Almost casually, she retrieved her shoe and put it back on.

'Do you believe that stuff?' Farrow was still weighing the gun in his hand, his attention now fixed on Aiken. 'About Daemons, and all that crap?'

Aiken's eyes were glittering in the green darkness, his current physical condition and demeanour a startling contrast to his previous cool. 'All I know is . . .' He swallowed hard, looking anxiously back down the corridor. '. . . that thing that he called the Berserker, it tore my men to pieces . . . I mean it *tore* them to pieces.'

'I don't believe it,' said Farrow, the smile widening on his face. 'None of it. Don't you see?' He turned back to the others. 'It's all some bloody trick. Everything that Draegerman's said. That thing back there from the Screening Room. All a stage-managed trick, like one of his fucking horror movies.'

'It's *real*,' insisted Gloria. 'It nearly got me back there.'

'Says who? You? How do I know that you're not acting out your part just like Aiken might be acting out his own part? Is that what you're doing, Aiken? Acting out the part, just to give us a good scare? You say this gun didn't stop the thing that was after you? Let's try something out.' And then Farrow aimed the gun back down the corridor and fired. The sound of the shot was deafening. A chunk of stone blew out of the wall twenty feet from where they stood; the ricochet seeming to scream its way endlessly into the darkness. Farrow shook his head. 'Well, I was wrong on one score, I suppose. These aren't blanks this time, I'll give you that.'

'Stop fooling around with that thing!' snapped Roy.

'Or what?' And Farrow raised the gun to point it directly at him, smiling again. Roy stood, fists clenched. Farrow laughed again and lowered the gun. 'So maybe it's a game, maybe not. But this little toy's real enough, so I think I'll just hang on to it, just in case anybody does play some more games with us.'

'Which way do we go now?' Boone looked as if he might weep again. 'Which *way*? We can't go back, and Aiken came from the direction we're headed.'

'There's two . . . no, *three* doors back there,' breathed Aiken, leaning back against the wall, eyes closed now as if he was fighting to conserve his strength. 'I came through one, and . . . and we don't want to go back that way. So maybe one of those other two . . . ? If I can just get my bearings, I might be able to find one of the exits. It's just that . . . it's . . . well, I thought I *knew* this place. But I fucking don't! Maybe if we stick together – yeah, that's it! If we all stick together, then we'll be okay, won't we?'

'You mean like the way we stuck together back at the Banqueting Hall?' said Roy. 'When that thing was breaking down the door?'

'Okay,' said Farrow, shoving the gun into his pocket and moving off around the corner. 'Let's find those doors. See if we can find a snake or a ladder.'

'I'll never play a board game again in my life,' said Susan.

They moved off.

THIRTEEN

'Kendricks?'

'It's too soon! I haven't had enough time . . .'

Silence on the line then; a silence that makes Kendricks's mouth dry out, makes his fingers tremble on the receiver. 'Well, all right . . . look . . .'

'I'm getting impatient.'

'Christ, Taylor! I've tried everything, used all my contacts and all my favours. And I've run up against a blank wall each time. He's got four main business and administrative centres in the city, but all the internal details are controlled by his own security force. All the recruitment details, all the business records are harder to get at than the gold in Fort Knox. Look, what about newspaper and library files? They've got lots and lots of stuff on Draegerman's history. Why don't you . . . ?'

'Information on public record about Mr Draegerman's activities is not what interests me, Kendricks. You know what I asked you for, so where is it?'

This time, when Kendricks speaks, he sounds on the verge of tears. 'I've tried to track down everyone involved with the construction of The Rock: the engineers, construction experts, power, maintenance, sewage. And I can't come up with anything. It seems as if every firm, every company and every person originally involved with the construction of The Rock has gone out of business, disappeared or died. And there's something else. Someone has systematically destroyed all the official records. So how can I . . . ?'

'Okay, that's what I wanted to know. Something told me it might be like that.'

Kendricks's relief is audible on the other end. He gives vent to a barely suppressed sigh. 'Draegerman's got this thing about terrorist attacks, or kidnapping. Seems he got some anonymous notes back in the seventies. Maybe that's the reason. All . . . all I know is that people seem terrified to talk, that Draegerman's got some kind of hold over some of our top politicians. And listen, Taylor – if I go on asking questions about Draegerman Enterprises, there's a chance that I might

154

suddenly go missing, too. So at the moment, I seem to have a choice between you and them.'

'Don't get pushy, Kendricks.'

'I'm not . . . I'm not . . .' *There are sounds of fumbling as Kendricks takes out a handkerchief and mops his sweating brow.* 'It's just . . . just . . . look, I've got two names. Just two names. And I don't know if they're any good to you or not. But you've got to promise to leave me alone if I give them to you.'

Silence at the other end.

'Taylor? Can you hear me? You've got to . . .'

'The names?'

'You've got to promise.'

'Cross my heart and hope to die.'

'You mean it?'

'Give me the fucking names, Kendricks.'

Kendricks swallows hard. 'The first one is Talbot. Jeremy Talbot.'

'And who's he?'

'You've got to . . .'

'WHO'S HE?'

'He owned an architect's firm! They were sub-contracted for some of the interior construction work on The Rock.'

'Where is he?'

'Bradleigh Nursing Home. He's been in there since The Rock was built. Had some kind of nervous breakdown while he was actually working there. He's still not right in the head – so you can't blame me for that, Taylor! If he's still Loony Tunes and can't give you want you want, you can't hold me responsible.'

'Don't tell me anything about responsibility. What about his company? There must still be records . . .'

'The company doesn't exist any more. There was a fire shortly after Talbot was committed. Sixteen people died in the building. No one knows what happened to anyone else who worked for that firm. Like I said, they disappeared off the streets – just like I'm going to disappear if I keep on sniffing around Draegerman.'

'Like I say, I know one or two fathers who would rather you disappeared altogether, Kendricks. What's the second name?'

'Fisher. Terry Fisher. He was a guard working for Draegerman's security firm. Had an accident or something. I don't know any of the details. But you're going to find it difficult getting to him.'

'Why?'

'For the past few years, he's been living at a place near to The Rock called The Pool. That's a really rough place, Taylor. Run by someone called Moss. That part of the city belongs to street gangs. And Moss controls them. So you won't get near unless you go in with a riot squad. So – those are the names, Taylor. Now, you promised. You said . . .'

'I never said a thing. Anything else I need, I'll get back to you. Oh, and Kendricks?'

'Yes . . .'

"As the police might say: "Don't leave the country".'

FOURTEEN

'Mr Talbot?'

The old man in the wheelchair turned only slightly from his window, just enough to take in the figure of the nurse standing in the doorway, leaning in and smiling that all-purpose smile. The smile was part of her stock-in-trade, masking her real activities and intent – things like putting bromide into his medicine and chemicals in his food which made him pee in his trousers. All part of the overall plan to humiliate him. But it never worked. He was well past any humiliation.

'Mr Talbot, are you decent?'

Lot more decent than you!

The nurse stood slightly to one side, and Talbot could see a man standing behind her. He too appeared to be wearing the same all-purpose smile.

'Your nephew is here to see you, Mr Taylor.'

Still not speaking, Talbot rearranged the blanket on his lap and turned away again to stare out of his window into the night sky. The newcomer pushed gently past the nurse with a look suggesting that he had never hurt a fly in his entire life.

'Uncle Jeremy.' Talbot was aware of the man approaching, now sitting on the chair beside him.

'Not too long,' said the nurse from the door. 'A first visit might be a strain.'

'Thank you,' said the man.

When the door snicked shut, the old man turned back to look Taylor full in the face. For a while, he studied him, chewing and nodding as if weighing up this newcomer's presence. At last, he asked:

'How are you going to do it?'

'I beg your pardon.'

Talbot turned, apparently disgruntled by this unacceptable response, staring out of the window again.

'How am I going to do what?'

'I don't have a nephew called Taylor,' said Talbot, still looking out of the window. 'I've never had a nephew, never had any family.'

157

'I only came up with that line because the people in charge told me that you never wanted to see anyone, never wanted to talk to strangers. That's why I pressed the family relationship bit. Then they told me that *you* wanted to see *me*. Which surprised me a little, since I thought I was going to have a hard time getting to speak to you.'

Talbot turned back again: 'Again, I ask you – how are you going to do it?'

'Do what?'

'Kill me,' replied Talbot gently, as if he was talking to a child. 'That's why you're here, isn't it? To kill me?'

'What makes you think I've come to do that?'

'Don't play games with me!' Now the old man looked furious. 'I've waited long enough, put up with enough.'

Taylor sat back in his chair, weighing the old man up.

'All right,' he said at last. 'All right, if that's what you think. That's why I'm here.'

Talbot slumped back in his wheelchair, closing his eyes. Incredibly, he now looked immensely relieved, a half-smile on his face. 'Good ... that's good ...'

Taylor looked around the room. Plain pastel walls. No pictures. No books. One bed and a window. There was nothing here that could help Taylor in analysing the man who sat before him. The room was like a prison cell.

'Do you know?' continued the man, opening his eyes again and with the half-smile still on his face. 'In the first four years, I used to dread your coming. Every day, waiting for you to come, every night lying awake. Waiting to see you standing there in my room. Now I know that's what he wanted, of course. He wanted me to spend my days like that, waiting in terror for you to come. Prolonging the agony. But I beat him, Taylor. If that's your real name, of course.'

'That's my name.'

The old man nodded, as if really appreciating the honesty. 'Yes, I beat him. Because I came to terms with it as I got older. I learned something that he would never have dreamed about. You see – you can't, you just *can't* live with fear all the time. Hideous though it is while you're experiencing it, it can't last forever. Given time, it can be burned out. Now, far from fearing you – I've been awaiting your arrival with pleasure.' Talbot held up his hands. 'Look at me! Eighty-nine years old, and nowhere to go. I'm tired, Mr Taylor. So tired. I don't care whether you've been told to do it quickly, or prolong my pain if you have the time and the opportunity. Just do it, please, and let me rest.'

'I haven't come to kill you, Mr Talbot.'

'So that's part of the plan, part of the torture?'

'No plan, no torture. I'm only here to ask if you can help me.'

Talbot's eyes were like glittering marbles. The half-smile had vanished.

'Someone very close to me has been kidnapped,' continued Taylor. 'I've reason to believe that it's Draegerman's doing and that he has her with him inside The Rock. Now I know that you were sub-contracted to do some interior work there and . . .'

'Get out . . .'

'I need to find out everything I can about the place.'

'*Get out!*'

'I can pay you for any information. If you need time to think about it, here's a telephone number where you can contact me.'

'GET OUT!' Talbot knocked the piece of paper from Taylor's hand to the floor.

And in the next moment, the nurse was at the door.

Four minutes later, Talbot was on a ventilator and Taylor was outside on the street again.

For a long time he stood looking up at the sky, as if searching for answers.

There were none.

So where the hell do I go from here?

FIFTEEN

That same sick-green light suffused the corridor beyond. This was another fifty-yard stretch, identical to the corridor they had just come down.

Farrow jammed the gun into the small of Aiken's back and shoved him forward. Unprotesting, Aiken moved ahead. The first of three stout wooden doors, with the familiar three-claw ring handle in the centre, was clearly visible to their left.

'This is where I came in . . .' Aiken waved feebly at the first door.

'So why shouldn't we take this one?' asked Farrow.

'It doesn't go anywhere, believe me. Even if you wanted to go that way, you can't now.'

'What do you mean?' Roy pushed forward, and now they were all standing by the first door at a respectful distance.

'Something happened in there as I was running. I think the floor caved in. I could feel it coming apart beneath me. I only just made it through the door in time.'

'I still think you're lying,' said Farrow, keeping his eye on Aiken and now moving quickly to the door. 'I reckon this is the way we should go.'

'I don't think he's lying,' said Gloria. 'Look at his face.'

'Well, no harm in looking, is there . . . ?' And before any of the others could react, Farrow had pulled the door open. Its squealing hinges made them all flinch, the sound echoing away to nothingness. Farrow edged carefully around the door to look. No one else could see what lay beyond. His face remained blank, even when he looked back at Aiken – and then he savagely flung the door wide to crash against the wall.

'See! I told you all, he's a bloody liar!'

There was no corridor beyond the door – only a small enclosed space, no bigger than a pantry. Water ran gleaming down the stone wall at the back of the cupboard-like space. There were no shelves, nothing to indicate just what this space might be used for.

Farrow stepped forward, gun raised as if to strike Aiken. 'So there's a corridor there? And the floor caved in?'

Aiken shrank back against the far wall. 'I swear! That's the door I came through. I couldn't have made a mistake ... couldn't ...' His eyes were wide with fear and astonishment. 'That was the door! That *must* be the door.'

Bobby edged carefully into the small enclosed space, slapping his hand against the innermost wall and then shoving hard. It would not budge.

'Solid as a rock,' he said, emerging again.

'Let's try the other doors,' said Susan, moving off down the corridor.

'And *you*!' snapped Farrow, pointing the gun at Aiken again. 'You stay in sight all the time.' He waved the gun and Aiken, still utterly astonished and casting anxious glances back to the 'cupboard', moved ahead with the others.

The second and third doors were at the mid-point of the corridor, ten feet or so apart; the same solid oak and same three-claw handle in the centre of each. From behind came a sound of muffled thunder, like a dam breaking. They hurried to the doors, and paused there – waiting for someone to make a decision about which one to open.

'Both,' said Jessica at last. 'Let's open them both.' Quickly moving to one, she gripped the handle and looked back at the others.

Roy moved to the other door.

'Right,' said Farrow, taking Aiken by the shredded lapel of his jacket. 'If there's anything behind one of these, you're going to get a bullet and then I'll feed you to whatever it is.'

'Now,' said Jessica – and they heaved both doors open. The same squealing of hinges filled the air, like the dying cries of some night creature. Jessica pushed away from the door, ready to run if anything should come. But there was nothing there, only another corridor spiralling away to the right. Draegerman's light scheme here was also different: this time the fixtures in the walls were shedding a lurid blue over the running-wet stone.

Behind Roy's door, they could see a flight of rough stone stairs carved out of the rock, spiralling away down to the left and out of sight; like the stairs in some castle turret, again with the new blue light.

'It's make-your-mind-up time,' said Bobby.

'Aiken.' Roy moved towards him. 'Which way would *you* go?'

'The corridor, not the stairs. Yeah, definitely – the corridor.'

'Why?' snapped Farrow.

'It curves away to the right, and I think that might take us down to where one of the outside Walkways meets The Rock.'

'How do we know he's telling the truth?' Boone was rubbing at the scar on his face again, as if it was giving him pain.

'I gave him the gun, didn't I?' implored Aiken. 'Why the hell would I give him a loaded gun, if I wasn't telling the truth?'

161

'What about that door back there?' Susan pointed to the first one.

'I swear to God I'm not lying. Honestly, I came through that first door into this corridor. But you don't know what this lunatic place is like! Sometimes there are doors where you'd swear there wasn't a door before. If anyone should know their way around this place, it's me. But when that thing was after us, it was as if everything had been changed around ... doors, corridors, passageways, everything. Look, you heard what Draegerman said back there. He wants me dead, too. Look at me, for Christ's sake!' He gave a broad sweeping gesture with both hands, emphasising his torn clothes, his gashed and bloody face.

'No,' said Farrow. 'I still don't buy it. We're going to take the stairs.'

'Wait a minute,' said Roy. 'Much as I hate this bastard's guts for what he thought he was going to do to us, I believe him.'

'That's your privilege,' said Farrow, seizing Aiken's lapel again and propelling him towards the staircase door. 'But we're going this way.' He paused then on the threshold, still holding on to Aiken and keeping the gun close to him. 'So who else is coming?'

No one moved to join him.

'It's all part of the bloody plan,' continued Farrow angrily. 'Can't you see that? Draegerman wants us to go the way Aiken says. It's all part of the act. So who's coming with me?'

'Not me,' said Roy. 'I'm for the corridor.'

'Me too,' said Susan, and joined Roy at the threshold of the other door.

'I've got the gun!' snapped Farrow. 'That makes sticking with me a safer bet.'

'Not in my books it doesn't,' said Jessica, joining the others.

From somewhere behind, a long way away, came the mournful banshee howl of the Berserker, still hunting, still searching. Aiken flinched.

'We're taking the stairs!' Farrow pushed the barrel of the gun up under Aiken's chin.

'I'll come with you,' said Boone, and moved to join Farrow and Aiken.

'Big deal,' said Farrow. 'You're a real asset, Boone. But I'm telling you – keep up with me, or I'll leave you behind. And as long as I've got this gun, you do as I say. What about you two?'

Without answering him, Gloria and Bobby moved towards the others.

'Suit yourselves,' said Farrow. 'But you're making a big mistake.'

In the next moment, he shoved Aiken ahead through the door. 'Ever hear of mules and minefields, Aiken? No? Well, you're my mule – and that means you go first in case there's something else waiting for us down there.' Their shadows loomed large and angular

162

as they turned the corner and vanished from sight. Bobby shut the door behind them.

'Anyone want to change their mind?' asked Roy.

No one answered.

'Okay, let's go.'

They started down the spiralling, rough stone stairs.

SIXTEEN

'That's as far as I go,' said the taxi driver, pulling in to the side.

Taylor had been watching the night-dark streets as the cab flashed by, noticing how the buildings and the stores and the apartment blocks became steadily more decrepit as they headed down towards the neighbourhood that surrounded Draegerman's Rock. Occasionally, he had caught sight of the edifice, but there was no vantage point down here that would give a clear view. And on the occasions when he had seen it, strangely not illuminated at all and only showing as a blacker-than-black outline against the sky, he felt a knot in his stomach about what might be happening to Susan somewhere in the man-made mountain crag. He forced himself to suppress the feeling. It was unprofessional, and it might slow him down if he gave in to it.

Now the driver was looking at the clock on his dashboard, and without turning around he said: 'That's twelve-fifty.' It seemed as if all street lighting, however irregular it had been so far, ceased to exist altogether beyond this street; as if there was some kind of invisible barrier between this neighbourhood and the dark streets that led down to The Rock's perimeter.

'So where's *The Pool*?' asked Taylor. 'I don't see it.'

Again, without turning, the driver said: 'It's about four blocks down. Then you take a right – that brings you to *The Pool*.'

'So why are we sitting here?'

'Because I'm not going any further than here. I don't know what business you've got down there, but I hope you know what you're doing. This place has been no go for as many years as I can remember. Guy I know was stabbed after taking someone just around that corner.'

'How much did you say?'

'Twelve-fifty.'

Taylor leaned forward in his seat, proffering a twenty, and the driver slid open the small window behind him.

And when their hands connected, Taylor dragged him clear out of his seat until his entire arm was through the aperture and his face was pressed up close against the glass.

'Now listen to me,' said Taylor quietly. 'I asked you to take me to *The Pool*, because that's where I want to go. Did you hear me say: "Drop me four blocks away from *The Pool*"?'

'Christ, my arm! For God's sake, you're ...'

'*Did* you?' Taylor yanked hard again, slamming the driver's face against the glass.

'No, no, no! I didn't hear you say that.'

'And did you say anything about not wanting to take me there when I first got into your cab?'

'No, I didn't! I didn't!'

'Good. So now I'm going to let you go – and you're going to take me where I want to go. And you're not going to try any more funny business, because if you do I'm going to punch my way right through that glass partition and tear your fucking arm off. Do you understand?'

'Please ...'

'Do you *understand*?'

'Yes, I understand!'

'Good.' Taylor let go of the driver's arm and settled casually back in his seat. The driver slumped over the wheel, gripping his left shoulder, breathing heavily.

'Whenever you're ready,' said Taylor.

The driver gunned the engine into life. The car roared ahead, past the last street light and into the darkness. Taylor watched his face in the rear-view mirror. Was that very real look of fear just to do with what he had threatened, or was he really so terrified of being in this badly-lit neighbourhood? At the fourth block, the taxi took a sharp right, and Taylor could see that there were oil drums in the street. Fires had been started in the drums, lighting the surroundings in stark, sharp-angled relief, making the shadows on either side loom and sway. At first Taylor could see silhouettes of people, standing there in the street backlit by the fires. But before the images had a chance to register, the shapes melted away into the darkness.

As the taxi roared down the street, Taylor could see that most of the tenements here had boarded windows. A car had been dismantled at the side of the road, its innards tossed around. The taxi jolted as they went over a wheel-trim. And now, at last, Taylor could see a half-circle of neon above a door on the right hand side: *T-e Po-l*. Even though two of the bulbs had burned out, this sight of neon seemed out of place, extravagant in an area where there was no other man-made light apart from the burning barrels.

The taxi driver executed a handbrake turn, the car spinning to face in the opposite direction, tyres screeching and leaving twin tracks of burned rubber on the corroded street surface.

'Thank you,' said Taylor. 'How much now?'

'Never mind the money,' yelled the driver, nervous eyes glancing around for signs of anything moving. 'Just get the fuck out of my car!'

Taylor dropped his twenty on the back seat and climbed out of the car, slamming the door. In the next instant, the car was roaring back the way it had come, tyres screeching again as it took a sharp turn.

And when he turned back to look for the neon sign, the street was suddenly full of silent figures, all standing and watching him, their shadows harsh and angular across the street, backlit by the burning petrol drums. They remained still and silent as Taylor walked slowly down the centre of the street to meet them. To the right, he caught sight of someone standing in the shadows beneath the neon sign. As he approached, the figure suddenly vanished inside.

Twenty feet away, Taylor stopped.

'I'm looking for Moss.'

'Got any money?' It was impossible to tell who had spoken. With the light behind and the darkness all around, the shapes were only silhouettes without faces.

'Not as much as I'd like,' Taylor replied. His voice seemed to carry in the street. 'But I don't have business with you. I'm looking for Moss. Someone told me I could find him in *The Pool.*'

'But have you got as much as *we'd* like?' asked another voice, ignoring the last part of Taylor's statement. Again, it was impossible to tell who had spoken. But now it seemed that the silhouettes were laughing quietly. Taylor did a quick head count. There were nineteen – not counting anyone who might be concealed in the doorways.

'Not enough to go around nineteen times,' said Taylor. 'But maybe enough for one or two. If they had balls enough to come over here and take it, that is.'

The figures were no longer laughing.

'I'm here to see Moss, that's all. And I don't want any trouble.'

'I think you're so scared right now that you're pissing in your pants,' said someone.

'Come on, then, let's have one or two of you.' Taylor's voice remained calm and resolute. 'If all of you come on at once, then you'll get it all and have to squabble about how you're going to split it up afterwards. But one or two, well, that makes it easier to divide up. You can divide up, can't you? Doesn't look to me as if any of you can read.'

The crowd began to move forward.

In the next instant, something *snicked* – and a switchblade had appeared in Taylor's hand. The sudden, rapid movement caught the figures off guard – and they halted while Taylor took a step *towards* them, holding the knife casually, as if he might be going to pare his fingernails rather than use it on anyone who might rush him.

His gamble seemed to have paid off as one of the two shadows who

166

had reappeared in the doorway beneath the neon sign suddenly stepped forward and shouted:

'Enough!'

The silhouettes in front of Taylor turned to look back at the sound of the man's voice. For the first time now, Taylor could see some of the faces in the firelight: none of them looked older than twenty. They waited while the man walked down to the street, joined now by the other shadow.

'Mr Taylor,' said the newcomer, and now it was Taylor's turn to be surprised. How the hell could this stranger know his name? He stayed where he was, kept his face impassive. The figure reached the street, stood for a moment as if appraising him, then beckoned. 'Please, come with me.' The others shuffled uneasily. 'It's all right. Mr Taylor and I have some business to discuss.'

Taylor casually closed his knife and put it away, walking slowly over to join the newcomer. 'You must be Moss.'

'Now how about that?' said the figure. 'We both know each other's names and we haven't even been formally introduced.' At last, Taylor could see with whom he was dealing. The man was in his late thirties perhaps; black African and wearing a multi-coloured waistcoat that Taylor was surprised had not shown up even in this darkness. He seemed fit; his arms were bare and he was wearing a sweatband, even though his hair was cropped close. His face and arms gleamed black in the firelight, as if he had been working out and the sweat had yet to dry. One of his front teeth was missing. Moss seemed to catch his look, and smiled.

'Used to be gold, but when I needed the cash, I pulled it out and sold it.'

'Times are tight,' said Taylor.

'Never been tighter and getting worse all the time.'

The other young men seemed utterly at ease now. Some were sitting on the kerb, smoking and talking, others carrying on with an argument that had started before Taylor's arrival. The air of menace was still there, but the immediate threat had passed. Even so, Taylor knew that he had to be on his guard when Moss said: 'Follow me.'

They walked back to the neon sign and, without turning, Moss plunged straight through the doorway and into the darkness. The other shadow nodded as Taylor passed. An Asian, perhaps late forties, with a face that looked as if it had been smashed up and refixed several times. Inside, the light was dim, but as Taylor's eyes became accustomed to it, he saw that they were passing through a bar. He fixed his sights on Moss's muscular back as the man moved quickly through, but out of the corner of his eye he could see shapes at the bar, silent as they passed. Several card games were in progress. Somewhere, a woman was singing – but whether this was for real, or from a jukebox, he could not say. Now they had turned a corner and Taylor was aware of the shadow behind him, probably the Asian guy from the entrance. They were passing several pool tables, the green-shaded lights above the baize the only details in the darkness. Faces peered up at them; someone paused before making a shot.

And then they turned again and Taylor saw a room with work-out equipment, barbells and a makeshift frame for squat-lifts.

'You work out?' asked Moss without turning.

'I try to keep fit.'

Moss laughed, a low and musical sound. 'Maybe I should have waited a little longer. See if you could back up your hard man's challenge.'

'No,' said Taylor. 'I think you came at a good time.'

Moss laughed again, opened a door and entered a small room where three men were playing cards beneath a single light bulb in the ceiling. The air was filled with cigarette smoke. The ethnic mix of the men was strange, if not downright unusual for an area that was supposed to be ruled by street gangs. One was clearly Chinese, another white (with one empty eye socket, it seemed), and the other was black. The mix seemed to reflect what he had seen since his dramatic arrival at *The Pool*. There was no common factor. He had never seen such a mélange of racial types before in this situation.

The door closed behind Taylor, and he turned to see that the Asian with the battered face had taken up position there with his back to it. The card game stopped when Moss pulled up a chair and sat at the table. The others turned in their chairs to examine the new arrival. There was no other chair, so Taylor stood where he was and concentrated all his attention on Moss. Clearly, Moss was searching his face for any sign of unease. After a long thirty seconds, he began to laugh again.

'Damn, you're good. Isn't he good, Lee?'

The Chinese uttered a grunt that could have meant anything at all.

Just as suddenly, the smile vanished from Moss's face. When he spoke again, his voice was deadly serious.

'You're a hard man, but you're a foolish man. Don't you know what it's like on these streets?'

'Let's just say I'm here on business.'

'Well, what business have you got on *our* streets?'

'I need some help.'

'We're not in the welfare business. Leastways, not the way you might think. The only people we help are our *own* people. That's the way it's been on these streets for a long time. Since the so-called authorities gave up on us, we have to look out for ourselves. So why the hell should we help you? What the hell do you want, anyway?'

'I'm looking for a man.'

'What man?'

'Terry Fisher.'

No one's expression changed, but Taylor could feel the chill suddenly deepening.

'What the *fuck* do you want with him?' asked Moss, eyes blazing.

'Cut him up and throw the bastard out.' The one-eyed card player turned away from the table in disgust, as if to rise.

Moss gripped his arm, and made him stay there. 'Know how I knew your name?' he asked Taylor calmly.

'Probably the same source as I got Fisher's name from, and yours. Kendricks.'

Moss nodded, smiling again. This time the smile was glacial. 'Yeah, Kendricks. He was sniffing around, asking some questions. He got the name all right, but that's all he got. You see, if anyone starts sniffing around me and mine, I have to ... take steps ... to make sure they don't have anything left to sniff with. Know what I mean?'

'I know what you mean. Perhaps I shouldn't rely on getting anything else out of Kendricks.'

'No shouldn't about it. Unless he's a good swimmer.'

'Difficult to swim carrying so much weight,' said the man behind Taylor. 'Should have gone on a diet before he started asking questions.'

'There's more than one person will be glad of that,' said Taylor.

Moss nodded, as if they now understood each other. 'Before Mr Kendricks left on his indefinite vacation, he gave me your name. In fact, it's surprising the amount of information he wanted to give me. Very keen, very eager. Got to find out a lot of things about you, Taylor. Some of it I liked – that's why you were able to get past our front door. But your reputation won't get you any further than this room if we don't like what we hear next.'

'I want to speak to Fisher. That's all. I want to find a way to get into Draegerman's Rock.'

There was silence then. And Taylor could feel the sweat in the small of his back.

'Let me tell you a story,' said Moss, sitting back. 'Once upon a time there was this guy who had spent time in prison, had been knocked around most of his life, could never find the right place, the right job. Just didn't fit in. Until he was recruited by Draegerman Enterprises as a security guard. Pay was good, but company was a little strange. A little hard, know what I mean? Seems that most of the security people on Draegerman's crew had some kind of form, had a certain taste for ... efficiency in the line of duty, let's say. That was okay, because at last he had a place to *be*. Then one night, while he was patrolling one of those Walkways, some kids on the neighbourhood side started to joke around. You know what kids are like. Shouting, yelling, a couple started to throw stones. No chance of hitting anyone, understand. Just horseplay. But then one of the bastards that's patrolling the Walkway

169

with the subject of my story just ups with his automatic and starts firing. Two kids get hit. One in the foot, still limping bad today. Another one killed outright. But our friend, the one I'm talking about, grabs this other guy and they have a heated argument. And during that heated argument, the guy who shot the kids goes over the edge of the Walkway.'

Moss paused, still looking without expression into Taylor's eyes.

'That's a long, *long* way down, man,' he continued. 'So, anyway . . . the other guards on that Walkway jump on our friend and kick the living shit out of him. Then they take him back into The Rock. And normally, that would be the end of the story.

'But then, three days later, when the fucking police aren't going to do anything – as usual – a guy is found wandering through the streets around The Rock. This guy looks in a very bad way. His clothes are torn, somebody seems to have cut him so bad that you can trace the blood-spill all the way back to one of the Walkways. He doesn't seem to care that he's in a *bad* place. His eyes are staring, and he's talking to himself, but none of it makes much sense – and sure as hell he doesn't know which way he's going.

'Before long, it happens. He gets rolled by a bunch of kids. They knock him down, can't find anything of any use to them on him – so they decide just to kick his head in for the inconvenience. But lucky for him, one of those kids is also one of the kids that was shot at from the Walkway. And he recognises this guy, 'cause he had his helmet knocked off in the fight, and it's difficult to forget that thick red hair. Redder now, with the blood stains and all, but white around the edges – like he's suddenly aged about ten years. So the kid stops them from stamping the guy flat, and they bring him to me.

'That was two years ago, and he's been with us ever since. That fucker up there in his tower, and the ones who work for him, they did something to him then. Something to his mind, something worse than torture. We still don't know how he got away. He once told us that he *flew* over. But that doesn't matter. What matters is that he's still suffering from what Draegerman did to his head. Suffering so bad sometimes that we've got to keep him high all the time, just to keep those blue demons away. So you see, the thing is, Mr Taylor – we look after our own.

'But the story doesn't end there. Because shortly after he came to us, Draegerman's people came looking for him. Bad move. For them. Like I say, up at The Rock, Draegerman might be *the* man, but down here on the streets . . . well, that's a different matter.'

The Chinese laughed. 'A *lot* different.'

'They tried to come heavy on us, tried to bribe us, then tried to scare our people. Result? We put six of their men in hospital, two permanently. And they never came sniffing around again. End of

170

story. So tell me, Taylor. Now that you know the score, why should we help *you*?'

'Because he's got someone in there,' said Taylor. 'Someone in The Rock with him ...' He stopped himself from saying 'someone I love', the wrong phrase in his present company. 'Someone I've been paid to get out.'

'Ahhh, money,' said Moss. 'Ever the professional, Mr Taylor. But I still haven't heard one fucking reason why we should help you.'

'But there *is* another reason why you should help me.'

'And that is?'

'Because I want to hurt Draegerman very badly. For personal reasons.'

'He means what he says,' said another voice.

An elderly woman had suddenly appeared from the darkened corner of the room. Her appearance startled Taylor, even though he forced himself not to react. The woman was perhaps seventy years old, her black face weatherbeaten, the eyes hidden almost completely in folds of skin. She was wearing something that looked like a brightly coloured pinafore dress. Instantly, the one-eyed card player swivelled out of his seat and held it for her. She groaned as she sat. 'These old bones ...'

'You want some whisky?' asked Moss.

'No, just listen to me. This Taylor-man, he's speaking from the heart. I taste it in my mouth. No more argument now. You listening?'

For reasons he could not properly discern, Taylor found himself swamped by a massive wave of relief at this woman's appearance.

'I'm listening, Mother.' Now why the *hell* had he called her that? But it was a good word, even so, because something that was almost a smile came and went on the aged, lined face.

'Good. You know why these streets are bad?' The old lady leaned across the table and pointed a finger at Taylor. 'It's 'cause of that thing out there, that thing that stabs up into the sky. Draegerman's Rock, they call it. Me, I got another name. Draegerman's *cancer*. 'Cause that thing isn't stabbing up into the sky at all. It's stabbing down *into the ground*. That thing he built, it's more than a house, more than a place for him to hide and live in. It's *him* – that thing that stabs into the heart of the earth. It's Draegerman hisself, dark heart and dark soul. And it's sucking all the good out of the ground. You can feel it every day that passes. It's sucking all the goodness and the love and the kind thoughts and the caring, right out of the ground, right out of the people who have to live around it. I don't care what anyone says, *that's* what's happening. And it's spreading, Taylor-man. Street by street, alley by alley, building by building – everything around that thing he calls The Rock is being sucked dry of the goodness, leaving only the bad behind.'

'You're talking Street Belief again, Mother,' said Moss.

'And that's the right word. *Belief*. 'Cause seeing is believing, and I've

171

seen it with my own two eyes. Now I've had my say-so. You take this man to see Terry. Anything that hurts The Draegerman helps us.'

Still expressionless, Moss stood up. Behind him, Taylor heard the Asian open the door. As Moss passed him, he said: 'Follow me.'

'Thank you, Mother,' said Taylor, nodding his head.

'You just get the girl out, and hurt him bad while you're doing it.'

Girl? Who'd said anything about Susan?

Taylor nodded again, and turned to follow Moss. The old woman's voice made him turn back.

'And just remember, when the time comes to start hurting The Draegerman, you might find you've got friends in *low* places.' The old woman started to laugh then, as if she had cracked the funniest joke in her life. Still apprehensive at what lay ahead, Taylor tried his best to return a smile.

Then the Asian pushed him gently from behind.

Taylor squinted through the gloom, saw Moss's powerful frame up ahead, and followed.

SEVENTEEN

Roy, Jessica, Susan, Gloria and Bobby wandered down the winding corridor in silence. They had no idea how long they had been walking. An hour? A day? Time seemed to have lost its meaning. Sometimes the corridor curved to the right, at other times to the left – but it was always heading downwards. When they came to an opening on their right, Roy got there first, turned and looked at the others. It was another corridor, this time heading upwards. No one discussed whether they should take the turning. Upwards meant back to the horror, back up into Draegerman's lair. Instinctively, they knew they must go down.

They continued slowly downwards. Hunger and exhaustion were now threatening to rob their strength.

Susan gritted her teeth, and concentrated on her feet. The kids were safe, they must be safe, and that was the only thing that mattered. Sara and Den would be there to look after them, and surely the police must be involved in her disappearance now. Surely those black-suited bastards couldn't just drug her and carry her out to a car without being seen by anyone? For once, nosey neighbours seemed a positive asset. No, someone must find out where she had gone. And then she thought back to the hideous things that Draegerman had told them all in the Banqueting Hall; about the other guests who had been invited to the Rock over the years. Surely he must have made up those stories, about what he had done to them and made them, in terror, do to each other? Susan's stomach heaved. No, that part of it surely could not be true. Maybe this was some kind of test, a test of their strength and their endurance – all of it some kind of fantasy, or living video game, or . . .

Susan forced herself to concentrate on the corridor ahead. Already she could feel the urge to retreat from the reality of their situation, could feel the potential relief from the ever-present fear in pretending that all this was not really happening. But it *was* happening, and she was not going to let that bastard Draegerman get away with it. She thought of the kids, and it gave her strength – and then another image supplanted it: an image of the kids crying and grieving and begging Sara and Den to tell them where she had gone, why she had run away. She tried to block this image from her mind, tried to concentrate instead on her need to be strong, to get through this alive and return home to them. Fists clenched, she glared at the corridor wall. It seemed somehow as if the very stones were trying to suck out every last ounce of her strength, replacing that strength only with fear. Gritting her teeth, Susan cursed Draegerman and carried on, fighting her inner battle . . .

Jessica struggled with the out-of-body feeling she had begun to suffer ever since they had started this new descent. Although her fear and anxiety were constantly with her, she had at first experienced something like minor relief when Farrow had decided to carry on through the other door and down the stairs. He had made it quite clear that he held Jessica responsible for their delay in getting out of this place, and now that he had a gun he might be in a position to do something about it. But the relief had been short-lived. Now it was as if the crowding fear had taken Jessica completely out of herself. At times, she seemed to be floating near the ceiling of this winding, dripping, green-lit corridor; watching herself and the others as they descended. And – more than that – she was utterly unable to think of their present plight at this moment from anything other than a reporter's perspective. Even from this curious floating position, she found herself examining the others, watching their movements, seeing their fear. Was this some defence mechanism on her part; examining the fear that everyone else was feeling, so that she would not have a chance to think about herself, and what might lie in store? Whatever the reason, there was a form of comfort here. She could see the copy even now, and it would make one hell of a story.

Hell, an inner voice seemed to say to her. *Yes, that's exactly where you are, Jessica. And the further you travel, the deeper into Hell you're going.*

She was shocked out of the floating sensation. Now she was back again with the others, descending silently. Was that voice an inner thought? Or did it seem more like Draegerman, somehow talking to her directly in her head? The very sound of that voice, the way it made her feel, threatened to bring the terror crowding back in on her.

'No,' she said aloud, and the others turned to look at her. She shook her head. 'Sorry, I was thinking out loud.'

But were they my thoughts? Or someone else's?

The floating feeling had returned, and now in her head Jessica could hear: *'As we descended in silence, each one of us was absorbed in our own thoughts, our own fears about what might lay ahead. Draegerman had promised us terrors, had talked at length about raising Daemons. But how much of this was actually true, and how much the delusions of a madman? After all, no one had seen the thing he called the Berserker up close. Susan had only seen bare glimpses of it, as had we all as something tore its way through the Banqueting Hall door. Even Gloria, who had been attacked by the thing, seemed unable to tell us what it had been like. Was it real? Or was it something from one of Jack Draegerman's movies? If we had a chance to look closer, would we really see that all we had to be afraid of was a man in a rubber suit, with the zipper clearly visible up the back? After all, illusion had once been Jack Draegerman's stock-in-trade ...'*

Fear is never an illusion, intruded the voice again. *It's a real response to something that hungers for your pain, your agony, and slow death.*

Jessica refused to listen, and continued: *'But the fear on everyone's face as we descended was real enough ...'* No, not that. No. *'We were determined to get out of that place even if it meant ...'*

Fear is never an illusion ...

No! *'We were determined ... determined ...'*

Fear.

'... determined ...'

Roy wondered what time of day or night it was outside The Rock. He checked his watch, only to find that it had stopped. Unknown to him, everyone else's watch had stopped, all at the same time. From the moment that they had arrived. He wondered how much time had passed. Was it day yet? He wondered whether Frank Wells had turned up at *The Wayside* as usual, looking for his free beer and an explanation of what the hell had happened the previous day. But that all seemed like a lifetime ago; in a different world, a different time. Roy cursed himself, remembering how he had felt when the helicopter first approached The Rock. As usual, it seemed that his first instincts were right, and he had ignored them. Would the Black Suits have allowed him to leave, if he had said that he was not going ahead with the invitation? Or had they received orders merely to pretend to go along with his choice, and then put a bullet in him when they were somewhere out of the way? No, now he knew that if he had insisted on leaving, then the Black Suits would have insisted he stayed. Draegerman's cover would have been blown, and maybe that would have spoiled some of the sick bastard's fun, but it was always intended that each of the guests should come. After all, they had drugged Susan when she said 'No'.

And do you believe that she didn't want to come? Now where the hell did that thought come from? *You've only got her word for it, Roy. Maybe she's here because she wants to be here.* That doesn't make any sense, Roy. Stop thinking like that. Just keep going and maybe we can find a way out ...

You'll never leave alive.

Shut the hell up, Roy! And keep going ...

Gloria searched her son's face as they walked. Ever since he had been born, she had spent time carefully examining that face to see whether he would turn out looking like his mother or his father. She had prayed to God that he would not be the spitting image of Jack Draegerman. Fortunately, he looked like neither of them. And that had given her some comfort. But now she knew that Jack had known all along that Bobby was their child. All that worry about Bobby going into the acting profession, the casting call, appearing in Jack's movies. She had been gloating then, when the fear had gone – but Jack had known all along, so the last laugh was undoubtedly on her. Unconsciously, she gave vent to a small, bitter laugh. Bobby looked over at her with concern, but she managed a fractured smile and shook her head, confirming that she was all right. Bobby nodded, put an arm around her shoulder, and they carried on. That embrace brought everything bubbling to the surface again. What was she feeling? Relief, joy at the reunion with her son, or just downright fear at what was going to happen to them both in this House of Horrors? Whatever, it threatened to burst out of her at any second like some kind of emotional dam giving way. She looked down, forcing the tears back. Her eyes misted, but she managed to pull herself away from the danger. Bobby could feel her body shaking. He did not look, but hugged her tighter as they walked.

Gloria damned Jack Draegerman to hell for what he was putting them through. Even though she could not explain the nature of the thing that erupted through the cinema screen, she knew instinctively that just pretending it did not exist would not make the terror go away. She believed him when he said she was meant merely as an hors d'oeuvre, an initial 'blooding' of one of the mothers. Well, this was one bloody mother who was not going to give up without a fight.

But you're going to die, a voice seemed to be saying in her head. *Don't you realise that, Gloria? And not only that, you're going to die in agony and terror – and no one will care.*

Gloria glanced at the corridor wall. Had that thought merely been her inner fear, bursting through in her head? Or had it come from somewhere else? It seemed such an independent thought, so malevolent, so intense and evil. She shook her head. *No, keep it together, Gloria. Keep going. There must be a way out of here. There MUST be ...*

Bobby held on to his mother, hoping somehow that he could generate strength within for both of them. No one knew what he was going through, everyone seemed to think that he had adjusted to this bizarre nightmare. But he had been fighting the shakes ever since he had emerged from his blur in the Banqueting Hall. He barely remembered the figures who had emerged from the darkness of that alley, certainly could not remember why he was in the alley in the first place. But he remembered he had felt good, then. That feeling had lasted for a long while. Vaguely, he remembered travelling in the back seat of a car. And then sitting in a large chair, in front of an open log fire. But now that he had emerged from the blur into this new and real nightmare, he knew that it would only be a matter of time before . . .

Before the shakes begin.

That wasn't my voice. That couldn't have been my voice.

Come on, now. This won't be the first time you've heard voices in the head, Bobby. This surely can't be the first time you've heard and seen things that weren't there?

Oh Christ, it's starting again earlier than I thought.

You need a fix, Bobby. That's a shame, because there's nothing here for you.

I can beat this. I know, this time, I can beat it.

How many times have you told yourself that before? How many times have you begged for it, sold everything just for a little bit of that white dust? I bet you've even sold yourself once or twice. Know what I mean, Bobby? Sold yourself?

'No!' Bobby suddenly stopped, clutching his midriff. It was as if the voice in his head had brought on the delirium tremens earlier than he had thought, as if it had conjured them up in order to make them worse. Gloria grabbed his arms, and now all the others had stopped to look back at him.

'No!' Bobby reeled and reached for the corridor wall. He missed, falling heavily to his knees. Susan had joined Gloria and grabbed an arm. Roy pushed forward, and Bobby could hear their voices, but they made no sense now. There was only the drug-voice in his head.

You can't run away from yourself, Bobby. You can't run away from what's inside your head. Don't you know that by now?

'No!' And this time, Bobby keeled over sideways. Faces swum in his vision, but he could not make out their features. There was only the overwhelming fear and the terrible pain in his stomach.

Can't run away, Bobby. Can never run away . . .

But he did run away, inside his head. Unconsciousness enfolded him. And in that great grey space there was no pain, no fear and no voice . . .

'All right,' said Roy. 'Perhaps we'd better stop for a while just to rest.'

Gloria hugged Bobby close to her, could still feel the violent trembling in his body even though he was unconscious. 'It's withdrawal,' she said. 'He'll be okay. He just needs rest . . .' She nursed him like a child, as if making up for lost years; hoping that her love could make him whole and better again.

Jessica looked ahead anxiously. She too was exhausted, but felt that they must go on. She began to say something, and then saw that Susan was sitting next to Roy on the cold stone floor. Instead, she raised her hands in surrender, slumped back against the other wall and slid to a sitting position, uncaring when a snag of rock tore her jacket at the sleeve.

There was silence then, while they listened for the sounds of a distant banshee wailing and roaring; something to suggest that the Berserker – or whatever it might be – had found them. But there was no sound, other than the small crooning noise that Gloria was making into Bobby's ear as she rocked him in her arms.

Seconds later, exhaustion had taken its toll in spite of the danger. They slept.

EIGHTEEN

A fight had started at one of the pool tables, and Moss nodded to the Asian behind Taylor. As Taylor followed him up a flight of uncarpeted stairs, he looked back to see the man striding through the darkness towards the troublesome pool of light. At his approach, the two men struggling there broke apart and looked conciliatory. Clearly, no one was prepared to argue any more.

At the third landing, two teenagers in shellsuits sat on the top step, drinking from cans of beer.

'Guards?' queried Taylor.

'No,' said Moss without turning around. 'Terry's here with us because he wants to be here.' The teenagers stood aside as they passed, then resumed their seats and their conversation. Moss moved to the only door on the landing and knocked.

'Terry?'

Taylor heard a muffled response from behind the door.

'It's Moss. You sleeping?'

Again, a muffled response.

This time, Moss opened the door and walked in. Taylor followed. The entire room was bathed in low red light from a single table lamp beside a large double bed. The rest of the furniture was a mass of formless shadows. Taylor closed the door, and when he looked back he could see that there was a man on the bed, sitting up, presumably naked. It was impossible to make out any details of his face. From somewhere off to the right came the sounds of hissing water and a clink of glass. Someone, somewhere was having a shower.

'This a bad time?' Moss asked.

The man on the bed shook his head, but someone in the hidden shower room offered a muffled reply. Moss crossed the room to where the bathroom door was hidden in shadow, and Taylor could now see a sliver of orange light on the floor, from under the door. Moss tapped on the door, and called through it: 'I asked if this is a bad time.'

'What the hell are you after?' asked a woman's voice, in a tone that was jokingly provocative rather than hostile.

179

'I'm after you,' said Moss, smiling. 'Didn't you know that?'

'Hear that, Terry?' asked the invisible woman.

'I heard it,' replied the shadow from the bed. 'A jealous man is a sad thing to behold.'

'You've got two minutes,' called the woman. 'That's all.'

Moss moved back to the bed, sitting on the edge. 'You heard the girl, Mr Taylor. That's how long you've got.'

The shadow took a deep draw on his cigarette and then waved casually to a corner of the room. Taylor moved there to find a chair hidden in the darkness. He brought it back and sat beside the bed.

'Taylor?' queried the shadow. 'Should I know you?'

'No.'

'Been a long time since I had visitors,' said Fisher.

'I can understand that,' replied Taylor casually.

'The fact that Moss allowed you in here means it must be important.'

'I'm told that you might be able to help me.'

Fisher paused then to take another draw, this time inclining his head towards Moss.

'He's cool,' said Moss. 'Mother says he's okay.'

Fisher nodded, then leaned back with a weary sigh. 'It's to do with Draegerman, isn't it?'

'Yes,' replied Taylor.

'You *from* Draegerman?'

'No. He's kidnapped somebody. Got her in there against her will. And I want her out.'

'In The Rock?'

'That's right.'

'Then she's never going to get out alive.' Fisher seemed to shudder then, drawing on his cigarette again. Taylor could see and smell that it was not an over-the-counter brand. When he turned his face to look directly at Taylor again, the red light spilled over his face and Taylor could see him properly for the first time. This was a man in his late twenties, but something about his eyes and the crow's feet there made him look as if he had seen Hell and come back.

'Yes she is,' said Taylor. 'If you'll help me.'

'How?'

'You worked for Draegerman's security people. You must know a way into The Rock.'

'Yeah. There are four.'

'You mean the Walkways?'

'That's right.'

'And there's no other way?'

'No, the sewer system is impregnable. Like a fucking maze, even if you could find the maps. Which you won't, of course. They're designed

180

in such a way to prevent anyone getting in there. I saw pieces of bodies floating around down there once.'

'The roof?'

'No chance. Draegerman's own helicopters have security-encoded strips in the fuselage. That guarantees a safe landing on the pad up there. If anything else tries to touch down without that inbuilt security coding, then two automatic cannons in the towers just open up and blow it away. Had a glitch in the equipment two months after I started there. Fella got out of the 'copter and had his head blown off. *Not* a happy situation. Everyone got a bonus that month to make up for it.'

'Then it's the Walkways.'

'Can't do it. Twelve men per Walkway. Six in the towers overlooking the gates and six in a security station at the halfway point on each Walkway.'

'Seems like the man's expecting a war,' said Moss.

'He just might get one,' said Taylor.

'I can tell you something about those Walkways, Taylor,' said Moss. 'Something that you don't know.'

'And that is?'

'The only way on to each of those Walkways is through the gates. Anything coming out of that gate or going into it always gets a reception from the kids who live around there. I know for a fact that one of Draegerman's black sedans was seen going hell for leather into there with two women in it. Maybe one of them was yours.'

'Dark hair, about twenty-five.'

'Yeah, could be one of them. But, I have to tell you, they didn't seem to be going in there against their will.'

'That must be her.'

'There's something else.'

Taylor waited. Moss had paused for dramatic effect.

'There's something going on in Draegerman's Rock,' continued Moss. 'I don't know what it is – but something's happening.'

'How do you know?'

'Because steel shutters came down in each and every one of those Walkway gates last night. And they haven't come up again. And my friends on the street tell me that some of Draegerman's people have been on the Walkways all night. They don't seem happy.'

'The Four Day Rule,' said Fisher. 'What do you know, it's finally happened.'

'Four Day Rule?' asked Taylor.

'It's one of the prime directives in the Draegerman security manual, written by the man himself when The Rock was finally completed, so I'm told. Drummed into all the new recruits – that at some time, without warning, The Rock might become sealed from the inside. No warning would be given. All the security shutters would come down, and there would be no way of getting in or out for four days. If it happened, we all had instructions to do nothing, to lie low and just wait it out. Four days after shutdown, The Rock would be opened again. Like I say, nobody knows why. Draegerman is ... well, he *is* who he *is*, isn't he? A bloody recluse, an eccentric – just plain crazy. There was lots of other weird stuff we had to observe. But the Four Day Rule was the big one. Strict instructions if and when it happened: no one moved, no one should try to contact anyone else. Just sit tight, wait for four days and hold the fort until it opened again.'

'So his people on the Walkway aren't stranded there?' asked Taylor.

'There's something in the handbook to cover that as well. They've got emergency supplies on the Walkways, they've got to sit tight and wait out the four days, just like anyone else.'

'I've *got* to get in there,' said Taylor.

The woman in the bathroom rapped on the door. 'Okay, that's two and a half minutes by my reckoning.'

'Sorry,' said Moss, rising from the bed. 'That's it.'

'Just one thing I need to know,' said Taylor. 'Just one.'

'Come on, man ...'

'I know Draegerman has two private helicopters. Neither of them are on the roof. So they must have a base somewhere else in the city. Where?'

Moss moved as if he was going to take Taylor's arm. Taylor swung to prevent him, and for a moment it looked as if both men might have a confrontation now in Fisher's room.

'Draegerman bought part of a disused military base twenty miles south of The Rock. If they're not being flown, and they're not on top of The Rock, they'll be there.'

Taylor and Moss relaxed.

'Thanks, Fisher,' said Taylor, his face betraying how he really felt for the first time since he had arrived in this inner-city hell. 'Thanks a lot.'

Moss moved to open the door.

Just before Taylor left the room, he heard Fisher call his name.

'Taylor?'

'Yeah?'

'For what it's worth – good luck.'

Taylor nodded grimly.

Moss shut the door and waved to the staircase.

Without looking back, preoccupied by what he knew he must do, Taylor descended.

NINETEEN

They had been descending this winding stone staircase for what seemed an impossibly long time. Aiken always went ahead, at Farrow's insistence, the gun jammed between his shoulder blades when he slowed down, Boone following nervously at the rear.

'This can't be right,' said Aiken at last. 'We should have reached the bottom by now.'

'I don't want to hear anything out of you,' said Farrow. 'Unless it's good news, like you suddenly remember where the hell we are.'

'I've never seen this place before. Believe me.'

'Believe you? Now haven't I already told you that I've got problems with that?'

'I've been thinking,' said Boone.

'Don't think,' said Farrow. 'Just shut the hell up.'

'Maybe this isn't the way,' continued Boone. 'Maybe the others were right after all.'

'I'm warning you, Boone . . .'

'No, listen to me. There's something else as well. I mean . . . that thing . . . the Berserker. Draegerman said that it was summoned principally to kill his employees. But look, Aiken's with us and if we stay with him, and it finds us . . . well, you saw what that thing can do. Maybe it's got Aiken's scent. Even if it does just want Aiken, what's to say that if we're around him when it comes, it won't just kill us as well?'

'You believe all that back there? Think about it, Boone. *Think* about it! We never saw it properly, even that stupid Gloria what's-her-name didn't see it properly, and she was supposed to be in the same room with it. Now I come to think of it, I'm sure I screwed someone in the back row when I was a kid, while one of his stupid horror movies was showing. Horror movies! Don't you get it? The bastard's mad all right, and he's got lots of tricks up his sleeve, enough to make it bloody dangerous to be here. But Daemons? I mean, devils and witchcraft and scary monsters? Give me a fucking break!'

'You're wrong,' said Aiken. 'You're wrong about that thing back there.'

'Did you see it?'

'Not properly, but . . .'

'You see, Boone. "Not properly", just like good old Gloria. I'm telling you, a couple of rounds from this . . .' Farrow held the gun up over his shoulder so that Boone could see it. '. . . and the guy in the rubber suit is going to start wondering whether he was paid enough.'

Aiken whirled on the stairs to face Farrow. The look on his face was enough to make Farrow momentarily forget that he had the all-important gun; made him stagger back one step and blunder into Boone. Aiken's face seemed suffused with rage.

'You're right, I didn't see the fucking thing properly. But we were shooting back into it when it came. Point blank! At least four of us. And we were running, and it was coming, and – don't you see? – we couldn't turn around to look. It just kept coming. And when it brought someone down, it was . . . it was . . . I could hear it tearing them to pieces, without even slowing down. Do you hear what I'm saying? We were firing backwards, point blank into that thing. Running and firing, running and . . . and it had no effect.'

'You acting again, Aiken?' snapped Farrow, grabbing him by his frayed collar. The fear in Aiken's eyes was not what he wanted to see. He wanted to see evidence of acting, wanted to believe that his assessment of their predicament was accurate. He did not want to see the look of naked terror on the face of someone who had been, until recently, completely in control. 'Maybe you just don't appreciate how pissed off I am with you. In fact, I'm getting so pissed off that I might just put a bullet through your head now and . . .'

'THEN DO IT!' screamed Aiken, thrusting his face into Farrow's, catching him further off guard. The utter fear and the stark honesty in those once commanding but now starkly terrified eyes so unsettled Farrow that he could do only one thing. He could only try to refute what Aiken was saying, deny the truth of his words, reaffirm his own strength, by acting in that instant in the only empowered way he knew.

Farrow smashed the gun into Aiken's face.

Aiken crumpled and fell down the stairs, hitting the stone wall hard and then rolling out of sight around the next left-hand turn of the spiralling stairs.

'What if he's right?' Boone's voice sounded strangled. 'You idiot, what if he's RIGHT!' He somehow pushed past Aiken, and scrabbled down the staircase in panic. The pathetic act of fear enraged Farrow further. He charged down the stairs, fully intending to bring the bloodstained gun-hand down across Boone's head. Boone had vanished around the bend in the stairs, and Farrow jumped four steps, shouldered the wall and leapt again.

'Look!' Boone had suddenly stopped, standing astride Aiken's prostrate form.

The staircase had ended. They were on level ground again.

Farrow shoved Boone ahead. Aiken struggled to his knees, and Farrow took pleasure in seeing that blood was oozing between the fingers of the hand he clasped to his face.

There was another corridor before them; the same dripping black stone, the same flagged floor, the same sick-green light. To Farrow, it looked like the corridor they had been walking down when Aiken had reappeared on the scene.

It is the same corridor, a voice seemed to say in his head.

Farrow charged ahead down the corridor.

'Draegerman! You bastard! Come on out! Come out and show your-self!'

He swung the gun up and fired into the darkness. The shot hurt their eardrums, made them all wince in pain, clutch their ears.

'Come on, then. COME ON, THEN!'

Something hit him hard; red pain exploded behind his eyes and engulfed him. And then Farrow lost consciousness.

And in his fractured dreams, Farrow sees his hated mother's face. He's seven years old and she's crying again, telling him that she doesn't know why his father vanished from their lives. She doesn't understand it, and she begs him to believe that it wasn't her who drove him away. She tells him that he can hit her if it makes him feel better. So in his dream, he does. But there's no satisfaction when he smacks her across the face, just as there was no satisfaction in the following years when she allowed him to brutalise her as much as he wanted (just as long as he didn't blame her). Farrow sees her writing the suicide note now, begging him to forgive her – and in his dream he snatches it away, begins to tear it up and then—

Draegerman's face suddenly swims into view. But this is a younger disguised Draegerman, because Farrow is still seven years old. And now, in this dream place, instead of hurling abuse at that hated face, instead of screaming his rage and fear, Farrow hears his boy-self plead: 'Why did you go away? Why weren't you THERE when I needed you?'

And Draegerman smiles then, and says: 'You've got the gun, you've got the power, you're my son. Not like that utter fucking weakling, Boone. No, not like him – you're stronger than him. You're the first and the best. I'm ashamed to admit I conceived Boone. But I'm not ashamed of you. You're my favourite son, didn't you know that?'

'Why weren't you THERE?' cries the boy.

'I'm here now,' says Draegerman. 'And so are you. That's all that matters.'

The gun is in Draegerman's hand now, and he bends down to give it to Farrow.

Farrow reaches up, takes the gun . . .

He woke on cold, hard ground.

He was in darkness, there was pain on the left side of his face and head – and the gun was not in his hand. Frantically, he scrabbled around, unsure of where he was, but knowing that he must have that gun. The movement caused great pain behind his eyes.

'Where is it? Where IS it?'

And then his eyes focused at last, and he saw Aiken and Boone sitting six feet from him, their backs against a stone wall. They had been sleeping, and Farrow's cries had woken them with a start.

'Where's the gun? Which one of you took it?'

'No one took it,' said Boone. 'It's still beside you.'

Farrow saw it lying on the ground by his side at last. He seized it, and then felt his face. There was blood there.

'What . . . ?'

'It wasn't me, or him,' said Aiken. 'You ran into a wall. Knocked yourself out.'

Farrow felt dried blood on his scalp, shook his head in an attempt to clear it – but this only made the pain worse. Struggling to his feet, he steadied himself with one hand against the wall. 'How long have I been out?'

'Can't say,' said Boone. 'My watch has stopped.'

'Maybe two hours,' guessed Aiken.

'And you didn't go on and leave me behind?' said Farrow. 'How touching.'

He looked at the gun in his hand, wondered why they had not taken it, killed him and moved on. Now he knew that Aiken was not acting a part or lying. The miserable bastard was too scared.

'Now, get up.'

He waved the gun and they climbed to their feet.

Farrow ran a hand over his grazed face and staggered down the corridor ahead.

The other two followed miserably.

TWENTY

'It's going to be tough,' said Taylor.

'Then what are we going to do?' asked Sara. It seemed that she had been weeping a lot since Susan's disappearance. Her eyes were perpetually red-rimmed. She sat on the sofa opposite Taylor, wringing her handkerchief into a twisted rope. 'The police don't want to know, and the kids . . .'

'I only said it would be tough, Sara. I didn't say that I didn't have something in mind.'

'So you've got some kind of plan?' asked Den from his usual place, standing in the doorway between the kitchen and the living-room. There was another can of beer in his hand.

'Like I said – I've something in mind.'

'Care to share it with us?'

'No.'

Den made a sound of disgust, screwed up the empty can in his fist and swung moodily back into the kitchen for another.

Taylor took something from his jacket pocket, leaned across and gestured that he wanted Sara's hand. When she held it out, he pushed something on to the palm. It was a small gold key. She looked at him in puzzlement.

'That's the key to a safety deposit box,' said Taylor. Reaching into his pocket again, he took out a small envelope and handed it to Sara. 'The details are in here. It's also the security key for a numbered Swiss bank account. If anything happens to me, the money in that account is yours.'

'Sounds like you're not expecting to come back,' said Den, from the threshold, fresh can in hand.

'No, I fully intend to get out of there alive – with Susan. But I'm making contingency plans. There's something else you may need to know, something about my long-term future . . .'

'Then what's wrong with another pair of hands along to help you?' interrupted Den, ignoring these last words, not realising that Taylor had been building up to that point, had struggled to tell them about what the doctors had warned him. 'Two have got to be better than one.'

'Not in this case,' said Taylor tightly. 'Look – I know what I'm doing. It's what I was trained to do, it's how I've lived my life. Maybe I don't know anything else, don't know any better. But that's what I *am*. You come along with me and you're only going to be baggage. I can't afford to be looking out for you.'

'I won't slow you down,' said Den angrily. 'I can look after myself.'

'You just don't see it, do you? What about killing? You prepared to kill somebody to get Susan back? Because maybe that's what you'd have to do.'

'I'd do anything to have Susan safe back home again. Understand? *Anything!*'

Taylor shook his head. 'Don't you bloody realise? I don't *know* you, Dennis. We'd never met before this happened. How do I know how you'd handle yourself for what I'm thinking about? How do I know that you won't screw everything up? Answer? I *don't*! Solution? You don't go. Look, if you're in love with Susan . . .'

'Don't patronise me, you bastard!'

'And don't be so fucking touchy, sonny. You want to come along with me, maybe end up killing, maybe end up *getting* killed – and you can't even take any straight talking without getting touchy?'

Den glared back at Taylor, but said nothing more.

'The point is – I believe that you love Susan, and that she loves you. Because Sara's told me so. But think about it, Dennis. I might not get out of this in one piece. If you're along, the same thing applies. And what the hell is Susan going to do if she and I get out of there alive, and *you* don't? What the hell is she going to think of me, letting *you* come along? She'll be back safe – and she won't have you. Great! A dead hero. It's Susan I'm thinking of, you bloody fool.'

Den tried to think of something to say in retaliation, but nothing suggested itself. He drank again, feeling utterly powerless and hating himself for it.

'So . . .' Sara's voice choked. 'So, when . . . ?'

'Tonight,' said Taylor. 'Or maybe early morning. I need sleep, and I've got two contacts to see. Two people who owe me favours, who can supply me with the . . . raw materials I need.'

Sara nodded, still wringing her handkerchief. 'Have you eaten?'

'No, and I could use it.'

Taylor watched as she stood and headed for the kitchen. Den stood aside and then followed her, moving to the draining board and bracing both hands against it, head down, trying to think. Sara put a hand on his shoulder and then moved away to make some sandwiches.

Taylor sat back, realising that he had missed his one chance to tell them about his future, or lack of it. Settling back in his chair, he decided that maybe it was for the best. If they knew, maybe they would doubt his ability to get into The Rock and rescue Susan. Why the hell had he wanted to tell them, anyway?

Sympathy?

He laughed quietly, a bitter sound unheard by the others in the kitchen.

He ran his hands over his face. For the first time, he noticed the multitude of scars on them. They seemed to belong to someone else.

As long as they do the job, he thought.

In the next instant, he was asleep.

TWENTY-ONE

'No, I don't believe it,' said Susan.

The others turned wearily to see that she had stopped and was looking at the corridor wall beside her. even though they had slept, they did not feel refreshed.

'What?' Jessica, who was closest to her, turned and tried to see what she was looking at. Roy, Gloria and Bobby were some way ahead. They waited.

'We've been this way before,' said Susan.

'We can't have,' said Jessica. 'The corridor has always headed downwards. Can't you feel the cant in the floor?'

'This patch of moss or slime, or whatever it is – on the wall.'

'What about it?'

'I saw it an hour ago. I'm sure I did. See? It looks like a face. That's why I remember it.'

'Come on,' said Jessica. 'We've got to keep moving.'

'But how do we know which way we're going?'

'So what do we do? Go back?'

Resigned, but still troubled by the patch, Susan followed Jessica until they had rejoined the others. The corridor curved to the left this time, and Susan kept her gaze riveted on the wall at about the same height at which she had seen the moss patch. If it reappeared again around this bend, she felt sure that she might yell out loud.

Thoughts of the boys, Den and Sara began to crowd into her head. Where were they now, and what must be going through their minds? She tried to push the thoughts away. She had to concentrate on getting out of here, no matter what. And even if this was the largest, craziest madhouse in the world, there must be a way out. If there was, they would find it. They *had* to find it.

She bumped into Jessica, and realised that the others had stopped. Roy was at the front, holding up one hand.

'Listen,' he said.

And now they could hear it; a low, rumbling sound coming from somewhere ahead. And something else – a slithering sound behind it.

'Oh God,' said Gloria. 'Is it coming this way?'

'No, wait.' Roy took a few hesitant steps forward, his hand still held up for quiet. 'No, it's not moving. It's not headed this way, whatever it is.'

'So what do we do?' asked Bobby.

'Well, we can't go back.' Jessica moved towards Roy, then put her hand to the corridor wall. 'There's a slight vibration.'

'Well, if we can't go back, we either stay here until it stops,' said Bobby. 'Or we go and see.'

'Stay here,' said Roy, walking on ahead. 'I'll go and look.'

'I'll come with you,' said Jessica.

'Look,' said Roy. 'If there is something up there, something dangerous, then at least only one of us is at risk if I go . . .'

'Cut the macho crap, Roy. We'll both go.'

'What the hell is it with you? I'm not trying to be macho. What I'm saying makes sense.'

'You're not our leader. I don't remember taking a vote on it.'

'Yeah? Well maybe you'd prefer Farrow and his gun . . . ?'

'I *prefer* to make my own decisions.' Jessica moved on ahead. Roy followed, shaking his head.

And then Jessica froze in her steps. Immediately, Roy could see why.

Shadows were looming and rearing on the right-hand wall. The shadows of something that could be man-shaped, but the crazy green light was distorting the shadow out of all perspective. It was heading down the corridor towards them, huge spindly spider-legs, a head that was grossly elongated, and shadows of arms that were three times the length of the body, now groping the slime-covered wall as it came.

There were other shadows moving behind the first; other monstrously distorted figures apparently groping blindly along the wall towards them.

Roy and Jessica backed away. The others could see the groping of the hideous shadows now, and also began to back away, as the sounds of grumbling, screeching gears filled the air like machines toiling in Hell.

'We're going to have to run for it,' said Roy. 'God knows what . . .'

And then the source of the first shadow blundered into view.

It saw them and halted.

Standing there, silently weaving on the spot, white face fixed on them.

'Bloody hell,' said Susan. 'It's Farrow.'

And now the others staggered into view: Boone and Aiken. They also looked stunned at the sight of them.

Roy pushed forward to meet them, halting only a few feet from where they stood as the others came up from behind. Farrow's eyes seemed blank, as if somehow unable to comprehend their situation. Boone fell to his knees again, curling up tight and moaning around his attaché case. Aiken was struggling to speak, but no words were emerging.

'How have you . . . ?' began Roy.

And then Farrow's face twisted into a mask of rage, and he swung the gun up towards him, screaming. Roy grabbed instinctively at his arm, and in the next moment Farrow had hurled himself at him, attaché case clattering to the ground. Both men collided with the far corridor wall, Roy hanging on to Farrow's gun-hand while the latter continued to scream obscenities at him.

The gun went off, blasting a series of reverberating echoes down the corridor, gouging a chunk out of the ceiling. Everyone else ducked instinctively, and then Susan rushed forward to grab Farrow's hair, yanking back hard. He roared at her in pain, and then Roy twisted the gun out of his hand, kicked him away hard – and stumbled back to his feet. Farrow scrabbled and clutched at the ground, finally pulling himself erect by clambering up the corridor wall. He looked set to launch himself at Roy and Susan again.

'*Don't* do it, Farrow!' shouted Roy breathlessly.

Farrow looked at the gun – and then hurled himself back at the corridor wall, pounding with the flats of his hand on the dripping-wet stone.

'Round and round in fucking *circles*! Don't you see it, don't you understand. Draegerman! These bloody walls have been lying to me! I'll . . .' He delivered a blow to the wall with each word. '. . . tear! Your! Fucking! Heart! *Out!*'

Finally, he collapsed to his knees, sobbing.

Roy lowered the gun.

'How long have we been down here?' Boone's face was still buried in his hands, his words muffled. 'For God's sake *how long*?'

Roy and Susan joined the others as Farrow rolled around, his back resting against the wall, head up and sucking in deep breaths of air while he regained his self-control.

Throughout, the sounds of rumbling and screeching had continued from afar.

'All right,' said Roy. 'Everyone just take it easy.'

'What's back there?' asked Susan. 'Farrow? You must have seen what's back there?'

'We heard it, but we came this way,' said Farrow. His voice was now much more in control, but sounded cracked. 'We came down a corridor, until it branched into this one. Then we heard the noise. We were just trying to get away from it, when we . . .' He pulled his knees up to his chest and lowered his head.

'So, it's back to square one,' said Roy. 'Let's go and see what we're up against now.' Jessica nodded and joined him. Together, they began to walk in the direction the sound was coming from. Susan hurried to join them.

'Me too.'

They followed the left-hand curve of the corridor, carefully and slowly.

Just before they vanished from sight completely, they looked back at the others. Farrow was still sitting with his head down. Aiken and Boone still seemed to be in shock, but Gloria and Bobby were standing with arms around each other, watching anxiously. Susan waved once, and then they turned and disappeared around the bend.

The sound was much louder now. It was obviously an engine or motor of some kind, and they could feel the rumbling sensation beneath their feet as they moved on. Now, to their left, they could see an aperture in the wall. As they drew level, they realised that it was another corridor: presumably the one down which Farrow, Aiken and Boone had come. They continued on past it, the corridor still curving left – but now there was new light on the opposite wall, heralding the fact that the corridor was about to end, and they were about to emerge into a new, open space.

'What's it going to be this time?' said Jessica.

'The Hanging Gardens of Babylon?' suggested Susan.

'Just as long as it doesn't have spiders,' said Roy.

And then they rounded the last curve and could see what lay before them.

'*Jesus* . . .' said Jessica.

They edged forward as the rumbling and slithering filled the air, sounding like a great waterfall. Occasionally, something metallic screeched underground – as if unoiled gears were being slowly jammed together.

'It's a . . .' began Jessica.

'. . . moving staircase,' finished Roy. 'An escalator.'

But like no escalator they had ever seen in their lives.

This was a moving staircase into Hell.

The corridor ended where they stood, opening out into a larger space which seemed to have been carved out of solid rock. There was no sign of brickwork, slabs or flagged blocks. No sign of any architectural forethought. This was like some underground cavern, rough-hewn from the rock itself. Overhead, twin green fluorescent strips arched away and then downwards out of sight, giving the familiar sick-green illumination to what lay before them. The staircase itself gleamed black, white and chrome. There were black, moving handrails on either side of the escalator, the steel sliding out from the stone floor on which they stood, moving forward for a dozen feet or so before resolving itself into steps and arcing away downwards into unknown depths. In construction, it looked not unlike every other department store escalator they had ever seen.

But with a difference.

With the exception of the plate-steel stairs, it seemed as if it had all been constructed out of cadavers and animal bones. As if some crazy sculptor had visited the slaughterhouse, taken all the bones and dismembered carcasses he could load into his trucks, and had then set about welding them together in this nightmare jigsaw construction, finally painting the entire blasphemous structure in black pitch. In places the pitch seemed to have worn away, or melted – leaving the stomach-churning sight of bones, ribs, cattle-skulls and musculature beneath; all welded in some hideous configuration that could only make sense to a madman.

As the steel plates slid out of the ground before them, trundled screeching to the brow of the staircase and then toppled downwards out of sight, the din gave them all the same feeling, a feeling they did not want to vocalise but which nevertheless shook them, all three, to the core.

It was as if this escalator were a living thing.

These noises – the rumbling, the thin screech of the steel plates and the clanking trundle of the hidden machinery that powered this nightmare construction – were not the sounds of machines and engines, cogs and pulleys. They were the sounds of some animal; some hideous living thing that was biding its time, waiting for them to descend. And an instinctive dread seemed to sap their strength as they stood there. This was a terrible, *terrible* place.

Roy moved forward, and put his hand on one of the black handrails. It slithered under his fingers, but strangely did not feel wet as he thought it might.

'What are you going to do?' asked Susan. Her hand went out to stop him.

But Roy did not listen to her, did not listen to the hideous fear-whisper inside which threatened at all times to debilitate him. There was only one means of establishing whether it was safe to go this way or not. He stepped on to the steel plates and, keeping his hand on the handrail, allowed himself to be carried forward.

'Roy, no!' Susan also stepped forward – but Jessica took her arm and held her back. Her face was grim, her mouth set in a tight line. Susan pulled free. Roy had almost reached the outermost edge of the escalator, the point at which the plates became steps. He began to walk backwards then, carefully keeping his hand on the rail. Walking on the spot, remaining in the same position, Roy jerked his head forward to look down the grim moving staircase.

'Roy!'

He held up his other hand to indicate that he was okay, and let the plates carry him a little further forward. At the very edge of the descent, he began to walk on the spot again. This time he could see all the way.

And then his heel caught on the edge of a plate, as the plate below dropped into a step.

He stumbled and fell.

'Oh no, *Roy!*' Susan lunged forward, but was again held by Jessica.

Roy twisted, grabbed for the handrail, and landed on his left hip. Frantically, hand over hand, he pulled himself erect even as the stairs bore him over the edge.

'Let me *go*!' shouted Susan.

Scrambling on all fours, Roy clawed his way back over the lip. Then, bracing one leg, he lunged back towards them like an Olympic runner from the blocks. Susan caught his arm, and all three staggered back breathless from the moving plates.

'Going down?' said Roy in the best elevator-operator voice he could manage.

'Christ, I thought you'd gone,' breathed Susan.

'Did you see anything down there?' asked Jessica. 'Is it safe?'

'Safe? God knows. I can see the bottom, though. It's maybe four or five hundred feet down, where the stairs flatten into plates and slide back under the ground. Beyond that, I can't say. It's too dark.'

'Wait here,' said Susan. 'I'll go and get the others.'

As Susan hurried back down the corridor, Roy slid down on to his haunches with a loud and relieved exhalation of breath. Jessica leaned against the stone wall, looking at him. After a while, Roy looked up at her again.

'So say it,' he said.

'Say what?'

'Tell me that was just another macho trick. That I was trying to show off my masculinity.'

'You've got me wrong,' said Jessica. 'I don't care what decisions you make that might affect yourself. I do care about people making decisions for me that might drop me in the shit. Simple as that.'

'Fair enough.'

'That was a brave thing to do.'

'Thanks.'

'But it was also a stupid thing to do.'

'Thanks again.'

'How do you feel? I mean, right now.'

Roy looked hard at her. 'I've got you sussed. At last, I've worked it out.'

'Worked out what?'

'You're interviewing me now! You're goading me, and trying to get a response. This whole bloody thing *is* a Big Scoop for you, isn't it? Every step of the way, everything that happens – you're making mental notes about it, writing everything down in your head. How each person is reacting, what they're thinking, what they're feeling.'

'You shouldn't have such a chip on your shoulder, Roy. We're all under a strain.'

'And don't you know it. Christ, I should have realised.'

'Now you're overreacting.'

'You're having just as much trouble adapting to what's happening here as anyone. Being the reporter gives you a way to sidestep everything. Maybe if you're an outside observer, bad things might not happen to you. After all, you're not really *here*, are you, Jessica?'

She turned away from him.

'All right . . . all right, I'll tell you how I feel,' continued Roy, 'I'm scared shitless, just like everybody else. I don't know whether we're going up or down or round in circles. I'm scared of every corner, of every turn in one of these corridors – expecting something to be waiting for us around every bloody bend. Do I believe that Draegerman's telling us the truth about Daemons, and that we're all marked for death? Yes, I do! Because *if* I do then maybe I can keep sharp enough to get out of here alive. If I don't, I'm going to end up dead. Pulling the bedclothes over our heads isn't going to make these bogeymen go away. There, now you've got the inside story of what's happening inside Roy Jensen's head. Happy with that? Or would you like me to write it all down for you?'

Jessica turned back to Roy. The confident smile on her face was infuriating. 'Give me the gun,' she said.

Roy looked at her angrily for a long time, then slowly stood. He pulled it out from the belt of his jeans – and then threw it to her.

'Here, you have it then!'

Jessica caught it, still smiling. She examined it briefly, as if somehow this might not be a real gun at all, but a toy provided as part of the fantasy they were all living. Then, just as roughly, she threw it back, taking Roy by surprise. He fumbled the catch, almost dropping it.

'What the hell are you playing at?' he snapped.

'I just wanted to see if you'd do it,' smiled Jessica.

'Like I said, you're playing games – and testing out the characters.' He shoved the gun back into his belt. 'Just watch out that something doesn't come up behind you when you're mentally writing up that newspaper story of your exploits in Draegerman's Rock.'

The sounds of scuffling feet and the shadows on the walls told them that the others had arrived. Susan was leading them. Boone and Aiken were standing quietly at the rear, and it seemed that Farrow had regained his self-control. Roy noticed how he looked at the gun in his belt, but he made no move to retrieve it. Instead, wiping one hand across his mouth, he moved past them all to look at the steel plates heading on out and over the brow of the escalator. It was clear from the look on the others' faces that they were feeling the same instinctive dread, revulsion and terror.

'You see anything down there?' he asked brusquely.

'Nothing other than Susan's already said, I expect.'

'What do you reckon, Roy?' asked Bobby.

'I've no idea. Better ask Jessica.'

'Touchy, Roy,' said Jessica. 'I wouldn't have expected that of you. Well, we've only two choices. Back the way we came or down there.'

'Three choices,' said Gloria. 'We could also go back from where Farrow and the others entered this last corridor.'

'No way!' snapped Farrow. 'We'll end up wandering around this place forever if we go back that way.'

'No, please,' said Boone. 'Not the way we came.'

'Aiken.' Farrow turned to him and Aiken shrank back again, as if expecting a physical attack. He seemed barely recognisable as the man they had first met. The gash in his cheek was suppurating. An unhealthy blue tinge had spread from the dried blood on his cheek across his face to his eye and ear. 'You ever been here before? You recognise this escalator?'

Aiken shook his head. 'No, I didn't . . . don't . . . no.'

'Can't tell you how grateful I am for all the help you've given,' said Farrow, hefting his attaché case.

'We have to go down,' said Gloria. 'What else are we going to do?'

There was silence then, while they all looked at each other, all of them hoping that someone might break the silence with another alternative that made better sense.

'Down it is,' said Roy at last. 'Who's first?' He looked at Jessica.

'Aiken goes first,' said Farrow. 'Remember what I told you about mules and minefields? Well, here's another chance to prove yourself useful.'

Aiken looked at the rumbling, screeching stairs and shrank back again.

'Come on!' snapped Farrow.

'No, I can't . . .'

Farrow lunged angrily forward to take his sleeve. But in a sudden burst of frantic energy, Aiken pulled away from him and fled back into the corridor from which they had come.

'I *can't*! It's mad going down there! Haven't you learned yet? Don't you know anything about Draegerman? That's the way he *wants* you to go . . .' Aiken halted then, whirling back to stand and stare at them. Farrow had also halted, angrily glaring at him but not intent on following him any further.

'Come back here, Aiken. Come back or I'll break your neck.'

'You'll all die on that escalator!' Aiken turned and ran again, back into the darkness. This time, Farrow moved forward.

'Let him go!' said Jessica.

Farrow turned and looked back at them. He nodded, and with one last glance into the darkness of the corridor as Aiken's stumbling footsteps faded into the distance, he walked slowly back to the others.

They stood in silence again, watching the steel plates slither and rumble away from them, listening to the clank and clatter of hidden machinery.

Who's first? The unasked question lay heavily between them.

Then, suddenly, Susan stepped on to the plates and grabbed the handrail, looking back at them. Roy quickly joined her, and then the others in rapid succession, with Farrow in the rear. They remained in a huddled pack as the plates moved out to the edge.

The plates slithered into steps, and suddenly they were standing at the top of some bizarre precipice, looking down the long, gleaming, serpentine staircase as it trundled downwards to the bottom platform – and God knew what beyond.

Going down? The remark froze on Roy's lips. There was no place for bitter humour now.

They were on their way.

Deeper and deeper, into The House That Jack Built.

TWENTY-TWO

The abandoned military base was not hard to find.

Even though it was only twenty miles south of the city, its location was sufficiently isolated to ensure that it had never attracted public attention. In the early years of its abandonment, local entrepreneurs had attempted to move in and strip out anything of worth: electrical wiring, heating systems, lead from the roof. But Draegerman had been quick to move, establishing his own security force when ownership had been guaranteed, ensuring that any damage was contained. The term 'military base' had always been a misnomer for this haphazard arrangement of concrete bunkers, storage warehouses and unused hangars. The small landing field had rarely been used, and was now overgrown. Almost since its construction, the base had been used as a maintenance depot and storage facility, of no real strategic importance. Draegerman's use of the facility was limited. Whereas the hangar, bunkers and sheds at the centre of the facility proved ideal, the rest of the buildings surrounding the inner core had been left unused and dilapidated. The perimeter fence was rusted but intact, and security had been restricted to one double-guard patrol when it became clear that no one was really interested in the place any more.

From his hidden vantage point, the figure in black had seen the double-guard patrol walk past, had watched them vanish into the darkness and knew that he had more than enough time to do what had to be done before they reappeared again. He chose a patch of shrubbery close to the fence. Using it for cover, he clipped the fence and peeled it back. The cutting was a lot easier than he had expected. Rust and lack of maintenance over the years made it a simple task. Waiting again, adjusting the black woollen balaclava, the figure wriggled through the gap and then kept low in the grass. Again, the long grass made for perfect cover. For a man who was security-conscious at The Rock, Draegerman was clearly not worried about security here.

Sloppy. Very sloppy, my friend.

Wasn't he the one who worried about terrorist attacks?

Don't count your chickens. This may not be as easy as it looks.

There was a hangar or storage shed directly ahead. It was clearly derelict, but beyond it he could see a glow of light, hear the sounds of movement. A jeep, perhaps? Darker than the night itself, the figure broke into a crouching run – heading for the hangar. Twenty feet from the rusted wall, the figure seemed to trip and fall into the long grass. Still hidden, the intruder brought his knees up to his chest, enveloping the gut-searing pain that enveloped his body.

Oh Christ, no! Not now, not now!

The pain should not have started yet. There had been twinges, increasing in severity – but nothing like the pain than now ate at his innards like some wild beast nuzzling and tearing at his intestines. Gritting his teeth to keep from yelling out loud in agony, he clutched at the pain as if he could wrest it out of his body and discard it. The doctor's words were echoing in his head now, a bitter mockery: *Just try to avoid stress ...*

He turned his face to the ground, ready to stuff grass into his mouth if he could not stop himself making a noise.

And then, just as suddenly, the pain was gone. Silently gasping for air, he lay there, looking up at the night sky. The moon was barely visible behind heavy cloud, something he had considered an advantage tonight. Flipping back on to his haunches, making sure that he was ready to go on, he surveyed the derelict hangar again.

And then ducked low when he saw the armed guard emptying his bladder against the western end. He really could not believe his luck. Maybe the pain had been sent to help him, because if it had not sent him reeling into the grass he would have reached the hangar just as the guard rounded the corner – and perhaps then it would have been all over. He waited until the guard had finished, watched as he zipped up and turned casually away, heading around to the other side and the source of the light.

Then he skimmed through the grass, crouching low and constantly looking around, until he had reached the darker night-shadow of the hangar wall. Still keeping low, he loped to the spot where the guard had been. Steam was still rising from the grass.

Something clattered in the sky.

He looked back to see the brightly lit helicopter skimming towards the base. It was coming in low, at about two hundred feet, obviously expecting to land. The wind from the rotor blades blasted into the side of the hangar, whipping the long grass around him into a frenzy. He lay flat in the grass, smelling urine, as the 'copter flashed overhead. The instant it had passed, he was up again, running low and fast around the edge of the hangar.

The helicopter was descending, about one hundred feet from the hangar, on to a roughly marked landing pad. Spotlights had been installed in the open concrete space behind the hangar to aid the pilot. Quickly, as the 'copter hovered over the pad, getting its bearing for landing, he glanced over at what looked like a Nissen hut, where three men stood watching the helicopter's final manoeuvres prior to landing. The nearest figure was obviously the armed guard Taylor had just seen, the next was wearing a pale green security suit, the other a sober black business suit – as if he was on his way to a funeral. Breaking cover while their attention was focused on the helicopter, he ran from the hangar to the nearest end of the Nissen hut, melting into its shadowed recesses. No sooner had he done so than two other men, also wearing the same sober business suits, moved into view to watch the helicopter land. One of them was even wearing a pair of designer sunglasses. Now Taylor could see another helicopter on an identical pad, fifty feet away on the other side of the Nissen hut.

As the helicopter finally landed in a blast of dust and air, Taylor slid along the wall of the hut towards the figures, who were shielding their eyes. While the rotors were still spinning, a figure hopped out of the passenger door. Another Black Suit, also wearing the ridiculous shades, but now swiping them from his face as he ran towards the hut through the blasting air, keeping low. The pilot remained in the helicopter; an indistinct figure, but wearing the pale green security suit and cap. When the Black Suit was still fifty feet away, he began to shake his head. Angrily, it seemed, he walked straight past the others and into the hut before they could begin to ask questions. The others followed, the guard propping his automatic weapon up by the door. Taylor slid along the wall until he had reached the edge of light shining from the window. He pressed one side of his face against the wall, holding the flat of his hand against the other ear to block out the sound of the rotor blades – and now he could hear what was being said inside.

'I told you, it's just the same.'

'What do you mean, just the same?'

'I told you on the 'copter radio. It was just like the last three times. We circled around, trying to get an answer from inside. Nothing. We put the 'copter down on the roof, tried the entry points and the security codes all came up blank. Not easy when you know those automatic cannons are trained on you. We just couldn't get into the fucking building. It's the Four Day Rule.'

'But aren't we supposed to get some kind of warning first? Wasn't that the idea? Look, I don't care what was said at the beginning, we've got to make sure, get the police involved.'

'Are you fucking joking? You know what Draegerman's like, know what we were told to do. It's the Four Day Rule. Been in the textbook long enough – and we've been reminded about it God knows how many times. It's not unexpected, we just have to sit tight and wait, like the man wants.'

'But we've got people still on the Walkways. Eric and Ken and

Thompson are all stuck out there. Never been off the radio since it all happened. It's just a matter of time before they switch frequencies and get on to the police themselves.'

'They've got emergency rations on the Walkways. Speak to them again and tell them to hold tight. Remind them of the textbook, what staff on the Walkways are supposed to do, and tell them to keep their hands off the fucking radios. One call to anybody on the outside, and they can forget working for Draegerman, forget breathing any more.'

'I still don't like it.'

'Then maybe you shouldn't have joined up. Just do your job, that's what you're being paid for – that's what we're all being paid for.'

'A job or jail in your case.'

'You trying to be funny?'

'Any time you feel like trying me on, just say so.'

'You little . . .'

'For Christ's sake!'

And at the sounds of a tussle from within the Nissen hut, Taylor ducked under the window and slid along the wall to the doorway. Standing then, he pulled off his black woollen balaclava, scooped the automatic weapon from the doorway and casually hoisted the strap around his shoulder. Keeping well out of the sight-line of the door, he stuffed the balaclava in his belt pouch, shifted the pack on his back so that the weapon hung better, and strolled towards the helicopter.

The rotors were slowing, but still spinning fast. The pilot seemed preoccupied with the dashboard before him, scribbling readings on to a clipboard in his lap. He looked up as Taylor approached. Taylor smiled and waved a hand. Unconcerned, the pilot nodded and returned to his clipboard, half raising a hand in return.

And then the 'copter door was sliding open and the pilot looked up into the barrel of the Uzi.

'No noise please,' said Taylor, looking back at the Nissen hut. Shadows danced and leaped inside. Even over the noise of the rotors he could hear glass smashing. Perfect. He climbed in, holding the gun under the pilot's nose and sliding the passenger door shut again. 'Got enough fuel for a return flight to The Rock?'

'No,' said the pilot nervously. 'Tank's nearly empty. That's why I'm taking readings.'

'You're a lying twat,' said Taylor, leaning forward to look at the gas gauge. 'The tank's three-quarters full. Okay, I know the rudiments of flying one of these things, so if necessary I can chuck you out while we're in the air and take over myself. So just be a good boy and do what you're told.'

'Yes, sir.'

'Take her up. Quick as you like.'

Taylor fastened the seat-belt clasp and twitched the gun barrel up in the air before returning it to the man's temple. Swallowing hard, the pilot began to rev the engine. The rotors began to spin faster. Taylor kept one eye on the pilot, the other on the hut for any signs that Draegerman's security people might be coming to the end of their misunderstanding. Clearly, the pilot was praying that someone would look over and see what was happening.

'Don't try my patience,' said Taylor at last. 'You don't need any more revs to take her up.'

'No, sir.'

In the next instant, the helicopter lifted from the landing pad. Sweat had beaded on the pilot's face, his eyes seemed glazed.

'Take it over to the next 'copter!' shouted Taylor. 'Bring it down low on the far side. But do it *fast!*'

The helicopter skimmed sideways across the airfield while Taylor kept his eyes on the hut.

'Not fast enough!' he snapped.

The machine drifted over the top of its companion, dropping close to the other side but well clear of the rotors.

Taylor threw back the cabin door, aimed his weapon – and the pilot's hand tilted at the controls in shock, enough to make the machine wobble slightly in mid-air, but not enough to spoil Taylor's aim as he strafed the fuselage and cabin roof of the other 'copter with his weapon. The sounds of detonation were almost drowned by the sound of the rotor blades, but half a dozen holes were punched into the other helicopter's petrol tank. The next half-dozen shattered its windscreen, punching through to the instrument panel.

'Now take it *up!*' yelled Taylor, sliding the door shut and turning to the pilot.

And as they swung left away from the damaged helicopter and hangar, gaining altitude, he could see that two men had suddenly appeared silhouetted in the Nissen hut doorway. They were frozen in position, staring upwards as the 'copter completed its swing. The last Taylor saw of them, they were both running across the open space to where the other helicopter was parked on the landing pad.

Seconds later, as they sped off into the night sky, Taylor whipped the personal radio headset from the pilot and dumped it on the floor. A thin crackling voice seemed to be gabbling something indeterminate in the earpiece.

'Let's not tell them where we're going,' said Taylor casually. 'Even if they can't follow us.'

'I've a feeling they may be able to guess.'

'Let's hope for your sake that they don't.'

Directly ahead, the moon tried to show its face from behind the night-dark clouds, making the chrome on the helicopter gleam in the darkness.

Taylor waited for the pain – but it did not come.

So much good luck so far.

How long would it last?

TWENTY-THREE

Keeping close together on the hideous escalator, Draegerman's guests looked anxiously in every direction as they descended.

Farrow kept his eyes on his feet, making sure that he was nowhere near the edges of the steel plate on which he stood. Instinctively, being last in the group, he knew that he should be looking back – just in case something should come out of the corridor behind him. But he had an aversion to escalators.

Back then, he had been travelling on one such escalator when another kid's scarf got caught in the gap between one of those steel steps as it had levelled out at the bottom. The scarf had been dragged under the grid at the foot of the escalator, dragging the child from her feet and turning her face bright purple as it strangled her. People had begun to scream then, and at the midway point on those stairs, Farrow *knew* what was going to happen. She would have her head ripped off down there in a scarlet explosion and everyone would pile up on top of each other at the bottom, unable to get past. Then the kids behind would fall on top of him when he fell and he would be fighting to get up as more people fell on top of them and then his scrabbling fingers would get caught between those steel plates and be snipped off just as neatly as if it had been done by one of those paper guillotines that Ma used in the stationer's store, and he would try to scream but then more people would crush him down, and he would be suffocating and then the weight of those bodies would press his *face* down on those slithering steel stairs and his *nose* would . . .

And if not for the quick thinking of the adult behind that child, literally tearing it from the child's neck, she would have strangled to death. Or worse. Farrow had never forgotten that moment, had always felt uncomfortable when he travelled on the damned things, always remembered that childhood phobia – and now it seemed that Draegerman had built this monstrous thing solely to make him sweat. If that was the case it was doing its job.

Step on a crack, that voice in his head seemed to say again. *Break your back*. Farrow lifted his head to glare around him. He glared at the hideous boneyard walls, and remembered the things he had dreamed when he had run smack into one of the corridor walls back there. He remembered the hate he felt for the father who had run out on them. And remembered how the voice from the wall – Draegerman's voice – had said: *But I'm here now*, as if this somehow made everything all right. That insidous voice was trying to make things better, trying to get on his good side, but that was not good enough for Farrow. The voice had misjudged the depth of his resentment, depths of which perhaps even Farrow himself had been unaware. That glare of pure hatred instantly dissolved the voice. It faded into echoes. But even in the fading there was a feeling that it might come back soon, and try again . . .

He looked down at his feet again, making sure they were centred.

Gloria held on to the black handrail at her side, even though she did not want to touch anything to do with this sickening travesty of a moving staircase. She tried to pretend that the sides of the escalator and the walls on either side were just some movie art director's stupid work for one of the tacky films she had been making of late. The hideous jigsaw of cartilage and bone and dripping tar and horns and grinning cattle skulls – all compressed, moulded and welded into shape – was not *real*. The descent was not real. She was acting, just until she could get to the bottom of the godawful escalator. Maybe she could be Gloria Swanson in *Sunset Boulevard*, just as the cops came to arrest her and she came down the stairs, insanely believing that the flash cubes of the attendant newspaper reporters drawn by murder were the flashes of attendant paparazzi. Well, Gloria could act insane too; just for a little while . . . *there! Head back, looking down, assuming that haughty air. Good, keep that pose, keep it juicy, just until you get down to the bottom and step off, just until . . .*

Bobby is your baby, said the voice in her head.

It was a voice that also seemed to come from those hideous walls.

And he's going to die. Bobby is OUR baby – and he's still going to die.

The voice in her head killed the act. Gloria began to tremble then, looking down at her son on the escalator.

Something seemed to move in the jigsaw of bone and cartilage and sculpted offal that formed the side of the escalator; just there, low down, between Bobby and herself. Gloria stared. It had been a brief, pulsing movement. But no . . . that couldn't be right. Surely nothing could be *alive* in that hideous mélange? Gloria forced herself to look away. They would be off this bloody escalator soon, and moving on towards whatever lay beyond. As her eyes moved over the bizarre walls on either side, something else seemed to catch her attention – something that made her gasp involuntarily. The configuration of bones and tar and ribs and whatever disgusting mess this contortion of graveyard 'sculpture' was supposed to represent had suddenly taken on a recognisable form. For the moment that she allowed herself to look, it seemed as if the design made sense. She was surely passing a twenty foot tall, hideously complex but recognisable figure from one of her own movies for Draegerman. It was the Swamp Water Woman, rising from the bayou, with her cloak of dripping weed and her snake-slit eyes, and her white, white face – Gloria's own face. Surely that was the crown of snakes around her forehead and in her hair, making her look like one of the Gorgon sisters? And the close-fitting reptilian body suit, glimmering green and black, the scales sculpted from the underbelly of an alligator, but still incredibly sensuous and showing off the wonderful figure that Gloria possessed back then.

Was that head turning down to look at her as she passed?

No, I won't look, thought Gloria, closing her eyes tight.

Don't look and it'll go away? said the voice in her head, taunting. *Just like the movies, Gloria. As always. Look away when the monster comes, or look at the screen through your fingers. That's the way, isn't it?*

I won't look.

Don't you know, yet? You're IN the movies now. You're here, in my house, and on my screen, playing to my rules. No use not looking, Gloria. Not here, not now. Because it won't do you any good. It won't go away, won't go away . . .

I won't look . . .

. . . won't go away, go away, go away . . .

Bobby stood in a stiff, crouched, cruciform position; stopping low and stretching his hands at either side so that he could keep one hand on either escalator handrail. His teeth remained gritted between tight lips, his attention fixed on the others just below him: Boone, Roy and Susan. The sleep back there seemed to have done him good, it had certainly got rid of the shakes for a while – but the dreadful hunger was already returning, and if it took hold and seized him the way that it usually did, he knew that he could never make it through. In the past, he had never allowed himself to get to this stage. As soon as the shakes began, he got high again as quickly as possible. Suddenly, he realised that he had lost two years of his life in that pursuit. When he tried to think back to what he had done, where he had been, a fragmented and distorted series of images paraded behind his eyes. It all looked so unreal, so . . .

That's because it IS unreal. Don't you see, Bobby? You've been right all along. This isn't reality. Look around you. Look at this crazy, bizarre escalator. Are you trying to tell yourself that it really exists, that Draegerman's Rock exists, that even Draegerman himself exists? Of course not. It's lunatic. You're on a bad trip. That's all. A bad trip, that's all. A bad trip, that's . . .

Bobby shook that bad dream voice away, the voice that sounded so much like the mad bastard who said he was his father, so much like the voice that had directed him in those cheap, exploitation movies so many years ago. Had that really happened? Like everything else now, his memories of that time were dim and fragmented. Yes, he had been in a movie, he was sure of it. Something called . . . called . . .

And Bobby looked in sick astonishment at the passing walls as they descended. The hideous jigsaw configuration of bones and tissue and sculpted ivory *did* have meaning after all. There was movement in there now when he looked closely, he was sure of it. The intertwining cartilage and sinew and tar was like a tapestry, and within the tapestry figures were moving. He stared at it in awe as it slowly unreeled and passed before him. He was seeing *himself* in there – on the set of the very movie he had been trying to recall. He could see three other actors on that set, people he had completely forgotten about. He could see the cameras and the cable and the studio technicians, could see the boom overhanging the scene they were about to film. And Jack Draegerman was in there, too – now standing with his back to Bobby as he watched, issuing silent instructions to the four people on set.

Now, Bobby could see the clapperboard: somehow much too large for real life, and the title of the movie they were shooting: *Speed Demon*. Yes, that was it. Now he remembered. A movie made in the eighties, but set in the fifties. A bizarre 'take' on the exploitation hot rod and rock'n'roll movies that were made back then – except that this one was also a horror movie. He remembered the scene they were about to shoot now: the teenage rockers have just had a drag race, and during that race one of the cars smashes into something that tried to run across the road. Something that had just emerged from a cocoon or something in the woods – that part of it had never seemed clear to Bobby from the script. He supposed that the thing had fallen to earth from outer space, the cocoon looked like it was supposed to be some kind of meteorite from the look of the full-size mock-up the technicians had built on the sound stage. And of course, that thing was the 'Speed Demon' itself – a guy in a rubber suit for the hand-held camera fight and murder scenes, but mostly an optical effect that took a further four months to put into the movie after principal shooting was finished. Now wounded, it turned its attention to the teenagers in the woods, knocking them off one by one. Christened the 'Speed Demon' because firstly, this thing was *fast*, plucking people off their feet and smashing them against trees and no one could see it come or go. And secondly, it could inject a certain substance into the bodies of its intended victims through its six inch talons. Not poison, not sulphuric acid – but good old amphetamines. This was one alien who could give everybody a good trip or a bad trip before it offed them according to the whims of the script. Bobby remembered laughing a lot on that movie, remembered how he and others in the cast had talked about their own drug-taking as research for the movie. And here it was now, a behind the scenes shot. And there he was, nodding his head as he listened to a much-younger Draegerman.

And now Draegerman was turning slowly away from the cast members.

The escalator continued on down . . . and Draegerman had turned from the Bobby on set and was looking directly at Bobby on the escalator, smiling in a way that he did not like at all. Now everyone behind the figure had faded away, just as if the studio lights had been killed one by one. Now, there was only Draegerman, walking towards him through that bizarre frieze on the escalator wall. His face was changing as he came, running and blurring as if the face was a water-colour painting and excess water had been spilled over the features. No, not a water-colour, after all. More like the special effect sequence that had shown the Speed Demon suddenly appearing beside one of its victims, as its nightmare insectile face began to assimilate and form behind the unsuspecting teenager who was backing right into its raised six-inch talons. Draegerman was raising his hands now, and those hands were also mutating and changing, the fingers elongating and sharpening as that mutating grin began to spread to cover the face that was no longer a face . . .

Bobby forced himself to look away from the horrifying visage; forced himself to look down at the back of Jessica's head – and all the way down he was aware that Draegerman the Speed Demon was watching him, and willing him to turn back and look, turn back and look, turn back and . . .

Boone clutched the attaché case tightly to his chest, lest someone or something might try to rip it from his grasp as they descended. He lived and breathed fear, could feel it in the others, every one of them. From the very beginning, he had felt their fear. And as this nightmare journey continued, he realised that he must balance that contagious nature of the fear all around him. It was there now, on every face. He studied their faces as they descended, knowing that even though they were trying to suppress their terror in their bid to escape, it was utterly obvious from each pale face that the fear was ready to leap screaming from their mouths at any moment. Boone swallowed hard, fingered the scar on his face and realised that it was the only part of his skin not sweating. He thought of what might lay ahead, and clutched the attache case even tighter to his chest.

Fear is what I want. More than anything, it is the emotion I want to exact from my Guests. You all must die, so that I can live. It's a very simple equation. But I want to feel your terror, want to taste your horror – just as my other Guests will want to taste it when they arrive. We have the same appetite, you see. It's a rare and refined palate. And of all the fear, all the anxious dread, all the nightmare anticipation that you are all feeling – yours, Boone, is the greatest. Hopefully, it will soon be unbearable. Greater terror by far lies ahead . . .

Boone shuddered then, staggered on the steps – and only Jessica's hand on his arm from the step below saved him from falling backwards. Boone mumbled a hopeless and hollow apology.

Jessica had been forced to switch off her mental recording of what she could now see. It was true that Roy Jensen had rocked what

209

little confidence she was able to muster in this hellhole, when he had accurately described just how she was trying to keep the horror of their situation at bay. Perhaps she had been unable to appreciate fully that she was using this ploy, and now the bastard had shown her the truth. Even so, it could work for her only as long as she did not allow it to get out of control, as long as she did not allow that mental ruse to dull her senses from reacting to any real practical danger that might emerge. No, she had stopped reporting and describing, because the horrifying sculpture and design of this escalator and the walls on either side had managed to touch a nerve deep inside which she found difficult to understand. She was not a religious person, but it seemed as if the design was, well, blasphemous. The word was hardly right, given her religious views, but it seemed to be the only word she could find that seemed to get anywhere near describing her reaction to this place. Something about it appalled the very core of her being. Now, she could no longer bring herself to look, so she stared at her feet and prayed that they would reach the bottom as quickly as possible. Only Boone's sudden stagger on the stairs had broken her out of that rigid position, but now she had returned to it – and refused to look up.

You're a reporter, Jessica said the voice in her head. *How can you turn away from the truth? Isn't that a travesty of your professional aim?*

I won't listen. Jessica shook her head, keeping her eyes fixed on the trundling metal plates beneath her feet.

Won't listen? But that's not YOU at all. At all times you're listening, analysing, looking for the right angle for your story. Don't you remember what you said at the Conference, how news reporters should first of all be brutally honest with themselves and their reactions to events if they wanted to make it big in this industry? Weren't you the one who said that even a passerby can't turn away from a horrifying road accident?

I won't . . .

And as the voice talked in her head, Jessica felt her defenses crumbling as it began to describe a scene so vivid that she could see it in her mind just as surely as if it were being projected on a cinema screen. She saw her newspaper office, saw first the headlines about *The Independent Daily*'s Jessica Morell suddenly vanishing, then another telling the readers that her body had been found. She watched the excitement of her colleagues, saw the mock-sincere horror of what had happened to her and knew that no one there cared a damn. She could see the outright glee on faces that were so delighted about their in-house story. She saw the Editor and the Deputy, putting together a tribute to her in the paper. It dripped with cynicism, and she saw the others laughing when they read it. Jessica tried to block out the sight, but could not. Instead, she was overwhelmed by a cascade of sensations.

She saw Jerry, her partner, screwing her best friend.

She saw a post mortem being carried out on her own body.

She saw the morgue attendant taking an interest in her body when the other staff had gone, saw him lifting the sheet from her body, saw him grinning and beginning to unbutton his shirt . . .

But worst of all, far worse than anything, she was shocked to her very core by the the horribly crushing realisation that shortly after her death, it would be as if she had never existed at all. And now Jessica knew, as that horror cut deep to her soul, that in her chosen profession she had fooled herself into believing that she was only interested in revealing the truth to the world. This was only a cloak. In reality, she wanted more than anything else to be remembered and revered for the things she chose to unveil and write about. Instead, she would be forgotten.

Utterly and undeniably.

Oh God, no. Please God . . . please God . . .

Roy kept his hand on the gun jammed into the belt of his jeans, keeping his gaze fixed on the bottom of the escalator. He tried to see beyond, but the downward curving slope of the ceiling hid everything from view. Maybe they had found the way out, after all? Perhaps there was an exit down here? In moments, they might all be on the outside of this hellish place forever.

Do you really think I'd let anyone out of here alive, after what you've all seen, after what I've told you all? Roy shook his head. This was the wrong time and the wrong place to let his imaginings run wild.

Imaginings? Is that what you think? Why don't you close your eyes, Roy? Then wish with all your heart that this is all a dream, that you've imagined everything? Then open them again for a big surprise . . .

Roy glared at the hideously decorated walls. Was that really Draegerman's voice? Somehow coming out of those walls and getting directly into his head? Gritting his teeth, he forced that insistent whispering to the back of his mind.

Susan clutched the handrail tight, as if that contact might confirm or refute the reality of her situation. How long had they been in this hellish place? She had slept once, but for how long? And how long since she had last eaten? Was her stomach cramped by hunger pangs, or was it simply fear?

It's fear, Susan.

Again, that voice.

And it will worsen. Far greater terrors lie ahead.

Susan clenched her other hand, until her fingernails pierced the flesh of her palm.

And when you're dead at last, I'll take away your children. They're my grandchildren, after all. And I have the power to do it.

Susan swore at that inner voice, tried to push it out altogether.

And when they're here with me, in The Rock, what fun we'll have together.

'You bastard . . .' The word slipped out. She turned then to look at Roy with something like guilt.

'It's okay,' said Roy. 'Believe me, I know how you feel. We'll . . .'

'*Wait!*'

The sudden yell from the top of the escalator sent shock waves thrilling through them all. Gloria stumbled and almost fell, but Bobby grabbed her arm and steadied her. They turned as one to see that a figure had appeared up there, now standing on the moving steel plates, but walking nervously backwards on the spot, as if desperately unsure about whether to allow himself to be carried downwards or not.

It was Aiken.

'Wait . . .' he said again, in a voice that was barely audible. As he walked on the spot, he cast anxious glances over his shoulder. 'There's something back there. I'm sure there's something back there in the corridor . . .'

'Oh God . . .' said Boone. 'It's the Berserker.'

Aiken suddenly decided, and began to hurry down the escalator to join them.

'Jensen!' shouted Farrow. 'Use the gun!'

'What?'

'Shoot the bastard. If it's up there, it's after him. Draegerman said it would go when the last of his employees was dead. Remember?'

Roy turned to look down. They were fifty feet from the bottom of the escalator, and now he could see that beyond the point where the moving steps flattened into steel plates again and slid into the solid rock floor, lay another of the hideously familiar green-lit corridors. He looked back and forth, from Aiken to the sliding steel plates below.

'Everybody *run!*' he shouted.

No one needed a second prompting as they clattered down the last fifty-foot stretch.

'Wait!' yelled Aiken. 'Wait.'

'Jensen, you fucking idiot!' Farrow's face was a mask of rage. He was the last one on the escalator, and that meant Aiken would reach him first. 'Shoot him! Before he brings that bloody thing down on us!'

Susan staggered on the plates at the bottom, righted herself and all but leapt from the escalator to the rock floor. The others clattered behind her, Farrow delivering a stream of oaths and curses when he too almost fell on the stairs. Roy whirled back, pushing Gloria and Bobby ahead of him, and came face to face with Farrow as he rushed towards him. Suddenly, the gun was in Roy's hand, with no idea that he had taken the decision to draw it.

'Give it to *me*, then!' snapped Farrow, groping for the gun as he stepped off the last of the moving steel plates. Roy seized him by the collar, using Farrow's own impetus to yank him to the side. Farrow staggered, tried to grab the gun and this time Roy shoved him hard

212

in the chest with the flat of his free hand. Farrow tottered back and fell to the stone floor.

'I'll *kill* you, Jensen.'

Angrily, Roy swung the gun round and pointed it directly at Farrow's face.

Behind them both, Gloria shouted: 'No!'

Roy looked at her, then swung the gun around in Aiken's direction as he blundered on down towards them. He had reached perhaps the three-quarter stage on the bizarre stairway.

'Go on!' yelled Roy, turning back to the others, but still keeping his gun trained on Aiken. 'Run for it.'

'SHOOT HIM!' screamed Farrow,

'Get the hell away from me, Farrow. Go on, everyone – run for it. If anything comes over the top of that escalator behind Aiken, I'll . . .

You'll do what, Roy? Shoot the Berserker? Didn't you hear what Aiken said about bullets not hurting it?

'I'll . . .'

Shoot Aiken? What makes you think it will simply go away if you do that? It's tasted blood, Roy. Maybe it wants some more?

'Just RUN!' yelled Roy – and this time they did just that, Farrow scrabbling to his feet and looking for a moment as if he might launch himself at Roy. Spitting at Roy's feet, he followed the others.

Aiken had only one hundred feet to go before he reached Roy at the bottom, and there was still no sign of anything up there at the top of the escalator. Maybe he had been wrong? The man had been broken by his experiences in The Rock. Could it be that he was seeing things in every corner, every shadow? Roy sensed movement to his left and whirled round to see that Bobby was standing beside him, eyes fixed on Aiken as he descended.

'What are you . . . ?' began Roy.

And then Aiken uttered a strangled cry from the escalator.

Roy looked back to see that, still fifty feet away from them, Aiken seemed to have fallen on the moving stairs. He was half lying, half sitting on the stairs, but with one hand still stretched upwards, clinging to the underneath of the moving handrail. The escalator was still moving, but Aiken seemed to be holding himself in the same stationary position. His other arm flailed for support as the steel-plate stairs moved beneath him. He kicked and thrashed, tried to turn – and then cried out in pain.

The escalator seemed to judder. The air was suddenly filled with a grinding screech, making Roy swing the gun up to the top of the escalator again, expecting the *thing* suddenly to appear there, ready to swoop down screaming upon them. But the noise was not being made by anything living – it was the grinding screech of gigantic cogs, wheels and pistons as the hidden machinery that powered this horrific escalator broke down. That ear-piercing shriek of the mechanism now sounded as if an entire scaffolding had suddenly fallen apart. As the ringing, echoing clatter of hollow iron poles finally ceased, the escalator slowed and then stopped altogether.

Aiken scrabbled to his feet – and now they could see that he was not hanging on to the underpart of the handrail. His right hand was somehow *caught* under there. He clambered to his feet and began to tug hard, trying to free himself.

He looked frantically over his shoulder at them, eyes wide in pain and fear.

'For God's sake, *help* me!'

Cursing under his breath, Roy shoved the gun into his belt, grabbed the handrail and began to ascend, two steps at a time. The sound of footsteps right behind him meant that Bobby was also coming. Aiken continued to tug furiously at his right hand.

Roy was only four steps away from him, was already reaching forward to help, when Aiken suddenly jerked upright, left arm and both legs rigid, his head thrown back so that he was staring at the ceiling. It was as if he had received an electric shock.

And then he began to scream.

It was one long continuous howl of agony and anguish, starting low and wheezing in his chest, now building and rising as if Aiken was trying to impersonate a wolf-howl, now erupting from his mouth in a shriek of distress. The sound paralysed Roy and Bobby. The agonised shriek was choked off in Aiken's throat, and now he slowly looked down, eyes bulging, at where his right hand was trapped. He began to sob.

Roy also looked.

Something had come up from beneath the handrail, from beneath the staircase itself. Something that looked like black and matted threads of string or weeds; threads that had intertwined around Aiken's hand and fingers. His hand was juddering – and blood was dripping from his fingertips. The matted threads were holding him tight, and Roy could see that they were *moving*, creeping and curling under Aiken's frayed cuff, crawling up his arm. There was movement under his jacket sleeve now; undulating, squirming movement as the threads hunted, encoiled and enwrapped. Aiken began to scream again, making Roy and Bobby back off down the steps.

The screaming was suddenly cut off in a strangled gasp as Aiken's other hand flew to his throat. His face was turning purple, the eyes bulging in horror, as the strangling threads erupted from his frayed collar with frightening and greedy speed to coil around his throat and part of his face. A small wisp of smoke curled from his face, and now Roy and Bobby could see with horror that the tendrils were burning and melting the flesh they touched, even now secreting some kind of acid as they attempted to burrow *under* the flesh of Aiken's face.

'For God's sake, *help MEEEEEEE . . .*'

214

And then Aiken's left eye popped beneath the squirming, burning weed and his shrieking reached a new pitch as he scrabbled at his face with his free hand.

Something beneath the staircase seemed to react to the screaming, something that sounded like a metal plate bending with a dull clank. The stairs beneath them seemed to quiver, and Roy looked back quickly to yell at Bobby, to tell him to run back. But before he could open his mouth the stairs beneath their feet suddenly fell away, each step dropping from horizontal to vertical.

Aiken fell screaming from sight as Roy twisted and groped at the handrail. His left hand caught it and he swung backwards with savage force against the sides of the escalator, his feet thrashing and kicking into the void below. Crying out, Roy kicked himself around and clutched the handrail with his other hand, jamming his foot against one of the thin metal ridges that had once been the edge of the step he had been standing on. It supported his body weight and he used it to stand upright, still clutching the handrail and looking back to where Bobby had been standing. He had been quicker than Roy, was in the same position as him now; both hands on the rail and both feet balanced precariously on the thin ridge of a step.

Aiken's screams had been cut off in the fall, but now they had begun again – only to be suddenly drowned by the sounds of the great cogs and gears and pistons juddering, clanking and growling into life beneath them. Roy looked down to see that they were both standing over the innards of the hideous escalator – innards that looked just as they sounded, as if they had been dreamed up and designed in some horrifying Victorian nightmare: huge iron rods and pistons gleaming with oil the colour of arterial-black blood, cogs that seemed ridiculously large, as if designed for some basic child's construction game but easily the size of a man, turning slowly, wreathed in steam, the edges razor sharp.

And Aiken had fallen into this hideous machinery, had fallen into this nightmare of steam, pistons and cogs – up to the waist. He flailed in agony trying to free himself, even though his left hand was completely smothered in the enveloping weed-like subtance, even though the left half of his face and head had also been consumed, was *still* being consumed. The cogs turned, the pistons slid into their shafted sockets – and Aiken was dragged down to his chest. He glared up at them both, his one eye wide and glittering, his mouth opening to scream for help; but there were no words, only a spout of red-black blood the same colour as the oil, erupting from his mouth in a spouting gargle.

But greater horror was rising from beneath Aiken.

From all around him, from beneath the escalator machinery, from beneath the hissing steam, something was rising in an engulfing mass. Roy and Bobby could only stare in disbelief at the swarming, undulating mass that somehow defied their eyes to make any sense of its constantly

215

shifting nature. It was as if the escalator machinery and its victim were being lowered into some hideous sea; something that seemed to be a thick, viscous liquid – but now was not. Something that seemed to be twisting, coiling clouds filmed at high speed – but now was not. Something that now looked like a huge mass of engulfing seaweed – the same voracious weed that had swarmed up Aiken's arm and dragged him down.

'Oh Christ,' said Bobby. 'It's that thing – the Berserker.'

All the time they had thought it was following somewhere behind them, all the time Aiken thought it had been hunting in the corridors they had travelled, it had been here, beneath this horrifying escalator into Hell; waiting for them, waiting for Aiken. And when it had scented him descending, it had reached up and found him.

'Move!' yelled Roy, leaning over to step on to the next thin ridge, moving hand over hand on the rail towards Bobby, who was still staring down into the rising mass, hypnotised by the sight of it. 'Come *on*, Bobby!' Roy was right next to him now, letting go of the rail and grabbing his shoulder. Bobby flinched, and then quickly began to follow Roy's example, clambering back down the last fifty feet of the inverted escalator, ridge to ridge, hand over hand.

Roy could not help but see as he moved that Aiken was being dragged down through the machinery into the thing rising from beneath it, arms still thrashing desperately for purchase. And it was impossible to tell whether Aiken, his one remaining eye almost popping out of his head, mouth wide in a silent scream, was being dragged into the machinery of the escalator or force-fed into the hideous writhing snake's nest that was the Berserker's mouth. Roy forced himself to look away as more of the hideous moss-covered tendrils slapped themselves over Aiken's face and head, finally dragging him down from sight into the undulating, all-engulfing mass. And as he vanished from sight, consumed at last by the chaotic, living, shape-shifting thing, Roy could see that it was still rising, still engulfing the machinery of the escalator. Rising now, perhaps, to take them both as they tried to clamber to safety.

'Bobby, come on! We've got to get off this damned escalator. *Now!*'

In his haste, Bobby stepped too heavily on one of the steel-plate ridges. His foot skidded and plunged him over the edge. Still clinging to the handrail, he swung in space above the quickly rising morass. A moss-covered tendril seemed to whip from the mass below, lazily curling and reaching for Bobby's dangling legs. It missed, and slipped back into the main body of the thing like a tendril of smoke. Quickly, Roy seized his arm and helped him to rise again.

Twenty feet to go and now they were not climbing down a slope – the escalator had evened out on its approach-run to the corridor.

Ten feet, six feet – and Roy felt something on his right shoe. Something that scraped and seemed to clutch at the rubber sole, as if he had stepped in clinging mud.

'Now, NOW!' Roy slapped Bobby hard on the shoulder.

Bobby leapt from the last steel-plate ridge, stumbled and sprawled headlong from the escalator on to the cold stone floor. Twisting back, he stood at the edge and held out both hands to Roy as something seemed to roar and hiss and erupt from the escalator behind Roy. He could not turn to look, could see before him that a gigantic shadow was falling over them, could see the wild alarm in Bobby's face as he saw what was emerging behind Roy.

And then Roy, with four steps to cover before he was safe, four thin steel ridges, launched himself from the escalator rail with both hands like some kind of demented tightrope walker trying his luck on parallel tightropes – and *ran*.

First ridge, and the impact shivered beneath his left foot.

Second ridge, and his right foot stamped hard to launch him again.

Third ridge, and his left foot came down too hard and he skidded from the ridge.

He was falling, cheated at the last, dropping through the aperture into the hideous maw below, to suffer the same agonising fate as Aiken. His hands clutched, he cried out aloud, voice hoarse and terrified – and Bobby suddenly seized his arm and yanked so hard that it seemed he might have pulled the damned thing out of its socket. The impetus pulled Roy forward across the last aperture. He fell heavily, on his hip and side – now kicking and scrabbling on to the cold stone floor as Bobby dragged him to safety.

In each other's arms they staggered and ran from the nightmare escalator, aware of the presence of the Berserker as it rose from the pit below. They did not look back, but kept on running, stopping only at the sight of figures ahead. It was Susan, Jessica and Gloria, running back at the sound of Aiken's hideous screams, despite the knowledge that they had to keep going or suffer a hideous fate. Farrow and Boone had gone on, and this did not surprise anyone. Gloria ran to support Bobby, and Roy tried to tell Susan and Jessica that they must keep running, but it seemed as if the last impact had knocked all the breath from his body. Instead, he could only shake his head and feebly pull at both their arms, trying to get them to hurry away.

'No,' said Jessica, looking back at the escalator. 'No, look. It's . . . it's *not* coming.'

Roy staggered and looked at her face. It was horrified, yes – but there was something else on her face, too; another expression, an expression that was matched by the look on Susan's face. He looked from one to the other, not understanding why they did not just simply run and get the hell away from this place. Then he saw that Gloria and Bobby had also stopped, were also looking back with that expression of horror . . . and awe.

Roy turned then – and saw.

The Berserker had consumed Aiken, body and soul. And there was a feeling, somehow a godawful, instinctive feeling, that it was as if Aiken had never existed at all. The awareness made Roy feel sick in a way he could not explain. And it was a feeling shared by the others; an instinctive reaction to the thing that was rising like the hissing, billowing clouds of a thousand storms from the innards of the escalator. Now it was a formless, twisting, hellish mass. Were there faces in there; dozens of screaming, changing faces? The faces of men, women and children, all screaming in agony? Did this thing somehow contain the souls of all that it had devoured? No sooner had their eyes focused on that aspect of the thing's being, than it had changed again. Now it was the thunderous spray from some subterranean ocean: a poisonous, erupting spray of foam and black-plumed water. Now it was the smoke from burning petrol, the fumes that might rise from some horrifying mass grave, where petrol had been poured on to the corpses and set alight. Now there were faces in the petrol smoke. Faces of things that could not possibly be human. It was all these things and none of these things – and they looked at it as it hovered above the escalator, now free of the underground machinery.

It was impossible to focus on the Berseker. Its existence was an anathema to humankind. Something about it *offended* the human eye's ability to construct it, as if the mind could not contain its obscene and shape-shifting characteristics. In trying to see it, they could not truly see it – only *feel* it. And that feeling was awe-inspiring, and sickening.

And instinctively now, they knew that it had got what it wanted: Aiken, the last of the Black Suits. All part of Draegerman's monstrous plan.

They watched as the Berserker simply began to fade from view. As it faded, it began to bellow and shriek; a sound far worse than any primeval monster on the edge of some stinking prehistoric swamp. A sound of sated malice, a trumpeting, screeching, hissing sound of vile satisfaction. Now it was only a billowing mass of dark clouds; grey, billowing storm clouds; the dissipating remnants of a storm that had moved on to some other plane. Soon, the clouds were mere wisps of steam – and the steam whipped and curled and vanished, just as the sounds of the thing's obscene screeching faded into a last dying echo.

Hollow and horrified, they instinctively staggered together, into each other's arms. It was as if the arrival and departure of this thing had sucked at their very humanity, had marked each and every one in some way that could only be healed and consoled in the company of other human beings. They stood together in a joint embrace, Roy and Bobby still breathing heavily, looking back to the inverted escalator – and the empty space above it. There was no apprehension that the thing might return. They all felt it in their souls. The Berserker had gone.

Without speaking, unable to say anything after what they had witnessed, they turned slowly and began to move off down the

218

corridor, still casting anxious looks back at the escalator, still reassuring themselves that the thing had gone.

Something hissed into life in the corridor wall. Something that buzzed, strobed and flickered.

As one, they flinched from the sudden eruption of light and noise, and then halted in their tracks when the familiar face appeared on the television screen, set eight feet high in the dripping stone wall.

'You see?' said Draegerman. *'All the time you thought it was behind you, when it was always ahead of you. Waiting. Now that it has tasted the last of my employees, has been fully blooded, it can return to where it came from. It has paved the way for the others I told you about. You've done well to come so far. I've been with you each step of the way, believe me. Sharing your fear. Yes, that's right – SHARING your fear. It's the finest, most refined of emotions. Remember what I told you? I've summoned a Daemon for each of you, have promised one of my children to each of them. If any one of you had been killed up to this moment, then my pact would have been broken – my arrangements for longevity null and void. And you could so easily have died. My Spider Garden. The Berserker – yes, the Berserker was on the scent of my employees, summoned to hunt and kill them all – but it would certainly have taken you if you'd been close enough to it. So you see, I really have been sharing your fear. In your case, fear of losing your lives and your souls. In my case, the fear of failure. Roy and Bobby, so close to death. Such sweet terror.'*

Gloria stood trembling, hands held rigidly at her side. She searched the ground for something – anything – that she could pick up and throw at the screen.

'Gloria, my darling,' continued Draegerman. *'You've come through this all so well. Maybe not so much of a surprise after all. You always were a gutsy lady.'*

'Shoot that fucking screen out!' Gloria yelled to Roy.

Roy shook his head. 'No, Gloria. We might need this gun for what's ahead.'

'You see? It seems that Roy's the one with the sensible head on his shoulders. He's the oldest of you, did I tell you? Maybe he's being the protective elder brother among you.'

'Go to hell!' rejoined Gloria, lips trembling.

'No, thank you. But welcome to mine. Gloria – the Berserker was summoned to take you first. One of the mothers of my children, remember? Had it done so, then it would have been able to complete its task of removing all of my remaining employees in The Rock a great deal faster than it did. Your soul, your energy, would have . . . how shall I say it? . . . fuelled that engine of destruction, made it a great deal faster. No matter now. It only slowed things up a little. In any event, one of the Daemons will no doubt take you as well. Not part of my pact – perhaps they'll look on it as a freebie?'

219

'Show your face!' shouted Gloria. 'Come out from hiding, you bastard!'

'Keep your temper, Gloria. Save your strength. As for hiding ... I'm always closer to you than you think. Now that the Berserker has paved the way, I can summon the other guests. I told you that The Rock has special architectural ... features. Well, now The Rock itself will do the summoning. I'd love to show you all, but it's unfortunately not possible. Just let's say that the four towers you've observed on the roof of this humble abode serve much more than the practical purposes for which they were designed. They will be beckoning. So – expect a little disturbance as that takes place. And remember, children. One Daemon for each of you. I'm afraid things are going to become ... rather nasty from now on.'

A snowstorm filled the screen. The snowstorm flurried, dwindled and shrank to a small white point of light. And then the screen was dark again, once more invisible in the face of the black stone wall.

Gloria dropped to her knees, head down. Bobby helped her to rise again. Roy took her other arm, and Bobby looked across at him as they helped her to join the others.

'Thanks for what you did back there,' he said. 'I nearly fell into that thing.'

'You didn't have to come after me,' replied Roy. 'So I should be thanking you.' Bobby nodded and looked back to where the television screen had blinked into life. 'Think we're going to get out of here?'

'Come on,' said Roy. Joining the others, they moved slowly off into the darkness, down the corridor.

TWENTY-FOUR

The Augusta 109 headed through the night sky, nose tilted slightly downwards in its forward flight. Weaving through the dark concrete canyons of office tower blocks, and over the glittering streams of traffic far below, it had finally reached the last open expanse of the city where developers feared, apparently, to tread. Now they were flying above the densely populated, run-down areas that surrounded Draegerman's Rock. It was impossible for Taylor to relate to the dark jumble of twisted streets and buildings and glowing neon. Were they really the same silent and apparently empty streets down which he had so recently been driven?

And there now – directly ahead of them – was The Rock.

A giant monolith, keeping watch over the warren of streets and run-down houses that surrounded the pit in which it stood. Still keeping one eye on the pilot, he tried to see where *The Pool* might be. It was impossible to tell in the dark, fragmented, badly lit jigsaw. The helicopter headed straight on towards the monolith.

Switching the weapon to his other hand, Taylor reached inside his tunic. The pilot saw the movement and began to lick his lips nervously. He had been sweating profusely ever since Taylor had emerged.

'What are you going to . . . ?'

And suddenly, Taylor leant across and clamped something around the pilot's left forearm. The pilot's hands twitched on the control column, and the Augusta 109 pitched in the sky before he could resume control.

'Just keep your eyes on The Rock,' said Taylor calmly.

'What is it?' The pilot looked at the metal band on his forearm. There was a square casing attached underneath, an LED display on the upper casing. The LED display showed a glowing *001*, now *002*, now *003* . . . 'What the *hell* is it?'

'Just a little insurance,' said Taylor. 'Now, tell me what's happened up at The Rock.'

'Me tell you?' babbled the pilot, still casting anxious glances at the electronic armband. 'I was hoping you could tell *me* just what the hell is going on.'

'I know that The Rock has been sealed off. I know about the Four Day Rule.'

'So what the hell can *I* tell you that you don't already know?'

Taylor leaned across again and jammed the gun under the pilot's chin. His head jerked back, but he kept looking forward in order to control the helicopter.

'No, honest!' he continued. 'Look, what I mean is . . . we were expecting the Rock shutdown . . . but we didn't know when . . . I mean . . .'

'You're not making a lot of sense,' said Taylor through clenched teeth. 'All right, so you're all trained and prepared for this shutdown. Now it's happened. So why the panic?'

'Some of us on the outside, heard . . . things . . . on the radios. Just before transmission from inside The Rock was blocked. There's some kind of jamming system in there, automatically cuts out any contact with the outside. But just before shutdown, a guy on the radio back there at the base thought he heard one of our own people . . .'

'Heard him what?'

'Heard him screaming for help.'

Taylor looked ahead. Draegerman's Rock was directly before them. Even in the darkness, he could see the strange channels and crevasses carved into the sides of the damned thing. The rococo design, the extravagant sweeping curves of stone, seemed as if they should make some kind of architectual or geometric sense – but they did not.

'Look,' continued the pilot. 'Look, I'm not being paid for this. I don't want any trouble. So whatever Draegerman has asked you to do . . .'

'You think I'm one of Draegerman's people?'

'Well, what else are you doing here? It must have something to do with what's going on. But I don't want any part of it. I'm just a hired hand, just . . .'

'You're going to put me down on top of The Rock.'

'We've been there. When the shutdown happened and we heard that screaming on the radio. We've been up three times, down on the roof three times. It's no good, you'll never get inside.'

'Why?'

'There are two main security points up there. Four towers at each corner of the roof, but only two have entrances built into them. And they're shut down, locked up tight. Won't take the security codes for access. Or so I was told. Listen, I've never had access to those codes – I *swear*! If I had them, I'd give them to you. But it would do no good anyway. You'll never get inside. Believe me.'

'Believe *me*. I'll get in.'

Now the helicopter was climbing, the face of The Rock filling their vision.

And the sight of the Rock face seemed to be doing something to Taylor inside.

Oh Christ, no!

Turning to keep his gaze fixed on the pilot, Taylor fought with the pain that the sight of The Rock seemed to have engendered within him.

Not so soon after the last time.

The pilot was busy with the controls, did not see the sudden contortion on Taylor's face as the fire clawed at his guts again. With his free hand, Taylor clutched at his stomach out of sight and tried to will the pain away; clutched as if he could burrow his scarred hand right into his innards and tear out the source of the pain.

The Rock face was suddenly gone. The helicopter had circled and risen above it.

And the pain also began to subside.

Taylor breathed out slowly, looking down now to see that they were circling the roof.

Thank God . . .

The four towers looked like some hideous parody of a gigantic crown; extravagant spines of rock jutted from the inner edges of the towers, all pointing towards the centre of the roof, with its two landing pads. But now, it seemed to Taylor that the four towers were like gigantic and monstrous fingers of stone. The Rock itself was an arm, thrusting out of the earth, and wasn't there a bulging parapet all the way around the top of that arm, perhaps three or four hundred feet from the roof, giving semblance to a wrist, and then wasn't that last three or four hundred feet like a fist, with the four towers like outstretched fingers of stone, reaching for the sky – ready to grab the moon, ready to clutch it from the night sky, clutch it in that huge stone fist and crush the essence out of it?

'All right,' said Taylor. 'Put it down.'

The pilot merely nodded, now wiping the free-flowing sweat from his face with his right hand and looking with anxiety at the metal sleeve that had been clamped to his other arm.

He began their descent.

Even Taylor could tell that they were not centred between the four pillars of stone and the rooftop landing pad. But before he could turn and say anything, the pilot had compensated, his face running with sweat, a mask of fear and concentration. Now he had reorientated the helicopter and they were dropping slowly and smoothly, dead centre. Taylor kept his attention focused on the pilot, aware that they were now within the clutch of the stone fist. He shrugged off the image, unable to allow any headroom for thoughts that were not concentrated on the job in hand. He had to remain calm and focused.

They seemed to be dropping too far.

Surely the four pillars were not so high.

But even as he glanced beyond the cockpit, the fuselage bumped softly.

'We're down,' said the pilot. The words seemed to come only with great effort. He leaned forward to switch off the engine.

'Keep it going,' said Taylor, reaching for the door at his side, sliding it open.

The pilot sat back, began to gesture at the device on his forearm. But before he could speak, Taylor leaned across and said above the noise of the rotors:

'That's just a little guarantee that you won't take off and leave me.'

'Yeah? Well what the hell IS IT?'

'A timed detonator, with plastic explosive in the boxed compartment. Enough to blow this 'copter out of the sky. There's about five minutes left. Just enough for me to do what I have to do. It switches off by numbered code, and unless you feel like sawing through your arm it won't come off. Keep the engine gunned, ready for a take-off. When I get back, I'll switch it off.'

The pilot's face was suddenly moon-white in the cockpit. He looked at his arm as if he might vomit at any moment.

'Where are the two entrances?' demanded Taylor. 'Which two of the four towers?'

The pilot seemed unable to speak, gesturing weakly out at the roof.

'There's only four and a half minutes left,' said Taylor.

'That one *there* – and that one *there*!' The pilot waved and pointed extravagantly, like a child eager to please. He had waved at the left-hand tower facing them, and the right-hand tower behind them.

Without another word, Taylor dropped quickly out of the helicopter, orientated himself, running dead ahead and crouching until he had cleared the span of the spinning rotor blades. The tower loomed ahead, now somehow more like a finger with its last joint curved inwards than ever before. Where the hell was the door on this thing, where was the entrance? Had the pilot been lying to him despite everything?

No – there was a door, built smooth and flush into the stone. There was a panel at shoulder height here, presumably a security-coded panel. It was black and featureless. Taylor did not even bother to try it. Instead, he unclipped the belt from around his waist, laid it on the ground and unfolded its contents: two double strips of plastic explosive. There was more in the small pack on his back. Glancing back at the helicopter on the pad, he set about jamming the long strips around the edges of the door, laying a double strip at its foot. It had been a long time since he had been called on to do a job like this, but his leathered hands had lost none of the old efficiency; scarred knuckles kneading the plastic into the barely visible aperture of the door frame. Jamming the detonators into the plastic at the base of the door, Taylor connected the timer, primed it for five minutes – and then, crouching low again, ran back towards the helicopter. The rotors were still spinning at take-off speed, the wind-blast on Taylor's eyes blurring his vision as he slid open the

224

door and began to climb inside. The pilot was turned away from him, apparently concentrating on the instrument panel.

'All right!' shouted Taylor over the noise of the rotors. 'Take it up!'

And then, as he began to slide the door shut, the pilot swept around in his seat. Taylor saw the blur of movement as a reflection in the plexiglass windscreen, tried to avoid it – but could not stop the pilot's elbow and forearm slamming into the back of his head. The blow was meant to knock him out of the helicopter; instead Taylor fell back from his seat into the passenger cabin behind, deliberately yanking the door shut as he fell, even as the pilot leapt from his seat and kicked out furiously with flailing legs at his sprawling body. Taylor tried to curl up tight, tried to haul himself around behind his own seat so that he could stand, but the pilot had fallen into the seat in the act of kicking out at him. Lunging forward, he smashed Taylor directly in the forehead. Taylor barely had time to register that the pilot had hit him with the same metal cuff he had managed to prise from his arm with the screwdriver from under his seat.

'It's a clock, you *fuck*!' screamed the pilot as he came over the top of the seat. 'No plastics in there, just a fucking *clock*!'

Taylor squirmed to retrieve the gun, but was shocked from his daze by the impact of the pilot slamming down on to his back, the breath whumping out of his body. The pilot reached for his neck, but Taylor squirmed again, trying to throw him off. Now the pilot was lying astride him, punching down at his head. Taylor's hands flew up to the pilot's eyes, thumbs hunting for his sockets. And knowing that Taylor had planted some kind of explosive on the roof, the pilot desperately tried to disable him as quickly as possible. The screwdriver was still in his other hand. Screaming when Taylor's thumbs found his eyes, he drove it down hard, stabbing it into Taylor's right shoulder.

And beneath them, beneath the helicopter, The Rock began to move.

The landing pad shuddered, the helicopter tilted, but the rotors continued whirling at take-off speed. The tilting motion propelled the pilot from Taylor's body and into the back of the cabin, leaving the screwdriver embedded in his shoulder. Groaning, Taylor struggled to stay conscious, feeling the pain like fire. Again, the helicopter tilted – but there had been no sound of an explosion. Had something happened to his eardrums, had he been deafened by one of the blows? Was the 'copter even now falling from the landing pad as a result of the blast? Still struggling with the pain, Taylor waited for the helicopter to tear itself apart when the tilting rotors hit the ground and shattered.

He saw the pilot clambering back to where he lay. His face was a mask of pain and rage – and he had retrieved the gun from the back of the cabin.

Taylor saw the barrel of the gun, thrust right down into his face.

He waited for the explosion.

The helicopter seemed to shudder again, and the pilot staggered back. Taylor was too dazed to move, unable to take advantage. He could only watch and wonder as the pilot fell back against the cabin wall. When Taylor touched the screwdriver embedded in his upper arm, a dark bubble of blood oozed through the fabric of his jacket and the pain overwhelmed him again. The pilot seemed to have lost interest in Taylor now that he had the gun. He staggered away from him, scrabbling into the front seat again.

'What the hell have you done?'

The Rock seemed to judder once more, jerking the pilot in his seat as he took the control column. There was no sound of impact; the pilot could see the door at which Taylor had been laying his charges, still intact. So what the hell was *happening*?

'What have you DONE?'

The pilot knew that his gamble to shove Taylor out of the helicopter before getting the hell off this damned Rock had not paid off. But it had been only at the last sweat-drenched moment, as he fumbled out of sight with the metal cuff, that he discovered he had never been in any danger. He moved the collective-pitch lever, increasing the speed of the blades for immediate take-off. He opened the throttle, jammed his feet down on the pedals. The helicopter began to lift.

'Oh *Christ* . . .'

And now the pilot could see what was happening, and could not believe his eyes.

The Rock *was* moving.

The four towers at either corner of the roof were slowly, impossibly, moving down and inwards. The helicopter was sitting in the palm of a hand, and the fingers of that hand were closing towards the palm. And even above the sound of the clattering rotors, he could now hear another *deeper* sound: a sound that was shaking the very fabric of the landing pad and the helicopter itself. As the helicopter continued to lift and the pilot kept his eyes on the slowly descending towers, the cabin was suddenly filled with the noise of grinding gears, of huge slabs of stone moving into place.

'It's not happening!' yelled the pilot.

In the back, Taylor clambered to his knees, face to the cabin window.

'It just CAN'T happen!'

The stone towers could not possibly be curling inwards like that. They should have crumbled and collapsed. Stone simply did not bend and curl that way. And now the pilot's sense of panic and unreality threatened to overwhelm him when he saw the movement that was taking place on the ground, off to the landing pad's right – and in the centre of the roof itself.

An aperture had appeared: a black, round aperture in the centre of the roof. The aperture was growing, keeping its perfectly round symmetry, but spreading and growing larger nonetheless. Was the roof caving in?

Taylor yanked the screwdriver from his arm and gasped in pain as it clattered to the cabin floor. His vision swam in and out of focus. Fighting to keep control, he too could see what was happening in the centre of the roof.

The roof was not caving in. It was *opening*.

The screeching and clanking of gears and pistons, the deep grumbling and roaring from beneath them, was the machinery operating the roof of The Rock. The circular opening was being created by the hidden mechanism; like some kind of gigantic kaleidoscope lens.

The helicopter was rising between the descending stone towers, the landing pad beneath them now sliding away with the roof as it opened.

And as Taylor struggled to look at his watch, to check how much of the five-minute timing was left, everything happened at once.

The plastic explosive at the base of the moving tower exploded with a flashing roar that drowned the sounds of the helicopter and the gigantic machinery below.

The fuselage of the helicopter tilted in the sky, the machine twisting and spinning in the blast. Taylor was flung back from the window to the cabin floor again as a chunk of rock exploded through the fuselage just behind him. The pilot began to scream obscenities at the top of his voice as he fought to retain control

A descending stone tower filled the cockpit windscreen, now looking more than ever like the finger of some stone colossus, ready to pluck the helicopter out of the sky and crush it in a massive stone fist. The pilot frantically tugged at the cyclic-pitch change lever, tried to correct the rate of their ascent.

For a moment, it seemed as if the blast of Taylor's explosives might blow them clear of the descending tower.

But then the tail rotors clipped the tower as it swung away, shattering and flying into fragments. In the next moment, the port elevator, tail rotor gearbox and ventral fin were torn from the fuselage.

'Oh CHRIST!'

The pilot fought like a maniac at the control column as two and a half tons of machinery pitched and twisted in the sky.

Taylor grabbed at a safety belt on one of the passenger seats, but had no time even to try to fasten it around himself. He clung to the strap with his good arm, saw the night-black sky through the hole in the fuselage and felt a hellwind blasting through the ragged gap. The fuselage juddered and he was flung into the air, still hanging on to the strap, momentarily in freefall as the helicopter whirled away from the roof, hopelessly out of control.

The helicopter had cleared the descending stone tower, and Taylor could see that they were falling away from the roof, whirling and twisting.

The stone face of The Rock filled the cockpit windscreen as they fell, like the side of some great concrete canyon.

Then something shattered the windscreen.

Taylor slammed into the fuselage wall.

The sound of the pilot screaming was the last thing he heard; that terror-stricken voice echoing away into nothingess as they fell into a roaring black pit.

TWENTY-FIVE

The corridor shuddered beneath their feet as if something had exploded somewhere within The Rock. They tottered where they stood, now clutching at the corridor wall as it subsided.

'The Berserker?' said Jessica. 'Oh God, it *has* come back!'

'No,' said Bobby. 'It's not that. It can't be that!'

Again, the corridor juddered underfoot. They could feel the vibrations in the walls. Gloria pulled away from the wall, as if the simple act of touching the stone could communicate some kind of evil contagion. The rumbling resolved itself into the familiar and unnerving sound of gigantic machinery; of huge pistons and levers, the rattling and clattering of chains as if a massive portcullis was being lifted somewhere.

Roy looked back the way they had come. He could still see the inverted escalator, but the bizarre Victorian machinery within remained silent and unmoving. Clearly, this noise was coming from somewhere else. As he turned back, there was another vibration; and this time, a thin layer of dirt and dust was shaken from the ceiling overhead.

'Oh God, no,' said Susan. 'The ceiling's going to cave in on top of us.'

'Back to the escalator . . . ?' began Bobby.

'No,' shouted Roy. 'We'll be trapped back there. We've got to go on.'

'But the ceiling . . .'

There was no more time to discuss the issue as the sounds of moving machinery and of hellish piston engines filled the corridor. They began to run and stumble down the green-lit corridor. There was a bend ahead, and bright light seemed to be shining on the furthermost wall. Was there another chamber ahead? Was that where Farrow and Boone had gone? The ground tilted beneath their feet again. Jessica almost fell, then regained her balance and was the first to hurtle around the bend.

Another impact, another deafening roar – and this time water began to sprinkle from the stone overhead. Roy fell heavily, skinning his palms, saw Susan stumble to a halt ahead of him, looking back.

'Go on!' he yelled, climbing to his feet. 'Go ON!'

Susan staggered onwards around the bend as he clambered to his feet and ran after them.

The light flooded his eyes as he reached the corner. The corridor ended just ahead. He could see an opened door set into an arch, through which the others had just passed. Had they reached the outside?

Now he could see the source of the light: a mediaeval-style torch, jammed into a bracket in the wall, its flame casting the light into the corridor behind. Beyond the circle of intense light it was dark again – but this time not with the sick green or orange tints they had seen so often. As he finally cleared the corridor, he could see the silhouettes of the others ahead: now no longer running, but walking slowly forward, as if somehow in awe.

Behind him, the corridor shuddered again.

The sounds of the gigantic cogs and pistons seemed to reverberate here. Although his eyes had yet to focus properly, Roy suddenly had the feeling that they had entered another large space. The sounds of screeching machinery shuddered to a halt, the echoing squeals bouncing and leaping from above. The quiet that followed was like the silence inside some vast cathedral.

At last, as the noises ceased altogether, Roy began to see where they had all emerged. It was another cavernous space, similar to the Banqueting Hall where they had all first met. He could see the Walkways and platforms high up in the vaulted arches, more of the strangely carved walls, the gargoyles peering down from massive stone columns that looked like gigantic prehistoric trees. There was a staircase rising to a platform high above ...

And there was the fireplace where a log fire had burned so bright, but now was only a cradle of glowing ashes ... and a banqueting table with four attaché cases on it ... and the flickering from dozens of television screens set into the wall at head height and above ... and the glittering shards of plastic or glass on the flagged stone floor where the hologram that was somehow much more than a hologram of Jack Draegerman had shattered and collapsed.

'You damned *idiots*!' Another figure was striding out of the darkness, his silhouette backlit by the remains of the distant log figure. He stopped, fists clenched at either side. The pose was familiar. It was Farrow. And there, just beyond him, kneeling on the floor with his head lowered – Boone. The others had halted now, were staring around them with the same dawning realisation and deep-rooted sense of horror and despair. 'You stupid, damned, *idiots*!' Farrow's raised voice caused more bouncing echoes, like invisible squawking birds.

'This can't be,' said Gloria.

'We were always heading down,' continued Jessica in a voice filled with unbelieving horror.

230

'We can't be . . .' said Susan.

'Oh yes we can,' said Farrow's silhouette through gritted teeth. 'We're back in the Banqueting Hall. We're back where *we damn STARTED!*'

PART THREE

HERE BE DAEMONS

News item from *The Independent Daily* September 26th.

Hopes are now fading that film actress Deborah Steele and her partner, the actor Perry Dillman, will be found alive following discovery of the wreckage of their Cessna aircraft in the foothills of Mount Keir. Search parties discovered the wreck of the aircraft on Tuesday, and have been searching continually since that time. With bad weather due to close in within 48 hours, reports back suggest that the aircraft appeared to have disintegrated completely on impact, despite the fact that weather conditions at the time were mild.

Ms Steele will be best known for her movies Autumn Song, The Story of Adele and Crying Crimson. She was currently filming for Draegerman Enterprises when the aircraft was reported missing . . .

ONE

Taylor had once dreamed that he was dead.

He had then been a professional soldier, long before his 'dismissal'; long before his new life as a mercenary, and with Sara's soothing presence in his life even further away. He and his other squaddies had been on a physical fitness training programme; the usual assault course stuff, the usual bastard of a sergeant instructor with them all the way, hurling insults as they ran, climbed and jumped. A rope swing had been rigged alongside a roped climbing frame. As Taylor had reached the top of the frame, fifty feet from the ground, he had leaned out to reach for the rope. Down below, the sergeant had called him a fairy – and that was all he could remember. No realisation that his grip had missed, nothing in his memory to suggest that he had fallen those fifty feet, the impetus of his fall broken when his legs tangled in the rope frame at the halfway point.

But that was when Taylor had first realised what death was going to be like.

He was floating in utter darkness, and his eyes were wide open. He could feel nothing beneath him, could feel no part of his body. Somehow he was unable to lift his hands to his face. And as he lay there, in that utter blackness, he remembered the climbing frame and the rope and the foul-mouthed sergeant instructor. When he realised that there was nothing in his memory after that, he knew then that he had fallen and broken his neck. He was dead. And this was what it was like.

No heavenly choirs, no Pearly Gates.

No sweet-faced angels consulting big books and weighing up the Good and Bad scales.

Just this unremitting, vast blackness – and the stark knowledge that this was what it was going to be like for him from now on. For eternity. Nothing to do but look back over his life. The ideals, the unrealised hopes, the failures, the mistakes. Constantly rerunning, over and over, forever and ever amen.

It was utterly horrifying.

He struggled but could not move, tried to will himself to lift

235

his invisible arms. The darkness seemed to be crushing down on him.

Oh God, I'm in my coffin. Underground. They've buried me and left me. Buried me and left me, buried me and . . .

He awoke with a start, drenched in sweat. Instantly, he realised that despite his sense of being awake in the godawful darkness, he had been dreaming after all. There was real pain now in his upper arm and the side of his head.

'Thank God . . .'

He was in the army infirmary, had been patched up after his fall. But what was that other stuff he had dreamed? Dreams of being a mercenary, of Sara and Susan, of someone called Draegerman. He wiped the blurriness away from his eyes with the knuckles of both hands, struggled to rise, and felt someone move to push him gently back down. At last, faces swam into view, and he realised where he was and what had happened.

'You're all right,' said Sara. She leaned forward again and pressed a cool towel over his forehead.

He reached up to touch her face and thought: *Please God, don't let her be a dream.*

Another face moved into view: Den, Susan's partner. He also had an expression of concern on his face. 'Welcome back,' he said, and tried to smile. Somehow, it would not come out right. Turning away from Taylor, he called to someone out of sight in the kitchen: 'He's awake.' Taylor realised that he was back in Susan's apartment, lying on the sofa in the middle of the room.

'Well, what do you know?' said a familiar voice, and Taylor turned to look as the figure moved into view, eating a sandwich.

It was Moss – the man from *The Pool.*

'What the hell are you doing here?' he asked.

'Wrong. You're supposed to say: "Where am I?" and "What happened?"' Moss strolled casually over, sitting on one of the upholstered chairs beside the sofa. He smiled, took another bite and settled down as if he owned the apartment. 'This is a great sandwich, Sara.'

Sara did not respond. Instead, she poured some water from a glass jug into a glass, ice cubes clinking. Taylor took it thankfully, drinking it down straight away, holding out the glass for more. Sara gave him two white pills to swallow.

'What are these?'

'For the stab wound in your arm. You had a tetanus injection while you were asleep.'

As Taylor drank again, his memory returned completely.

'The helicopter,' he said simply.

'Some of my people saw what was going on up there,' said Moss. 'Didn't I tell you that we've always got our eye on The Rock? Didn't

236

see it myself. I was . . . otherwise engaged. But I'm told the air display was really something.'

'The Rock,' said Taylor. 'It . . . *moved.*' He looked directly at Moss, his expression demanding confirmation.

'It moved,' said Moss, and this time his voice was deadly serious. 'Difficult to see too much up there, but the towers moved all right. They sort of . . . folded in towards the roof and then stopped. They look like four big black fingers, trying to make a fist.'

'I don't understand why I'm not dead.'

'Neither do I,' said Moss. 'While Sara was fixing you up, I couldn't help but see. Taylor, you've got more scar tissue than tissue. With your clothes off you look like a mass of scars just stitched together.'

'I cut myself shaving.'

'How many times you been shot?'

'Five.'

Moss whistled and bit into his sandwich before continuing. 'No one knew that it was you up there, even though we knew you'd got something planned. What happened up there when the 'copter was trying to take off? An explosion?'

Taylor nodded.

'It blew the tail of the 'copter against one of the towers,' continued Moss. 'Smashed the rear section right off. 'Copter went over the side of The Rock. That's when your air display really started. For a while, everyone thought the 'copter was going straight down into the moat around The Rock.'

'The fact that I'm here means it didn't?'

'No, the guy at the controls managed to get it away from The Rock and into . . . *my* territory. Some sight. Cartwheeling all over the sky. He tried to put it down on one of the roads. Didn't work. We're not sure what happened after that. Reckon one of the rotor blades hit a building on the way down, then the 'copter just about tore itself to pieces. By the time I got there, it was all over. One Draegerman Security Augusta 109 helicopter smack in the middle of Pyrannon Street – looking like a pile of smoking junk. One of the tanks had ruptured in there, a fire had already started. Everyone down there who'd come to look had smiles on their faces, waiting for the fireworks to start. That won't surprise you, since you know we never started a fan club for the man. Lucky for you I sent some people in there. And, by God, look what we found all messed up in the back of that junked 'copter. Mr Taylor himself.'

'The pilot?'

'Dead. Smashed up pretty bad. We left him in there when it finally burned up. But, let me tell you, your street cred is running high at the moment, Mr Taylor. Mother sends her regards. Might start a fan club for *you.*' Moss seemed to find this last remark particularly funny and almost choked on his sandwich.

Taylor turned to Sara. 'How did they know about this place? About you?'

'Give me a little credit,' continued Moss. 'Some fella just walks into *The Pool*, starts asking questions, wanting help – and we're *not* going to be able to check him out? Sorry if it offends against your professionalism, Taylor, since I know you want your movements to remain as secret as possible. But *we* control the streets around Draegerman's Rock. At the very least, we're organised.'

'They brought you here,' confirmed Sara. 'With a doctor. One of their . . . own people, he said.'

Moss laughed again, returning to his sandwich. Now his mood had changed again. This time he was deadly serious: 'Now we know who you're trying to get out of there. You weren't shitting us around, so that's good. And you're doing it because it's personal, maybe that makes it even better. Thing is, you've tried to get into The Rock and it didn't work. But all that business up on the roof hasn't gone unnoticed. A Draegerman helicopter falling out of the sky? Fireworks on the roof? Police have taken a big interest. Questions are being asked. Now there's more heat on the streets. So what are you going to do?'

'Christ, Sara,' said Taylor, bowing his head. 'I just don't know.'

'Maybe now that the police are involved, I mean *really* involved . . .' Sara struggled to control the tears. 'Maybe now they'll be able to find out what's happened to Susan . . .'

'Don't count on it,' said Den tightly. 'They've done shit-all, so far.'

'I need time to think,' said Taylor. This time he did sit up, despite Sara's protestations.

'Whatever you do,' said Moss, 'I'm a part of it.'

'I work alone.'

'Don't be fucking stupid,' said Den. 'You're all chewed up. You're going to need help.'

'So the man says *I work alone*,' said Moss. 'How many John Wayne movies have you seen?'

'This isn't a fucking joke, Moss.'

'Yeah? Well believe me I'm not joking when I say that Mother gave me instructions. God knows why she likes you, but she does. And you should be *very* grateful for that. She told me to tell you that I'm tagging along for the rest of this ride whether you like it or not . . . and so is *he*.' Moss pointed at Den, whose face registered surprise. 'That's what Mother said – and Mother knows best.'

'I've already told him that he can't . . .'

'Well *un*-fucking tell him, then.'

'Why the hell is it so important?'

'That doesn't matter. Maybe it's because he's a black brother. Maybe Mother just likes a good love story. But think about this, Taylor. *Think* about it. Since you turned up, there's been a feeling on the

238

street. A feeling that maybe now's the time to rid ourselves of Mr Jack Draegerman and his Big Rock Candy Mountain. It just might be that you're going to get a great deal more help than you could ever imagine.'

'Someone wanted to speak to you,' said Den. 'While you were ... away. He said that you'd given him this number, if he ever changed his mind about talking to you.'

'Who?' snapped Taylor.

'Someone called Talbot ...'

'Talbot!' Taylor began to slide from the sofa, taking Sara's arm for support.

'So who's he?' asked Moss, cramming the last of the sandwich into his mouth.

'He helped to build Draegerman's Rock. Acted as if he was out of his head when I went to see him. Where're my clothes?'

'Over there,' said Moss. 'We brought some spares from your motel room.'

'So you know where I'm staying? Seems I can't make a move and you know about it.'

'I'll take that as a compliment. Now come on, get ready, and let's go see this man.'

Taylor looked as if he was going to say something else, was going to make another statement about working alone.

'You going to throw me on the floor again?' asked Den.

'No,' said Taylor. 'No ... just ... just don't slow me down, that's all.'

Moss laughed and said: 'Feet, don't fail me now.'

Outside, the sky grumbled with the promise of an approaching storm.

TWO

'It's you,' said Farrow, stepping forward.

Slowly raising his hand, he pointed at Jessica.

'It's been *you* all along. You said we should go down, so we went down and down – and now we're right back here again. It's your fault . . .' He took another step forward.

'Calm down, Farrow.' Roy moved to take the gun out of his belt.

'Leave it,' said Jessica. 'Let him try if he wants to.' She stood her ground.

'Maybe she's a karate expert,' said Susan, stepping forward to join her. 'Ever think of that?'

Farrow halted, glaring at them. They could feel the hate and anxious frustration radiating from him. Whirling away from them all, he vented a yell of frustration at the overhead rafters. As the echoes chased each other, he strode away again, shoving Boone roughly to one side with a foot as he passed. Boone sprawled, still clutching his attaché case, his face more miserable than ever. They watched Farrow stride to the banqueting table, slam his attaché case back down and grab a bottle from the table before throwing himself into the chair that Bobby had been sitting in for so long when they had first arrived.

'Oh God,' said Gloria. 'Look, there's something to eat and drink.'

They hurried past Boone to the table. Farrow kept swigging from the bottle, glaring into the ashes in the fireplace. They fell on the food and the trays of drink like ravenous animals. From behind, Boone staggered to his feet and joined them, taking handfuls of cold meat from a platter.

And as they ate and drank in silence, ignoring the other attaché cases, they all looked around the Banqueting Hall, trying to convince themselves that they were in a different place after all, and not where they had started from. But all the details were as before: the thick columns of black stone supporting the swooping arches overhead; the iron rings and three-claw devices in the walls; the television screens with their hissing snowstorms, thankfully devoid of that mocking face or any of the man's movies. Roy realised that the door through which they had re-emerged into this place was the door that Aiken and his

240

colleagues had used to flee from the Berserker. That door had been locked – but had been opened again. Who could have done that, other than Draegerman? The door from the platform at the top of the stairs lay on the ground not far from them, torn from its hinges and thrown back into the hall by the Berserker, the wood punctured and torn by vicious talons. And when Roy looked back up the staircase, he could see shredded strips of wood littering the stairs. The door to the spiral staircase, which Roy and Farrow had descended on arrival, had been blocked by a solid steel shutter.

Something else lay at the foot of the stairs, as if it had fallen from overhead. Something that looked like a cinema projector; now a shattered mass of metal. Had this been part of the equipment that had projected Draegerman's hologram down to them?

'This can't be right.' Boone had found his voice at last. 'We *were* going downhill most of the way, even when we split up. We can't possibly be back here.'

'What do you say, Farrow?' asked Roy. 'No point blaming Jessica for something we all decided to do.'

Farrow cursed under his breath, spat into the fireplace and took another drink.

'The machinery,' said Bobby. 'Under the escalator.'

'What about it?' asked Susan.

'I don't know. I just had this crazy thought. It doesn't matter.'

'Crazy or otherwise,' continued Susan, 'let's hear it.'

'Well . . . the parts I remember. I mean, about us getting out of here and heading downwards. Down those orange and green corridors.'

'Yes?' prompted Jessica.

'Well . . . we heard the sounds of machinery and gears and crashing chains most of the time, didn't we? I mean, it seems to me I remember those sounds most of the time we were moving.'

'That's right,' said Roy. 'The noises were always there. What about it?'

'And wasn't Draegerman supposed to be an architectural genius, I mean apart from everything else he's known for?'

'Make your fucking point,' said Farrow from his chair, taking an interest at last.

'What if there's machinery everywhere – in the ceilings, under the floor, behind the stone walls of these corridors? What if the sound we hear is that machinery, all operating behind the scenes? Every time we enter a corridor, what's to say that machinery isn't set into operation as soon as we set foot in there?'

'Why?' asked Jessica. 'What would that machinery be doing?'

'I was on a ship once, a long time ago,' continued Bobby. 'Making a movie. One night we had really high seas, and I had to walk down a long corridor to my cabin. Every time the ship hit a big trough or started climbing a wave, it did crazy things as I was walking. Sometimes it felt like I was walking uphill, sometimes like I was walking downhill. But all the time the corridor just looked as if it was going straight ahead to me. That makes me think . . .'

'What, for fuck's sake?' snapped Farrow.

'What if the machinery is slowly and subtly *tilting* corridors and passageways up and down when we're moving along them? Could be like that ship I was on, couldn't it? So – sometimes we think we're heading down, but we're not. He could be leading us round in circles that way.'

'Bullshit!' said Farrow. 'When you feel you're walking down, you're *going* down. It's called gravity, you stupid little shit.'

'So what do *you* reckon?' snapped Roy. 'You were the big man at the beginning. What the hell do you have to say? You got any better explanations for why we're back here again?'

Farrow drank again and did not reply.

'It doesn't really make sense,' said Jessica. 'But since Bobby's suggestion, I've had these strong images in my mind.'

Their silence meant that they wanted her to continue.

'There was an artist called Escher, and he created these lithographs and woodcuts of men – and creatures – constantly walking up staircases that never end. You must have seen some of them. Staircases with impossible angles and perspectives, so that whoever is ascending always ends up at the bottom again, starting up. Water that flows uphill. Oh God, what are they called . . . ? *House of Stairs*, that's one. And *Ascending and Descending*. Oh God . . .' Jessica's face had taken on a ghastly hue. 'Is that was this place is based on . . . ?'

'*So up is down and down is up,*' echoed a ghastly and familiar voice. '*That's an interesting theory – and very nearly true.*'

The dozens of television screens in the dank, black walls suddenly fluttered into life, casting dancing shadows across the Banqueting Hall floor, chasing over black stone columns like living things looking for a place in which to hide from the light. The image settled. But although the sudden eruption of sound and flickering light caused them all to recoil, no one said a word when they saw the hated face again. No one spoke, because the face seemed to have undergone some horrifying change since they had last seen it. There was something not *right* about it. Had he been injured? What had caused the dark grey shadow on the right side of his face, the shadow that crept from his temple, down past his eye – dragging that eye, somehow? Boone's hand went nervously to his own face as he looked. The shadow continued down over Draegerman's face, highlighting his cheekbone with dreadful prominence and making the cheek and mouth on that side seem somehow sunken. It seemed to have melted away the flesh on that side of his face, leaving only a parchment-grey covering of skin which stretched over and highlighted the skull beneath. Despite this dreadful change, whether or not it was an injury or some terrible creeping disease, Draegerman appeared uncaring. His face still held that taunting smile, a smile made even worse by the shrunken lip on the right-hand side, curling back to expose skull-like teeth.

'What?' said the dreadful face, wet eye glimmering in a sunken socket. 'No yelling, screaming or bad language? No throwing things at the screen?'

They stood and looked, and listened.

'What well-behaved children you are. A credit to any loving parent.' Draegerman laughed then, the sound echoing and ringing in the Banqueting Hall. At last, he composed himself, his hand moving to the hideous mockery of a mouth in what seemed to be a parody of good manners: a genteel and polite brush of the fingers across the lips, as if to sweep away a crumb of food at a dinner party. Now, a polite cough – and the eyes continued to glimmer with inner satisfaction.

'And did you know that I'm not the only one who thinks so highly of you? Someone among you has an admirer out there in the so-called real world, beyond The Rock. Someone actually tried to get in here. Can you believe that? Now who among you is so popular that someone might risk their life to save you? Something to think about, isn't it? I'm afraid to say that whoever or whatever that person was, he or she was not successful. Still – it's time, I think, to up the stakes in our game.'

Draegerman paused, head cocked to one side as if waiting for an interruption. Again there was that dreadful smile.

Roy looked as if he might do something. He took a step forward, then stood back again, turning to grip the edge of the table. He seemed to be controlling his rage.

'Do you know how long you've been here with me? Do you know how long you've been my guests in The Rock?'

Draegerman paused again, awaiting a response that did not come.

'Three days. Can you believe it? Wouldn't you say that time passes very quickly when you're enjoying yourself?'

Now he seemed deeply disappointed that his latest appearance had not elicited any reaction. His face changed, the revolting smile vanished, and now he looked more like half a death's head than before.

'No matter. That final beckoning by The Rock has been made. And the first of my guests of honour has arrived. Do you hear that, children? The first has arrived.'

'Roll out the red carpet,' said Gloria in a hollow voice.

'Keeping you in complete ignorance spoils the fun,' continued Draegerman. 'So here's some more information to keep you sharp. If you were paying attention, children, you'll remember that I told you there would be six Daemons, one for each of you. It doesn't matter which of you is taken first – and Gloria can be taken by any one of them, since she doesn't

243

matter in this game. Are the rules clear so far? Good. Now let me tell
you something about our guests of honour . . .'

'You lying bastard,' said Farrow from behind gritted teeth. He seemed
not to be hearing anything the face on the television said. The very
sight of the hideously damaged but familiar apparition seemed to have
overwhelmed him; the fury continued to rise and build as he stood up
from his chair and took a deep swig from the bottle.

'They aren't what they seem. That's something you should know. And
would you believe it? I've nearly given too much away by saying that. No
matter. Just be careful where you walk, or what you touch. You could
walk right past one and never know it. Be careful of reaching for that
door handle or sitting on that chair. Listen to me, so enthusiastic that
I'm all but giving the game away. But you should know this – they are
not human, and never have been. Also, they are subject to restrictions
of movement, like chess pieces on a board. In their own hellish plane,
there is no restriction, but here in this worldly plane there are sometimes
places they can't go and things they can't do. Isn't that some kind of
comfort for you? Generally, kids, they'll lie in wait for their prey – that
is, you – like a trap-door spider. Think back to that Screening Room,
Gloria. Why do you think the Berserker took the form it did? Doesn't
that tell you something? But now I'm REALLY getting carried away, all
but telling you everything you need to know. Just let's round this little
chat off, children, by reminding you that as soon as one of my guests
of honour takes one of you, CONSUMES one of you – it can return to
where it came from. And when the sixth guest is satisfied, my side of
the bargain will be complete, they'll have what they want and I'll have
what I want. Between now and then – lots and lots and lots of FUN.
What do you think?'

'What do I think?'

Farrow's voice began quietly, his chest seeming to swell as his
rage grew.

'What do I *think?'*

He began to walk slowly towards the first of the television screens.

'WHAT DO I THINK!'

His slow walk suddenly became a lunge, and with a great roaring
cry that filled the Banqueting Hall he launched himself over the flagged
floor, holding the bottle like a club. No one was inclined to stop him or
get in his mad way. Still running, he hurled the bottle high at one of the
television screens. It missed its target, shattering on a black stone wall.
Still roaring, Farrow lunged back to the table, gathered up an armful
of weapons – bottles, goblets, plates – and, in a welter of spilled food
and slopping wine, charged back to the screens. Draegerman burst into
laughter as Farrow began to throw his makeshift arsenal. The laughter
erupted from the dozens of flickering faces set into the walls, and
seemed to fuel Farrow's berserk actions. Plates clattered and smashed

to the floor, missing their targets. And then one of the lowest screens suddenly imploded as a wine bottle found its mark. Blue sparks and smoke fell in a cloud from the innards of the screen. Farrow yelled in triumph, eliciting redoubled laughter from Draegerman – and redoubled rage then from Farrow. Now he was scrabbling at the floor, grabbing at broken shards and flinging them impotently at the screens.

The others shrank back when Farrow suddenly threw back his head, flung his arms wide and screamed like a wild beast. Still keeping well away, they watched as he turned and hurtled past them, eyes wild and staring, foam flecking his lips. With the laughter still mocking and echoing all around, he reached the stone stairs leading up to the balcony. They turned in horror to watch as he ascended the stairs like a madman, clawing at the stone wall by his side, lurching three steps at a time. When he reached the balcony, he stumbled – and it seemed that he must fall to the side, arms pinwheeling, crashing over the flimsy safety barrier to the cold stone floor a hundred feet below. But he regained his balance, flung himself forward – and in the next instant had vanished through the shattered door frame beneath the familiar Gothic arch. In seconds, the sound of his running footsteps and his sobbing breath had been swallowed by The Rock.

His attaché case filled with money was still on the banqueting table.

The laughter continued.

But as they turned back to the screens, the image was suddenly dissolving into a swirling snowstorm.

With a one-note musical snap! the snowstorm shrank to a single white spot in the centre of the myriad screens.

Now, there was only darkness.

They stood looking into that darkness for a long time.

'Three days,' said Boone at last, breaking the silence. 'He said we'd been in here for three days. How can that be?'

'Don't think about it,' said Roy. 'Just think about how we're getting out.'

'His face,' said Susan. 'What the hell was wrong with his face?'

Boone's hand strayed to his own face, and Susan looked down, feeling guilty.

'What did he mean?' said Jessica. 'About someone on the outside trying to get in? Does anyone know what that might mean?' No one answered.

'Daemons,' said Susan. 'Anybody believe *that*?'

'Maybe not before,' said Gloria. 'Maybe not even when that thing came out of the cinema screen after me. But after what we saw back at that escalator – I mean, we *did* see it, didn't we?'

'We saw it,' said Bobby.

'Well, I'm inclined to believe anything's possible now.'

'Let's just stay the hell where we are,' said Boone. 'He *wants* us to keep moving, don't you see that? That way, we'll walk straight into ... whatever in hell is out there waiting for us. But if we stay here, someone's bound to come and find us, aren't they? There's food here. Not much, maybe. But enough to keep us for a while if we spread it out. And drink. Listen – he said those things, those Daemons or whatever, are just lying in wait, like trap-door spiders. They can't move around in this ... this plane, yes, that's the word he used, the way we can. So all we have to do is sit tight ... If what he says about everyone else in here being dead is true, someone *must* notice that people are missing and come looking. Isn't that right?' Boone was exuding desperation, finger constantly caressing the scar on his face, as if the sight of Draegerman's corrupted face bonded them, and he was anxious to wipe his own scar away.

'Makes sense to me,' said Gloria.

'At least let's have some time to think,' concurred Jessica.

Roy was still looking up the staircase to the shattered doorway, as if expecting Farrow to return. He turned back to them, said nothing, but nodded assent.

'What about us all being his kids?' asked Susan. 'Do we believe *that*?'

'Never had brothers and sisters,' said Bobby, holding his mother tight around the waist. 'Now look at us. One big happy family.'

Slowly, anxiously, and always keeping one eye on the dark, unknown recesses of Draegerman's Banqueting Hall, they began to trade and share family histories.

THREE

They had travelled mostly in silence since leaving Sara behind at Susan's apartment. A car had been arranged. Whether stolen or not no one seemed concerned. Moss had cracked one joke, about himself being a hired chauffeur. Neither Taylor nor Den had laughed as he mockingly held open the door open for them and they climbed into the back. Their silence had made Moss laugh long and loud. He seemed to be the only one with a sense of humour these days, told them so as he climbed laughing into the driver's seat and they sped away into the city's night-shadowed places.

At once, Taylor had taken off the makeshift sling that Sara had made for his screwdriver-damaged shoulder. He had handed the scarf to Den, begun to flex his fingers, and Moss had laughed again from the driver's seat, saying something else about scar tissue and hard men. They were the last words spoken.

Forty minutes later they had arrived at their destination, sliding into the nursing home's car park.

Again without speaking, they made their way to the central entrance.

The nurse who received them remembered Taylor from his first visit. She was still not well disposed to his initial deception and for a moment it looked as if she might try to throw some bureacratic reason at them for not being able to visit.

'I know it's late,' Taylor pre-empted her. 'And I know that there are three of us. But Mr Talbot rang *me*, not the other way around – and if this is a retirement home and not a prison, I think we should be allowed to see him. Don't you?'

The nurse's face looked as if it were carved from granite. Behind him, Moss gave vent to another barely disguised laugh.

'Follow me.' The nurse turned and headed off down the corridor without waiting for them. Taylor knew the way, at one stage almost overtaking her in his concern to find out what Talbot had to say. The nurse glared, and he held back, deciding not to overplay his hand.

Even before the nurse had knocked, a voice from inside said: 'Come in.'

247

Unmistakably it was Talbot's voice, and the sudden invitation startled the nurse, her hand frozen in the act of knocking. She opened the door.

'It's Mr Taylor again, Mr Talbot, and he's brought ...'

'I know. Thank you, yes. I sent for him.'

Pausing only to transmit another deep-freeze expression, the nurse ushered Taylor, Den and Moss into the room, closing the flimsy door with unnecessary force.

Talbot was sitting in the seat where Taylor had left him, by the picture window. He was wearing the same dressing-gown, the curtains were open and the picture window was a portrait in black. He seemed to have aged a further twenty years since Taylor's first visit.

They stood for a moment in the centre of the room, while Talbot surveyed the two men that Taylor had brought with him. Taylor waited to answer any questions about them, but did not have to do so. Instead, the old man nodded at the two chairs on the other side of the room. Moss took one and Den the other. Taylor sat on the edge of Talbot's bed.

After a while, Talbot said: 'Something happened up there on The Rock.' His voice was like rustling parchment, as if the sudden storm of fury that he had initially vented at Taylor had ruined his vocal chords.

'That's right,' said Taylor.

'Was it you?'

'Right again.'

Talbot nodded, pausing again while scrutinising Taylor's face.

'You tried to get in,' he continued. 'And it didn't work.'

'Three out of three.'

'Who's in there? Why is it so important that you get them out?'

Before Taylor could reply, Den interrupted: 'My partner, Susan. We've got two kids – and that bastard has got her in there.'

'It wouldn't be the first time that people have gone to visit, and vanished off the face of the earth.' Talbot turned back to Taylor. 'So what's your interest?'

'Family,' said Taylor. The word felt somehow awkward on his tongue.

Talbot nodded again, as if this last answer completed the puzzle.

'You know what happened to my company, shortly after I ... became ill?'

'Yes,' said Taylor. 'There was a fire.'

'It wasn't just a fire. My main office was bombed. Sixteen people killed. But you won't find any mention of a bomb in the official reports at the time. All the reports are gone. Missing or destroyed.'

'I know that.'

'Shortly afterwards, things started to happen. My company accounts were audited, and discrepancies found. Accusations of corruption and

248

bribery. None of it involving Draegerman Enterprises, of course. My chief accountant committed suicide. Or so they say. I know for a fact that he was murdered, and his death faked to look that way. All of it done to discredit my business, ruin me – destroy everything. It would have been so much simpler just to implicate me, and then fake my own suicide.'

'So why didn't he?'

Talbot gave a fractured smile. 'You don't know Jack Draegerman. That's not his way. Believe me, I've spent many years thinking about it. He much preferred that I live out the rest of my days like this, in fear. Mr Draegerman, you see, has a thing about fear.'

Talbot paused to look out through his window into the night. He seemed to be looking for The Rock.

'Ever hear of sick building syndrome?' he continued. 'Well, believe me, that thing he calls The Rock is sick, just as sick as his own mind. God help me, I helped build part of it, so I know what I'm talking about, Mr Taylor. Listen, do you know how long it took Draegerman to build The Rock? Four years. Want to know something else? It's not architecturally possible for that place to have been built in that time scale.'

'But he *built* the place, didn't he?' said Moss. 'So what's your point?'

Taylor glared at him, aware of how fragile their situation might be.

'I wasn't solely responsible for the construction. There were many contractors and sub-contractors involved. No single person ever really got to find out what the complete internal layout of The Rock comprised. Draegerman's obsession with secrecy was intense. My involvement lay strictly with foundations and basic structural design. But he was creating cavernous spaces and chambers in there which would have put Piranesi and Gaudi to shame. Never admitted to his influences, never been reported on. But I know what I saw. One night, I was so curious about the construction that I managed to slip away from what my own team were working on to see what else was happening. This wasn't easy, because Draegerman had his security force already there on the job, making sure that no one trespassed further than their allotted area of work. But I did manage to get access to one of the chambers above. And I'm telling you now – *no one* could have built and designed the gallery and chamber I saw. Not in the time available, and not with the equipment on hand. I didn't manage to stay long, had to slip away again. But what I had seen intrigued me. I started to check out some of the confidential records, again not an easy task. And I found out something else, about some of the raw material that Draegerman was using to build The Rock. There was a lot of newspaper coverage back then, about the activities of Draegerman Enterprises. Specifically in relation to oil development programmes abroad. During the acquisition and purchase of land or drilling rights, Draegerman upset a lot of conservationists and

249

historians by buying up and destroying important archaeological sites. Ancient ruins, temples and the like. But I found something very curious about this whole business when I checked through those records. You see, those sites hadn't simply been demolished and razed. They'd been carefully *taken apart*. And that raw material had been shipped back here in secrecy. Draegerman was using the stone, using the remains of places like Tempra Abruzza, to help build The Rock. Some of those corridors were being reconstructed from the stone of a pagan temple, some of those galleries from the stonework of a demolished shrine. I was convinced ... I'm still convinced ... that Draegerman thought that the stone was ... well, *mystical*. There was something else. Based on what I'd seen in those other corridors and galleries and chambers, none of the contractors or sub-contractors on that job could have carried out the work I had seen. It was just not possible.'

'So what are you saying?' interrupted Moss. 'The place was designing *itself*?'

Talbot fixed Moss with an intense stare. The stare soon glazed, as if he was thinking back again.

'That's perhaps how Draegerman got on to me. He must have found out about my unauthorised access. Everything else after that is as I've told you. But listen to me, Taylor. I'm not rambling. I'm making a point. Even if you *do* get into The Rock, be very, *very* careful. There is something *wrong* about the place. I could feel it then, still feel it now. You see, I saw something else in there – in the brickwork – something that couldn't ...'

He seemed to crumple then, slumping back in his chair. Den moved uneasily, looking around for a patient alarm by the side of the bed.

Talbot seemed to rally again.

'Never mind what I saw,' he went on, stroking his forehead with a trembling finger. 'The thing is, enough is enough.'

'You mean you'll help me to get inside The Rock?' asked Taylor.

'There are no maintenance plans left, no engineering reports, no architectural designs.' The old man coughed, the action seeming to rack his entire body. 'Whatever hasn't been destroyed will still be up there in The Rock, I expect. But there *is* a way in there.'

The old man coughed again, and now it seemed as if Taylor's cool was breaking. He shuffled forward on the edge of Talbot's bed, eyes glittering, looking at any moment as if he might suddenly lunge forward, take the old man by the shoulders and shake the secret out of him.

'I've been sitting here waiting for death, ever since my breakdown. Draegerman knows that. When you first came, I thought he had sent you. Now I know differently. Perhaps, just perhaps, the mad bastard never intended to kill me at all. Maybe he knew I'd sit here wondering and waiting for death to come and that finally my heart would just give out under the strain. Maybe he laughed sometimes when he thought of it. My own fears killing me, day by day, hour by hour. But now, it's time to help turn some tables. I'm going to help you, Taylor. Your cause isn't mine, but I'm going to help you. There's one condition.'

'What's that?'

'If you do get in – and there's no guarantee that you will – you have to promise me one thing.'

'Yes?'

'That you'll kill Jack Draegerman.'

'*I'll* kill him!' interrupted Den again.

'Amen,' said Moss. Again, there was no hint of a smile on his face. Taylor had not answered.

'Well?' asked Talbot.

'Three of us going in,' said Taylor. 'Three chances that Draegerman won't be entertaining any more guests in the future.'

Talbot nodded again and pointed to his bedside cabinet. Taylor moved quickly across the counterpane and opened the door, looking back. Talbot nodded again. Inside, Taylor found a folded sheet of paper. As Talbot gestured impatiently, he began to open it up on the counterpane. Den and Moss moved quickly over to have a look. Now Taylor could see that Talbot had taken all the small pages from an ordinary notepad, had torn them out one by one and then sellotaped them all roughly together until there was a four-foot single sheet.

There was a hand-drawn map on the large sheet.

'The sewer,' said Talbot. 'It's the only way in. A hideously complex maze.'

Taylor looked up at Moss, remembering their conversation with Terry Fisher and his confirmation that no one could get in that way.

Saw bits of bodies floating around down there once . . .

'I've drawn that map by hand,' said Talbot. 'I designed the bloody thing, so I know what I'm talking about. All those years, sitting here waiting for death, sometimes I'd go over and over things in my mind. That's a complete map of the way in. The entrance you want starts from an industrial canal on the west of the city. It's marked. Christ knows how long it will take you to get to the centre. But when you do, there's a main central duct. Climb that and you're into The Rock.'

Taylor punched the map on the bed. 'That's *it!*'

'Don't get too bullish. It's been a long time. Anything might have happened in there since it was built.'

'Like what?' asked Den.

'Tunnel cave-ins, for example.'

'Yeah, but if there was a cave-in you'd have a . . .' Moss struggled to find the right phrase, but could only think of: 'Shit build-up, or something. It would have to be cleared or Mad Jack starts getting poo-poo-all over his nice clean floors.'

'Not necessarily,' continued Talbot. 'Like I say, it's a horrendous maze

251

down there, and we had security in mind when it was built.' He gave an ironic laugh, the breath wheezing in his lungs. 'Yes, I was even asked to think about ways of preventing just what you're going to do now. That's why the system is such a vast complex. Think about it. How many people are going to need to take a leak in Draegerman's Rock. One? Ten? Twenty? A hundred? Not enough to warrant what was constructed under there, that's for certain. One sewer pipe would do it. But the fact is, for security reasons, that central duct I've just told you about was tied into the sewer system of the *entire city*. Even the city engineers don't know to what extent.'

'Shit!' said Moss. For the first time his epithet was entirely appropriate. 'Hope everyone in the city doesn't decide to flush the pan at the same time when we're down there.'

'The thing is, gentlemen,' said Talbot, 'you don't really have time to engage in a technical discussion about sewer layout and drain construction. That map will get you inside, depending on whether or not there have been cave-ins or silt build-up.'

Taylor folded the map, placing it in his inside pocket. When he stood, so did the other two.

'Remember,' said Talbot. 'A promise is a promise.'

Taylor nodded. Den had already moved to the door, had opened it and was waiting anxiously. Without a further word, Taylor turned and moved to join him. Den was hopping from one foot to the other. For a moment, it seemed as if Taylor might turn back and say something. Instead, head down and looking away from Talbot, he nodded again and left the room. Den followed quickly.

The last to leave, Moss leaned back into the room from the doorway.

'You really helped build that place, old man?'

'God help me. Yes.'

'Well, let's see if we can't *lower* the tone of the neighbourhood.' Moss smiled, and then was gone.

And later, when the corridors of the nursing home were dark and quiet, Talbot wheeled himself closer to the picture window again and strained to see the outline of the hated construction against the night sky. The work he had undertaken on The Rock was perhaps his major architectural achievement – and a constant reminder of his fear.

After a long while, he said: 'Damn you to Hell, Jack Draegerman.'

And then, opening the bottle in his lap with trembling, arthritic fingers, he poured out the contents and began carefully to place the sleeping pills in his mouth, one by one. A half-hour later, the entire contents of the bottle had been swallowed and washed down with water.

Talbot settled down to his vigil by the window, still looking in vain for the monstrous outline.

Soon, a darkness deeper than night had crept up behind his eyes.

FOUR

Farrow stumbled and ran ahead, reeling and clutching at the corridor walls.

The madness had somehow wrenched his soul out of his body. Farrow, the *real* Farrow, was floating in the air above the figure that thrashed and flailed and ran below. He had watched himself hurling plates and bottles and cutlery at those television screens from afar; had watched that wild, deranged figure clawing its way up the staircase. Detached, he watched himself plunge ahead down the corridor. Now, it seemed that his manically possessed body was not running at all. Instead of a corridor, he was in a vertical mineshaft, dropping away into the bowels of the earth. The sudden change of perspective snapped the wraith out of the air and transplanted it instantaneously into the wild beast below.

You're the one! hissed the voice from the walls as he fell. *You're my favourite son!*

'LIAR!' screamed Farrow as he flailed and clutched at empty air.

It's you! You're the one! The only one!

Farrow screamed the voice out of his head.

He ran.

And fell.

Ran again.

And now somehow he was on his hands and knees, sobbing like a child. The palms of his hands were skinned and bleeding, leaving smears on the bare stone floor. His trouser knees were torn and bloodied. Was the madness abating? Was it leaking out of his body with every sob? Some rational part of him was returning, and he remembered Aiken, Draegerman's number-one henchman, running terrified through the vaulted halls and mindless, twisting corridors of this mausoleum maze. He would *not* become like Aiken. He would *not* lose control. The sobbing ceased. Now his breathing was under control. His face was soaked with tears. Roughly, he wiped them away, leaving a bloody smear on his cheek.

He looked up at last.

He could see the shattered remnants of a door lying on the corridor floor. Had the Berserker broken through that door at some stage?

Something moved to his left, only inches away.

Something that squealed, like a small animal being crushed under-foot.

Fear froze his soul. He could not even turn his head to look at the indistinct movement. Was something standing over him, watching? Was it, even now, reaching down to take him? The thin, hideous screech ended. The movement stopped.

And now, without any awareness of physically having moved, Farrow found himself crouching in fear against the far corridor wall, curled foetus-like, staring back through a nest of fingers at what had moved.

It was a door. Nothing more.

It had opened beside him as he had knelt there, the screeching sound made by the unoiled hinges. The door was like all the other doors in this hideous place. Thick oak, obscene carvings around the frame and that three-claw device in its centre: the door handle.

The door swung inwards again. This time, it was only the sound of old hinges, and not a thing of terror.

He tried to think back to the words Draegerman had spoken from these television screens. Had they been warnings? He could not remember. The madness had driven the sense out of the words as he had flailed and thrown anything he could get his hands on at the screens.

There was something inviting about this door, something beyond it which seemed to be deeply enticing. Before he was aware that he had made the decision, Farrow was standing at the door. This was the second time he had moved without being aware of it, and he felt like a piece on a chess board. Even now, part of him – a deep, *deep* part – seemed to be trying to warn him. But it was a small voice, getting smaller by the moment. Farrow pushed the door completely open, until it bumped against an internal wall.

He walked in.

And although his first perception of this bizarre room should have encouraged the small, terrified voice inside to erupt, screaming a warning, he felt no fear.

It looked like a torture chamber.

The walls of the room were much the same as all the walls inside The Rock. Carved blocks of black stone. The floor, as ever, was flagged with the same stone. There were lanterns set high in each corner, spilling red light downwards. Vaguely, Farrow wondered which film set Draegerman had taken the lanterns from.

My Jack the Ripper movie, said a vague voice inside. *'Jack's Back Again.' They're Whitechapel lamp standards, can't you see?*

There was equipment in here. Equipment and . . . devices. But Farrow could make no sense of what he was looking at. What had at first seemed to be a mediaeval rack, maybe another prop from a movie, was now clearly a bed. There was a stained mattress, with a coiled nest of leather straps in the centre. At the head of the bed was some kind of wooden wheel with handles like a sailing ship's wheel. In the centre of the chamber was something that looked like a cross between a weight-training frame and a kids' climbing frame. It reminded him of the days when he used to work out in the gym, and had something like self-respect. The skeletal-tubed frame was fronted by two vertical bars. Between the two bars was a small bench, and as Farrow moved closer he could see that the bench had a leather covering. But he had never seen leather that colour before. Its texture was wrinkled and stretched like leather, but it was the colour of human skin. There was a small hole in the centre of the leather seat, as if it could be used as a commode. At shoulder height to anyone sitting on the bench was a parallel bar supported by the two verticals. Was that the bar from which a barbell and weights would be carefully eased on to the shoulders of a weightlifter? No, there were no brackets on which the weights could be rested. Instead there was what seemed to be a collar in the centre of the bar, perhaps to fit someone sitting on the bench. The strap was studded like some kind of dog-collar, made from the same leather as the seat, and with a curious screw-tap on one side.

Farrow suddenly became aware that there was music. Had it always been playing, ever since he had first stepped into the room? It was low, barely audible – but now increasing gradually in volume as he made a conscious effort to listen. A low, growling and distorted bass guitar. A muffled and distorted lead guitar being played very badly by someone who desperately wished they were Jimi Hendrix. And a corny drumbeat behind it all, very middle-of-the-road seventies stuff. Farrow looked for speakers, but could see none. He felt as if he was floating again, distanced from it all. Was the music playing only in his head? Where had he heard something like it before? Now there was a woman's voice. Was she singing, or just moaning? It reminded him strongly of something, but he could not trace the memory.

He explored further.

There was another bench with straps, this one in a 'Y' shape. Would someone's torso be strapped on to the lower half of the 'Y', their legs strapped to each of the upper sections?

Strobing white light flickered over his face. He held up a hand to his eyes and became aware of a whirring sound, like an old cine projector. The light was coming from a small slit on the other side of the chamber, from an aperture set eight feet high in the stone wall.

'*She Wasp!*' said a man with melodramatic conviction from behind Farrow. He whirled round to see that an image was being projected on to the chamber wall behind him. '*A nightmare of terror erupts from the screen to haunt you for ever!'* Farrow saw his silhouette in the middle of the image and stood aside as dramatic music blared from invisible speakers. Now he could see that this was a black-and-white movie. A very attractive woman with long dark hair was clawing her way through a studio jungle, not unlike the one Farrow and the others had found themselves in. *'An expedition into Green Hell,'* continued the voice. *'And an encounter with horror!'*

Farrow turned from the flickering image as a swarm of hornets appeared around the woman's head, and she began to flail at them – her screams filling the soundtrack. He moved back to the 'Y'-shaped bench. To the side was a medical trolley, with instruments neatly laid out. A garment had been hung on one corner of the trolley. Standing between the legs of the 'Y', Farrow unhooked it and examined it. It was a leotard, fashioned from black leather and with the same studs that he had seen on the dog-collar. There was a hollow plastic tube between the legs, like some kind of see-through penis, the hose open-ended.

'You say you love me, Tommy,' said the dark-haired woman from the screen behind him. *'But would you let me love you to death?'* Suddenly, a young man was screaming as a buzzing sound filled the soundtrack. There was another burst of melodramatic music.

'In her eyes – desire!' came the melodramatic voice once more. *'In her veins – the blood of a lusting She Wasp!'*

Farrow leaned over to look at the instruments on the trolley. Were they drill bits? He touched one of them and immediately pulled his fingers away. He had felt something then; like a small electric shock. But the feeling had not been unpleasant.

'Starring Deborah Steele,' announced the narrator. *'In her most amazing role yet!'* Dramatic music swelled, and suddenly the image and the flickering light vanished. Now there was only the rock music.

Still holding the leotard, Farrow realised that the gauge on the drill bits matched the hollow tube. He picked up one of the bits, shuddering at the shock again, and then instinctively pulled down the metal collar between the base of the drill and the bit. The ragged point began to whirl, emitting a grinding noise.

At the sound of the drill, the light in the chamber changed, now strobing and muted and dull. The music was much louder, and as Farrow looked it seemed as it the shadows were swooping and diving and unfurling all around him for a special purpose.

The whirring sound and the flickering light had begun again. Still holding the drill bit, Farrow looked back to see that a colour image was now being projected on to the chamber wall. This time, it was news footage.

'Deborah Steele,' said a different man's voice. *'The Hollywood actress.'* The dark-haired woman that Farrow had seen in the trailer was standing at the top of an aeroplane stair-flight, waving back to an invisible crowd.

'... *is missing, feared killed in an aeroplane crash.*' The image changed, showing an aerial shot of burning fragments scattered in the trees. '*The search continues both for Ms Steele and her pilot, Perry Dillman – also an actor. Search parties say that there is little chance of finding either pilot or passenger alive ...*'

Farrow turned away from the screen to look at the swooping, diving, living shadows. The movement was hypnotic, and he continued to stare as a montage of clips from the movies of Deborah Steele began to appear on the chamber wall. Most of the clips showed the actress at her most alluring, and in various stages of undress. But Farrow continued to stare at the swooping shadows. Like living things they seemed to be directing his attention towards ... what?

Towards one of those three-claw devices that he had seen so often used as door handles and decoration all over The Rock. Except that this three-claw device was fastened in the centre of the wall on the other side of the bench. Was it a door handle? No, now he could see that it was fastened in the rough-hewn stone wall, and although he stared hard, he could see no sign of a door frame. The shadows continued to oscillate and swoop, the light strobing and undulating to the music. The shadow of the three-claw device also undulated, writhed and bulged, making it seem that the device itself was alive and trying to disengage from the wall. The sight drew his eyes.

'*Love me, Jack,*' said Deborah Steele from the chamber wall behind Farrow. '*Tell me that you love me, and I'll never go away.*'

Again, Farrow was moving without consciously having decided to do so. Dropping the leotard back on the trolley, he moved away from the bench and towards the three claws in the wall.

'*I can't live without you,*' said Deborah. '*I'll do anything if you let me stay.*'

Slowly, hesitatingly, Farrow reached out.

And then Draegerman's face appeared on the hidden screen in the wall behind him.

Go on, you know you want to.

No ...

What brought you in here, if you were so scared? You came because you wanted to come.

Farrow's fingers had almost touched the device. Was it a handle, or not?

Come. That's a good word. Means all sorts of things, doesn't it? Don't you want to come ... to whatever's in there?

Yes ... I mean no ...

Come on ...

Unbidden, a childhood memory flashed in Farrow's mind.

He was six years old, in the dark. He had heard bad things in his dream, had climbed from bed and was looking for his mother's room.

The darkness was all around, and he was fighting back tears as he fumbled through it, arms outstretched and praying that his groping fingers would not find the invisible face of a ghost. He was so dry, needed something to drink, and it seemed that he had been walking forever. Did night-time make things further away? Now he could see the faint outline of her bedroom door, and another darkness beyond. But something was wrong as he touched the door frame and stepped into her room. His mother was thrashing and moaning and giving small cries. Was she ill? Overwhelmed with fear, Farrow called her name and ran into the room.

And suddenly her thrashing head turned from the bed to see him coming. Her face was sweating, her hair lying lank across her face – and that face had become a mask of horror as he approached, wanting to help her. The bedclothes were alive. Yes, that was it. They had come alive and had wrapped themselves around her, suffocating her and strangling her. He grabbed at the edge of the nearest blanket and tried to pull it off. But at that first touch, they suddenly flew away. And there was someone . . . *lying on top of her*. That figure also turned its face, and now with a thrill of terror, he could see that it was the man he had been told to call Dad, the one whom he so rarely saw, the one who had not been there when he had gone to bed that night. And the face turned to glare at him in a way that froze him to the spot. It was a face so bestial with rage at being disturbed while feasting on his mother that it completely traumatised Farrow – traumatised him so much that his youthful mind had never seen the face again, even in his worst nightmares, was simply unable to contemplate it. The man called Dad would be gone forever from his life the following morning, and that face would be changed and mutated in Farrow's subconscious to the point where the prime source of his nightmares would be constantly masked to protect his mind.

Which was why Farrow could never remember his father's face.

But he remembered it now, remembered as he reached for the three-claw device, (blanket), remembered to the extent that urine was running down his leg just as it had when he was six years old.

Finally, he recognised the face.

It was Draegerman. The face on the television screen. Back then, twenty years ago, the face had somehow been disguised. There had been a moustache and beard then, and the hair had been red. But even twenty years on, it was still the face of his father. So successfully had he blotted out the face he had not even recognised it when Draegerman made his first appearance in the Banqueting Hall. Now Farrow's mind had been stripped raw.

And in that one instant of memory, as his hand reached for the invisible door which had also somehow become the forbidden bedroom door, he was shocked out of the seduction. He lunged away from the three-claw handle and collided with the trolley. It spun away, clattering on its castors. He whirled as the music surged.

Uttering hoarse cries of terror, as the small inner voice of warning suddenly became a screaming, terrified banshee, Farrow lunged back across the chamber towards the door. But somehow it was as if he were in a nightmare and could only move in slow motion. His limbs were heavy and he could hardly move his legs. He saw the door and the corridor beyond, raised his heavy arms, groping at the air.

'*Be good to me,*' said Deborah Steele. '*And I'll be good to you. Anything you want, anything at all. Love me. Be my baby.*'

And something *moved* on the bed in the centre of the room.

Something that was not a swooping shadow.

Something that uncoiled and rose like a cobra from the mattress.

Farrow saw it as he stumbled slowly to the threshold, watched in horror as one of the leather straps seemed to hang there in the air, swaying in time with the insane music. It began to turn, and Farrow knew in that moment that it was *looking* for him. Screaming, the sound of his voice also horridly slow and dragging, he fell headlong over the threshold in his desperation to get out.

With the sound of a cracking whip, the leather strap uncoiled and flew from the mattress like a striking snake, just as Farrow scrambled on all fours into the corridor. Only one foot remained inside the chamber – and at lightning speed the strap coiled around his ankle, tightened and yanked.

Farrow clawed at the stone floor. Still fastened to the mattress, the living leather strap coiled tighter around his ankle ... and began to reel him in. Farrow kicked and thrashed on the floor, clawed at the ground. His fingers raked the gaps between the stone flags, breaking his fingernails.

Pleasssse, implored a voice that sounded like Draegerman's voice, but was not. *Please stayyyyyyy!*

The strap strained at his ankle, but Farrow clung tight to the ground.

I can't come to youuuuu, said the thing that was trying to copy Draegerman's voice. *So please – come to meeeee.*

'Get *off* me!' yelled Farrow in terror. 'For Christ's sake, GET OFF ME!'

Look what I can give you, said the voice. *FEEL what I can give youuuu.*

And then Farrow felt what he had felt when touching the drill bit.

Now there was no need to fear.

He ceased to thrash, the leather strap ceased to tighten.

The same electric thrill was transferring to his leg from the strap itself. A warm, caressing, surging thrill. It was beyond description, but it was deeply arousing.

259

And as it surged and enveloped him, he could suddenly see everything in the chamber clearly. The music and the laughter were all a part of it, no longer discordant. As he looked from the mattress to the frame to the other devices in the chamber, Farrow at last realised to what purposes they could be put.

'Yes ... yes ... now I see ...'

The possibilities were endless.

The leather strap on his ankle felt warm to the touch, warm and *alive*. He could feel its pulse.

'Yes ...'

Straight, hetero, gay, bisexual; none of it matters, said the voice, now sounding completely like Draegerman. *Only the YOU of it matters. Nothing else. It doesn't matter what you do, doesn't matter who suffers. It's time to have pleasure in return for everything you've been through. Haven't you suffered enough? Haven't you suffered on those streets in that fucking institution they said would rehabilitate you, at the hands of that fucker who called himself your uncle? It's time to be paid back, son. Time to PAY back. Time to get your due returns for what you've been made to suffer.*

The leather strap uncurled from his ankle. Now it was being drawn back to the mattress, and as Farrow watched, it was as if he was seeing that bed and mattress through a heat haze. The contours and shape of both the mattress and bed seemed to waver and shimmer. Instinctively, he knew that what he was looking at was much, much more than a piece of bedroom furniture. The leather strap was yanked back to the centre of the bed. It curled and settled in the centre of the nest made by the other straps.

Farrow slowly stood up, still aroused; knowing that Draegerman had entertained selected guests in this room over the years. Could he hear the screaming of those guests, somewhere in the pounding music? Now, he was also ready to entertain.

Like father, like son, said the voice.

Whatever was in that room could not venture beyond it into the corridor. But between the fury and the madness of his flight from the Banqueting Hall and his arrival in this hideous chamber where so much had been promised, Farrow's soul seemed to have been flooded with the dark essence of his father. And if his father had entertained guests in this chamber – then he would carry on the family tradition.

Now that you know, come inside to me.

'So much better with two,' said Farrow.

Come back inside ...

'No,' said Farrow, standing back. 'Not yet.'

Please come to me ...

'I will, I will. But not yet. Like father, like son. Right, Dad?'

No, don't wait. Come to me now ...

For the first time, Farrow felt truly bonded with his father. He began to laugh then.

'So much better with *two*!'

Come back . . .

Eyes sparkling with expectation and intent, Farrow turned back in the direction from which he had come.

FIVE

'So I never knew him,' finished Susan. 'Just what my mother had told me. All about the great romance with the travelling shoe salesman, her own father's dislike of the man, how he would have nothing to do with the sudden whirlwind marriage. Her father died three months after they were married. She's convinced he died of a broken heart, and I think it's that more than anything that made her so bitter when Dad ... I mean Draegerman ... left. I was nine months old, so I can't remember him. My mother didn't have any photographs.'

'Is that coincidence?' said Roy. 'The fact that none of us has a photograph of the man? Or was that something he was aware of, planning against, even then?'

'Everything else seems to have been carefully, cold-bloodedly planned,' said Jessica. 'It makes sense that he would have planned for every eventuality.'

'Control,' said Gloria. The word came out like a sigh. 'He always was a control freak. Any of you read about an actress called Deborah Steele?'

'Something ...' began Jessica. 'She ... that's right. She went missing, at the height of her career.'

Gloria gave a bitter laugh. 'Well, I don't know about height exactly. Most of her movies were Joan Crawford ham, six inches thick. But she certainly thought she was a big star, even if the box-office takings didn't agree. I worked with her once. Never again. But she worked for Jack Draegerman just before she did her vanishing act. It was a film called *She Wasp*. Typical J.D. picture – woman stung by swarm of South American hornets gets home, turns into a queen wasp at night, flits around back alleys and drive-ins screwing and eating any teenager she can get her stinger into. Real try-out for method acting.'

'Nice,' said Boone. He had taken to sitting in the high-backed chair, clutching his attaché case as if someone might try to take it from him.

'But there is a sting in the tail,' continued Gloria. 'Apparently she caused merry hell on set, making it clear to everyone that the project was well beneath her talent. Said that the movie he was making wasn't what she had expected after reading and accepting the script.' Gloria gave a quiet laugh. 'I saw the first draft of that script. She knew what she was doing, and she had to pay the rent. Believe me. But there was a lot more going on than met the eye. The thing is, she and Jack had an affair when she was still a big name and he was just starting to make movies as a rich boy's hobby. He finished the affair, and she resented the fact. Made it plain from day one on set that she was going to get her own back.

'Then she went missing, presumed killed. Her new boyfriend was a pilot, and a week before shooting was wrapped, they found their Cessna – or I should say, they found *pieces* of the Cessna, scattered around the mountain range they'd been flying over. But they never found poor old Deborah or her boyfriend. Draegerman finished the movie with a stand-in wearing her FX make-up.'

'That's a good story,' said Jessica. 'But how does it tie in with us?'

'It doesn't tie in with us – it ties in with *me*. There was some talk, and I believe the people who did that talking, that Jack Draegerman got so pissed off with Deborah Steele's behaviour on set that he *arranged* for her to go missing. Like I said at the start, Jack was always a control freak.'

Gloria turned to Bobby.

'That's why I couldn't tell you about your father. That's why I didn't tell Jack that I was pregnant with you. If he could arrange something like that for Deborah, what the hell would he have done to us? That's what I was thinking then. In the event, the bastard knew all along that I was expecting his child. I wonder when he first started making plans to sacrifice his kids . . . ?'

And with that last sentence, it seemed as if the fear and anxiety had returned in full measure; threat crowding in on them from every corner, from every shadow. During the time they had discussed their pasts and Draegerman's part in them, they had momentarily given themselves a brief respite from the fear. Now it had returned.

'All right, all right,' said Susan, reacting to the deep chill that had settled over them once more. 'Let's think about this. Who knows that we're here? Let's go through it, one by one.'

'My deputy editor,' said Jessica. 'Hell, practically everybody on the staff. Draegerman's Black Suits made a big impression when they marched right into the office. Everyone will know I got an exclusive, and my bosses must be wondering why I haven't touched base yet.'

'Just one man,' said Roy. 'An old guy at the place where I work.'

'Christ knows,' said Bobby. 'I don't even remember how I got here.'

'I made a big exit from the studio where I was working.' Gloria began to speak with enthusiasm, thinking back to how one of Draegerman's men had shoved the director to the floor. Then she remembered something else, and she finished the sentence on a miserable low. 'But no one knew where I was going ...'

Susan turned to Boone.

'No one knows where I am,' he said miserably.

'And I was kidnapped,' said Susan. 'So no one will know where I was taken, unless some passer-by saw me being bundled unconscious into a car. And we can't rely on that. So it seems to me that Jessica's people are our best bet. Draegerman said it's been three days. Someone *must* come looking for us.'

'He said that someone had already tried to get in,' said Roy. 'Who the hell could that have been?'

'*Someone who doesn't matter,*' said two dozen television screens.

Shadows leapt and danced as the screens flickered into life.

Susan refused to give in to the strength-sapping fear she had felt during Draegerman's last message from the screens. Seizing a brandy bottle by the neck, she spun from the table, ran three quick steps and hurled it savagely towards the nearest bank of screens. The bottle exploded on a stone pillar. The sound of its impact and the glittering spray of glass fragments and alcohol was somehow satisfying. Breathing heavily, she came back to the table again, sitting on the edge, hands clutching the rim.

'*It's been interesting,*' said Draegerman. '*Listening to you chat. But I'm afraid events have moved on, and I really can't afford to have you sitting around chewing the fat.*' This time, there was no taunting smile on his face. Was it because of the terrible creeping shadow, which now seemed to have spread further? The flesh on his forehead seemed to have furrowed like old bark, there was no pupil in his remaining eye – although it was clear that he could still see them all. Even though his lips had withered and shrunk back from his teeth, the death's-head grin now looked more like a hideous expression of pain. '*Perhaps I've over-indulged myself in the early stages of this plan. Understandable, since it's been so long in the preparation. But now it's time to make up for that. Clearly, you intend to sit tight and try to avoid my other Guests. That will never do, I'm afraid.*'

'Go to Hell, you bastard!' yelled Bobby.

'*You keep on saying that. Does that mean you're constantly missing the point of the exercise?*'

'For Christ's sake!' yelled Boone, suddenly leaping up from the chair with the attaché case clasped to his chest. 'Let us out of here!'

'*So – if you won't move ...*'

Draegerman's grimace widened, and this time the death's-head face *was* smiling.

'*I'll have to move you.*'

And on his last word, something seemed to groan underfoot in the Banqueting Hall. A long, shuddering groan of stone on stone. They could feel the vibration beneath them. Bobby grabbed for Gloria in alarm, and Susan whirled away from the table. Jessica stood frozen, hands in the air, looking down at her feet, just as she had done in Draegerman's spider jungle. Boone clutched at the high-backed chair for support with one hand, refusing to let go of his money.

'What are you doing, you bastard?' Roy took Susan's arm when it seemed that she might lose her balance.

'*Wait and see,*' said the two dozen death's-head faces of Jack Draegerman.

There were other sounds now. Sounds with which they had all become familiar during their endless wandering in the Rock's corridors. The sounds of great chains being dragged behind the massive walls; of huge gates being drawn open; of windlasses suddenly released from their holding brackets, spinning and clattering wildly as drawbridges were lowered or raised. The shuddering, groaning noise had now become the roaring of an avalanche, or of a tidal wave headed their way. They spun wildly at each new tumult of sound filling the chamber, expecting at any moment that great gushing explosions of seawater might suddenly explode through the doors and the Gothic arches of this unholy place, sweeping them away in an ocean of foam, dashing their bodies to pieces against the black stone walls.

Draegerman remained silent, watching everything.

The stone slabs beneath their feet shifted, as if in a sudden earthquake tremor.

They reeled and clutched for support.

Overhead, clouds of dust and a small rain of powdered stone began to fall.

'Oh good Christ, look!' said Boone, pointing to the centre of the jagged floor.

Something was happening there. A dark, circular opening had suddenly appeared. As they watched, it began to widen as the sound of stone grating on stone grew louder. Now it was like some black, slowly spinning whirlpool. The segmented stone slabs that made up the floor around it were sliding and parting and folding in on themselves like some huge kaleidoscope lens. The floor juddered again, as the slowly opening aperture spread to one of the massive black columns supporting the ceiling. As one, they began to back away from the banqueting table, towards the stone staircase. No one spoke, their breath taken away by the awesome sight before them.

'The stairs!' yelled Roy. 'Quick, before the ceiling comes down!'

Surely that *must* happen as the aperture reached the massive stone column? Surely it would collapse into the abyss that was now yawning in the centre of the floor, bringing the roof down with it? They turned and ran for the stairs. But even as they stumbled to the foot of the staircase, the stone slabs at the base of the pillar slid away as the black

265

hole grew larger – and now they could see that the pillar extended far beneath the opening floor. The aperture was yawning and sliding around the great carved buttress which had seemed to serve so little purpose before. Halting on the staircase, they turned to stare in amazement as the flagged stone floor rippled around the base of the buttress, like some wave of stone, the slabs sliding back and away to reveal that the buttress also continued downwards beneath the floor; a great slab of rock implanted hundreds, perhaps thousands of feet below.

The staircase began to groan and shudder. A thicker cloud of dust gushed down from above. In that moment, Roy and Bobby had the same premonition. Was this stone staircase like the monstrous staircase from which the Berserker had erupted to take Aiken? How long would it be before the stairs turned inside out and dropped them into the yawning maw of cogs and wheels and pistons and hideous teeth below?

The slowly spinning, yawning black hole was sliding and spreading; devouring the very floor on which they had stood. Soon there would be no floor left at all. Only a mind-staggering chasm into the depths of The Rock.

The outer edges of the chasm had reached the foot of the staircase. They could see the stone flags grinding and sliding away all around the staircase as they kept moving upwards, mindful that the shuddering of the stairs could pitch them over the edge at any moment.

And now, with the logic of nightmare, it seemed that Draegerman knew of Bobby and Roy's premonition. With a slow, ghastly and remorseless rumbling of stone, the staircase on which they were staggering began to slide sideways *into* the wall on their left.

Jessica stumbled and grabbed at the handrail, and in the next moment Susan had her arm and was dragging her up.

'Keep moving!' yelled Roy.

'It's not possible,' Boone stuttered over and over again. 'It's just not *possible*.'

They had reached the halfway point on the hideously moving stairs. Once twelve feet wide they were now perhaps only eight feet wide, and still shuddered and slid sideways towards the wall as they scrambled for the balcony ahead.

'He *can't* kill us!' shouted Bobby as they ascended. 'He wants us for his bloody Daemons, for his pact . . .'

As if in answer, something roared and bellowed far beneath them, from the depths of the pit that had opened up in the Banqueting Hall.

'They're down *there*!' screamed Boone. 'Don't you see? They're down *THERE*!'

The stairs juddered and slid. Somewhere behind them, something fell from the overhead Walkways, dashed itself to pieces against a black stone wall and then plummeted, disintegrating, into the blackness. Roy had a vision then. There were great gaping maws somewhere down

266

below, just like the maw of the thing that had risen from the opening escalator. Cavernous jaws and slavering teeth, writhing and contorting, waiting for the staircase to slide finally into the wall – pushing them all into the void. One for each of the hideous maws.

'For *Christ's sake!*' he yelled.

The stairs beneath them were gaining speed as they slid into the blank rock wall to their left.

Something else crashed and echoed from far below, followed by a distant bellowing. Had that unseen thing falling apart and crashing into the chasm smashed into one of the waiting mouths? Was that bellowing a sound of rage and disappointment as the hideous maw spat out shattered concrete and splintered wood?

The stairs were now three feet wide.

With a cry of relief, Susan and Jessica reached the top, staggering on to the balcony.

Roy joined them, seized Gloria's arm and dragged her with him as Bobby pushed from behind. Boone was making a sobbing noise as Bobby reached back and grabbed him by the collar.

In the next moment, they were all standing on the balcony.

Breath sobbing in their chests, they watched in horror as the stairs that they had been frantically ascending finally juddered from sight into the wall. Just before they vanished altogether, there was a ringing metallic clatter – and the metal stair-rail was instantaneously and neatly shorn away from the edge of the steps. The hundred-foot length of rail turned lazily end over end, hit the chasm wall below and struck sparks. The shivering clang echoed back to them as the sparks died and the rail vanished into the utter darkness of the pit.

And then the staircase was gone, as if it had never existed.

They gazed in horror into the gaping chasm that had replaced it.

The Banqueting Hall had ceased to exist, its floor gone for ever.

Roy looked back to where the log fire and table had been. It was a bizarre, surreal sight. There was no sign of the table itself. It had fallen into the pit, together with their attaché cases. But the fireplace was still there. A small square aperture in a great column of black stone that stretched away below, like the rest of the stone pillars in this cavernous space, into the utter blackness of the chasm. Gushing clouds of dust and powdered rock filled the vast space.

They turned from the terrible sight, now looking at the platform beneath their feet, feeling the shuddering, settling sound of moving stone all around them. Would this balcony support them, or would it too suddenly detach itself from the black rock wall and send them plummeting to whatever lay below. From the depths, they heard the faint and shivering echo of the stair-rail finally hitting bottom.

Roy hurried across the platform to the entrance that led to the spiral staircase. He slammed his hands against the steel shutter that had completely sealed it off.

'It's no use. We'll never get through this.'

On the threshold of the shattered door through which the Berserker had erupted, Gloria clutched at the frame for support and shouted: 'But he *wants* us to go this way, don't you see? He *WANTS* us to go this way . . .'

Bobby prised her from the splintered frame.

'What choice do we have?' he shouted.

Without looking back, they staggered through the shattered door and into the corridor ahead. The stone beneath them and the ceiling overhead still shuddered and groaned.

But something impossible was happening to the walls on either side of the corridor.

Something which, despite the overwhelming terror of what had happened behind them, prevented them from moving any further forward. Despite the fact that the balcony might also be subject to the same impossible architectural manipulation by Draegerman and might at any moment collapse, sending them all whirling into the dark void below – they could not move.

Because the walls on either side were moving.

With that horribly familiar, slithering, grinding sound of rough stone on rough stone, the walls were *moving*. From ground to ceiling, they were moving upwards at a steady pace. The ground and the ceiling were perfectly still. But the walls were emerging from ground level, slithering upwards on either side and vanishing past ceiling level.

Even now, a door appeared in the wall to their left, emerging twenty feet from where they stood. The same oak door with which they had become so familiar in this hellish place, the same three-claw handle even now clacking back into place as the door reached its midway point and some unfathomable device pushed it out of its slot once it had cleared the floor. They watched this surreal movement, unable to comprehend, as the door rose from the floor and then passed upwards towards the ceiling. Another clack and the three-claw handle had withdrawn into its slot again before the door slid up into the ceiling and beyond – and now another door had suddenly appeared ten feet away from them, in the right-hand wall. It too began its steady ascent.

Still unable to understand how this was happening, each of them was hideously reminded of what Bobby and Jessica had said about tilting corridors, ships' passageways and water that could run uphill. Was this just one small example of what had been happening while they had descended the corridors in their futile attempt to escape? The door on the right had gone – another, fifty feet on the left, had appeared. It climbed, and Gloria gave vent to something that might have been a laugh.

'Piano roll,' she said. 'It looks just like a piano roll.'

'What . . . ?' Bobby put an arm around her.

'The doors are keys in the roll,' said Gloria. Her face was white, like a mask. 'See?'

There was a new sound in the corridor now. Something below that low, stone-on-stone mill-wheel grumbling as the walls moved on either side. This was a metallic screeching, somewhere behind the moving walls; the thin screech of metal on metal. It was a sound from some hellish foundry where engines of destruction were welded and forged by daemonic hands. This was the screeching of Talos the Bronze Giant's limbs as he moved ponderously and remorselessly through the gigantic caverns below.

'No,' said Jessica simply. Roy turned to look, saw her shaking her head, saw an impossible smile on her face – as if she had just declined an embarrassing offer. 'No,' she said again, and this time laughed.

'It's *happening*!' snapped Roy, thinking that she was referring to the architectural impossibility of the moving walls. 'Saying "no" doesn't . . .'

Then Jessica seized Roy's arm, twisting him to the side and pointing back down the corridor.

'Oh, Jesus Christ,' said Susan. And now they could all see what Jessica had seen, realised what the onset of this new sound meant.

The far wall of the corridor, the one facing them now, was also moving.

There had once been a right-hand turn at the end of the corridor, a turn that Farrow had taken as he plunged insanely on into the depths of The Rock.

No more.

The black, dripping stone wall was coming towards them, filling the corridor just as surely as a ramrod filled the barrel of a musket. It was moving at the same pace as the walls on either side. They watched – hypnotised and fascinated – as it came on.

And when something behind them suddenly shattered and gave a scream of twisted metal, they also cried out in unison, the shock making them stagger into the corridor. In the next moment, the balcony on which they had been standing was shorn away from the wall. It dropped away into the void.

'This can't be happening!' wailed Boone again, still clutching his attaché case as if it were a protective charm.

'It's what he wants,' said Roy grimly, nodding his head. 'Brothers and sisters, it's what that bastard Draegerman *wants*!' He strode ahead down the corridor, ignoring the giddying effect as the doors climbed the moving walls on either side. Now he was running and Susan yelled a warning as he threw himself forward at the slowly advancing wall. He hit it hard, with both hands flat against the black rock, and braced

269

his feet, trying to shove back. His feet skidded on the rock floor as the wall came on. Roy turned, throwing himself back against the advancing wall, tried to find some purchase in order to stop it. But the wall came on remorselessly and again his feet skidded as it pushed him forward. Cursing, Roy turned, kicked the black stone impotently, and then ran back to the others.

'What?' Boone blurted helplessly. *'What?'*

'We've got to take one of these bloody doors. One of the doors climbing the walls.'

'What . . . ?' Boone bent double, hugging his attaché case, no longer able to speak.

Quickly, Roy moved to a door that had appeared in the left-hand wall. He confronted it, looking back at the approaching wall, turning to watch again as the door before him ascended the wall. The three-claw door handle clacked into place as it cleared floor level. He watched it rise.

'If we don't take one of these doors,' he said, 'that far wall is going to just shove us out through the archway gap . . .'

Boone uttered a strangled sound. The others said nothing, but stood watching Roy silently.

The door handle had reached its normal level. Roy lunged forward, twisted it and yanked. The door opened out into the corridor and, as it swung wide, they could all see that – impossibly – there was another corridor beyond.

'There's a way!' yelled Roy, again checking on the approaching wall. 'See?'

He tried to slam the door, but was too late. His grip was mistimed and he staggered away as the open upper edge of the door reached the ceiling.

'Look OUT!' yelled Bobby, and Roy barely had time to dodge aside as the open door was torn screeching from its hinges as the door frame continued its ascent beyond the ceiling. The wood splintered with a screech that drowned out all other hellish sounds in the corridor. They flinched as a hail of split wood exploded in the corridor, stinging their flesh and hands, which flew protectively to cover their faces. A board from the crushed door span clattering past Roy as he ran back to join the others.

The doorway was gone.

And the trundling, screeching wall was less than eighty feet from where they stood.

Another door had emerged in the right-hand wall. Bobby ran to it and crouched before it, waiting for the three-claw handle to emerge. He gestured quickly to Gloria to join him, face grim. As Gloria staggered to him, he grabbed the handle and tugged. But the bottom ridge of the door had not cleared the floor yet, and the door would not open. Bobby cursed as the others clustered around him.

'There's not much time,' he said. 'We've got to be quick . . .'

And in that moment, the door juddered open as the bottom ridge cleared the floor. Bobby reached for his mother, ready to drag the door fully open and push her through first.

But Boone, uttering a strangled cry of fear and desperation, suddenly lunged at Gloria, pushing between her and Bobby.

'Boone! You crazy . . .'

Roy tried to grab him, but in the man's headlong lunge for safety, he had shouldered Bobby to one side. Bobby collided with Roy and sent him staggering back into the corridor. Boone groped around the edge of the door as it rose.

And then Susan punched him full in the face, shoved Gloria ahead through the door and tried to grab the outer edge to swing it wide for the others. Boone staggered and fell to his knees, emitting high-pitched keening sounds.

The bottom edge of the door, and the corridor beyond, were now at waist height from the ground.

'Don't wait!' yelled Roy from the floor. 'Just GO!'

And in the next moment, Jessica had vaulted up on to the threshold. She hung there struggling, legs kicking as it rose. From beyond, Gloria grabbed her hand and began to pull her inside. But it seemed as if Jessica was somehow trapped there. Susan launched herself at Jessica's legs, seized them and began to heave upwards.

The door continued its ascent towards the ceiling.

In seconds, Jessica would be cut in half.

But with a cry from beyond, Gloria hauled Jessica into the corridor with her. One final kick, and she had cleared the threshold. Susan whirled on Boone, the threshold now too high to reach.

'Boone, you *bastard*!'

It was too late for anyone else to reach the doorway. In another moment, the opened door would shatter to pieces against the ceiling, just as the other one had, filling the confined space with another potentially deadly rain of splintered shrapnel. Bobby heaved himself at the door, Susan completed its swing, and the door slammed shut just as its upper edge reached the black stone ceiling.

The door slid into the ceiling.

Gloria and Jessica were gone.

The advancing wall facing them was perhaps forty or fifty feet away. Bobby stayed where the door had been, crouched and waiting.

'What the hell are you *doing*?' yelled Roy.

'The same door might come back in the same place.' Bobby's eyes were wild. 'We can still get to them . . .'

'You idiot!' snapped Roy. 'We don't know that, and we haven't got time to wait. That bloody wall's going to push us out over the edge in the next minute.'

271

Boone had scrambled to the other wall, was crouching there as another door slid into sight before him. He was making low, babbling noises as the door rose. As they turned to look, he seized the door handle as it emerged from below ground level and began to twist and yank at it even though it was not yet possible to open the door. Angrily, Roy twisted towards him and put out an arm to restrain him. In his frenzy, Boone slapped out at him, eyes blazing – and in the next moment the bottom edge of the door had cleared the floor and he had yanked it open.

The facing wall still trundled on towards them. There was perhaps thirty feet between themselves and the wall; no time to pick another possible exit.

Boone threw himself into the corridor beyond, stumbled and fell headlong. Roy jumped up as the threshold began to rise, leaned back and reached for Bobby, who was still standing in the centre of the corridor looking back at the other wall, as if willing the door that Gloria and Jessica had taken to rise from the ground in the same spot.

'Come *on*!' yelled Roy, hand still held out and downwards.

'No, wait . . .'

'Bobby, get out of there now!'

His feet were now at waist height to the corridor from which he had come and Roy had to crouch down, still keeping his arm outstretched to Bobby. In another moment it would be too late.

Uttering a cry of frustration and rage, and with the trundling stone wall only ten feet away, Bobby threw himself across the corridor and reached up to grab Roy's arm. Roy braced himself and tugged. Bobby hit the edge of the threshold and the impact knocked the wind out of his body. Roy cried out too, feeling his grip slip. But then Bobby kicked at the wall, found purchase – and heaved himself into the corridor.

Roy backed up into the darkness, dragging him clear.

It was pitch black inside this corridor, the only illumination coming from the corridor from which they had just escaped. Even now, that dim outline was vanishing. As Roy staggered back into the darkness, still hanging on to Bobby and dragging him over the rough ground, there was a grinding, screeching crash of pulverised wood from the now vanished oblong of faint light. The open door had been torn from its hinges by the ceiling and had splintered apart.

The doorway vanished.

As the corridor in which they crouched began to rise, they could see only the faint glistening of water on black stone where the door had been. They lay in the darkness, listening to the sounds of invisible pistons gasping and pounding in the depths, to the sounds of millstones grinding stone to powder and of the continuous rattle and clatter of impossibly gigantic gears, pulleys and levers.

Gasping for breath, they lay as if in the belly of a monstrous mechanical beast.

After a while, Bobby began to weep.

The sound brought utter desperation to Roy's soul. He crammed his clenched fists against his eyes as they lay there. Drawing in two lungfuls of stale air, he suddenly threw back his hands and yelled into the blackness.

It was the sound of defiance; harsh, animalistic and filled with rage.

It echoed and bounced in the darkness, ricocheting off into the vast depths of wherever they now found themselves.

Then the sound was gone.

Swallowed whole in the depths of Draegerman's Rock.

SIX

Outside, in the night, police and fire sirens were wailing like lost souls.

'It's started,' said the black woman they called Mother, coughing a racked smoker's cough. She leaned over to drink from the glass tumbler in front of her. Vodka, gin or just plain water? It was difficult to say. 'Yes . . . it's started.'

'I need weapons,' said Taylor. 'And equipment.'

'That's not a problem,' said Moss.

'The stuff I had in the helicopter? Did any of that survive?'

'They didn't have much time to drag you out. Just the plastics you had in your belt, and an automatic. Surprised it didn't blow you to pieces.'

'I've used up most of my debts and favours. Don't think I can use any more of my contacts to get what I need.'

'Like he said . . .' The black woman took off her spectacles and began to polish them with an embroidered handkerchief. 'We can get you what you want. That's not a problem.'

'So tell me,' said Moss. 'Give me a list.'

'We'll need to travel light. Skin-diving wet suits, but no aqualungs. We need two small portable oxygen canisters each that can be hooked to face-masks. A spare mask each. Waterproof duffel bags, the kind with straps for each shoulder. Automatic, semi-automatic weapons, or both. Glock or Ingram nine-millimeters will do. Phosphorous grenades. More plastic explosive, timers and detonators, if you can get them.'

'Travelling light? Could have fooled me.'

'We don't know what we're up against when we get in there.'

Mother laughed, still polishing her spectacles. Without looking up, she said: 'I knew there was something about you the moment you first walked into this room. Knew it was going to lead somewhere, but never dreamed it might have something to do with Mr High and Mighty Jack Draegerman. Now things are going to take their course . . .'

From somewhere outside, somewhere a long way away, came the

sound of a muffled explosion. Everyone in the room except Mother looked at the door.

'Hear that?' she said nonchalantly, still polishing. 'That's the sound of the changes. Had to happen one day, and here it is.' Carefully, she replaced her glasses, then leaned forward across the table until the overhead light made the lenses reflect and glint. Taylor could no longer see her eyes. 'Remember what else I said? About Draegerman's Rock? How it's been sitting there for all these years, sucking the goodness out of everything around it? Well, sometimes you can only keep people *down* for so long. They can take every kind of shit that's thrown at them for a long time. But then something happens, could be something small, maybe even trivial, but then when it happens, it's like ... like the tide turns. Instead of coming in, it's going out. And the sounds you can hear out there now, Mr Taylor, are the sounds of that big tide going out. They've had enough, and there's nothing I or any of these gentlemen can do to stop them taking to the streets and having their say.'

Taylor thought back to the streets around The Rock; the streets that had been so strangely derelict and deserted on his first visit. Those streets were no longer deserted, and he remembered how the crowds who had suddenly emerged had pressed around their car as Moss drove them back from the residential home to *The Pool*. The looks of hostility on his arrival had turned to smiles of greeting when Moss was recognised. Taylor remembered hearing one acne-scarred teenager with green hair ask: 'Is *that* Taylor ... ?' There had been real awe in his voice. Moss had laughed then at Taylor's baffled expression as the car moved slowly on through the cordons, and the crowds had re-formed their barrier.

'They think you're a hero,' said Mother, as if she had been reading his thoughts. 'Hijacking a Draegerman security helicopter, landing on The Rock, blowing a hole in the roof with everybody down below watching the fireworks.'

'I didn't blow a hole in the roof. I don't think the plastic even dented the bloody thing.'

'That doesn't matter,' continued Mother softly. 'It's what *they* think out there that counts.' Moss gave a small low laugh, and Mother turned her head to look. Moss was quiet instantly. 'It doesn't really matter now who or what Jack Draegerman is or what he's doing or what he's done. He's come to stand for something that these people hate. They're down here, trying to make a living, trying to get by and constantly being ground underfoot. This is a no-man's land because the system's let them down. So they've had to try and arrange their *own* society here. For the most part, it works. But it's fuelled by resentment, by hate, by the knowledge that they've been abandoned. And there's a constant reminder for them all, every time they open a window, or look up for some clear sky.'

275

'The Rock,' said Den.

'Now there's a man who understands,' said Mother.

'I understand as well,' said someone from the darkness beyond the table and its pool of light. Taylor recognised the voice immediately. It was Fisher, the young ex-security employee. He turned to see where he was, but Fisher remained beyond the circle of light. 'I understand it better than anyone here. I want to go with Taylor and the others.'

'No,' said Mother simply. 'It's been decided.'

'But I used to work for him. I can . . .'

'Mother said "*No*",' snapped Moss, then gently: 'We know how you feel . . . but it's been decided.'

'You can help with the . . . diversion,' said Mother. 'On the streets.'

'Diversion?' asked Taylor.

'Like we said, now that our friends the authorities have started to take notice of what's going on at The Rock, they've sent in the police. Our people are already making it difficult for them to get anywhere near the place. Fires have started elsewhere around The Rock – enough to keep the city's fire tenders all tied up and roads blocked for hours. See what you've started, Taylor? Take advantage of the time it buys you.'

Mother had been leaning back in her chair during this last exchange. Suddenly, and with a swiftness of movement that was unnerving, she jerked forward and pitched something into the centre of the brightly lit table. They rattled and clattered to a halt.

Three yellowed dice.

Mother leaned forward to look. Instead of numbers, these dice had representations of playing cards on each surface.

'A King of Diamonds, an Ace of Spades . . . and Jack of Hearts.' She laughed. 'Perfect. Taylor, you're the King, and your boy there is the Lover, the Jack.'

'And the Ace?' asked Moss. 'That's me.'

'Well,' said the black woman, 'two out of three isn't bad.'

Moss looked at her uncertainly, and she began to laugh.

'Does that mean . . . ?' Den had started to talk without realising that he was going to ask a question. 'Does that mean that Susan's okay, that we're going to make it in there?'

'Well, you don't see three Black Jacks, do you? That's something.' Mother stopped laughing then, and just looked at him.

'I don't understand,' said Den.

Silence hung heavily in the air.

'I mean . . .' he continued hopelessly. 'Will we get out of there alive?'

'Hell,' said Mother at last, 'we've all got to die some time.'

She laughed again, and when the laughter brought on her smoker's cough once more, she drank from her glass and sat back.

There was no more to be said.

'Okay,' said Moss. 'Let's go.'

SEVEN

Gloria and Jessica crouched, waiting in dread as the grumbling sounds filled the corridor.

There was no light in here, no way to know from which direction any threat might come. So they had remained in almost the same positions in which they had fallen; twenty feet from where they believed that hidden door to be. Would it open again? Would they find themselves back where they started, or would the door open to reveal some further horror? Having seen the Banqueting Hall floor suddenly cease to exist, watched doors rise like elevators in walls, and clambered into what seemed to be a constantly rising, pitch-black corridor, they could not even be sure that the solid rock beneath them would remain solid for very much longer. Teeth gritted, fingers clutching at the cold black rock beneath them, they crouched, and waited ... and listened. It was impossible to tell how long the grinding noise continued.

But when it stopped, Gloria put out a hand to touch Jessica. The contact made her flinch.

'Sorry!'

'God, what next?' hissed Jessica. 'What has that bastard got in mind for us *now*?'

'Do you think ... do you think the others got through?' Gloria could barely speak, anxiety for Bobby's fate constricting her throat. There was no answer, but Gloria could sense that she was shaking her head. Whether that headshake meant 'No' or 'I don't know' Gloria was unable to guess.

They waited in silence for some further development. But the door did not suddenly slide open to admit some further terror. Now there was no sound, other than their own anxious breathing; sibilant and strained in this confined space.

At last, Jessica said: 'We can't just stay here.'

'What ...' Gloria struggled to get the words out. 'What do you think we should do?'

'What else? Head in the opposite direction and hope we can find a way out.' Jessica rose to her feet slowly. It was impossible to tell in this darkness how high or wide the corridor might be. But when she carefully straightened up, her head did not meet any obstruction. She helped Gloria to stand. Blindly, they groped for the nearest cold stone wall, then slowly turned in what they believed to be the opposite direction from the door.

'You okay?' asked Jessica.

'Fine and dandy.'

'Give me your hand. Good, now keep your other hand in front of you – well out in front. We don't want to smash our teeth on anything we might walk into. And keep your steps slow and careful. Let's do it like this – you step forward and stop. Then I'll step forward and stop. That way, if you step into a gap or a hole or something, then I'll be able to haul you back. Same for me.'

'Okay . . . let's go.'

Slowly and carefully, they began to move down the corridor.

The darkness remained inpenetrable, their eyes unable to focus on any detail.

When Gloria spoke again, it could have been ten minutes or ten hours later; their sense of time in this Stygian nightmare was utterly lost.

'I don't understand it.'

'What?'

'This corridor. The door back there. The way the walls and the doors were moving up like those old-fashioned elevators. I don't see how Draegerman could design something like that.' Gloria had to speak, had to break this awful silent darkness with *something*, her thoughts of Bobby's fate were too much to bear.

'There are lots of things in this godawful place that don't make sense. Doesn't stop them being there though, does it?'

'Part of me wonders . . .' Gloria's voice dried up.

'Wonders what?'

'Wonders whether it wouldn't be best to just end it here and now.'

'What do you mean?'

'I mean maybe we should just beat our brains out against the wall, cheat the bastard.'

'No, we've got to go on.'

'Is that the crusading reporter talking?'

'No, just someone who wants to get out of this madhouse alive.'

Gloria stumbled. Jessica froze, hanging on to her arm.

'It's okay. There's nothing there . . .'

They carried on through the darkness.

'The others will have made it,' said Jessica.

'Yes,' said Gloria. Her voice carried no conviction.

'You didn't like me when we first met, did you?'

Gloria was silent for a while; taken aback by this sudden and unexpected turn in the conversation. 'Did I give that impression?'

'Yes.'

'Then I'm sorry. I keep pretending that I'm a movie star. I've got this been-there, done-that attitude. It pisses people off sometimes. But it's just a defensive measure. In reality, I've been living under the shadow of Jack Draegerman these past twenty-five years. Always with my defences up, making me wary. Living with a secret horror. Now it looks like I'm playing my part in a real-life horror movie. Might be ironic, but I can't find anything to smile about.'

'This is one story I'd rather not be covering, believe me.'

'Do me a favour. If we do get out of this, and you do sell the film rights – make sure you cast my part ten years younger and in full make-up at all times.'

'Don't worry, we'll get through this – and you can play yourself.'

'Want to know something funny?'

'I don't think I can remember how to laugh.'

'Something good has come out of this. If not for this whole fucking nightmare, I don't believe I would ever have found Bobby again.'

They carried on in silence.

'Damn you to *hell*, Jack Draegerman!' Gloria's sudden yell in the darkness sent shivering waves of fear like an electric shock through Jessica's body. 'Now that I've found him again, you'll *never* take him away from me!' Jessica could feel Gloria trembling, now taking deep breaths to steady her nerves. She seemed to have found renewed strength. '*Never!*' she hissed under her breath.

'Fuck you TOO!' yelled Jessica – and this time it was Gloria's turn to flinch.

Gloria began to laugh then as they moved, gripping Jessica's hand tight.

And then her foot came down on empty space.

She lurched forward, twisted – and Jessica was unable to compensate for the sudden shift in balance between them. She was dragged with her, and in the next moment, Gloria's other leg had knocked Jessica's feet from beneath her. With a cry of surprise and shock, Jessica fell on top of Gloria and both women were suddenly tumbling down a rough slope.

'Oh *God* . . .' Gloria scrabbled at the ground as they fell, could find no purchase, and had the breath knocked from her body as Jessica rolled heavily across her. Jessica's knee came up under Gloria's chin, the impact stunning her. And when Jessica's head hit the ground again, sparks exploded behind her eyes. Then there was only the darkness.

In a flailing tangle of limbs, they fell.

EIGHT

'Are you all right?'

Jessica came out of her fractured sleep like a diver struggling to the surface for air. Her wrists were seized as she tried to claw her way out of the nightmare.

'It's me! Take it easy! It's only me ...'

And God, oh God, how she had wanted to wake from this living hell to find that she was at home, or even in a hospital bed. How much better that would be, to know that she had been hit by a car crossing the road to the newspaper offices and was now waking in a hospital bed to be told that it was okay, everything was going to be fine and there was nothing left to worry about. But she was still in Draegerman's Rock, still living the nightmare, and there was no escape.

Gloria leaned back, letting go of her arms now. With a great sigh, she sat back.

'I'd trade two broken legs and a broken arm just to be out of this place,' murmured Jessica.

'What?'

'Nothing ... I'm just ... nothing.'

Jessica's eyes were hurting and there was a lump the size of a duck egg on the back of her head. She could feel dried blood there. How long had she been out?

At last, Jessica realised that she could see.

'I know,' said Gloria, pre-empting what she was about to say. 'God knows how far we fell, but I reckon we came down there ...' She pointed behind them, and when Jessica turned to look, she could see a flight of rough stone stairs winding up a passageway and out of sight into darkness. They were lying in another corridor, and there were the usual lamp brackets set high up in the wall. Orange light this time, rather than green. Did that mean something? It looked the same as all the other corridors they had travelled down since their arrival in this place, and stretched away fifty yards before curving out of sight. It looked like a main thoroughfare, unlike the smaller corridor from which they had fallen. 'We were both knocked out, I

280

think,' continued Gloria. Jessica turned back to see that Gloria's nose had been bloodied; she was dabbing at it with a scrap of handkerchief that had miraculously remained in the sleeve of her blouse.

Jessica groaned, rubbing her eyes. Fear had returned to eat at her insides like nausea. She struggled against the compulsion to vomit; it would only make her feel worse than she already did. There was a noise in her head; a scrambling, pattering noise that sounded like ... like ...

'Listen!' hissed Gloria. 'Can you hear it?'

So the noise was not in her head at all. Jessica strained to listen.

'Footsteps,' she said. 'Someone's running. This way ...'

Light suddenly began to flicker off to their right, where the corridor curved away into darkness. Light was dancing on the far wall, shadows were leaping as the sound of the footsteps grew louder.

'The others?' Gloria moved forward, straining to see. 'Maybe they've found us.'

'And maybe it's something else.'

They shrank back into the shadows, staring intently. The sounds were really close now. Someone was definitely running in their direction. Gloria's intake of breath when they both saw the elongated silhouette of a human figure on the far wall was like the sound of hissing steam. In the next moment, the figure staggered around the corner breathing hard, clutching at the corridor wall.

It was a man. He was holding a rough torch of some kind, orange flame billowing from a thick knot of fuel-soaked linen. Sparks dropped from it as he stood there, drawing breath.

'Jessica ... Gloria ...'

'Oh God, it's Roy!' Gloria stepped out of the shadows. 'We're here!'

Now the light was shining on the figure's face as he gasped for breath. Unmistakably, it was Roy Jensen – and by the expression on his face he was a very worried man indeed.

'Thank God ...' he gasped, beckoning to them with the torch. 'Come on, we've got to get away from here.'

Gloria and Jessica stumbled down the corridor towards him.

'What happened?' stammered Gloria. 'Is Bobby all right?'

'He's fine,' said Roy, pushing himself from the wall as they reached him. 'We got away. But thank God you're here. We split up to look for you.'

'Where are the others?' asked Jessica.

'Follow me,' said Roy, turning quickly back in the direction from which he had come. 'We've got to get back to them as quickly as we can.'

'How did you get away? Did you ... ?'

'No questions!' snapped Roy, cutting Jessica off. 'Just follow me, and save your breath!' He began to run on ahead, holding the torch high.

Their gaunt shadows danced and leapt over the corridor walls as they followed. Roy's sense of urgency had communicated itself instantly to the two women. Still aching, stil feeling weak and both with an inner gnawing of fear, they staggered on behind him. The corridor stretched ahead for another fifty yards before curving to the right again. Roy looked briefly back to make sure they were still following, and then pressed ahead.

As they turned the next corner, feet clattering on the stone flags, both Jessica and Gloria suddenly staggered to a halt.

There was yet another fifty-yard stretch of black stone corridor beyond. But the floor here was wreathed in curling fog. Roy had kept on running, his passage causing swirling shrouds of fog to billow around him. Now he too staggered to a halt, turning to look at them.

'Come *on*!' he yelled, face still a mask of anxiety. 'We don't have time for this. It's fog, that's all. It's all over the place.'

Reluctantly, Gloria moved forward.

'Will you COME ON!'

And now both women were running again, rushing through the calf-high undulating blanket of white. Now the sounds of their footsteps on the stone floor seemed to be swallowed by the mist. It was freezing cold.

Roy reached another corner and paused briefly to make sure that they were catching up. Then he plunged on ahead, still with the torch held high. This time, the corridor was curving to the left.

'How much further?' gasped Jessica, and a wisp of fog curled into her throat. She gagged. It tasted not only cold but somehow bitter.

'Nearly there,' called Roy. 'See – just up ahead.' He gestured with the torch, sending shadows chasing over the walls again.

The fog enveloped the stone floor in another identical corridor, but at the midway stage was another of the familiar oak doors with the three-claw handle in the centre. Roy speeded up, hurtling ahead and scattering the fog around him. Without pausing, he seized the handle of the door and yanked it open, the incoming draught of air scattering the fog completely in all directions. In the next moment, he was through the door and it slammed against the inner wall with a hollow, echoing boom.

Gloria reached the doorway first, rushed through and then halted so suddenly that Jessica almost collided with her.

There was another bizarre sight beyond the door.

Something that, by rights, could not be.

They had emerged on to what seemed to be a dilapidated wooden jetty. Some of the boards were covered in algae, others plainly rotting. In some places, the boards were missing altogether. Black water glinted below the gaps. Beyond the jetty, which was perhaps twenty feet long and fifteen feet wide, was a dark expanse of water. The fog they had encountered in the corridor was also curling on the surface of the water. Moss and vegetation occasionally sprouted from the water near to the jetty, but two or three hundred feet out a great tangle of vegetation hid everything beyond from sight. The darkness, the fog on the water and the silently weaving fronds of vegetation hid any indication of how large this bizarre new chamber might be.

Jessica stepped around Gloria to look in amazement. The fog was swirling in a thick mass to their left and right. Overhead there was nothing but darkness.

Roy was standing with his back to them, on the edge of the dilapidated jetty. Without turning to look at them, he suddenly grabbed at a makeshift wooden ladder resting against the edge of the jetty and started down towards the murky water. They watched him descend – and then he suddenly stepped off into the water. Gloria gasped and pulled back. But the water came up only to his knees. Before they could react, he was surging on ahead, holding the torch aloft.

'Are you kidding?' yelled Jessica. Her voice seemed dead and oddly flat.

'Come on,' said Roy without turning. 'The others are waiting on the other side. It's safe there.'

Jessica shrugged and moved to the edge. Carefully, she followed him down, dipping one foot into the water and wincing at the cold. She held her breath, and then pushed herself off into the water. Silently, Gloria descended. In the next moment, both women were in the murky water, and they began to follow in the furrowed ripples of water and fog that Roy was leaving behind him. Up ahead, perhaps twenty feet from them, they could see that the water was still knee-deep on Roy.

'This reminds me ...' began Gloria, and then felt something snag her foot. She cursed, kicked the weed free and struggled on.

'Mangrove trees, creepers and ferns,' said Jessica, ploughing on through the water. 'Up ahead on those tangled mud banks. That's what they are.'

'Yeah, I thought so.'

'Remind you of what?' continued Jessica.

'This is like some kind of ... bayou, or something. But more than that. It's not ...' Gloria was silent then, shaking her head. And when Jessica looked at her, she noted a deeper sense of unease than she had seen before. She changed tack, shouting up ahead to Roy: 'How far, Roy?'

'Not far,' he replied. 'Just up ahead. Any moment now.'

'Bobby! Where are you?' yelled Gloria. Again, the sound of her voice was flat and unreal. She stopped in the water, staring ahead. 'Oh no ...' she said under her breath. Jessica was marginally ahead of her. She stopped to look back when it was clear that Gloria was no longer following.

'What is it?'

'It's unreal,' said Gloria.

'You're telling me. *Everything* about being here is unreal.'

'No, I don't mean that.' Gloria's face suddenly seemed much whiter than it had before. 'I mean this place. This bayou, this swamp or whatever it is. It's not like a real place. It's like . . . a film set.'

'Come on,' said Jessica, moving on but still looking uneasily back at Gloria, who did not move.

'This is like a studio tank. Look at it. Water that should be deep, but isn't. How many times have you seen this in black and white at the movies? How many times have you seen something like this and known all along that it was an indoor set . . . that the actors and actresses weren't outside?'

Jessica turned angrily to face the front, not wanting any renewed fear in Gloria to slow her down when they were so close to the comparative safety in numbers that lay ahead, no matter how tenuous that 'safety' might be. She halted, foam surging around her legs.

Roy had also halted up ahead. He was standing, stiff and straight and still, with the blazing torch held high. Had he seen something? Was something wrong?

'What is it?' hissed Jessica, moving to one side to see if she could catch sight of what it was that had alarmed Roy. There was nothing to see but the swirling fog and the tangle of creepers and vines up ahead.

'I know this place,' said Gloria. Now there was a sound of utter resignation and weariness in her voice.

'Roy, what can you see? Is there something . . . ?'

'It's a movie set, Jessica. It's just like the set from one of *my* movies.'

'*Which movie?*' said Roy, again without turning.

The sound of his voice filled Jessica with a deep sense of horror. She staggered to a halt, staring at his back. Because the voice that had issued from the man ahead was not the voice of Roy Jensen. More than that – oh God, much, *much* more than that – the voice could surely not belong to anything that was remotely human. It was a low, malevolent and deep-bass travesty of a human voice; the very sound of it was tainted and deeply repellent.

'Roy . . . ?' Jessica backed away.

'*Which movie, Gloria?*'

The sound of the voice did something to Jessica's soul. It made her want to fold up, fall to her knees in the water and weep. It engendered desolation and despair.

'One of my movies for Jack Draegerman,' said Gloria. And it was clear that she too was feeling the same sickening horror and desperation inside. '*Swamp Water Woman.*'

Roy turned in the water to face them.

He was grinning, head down low, looking at them both from under

284

eyebrows that seemed somehow saturnine. And in that moment, Gloria remembered the hideous decoration on the walls of the boneyard escalator; that sickening mélange which she could suddenly see was a huge representation of herself in full make-up from Draegerman's movie. Because Roy's eyes were somehow now the same as the eyes of the figure in that hideous tapestry.

The fog was rippling and moving on the surface of the filthy swamp. Jessica watched in horror as it suddenly began to sweep, to *pour* across the surface towards Roy as he stood there unmoving, with that fixed grin on his face. She turned in the water to look at Gloria, as if expecting her to resolve what was taking place. White-faced, Gloria also stood transfixed as every wisp, every wraith-like veil of fog was sucked over the water towards Roy. It began to swirl and gather density around his legs, undulating and rising there. Gloria had another movie image in her mind now. This was like a speeded-up film *in reverse*. It was as if the figure of Roy had itself emitted the fog, and it had spread to cover the entire surface of this studio-set swamp. Now the film was being run backwards, at ten times the speed, and the fog was returning to its source.

Gloria and Jessica, still speechless with horror, could see that the fog had cocooned Roy's legs to the thighs. A thick white mantle of cobweb had formed there – and was rising quickly. Roy's smile began to widen as the fog crept swiftly and hungrily around his waist.

'It's not . . .' Gloria struggled to speak, as if the words could eradicate what they were seeing before their eyes. 'It's not Roy.'

The fog swirled, gathering speed as it climbed, now engulfing the figure's waist; swarming around his outstretched arms; undulating over his grinning face. As the fog engulfed the torch in his right hand, the flame was instantly extinguished. The hissing of the drowned torch seemed to go on and on – now becoming something else, something altogether more sibilant and malevolent. It grew in intensity, like the sound of a pressure cooker, something at boiling point that must surely explode. The water around this pillar of rolling, undulating fog was rippling violently.

Jessica thrashed back through the water to Gloria, the fear of imminent threat breaking her out of her enervation. Still wide-eyed, Gloria put out a hand towards her. Their hands connected and . . .

And then the fog-pillar was suddenly blasted away with a great roaring sound; as if some film studio wind-machine had been switched on behind them.

'Oh good God . . .' Jessica's fingernails pierced the skin of Gloria's palm, but Gloria felt no pain, could not react. She could only stand in the rippling water and stare at what had emerged from the cocoon of mist. Gloria Pernell, film actress and star of Jack Draegerman's *Swamp Water Woman*, could only stand and stare at her own creation suddenly made real.

The arms were spread wide, just as she had seen in the decoration on the escalator wall, just as the figure had stood in its pose for the cinema poster: the cloak hanging around her shoulders like a bat's wings or a vampire's cowl, fashioned from the dripping swamp-water weed from which the nightmare figure had risen; the savagely long fingernails, with the ridiculous blood-red varnish; the black-green gown fashioned from scales which hugged the sensuous figure tightly, rotted in places by the swamp water. Gloria could see, despite the horror, that the figure's waist was just as slender as her own had been back then when the movie was made.

The face was her own – yet not her own.

White as a corpse ten days in the water. Eyes with no irises, only the thin yellow slits of a reptile, unblinking and fixed on the two women before it. The tangled crown around the brow, of weed and barbed wire and small, slime-coated living things that writhed and coiled and tried to squirm free from the hideous head decoration. The long black hair around the shoulders, also matted with dripping green swamp weed.

The thing screeched as the last tattered veils and shrouds of fog dispersed behind it. Something long and thin and black as a snake writhed from between the lips, caressed the thing's lower face and was instantly withdrawn, briefly flickering over two curved, sharp reptile's fangs before vanishing. It was the forked tongue that Gloria had never been able to hold in her mouth when they were shooting, a special effect that had to be added later because of her discomfort – now real and living and flickering in a hideously serpentine manner that would have pleased Jack Draegerman utterly.

'Cut!' said Gloria, some inner part of her reacting to the nightmare, trying to rationalise it on its own terms. Now, would the horror that was the Swamp Water Woman relax her pose, spit out the tongue and say: 'Thank Christ for that, has someone got a cigarette?' Would the stage technicians suddenly come ploughing through the water to help them all back to dry land? Would the sound-boom suddenly dip into view from overhead?

The thing laughed manically: a horrid gargling of swamp water in its lungs. Green bile spilled from the lips. And then it dropped away with ferocious swiftness, plunging into the water as swiftly as if some underwater trap-door had opened beneath where it stood. A plume of spiralling, dirty-green swamp water erupted from where it had vanished soaking Jessica and Gloria to the skin – at the same time releasing them from the thing's hideous gaze.

They were left alone, standing in the middle of this surreal swamp holding on to each other and staring at the place where the thing had vanished; their balance shifting as the great ripples caused by its sudden disappearance troughed around their legs.

'It's still here,' said Jessica, scanning the surface. 'It's still here under the water.'

'Come on!' Gloria dragged Jessica with her as she whirled around. Together, they began to plough back through the swamp water. The dilapidated jetty and its makeshift wooden ladder were perhaps fifty feet from them. Above the jetty, the oak door was still open.

Something made a ripple in the water, away to their left; like something nibbling at the surface. As one, their heads jerked in that direction.

'Go on then, you bastard!' yelled Gloria. 'Play us the *Jaws* music!'

Jessica looked at Gloria as if she had lost her mind. Her face was still white, mouth set firm. But now there was more anger than fear in her eyes. Something snagged her foot then, and Jessica cried out aloud. Gloria heaved her forward, and she managed to clear the obstruction.

'It was . . . was *you!*' Jessica managed to gasp as they staggered on, thrashing through the water.

Gloria nodded grimly.

'But it can't . . . I mean . . . it won't . . .'

Something splashed off to their right this time, another wave of ripples, but there was still nothing to see.

'Dry land,' said Gloria, refusing to look at this new disturbance on the water, focusing ahead. 'We've got to get back to dry land. To the jetty. The Swamp Water Woman needs to be standing in water, she can't live on dry land.' She was nodding her head extravagantly as they splashed onwards.

Jessica stared anxiously at the oak door, the part of her that knew of nightmare and its logic *willing* the door not to swing slowly closed, trapping them.

Fog was starting to spread and ripple on the surface of the swamp, its tendrils curling through the ferns and the creepers and spilling out over the water behind them. Jessica glanced back, moaned and flung herself forward with renewed vigour.

And then they had reached the jetty ladder.

Gloria braced her arm on the ladder as Jessica drew level.

'You go first!' she shoved Jessica on to the ladder, looking back across the swamp. Jessica began to climb, and as soon as Jessica's heels had cleared her face, Gloria began to climb too.

'Dry land,' said Gloria breathlessly. 'We've beaten it.'

And then something exploded through the rotting timbers before them; something that erupted with roaring force, a geyser of stinking black mud and a torrent of swirling swamp water. The ladder and surrounding timbers shattered and flew apart, and in the same instant Gloria and Jessica were flung back from the disintegrating jetty, the force of the eruption hurling them into the water from which they had just clambered.

Jessica thrashed and clawed at the enfolding, surging green-black water. It had erupted into her mouth and lungs. Her arms were tangled in weed, and as she clawed blindly to break to the surface, the weed also became tangled around her legs. Instinctively she tried to scream, and sucked in more of the muck. She felt the ground beneath her, remembered instantly that the water here was not deep, and then braced her feet. Straightening her body, she surged out of the water. Spume erupted from her mouth as she clawed at her head and face, tearing away the cloying green weed. She could not see, could not breathe, and there was a great roaring and screeching sound in her ears as she felt something solid beneath her fingers – a shattered spar from the jetty. She clutched it, felt its solidity beneath her, and then vomited the swamp water from her lungs. Coughing and gagging, she tore the last of the suffocating green slime from her eyes.

The jetty had all but been destroyed, splintered spars jutting from the wall beneath the oak door, dirty water lapping and foaming around the driftwood that floated there. The surface was littered with rotted debris, and Jessica was clinging to a spar that was still rooted in the bed of this studio swamp. But as she hung over the broken stanchion, all she could see were the two figures before her.

Gloria was standing with her back to Jessica, perhaps twenty feet away. The same cloying weed was in her hair and on her shoulders, but she was standing straight and silent, thigh-deep in the water and looking up . . .

Looking up at the thing that stood not six feet in front of her, the thing that now seemed to tower over her – the face of the Swamp Water Woman. It was a travesty of Gloria's face, now looking down on Gloria with its white and evil grin. The snake tongue flickered around its lips and was gone again.

Jessica's sense of logic was fractured once more. The thing they had thought was Roy, the thing that had led them into this place and then *changed* to become Gloria's fictional creation, had been Roy's height, his weight and size. But now this thing which had surged up from impossibly shallow water and destroyed the jetty, was at least twice Gloria's size. As Jessica watched, it opened its arms wide as if to take Gloria into its embrace, and as it did so its face began to change again . . .

And Gloria could only stand there, and look up in dread fascination at her own face; could only remember, as those features began to change again, how Jack Draegerman had said to her:

'We're going for double exposures, Gloria. Just like the old Lon Chaney Jnr werewolf movies. Frame by frame, we add just a little more make-up as we go on. Takes some time, but it's worth it . . .'

And Gloria looked up and watched as the face changed, as the scales crept up from the neck and over the cheeks and across the forehead as the Swamp Water Woman underwent her final transformation for the climax of the movie; now more reptile than woman. She watched the hairline recede as the forehead swept back and her skull became more like a snake's than ever, watched as the eyes bulged and the thing dislocated its own jaws prior to swallowing its prey . . .

. . . and remembered how Jack had said: *'Of course we can't use a fucking stand-in for the double exposures, Gloria. Or a dummy. For God's sake, we're trying to get a little reality into this thing. This is the big finish . . . the . . .'*

'Big finish?' said Gloria in a small voice.

Above her, the thing shuddered. Was it laughing? It seemed to look away from her then, over her head to something that was in the water beyond.

And Jessica cried out involuntarily as the thing fixed her with its reptilian gaze.

Would you rather it was YOU?

Jessica knew that the thing was speaking to her, even though its hideously dislocated jaws had not moved. And instinctively, all she could find to say was: 'Please God, not me, please God, not me, don't let it be me . . .'

The thing shuddered again.

Something flew from the swamp water beside it, something that erupted with a splash of foam and sped towards Jessica. Crying out again, she threw herself away from the spar to which she was clinging. Water surged and foamed around her. The thing that flew whirling through the air had a leather strap, that strap now looping around the upper edge of a shattered spar jutting from the stone wall, a spar that had once supported the floor of the shattered jetty.

Now Jessica could see that it was her dictating machine, lost somewhere in the flight through Draegerman's House of Horrors. It hung by its leather strap from the spar, six feet below the threshold of the door into the corridor.

Do you remember how to use this?

Jessica looked back to see that the thing was still looking at her, its face now beyond anything human, but still with a travesty of a grin. The serpent tongue flashed again and was gone.

Don't you trade in misery, Jessica? Isn't it your role in life to detail and report on the woes and the fears and the pain and the agony?

Jessica tried to speak, tried to deny the very existence of the thing. Gloria had not moved, still stood staring up at the hideous apparition that towered over her.

Get the dictating machine.

Jessica looked up at it, dangling from the leather loop.

Don't you know what I want? Don't you know why I'm here? Not for

Gloria, but for one of the Draegerman spawn. Didn't he tell you? We came to an arrangement . . .

'Oh God, not me, please not me . . .'

Then get the machine. Show me how well you can do your job.

'No . . .'

But Jessica was moving through the water, pulling herself past the shattered debris, fingers outstretched towards the dictating machine dangling by its strap.

You can die with pain. Or without pain. Show me how well you can describe torment and agony, Jessica. Report what you're about to see, and perhaps I will be kind to you . . .

'. . . not me . . .'

She pulled herself up on to a broken stanchion, the filthy water surging from her soaked dress. Hand trembling violently, she leaned up and tried to reach the dictating machine.

And Gloria turned then, her face a mask of terror and pleading.

'Jessica, help me. Please.'

'Oh God, not me . . .'

Jessica pulled herself up to the spar, bracing her feet on more shattered remnants of the support structure still jutting from the chamber wall. Clinging there, she unhooked the dictating machine from where it hung. Putting it to her mouth, she pressed the record button.

'Jessica, after everything we've been through together. For the love of God.'

The Swamp Water Woman shuddered, its claw-hands descending to rest lightly – even gently – on Gloria's shoulders.

Against her will, her face still shocked and white, her eyes glazed at the inevitability of what was about to happen, Gloria turned back to face the thing.

Begin . . .

'Gloria . . .' Jessica gagged, clinging to the spar, and then continued. 'Gloria Pernell could not . . . could not believe that fantasy and reality had become so seamlessly . . . seamlessly fused . . .'

Continue . . .

'The thing's head descended,' stammered Jessica. 'The jaws unhinging even further, and now . . . now that spell which had held Gloria so still was suddenly broken . . . she began to struggle . . . and then . . . and then . . .'

And then the screaming began.

NINE

There was only the faintest illumination in this corridor. Enough to see the huddled silhouettes who lay or crouched on the hard, cold ground. Enough to see the faint glistening of water as it ran down the walls.

Bobby had stopped weeping and now his body was racked with shivering as he crouched on his haunches, head in hands and back against the stone wall. Roy supposed that he was suffering from the shakes again, but there was nothing to be done for him. Susan sat next to Roy, and he was grateful for the warmth of her body. Once, she had turned to him after he had vented his impotent, echoing scream of rage, as if she wanted to say something. Instead, she had shaken her head and looked down.

Boone, as usual, was sitting apart from the others, arms resting on the attaché case across his knees.

The sounds of the hidden pistons and gears and pulleys suddenly grated to a halt.

Tense, they waited for something to happen.

Roy felt a deep enervation overcome him. He tried to rise, tried to say something, tried to make some kind of decision. But nothing would come. He was sapped of energy. Let this damned corridor tilt and spew them into a bottomless pit, let the ceiling cave in – there was nothing he could do about it. He wondered whether *The Wayside* was open for business, wondered whether Frank or the owners had called the police when he failed to show up for work. Perhaps a new bartender-cum-dogsbody had been hired to take his place already. That all seemed a million miles and a million years away; another life, another place.

And then Bobby stood up, using the wall behind him for support. Still shaking, he pushed himself away from the wall and tottered past them in the darkness. Roy wanted to ask him where he was going, wanted to rise and go after him. He could do nothing but watch as Bobby staggered past. But he was not heading off down the murky corridor; his steps were weak, but they had a purpose. Directly opposite Boone, he stopped, weaving from side to side.

Roy saw the silhouette of Boone's head look up.

291

Bobby stood there, weaving, looking down.

'What?' asked Boone in a cracked voice. 'What the hell do you want?'

The sound of Boone's voice seemed to act as just the goad Bobby was looking for. He lashed out with one foot, the blow hitting Boone on the side of his face and slamming him back against the corridor wall.

'It was you,' said Bobby shakily.

Leaning forward to brace both hands on the wall, he kicked out at Boone again; this time the blow took him in the ribs. Boone cried out, crumpled, hugging his midriff.

'You! You screwed it up ... the others could have got through that door ... but you ... *You!*'

He lashed out with his other foot, and this time Boone sprawled in the corridor, his attaché case clattering from his grasp.

'Bobby, no!' Susan was on her feet, pushing forward between them. 'He's just more scared than we are.'

'*More* scared!' shouted Bobby, whirling on her; and the force of his rage made Susan stand back. 'More scared than *me*, for instance?'

Now his rage was directed at the man on the ground again as he scrabbled for his attaché case.

'Boone, you make me sick – and if my mother dies as a result of what you've done, I'll kill you. Do you hear that, I'll fucking *kill* you!'

Just before Boone could reach his attaché case, Bobby staggered forward again and kicked it hard. It clattered away down the corridor. Boone cried out, as if the blow to the case had been worse than the blows to himself. On hands and knees, he scrabbled after it.

Spent, Bobby swayed and groped at the wall for support. Susan moved quickly forward to take his arm, and helped him to sit again.

Boone grabbed his case, scrabbled to the nearest wall and held it firmly in his lap. Looking back at the others, he opened it to check the contents.

And then light flickered in the corridor; there was a sickening and familiar crackle of static. Boone froze, the lid of his attaché case still open, the light playing over his face.

'Oh, *shit!*' said Susan.

Roy turned to see that another screen had flickered into life, almost directly opposite Boone, set into the corridor wall at about head height. The screen had been carefully placed. Even in the tight confines of the corridor, it was possible for everyone to see the hated face that appeared there.

But something seemed to be affecting this transmission; the static-snow flurried and buzzed, the face seemed about to come into focus, then vanished back into the snowstorm. The familiar voice said something they could not hear properly – and then, at last, the image resolved itself.

The creeping shadow had now covered Draegerman's face. His eye sockets were hollow, rheumy eyes glinting within. The cheeks looked sunken and drawn and this time, when he talked, they could barely see his lips moving.

'Very resourceful. All of you.'

The voice sounded somehow breathless.

'And no, there was nothing beneath the hall floor. All the Daemons lie ahead, waiting for you. But let me give you ...'

And then static filled the screen again, dissolving Draegerman's image. Once more, the image sharpened.

'... give you some more clues for this game. Our guests have no physical form in this plane, but they need physical form to materialise in our plane. I've helped them to find that form. The act of summoning means that I have had to open myself up to them, to allow them access to the inner creative me. And they have drawn on me – drawn on my inner mind – to find things there on which they can anchor their physical materialisation. Think about that, children. Think carefully.'

'And what if we just stay here?' said Roy. 'Stay here and die?'

'That wouldn't be sensible. Don't you know that this place, this Rock, is ME? I can do so much with it. You saw what happened to the Banqueting Hall floor. Don't you know that I can arrange to move you from that corridor very easily?'

'It's no use,' said Susan. 'We'll have to move ...'

'Now you're being good, children. And remember – I'm with you every step of the way.'

Draegerman's image dissolved, the snowstorm filled the screen – and then the light died altogether, plunging them back into the gloom.

Roy clambered to his feet, moved across to Bobby and helped him to stand. He was still shaking, but the tremors were less violent. He gazed with hate at Boone, who snapped the lid of his attaché case shut and stared at where the television screen had blinked into life.

'Come on,' said Roy. 'Maybe there's a chance. Maybe there is a way out if we just keep trying.'

'And look what happened last time we thought we were going down,' said Boone. 'No, I'm staying here. I'm not going to just walk blindly into something like that Berserker thing, or whatever in hell it was.'

'Then how are you going to spend all the money in that attaché case of yours?' asked Bobby. 'You snivelling little shit. I should just kick your head in. Then Draegerman's pact with whatever these things really are will be screwed, won't it?'

'You can please yourself,' said Roy to Boone. 'Stay if you want to. It's your affair.'

He moved to help Bobby walk, but Bobby shook his head and

293

walked on ahead down the corridor. Susan joined Roy as they passed, leaving Boone sitting on the floor, attaché case across his knees, head in his hands.

They had gone no more than thirty feet in the darkness, when Boone suddenly pulled himself upright and hurried after them. No one acknowledged his presence.

After a while, Susan said: 'Want to hear something bad?'

'You mean it gets worse?' said Roy.

'Much worse.'

'Then what?'

'I think I've laddered my tights.'

Roy looked at the silhouette of her face as they walked. He laughed then. It was a good sound. Bobby joined in and now Susan was laughing. They could not understand why they were laughing in this godforsaken place, but it felt good. Good and clean.

Behind them, Boone followed with his head lowered. He made no sound.

Slowly and carefully, they carried on down the corridor.

TEN

Jessica ran in terror.

Her shadow leaped ahead of her, and as her arms pinwheeled for balance at the corner of this corridor, the shadow performed a mad dance on the wall. Sobbing for breath, she paused there for breath; hardly daring to believe that she had somehow managed to get away from that terrible place.

She had done as the thing had requested.

And at a point where she believed she must lose her sanity altogether, when the thing had become so preoccupied in its hideous feasting, Jessica had feverishly clambered from the shattered spar jutting out of the chamber wall to the door above, still dictating into the machine, believing that the thing would see her movement at any moment, discard what it was doing and surge through the filthy, littered swamp water to take her.

But somehow, she had climbed to the threshold.

And now she was running.

Tossing her sodden hair away from her face, she turned and ran ahead down the next corridor. With each step, one word was dragged out of her sobbing body over and over again.

'Please . . . please . . . please . . .'

In her mind's eye, she could see only one thing: Gloria's face as she turned back to her and said: *'Jessica, help me. Please.'*

'Oh, Gloria, I'm sorry . . . sorry . . . please . . . please . . .'

Jessica, after everything we've been through. For the love of God.

'Oh GOD!' Jessica's hands flew to her face as she staggered on, as if she could tear what she had seen out of her mind and hurl it away. And it was only then that she realised she was still holding the dictating machine. With a cry of anguish, she unhooked the leather cord and threw it back down the corridor. It smashed to pieces against a wall. She blundered away again and kept running. At the next corner, she leaned with her back against the wall for a moment, trying to control herself. She looked back again, breath sobbing in her throat. Could she hear anything back there? A sibilant hissing sound? Something wet gliding over the flagged stone floor of the corridor, something coming to find her now that the feasting was over?

She turned and ran on again.

And then something stepped out in front of her.

Before she could utter a sound, the figure drew back its fist and punched her hard on the side of the head.

Jessica fell senseless to the corridor floor.

'Poor baby,' said Farrow, grinning. 'Want to come back to *my* place?'

Stooping, Farrow picked her up and slung her unconscious body over his shoulder.

ELEVEN

'Here?' asked Den, looking over the waist-high concrete buttress into the filthy water below.

Taylor leaned over, and scanned the river.

Dilapidated warehouses and factory storage facilities lined the river here, and had provided perfect cover for them. No one in their right minds would be down here at this time of night, and Den had said so when they had parked the car and made their way down the concrete ramp. Taylor and Moss had simply looked at him. Den had taken their reaction sullenly, as if they were deliberately misunderstanding and denigrating his commitment to getting Susan out of that hellhole alive. He resolved to make no further comments. It had not taken long to follow this stretch of river to the point marked on Talbot's map.

At last, Taylor spotted the wire grille set into a recessed gulley, ten feet below them. Dark brown water was gushing from the grille into the polluted river.

'Nice,' said Moss, peeling off his shirt and trousers.

The others followed suit, and soon all their clothes had been bundled up into a black plastic sack which Moss carefully hid out of sight behind a crumbling factory wall behind them. Now all three men were standing in the skin-tight black wet suits that Moss's contacts had provided at short notice, as required by Taylor. Each of the three had a waterproof satchel with arm-straps, containing two small portable cylinders of oxygen with enough air in each for thirty minutes, two face-masks, and an Ingram nine-millimetre machine pistol with armrest. They had been unable to obtain more plastic explosive at such short notice, but someone had come up with two phosphorous grenades. Both of the latter were in Taylor's satchel. Each man had a waterproof torch in his belt. Taylor alone had a belt with several large waterproof pouches, one of which now contained Talbot's map, a small crowbar, and rope.

There was no need for the latter. The concrete bank above the river sloped downwards to a small inlet, and three feet below the rim was the iron grille. Quickly, Taylor moved down to the inlet and sat on the bank. The others watched as he lowered his legs over the side. Looking around, he kicked flotsam away and then carefully let himself over the side and down into the murky water. It was waist-deep. No sooner had he done so than the distant sounds of police sirens came to their ears. From somewhere far away, over the city skyline, came the muffled sound of a great retort. An explosion? The silhouette of the skyline was suddenly thrown into relief. When the initial flash disappeared, the sky was glowing orange.

'Looks like your people are keeping the police busy after all,' said Taylor.

'Mother's little helpers,' said Moss, and quickly followed him into the water.

Teeth gritted, Den followed suit.

Taylor waded through the poisonous yellow foam to the grille. Taking out his waterproof torch, he shone it inside and the beam played on the sewer tunnel beyond. Inside, he could see a raised shelf on the left; a walkway, presumably. He tested the grille. Hand over hand, he examined the rim of it, scraping away years of residue to find the fixing screws. Handing his torch to Moss, he took a screwdriver from one of the waterproof pouches and began to unfasten it. Behind him, Den weaved impatiently in the water, feeling the mud shift beneath his feet. He turned to look back over the polluted river in which they stood. It seemed as if every factory along this stretch was spewing its industrial excrement into the river.

After what seemed like hours to Den, Taylor yanked out the final screw and pulled. The grille was still fastened underwater, but Taylor bent it back towards him at surface level. Moss joined him and together they prised it from the opening, knelt on the upper rim and pushed it further down. Finally, using their feet, they managed to shove it down even further until the screws under the water popped out. The grille slid to one side.

Taylor took his torch and forged through the water into the mouth of the sewer pipe. He stood there, submerged up to his waist, shining the torch into the darkness. The curved ceiling overhead was perhaps ten feet from their heads. When they did scramble up on to the shelf they would have to stoop as they moved forward.

'How far?' asked Moss, purely to break the silence. His voice echoed over the rushing of the water.

'Three long, twisting miles,' said Taylor.

'Three miles of shit, more like.'

Den said nothing

Taylor moved to the concrete shelf, braced both hands on it and hauled himself out of the water. He stood and waited while Moss and Den joined him, shining the torch ahead. As Den climbed up, he put his hand in a human turd. Taylor smiled at him, waiting for a comment. Still saying nothing, knowing that their eyes were on him, Den silently leaned back down and washed it off in the dirty water.

Taylor nodded.

'Shall we go?' asked Den.

Taylor stood aside and made a theatrical gesture to the effect that he should pass.

Three torch beams played on the walls and ceilings.

When they had reached the first intersection of sewer pipes, consulted the map and turned left, the torch beams vanished from sight.

Darkness returned.

Now there was only the sound of rushing water.

Soon, the denizens of the sewer re-emerged from their hiding places – and began scenting the concrete shelf on to which these human interlopers had hauled themselves.

Dozens of small black shapes began to swarm on the shelf.

After a while, they began to follow the scent.

TWELVE

When Farrow turned into the familiar stretch of corridor, the door to the room where he would find transcendence was already open.

Now that he was bonded with his father, it seemed that he was at one with the very fabric of this house. No longer did he have to wander these endless corridors, lost and not knowing what was around the next corner. Since that transcendence, it seemed that every turn he took, every door he opened, was leading him straight back to the place where he had been made whole; to the place where he had been enlightened by the spirit of his father.

Like father, like son.

The phrase had a deep resonance which made Farrow feel complete for the first time in his life. Jessica groaned as he hurried towards the door. He shifted her weight on his shoulder, and she moaned again.

'Not yet,' whispered Farrow. 'Not just yet.'

He shoved the door wide and entered.

It was just as he had left it; just as he remembered: the room that looked like a torture chamber, but which was much, much more than that. Farrow stood for a moment, re-examining the equipment and wondering just how many guests his father had entertained here over the years. Now he *knew* that of all offspring, he alone was the chosen one; chosen to continue the family traditions. Licking his lips in anticipation, he surveyed the carved blocks of black stone, the movie-set lanterns set high in each corner, spilling blood-red light downwards.

He looked at the bed that seemed more like a mediaeval rack and wondered if he should start there. The nest of snake-like leather straps lay piled in the centre, unmoving. There was so much here; so much pleasure to be obtained. Striding into the chamber, he swung Jessica from his shoulder and let her fall heavily on to the stained mattress. She groaned again as she sprawled there, and Farrow stood over her, watching and smiling.

'So much nicer with two.'

As he spoke, the music began again. Just as before, low and barely audible at first; now increasing gradually in volume. That same low, growling and distorted bass guitar. Then the muffled and distorted lead guitar, by the wannabe Jimi Hendrix. Farrow began to nod his head in time to the music as the corny drumbeat began. At last, he knew what the music was supposed to be; remembered where he had heard it before, or something very like it. It was the music he had heard playing in numerous seventies porno movies. It was playing for him, playing for Jessica. His father, Jack Draegerman, was famous for the movies he had made. Didn't it make sense that he should act out his own porno movies in this chamber? Didn't it make sense that his father had gone to the very limits in his search for transcendence through indulgence? And now, like father like son, Farrow would be starring in his very own movie. Farrow . . . and his co-star, Jessica.

'Want to be a star?' he asked, grin widening as he began to sway to the music. Smacking his hands together, eyes glittering, he turned again to look around the chamber. The hidden projector flickered into life and the trailer was projected again, on to the chamber wall.

'*She Wasp! A nightmare of terror that will haunt you forever!*'

There it was again, the melodramatic music that clashed with the porno music but was somehow not discordant – only more exciting.

Farrow still did not understand what relevance this missing actress, Deborah Steele, had for his father. Maybe he just liked looking at the woman up there on the screen while he was . . . while he was entertaining a Guest.

'*An expedition into Green Hell. An encounter with horror!*'

Something moved to his right. Farrow turned to look. For a moment, it seemed that the rack that was also a bed had . . . shimmered. It was as if the outline had somehow become distorted. He rubbed his eyes, still grinning and dancing. No, it was solid enough. Perhaps he was becoming over-excited? Jessica moaned and moved on the mattress.

'Getting to you, Jessica? You getting hot already?'

From the screen, Deborah Steele screamed in terror.

Farrow looked around again, decided – and strode back to the mattress. Jessica was beginning to sit up. In the next instant, Farrow seized a handful of her hair and dragged her from the mattress. Jessica screamed in pain, twisting and grabbing at the hand in her hair.

'*You say you love me, Tommy. But will you let me love you to death?*'

Hanging on to his wrist, Jessica thrashed, but could only cling on as Farrow dragged her to the 'Y'-shaped bench. He was still grinning, but his glittering eyes reflected a deep inner well of hatred as he pulled her to the open part of the 'Y'. Jessica tried to rise, got to her knees – and then Farrow pulled her up the rest of the way and, still with a fist ravelled in her hair, hit her back-handed with the other. Stunned again, Jessica fell back onto the bench. In a matter of moments, he had strapped her arms to her sides on the table. Spittle fell like gossamer

301

from his lips as he finished. Jessica's eyes began to focus at last. For the first time, she could see her assailant.

On the screen, a young man was screaming.

'Farrow! You bastard ...'

'Now we *know* that's not true,' said Farrow through gritted teeth.

He slapped her across the face, and blood flowed from a cut lip.

'Because we know who our daddy is, don't we?'

He seized Jessica's leg, and she lashed out with it and caught him off guard. He stumbled and almost fell, but seizing the leg again in rage, he slammed it down on to the bench and strapped it. Yelling hoarsely, Jessica tried to ram her free knee between Farrow's legs.

'*In her eyes – desire! In her veins – the blood of a lusting She Wasp!*'

'Naughty, naughty,' said Farrow, and then strapped her other leg to the bench. Jessica twisted her head from side to side, still yelling at him. Farrow stood back, standing in the centre of the 'Y', between Jessica's legs. He was breathing heavily, now stepping forward to press his crotch between her legs, grabbing the outside of her thighs with both hands.

'*Starring Deborah Steele in her most amazing role yet!*'

'Oh, no ...' Jessica realised his intent with dawning horror.

Farrow licked his lips, eyes glittering.

'Always wanted to go down, didn't you, Jessica? Always leading the fucking way, always in control, always knowing better than anyone else. And where did it get us? Back to square one. Have you got any idea how angry that made me? Any idea what I'd planned for you? No? I've seen your kind before, Jessica. Seen you cruising by in your chauffeur-driven cars, talking your business-talk into your fucking portable telephones, or giving out your rich-bitch instructions. I've stood on the streets in the rain watching you and your kind, cruising on by to your high-society business dinners.'

'Farrow, for God's sake!'

'Time to teach you a few lessons, rich bitch.'

He stood back again, now looking at the medical trolley by his side, with its instruments laid out neatly on the tray.

'*Deborah Steele,*' said the news announcer, '*the Hollywood actress, is missing feared dead ...*'

'Now I'm going to show you what going down really means.'

He leaned back and plucked the black leather leotard from the trolley and began to take off his shirt.

'Please, Farrow. Look ... I just want to get out of this place ... just like you ...'

Farrow laughed and Jessica could no longer see what he was doing, but she could hear the rustle of his belt, his trousers.

'What makes you think I *want* to get out of here any more?' laughed

302

Farrow. It was a harsh and bitter sound. 'Maybe I want to stay, after all. Ever thought of that?'

'We've got to find the others . . .'

'Fuck the others,' said Farrow. 'But first . . .'

The distorted music had reached a new pitch. A female vocalist had joined in, was moaning along with the music. The collage of film clips continued on the screen. And from where Farrow stood there was a new sound, like leather being stretched. He grunted in effort. Jessica tried to look up, but still could not see what he was doing.

'Farrow . . . let me . . . I'll give you . . .' In helplessness and rage, Jessica screamed aloud then, at the top of her voice, shaking her head from side to side. Her arms were tightly bound by the straps. It was impossible to move them.

Then Farrow stepped forward again, between her legs.

He was wearing the skin-tight black leather suit. There were studs at the seams; down the arms, at the belt, and below the belt.

'For God's *sake*, Farrow! What the hell are you . . . ?'

Farrow grinned again and leaned over the trolley. He picked something up and seemed to wince, as if the very touch of the object had sent some kind of electric shock through his body. But now he was smiling again as the thing in his hand began to emit a harsh electric buzzing.

'Farrow! Let me UP!'

'Want to screw, Jessica?'

The lights in the chamber suddenly changed. They began to strobe and flash, sending shadows swooping and diving all over the black stone walls.

'Time for your lesson,' said Farrow, bringing the whirring thing down towards his crotch.

And then Jessica suddenly froze on the bench. Farrow laughed aloud, looked up to watch the terror on her face as he began – but then saw that she was not looking at him any more. She had twisted her head away from him, and was looking over to the left. The look of horror on her face and in her eyes was directed at something over by the door, something that had even overwhelmed the horror of Farrow and what he was about to do.

He followed her gaze.

Jessica could not control the feeling that enveloped her, and began to shiver uncontrollably.

Because the shape-changing thing was at the door.

It was the thing that had looked like Roy, then Gloria, and then that monstrous shape from Draegerman's movie.

It had changed again, back to Roy.

It stood there at the threshold, arms braced in the doorway, glaring at them.

But maybe this was best; to die as Gloria had died, rather than at

303

the hands of Farrow and the insane torment that he had planned for her. Jessica could feel herself drifting away, could feel coldness creeping through her limbs. Please God, would she die before the thing could get to her?

The thing screamed, a bellow of rage.

But it had not opened its mouth, and Jessica's body was suddenly jarred as Farrow lunged away from the bench, almost tipping it over in his rage.

And in the doorway, Roy raised the gun and pointed it directly at him.

'Stop right there, Farrow!'

But Farrow, still screaming like a wild animal, seized the trolley and whirled it from where it stood. The instruments on the upper tray flew through the air, clattering to the stone floor. Using the upended trolley like a shield, he charged across the room at Roy. Startled by his bestial screaming and violent attack, Roy dodged into the room and fired. The shot punched a hole through the trolley, missed Farrow's head by an inch and then screamed ricocheting around the chamber. In the next instant, Farrow and his trolley smashed into Roy. They fell thrashing together to the floor, Farrow grabbing at the gun. There was a sharp tearing pain in Roy's side.

'*Roy!*' Someone else was shouting from the corridor outside, footsteps clattering on stone.

Still screaming his rage, Farrow elbowed Roy in the face. With feral strength, he wrenched the gun out of his hand. Staggering to his feet, he threw himself backwards, his weight slamming the door shut. In the next moment, he had thrown the bolt – and the door instantly juddered as weight was put against it from the outside. There were muffled voices in the corridor as someone began to pound at the door with the flats of their hands.

'Roy!' It was Susan's voice. 'For God's sake, what's *happening*?'

On the floor, Roy shoved the trolley aside and started to rise.

'Someone else who needs a lesson,' said Farrow, grinning his insane grin. He raised the gun, pointing it at Roy's face.

The music pounded.

The swirling lights made shadows leap and crawl around them.

'Come on, then!' yelled Farrow. 'Try to take it off me! You were the big man, always wanting the fucking gun. So come on. Take it if you've got the guts!'

Roy looked around him. There was nothing he could do.

Snarling in disgust, Farrow pulled the trigger.

The hammer fell on an empty chamber – and Farrow's look of rage and disgust instantly turned to a childish look of stupidity, at the impossibility of what had happened. Roy seized the punctured trolley and lunged forward, swinging it in a wide arc. Farrow was still looking

304

at the gun in his hand as the trolley smashed across his upper torso. The impact slammed him against the door, and the frenzied attempts of those on the other side were renewed as Roy seized him by the neck. Farrow clawed at his eyes then, and both men staggered back into the chamber.

Jessica tried to scream, tried to yell at someone to help, but something was wrong. Something deep down, something that had to do with Gloria's death – and what she had done, instead of trying to help her. It was as if everything special and good, everything that made Jessica human, had been drained out of her back there in the studio swamp. Farrow's attack had only served to complete that trauma. Helpless, now no longer able even to struggle against the binding straps, Jessica could only lie there trembling and watch as Roy and Farrow fell to the stone floor in a ferocious embrace.

Something was happening to the strange bed with its sailing-ship wheel and its nest of leather snakes in the centre. Jessica's eyes were drawn hypnotically to the blurring outline of the bed as the two men struggled and writhed on the stone floor. It was as if a sudden heat haze had risen between Jessica and the bed, a haze that was making the bed's shape distorted and fractured. Jessica kept on watching as the bed began to dissolve from view.

Love me, Jack, said Deborah Steele from the chamber wall.

Farrow still had the gun in his hand, tried to use it as a club as he lay astride Roy. But Roy grabbed his wrist, sank his teeth into the bare skin and twisted his head. Farrow screamed, the empty gun clattered across the floor, and a splash of red sprinkled the leather sleeve of his bizarre suit, spattering Roy's face as he twisted on the floor, throwing Farrow off balance.

'Be my baby,' purred Deborah.

Jessica watched as the outline of the bed blurred to the point where every aspect of its detail was a confusion of shimmering light. Were the things that looked like leather straps in the centre of the bed alive? Were they twisting within that formless mass like snakes? The shimmering effect was hurting her eyes. She blinked, and then the bed was no longer there. Instead, it had become something that increased her violent inner trembling. For a moment, she could not breathe, could feel a pounding inside her that was even louder than the distorted, wailing music. In the bed's place was a formless, twisting cloud of fog. It was the same undulating fog that had flowed over the surface of the studio swamp; the same living fog that had swarmed into the thing that looked like Roy and had transformed him into a living cine-nightmare. Jessica saw it hanging in the air, occupying exactly the same position as the bed. The curling, poisonous wisps seemed to undulate and to watch as . . .

'Tell me that you love me, and I'll never go away.'

. . . Farrow brought his knee up between Roy's legs. The blow was

305

off centre but effective enough. Roy yelled in pain and was flung from Farrow's prostrate body. Farrow scrabbled to his feet, clutching at his torn wrist and leaving a bloody smear on his chest. Roy gagged on the floor, clutching at his genitals with one hand, trying to push himself to his knees with the other. Uttering another feral cry, Farrow ran at him. Roy tried to twist away, but could not move quickly enough. Farrow kicked him in the stomach, the blow flinging him over to crash against the foot of the weights frame. The iron structure rattled and creaked as Farrow rushed in and . . .

'I can't live without you.'

. . . Jessica saw the fog begin to unfurl and creep through the air, away from the spot where it had materialised, drifting with a fearful sense of purpose towards the two figures in the centre of the room . . .

'I'll do anything if you let me stay.'

. . . and Farrow tried to kick out at Roy again. Roy thrust himself backwards into the frame, kicking the bench towards Farrow as he approached. Savagely, Farrow bent down and grabbed it, flinging it away across the chamber and lashing out again at Roy as he twisted behind the metal supports. Roy lunged forward and seized the rubber hose between Farrow's legs and yanked hard. Farrow tottered on one foot, clutched at the frame for support – and in the next moment, the entire frame rocked on its supports. Roy yelled aloud, yanking again, and Farrow was forced to grip at the parallel bars with both hands as his centre of gravity was shifted. The frame – for whatever purpose the damnable thing had been invented – could not take his weight. With a screech, it tore from its ground supports and Farrow fell away from Roy, taking the structure with him. A metal bar tore from the support where Roy lay, the rough edge scoring a wound across his cheek and temple. Roy clambered out of the collapsing framework as Farrow, yelling in rage, brought the structure down on top of himself. The supporting metal poles fell apart at the joints, the parallel bar pinning Farrow to the ground. He struggled beneath it as Roy knelt watching him, gagging at the pain between his legs, and trying to regain his strength, and . . .

'Be good to me. And I'll be good to you.'

. . . Jessica wanted to scream, wanted to give vent to the fear inside, but was struck mute as the rolling, coiling fog paused in mid-air behind the combatants. She knew instinctively that it was watching the struggle, watching and thinking. Then, as suddenly as if a blast of icy air had invaded the room, the fog swept away from them, snaking and streaming across the chamber. Jessica watched wide-eyed as it streaked to the chamber wall, pooled there as if waiting for the last of its wraith-like, straggling wisps to catch up – and then began to roil along the wall towards her, undulating and crawling as . . .

'Anything you want, anything at all. Love me. Be my baby.'

. . . Farrow kicked the parallel bar away from him. Roy could feel its shivering, ringing impact on the stone slabs beneath him. He clutched at the shattered remnants of the frame-base, tried to wrench one of the twisted poles free to use as a weapon. The bar remained stuck fast as Farrow stood erect, blood dripping from his crimson fingers to the floor. His face was spectrally white, the swooping shadows in the insane chamber making him look inhuman in his rage. Roy tried to rise, still wrenching at the iron pole. It would not come free from its socket. He paused then, as the wretched music wailed and howled and shadows chased shadows. But Farrow did not scream with rage again, did not launch himself over the wreckage of the frame with bloodied claw-hands outstretched. He simply stood, smiling his ghastly smile and with the blood dripping from his hand. Slowly, he began to back off. Was it over? Had Farrow had enough? Roy still could not rise, the pain sickening and crippling in his loins. Farrow bumped into the chamber wall behind him, his ghastly smile still intact. Slowly, he turned his head to look at something projecting from the wall to his right, at shoulder level. He reached for it, pulled it out of its clamp on the wall – then turned to look back at him. Roy crawled away from the frame-base and its still firmly fixed metal rod, looking for something else to use as a weapon – *anything* else – when Farrow began to walk slowly forward again. The object he had taken from the wall was now clearly visible.

It was a mediaeval mace-and-chain.

But this was no harmless movie prop. This was a bound-leather handle connected to a twelve-inch length of thick chain, attached in turn to a spiked metal ball. Farrow twisted his wrist and the metal ball whirled in a tight, vicious circle around the handle. He stepped over the ruined frame and Roy looked around desperately for something with which he might protect himself as . . .

. . . Jessica realised that she had stopped breathing and sucked in air at last in fast, short intakes that sounded like sobs of despair. The undulating patch of fog had stopped crawling along the wall towards her. It paused mere inches from where she lay, at a point in the wall where one of the three-claw handles projected from the brickwork. Jessica could not reflect on why there was a door handle where there was no door. The fog and what it could potentially become was all that occupied her mind, the sounds of the combat to her right hardly registering at all. As the lead guitarist in the hellish soundtrack screeched into a solo for damned souls, the fog suddenly began to seep *into* the wall – and Jessica could see that there was, after all, a door of sorts there. The fog had found the almost invisible door frame, was even now vanishing into the brickwork. Jessica was still sobbing when the last tendril of the wraith-like mist vanished into the wall and . . .

. . . Roy hobbled to his right, to where Jessica was strapped to the bench. He had seen the instruments falling from the medical trolley when Farrow had upended it and used it as a shield. If he could get there, and find something on the floor . . . ? But it seemed that Farrow had second-guessed him. He darted around the remains of the frame, quickly stepping between the other two. Roy could see Jessica on the bench. Her head was turned from him, he could see her chest rising and falling quickly. Was she *staring* at the wall? Farrow strode forward then, whirling the mace-and-chain around his head. And in Roy's mind now, he heard Frank Wells from *The Wayside* say 'Only two ways to go', before he took the initiative and started the fight with the bikers. Stay and take it or . . .

'*Love me, Jack,*' said Deborah Steele. '*Love me to death.*'

Refusing to allow the pain to debilitate him any further, putting everything he had into the effort, Roy threw himself forward from his crouching position with arms outstretched. Farrow was already coming on fast. Roy's sudden lunge took him directly under the vicious whirling circle of the mace-and-chain. He grabbed Farrow in a body-hug, the force of his charge whumping the air out of Farrow's body. Both men collided with Jessica's bench. The impact span the bench away, and this time Jessica was able to yell aloud as it suddenly tipped on to its side, the impact jarring her body. She lay there helplessly, facing them as the two men fell heavily to the floor. Farrow could not bring the mace-and-chain to bear; instead he rammed the handle-grip against the side of Roy's head. Roy grabbed for it, then his other hand groped at the ground beneath them. Something sharp scored his fingers. He gripped it, pulled it aloft – a wicked, ragged-edged drill bit – and now Farrow had dropped his own weapon to seize Roy's wrist as Roy tried to bring the bit down into his face. Farrow dragged a leg up beneath Roy as they squirmed in their death embrace on the floor, got his knee to Roy's chest and dragged him over to the side. Now he was on top of him, still with his knee planted in his chest as . . .

The wall behind them began to open.

Now there was a door where there had previously been no door. The three-claw handle was turning, and a four-foot-wide, six-foot-high section of the brickwork was slowly opening into the chamber. Jessica could see the hideous fog rolling and undulating in the recess behind the door. And a figure was emerging slowly from the fog. It was the silhouette of . . . a woman? The figure itself was unmoving, resting on some kind of platform at floor level, a platform that was sliding out of the recess. It was raising both arms as it emerged, arms clad in black leather gloves, studded like the suit Farrow wore. There was something mechanical about the movement. The fog remained in the alcove as the platform slid from it, revealing the figure as it trundled up behind both men on the floor . . .

And somehow, Jessica was able to scream then. It was a scream of denial that terror could be heaped on terror in this way, a scream that tried to gainsay the dreadful shattering of self that had taken place within her. It was also a scream of recognition.

The figure on the trundling platform was that of a woman. A woman dressed in a black leather corset, cut low to reveal cleavage. With spider web lace from the black-leather studded collar around her neck to her shoulders. With black leather gloves covering her forearms and thigh-length black leather boots. The hair of this dominatrix was black and lustrous, falling over her shoulders.

It was Deborah Steele.

Dead and embalmed; thin yellow flesh stretched hideously over the once-beautiful face. It was a face that was still recognisable from the newsreel footage and movie clips that were showing continuously on the chamber wall, even though the eye sockets were black and empty. The mouth was pouting, with bright red lipstick and gloss. Even though the cheeks were hideously sunken, an attempt had still been made to apply rouge. The head was cocked to one side in a parody of some winsome expression. The arms remained outstretched, desiring an embrace. Deborah Steele, troublesome film star kidnapped by her former lover and present director, her death meticulously planned and staged. Now dead and preserved as some hideous and depraved parody of a sex doll, no longer able to make trouble or answer back. An automaton, existing now only for the gratification of her master.

Jessica's scream had an instantaneous effect on the two struggling men, both faces twisting around to look at her. Seeing the look of terror on her face, and now becoming aware of the trundling movement behind him, Farrow brought all his weight to bear on the knee that pinned Roy to the floor. Roy cried out in agony as Farrow lurched backwards away from him, spun around – and came face to face with the hideous love-doll, arms outstretched as if to take him in an embrace.

Farrow screamed, staggering to one side, away from its clutch.

The doll juddered to a halt and Farrow could only stand there, mesmerised, as the embalmed corpse of Deborah Steele cocked its head towards the other shoulder, some mechanism within the platform and wired through the body making a ratcheting sound as it did so.

'*Love me, Jack.*' The doll's lips did not move, but somewhere within it a tape recorder had been installed, the words edited from lines of dialogue Deborah had spoken in various movies, words edged with crackling static. '*Tell me that you love me . . . and I'll never go away.*'

Farrow stood staring at the apparition on its moving platform, a hideous mélange of taxidermy and animatronics.

'*Can't* (click) *live without you . . .* (click) *. . . Jack. I'll do anything, if you let me stay.*'

And Roy seized Farrow by the shoulder from behind, bringing the blunt end of the drill-bit attachment down across his head. Farrow grunted and fell on the spot, sprawling at the feet of Draegerman's hideous love-doll.

'*Be good to me . . . and I'll be good to you.*'

Roy staggered back across the chamber to where Jessica lay. Breathing heavily, pain racking his body, he seized the straps that were binding her torso and tried to unbuckle them. Still struggling with the buckle, he began to hack at the straps with the sharp edge of the drill bit.

'It's okay . . . okay . . .'

The others in the corridor were still hammering on the bolted door. The shadows still swirled madly to the cacophony of music, and Deborah Steele cocked her head back to the other side with an audible sound of inner gears and pulleys, promises of love and obedience still issuing from the hideously pouting mouth. Farrow lay as if he was worshipping at her feet.

But Jessica's eyes were fixed on what was happening back in the recess from which the late Ms Steele had emerged. The fog was curling slowly out of the aperture back into the chamber, tentacles of mist groping and feeling their way along the elaborate platform device on which the doll stood. The strap around Jessica's waist came free, and she clutched at Roy's shoulders for support as he began working on the straps that bound each of her legs.

'Roy . . . Roy . . .'

'It's okay. You'll be free in a moment. It's all over.'

'It's . . . not all over. For God's sake, look!'

And Roy looked back as one of Jessica's legs slid from the frayed straps. He saw the fog creeping into the room.

'It's alive,' hissed Jessica. 'That fog. I've seen it before. It's *alive*.'

Grim-faced, Roy tore the last buckle away and Jessica was free. Groaning at the assortment of pains that Farrow had inflicted, he stood, pulling Jessica up with him. The fog was completely out of the recess now, and was enveloping the love-doll as it cocked its head again.

'*Anything you want, Jack . . . (click) . . . anything at all.*'

Arms around each other, Roy and Jessica staggered across the chamber to the bolted door. Jessica cried out again as they moved, and Roy looked over his shoulder to see that, somehow, the pulsing mass of ectoplasm was streaming into the empty black eye sockets and mouth of Draegerman's plaything. Faster than he could have believed possible, the fog had vanished into Deborah Steele's body. Now her voice began to slow down as if the freezing fog was damaging the internal mechanisms.

'*Anything you waaaant, Jaaaaaaaack . . .*'

Roy threw the bolt back on the door, and Bobby almost fell into the chamber. The others were pressing close behind. Boone, as ever, kept himself far back against the corridor wall. Susan saw Roy's battered and bloody face.

'What the *hell* happened to you . . . ?'

Roy pushed Jessica ahead, almost into Susan's arms. Bobby was looking into the chamber in awe and wonder. Roy leaned back to grab him by the sleeve and pull him out.

'We've got to get away from here!' yelled Jessica. 'Something *bad* is going to happen . . .' The force of her panic pushed them all out into the corridor.

'Where's my mother?' Bobby took Jessica by the shoulder, looking back into the chamber and seeing no sign of her.

On the floor, Farrow began to rise groggily to his knees.

'Where's my *mother*?'

Jessica could only shake her head. Face wild with anxiety, Bobby began to shake her. Roy grabbed at his arm, tried to wrest him away.

And in the chamber, the living corpse of Deborah Steele suddenly wrenched one leg free from its supporting mechanism with a sound like tearing cloth. The arms lowered, then gripped the supporting bar at waist height as it wrenched the other leg free. The mouth was no longer pouting. It was stretched into a skeletal grin, the withered thin flesh of the face tearing at each corner of the mouth, giving the thing a leering smile. In its eyes sockets, two orbs of fog undulated and glowed.

Shadows chased and swarmed over it. In a stiff and horrible travesty of a seductive pose, it brought its glove-clad hands up over its thighs and hips, and then raised them to its face. Now the stiff, claw-like fingers were moving behind its head, throwing out the long black hair behind. It tossed its head with a sound of ripping cloth as the black tresses of hair fell over its shoulders.

Still crouched on the floor with his back to the doll, Farrow became aware of movement and looked over his shoulder.

The living-dead face of Deborah Steele looked down on him, smile widening to reveal the skeletal teeth.

'*Love me, Farrow*,' said the thing.

And this time the voice was not a tape.

'*Be my baby*.'

Farrow uttered a strangled sob of terror. Still on hands and knees, he scrabbled away from the thing towards the chamber door.

The Daemon stepped down from the platform behind him.

'For God's sake!' hissed Jessica, pushing Bobby away as he tried to shake the answer to his question out of her. 'We've got to get away from here. *Now!*'

'Help *meeeeeeee!*' shrieked Farrow, as he scrabbled towards them on his hands and knees. His eyes were wild and staring, foam flecked his lips.

311

Behind him, the Daemon took three quick and fluid strides, reached down and seized the collar of his leather suit. Refusing to look back, face rapidly turning crimson as he still scrabbled to get away, Farrow opened his mouth to scream again for help. But the grip on his collar choked the words in his throat.

The others saw at last what was happening and stood rooted to the spot as they gazed at the hideous travesty of a face with its burning, luminous eyes. As it held Farrow on the ground, it looked slowly up at them. Jessica flinched and moved back against the wall. The horrifying face was begining to change. The fog in its eyes suddenly swarmed from the sockets, began to envelop the thing's head. Now the visage was covered in a spider's web of ectoplasm. Jessica unconsciously held out a hand as if to ward off what might happen next.

The mask of fog undulated and curled as they watched.

And then suddenly dissolved and parted like steam, wraith-wisps flying apart and vanishing – to reveal the changes that had taken place there.

'Oh God, no . . .' said Susan.

Everyone in that instant recalled what Gloria had said about the movie that Deborah Steele had been working on when she disappeared. *It was called* She Wasp. *Typical J.D. picture – woman stung by swarm of South American hornets gets home, turns into a queen wasp at night, flits around back alleys and drive-ins screwing and eating any teenager she can get her stinger into. Real try-out for method acting.*

The corpse-face of Deborah Steele had become as one with her role for Jack Draegerman. The mask of fog had created something that would perhaps have been the envy of Draegerman's special effects crew, but which now struck dread and fear into the others' hearts as they stood and looked. The head was the head of a wasp: the black multi-faceted orbs that were eyes, the chitinous yellow armour of the head, the horribly working and greedy mandibles. But there was still about that frightful mutation the essence of Deborah Steele; her long black hair still hung down from that dreadfully changed visage and over its shoulders. But above all, there was the dreadful essence of the thing that had used the fiction to create the flesh.

'*We want to be alone,*' said the thing in a hideously cracked voice, the mandibles and mouth-parts chittering and drooling.

Farrow threw out a hand towards them, now scrabbling with the other at his throat as he straightened, brought to his knees by the thing which stood over him. It looked down at him again, tossing its black hair and laughing. It was a hideous and sickening sound.

'Please . . .' Farrow managed to squeeze out, eyes bulging in terror.

'*Come on, honey,*' said the Daemon. '*Let's screw . . .*'

The Daemon looked quickly up towards them all again, and something flew from its jaws, something that looked like a flashing tentacle of the hideous fog. The sudden movement made them all shrink back.

And in the next instant, the chamber door swung savagely shut, the shuddering crash echoing away down the corridor in which they stood. Behind the door, the sounds of the porno music were muffled.

'We've got to get *away*!' Jessica pulled herself away from Bobby.

'What . . . ?' Susan could find nothing to say. She weakly pointed at the door, unable to accept what she had just seen inside.

Roy moved instinctively to the door.

'Are you *mad*?' shouted Boone.

Susan grabbed his arm, dragged him away.

And then the screaming began from within.

'There's nothing we can do!' hissed Boone, eyes bulging from his head. 'Nothing!'

The sounds behind the door continued. Hideously fearful, shrieks of utter agony. Those shrieks died into a low dreadful moaning.

Now there was a sound like tearing leather – and the shrieking began again.

'*Love me Farrow*,' implored the hideous voice.

There was nothing they could do. Sick with horror, they staggered away as the sounds of Farrow being loved to death filled the corridor.

PART FOUR

MAELSTROM

Extract from *Cinefacts*: November issue.

Sick, sick, sick!

*What is it, I asked myself while sitting through the 'unauthorised'
Jack Draegerman Retrospective Film Festival that makes
decent-minded critics heap such lavish praise on movies which were
regarded at the time of their initial release as 'gross', 'perverted' and
'vomit-inducing'? What is it that makes presumably decent-minded
cinemagoers flock to see such unmitigated garbage? I would like to
think that it's the ridiculous hype surrounding the rediscovery of
Draegerman's so-called lost movies, and that it's another passing
fad. But with several of the big-name directors now heaping praises
on his movies and – God help us – planning remakes, I can only
presume that some people simply get their kicks from watching such
sadistic nonsense.*

*At first, I was willing to believe that there might be some camp
value in movies made in the seventies and eighties but deliberately set
in the 1950s, complete with all the clichés, over-acting and monsters
in zip-fasteners that seem to be remembered so fondly (albeit not
by me, I hasten to add. I outgrew such childish horrors at a very
early stage).*

*But where is the camp value in seeing such a formerly respectable
actress as Gloria Pernell being eaten alive by what looks like a monstrous
leech in Cape Sinistre? What humour is to be obtained from such
disgusting and such horrifying effects? Who gives a damn whether
teenage suicides can haunt the highways to such nauseating effect in
Hot Rod Hell? If this is a camp take on movies that were already
camp, why aren't the audiences paralysed with laughter? Whether or
not the torture-rituals in Macumba are actual documentary footage
or faked seems to me to be beside the point. If it is faked, then in
my view it reflects badly on an audience's requirements by way of
'entertainment'. If it is actual footage, then not only does it discredit
everyone involved but must surely require official investigation and, if
necessary, prosecution.*

She Wasp *takes the sickness to new depths, using the well-worn
genre staple of man-into-beast or in this case woman-into-insect. I
was quite unprepared for the clinical attention to detail by which
Draegerman's title creature attacks and consumes its victims. And
for those who have praised the so-called 'stinger-attack' sequences for
'wild-life documentary reality', it seems to me that the real victims
are those whose gullibility and utter lack of taste have led them to
heap praises on such crass, sick wastes of celluloid.*

The retrospective finished with a showing of the movie which has caused the hoo-hah and which has turned over a very nasty stone to reveal the Draegerman talent in all its glory: A Multitude of Sins. *I have never in my life walked out on a movie, have always held to the belief that it's a critic's duty to at least sit through a movie in its entirety without passing verdict. But I'm afraid that this was a rule I had no compunction in overturning on viewing only the pre-credits sequence. After hours of watching such atrocity, I had no intention of taking any more.*

If this is the future of the horror movie, God help us all. Why not take it one step further? Bring back gladiators and arenas. It seems to me that the audience with whom I viewed the film had everything in common with the ancient spectators of that sport. If you're looking for any sense of film-craft, taste or basic morality – leave well alone.

Sick, sick, sick!

(Ed: For the record, the Draegerman canon comprises: Swamp Water Woman/Cape Sinistre/At Death's Door / Macumba/ Ten Little Mannikins *(lawsuit settled out of court with the estate of Agatha Christie)/* A Multitude of Sins / Speed Demon/ Hot Rod Hell / Jack's Back Again / She Wasp / Spider Venom /Somewhere South of Midnight. *P.S. Take a sick-bag.*

ONE

They had been in the sewer system for two hours when Taylor found his first real problem with Talbot's map.

For the most part, the main pipes down which they had travelled had been more or less the same as the first: concrete walkways on either side, wide enough for one man at a time and with the ceiling usually at about head height. Changing direction at crossroads and intersections of waste pipes had been the only real difficulty, necessitating stepping down into the sludge – some of it shin-deep, but most of it waist-deep – before reaching the other side. There were strange sounds down here, too; sounds that made no sense. Sometimes, they sounded like someone calling. At other times, like the echoes of steel doors slamming; and constantly, whether the sludge in these pipes was moving or not, there was the sound of running water. They had not spoken a great deal since their first entry through the grille; but when they did, their voices seemed to echo interminably.

Now Taylor had stopped at another crossroads and was looking at the map. From his expression it seemed clear that it did not correlate with what Talbot had drawn. The main pipe down which they were travelling curved left, but at this intersection another smaller pipe led straight on, with another to the right.

'It must be this one,' said Moss, after a while. 'To the left.'

'Why must it be?' asked Taylor, eyes still fixed on the map.

'Because a sewer rat couldn't get through the pipe ahead, or the pipe on the right. Look at them. Neither have got concrete walkways, and the shit is almost up to the ceiling on both.' Moss began to move to the left.

'Wrong way,' said Taylor quietly. 'We've got to go ahead.'

'Are you fucking *joking*?' demanded Moss.

Taylor looked up. His face remained calm. 'Remember what I said? About doing this alone? Either one of you change your mind and feel like heading back, do so. But the only way is straight on.' Without another word, he shoved the map into the waterproof belt around his waist and then sat on the concrete shelf, adjusting his equipment. Moss looked

319

at Den, as if expecting some kind of back-up. Instead, Den sat next to Taylor and waited. Taylor looked up at him, and nodded again.

'Okay, you've got masks in your packs. I suggest you put them on. And take out one of those oxygen cylinders. There's enough space for headroom through there, but we don't know if there are any methane gas pockets. We walk into one, and we won't walk out of it again unless we've got some clean air. Here . . .' Taylor showed Den how to adjust the air intake from his portable oxygen cylinder into the mask. He looked up at Moss when he had finished, expecting him to make some kind of decision about going on or turning back.

'Shit!' exclaimed Moss.

'And lots of it,' added Den.

Grudgingly, Moss sat down beside them. 'Show me.'

Taylor went through the routine again. When he was sure that they both knew what they were doing, he slithered over the edge of the concrete shelf and into the foul black water. Den followed him instantly. The water was chest-deep.

'Don't we need ropes, or something?' asked Moss. He stretched one leg down into the water, as if testing bath temperature.

'No,' said Taylor. 'I'll lead the way. Den, you put one hand on my shoulder. Moss, you put yours on Den. Anyone feels a hand slip away, the others turn back to help. Simple as that.'

'How far is it?' asked Den.

'About a hundred and fifty feet. Not far.'

'Far enough,' said Moss in distaste.

'Masks,' said Taylor, and they all put them on, turning the air valves on their cylinders.

Taylor then turned and ploughed through the water to the entrance to the pipe ahead. Turning again to make sure that the others were right behind, he gave the thumbs-up. Den smacked his hand down on Taylor's right shoulder, waited until Moss had done the same to him, and then tapped Taylor's left shoulder to signal that they were all ready.

Taylor moved on into the pipe.

There seemed to be nothing solid under their feet. Just a bed of ooze into which their feet sank to the shins. The rippling black water came up to their chins, the roof of the pipe perhaps eight inches from their heads.

Den forced himself to remain calm, unable to cast aside an image of himself suddenly putting down his foot and sinking instantly into the quagmire beneath. He could see himself being sucked into some kind of pothole, arms waving, fingers grasping, the mask being torn from his face. He could imagine the others up above somewhere, scrabbling down through the black ooze in vain to find him. He tried to supplant it with another image; an image that reminded him forcefully of why

320

he was here and why he was going through this hellish experience. It was an image of himself at the local municipal swimming pool, teaching Carl and Bennet to swim while Susan sat at the side, watching over their clothes, reading a magazine and looking up occasionally to smile. Carl wasn't keen on the water, had a thing about getting his head wet – and Den had been spending time trying to reassure him, showing him how to breathe, how to hold himself in the water, building his confidence. How could he talk about confidence to Carl if he did not have confidence in what he was doing now? And that image of Susan was strong and pure. He concentrated on it now, kept her smile firmly in the forefront of his mind. He would get through this bloody sewer and find her. There was no alternative. He kept his inner eye on the face he loved, and his breathing calm and regular.

Miraculously, Taylor's torch beam suddenly shot off into the darkness ahead to reveal a large, open chamber.

They were out of the tunnel.

Taylor forged ahead, swimming to the concrete shelf; turning now to let his beam play on the water where Den and Moss were emerging, careful not to let the beam shine in their eyes and cause any kind of panic at the last moment.

In seconds, Den and Moss had joined him. Taking off their masks, they climbed up the concrete shelf to sit on the side, water runnelling and splashing back into the pipe.

'Switch off your oxygen,' said Taylor. 'We'll need every bit we've got if there are any more pipes like that one.'

'How many more are you expecting?' asked Moss. 'Or doesn't the map tell you that?'

'The map tells me about the system in here. It doesn't tell me the water levels.'

'You mean it doesn't tell us how deep the shit is,' replied Moss.

'Didn't you know we were in deep shit from the beginning?' asked Den.

'I was wrong about you,' said Taylor at last, looking at Den.

'Don't do me any favours,' he replied.

'I'm not. There's worse ahead of us. But I was wrong about you, and I wanted you to know that before we go any further.'

Den looked down, adjusting his mask before putting it away in his waterproof satchel.

'Want me to play a violin?' asked Moss.

'No,' said Taylor simply, standing again. He shone the torch down the tunnel ahead, took out the map and after a brief look said: 'Well, gents. Let's take another walk.'

Silently, they followed him into the darkness.

321

TWO

Fisher walked through the streets, watching the trouble escalate all around him. Somehow immune from it all, he watched the kids psyching themselves up, gathering on the corners, marching with as much street-swagger as they could muster towards The Rock.

As usual, he was high; and as he walked through the night, he felt as if he was floating two feet above the pavement. He was untouchable, nothing could harm him. Even so, some deep inner voice wondered what it would be like *not* to be taking drugs every waking hour. He knew that there was no way on God's earth that he would be walking so cheerfully, observing the ruckus all around so casually. Because without those drugs, the terror would consume him. It was a complex, though muddled, situation in his head. Part of him knew that he was dependant on the drugs to keep the fear at bay, another part wanted not to be taking drugs at all. Part of him admired and was deeply grateful for the drugs and protection that he was given; another part of him hated the fact that he was living as he did, and in turn that hatred spilled over to the people who were protecting him. Was he being used as some kind of instrument in a power play? Was the fact that he was being sheltered after saving those kids from the Walkway on Draegerman's Rock supposed to show how caring and loving and generous and *loyal* these people could be? On the rare occasions when he had been out of his room, he had felt as if he was on display; a living symbol to all who saw him of something that he could only barely grasp in his drug-induced state. But tonight, these questions were not at the forefront of his mind.

He had slipped away without telling anyone else back at *The Pool*, not even Tanya – the girl who said she loved him, but of whom he was so deeply unsure. Even in his torpor, he had been aware of the feeling that had been building since Taylor's arrival on the scene. He could feel the agitation in the air; the feeling that something big was about to happen, something that everyone wanted a part in. Tonight, it seemed as if everyone he saw or spoke to was at boiling point. So, he had slipped open his window and made his way down the fire escape at the side of the building.

He had never been on these streets without an escort, ever since his arrival in the neighbourhood. Even drugged, that fear had crowded in on him. But tonight was a different thing altogether, because he too had fallen prey to the same need for street action that was agitating everyone in the neighbourhood around The Rock. Except that it was much more personal for Terry Fisher.

Taylor's arrival had done something to him inside. Even now, his memory of the man standing in his room, just standing and asking questions, had done something to him. Then, the time when he had sat at the back of the Business Room, a rare privilege, as Taylor had been questioned by Mother. That same feeling had made him suddenly want more than anything else to be going with Taylor and the others into The Rock.

Fisher could not remember anything of what had happened to him when he had been taken back into Draegerman's Rock. By all accounts, it had been two weeks between the time that he had saved those kids, been beaten and taken back inside The Rock to the time when he had been found wandering the streets, half insane. His experience in there had put him into his current state, but as a mental defence, his subconscious mind refused to release any details of what had gone on. Even his dreams, even his nightmares, betrayed no clues or symbols. He felt sure that if he *did* remember, then he would surely die insane. And God, how he *hated* Draegerman. It was a hate which had been dulled, sedated and distant. But Taylor's arrival had brought it out of the fog, stood it in the forefront of his mind – and honed it to a razor edge. It was the only real focus in his mind.

He walked and watched as a mixed group of people stood cheering and throwing empty beer cans at a derelict house as it was torched. When flames suddenly gushed through the front windows of the house in a blossom of angry orange flame, that crowd had at first reared back, then began cheering as the fire really took hold. He stood for a long time then, watching the house be consumed by the fire. After a while, it seemed that the flames were alive: some monstrous and voracious animal, chewing up the plaster and the brickwork and the wooden beams; coughing and gagging out sparks through the ruptured walls and windows. Fisher had watched those sparks gush skywards in a dissipating cloud, watched the last of those sparks trail away into the night sky – and had seen the silhouette of The Rock as the last of those sparks had died in the air.

He wished with all his heart that a similar beast would devour that building.

Perhaps tonight would be the night. The crowds on the street were ready for it.

He shrank back into a doorway when the fire tender announced its arrival by klaxon. He knew that the crowds here would be waiting for it.

He was right – they rushed to meet it at the corner of the street, causing the vehicle to swerve and mount the pavement. In the next moment, the crowd were throwing everything at the tender that they could get their hands on: rubble from the derelict houses on this stretch, railings torn from the frontage of the houses, beer bottles, planks of wood. Yes, tonight would be the night, he felt sure of it. The beast that he had seen eating that house would not be held back. It had been set loose by the crowd, and if he had anything to do with it, he would try and direct that beast to the place which had stolen his life.

He watched the crowd draw strength and boldness from the fire tender's rapid departure. And when that crowd surged down the street, past that blazing building in the direction of The Rock, Fisher was running with them now, still two feet above the pavement, but with the sure and steadfast knowledge that he would be a big part of the things to come.

THREE

They huddled together on the stone floor of another corridor.

It could have been the same corridor, the same fifty-yard stretch of black stone, with water glinting in the hideous orange light. The only sounds now were those of their own ragged breathing. It seemed that no one could find the strength, energy or inclination to utter a word.

They had no idea how far they had run from the Chamber of Horrors where Farrow had met his hideous demise. The flight had been made in utter panic and desperation; the simple need to distance themselves from what had gone on behind the closed chamber door. Jessica had led, stopping only when her strength had finally given out. Terror and relief had given her added impetus, but finally she had fallen, skinning her knees – and then she had collapsed. The others had staggered to a halt then, milling in confusion as Roy propped Jessica against a buttress that was not running with water, seeing if he could do anything to tend her knees. Only Boone seemed to want to go on, still fearfully clutching his briefcase. Finally, even he had sunk to the ground.

Jessica awoke from her daze with a start, hands flying out and clutching at Roy as he tried to wind a handkerchief around one of her knees. Her eyes were wide with fear, fixed on a point somewhere beyond Roy. She said nothing, the only sound her tortured breathing. Roy grabbed her hands, pressed them down.

'All right! We got away. It's gone. You're all right.'

She slumped back against the buttress, eyes focusing at last. With that focus came some relief, but even now the fear was rebuilding within.

'You don't understand. There's another one. There's another of those things back there . . .'

'Yes, we know. And according to Draegerman, there are *five* of the bastards lurking somewhere in this house. One for each of us.'

'But I *saw* it . . . it's back there . . . in the swamp . . . in the . . .'

Bobby hurried towards her, crouching down on his haunches as if there were some threat above. His eyes were wild. Clearly, he had been waiting with some agitation for Jessica to come round again.

'My mother,' he said as he drew close, taking one of her arms.

'Where's my mother? She wasn't back there in that room with Farrow and that thing. Tell me she wasn't back there . . .' Jessica tried to pull away, turning her face from Bobby as the utter horror of what she had seen and what she had been made to endure consumed her once more. Bobby reacted in anger, grabbing her arm again. '*Tell me she's still alive!*'

Roy grabbed Bobby's arm and tried to prise him loose, but he clung to her, shaking her now.

'*TELL ME!*'

The ferocity of his voice seemed to provoke an equal ferocity in Jessica.

'She's *dead*! I was *there* and I *saw* it! Do you understand, one of those things killed her! One of Draegerman's Daemons!'

The colour drained from Bobby's face. He slumped back, eyes still fixed on her face. When he spoke again, his voice was quiet and trembling.

'No, that's not right. If there was a Daemon, it should have taken you. That's what he said. One Daemon for each of the children. It should have wanted you, not her . . .'

'It DID want me! But it got to Gloria first.'

'But why would it want her first – why wouldn't it want you? *You're* his child, it should have wanted you . . .'

'I don't know.' The sight of Bobby's face and the knowledge of what she had done began to overwhelm Jessica. Tears were coursing down her cheeks; an inner floodgate had been opened. 'I don't *know*!'

'You left her there, didn't you? It should have been you, but you left her there.'

'I didn't leave her. It took her and then it was going to take me.'

'You left her to die.'

'No, I got away,' pleaded Jessica. 'What else could I do? I was *next*, for Christ's sake. I only just . . .'

'*Really, Jessica,*' boomed a voice in the darkness. '*Why don't you tell them all what really happened? I'm so disappointed in you.*'

The sound of Draegerman's voice shocked them all into silence. But there was no screen here, no sign of the familiar flickering snowstorms and hissing of static. They scanned the corridor, peering at the dripping stone walls.

'*There's nothing to see,*' laughed the voice. '*Not this time.*'

Bobby leapt to his feet, fists clenched.

'Show your face, you bastard! What have you done to my mother?'

'*Do you always need to see me, just to convince you that I'm always here? How many times have I got to tell you? I'm with you every step of the way, watching your fear, feeling your terror.*'

'Where's my MOTHER?'

'*Jessica has only told you part of the truth, Bobby. The part about Gloria being dead. Why don't you ask her about HOW she died?'*

Bobby spun around, looking down at Jessica. 'So what does he mean? What the hell is he talking about?'

Jessica tried to speak, but could not. Roy stepped between them, and now Susan had risen to take Bobby by the arm.

'Don't listen to that lying bastard,' she said. 'He's playing with us, playing his sadistic mind games.'

'So ask Jessica. Ask her to tell you the real truth.'

'Well?' Bobby was trembling.

'Don't listen to him!' snapped Roy.

'We followed one of those things. We thought it was Roy. We followed it through a door, into a Studio Swamp.' Jessica's eyes sparkled with tears in the darkness.

'A Studio Swamp? Really, Jessica?'

'What do you mean, "a swamp"?'

'There *was* a Studio Swamp!' Jessica's voice was trembling. 'Draegerman can do anything he wants in this hellhole, could have built *anything*. Like that jungle place with the spiders, like that hideous escalator. Look at me, I'm still soaked to the skin by the filthy water from that swamp. And that thing – that Daemon – turned from Roy into something out of one of Draegerman's movies. Something that Gloria played years ago. It *became* what she played! Just like what happened back there to Farrow. You saw what happened in that room. That thing became what Gloria called the "She Wasp". These things can change, can become anything they want . . .'

'She's still alive,' said Bobby, ignoring what Jessica was saying. 'That's what you both mean, don't you? She's not dead. That's the real truth of it. She's back there somewhere, where you left her.' He pulled free from Susan and strode past them, heading down the corridor.

'Come on, Jessica. He's so slow on the uptake. Now don't you deal with the truth? Isn't that your job in life? To report the facts? Come on – own up. Let them all know what really happened back there.'

Roy strode after Bobby, grabbing his shoulder. 'Don't listen to any of this. Let it go, Bobby. Gloria is dead – and it's that mad bastard's doing.'

'I've got to find her.'

'We've got to stick together, find a way out.'

'Not without her.' Bobby shrugged off his hand, pressing on.

'Then I'm sorry,' said Roy, and threw himself against Bobby, using the weight of his body to knock him to the corridor floor, now gripping him in a bear-hug from behind. Susan ran to them, tried to grab one of Bobby's thrashing legs. His boot raked her shin and she cried aloud, finally dropping her own weight across the legs and pinning him to the floor.

327

'Listen!' she shouted. 'If Jessica says she's dead, she's dead!' Bobby tried to lash out at her, but she caught his wrist and pinned it. 'Why would she lie about that? And if you go looking for her, you'll be next. It's what that bastard wants!'

'It's here!' shouted Boone from somewhere behind. Susan twisted to look back. Boone was perhaps twenty feet from them, still clutching the ever-present attaché case under one armpit and reaching up the opposite corridor wall, to something at shoulder height. Cursing, he put the attaché case down, then lunged back with both hands to seize what he had discovered there.

'Did I lie about the Berserker? Did I lie about the Daemons? Did I lie about . . .'

With a small cry of triumph, Boone wrenched something from the wall. The corridor was suddenly filled with the sound of static and Draegerman's voice died away in crackling dissolution. Boone wrenched again, and now they could see that he had discovered the hidden speaker. With a third and final yank, the wires were torn loose – and he threw it from him. It smashed on the corridor floor and Boone staggered back to lean against the wall, mumbling muffled curses.

Bobby began to weep again, his struggles diminishing as Susan tried to calm him.

'Take it easy, Bobby.' Roy loosened his grip. 'Take it easy.'

Bobby was shuddering now, another onset of the shakes; but now it was clear that he was not going to take off on his own.

From behind, there was another crash. Susan jerked backwards to see that Boone had advanced on the shattered speaker, was kicking the remnants away down the corridor in one last act of rage.

Jessica held her head in her hands. Draegerman's taunting, his knowledge of what had happened in the Studio Swamp that did or did not exist, was further damaging her hold on reality. Gripping her knees, she sat in the darkness and struggled to find herself, struggled to find what seemed so irreconcilably lost.

FOUR

Moss saw the body floating down the sewer pipe towards them, and waited for Taylor to say or do something as he led the way down the corridor shelf.

Instead, Taylor walked straight on. Moss could not believe that it had escaped his attention. Now Den had seen it and he turned back to look at Moss as they moved on. Moss shone his torch down into the water, and remembered what Terry Fisher had told Taylor about the bits and pieces they might find down here.

'It's a dog,' said Taylor, without turning around.

Sure enough, as the beam of Moss's flashlight shone over the mass, they could see that what they had first taken to be a jacket was a black bin-bag. The forepaws of the animal had been tied with what looked like wire, but it had still managed to scratch its way through the shredded plastic when it had been dumped down the manhole. It floated noiselessly past them as they reached the end of the sewer pipe.

Taylor stood at a new crossroads, consulting the map. Nodding, he turned left, and as the others caught up with him they could see that they had embarked on another stretch of sewer pipe, perhaps a hundred yards long. There seemed to be some kind of pollutant in the water, perhaps a chemical spill. As their flashlights skimmed the surface, it reflected back whorls of blue, purple and green. The walls and ceiling of this tunnel were encrusted with something that looked like rust but had the consistency and matted density of fungus. Curiously, there was none underfoot – but Den kept well away from the stuff on the wall to his left, preferring to walk on the shelf-edge by the water. Excrement was one thing, but he felt uncomfortable about any of that stuff rubbing off on him. He looked back to see that Moss had been watching him. There was a big grin on his face that Den did not like one little bit.

Taylor suddenly halted up ahead.

They stopped too, waiting for him to say or do something.

Instead he sank down to one knee and clutched at his stomach.

Now he was doubling over. Moss and Den exchanged looks. Den

ran forward when he saw the grimace of agony on Taylor's face as he clutched at himself, as if trying to force the pain back inside.

'What is it Taylor? What's wrong?'

'Nothing ... nothing ...'

'Well, it sure as fuck is *something*!' snapped Moss as he approached. 'Don't tell me that the Iron Man is going to finally collapse on us?'

Taylor shrugged off Den's proffered hand. He swallowed hard and began to rise again.

'No one's going to collapse, Moss.'

'You sure? I'd prefer to be able to get out of this shit-hole alive, and since there was never any map-reading classes where I come from, I hope you're not going to ...'

'Shut up, Moss!' snapped Taylor. 'It's nothing.'

He stood up, the pain vanishing from his face. He turned and carried on as if nothing had happened. Moss shrugged and held his arms open in a *So what did I say?* expression.

Den followed close behind Taylor, wondering just what the hell was going on. He kept watching Taylor's back, and wondered what he would do if the man suddenly keeled over and fell into the sewer water. The prospect was not encouraging. Den pushed it to the back of his mind and thought back to the factory and his workmates, wondering what they would be doing now; wondering if he would have a job to go back to if he ever got out of this place with Susan alive. Management had been unhappy about his sudden leave without absence from the ten-hour forklift shift.

No 'if' about it, Den. Just keep going. Do whatever Taylor says, and we'll get her out of here.

'Wait a minute!'

Moss's voice hissed sibilantly. Den and Taylor turned to look back at him.

Moss was looking back the way they had come.

'What is it?' asked Taylor.

Moss held up his hand for silence, cocking his head to listen. He looked back again and shook his head. 'Nothing, nothing. Just thought I heard something ...'

'Something like what?' asked Den.

'Hissing or scratching or something. From behind us. But there's nothing there now. It's this fucking place and its noises, that's all.'

Taylor turned and started walking again, his flashlight playing over the fungus-encrusted roof. Was he concerned about what he saw there? Den shook his head as he followed. Nothing seemed to bother Taylor down here; his face had remained stoic and impassive ever since their arrival, even when he had been telling Den that he had been wrong about him. That stoicism, that blankness of expression, could have meant anything. Den presumed that he had passed some test at last.

330

that Taylor was trying to say that he was all right after all, and not just some love-struck passenger who was going to get under his feet all the time. But with Taylor, it was difficult to tell. Expressing emotion did not seem to come high on his agenda. Den was still puzzling when Taylor reached the end of the sewer and suddenly stopped.

He did not consult his map.

He simply stood and looked, his flashlight beam directed up ahead – into the sewer system around the next corner.

Den could see Taylor's blank, expressionless face in the flareback. But he knew that something Godalmighty impressive had stopped Taylor in his tracks.

'What?' he asked, pressing forward. There was not much room to pass on this part of the shelf, and Taylor remained where he was. '*What?*' demanded Den again, and this time Taylor moved on enough to allow Den to see. From behind, Moss had hurried to join them, spurred on by the urgency in Den's voice.

Now they could all see what lay beyond, and stood looking in awe.

At first, it seemed that the sewers had ended, opening up into a great open chamber. But this was more than just a chamber; this must surely be some sort of natural cavern. It reminded Den instantly of a photograph he had seen years ago, just before he had been expelled from school. It was a photograph of the Carlsbad Caverns – and here they were now. Huge stalagmites emerged from the sewer water, meeting the stalactites descending from above to produce massive hour-glass shapes. Great clusters of petrified sediment hung from the rock ceiling, looking like giant ragged teeth, or perhaps the encrusted pipes of a giant cathedral organ. Huge ridges of multi-coloured material swept up from the water to form elaborate islands that looked like bizarre coral reefs. Water dripped constantly from overhead, raising a constant mist of spray from the water below.

But this was not a cavern.

This was the sewer beneath Draegerman's Rock.

And that first flash of remembrance, back to the forgotten natural history textbook in the school library, was almost instantly dispelled. The material that engulfed the sewer was the same colour as the barnacled rust-fungus on the walls and ceiling of the sewer tunnel down which they had just come, albeit in varying shades. It was the same material which had engulfed this part of the sewer, erupting from the walls and the ceiling and the very sewer channels themselves like some gigantic and hideous, cancerous growth.

'Where's The Rock?' asked Moss. 'On the map.'

Taylor was still looking at what lay ahead, at the monstrous and chaotic blockage of what might or might not be petrified stone. Slowly, he kept scanning the beam over the ridges and web-like arches, reaching into his belt for the map and then flipping it loose from the waterproof

331

pocket. He opened it out and now brought the torch to bear on it as Moss and Den's own torch beams played over the sewer cavern. Moss had the impression that Taylor did not need to look at the map to answer the question.

'The boundary starts here, doesn't it?' asked Moss. 'Where this . . . stuff . . . begins?'

Taylor nodded. He flashed his own beam out across the chamber. 'This is supposed to be another cross-section where four channels meet. Same as one we passed back there. But it looks like this stuff has . . grown here, and covered over the three other outlets.'

And Moss was suddenly reminded of Mother's words to Taylor back at *The Pool*, about everything around The Rock being sucked dry of love and goodness.

And here it was before him now. Evidence of Mother's instinctive feeling.

The roots of Draegerman's Rock, spreading down into the sewer water and through the wall, searching for vitality, searching for the goodness that it needed to keep it growing and for the nourishment that would keep it alive.

'So we can't get in?' asked Den.

Taylor's torch beam continued to play over the stalagmites and the funnels of stone. Suddenly, it stopped, and Taylor moved down the concrete shelf carefully to get a better look at what that beam had highlighted. The same rust-barnacles were growing on the shelf making the surface rough and uneven; his footsteps sounded harsh and brittle here, as if he were walking on barnacles or popping seaweed.

'Yes, we can get in.' He looked at the map again, then shone the beam between two ridges of the hideous petrified growth. Den moved forward. At last, he could see what Taylor had seen: a patch of brickwork, a square metre of sewer wall that the growth had not covered over.

'Shit!' exclaimed Moss. 'There it is again.'

They watched silently as Moss moved back to the junction, looking around the corner and back down the sewer pipe through which they had just travelled. This time, instead of listening and shrugging, he straightened. When he looked back at Taylor and Den, they knew that he had *seen* something. They walked quickly back to him.

Something was happening to the water back down that sewer. Moss was shining his torch onto the rippling black, blue and green of the surface. And now Den and Taylor could see that something was disturbing the surface; something that was causing a myriad series of rippling mini-waves. And as they listened, a sound was growing louder as the the movement of the water became more agitated.

A hissing sound.

A sound of scrabbling movement.

A thin, high-pitched squealing and rustling.

'Guess what lives in sewers?' asked Moss grimly.

And in the next second, a squirming mass of rats erupted into the light of their combined torches. A hundred yards back, they were swarming from a tunnel mouth, spreading like a black living carpet on the concrete shelf; others thrashing and swimming in the sewer water itself – the source of the agitation on the surface. The torch beams reflected hundreds of pinpoints of light in the frenzied mass: the eyes of the swarm. Now a great chittering filled the air as they approached, the human scent strong and appetising.

Den watched in horror as the rats in the water came across the floating carcass of the dog in the black bin liner. The corpse was now alive with squirming, squealing, thrashing movement. A spray of sewer water surrounded the ragged form; the water was alive in the pack's frenzy to tear every shred of decayed flesh from the waterlogged package.

'Jesus . . .' said Moss, backing off. He swung the waterproof satchel from his shoulders, fumbling with the fastenings to take out his automatic weapon. Taylor put a hand on his arm to stop him.

'Keep your machine pistol in your pack until we get inside The Rock.'

Then he moved calmly past, face expressionless. He began to walk back towards the advancing horde.

'What are you *doing*, Taylor?' yelled Den. And the sound of his voice resulted instantly in a dreadful surge of anticipation and excitement in the rushing black wave on the concrete shelf. The squealing and chittering filled the rank air.

Taylor swung his own satchel from his shoulder, opened it and rummaged inside as he moved. Then he took something from it and examined the black metal object in his hands. A jerk of movement, and something clattered on the concrete shelf at his feet. Quickly now, he hurled the object in his hand back along the shelf towards the rushing black mass. It bounced and clattered towards them: a black sphere no bigger than a handball. Then he turned; no longer casual and apparently carefree, lunging back towards them and shouting:

'Back around that corner! *Now!*'

And no sooner had they all rounded the curve than the phosphorous grenade he had thrown exploded on the shelf with a dull *crump!* that they could feel beneath their feet. A great, searing flash of white light was followed instantly by a great roaring sound. The sewer water suddenly reflected a mass of white flame and tracer sparks; shadows leapt and reared over the cavern's arches and pillars.

Taylor looked back around the corner, and so did the others.

It was a portal into Hell.

The surging black mass had become a twisting, thrashing mass of flame. Even now, the mass was breaking apart as dozens upon dozens

333

of rearing, burning shapes leapt into the air. Great gouts of white flame filled the sewer tunnel where the horde had been. Liquid fire was burning on the surface of the water, filled with thrashing, squirming balls of fire. And beneath the sounds of the roaring inferno, they could still hear the screaming and the squealing; now no longer the sounds of dreadful hunger, but those of agonising, flaring death.

'You are the *man*!' said Moss in awe.

'Wait,' said Taylor.

'I mean, fucking *hell*, you are the *man*!'

'Get back from this wall!' snapped Taylor, and now he grabbed both men, dragging them back around the corner into the cavern and away from the blazing tunnel that had once been a sewer full of ravening death. Moss's look of awe vanished when he saw that Taylor was concentrating on something that was going on in or around the wall by which they were standing.

'Now what?' asked Den.

'I don't like this.'

'Don't like what?'

'Just get away from the wall. I've got a feeling. A bad feeling about . . .'

Another sound stabbed the air: the sharp, one-note, piercing shrill of a klaxon. Then a sound of crackling static; a sound that was clear even above the surging of flame and the squealing agony of the horde beyond. The static vanished with a loud clatter – and then a voice stabbed out of nowhere.

'This section of the network is not subject to city authority maintenance. Any work herein is authorised specifically by Draegerman Enterprises. No such authority having been granted, your presence here is unauthorised and therefore criminal in intent. By agreement with City Ordinance 7/13/99 as approved by Public Works Committee and endorsed by the City Council, Draegerman Enterprises reserves the right to protect its own property utilitising reasonable force to do so.'

'Away from the *wall*!' yelled Taylor.

And in the next moment, the walls shuddered under great pressure.

Like the blade of a huge guillotine, a steel door slid from an aperture in the ceiling overhead. It fell under its own tremendous weight, released from the security apparatus that had kept it in place overhead. Completely filling the sewer tunnel, it crashed savagely into the water and through an aperture in the concrete shelf on which they were standing, raising a small tidal wave at its base. Den was jarred from his feet. He plunged from the shelf and into the sewer water. Moss staggered, but Taylor caught his arm and flung him back against the wall. The shock of the steel door's descent and the explosive roar of its impact shook the concrete shelf. The blazing tunnel beyond was now cut off completely – and the door

334

had come down where Moss and Den had been standing only a second before.

As the tidal wave swept through the cavern, huge chunks of the petrified growth cracked and shattered on the other side of the cavern. Two further steel doors had come down in the other overgrown tunnels beyond this encrusted intersection, severing arches of stone and pillars of the disgusting mass. They crumbled and collapsed into the sewer water, sending up great sprays of filthy water.

Taylor jumped feet first into the sewer, just as Den rose above the thrashing water. In almost the same action, he grabbed Den by the arm and hoisted him, gasping, back to the side of the concrete shelf. They clung there, Moss sheltering on his haunches, as the reverberating crash of the security doors finally died, and the last of the toppling towers of petrified sediment fell.

'Shit!' hissed Taylor. 'The bastard has *detectors* down here. That firebomb triggered them off. So much for Talbot's map.'

'How come he didn't know about that?' gasped Den, clutching at the side.

'Probably built and installed after he'd gone. That's the only answer.'

Even as the echoes died, a new sound erupted into the cavern. Moss leaned over the edge to help them climb as the sound increased in pitch and volume.

It was like an avalanche; a great thundering pressure which was now shaking the concrete shelf and stirring up choppy waves on the surface of the sewer water. The shuddering was making further chunks of the cancerous growth split and crack and fall into the water, like icebergs splitting apart in the Gulf Stream.

'Now what?' shouted Moss, flashing his torch beam around the cavern. The other two followed suit. And as if prompted by his words, two huge cataracts of water exploded into the cavern from right and left, from perhaps a hundred feet above, gushing downwards from two outlets in the sewer wall that had been hidden by the stalactites. Several of the jagged growths blew apart in the thundering explosion. Now the surface below was an exploding riot of water.

'Clever,' murmured Taylor, his words drowned by the twin waterfalls of stinking sewage. 'Very clever, Mr Draegerman.'

'What?' yelled Moss, when he saw Taylor's lips moving. He grabbed him by the shoulder as he yelled, eyes wide in alarm.

'It's part of his security protection!' shouted Taylor over the din. 'Talbot was wrong when he said this was Draegerman's weak spot, the only way in! The bastard second-guessed him! Those two outlets up there are diverted main drains, probably from the city sewers! Triggered by the sensors, no doubt by the firebomb!'

'You mean . . . those steel doors have locked us in!'

335

'Yeah, and those outlets are going to fill the chamber. He means to drown anyone who gets this far.'

'So you and your firebomb did this?'

'So what do you prefer, Moss? Drowned in shit, or eaten alive by rats?'

'So come on, Mr Indestructible! What the fucking *hell* are we going to do now!'

Moss could not believe his eyes when Taylor smiled back at him.

Already, the sewer water was lapping over the concrete shelf as the levels rose in the chamber, and Taylor was smiling as if this was a jaunt in the countryside: a mere Sunday afternoon stroll.

'Follow me!' he said, and he took out his face-mask, strapped it on and stepped over the side of the concrete shelf into the sewer water. Moss and Den watched in disbelief as Taylor was engulfed in the water. Then he surfaced again, and began to swim across the chamber, through the erupting water and towards the far side where the petrified growth formed a ridged beach, leading up to a webbed, arched whorl of petrified stone and coralled pillars. As he swam he held the flashlight ahead of him, the beam picking out the cascading water and the looming, rearing shadows of the bizarre structures of this underground nightmare.

Suddenly Den began to nod his head, understanding at last.

'The brickwork over there!' he yelled to Moss. 'Where Taylor's shining his torch.'

Moss saw the square metre of brick wall, and in the next moment both men had put on their masks and followed Taylor into the water, lunging through the thrashing foam, their flashlight beams playing ahead.

Taylor reached the coral beach, hoisted himself up on to it even as bits of the disgusting mass crumbed in his grip and fell dissolving into the water. Sewer water streaming from him, he pushed himself through the two ridges of growth to the wall and placed both hands against the bricks, as if his fingers could detect safety on the other side. Den could see the water level creeping up the beach as both he and Moss reached it at last. The growth felt disgusting to the touch. Its texture, the way in which it had cloyed, gelled and hardened, was more than just an affront to the eye. It registered on levels deeper than mere physical revulsion and in ways that Den could barely understand. Looking at Moss, he could see that he felt the same way. Taylor was clenching two lengths of black wire between his teeth. Reaching into his belt, he was taking out more material, now throwing two cellophane packets to Den and Moss.

'Open them!'

Moss nodded and began to tear his packet open. 'Plastics?'

Taylor nodded and began to work on the wires, now making the connections with the detonator he had taken from another pouch in his belt. Den tore open his packet. And as both men passed the pliable material to him, Taylor began to roll and knead lengths of the material all along the base of the brickwork, where it vanished into the coral. It was the explosive remaining from his attempt on the roof of Draegerman's Rock.

The water had reached them. It lapped around their shins, and when Den flashed his torch beam back across the chamber he saw that the concrete shelf had vanished into the water. The two thundering cataracts from above showed no signs of abating.

'Right!' yelled Taylor, priming the detonator and timing device. 'We've got three minutes. Follow me!'

Splashing along the beach-shelf, away from the brickwork, he headed for a thick clump of the material which hung like a petrified waterfall from the ceiling. The mass bowed in the middle, in the shape of an hourglass, and was at least thirty feet thick. Beckoning to the others, he swung around the pillar, splashing back into the sewer water. Still clutching the pillar, he pushed out and swam around its base, waiting for the others to follow suit. When they reached him, he guided them past him into a protective niche in the swell, then swam back around so that he could see the beach and the exposed brickwork.

The water level was rising faster than before. It would surely keep rising until it had reached the roof of this sewer-cavern and had completely flooded the chamber.

Grim-faced, Taylor looked back at the others and motioned for them to keep their heads down. He had used all the plastic explosives on the wall. There would be no more material for a second attempt.

At first, he thought there had been a misfire or a bad connection. He could feel the great thundering and shuddering of the two cataracts in the very substance of the pillar to which he clung, but could neither hear nor feel anything like a controlled explosion from the exposed patch of brickwork on the other side. But in the next instant, the churning sewer water across the chamber suddenly erupted into an even greater showering cascade as rubble and shattered chunks of the growth were punched out across the surface. The coughing roar of the explosion had been drowned by all the other noise in the huge sewer-cavern. A split second later, blue smoke gushed out across the surface of the foaming lake, and Taylor surged back around the pillar to look.

The blast had blown a hole four feet square in the wall.

Great cracks had appeared in the petrified fungus growth around the smoking hole, and Taylor looked up in alarm when it seemed that part of the overhanging structure was swaying. But he could not be sure whether this was the case, or whether the mist and spray being thrown up in the chamber were simply obscuring his vision. There was no time to hang around and debate. Waving quickly to the others, he thrashed around the pillar to the beach; a chunk of the growth had broken away from the foaming ridge and was floating out across the thrashing surface, turning slowly end over end and sinking with a hiss.

They scrambled out of the water back on to the beach, ran to the smoking aperture and peered inside. Smoke still gushed and curled in the darkness beyond. But even as they looked, a draught of cold air was dispersing the smoke, blowing it towards them. They waved at it until all the clouds had dispersed.

'Come on!'

Taylor grabbed a ragged edge and pulled out more of the fragmented bricks. Without pausing, he shone his flashlight beyond and climbed through the ragged gap, vanishing into the darkness. Moss quickly followed.

Den began to climb through and then looked back into the chamber. How long would it be before the water level reached the hole they had just breached in Draegerman's defences? They were far from safe yet, and he hoped to God that they had not just made themselves an exist from the flooding sewer into some blind alley; an alley that would soon fill with water just as surely as the chamber they had left was going to fill with water. He pushed himself through the gap.

They seemed to be in an enclosed space, the beams of their torches shining on a concrete ceiling above, perhaps ten feet from their heads. Despite the great roaring behind them, Den could hear Moss and Taylor breathing heavily, could see the two men standing just ahead. Moss continued to play his beam around him, but Taylor had dragged Talbot's not-so-complete map from the waterproof pocket at his waist and was examining it with the torch. Den joined Moss, also flashing his beam around.

They were in some kind of concrete culvert: ten feet high and perhaps twenty feet wide. There was a gulley ahead of them, sloping upwards. And when Den shone his torch up there, he could see that water was running down the culvert towards them, vanishing into an aperture at their feet, perhaps two feet wide. He wondered what would have happened if one of them had put a foot down there in the darkness. The prospect of a broken leg at this juncture did not bear thinking about. The water seemed clear, untainted by sewage. He could not begin to think what this construction could be.

So who needs to be a sewer expert? We're in, and that's the main thing.

'Can't see the top,' said Moss, still shining his flashlight up the steep gulley. 'That's some steep climb.'

'A quarter of a mile,' said Taylor. 'We follow this and it'll take us right into Draegerman's basement.'

'Anybody else relieved to be out of that shithole back there?' asked Moss. 'Or am I overreacting?'

'Well, if we're going to climb,' said Den, 'I think we should start.

Any second now, and that sewer water is going to follow us straight through that hole you've blown.' He looked at Taylor for confirmation, even began to move forward in anticipation that the other man would grunt assent.

But Taylor was not moving.

He had finished looking at the map, had placed it back in the waterproof pocket. Now he was simply standing and shining his flashlight into the water that was running down the concrete gulley. Then he began to shine it up and down the steep stretch, the beam glinting on the water.

And for the first time since Den had met him, Taylor had an expression of *doubt* on his face.

'What is it?'

Den moved towards him, using his own flashlight on the gulley and the water and the ceiling overhead. Was this some new source of threat which he had not seen? Concerned now at the expression on Taylor's face, he said tightly: 'For Christ's sake, Taylor. *What is it?*'

'The water,' said Taylor tightly, continuing to play his beam over the running surface.

'What about it?' demanded Moss. 'Come on, Taylor. Tell us what the hell's the matter?'

'I don't know . . .'

'You don't *know*? Then what the hell is the matter with *you*, man?'

'Nothing wrong with me,' replied Taylor. 'But there's sure as hell something wrong with this water.'

Both of the other men were playing their torch beams across its surface, unable to see what Taylor meant.

'So *what*?' demanded Den.

'Look again, and tell me I'm wrong . . .' continued Taylor.

He flashed the beam up and down once more, this time letting it rest on the water passing them before it fell into the narrow aperture in the ground.

'. . . but this water isn't running downhill.'

And now they could both see what Taylor saw. Unable to speak, they stood in the darkness, letting their torches shine on the surface of the running water, unable to believe their eyes. It could not be possible.

But Taylor was right.

The water was flowing *uphill*.

FIVE

Fisher stood like a ghost and watched as the crowd overturned the police car.

It was the second time he had seen it done that night. The first time it had been by the crowd who had torched the abandoned building and then frightened off the fire tender that had turned up to see to the blaze. He had run with the crowd then, for how long he had no idea. His body was still floating above the pavement, still apart from everything that was going on around him. But eventually that first police car had screeched around a street corner, then halted. As the crowd surged forward, the officers inside had decided to bluff it out and cruise straight on through them at a sedate and authorative pace. It had been a bad mistake.

In moments, that crowd had fallen on the police car. Perhaps the two men inside would have stood a chance if the driver had decided to floor the gas pedal and roar on through that tangled knot of civilians, regardless of who may have been run over in the process. But apparently too civil-minded to allow themselves such a renegade course of action, the car had slowed and halted – and the crowd had descended on it, rocking the vehicle from side to side on its suspension. Fisher had no idea what really happened next. He could not remember whether he had heard screaming or whether it was just the sounds of other police cars and their sirens out there somewhere in the night. But when the car finally turned over and its windows smashed out into the road, the two policemen inside were no longer to be seen. He had watched the crowd as they began to smash the car's bodywork with anything they could use as a weapon – but the drivers were gone as if they had never been there. When the crowd tired of beating the car panels and smashing the windows, someone had set fire to the overturned interior, and they had surged away from the vehicle as it was engulfed in an orange-black petrol-cloud of flame and smoke. Cheering, the crowd had moved on.

Fisher had not run with them. Instead, he found himself drifting in another direction. He could hear more shouting, more sirens. Somewhere, someone was singing. It sounded like a blues number, eerily out of place on these violent streets. Rounding a corner, he saw the second police car. It had been rammed off the road by a battered lorry carrying steel beer barrels. The truck's load had fallen away in the collision, and the barrels were rolling and clattering all over the street. Although armed, the two police officers who had been in the rammed car were taking no chances. They had pulled themselves out of it and were crouching on the steps of a graffiti-covered apartment as the crowd surged on the street before them. They stayed there, strangely aloof from that crowd as it descended on the truck and the police car. While one officer held his weapon levelled at the milling crowd, and was completely ignored – the other was radioing in for support to central headquarters on his handset.

It seemed that every ethnic group and all age-levels were represented here. It was as if everyone in the streets around The Rock had finally emerged to take vengeance for every ill done to them over the years. Some were rolling the beer barrels away, presumably for consumption, unware that the damned things were empty. Others were climbing over the truck, while another group had descended on the empty police car; tearing out its radio and slashing the seats.

Fisher saw the car finally turn over. It swivelled and span on the road as it was upended. This time the windows were intact on impact, a situation soon remedied by the yelling people who clambered over it. Fisher drifted away again, feeling himself being pulled by an invisible force. He rounded another street corner, and knew at last with undoubted certainty what was acting as the magnet.

Two city blocks from the corner he could see the concrete gates that gave access to a Walkway. And beyond the gates, towering over the surrounding neighbourhood, stood Draegerman's Rock. It was drawing him in. But there was no fear in Fisher, just a brimming feeling that he was about to participate in something that would affect that gigantic structure. He was being drawn to that place again after all these years because now, with the streets erupting into violence, he was going to be able to pay them back for the life they had stolen from him. He remembered the living firecloud that had consumed the abandoned building, wanted more than anything to lead that fire-beast to The Rock.

'What?' he asked the streets, arms held wide and looking for the key. 'What am I supposed to be looking for?'

There were crowds of people down there at the Walkway gate; milling and jeering and throwing things at the buttresses. People streamed past Fisher even now, ignoring his pleas; running onwards down that street, gesturing back to others to follow and join their ragged revolution. Fisher floated after them, drawn inexorably towards that gigantic and imposing shadow.

And as he flew with that crowd, three things happened as if in answer to his plea.

He had reached the end of the first city block, could hear the wailing of sirens and something that sounded like an explosion from the west. Smoke began to drift across the street, making him cough, stinging his eyes. He could see the crowd ahead, drinking and laughing and jeering. Someone threw a red and white striped traffic cone at the closed gate in a hopelessly impotent but defiant gesture. Suddenly, like a shoal of fish swarming and parting before a predator, that crowd surged back from the Walkway gate. Parting in the middle, the crowd headed for the sidewalks on either side; scattering and diving for cover. Then, Fisher heard the gunshots.

Suddenly, he was lying in the middle of the road. There were others all around him, all instinctively diving to the ground for cover as more gunshots ratcheted and echoed down the street. Fisher looked up to where he knew a guard post would be; beyond the blank concrete gate and in one of the two secondary towers behind, the towers which flanked the Walkway and also served as supports for the road on the neighbourhood side. He saw a flash of light from the upper aperture of that tower on the left. So, there was a security man in there . . . and the concrete Walkway gate was closed and . . . suddenly, a fog drifted from Fisher's mind and he remembered again.

'The Four Day Rule. The Rock's shut down.'

Fisher remembered a superior security officer telling him: *Nobody gets in and out during that time* . . .

Fisher looked up again, saw another flash of light, and this time saw puffs of smoke punching out of an apartment wall on the left as bullets raked the building. When he looked back to the Walkway gate, the second thing happened.

He saw familiar graffiti on the blank concrete face, about four feet from the ground. It was too dark to see properly, but then someone must have heard his thoughts, because a shadow flung a burning rag at the concrete wall. A burning rag that arced through the air, then shattered and spread a pool of fire on the road in front of it. It was a petrol bomb – and the flaring light directly illuminated that graffiti so that Fisher was able to see clearly.

Dee-Man is a Dead Man.

Fisher remembered that graffiti. This was the Walkway he had been patrolling when the bad things happened. This was the Walkway where he had saved the kids. The knowledge burned inside him like an inner fuse. That petrol bomb had also lit something inside him.

He turned his head to the right as people ran past him for cover – and saw the demolition site. Another abandoned building was falling apart. It looked like the skeleton of a grocery store. Perhaps the place had started to cave in, maybe it was a threat to passers-by? Whatever, there was a crane on the far side of that semi-demolished building; the wrecking ball and chain hanging from the jib was swaying and creaking.

But on the near side, parked on the remains of a cracked sidewalk, was the third thing – the last remaining part of the mystery. The solution to everything.

It was a bulldozer.

And at the sight of it, everything came together. The reason that Fisher had been drawn out onto the streets tonight. He had been meant to see these things and had been meant to find this place.

Slowly, he stood up, still facing the Walkway gate. Others lying on the road or scrambling away on all fours turned to look at him.

'Someone's knocking on your *door*, Mr Draegerman!' he yelled.

Turning, he strode towards the bulldozer.

He climbed up to the cabin, punched a hole in the door window and leaned inside to open it. He had gashed his hand in that action. Blood streamed from his knuckles, but he felt no pain. Climbing inside, Fisher found the control panel just behind the seat on the right hand side. There was no ignition key in there, nothing to start the engine.

'All *right*!' said an enthusiastic voice, and Fisher looked up to see the teenager hanging in that doorway. White, wearing a black woollen balaclava which was rolled up above his eyebrows at the moment, about fourteen years old – his eyes were sparkling as he ignored Fisher and dropped away from the cabin. As Fisher watched, he yanked a panel out of the bulldozer's side, just below where Fisher was sitting, leaned in and started to do something with the wires in there.

'Turn the ignition!' shouted the teenager, head still in the aperture.

Fisher twisted the handle, and the engine coughed into life.

Turning to face front again, Fisher experimented with the basic controls as the bulldozer roared with potential energy. He found the handbrake and throttle on his left, together with a lever sitting in a vee-shaped aperture. When he pulled the lever back, the tractor suddenly lurched backwards. Forward, and the bulldozer jerked forward, snorting angrily. He could see symbols there – a hare for fast, and a tortoise for slow. There was another handle-lever on his right. When he pushed it down, the bulldozer's blade descended. Up, and the blade came up.

Grinning, Fisher yanked the left-hand lever back, and the machine snorted and trundled back off the shattered pavement into the road. In his wing-mirror, he saw the people who had been lying in the road suddenly clamber to their feet and run. But some of the figures were running *towards* the bulldozer now as Fisher brought it to a halt, and then slammed into forward gear. The teenage kid who had hot-wired the bulldozer jumped up into the the shattered doorway, yelling encouragement to the others who began to jump and clamber aboard the snorting beast. Then Fisher yanked on the levers again and the machine swivelled in the road, its tracks slewing on the tarmac.

The bulldozer was in the middle of the street, facing the Walkway gate about one block's distance away. People up there were looking back and yelling as the bulldozer coughed and snorted exhaust fumes angrily from the pipe above the cabin.

Fisher yelled too, and pushed the black handle forward again.

Then he raised the bulldozer blade higher, a gesture of aggression and defiance which had its clambering passengers yelling and waving their fists in the air.

'Knock-KNOCK!' yelled Fisher.

The bulldozer roared forward, down the centre of the street towards The Rock.

SIX

Both Susan and Roy had been holding Bobby between them, gripping his arms as they sat in a huddle together on the corridor floor. His face had a deathly white pallor, but the shaking fits seemed to be easing. His flesh felt cold, but he was drenched in sweat, and they had been holding on to him as much for moral support as to prevent him from suddenly breaking free and going off to search for his mother. Despite everything, Roy could not forget that Bobby had come back to help him on that hideous escalator, when Aiken had fallen prey to the Berserker.

Boone had finally ceased smashing the remains of Draegerman's wall speaker to pieces, had sullenly found himself a dry spot – away from the others as usual – and slumped down into it, mumbling imprecations under his breath.

Jessica was still sitting against the wall, with her head in her hands. Roy watched her for a long time, thinking back to the horrific encounter with Farrow and the thing that had taken him, and then to what might have happened in what Jessica had called the Studio Swamp. When it seemed that Bobby had drifted off to sleep, Roy eased himself away and climbed to his feet, groaning. He felt a bad pain in his side again, and tried to shrug it off.

Jessica looked up at the movement, her face blank.

'We have to talk,' said Roy when he saw that she was awake.

No one answered.

'About what happened back there to Farrow.'

Jessica shook her head and looked down again.

'I want to understand what we're up against. If we understand it, maybe we can ... I don't know ... *do* something about it.'

'We're going to die,' said Jessica.

'Shut UP!' hissed Boone. When they all looked over at him, he cast his eyes down like a child being admonished in class for his outburst.

'That thing in the chamber, the thing that killed Farrow,' continued Roy. 'Was it the same as the thing you say killed ...' He looked back at Bobby. He was still asleep. 'I mean, was the thing you saw in that Swamp, the same as the thing that killed Farrow?'

Jessica rubbed her hands over her face, as if washing in invisible water.

'The thing in the Swamp changed its shape,' she said. 'So did the thing in that chamber.'

'But was it the same thing?'

'I don't know. Maybe it was ... no ... no.'

Jessica had automatically begun to dismiss whatever it was that Roy was beginning to ask. But as she spoke, she suddenly realised that despite the overriding terror of her encounters, there had been something different about the two horrific creatures that had killed Gloria and Farrow.

'Yes,' she said with strength returning to her voice. 'Yes. They were different. They weren't one and the same thing. They ... *felt* different.'

She struggled to remember what it was that made her so sure. Had it been a scent? Something in the way the things had spoken? No, it was something altogether more subtle than that. It was an instinctive human response to the presence of something so alien, so horribly *wrong*. She had instinctively felt the individuality of the things despite their shape-changing abilities.

'I can't explain it properly. But the thing in the chamber *wasn't* the thing from the Swamp. The thing that killed Farrow was already there when you arrived. Look, I know this is bloody crazy – but there was a bed or a rack in there. With leather belts and a thing at the head that looked like a ship's wheel. Didn't you see it?'

'I didn't have a chance to browse.'

'Well, it *wasn't* any of those things. It was a Daemon. When you and Farrow were having your difference of opinion, I saw that bed change; saw it dissolve. It was like smoke or mist, floating through the air. But it was the Daemon, I swear it was! It went into the wall and then got into that ... *other* thing.'

She shuddered, wiping her face once more with the washing motion. 'But the thing in the Swamp and the other in the chamber were two different creatures.'

'Right,' nodded Roy.

'Why?' asked Susan, still holding Bobby. 'What are you getting at?'

'I'm thinking back to what Draegerman said about these things. When he conjured them, or whatever in hell he did to get them here. He said something about their movements being limited in this physical plane. Don't you remember that?'

'He said: "Like trap-door spiders",' continued Susan.

'Right! Look – if Jessica says that the thing in the Swamp was different from the thing in the chamber, maybe that's a clue to something that might help us.'

'What are you talking about?' asked Jessica wearily.

346

'Think about it. Why didn't that Daemon follow you, when you ran from the Studio Swamp? If we believe what Draegerman said about what they're here for . . .' Again, Roy checked to make sure that Bobby was still unconscious. '. . . then it really wanted you. Not just you, but any one of us. His children.'

'It got to Gloria first,' said Jessica, voice trembling again. 'There was . . . nothing I could do. *Nothing!* I managed to get away, to escape . . .'

'But why didn't it come after you when you escaped from that room?'

Jessica found herself unable to look at the others as Roy continued.

'It didn't follow after you, Jessica – because it *couldn't* follow after you. Maybe it couldn't leave that room. Maybe the thing in the chamber couldn't leave that room either. Don't you see? If these things are limited in their movements like that, there might be a chance for us. There might still be a chance to get out of here if we're careful.'

'No,' said Jessica. 'The thing that looked like you came out of that chamber to find us. It led us back there. So it must be able to move around.'

'The Berserker,' said Susan. 'That wasn't confined to one place. It could move where it wanted.'

'But Draegerman *told* us that the Berserker wasn't the same as the others. Don't you remember? He said that it had been conjured for a special purpose. To hunt down and kill all of Draegerman's employees in The Rock. When it got Aiken, it got the last of them – and then it went back to wherever in hell it came from. But even if that thing from the Swamp *did* come out to lure you there, why didn't it follow you out again? Perhaps it didn't because it *couldn't*. Maybe that's why Draegerman has always been herding us. Pushing us on to where these things are, because they *can't* come to us.'

'And he's still doing it,' said Boone in a flat voice. 'He's doing it now.'

Roy looked at Boone, expecting him to say more. Instead, Boone pointed down the corridor, back in the direction from which they had come.

They looked back.

And what they saw there had Jessica immediately on her feet, staggering across the corridor to the others, eyes wide with renewed fear.

'Oh my God, *no* . . .'

Fog was creeping around the bend in the corridor. Wisp-like tentacles of mist were spreading and blanketing the cold stone walls.

'You're wrong, Roy,' said Jessica, shaking her head. 'Dead wrong. Those Daemons can go where they want. They're not just stuck in Draegerman's movie sets and his rooms.'

347

'It's fog, or mist, or something,' said Roy. 'That's all.' But his voice belied the dreadful doubt inside.

'It's not,' said Jessica. And now Susan was shaking Bobby awake, pulling him to his feet. Boone was also standing now, already backing off down the corridor. 'It's none of those things. Didn't you see that fog back there in the chamber with Farrow? It's one of those *things*. Looking for us, hunting for us . . .'

Already, the walls of the corridor by the corner were shrouded and obscured by the creeping mist. Silently, the tentacles of fog were creeping over the ground, the ceiling and the dripping stone walls towards them.

Bobby was awake again, now clinging to Susan's arm as they slowly continued to back away. The mist rolled over and enveloped the shattered remains of the wall speaker.

'All right!' said Roy angrily. 'I was wrong, and that bastard Draegerman was lying again!'

'We're *never* going to get out of here!' It seemed that Boone was on the verge of tears.

'Save your energy!' said Susan, eyes still on the creeping fog. 'And run!'

They staggered and ran off down the corridor.

The chase was on again.

The creeping fog slowly followed.

SEVEN

They continued to climb the steep sides of the concrete culvert, Taylor leading the way and the othes following.

There had been no time to discuss the water that flowed in the culvert, no time to question the evidence of their eyes; but as they climbed, flashing their torch beams on the walls and the stone ceiling, their eyes returned to the darkly glinting liquid. Each time they looked, they expected the uphill flow to have been rectified, expected that it would now be flowing the right way, downhill. Surely it must be a trick of the flashlight beams in the enclosed space? But no matter how they tried to rationalise the impossibility, neither Den nor Moss could forget the way in which, just before they had begun their long climb, Taylor had stooped to put his hand in the water. No one had spoken as it flowed *up* over his fingers. Taylor had simply shaken his head, and they had begun their ascent.

The noise of rushing water filled the narrow space, but when it became a loud and coughing roar, they turned, all shining their beams directly back down the way they had come.

The water from the sealed chamber was erupting through the ragged aperture that had been blasted in the wall; churning and foaming at the bottom of the culvert. Den wondered what would happen to the water from outside when it got into the culvert. Would it *also* ignore the basic rules of gravity and begin thundering up the slope after them? They stood and watched as the thundering torrent swirled and churned at the culvert's base. It was rising, slowly and surely filling the space in which they had been standing, but showing no signs of hurtling after them like some sort of crazy reverse waterfall.

Taylor's beam swung away, and the others turned back to see that he had begun climbing the slope again. They followed.

Den shone his torch ahead of Taylor, trying to see if there was any end in sight. The beam sharply outlined the way ahead, but was then diffused into darkness. Clearly, the summit was some considerable way off.

Taylor's foot slipped. His beam wavered.

'Don't fall back on me, man,' said Moss. 'It's a long way down and I've had more than enough dousings for one day.'

In the next moment, Taylor fell forward, face down. The flashlight fell from his hands, bouncing and clattering down the culvert past Moss and Den. The lens cracked and broke, the light was extinguished and now the shattered remains of the flashlight went bouncing and tumbling away from them into the darkness.

'Taylor!' Den lunged forward, grabbing his leg lest he should suddenly roll over and follow the flashlight, tumbling down the culvert.

'What the bloody *hell* . . .' grunted Moss, and scrambled up from behind to join them.

Den turned Taylor carefully over on to his back, placing the flashlight on the ground so that it shone over his face but would not follow the other into the darkness. Taylor's face seemed spectrally white, but that was probably the torch beam. His breathing was shallow, and when Den slapped his face to rouse him, he grimaced and curled over, hugging his stomach just as he had done earlier. He stayed in that position, showing no signs of recovering. Moss struggled alongside, also shining his beam directly into Taylor's face.

'He's hurt,' said Den. 'He must be hurt.'

'Of course the bastard's hurt,' said Moss. 'Smashed up in a helicopter, stabbed. A whole mass of fucking scars just stitched together. But he'd better not give up on us now. I've got every intention of getting out of this place alive.'

Den fumbled at the collar of Taylor's wet suit, then tried to unfasten the front. He shook him by the shoulder again, but Taylor did not react. His face was still screwed up in pain, teeth clenched. Moss leaned over Den and smacked Taylor's face hard. Den grabbed Moss's wrist and yanked him away. Moss shoved him hard so that he almost fell into the culvert at their side. Anger swelled inside Den as he scrambled back. When he spoke again, the rage made his voice tremble.

'Just what the hell are you doing here anyway, Moss?'

Moss was still shining the beam directly into Taylor's face. 'You get lippy with me, boy, and I'll have to give you a good slapping.'

'Oh, yeah? So let's just you and me have it out now, and let Taylor die.'

'Who says he's going to die?' The very suggestion alarmed Moss. He shook Taylor hard with his free hand. 'What's wrong with the fucker anyway?'

Taylor moaned and tried to sit up.

'So why?' continued Den. 'Come on, I want to know. I mean, I know why I'm here, and I think I might even understand what Taylor's doing here. But you. You don't make any sense at all.'

'Mother sent me. And good boys always do what their mother tells them. That's all you need to know.'

'Fuck you. That's no answer. For me and him, it's personal. We'll do anything to get Susan out of here alive. But there's nothing in it for you. Nothing at all.'

'Nothing except the promise that Taylor made. I'm here to see he keeps it. That's all.'

'Yeah,' said Den with disdain. 'Yeah, a *promise*.'

'That's right.' Moss's face was fixed and deadly serious. 'Draegerman is going to die. And if Taylor doesn't see to it, then I will.'

'So what have *you* got against Draegerman?'

'You really want to know? Okay, I'll fucking tell you. I grew up on the streets around The Rock. I've seen what happens there. And the only reason that it's a cesspit is because the system *allows* it to be a cesspit. And the people at the top are people like Draegerman. They only stay at the top because they keep people like us at the bottom.'

'Well, pardon me,' said Den. 'Here I am thinking you're a gangster, and all the time you're a fucking revolutionary, fighting for the people's rights.'

'The time's right. We're going to bring the bastard down. And when we do bring him down, all the other rich bastards like him will start thinking twice. *He's* the reason behind all the bad stuff going on out there. In every country, every city, all over the fucking world, you'll find people like him – sucking everything good out of the streets and never giving anything back but token gestures so that the fucking establishment can tip their fucking hats and say: 'Well, look what he's doing! Yeah? Well I've spent all my life on those streets and the only reason that me and mine are surviving at all is because we've not sat back and waited for the bastards to screw us. We've taken what we needed, and we've kept them *out!*'

'Don't talk to me about hard times on the street, Moss.' Now Den's voice was quiet and measured, no longer trembling with rage. 'I've been there. I've grown up on streets like that. And everything I got out of life that was any fucking good was what I worked for and cared about. I lived by the rules, played it straight and I've got nothing to complain about. My brother was like you, and he took the easy option. Dead at nineteen, a fucking heroin addict. So next time you're raking in the profits from your street dope peddlers, just remember what I'm telling you: You're no fucking solution, *you're* the fucking problem.'

Moss lunged across Taylor's prostrate body, his flashlight beam swinging crazily over the walls and ceiling. In that same movement, he seized Den around the waist and slammed him backwards over the narrow rim of the culvert and into the water. He brought the full weight of his body to bear on Den, pinning him down by the throat. They lay there with the shallow water swirling *up* around them, face to face.

'We get out of here alive,' said Moss through gritted teeth, 'and I'll take you on a conducted tour of my neighbourhood, you little shit.

351

You'll find that those streets are clean, and the reason that they're clean is that me and mine *made* those fucking streets clean. The only shit being peddled was white boy's shit. Hear that? *White* dealers! And where does most of the money from that go? Straight on up to the big white bosses – just like Draegerman and his kind!'

Den lunged up to jam his flashlight under Moss's chin, illuminating his face like a Halloween mask as he pushed him away. Grunting, Moss leaned down, squeezing the breath out of Den, who thrashed beneath the heavier man.

Then Moss made a guttural sound, a grunt of pain, and flew back from Den, landing on his back on the concrete slope. Den rolled out of the water, choking and rubbing his larynx, to see that Taylor had recovered, had seized Moss by the neck and hauled him backwards. Moss scrabbled to his knees, saw that Taylor had recovered, and remained crouched there, deciding against throwing himself back at Den. Taylor waited to make sure that the struggle was over, then sat back on the slope and rubbed his chest and stomach with one hand. When he grimaced this time, it was as if he was suffering from mild heartburn.

'For a fella who's dying or almost dead,' said Moss, 'you've got a hell of a grip.'

Taylor nodded. 'Save it . . . save it for later.'

'What the hell is wrong with you?' asked Den. 'That's the second time, Taylor.'

'You're not going to die on us are you?' asked Moss.

'Yes,' said Taylor simply. 'I'm going to die. But now now. Maybe not a month from now. But soon. The point is, we've a job to do. And I'll see that it's done.'

'Fucking great!' snapped Moss. 'Why didn't you tell me that *before* we crawled into this fucking toilet?'

'Because the chances are that you wouldn't have given me the help I need.'

'Too right we wouldn't!'

'Then the case rests. The fact is, we're here. So let's get on with it.'

'What is it?' asked Den. 'What's wrong with you?'

'Cancer of the colon. Doctor gave me a few months.'

'You're something else, Taylor,' said Moss. 'The streets needed a hero, and you're it. So in a couple of months they're going to have a dyed-in-the-wool fucking martyr as well. But just don't go collapsing or keeling over again until we're out of here. Right?'

'Give me your flash, Den.' Taylor held out his hand.

Without question, Den handed it over.

Taylor shone it down past them, at the torrent that gushed far below. Then he swung it uphill.

'Shall we go?' he said simply. He turned from them and began to climb as if nothing had happened.

Still rubbing his neck, Den followed.

Shaking his head in disbelief, so did Moss.

EIGHT

'There's no end to this!' Susan suddenly yelled. 'Never an *end*!'

They had paused at the next corner, looking back along the corridor. The fog was still there; still creeping along the walls, its gauze-like tendrils curling and groping through the air. It was coming at the same pace; slowly, almost languidly, but with what seemed to be a horrible confidence, a dreadful certainty that it would find them at last.

'We just keep running and running ... and there's still never any hope of getting out of this place!' Susan jammed her knuckles into her mouth, trying to control the inner terror. Roy gripped her shoulder and she looked at him. He was trying to reassure her, but the strained look of fear was deeply etched in his face.

'So what do we do?' Boone's voice held traces of a taunt within it. 'Just stay here and let it get us?'

'Maybe that's the only way!' snapped Susan, diverting fear into anger. 'At least we'll be cutting off that bastard's pleasure in seeing us suffer. We should just get it over with now. Finish it!'

'Stop,' said Roy, squeezing her shoulder again. He never took his gaze from the thickening cloud of fog behind them as it slowly crept and filled the corridor. They pressed on. Bobby was a little way ahead, leaning on the corridor wall; and now Susan moved quickly towards him, as if helping Gloria's son was another way of diverting the gnawing fear inside her. Bobby allowed her to sling his arm over her shoulder. Roy took his other arm, and they moved off again. Boone shoved roughly past them to take the lead as usual, putting the main crowd between him and any following threat.

'Devil take the hindmost, eh, Boone?' said Roy.

Boone did not answer. Still clutching his attaché case, he hurried ahead.

Jessica had been silent during this latest flight, but kept looking back over her shoulder. There was fear in her eyes, but Roy could not help thinking that something else was going on in her mind.

'What is it?' he asked as they moved.

354

Jessica shot a glance at him, then back at the fog. She shook her head. But clearly, she was puzzling over something.

'Come on, Jessica. Tell me. What is it?'

'It's ... I don't know ... there's something. Something different.'

'About the fog back there? What's different?'

'That's just it. I don't know. But something ... something ...'

The fog suddenly billowed and curled outwards, as if blown by a gust of wind. Jessica gave a small cry of alarm and the others reacted by hurrying their pace. Roy turned to look back, and strained to see if there were any shapes hidden in the mist. Was there anything in there that might be using the fog as a cover to pursue them? Still looking back, he ran into Boone, who had suddenly stopped. Bobby staggered and almost fell. Susan cursed and pulled him out of the way.

'What the hell ... ?' began Roy, then saw what it was that had made him stop.

'Oh, sweet Jesus.'

The corridor ahead continued for perhaps twenty yards before curving out of sight to the left. Once again, it could have been the same corridor they had been travelling down ever since their first flight from the Berserker. The same dripping black stone, the same hideous orange lights set high on the wall.

But around the left-hand curve, tendrils of fog were creeping and drifting towards them.

Susan hung on to Bobby and felt his trembling begin again. She could not look at what lay ahead. Biting her lip, she stared down at the ground and prayed that this was all just a hallucination. When she looked up again, she did not look directly ahead. Instead, she looked at Roy. He was standing straight and still, his white face etched with ever-present fear. Boone was standing like some store dummy, with the attaché case clasped to his chest. The scar on his face seemed suddenly vivid, as if the scar tissue was draining all the blood from his face. Jessica was standing at the far wall, arms spread wide against the brickwork behind her, now looking frantically from left to right.

'No,' said Susan simply. 'I won't look.'

But she looked anyway.

The fog was surging around the corner ahead now, its clutching tendrils creeping along the walls, the floor and the ceiling.

When she looked behind, the fog that had pursued them had begun to creep around the last corner. Draegerman's Daemon or Daemons had found them. They were hemmed in and there was no escape.

Boone sank to his knees. He began to mumble. Was he saying prayers?

Roy moved towards Susan and Bobby, holding out his hand to Jessica. She moved away from the wall to take it, still glancing back and forth at the approaching fog. They huddled together in a knot around Bobby, who kept his face down-turned.

'Together,' said Roy. 'At least it's together.'

And as if drawn by the anguish in Roy's voice, the fog suddenly gushed in on them from both sides. They were instantly shrouded in a deep-chilled mantle. It was a coldness that stung their bare skin and froze the sweat on their bodies. It rolled and curled and gushed, enveloping them as smoke might have engulfed those burned at the stake. Despite the cold, they waited for the flames of Hell to envelop them in all their agony and soul-searing hunger.

And then Jessica said: 'It's not ... it's not ...' She could barely speak.

But was she trembling with fear, or with some other emotion?

'It's not the same,' she finished. 'This fog is *not* the same.'

'What ...?' Susan felt the coldness seep through their joint embrace, felt the fog curl around her face, trying to creep into her mouth.

'I mean it's *not the same*!' Jessica suddenly pushed out of the circle, her movement causing the fog to swirl and part. Her eyes were wide. And now she was flailing out with both arms, scattering the wraith-like tentacles that surrounded them.

Susan also let go of Bobby to lash out, and watched as the fog parted before her face. Bobby had begun to laugh quietly, but it was a sound of utter desperation.

'It's only fog!' shouted Jessica, still flailing out. Tears streamed down her face now. 'It's not a Daemon. It doesn't *feel* the same as the other times. Thank Christ, it's just *fog*!'

'You mean we've been running from *nothing*?' demanded Boone angrily.

'The fog back there in the Studio Swamp ...' Jessica whirled again, slapping out at the chilled air. 'And the fog in that chamber with Farrow. They both had personalities, both had different essences. But this is .. dead. It's just plain fog.'

Boone charged ahead down the corridor, the fog swirling around him.

Bobby continued to laugh, but it was not a sound of relief. It still contained that note of utter desolation. Eyes brimming with tears, Susan hugged him tight. Roy turned to brace both hands on the cold stone wall.

'I thought that was it,' he breathed. 'I really thought that was *it*!'

From ahead, Boone called: 'I think you'd better come here.'

Feeling weak and drained, they moved slowly ahead to catch up with him. His voice had been flat and unemotional. No need to worry about further threat. They could see him now, standing up ahead in the thick fog, a vague silhouette. And as they moved, they could see also that he seemed somehow illumined. Was there a new source of light ahead, around the corner of the corridor? A way out? They reached him, standing at the bend. For the second time, they saw what he saw – and for the second time, they were speechless at the sight of it.

The corridor ended around the bend, opening out into another large chamber. This was a chamber filled with the same undulating, all-enveloping fog. It swirled before them, drifting and eerie. But it was not the fog itself which caused them to halt and stare numbly. It was the landscape before them. Because this time, they had emerged not into an impossible interior jungle, or a studio swamp, or some hideous S&M torture chamber – but into a street.

The fog obscured the buildings, swirled around the roofs of the terraced houses off to their left, a terrace that vanished into darkness. Directly ahead of them was an alley. A stone arch swept over the alleyway and as they looked they could see that there were cobbles on the ground. A nineteenth-century street lamp fought to maintain its fuzzy illumination through the fog-clouds that curled towards them down the alley. It was impossible to see any great detail through the arch, but there was a bare outline of iron railings and the steps and porch of what looked like an old-fashioned town house. To the right of the arch they could see what appeared to be the blank wall of a warehouse.

'Studio fog,' said Jessica, nodding her head. 'That's what this stuff is. Studio fog. Real fog doesn't move and swirl like this. Only the stuff that's made and blown by a machine.'

Her words seemed flat and hollow in this place, as if sound had difficulty in penetrating the miasma. But even as that impression registered, there was another sound to confound the assumption and their expectations. It was the distant but unmistakable sound of a horse's hooves on cobbles. It was the sound of a nineteenth-century hansom cab, out there on the street beyond the fog.

'Another movie set,' said Roy. And everyone recalled the previous conversation, remembered Roy's words about the possibility of the Daemons' movements being restricted to Draegerman's movie sets. The fog had gushed into the corridor, and moved them on; once again, Draegerman had managed to herd them all in the direction he wanted. And if Roy's surmise was right, they were once again in the potential lair of another of the hideous Daemons.

The sound of the hansom cab clattering past on the cobbled street faded and vanished. No one questioned that it was a recorded sound effect somewhere out there in the fog.

'I'm going back,' said Boone simply. 'I don't care what anyone says, I'm not going in there. I'm going back into that corridor . . .' He backed away from the others. No one felt inclined to convince him otherwise.

And then Susan said: 'Oh, no. No, I won't believe that. No, that's not right.' She was shaking her head and looking away, as if trying

357

to avoid some terrible internal voice which had just told her a terrible secret. She moved away and began to follow Boone.

'What won't you believe?' Roy was darting anxious glances from Susan back into the fog-bound alley. *'What?'*

And then they all started in alarm when a thin screeching sound came from behind them. It was the sound of someone in distress; someone whose sanity seemed under threat. Susan recoiled and Roy lunged past to find Boone. The fog rolled around them, and Roy saw Boone standing where the corridor opening had been. For some reason, he was standing up close to the stone wall at the side of the corridor entrance, the ever-present attaché case now lying at his feet. He was slapping the bare stone wall with both hands. And now Roy could see that it was Boone who was making the thin, keening sounds of distress.

'Boone, what the hell are you doing?'

Boone did not answer. He continued to slap the stone walls.

Roy moved to pull him back, looked over to his right – and could not see the corridor entrance. Was the fog so thick here that it was covering the entrance? He lashed at the air, making the fog part, and saw only bare black stone. He threw himself at the wall, felt its coldness, went hand over hand to his right, away from Boone, expecting to find the entrance at any moment.

There was no entrance.

Because now, there was no corridor.

'No, that's not possible. That isn't possible.'

Roy moved quickly back to where Boone was pounding at the wall.

'Oh Christ,' said Jessica from behind when she could see what was happening.

Roy passed by Boone, kept running his hands over the stone, moving to the left. No, the corridor could surely not have been so far over in this direction.

'It was here!' sobbed Boone. 'It was *here*, and now it's ... it's ...' He could not go on. He pressed his face up close to the stone, as if hoping that it would suddenly absorb him, suck him through to the other side.

'I didn't hear anything,' said Jessica weakly. 'No gears, no wheels, no pulleys. It can't just have gone ...'

'Well, it has!' Roy ran back to join them, leaving Boone where he stood.

'I know what this is,' said Susan, again struggling to remain calm, fighting her inner voice. 'I've seen this before. I know I've seen this before. With Den, at the cinema. Years ago. We'd been out clubbing. Sara was looking after the kids and we decided to take in one of those late-night horror shows. I remember now. It was one of *his* movies. Look

... there!' She pointed to the left of the arched alleyway. 'See there – it's a street sign.'

Roy peered through the murk at the sign which was almost obscured by the swirling fog.

'White ...' he began.

'Whitechapel,' finished Jessica. 'It says "Bucks Row, Whitechapel".'

'What was the movie?' asked Roy in a flat voice, without turning back to look at them.

'It was about Jack the Ripper,' said Susan. 'Jack-the-fucking-Ripper! And the movie was called *Jack's Back Again*. And it was *sick*. It was in black and white, so I remember Den and I booed at it, got shushed by the people in front. But then when it started, it was just ... it was one of the sickest things I've ever seen. We were expecting some old, hammy horror movie. But it was ... was ...' Susan could not find the words to express her feelings. 'It ruined our night. We left before it finished.'

'Well, let's leave before it *starts*,' said Roy, and stepped forward on to the cobbled street.

Boone staggered towards them, away from the wall.

'Can't ... can't ...'

'Look, let's not waste any time arguing the point. We're *here*, right in the middle of this bloody movie set or whatever the hell it is. And we know it can't go on for ever, so the best we can do is get out of here, find another exit and get the hell out of this place as fast as we can.' Roy stepped back, touching Susan's shoulder.

Again, they could hear the sounds of a horse's hooves on cobbles. It was the same recording.

'But ...' Boone began to wave his arms ineffectually, now looking back in the vain hope that the corridor entrance would suddenly have materialised in the fog.

The others did not speak. With silent resolution, they banded close together – Bobby again held in the middle and beginning to tremble violently once more.

As one, they stepped forward on to the cobbled street. Boone hastily joined them at the rear.

'Which way?' said Roy. 'What does everyone think?'

'The quickest and the shortest way looks to be straight ahead down the cobbled street, under the arch,' said Jessica.

Susan had been looking at the terraced houses to the left. 'But that could be the way he wants us to go.'

'That warehouse wall seems to screen everything off on the right.' Roy was peering back that way, through the fog.

'Couldn't we just follow that wall around, on the outside?' asked Susan. 'See if we come to another corridor?'

'No, look. The bare stone wall ends where that warehouse wall

359

begins. We couldn't get around that way ... and over to the left, by those terraces there – that looks like a hell of a long way round. What do you think?'

'Ahead,' said Susan at last. 'Like Jessica says. The sooner we get to the other side of this place the better.'

The fog enveloped them as they headed for the arch.

Their footsteps sounded flat on the cobbles. It was a horribly vulnerable sound. In moments, they had reached the pavement on the other side. The arched alleyway lay beyond. Overhead, the sign was clearly visible now: 'Bucks Row, Whitechapel'.

The fog swirling in the mouth of the arch looked like the great grey whorl of some immense spider's web. Was there some hideous parody of a spider waiting for them in there now, waiting for them to enter? Fighting off the hideous image, Roy led them on through the arch. And as soon as they had passed beneath it, another sound reached their ears, as if their presence had triggered further effects for this living movie.

It was the sound of a hurdy-gurdy. The staple cliché of all the fogbound-Victorian-streets-of-London movies they had ever seen over the years. It was even playing *Molly Malone*, and to Jessica there was a horrible irony about the choice of tune and its refrain of "Alive, alive-o."

They continued down the cobbled alley, looking anxiously about as they moved from side to side. They could see the rough brickwork of the walls on either side, the worn and cracked steps leading up to forbidding doorways. This was no real-life Victorian street. This was some studio art director's version of such a street; designed for the most horrid of horror movies. The doors hidden by fog and shadows were either too small or too large. Just like the doors, the angles of the shaded windows were all wrong. They could not possibly have been designed for practical use; the planes and perspectives were irregular and obeyed some insane perspective. Jessica remembered a childhood viewing of the silent movie *The Cabinet of Dr Caligari*, and knew now what that studio designer had in mind for this set, albeit on a more subtle, yet vastly disturbing level.

'Wait,' hissed Roy. He slipped away from them. The others were reluctant to let him go, clinging to the naive view that simple safety in numbers might see them through anything that might happen here. Quickly, he ran to a set of railings to their left; irregular railings that fronted what seemed to be a lodging house. Looking anxiously around, he seized one of the railings – and yanked hard.

It came away easily in his hand.

'Shit!'

He hurried back to join them, hefting the spiked railing like a spear.

'It's only painted wood. I thought it would be iron or steel. But it's a movie prop, like everything else.'

'Maybe these houses are just façades,' whispered Jessica. 'You know, wooden frontages. Maybe there's a way out behind one of them?'

Roy shook his head. 'I could see rooms behind the windows of that place over there. I think it's best we press on.'

The sound of the hurdy-gurdy died. Again, an invisible hansom cab passed close by and was swallowed by the fog.

Susan looked back in the direction from which they had come. The archway was faintly illumined by the hidden street lamp beyond.

'Oh.' She turned quickly back.

'What?' Roy jerked back to look at her.

'I thought . . .'

'*What?*'

'I thought I saw someone back there by the arch. Thought I saw a shadow in a cape . . .'

They were all looking back as they hurried onwards now. There was nothing to see but the swirling fog; the grim and bare outlines of the arch and the walls.

'Someone's laughing,' said Boone tightly.

'I can't hear anything,' said Roy.

'I tell you I heard someone back there in the fog, *laughing*.'

'How far is it, for God's sake?' Susan stumbled on a cobble and cursed, Bobby's weight hanging heavily on her.

'Still can't see much,' said Roy, holding the spear out before him; now turning back to look for the arch and any sign of someone following them back there.

'I heard it again,' said Boone, pointing over to their left. 'Laughter.'

They looked over, saw that Boone was pointing to what seemed to be a pair of large stable-doors. There was a sign above then: Johnson The Distillers.

'Still can't hear anything,' said Jessica.

'I heard it, I tell you! I *heard* it!'

They moved on. And now it seemed that they had reached the end of the cobbled street. Was the fog simply obscuring any further mock buildings on either side of the street up ahead, or did the movie set really end here? Was there another corridor beyond the swirling grey clouds ahead? Bobby's head still hung down on his chest. Now they were all but carrying his trembling body. Susan shifted his weight and Jessica moved to compensate. Roy leaned back to help and . . .

'*Help me . . .*' said a voice from the fog up ahead.

As one, they stopped dead, whirling to look at the swirling mass before them.

'I heard *that*,' said Roy, looking back. Both Jessica and Susan nodded their heads vigorously. They had heard it too. Boone just stared ahead, mouth open.

'*Please help me* ...' The voice, at first seeming distant, was now alarmingly close and horribly plaintive.

Roy held out the railing in both hands like a lance.

'Look, if we have to ...' He glanced back at them, tried to assess where there night be a short cut to the terraced houses which they knew to be over to the left.' ... if we have to make a run for it, I'll try ... try to ...'

A shape materialised in the fog up ahead.

'*Help me* ...' And now the voice was close, and obviously a woman's voice. A woman in deep distress.

The fog wreathed the figure. But it was unmistakably the figure of a woman, holding both arms across her chest. The gesture might be one of pain, or that of a dead person laid to rest. Was it a dead person, even now drifting through the fog towards them? Was it walking? Or was it floating horribly through the air to meet them?

'*Please, Bobby*,' said the figure, in a sudden and shockingly familiar voice. '*Please help me, baby.*'

The spectral shape ahead was no more than twenty feet from where they stood.

But it was Gloria.

Impossibly, Gloria Pernell stood wreathed in the hideous fog and held both her arms out towards them in a welcoming embrace.

'Mother!' Bobby was suddenly rigid, no longer hanging limply between Susan and Jessica.

Now it seemed that Gloria was standing over some hidden vent in the ground; a vent from which the fog was gushing, enveloping her body, snake-like gauze tentacles curling around her waist and outstretched arms.

'No colour,' said Jessica weakly. 'She's black and white ...'

There was no vestige of colour in Gloria's face; it seemed perfectly lit for a Draegerman *Gothique-noir*, eyes hooded and shaded, lipstick black as licorice. Her clothes were the same as before; but this time only in shades of grey. Gloria's black hair was flowing like the fog around her face. The hair seemed alive, like the living serpents that crowned the Gorgon's dreaded stare. And Jessica did not have to say anything to remind the others about her instinctive feelings in the presence of a Daemon – because now they were all feeling it. They could all feel the revulsion, the fly's inner dread of the spider.

'*Bobby, darling. Help me* ...'

Bobby struggled to be free, and succeeded in wrenching his arm clear of Jessica's grasp. Susan clung tight, preventing him from surging ahead. Roy stood back, planting one hand on his chest and hissing:

'It's not her, Bobby! It's not your mother!'

'You're a lying bitch, Jessica,' said Bobby tearfully as she clung to him. 'You said she was dead ...'

362

'And she *is* dead, Bobby! Can't you feel it, can't you *feel* that it's not her?'

'Let me go! She needs me!'

'Bobby, stop it!' Susan tried to loop her other arm around his neck. Jessica had grabbed his elbow again, face white and staring at the thing that was not Gloria.

Slowly, gradually, the hideously colourless figure was coming towards them through the fog. And it seemed that it was not walking, but *gliding* over the cobbled street, arms outstretched.

'*Someone come and keep me warm.*'

'Let him go to her!' stammered Boone.

Bobby grabbed for the railing in Roy's other hand. Roy twisted away, clenching his fist in Bobby's shirt front as Susan and Jessica struggled to hold him.

'Let him go!' Boone backed off from them, eyes glued to the approaching figure. 'If it takes him, it'll leave us alone!'

'Boone, you shit!' snapped Susan. 'Help us . . .'

'Run!' yelled Jessica, dragging Bobby, trying to pull him backwards. 'Everyone just *run!*'

And then somehow Bobby yanked the railing out of Roy's hand. Roy fell, a handful of shirt ripping away from Bobby's collar and chest. The fog gushed over Roy's body as he struggled to rise, but the violence of Bobby's action had torn him free from Jessica's grasp. He stumbled over Roy, following him to the ground in an awkward tumble, and Susan also lost her balance, falling heavily to the side and landing painfully on her hip. Before anyone else could react, Bobby leapt to his feet, fog swilling around him – and holding the railing like a spear, jabbed it at the others as they struggled to rise and reach him.

'Keep away from me!'

The spear smacked across Roy's forearm as he tried to reach him. He cried out in pain. Hugging his arm, he scrambled backwards. Jessica had moved to Susan, was helping her to stand, and Bobby kept lunging at them as he backed away.

'For Christ's *sake*, Bobby!' shouted Roy.

'She's alive!'

There was a horrifying inevitability about what followed.

Bobby threw the wooden railing to the ground. It was engulfed in the swirling fog. His face was a riot of confusing emotion; shock, defiance, and above all a desperate eagerness to show that everything was all right and that the others were wrong. Uttering a short bark of a laugh, he turned and lunged backwards, arms spread wide . . . unaware that the thing that looked like Gloria Pernell was right behind him, arms outstretched.

'Oh *Jesus* . . .' Jessica could not look, burying her face in Susan's chest.

363

Susan and Roy could only stand and look with white, shocked faces as Bobby was taken in the Daemon's embrace.

Could they have been wrong? Could their terror have confused their instincts? Because Gloria was not turning into some ravening beast, was not changing in the way that Jessica had seen that other thing turn from Roy into one of Draegerman's fever-dream creations. Bobby had been taken into Gloria's loving embrace, her arms around him. He in turn was holding her around the waist, his face buried in her shoulder, his eyes wet with tears, his face contorted not in pain but with vast, flooding relief; the relief of a lost child in the arms of its mother again. And now, somehow, they were turning, spinning slowly around and around on the same spot as the fog swirled and caressed. It was like some slow, languid waltz – except that neither Gloria nor Bobby's legs were moving at all. They were standing on some pedestal hidden in the undulating fog, dancing their slow *danse macabre* to an uncanny melody that no one else could hear.

Slowly, slowly, they were moving away from them into the fog. Turning and turning, loving and tender; reunited at last.

And then they heard the music: not a waltz at all, but a faint yet melodramatic orchestral piece, seeming to come from all around. Now growing louder as they danced. It was a full orchestra: a swelling and urgent flurrying of strings; now a stabbing three-note statement by the brass section; now a thundering of drums. And somewhere within that great and overly dramatic movement were the sounds of a small, 1950s jazz combo which was intergrated with the music, but desperately wanted to break free. They had heard this kind of music before; had heard it many, many times in the past – on late-night television or in the darkened cavern of a high-street cinema. Soundtrack music, without doubt – from a Draegerman movie.

When the narrator's voice started, it seemed to be accompanied by a hissing static, but the rising, swelling music had become horribly expectant.

'*Six teenagers looking for kicks.*' And from somewhere within this multi-layered soundtrack came the sound of revving motorcycle engines. '*Instead, they found only terror. Looking for thrills, they found only . . death.*' Somewhere, an actress screamed. '*And an unimaginable terror from beyond called . . .*' The orchestra blared stridently. '*The Speed Demon!*'

And in the space of one slow turn in their dreadful dance, as Gloria's back was to them, they could see a blurring jumble of movement around her head. Bobby's face was still buried in her shoulder, her hands around his waist. But as she turned to face them, they instinctively shrank away. Gloria's ghostly black-and-white visage had become the reptilian obscenity that Jessica had seen back in the studio swamp: Draegerman's Swamp Water Woman. A forked

364

tongue tasted the air around her face and whipped back between the hideous lips.

Another slow turn, and Bobby was still weeping into the thing's embrace. And again, there was a rippling blur of motion around the snake-thing's head.

And this time, when the thing turned to face them, the hidden orchestra delivered another musical 'sting', and the bass voice melodramatically announced:

'*Starring Bobby Pernell, in his most exciting role yet.*'

And the others looked on the face of the Speed Demon.

The snake-woman's head had swollen to twice its size, stretching and reforming from its reptilian shape into something rounder but no less hideous. Now, suddenly, there were large black, pointed ears. Coarse hair now covered the glistening reptilian skin. The snout had shrunk back into this new face to become a bat-like triangular cavity, tight black-rubber skin peeling back from the thing's mouth to reveal ragged, glinting teeth dripping with saliva. Glass-bead eyes caught sparking red-light – and in the next instant, the thing had raised its hands from Bobby's waist and held them high above his head. The hands had become talons, and their multi-jointed claws were also somehow hypodermic needles. Bobby still clung to his mother's waist, still had his face buried in a shoulder that was now covered in bristling black hair; a change that he seemed not to have noticed.

The thing did not have claws. Its multi-jointed fingers ended in what looked like hypodermic needles.

As they turned again, the thing stabbed its hands downwards.

The hypodermic fingernails plunged through the back of Bobby's shirt as the thing hugged him even closer.

The orchestra enhanced the violent movement with another stab of strings, followed by a flurrying, hideously expectant trilling of clarinets and other woodwind. Bobby threw his head back in silent agony as they continued to turn slowly in their hideous dance. They could see his face as the thing's powerful, black-furred back turned to them once more.

'*They were looking for speed, looking for thrills,*' said the voice. '*But this time, they got all this . . . and more!*'

The music swirled. The fog wreathed them in its loving, clinging embrace.

They turned in their dance.

And Bobby's expression of agony had changed, as the drugs injected into his system by the thing's hypodermic claws took instant effect, softening into a raptured expression of bliss. He clung tight to the thing that held him, squeezing its waist even tighter as the hideous tails kneaded and worked. And Bobby opened his mouth in ecstasy, head still held back, as his system was flooded with what it was craving. The last and fastest high in his life, the thing's chemicals speeding supernaturally through his veins as they turned again in their dance.

'I can see ... can see ...' And Bobby seemed to be choking on his laughter as he fumbled with one hand at the thing's side. The Speed Demon slowly raised and held back its head as he groped.

'I can see a *zip fastener!*' His laughter ebbed away as his fingers found something in the thing's side, and he pulled down. The Speed Demon's side seemed to open up from underarm to waist and then ...

Something like a hideous, glistening serpent erupted from its glutinous intestines, fastening on Bobby's hand. His laughter turned to screams of pain as the thing hissed and writhed. He jerked his hand away, but the thing flew back like a striking snake. In three quick jabs, almost too quick to see, it had bitten off three of his fingers. Bobby's hand erupted in a red welter. Mouth open in shock, he looked at his hand, and then turned back to look at the thing – just as it buried its hideous glistening bat-snout between his back-flung head and his chest; its face seeming to engulf his throat utterly.

Bobby tried to scream but could not. His mouth was wide in agony and horror once more as he swirled around in the dance. The thing guzzled and worried at his throat, still clutching him tight with both claws embedded in his back. Blood was leaking from the hypodermic nails now; streaming down his shirt and legs. And when Bobby turned to face them again, his mouth was opening and closing slowly, his eyes glazed. The thing that had erupted form the Daemon's side was burrowing into his chest. His shirt was alive with movement. In the next moment, a black torrent of blood filled his mouth and then erupted around the sides of his face.

'Oh my *God!*'

Filled with horror and fear, but also with an intense rage at his own feelings and inability to act, Roy groped in the swirling fog at his feet. He found the wooden railing, lunged back to his feet and uttered a loud and horrified cry, so intense that the others flinched from him as he took two great running steps – and flung the wooden railing directly at the thing. He fell to his knees in the fog.

The Dance of Death was still being enacted.

The music was still playing, swirling strings matching the swirling fog.

The thing was still hunched forward, feeding on Bobby.

And as its back turned to them, the railing embedded with all the force of a javelin in its right shoulder blade.

The effect was instantaneous.

The thing's head snapped back in a flurried spray of blood. It emitted a great shrieking sound, feral and enraged and agonised, as the railing shivered in its back. The orchestra speeded up and then droned to halt – as if someone had pulled the plug on hidden recording equipment.

366

The fog immediately around the two figures seemed to be writhing and curling at great speed, like footage of some billowing, volcanic cloud. The fog was at once *darker* than the fog that engulfed the rest of this bizarre studio set. The figures were still turning in their dance, and now the others could see that the tip of that railing was protruding from the front of the thing's shoulder. It let go of Bobby's inanimate body with one claw and scrabbled at its back. Bobby sagged, a bloody and feebly moving mass. Then the thing found the protruding javelin, seized it from behind and yanked hard, dragging it out of its shoulder in a gout of black blood. It shrieked again and lowered its head.

It fixed them with its red-marble eyes.

The bat-ears were stiff and erect, as if the thing was bristling with rage.

Roy shrank back to the others.

Boone was already running back towards the archway.

And then, shrieking again, the thing cast the railing aside, seized Bobby with both hands – and was gone.

The fog spun and curled on the spot where both figures had been, like some kind of smoke whirlpool.

In the next instant, something seemed to be hurtling down on them in a rush of air. Something so fast that it was invisible, something so fast that it knocked Roy, Susan and Jessica flat to the ground as it passed over them, sending up a great wave of gushing fog, a wave of fog that spread tidally, erupting over the sidewalk to either side.

Another rush of wind.

And Roy struggled up in a daze to see . . .

Something crouching in the bizarre angular doorway of a fake barber's shop on the other side of the street. Something that was holding a limp and dripping form. Something that vanished even as the image registered. Another great rushing of air filled their ears and a fake length of fencing thirty yards behind them on the other side of the street suddenly split apart as if something had collided with it. The false wooden railings clattered to the cobbled street in a jumbled, toppling mass as the fog around them suddenly gushed high, and the running figure of Boone was slammed to the cobbled street from behind by the invisible, rushing something.

Fog swirled in the archway as the thing sped invisibly from sight with its prey.

Boone struggled groggily to his feet.

And from somewhere, they heard a distant, dying scream.

It was Bobby – screaming his last, as he was borne away into the dark canyons between this world and the next.

Jessica began to weep. So did Susan. They fell to their knees, unaware that the fog was suddenly evaporating all around them. Roy staggered back to where they knelt. Stunned and sickened, he stared along the cobbled street to where Boone was walking in circles, hands held out at his sides and looking up as if expecting to see answers to all his questions written in the dissolving fog.

When the scream died forever, Roy sank to his knees beside them.

At that moment, all he could remember was that Bobby had come back to save him on the hideous escalator when he could have run for it and tried to save himself.

They held their arms around each other and mourned him.

And Boone looked at them, uncomprehending. At last, he sat on the kerb of the cobbled street and watched as the fog gradually disappeared.

NINE

The bulldozer snorted angrily as Fisher revved the engine. Smoke so thick that it was almost solid pumped out of the exhaust pipe behind the cab, making one of the passengers squirm away from it, to get a better footing above the caterpillar track. Fisher had gained six such passengers now. One had even tried to climb up on to the raised 'dozer blade, but had looked down beneath him, imagined what would happen it he fell between the blade and the cab, and decided against it, clambering back to hang on the window at the driver's side. Fisher was unconcerned. His eyes remained set dead ahead.

Slowly, remorselessly, the bulldozer headed down the centre of the street towards the Walkway gate.

Fisher was barely aware that people seemed to be cheering and yelling from the streets as the machine coughed and snorted and ploughed on; did not answer the yells from the many faces that jumped up to look at him, then pulled away again.

'You going to knock down The Rock? You going to push it over, man?'

Fisher did not answer, but someone scrambling over the cab roof yelled in response: 'You bet your life we are!'

'Come on, then!' yelled someone from behind, leaning in to slap Fisher across the back.

'Dee-man is a *Dead* Man!' someone began to shout from the darkness on the other side of the street, and his shout was taken up by others. Soon, it seemed that the entire street was chanting: 'Dee-Man is a *Dead* Man! Dee-Man is a *Dead* Man!'

And that chanting seemed to bring images flashing into Fisher's mind. Images of himself, from years ago, flashes of his own face in agonising pain. Images of someone holding him down and strapping him to a chair; someone else tying his arms and legs with leather straps, someone else standing before him with a hypodermic syringe . . .

'Dee-Man is a *Dead* Man! Dee-Man is a *Dead* Man!' . . . and now someone had seized his twisting head, was making him watch while that hypodermic was jammed savagely into his arm. *You nigger-loving*

369

bastard, said someone from behind. *Enjoy your dreams. You've just guaranteed yourself the worst trip that anyone's EVER been on . . .*

'Dee-Man is a *DEAD MAN!*'

Suddenly the cab windscreen exploded, showering Fisher with glass. One hand flew protectively to his face, and the passenger who had tried to climb up on to the blade yelled and dived from the cab to the street.

'Shit!' yelled another voice from behind, and Fisher could hear someone scrabbling across the cab roof.

Then he heard the retort of the gunshot that had come through the windscreen. The security guards in the tower had now taken a definite interest in the bulldozer. But Fisher would not be deterred. He grabbed the lever on his right, and raised the blade higher. No sooner had he done so than another bullet spanged against it, ricocheting with a thin scream into the night. There was a mad scrabbling movement all around the cab, but Fisher was uninterested in the plight of his passengers. Centring the 'dozer in the middle of the street, he kept the accelerator handle pressed forward, and the machine trundled on at its slow but steady pace.

Another three bullets impacted on the blade in quick succession.

Someone shouted from the darkness: 'Who's driving the fucking thing?'

And someone else, still clinging to the back of the bulldozer cab, yelled in reply: 'Don't you know, man? It's *Taylor!*'

The word seemed to act like an electric shock on the street. It was being passed to those who had sought refuge in the shadows, spreading like wildfire to those behind shuttered windows and barred doors. As the word spread, and the shadow-crowd became more excited and agitated, Fisher just smiled grimly and pressed on.

There was a sudden fusillade of shots from ahead. One of the security men in the tower was using an automatic weapon. Someone screamed from behind. But Fisher did not turn around. The rim of the Walkway gate was in sight, and the top of the security tower on the left. He raised the blade slowly and gradually to maintain his protection. He had almost reached the Walkway, a fact heralded by a revived cheering from the street crowd.

A female voice, somewhere close in the darkness, yelled: 'Go, go, GO!'

And then the entire cab jarred, pitching Fisher forward, as the blade rammed into the sheer concrete face of the gate. He kept the lever pressed forward, the engine roaring like some prehistoric animal, the exhaust belching fumes. The caterpillar tracks began to spin, kicking up dust. He heard more automatic weapon fire, and looked back to see that he had no more passengers and that bullets were raking the street a good twenty feet behind the bulldozer. From this position the bulldozer was so close to the concrete face the security guards could

370

not get a proper aim. The street seemed deserted, but beyond the pale street lights he could still hear the chanting and shouting of an invisible crowd. He faced front again, ramming the gear lever into reverse and backing away from the wall, at the same time lowering the blade to mid-position. A bullet tore into the roof, and Fisher realised that he had backed into their sights again. Flooring the accelerator, he rammed the dozer back towards the gate. This time the impact was more pronounced. He *felt* the concrete face give, saw a gaping crack chase from the blade to the concrete buttress to his right. Again, he kept the lever hard forward until the tracks spun and the smell of burning rubber filled the air.

'Dee-Man is a *Dead* Man, Dee-Man is a *Dead* Man!' Again the chanting came from the darkness.

Fisher reversed again, then ploughed back. The crack widened; a chunk of concrete fell forward when he reversed once more. He needed more leverage, needed a better run at the gate than the safety margin of twenty feet behind. Grimly, he reversed back into the sights of the tower. Instantly, the 'dozer was sprayed with machine-gun fire. The metalwork of the cabin roof and the struts supporting the blade were suddenly alive with exploding shrapnel and smoke. A bullet tore by Fisher's face, giving him a livid friction burn from ear to chin – but miraculously he was unhurt as he rammed the advance lever forward once more and the 'dozer thundered back into the gate. The gap widened further. A great crack like a fault-line chased to the top of the gate, the concrete around it caving in and falling on to the blade. The impact of the toppling masonry on the blade tipped the bulldozer forward. For a split second the cab tilted so far that the rear of the machine was lifted from the ground, the tracks roaring wildly in the air. Then, with a heavy crash, it fell back.

That Walkway gate was coming down.

And the crowd behind him was cheering wildly as Fisher reversed the bulldozer out of the still-toppling concrete. The machine slammed forward again; dust gushed over the blade and through the shattered windscreen, into the cab, choking Fisher.

The choking dust cloud was gushing out over the street and in towards the Walkway as the security guards began to fire wildly into it.

Reversing and then lunging forward Fisher could see the leering face of the man who had injected him. The face was looming out of the dust cloud, and Fisher reversed again, roaring forward for another shuddering impact and a great cheering from behind. Now, he remembered the security man's name: Aiken, a sadistic bastard.

Another reverse, and a stray shot ricocheted from the cabin roof again. The bulldozer roared into the dust cloud and Aiken's grinning face instantly shattered and dispersed. Fisher kept the lever rammed forward, and the blade ploughed into the ragged gap that had been made in the Walkway gate.

This time, the gate crumbled and collapsed with a shuddering roar and another gushing cloud of concrete dust. Fisher slammed into reverse, and the bulldozer screeched back on to the street in the cover of the dust cloud. The gunshots from beyond seemed only sporadic now, as if the collapse of the gate had destroyed the security guards' confidence. Fisher choked and gagged as dust swirled in his cabin. He lashed out at the air to clear it. At last, he could see the way ahead. The gateway was down.

'Someone's knocking at your door, Mr Draegerman!'

The bulldozer trundled forwards, over the mound of rubble ahead, kicking up clouds of dust from its caterpillar tracks.

And from behind, Fisher became aware of a great roar of noise as the street people who had been taking cover in the doorways and stairwells and shadowed places broke from their hiding places and ran into the gushing dust cloud that the bulldozer had created. There should be lights ahead, hanging on the suspension cables that held the Walkway in place, but there was only darkness. Fisher could see the Walkway over fifty feet away, stretching out over the seemingly bottomless moat that surrounded Draegerman's Rock. It was flanked on both sides by security towers, from which the gunfire had been coming. Fisher saw movement in the control box at the top of the left-hand tower. In the next moment, the machine lurched and trundled on over the mounded rubble, slamming onto the flat concrete platform beyond.

The security guards up there were waiting for him.

No sooner had the blade blocked the sight of the tower summit from view than an ear-shattering fusillade of shots exploded from beyond. The metalwork of the blade and the struts and the steel shields protecting the front of the caterpillar tracks were blasted in a riot of deadly shrapnel. Fisher kept the blade high, struggled to line the bulldozer up with the Walkway ahead, but the 'dozer began to slide to the right. The blade tilted low and Fisher fought with the controls as the rubble slid beneath the tracks.

He waited for the shot that would end it all.

But the bulldozer lurched back into position, dead centre and aimed at the Walkway. From behind, some of the street people had begun to clamber through the ragged gap, running up behind to use the bulldozer as a shield. Now Fisher became aware of a ragged return volley of small-arms fire from behind, enough to make the security guards keep low in their control box and stop the merciless onslaught of automatic fire from above. The bulldozer snorted and trundled between the two security towers in its own dust cloud, and now Fisher could see the Walkway dead ahead. Five hundred yards away, where the Walkway met the face of Draegerman's Rock, was another entrance. Fisher laughed aloud and kept the advance lever jammed forward. This time, he would take the 'dozer straight through that concrete door. He would punch a hole big enough in the concrete face to let in an entire army of street people.

And then the lone security guard in the right-hand tower – the tower from which there had been no fire so far – leaned out of the side window and let loose a single round from his rifle.

It ricocheted screaming around the interior of the cab, punching through the top of Fisher's left thigh before tearing a hole in the cab floor. A fountain of blood jetted into Fisher's lap as he lurched forward in his seat, grabbing at the wound. The bulldozer ploughed on, but slewed to the left. Shouting in rage and pain, Fisher fumbled with bloody hands to pull his belt out of the waist band of his jeans. Dragging it under his leg and yanking at the steering lever with his free hand to put the bulldozer back on its centre course, he looped the belt through the buckle and pulled hard. The pain made him scream again, but the fountain of blood bubbled down to a slow oozing of red.

There was a gunshot from behind. Then a rattling of automatic fire. Someone back there had managed to get their hands on an Uzi. Fisher saw the right-hand tower's security box window explode into a million glittering fragments; saw the man who had shot him, in full Draegerman security uniform, catapult backwards out of the window, still clutching his weapon. There was cheering again, and more intense fire from behind. The street people were giving him covering fire and chanting:

'Tay-*lor*! Tay-*lor*! Tay-*lor*!'

'The name's Fisher,' he replied through gritted teeth as the bulldozer hit the Walkway ramp and pressed on.

But then something slammed into him from behind, pitching him forward in his seat. The rear window had imploded, showering him with glass. His grip on the belt loosened, and the fountain of crimson began to spout from his leg again. He could hardly breathe, thought at first that it might *not* have been a bullet, but then lurched around to see what he had feared. There was no cover to be had from the bulldozer now. The security men in the control tower had a clear view of his back as he trundled along the Walkway. He fumbled at his back, and felt a gaping wet hole there. His hand was almost black with blood when he brought it around to his face. Strangely, there was no pain. He merely felt winded. There was a flash of light from the tower, and a shot screamed from the metalwork at the back of the bulldozer. Fisher dragged at the controls again. Something zipped stinging past his face, shattering the right-hand window. It felt like a stinging slap, but he had lost an ear.

A great numbness was creeping over his body.

He had covered less than fifty yards of the five hundred that would take him over the other side to Draegerman's Rock.

But when a light flashed from the small concrete pill-box that was a security station at the midway point of the Walkway, and something slammed into his left shoulder, smashing him back in his seat, Fisher knew that he was in trouble.

The numbness was rapidly becoming a fierce rigidity. Fisher knew that soon he would not be able to control the 'dozer. Even now, it was shuddering to a halt on the Walkway. He shook his head, tried to clear his blurred vision, and heard another shot slice singing through the night air.

There was a pause then, as the bulldozer sat snorting angrily on the Walkway.

From behind, the street people were keeping up their own onslaught on the tower.

'Tay-*lor*! Tay-*lor*! Tay-*lor*!'

'It's Fisher ...' He spat blood, darkening his chin.

He would never make the other side.

And then he knew what he had to do.

Grimly, Fisher leaned forward to seize the controls, jamming the gears into reverse. A shot from ahead screamed from the blade, and then the bulldozer swivelled around on the Walkway, tracks screeching on the concrete. He wrestled with the controls, the exhaust pipe belched more smoke and the engine roared angrily. Fisher's fingers were starting to tighten and a great coldness was descending on him. How much longer could he keep control?

The bulldozer swung back the way it had come, making the manoeuvre in several jerking turns, as if the machine itself was a mortally wounded beast. Coughing and roaring, it began to trundle back, blade raised for a protection that now seemed barely necessary.

And with its return, it seemed that the spirit of those who had followed its dust cloud into Draegerman's domain was fragmenting. Still firing ragged volleys up at the left-hand tower, they began to fall back over the mound of rubble that had been the Walkway gate.

The bulldozer was heading back, aiming for the fallen gate.

And the guards in the tower were taking full advantage of the crowd's retreat to concentrate their firepower once more on the great lumbering beast. They would make sure that it did not get past them.

Too late, they realised Fisher's full intent.

With a great lurch, the bulldozer juddered off the ramp and headed for the tower itself.

The machine was alive with movement as bullets raked the bodywork. But the fire could not stop the inevitable. Fighting for control of his own movements like some bloody, ragged puppet, Fisher jammed the throttle wide open and lowered the blade.

The bulldozer slammed into the tower.

Instantly, the firing from above ceased. Snorting, the bulldozer retreated and then lunged forwards again. This time, it seemed that

374

the tower swayed. Down below, Fisher could not be sure whether he could hear the sound of men screaming in their attempts to get away, or whether it was the hissing, buzzing sound that filled his head. Detached, and with rigidity now almost overwhelming him, turning him to stone, he reversed and – eyes wide – rammed the bulldozer forward again. This time he felt the shuddering crack reverberate through the cabin. Mouth filling with blood, he reversed ... and watched as the tower began to topple. He could see it coming and wondered vaguely whether it was going to come down right on top of the bulldozer. Lazily, and with the groan of a falling tree, the tower fell, exploding in a gigantic dust cloud at the base of the Walkway.

Fisher watched the dust cloud rear like a gigantic but formless night animal. As it dissipated, he could see how the suspension wires supporting the Walkway were shaking wildly in the air. Was the road surface moving? And could he finish what he had to do? He wished that he could hear the crowd chanting for Taylor, because now it didn't matter a damn. He just wanted to hear them behind him, urging him on. But there was no sound and no gunfire. A dreadful, eerie silence had descended on the Walkway after the collapse of the tower.

Please God ... thought Fisher. *Give me time* ...

The bulldozer juddered and lurched on the rubble that it had created; snorting and bellowing and coughing its ragged black exhaust smoke.

And there was no volley of gunfire, no defence, when the bulldozer rammed the second tower. Fisher slumped over the controls, overwhelmed by the feeling that he was filling up with blood. Didn't that make sense? Wasn't that why it was leaking out all over the place? The level had reached his neck, and was flowing out of the holes made by the bullets. When it reached his eyes and filled them, then it would all be over. Shouting against the rising tide, he reversed the bulldozer from the wall of the tower.

Reverse – and *forward*! Fisher tried to swallow the blood. But there was no more room inside.

Reverse – and *forward*! Something cracked somewhere, but Fisher kept the lever handle pressed forward. The caterpillar tracks spun and bared and gushed concrete dust. Another juddering crack.

Reverse – and Fisher saw the tower tilting, and thought: *Can't get the people these days. Can't get good builders. Look at that.* Then he fell forward over the controls, and the bulldozer lurched across the rubble.

Wonder what those kids' names were? The ones on the Walkway. Always wanted kids, never had them but it would have been ...

And then the blood filled his eyes as the bulldozer slammed into the tower.

The tower shuddered and groaned as the blade jammed through the

375

brickwork and into a central stanchion. The entire structure came down on top of the bulldozer, slewing sideways to shatter in an explosive roar on the spot where the first tower had come down. Something beneath the Walkway base snapped with the sharp metallic bark of a hand grenade. And in the next moment, great snaking cables of high-tensile steel erupted from the concrete, racing away along the Walkway like gigantic fuses, heading for The Rock. From the central security pill-box figures shrank back as the underground cables whiplashed past in a frenzy of erupting concrete dust. Then figures could be seen running like hell both towards and away from The Rock in confusion.

The supporting platform connecting the Walkway to the neighbourhood side shuddered and cracked. The rubble of the two towers and the shattered bulldozer seemed to shift and roll.

And then the supports caved in and collapsed, the entire Walkway platform crumbling and tearing away in a shuddering, roaring avalanche of disintegrating concrete and reinforced, pre-stressed steel cable.

The Walkway base, the rubble of the collapsed towers and the remains of the bulldozer fell into the pit that surrounded Draegerman's Rock with the sound of an earthquake. The streets on the neighbourhood side were shaking, the ground heaving as the roaring avalanche continued. Street people were yelling and shouting and running for cover once more; it seemed that the entire city was going to collapse on them. Telegraph wires waved crazily in the air, windows in apartment blocks cracked and fell apart.

And as the platform vanished into the pit, the disconnected Walkway fell from the neighbourhood side, its immense five-hundred-yard length dropping like a gigantic pendulum, still attached by the high-tension cables to the The Rock's side. The Walkway swung down with groaning, shuddering roar, the screams of those still on it drowned by the immensity of the destruction. It smashed with full force against the side of The Rock below ground level, punching a huge aperture in its concrete side. Hundreds of square yards of reinforced concrete slid away in sheets like the collapsing face of a volcano, a great avalanche of debris erupting as the shattered Walkway tore free and disintegrated below.

The moat filled with gushing canyons of dust and smoke.

The ground all around The Rock shuddered and groaned.

Silence.

Then the noises of internal shuddering. Of things that might be falling apart in the Rock.

The crowd was suddenly silent in awe.

And then the chanting began anew, with vibrancy and a renewed emotion.

'Tay-*lor*! Tay-*lor*! TAY-LOR! *TAY-LOR*!!'

TEN

Taylor staggered and grabbed at the concrete wall, his flashlight beam arcing wildly through the air as the culvert shuddered beneath his feet. His foot skidded and he fell cursing to one knee.

Den fell flat, slamming both palms down on the steep incline. The impact knocked the breath from his body and he whirled to look down at Moss. He too had fallen to both knees, gripping the concrete rim of the culvert, the water surging impossibly up and over his hands and rising into the darkness. His eyes were wide in alarm, at first seeming to expect that this impact was a result of something Den had done, as if he might come hurtling down on top of him at any moment.

The shuddering continued beneath them; a deep, grumbling vibration as if an avalanche or tidal wave was on its way. Den whirled again to look up at Taylor.

Still clinging tight to the culvert wall, and in answer to the unasked question, Taylor said: 'I don't know. Maybe the sewer below.'

They strained to listen, Taylor shining his flashlight down. Moss also shone his torch, but they had climbed too far for the beam to show them effectively what was happening below. Both beams illuminated the concrete stretch for a hundred feet or so, but beyond that the light was diffuse and it was impossible to make anything out. They could still hear the faint thundering of water.

'Maybe the wall we blew out has collapsed,' volunteered Moss.

Taylor shook his head. The ground beneath them was still shaking and now a cloud of concree dust was drifting down from the ceiling above.

'It's bigger than that, whatever it is.' He shone the beam up at the ceiling. Calmly, he said: 'Might be a good idea to get a move on. Don't want this coming down on top of us.'

'Why can't you ever say anything cheerful?' said Moss, scrambling to join them.

Den had risen and followed quickly behind Taylor as they began a renewed and hurried ascent through the darkness.

ELEVEN

Night had gradually become day, although they seemed unaware of
One by one, slowly and gradually, lights were coming on in the ceiling
the great chamber; just as surely as studio lights would change artific
night to artificial day.

After a while, Boone walked slowly and awkwardly towards the
'The fog,' he said weakly. 'It's going . . .'

Roy, Susan and Jessica came out of their embrace, still kneeling
the cobbled street. What had once been an all-enveloping blanket
undulating greyness had dissipated around them to a rolling carpet
ground mist; still looking for all the world like the ground mist th
might swirl and shift and undulate on the floor of a studio set. For
moment, the horror was over; but Draegerman's cinematic flourish
remained.

Bobby was gone.

They stood together, and Boone shuffled uneasily, as if emba
rassed.

Looking up, they could see gantries of lights hanging from bla
steel brackets and walkways. Now, all the lights were shining.
one questioned how and why they had come on. It was just anoth
of Draegerman's carefully controlled environments. This was anoth
chamber that seemed to have been hacked out of black rock, a cave
wherein Draegerman had created more of his hideous fantasies.

As they looked around, the cobbled streets of Whitechapel were
longer dark and mysterious places where unknown horrors lurked a
threatened. They could see the cobbled street down which they h
walked, could see the archway which had seemed so threatenir
Clearly, the archway was constructed from cardboard or plywood; t
bricks were obviously hand-painted. Beyond this street and its angu
doorways and painted windows, they could see the row of terrac
houses. The houses were merely plywood façades with gardens a
fences out front, the frontages held in place by thick wooden props fro
behind; and behind the props were the bare stone walls of The Roo

'Look,' said Susan.

378

They turned to see where she was pointing.

Directly ahead, in the direction in which they had chosen to walk and from where the Gloria-Daemon had emerged, there was another entrance in the rock face. It looked just like the tunnel-corridor that had led them into this place.

Now, it seemed to be their only way out.

Once again, it would be the way Draegerman wanted them to go.

Hollow, emotionally empty with horror, Roy turned back to Boone. He was fingering his scar and clutching his attaché case as usual. When Roy looked at him, he flinched as if expecting a physical attack.

'Boone, you ... you ...' Roy could not find the words, but now his accusing look was mirrored by those of Jessica and Susan. They too could hardly bring themselves to speak.

'It wasn't my fault, was it?' stammered Boone. 'I'm not responsible, am I?'

'Boone,' said Roy again, in a strained and tired voice. 'I should just ...'

'He ran to her ... I mean ... You couldn't stop him ... there was nothing ...'

And as Boone backed off, he suddenly slipped in something on the ground. His foot skidded and he almost fell, keeping a tight hold on his beloved attaché case. He looked quickly back at Roy, waiting for the attack. But Roy seemed more interested in the substance in which Boone had slipped.

'Look at that.'

He walked over, kneeling down to look at the trail on the cobbles. It was a thin, glinting substance – black as engine oil. He touched it, then quickly withdrew his fingers, uttering a sound of disgust. Wiping his fingers on a cobble, he stood back and then began walking away from them, following the splattered black trail. At the spot where Roy and the Daemon had performed their *danse macabre*, he knelt again.

'Come and look at this.'

Susan and Jessica walked over to him, kneeling to look at what he had found.

It was more of the thick black oil. But this was not a thin trail; this was a glinting splash of the stuff.

'What is it?' asked Susan.

'I think it's blood.'

'Oh God, Bobby ...'

'No, not Bobby. Look at this stuff. Look at this stuff. It looks like diesel oil, but I think its blood from the thing that killed him. Look at this, there's a great splash of the stuff where I got it with the railing ... and here ...'

He hurried to where the railing was still lying on the cobbles. He picked it up, grimacing again when he saw that the point and at least two feet of the rail were coated with the same black liquid.

379

'You see? This is where it bled from the wound and there . . .'

He walked back towards Boone, following the trail on the cobbles. Boone flinched again as he walked past. 'Then it stops and . . .' He remained where the trail ended, then looked at the spot where the had seen the shadow appear on the steps across the street. He hurried over to the steps, looked down and nodded. Then crossing again to the demolished railings, he knelt and nodded again. 'It's on the stairs over there, another splash of it here. Then it . . .'

He looked back at the arch, waving his hand and grimacing at the reminder of Bobby's dying cry of distress.

Rising, he walked past Boone to join the others, still hefting the black-tipped railing.

'Do you see what I'm getting at?' he asked, examining the blackened point. The others did not answer but waited, listening. 'I hurt the thing. It bled. And if they bleed and can be hurt – then maybe we can protect ourselves against them. It's like you said, Jessica. There's something about these things, when they make an appearance. You feel as if . . .'

'As if you're powerless,' finished Jessica. 'As if the very fact that these things exist means that they're invulnerable, that there's nothing you can do to stop them.'

'I felt like that when I saw the Berserker,' said Susan.

'Right,' said Roy. 'But that's something they're able to do to emotionally, to rob us of strength, weaken us, make us hopeless. But the thing . . . the bloody *thing* that took Bobby was in agony when the railing went into it. So maybe . . . maybe we can fight back.' He heft the railing again to emphasise his point.

'But you don't know that . . .' began Boone.

'We don't want a fucking *word* out of you!' snapped Susan, her voice trembling with emotion. 'Not so much as a word, Boone. Or so help me I'll take that railing and ram it down your *throat* . . .' Her words almost ended in tears. Angrily, she wiped her lips with the back of her hand. Boone was silent.

Something rattled overhead.

They looked up to see that one of the light gantries was shaking its bracket, perhaps a hundred feet overhead. As they watched, the shaking became more violent and seemed to be spreading to the other gantries. There was another sound now; a rumbling, rushing sound growing louder . . . growing nearer.

'Oh Christ,' said Jessica. 'What now?'

The gantries seemed to be shaking themselves to pieces. One of them over by the fake terrace houses jarred loose from the ceiling. The massive bulbs within exploded in a shower of sparks, wiring ripped loose from the supports and in the next instant the entire gantry toppled end over end from the ceiling, smashing on to the terraced façades.

Beneath them, the ground suddenly lurched. One quick and convulsive shudder, like an earth tremor. Boone cried out in abject panic, whirling on the spot as the others staggered to regain their balance. More of the light fittings began to explode, and suddenly there was a rain of sparks in the air.

'Run for the tunnel!' yelled Roy. 'I think this bloody roof is coming *down!*'

The ground shuddered again, and the roaring filled the great chamber. Staggering, they began to run over the cobbles towards the tunnel entrance. Behind them, the arch fell over backwards with a great plywood *whap!* and a cloud of dust. The fake houses were rattling, shuddering and falling apart. The lamp standard behind the arch suddenly toppled over and shattered on the cobbles.

And even above the sound of the thundering earthquake or avalanche, they became aware of another familiar and dreadful noise. It was the sound they had heard in the tunnels and corridors as they had wandered through Draegerman's hellish abode. It was a screeching of massive gears, wheels and pulleys; a shuddering creak of hidden machinery. But this time, there was a difference. This time, there was a sound of disintegration. The gigantic cogs, the monstrous wheels and pulleys and gantries and windlasses, were grinding in protest as they fell apart behind the scenes. Something hidden made an ear-splitting, explosive crash, and was followed by an immense shattering of glass.

Behind them as they ran, they could hear the sounds of the invisible hansom cab, the recording ridiculously speeded, then the sounds of the hurdy-gurdy followed by a stuttering crackle as the hidden recording was torn apart.

The ground shuddered again, and this time the impact threw them to the ground. Roy whirled back to see a barrage of lights tear free from the ceiling and come crashing down on to the set of the cobbled street from which they had come. It exploded on impact with the ground, showering the fake houses on both sides with sparks. A fire immediately sprang up on the roof of one of the surreal houses. The air was filled with smoke and dancing sparks, and when something else crashed from the roof over by the terraced houses the entire façade disintegrated.

They scrambled to their feet again, running madly towards the corridor.

Roy reached it first, and turned back at the entrance just as Jessica and Susan rushed past him. Boone was still twenty yards out, struggling to catch up, his face a mask of terror. Something exploded behind him and he cried out again, arms flailing for balance.

'I should just ...' said Roy grimly, then ran back out to help him.

Boone looked up in terror when he saw Roy running towards him. He stopped, staggering and holding up his hand as if to ward him off.

'You stupid bastard!' Roy seized Boone's outflung arm and dragged him towards the tunnel mouth, finally flinging his arm over his shoulder and half carrying the man until they had plunged through the corridor mouth to join the others. He threw the arm from his shoulder, as if disgusted with himself that he had decided to help Boone. The two women said nothing. They leaned against the shuddering corridor wall, breathing heavily.

'We may not be safe, even in here,' began Roy. 'We'd better get further back before ...'

'Look out!' Jessica seized Roy's arm and dragged him back.

At that very second, a light gantry crashed down across the mouth of the cave, shattering on impact and gushing smoke and sparks. They staggered away from the entrance, looking back as more of the overhead gantries fell on top of the first with a rending, exploding impact.

Fifty feet into the tunnel, with its familiar dripping stone walls and shuddering orange lights, they stopped again to get their breath.

'I don't think ...' breathed Roy. 'Somehow, I don't think ... that Mr Draegerman planned that one for us at all.'

'Someone tried to get in,' said Susan hopefully. 'Didn't he say that to us earlier? Someone had been trying to get in. Maybe they have. Maybe they just *have*!'

Jessica leaned back against the wall, struggling for breath.

Roy looked back at the blocked tunnel entrance, weighing the Daemon-blooded wooden railing in his hands.

Boone could not speak. He was shocked into silence, his face white, his scar livid.

But Susan's face was filled with a crazy and bright spark of hope.

With the walls and floor still shuddering, and the sounds of disintegration and collapse still echoing, they turned slowly and began to journey onwards.

Towards yet more horror – or was there now real hope?

TWELVE

'I can see the top,' said Taylor, and Den looked up past him to see that his torch beam was playing on the ceiling, and that about fifty feet from where they were climbing the ceiling was no longer slanting upward. Instead, it straightened at a sharp angle.

The concrete beneath their feet had continued to judder and shake during their ascent, and Den had lost any concept of how long they had been climbing. The muscles in his calves ached from the continual stooping posture, and there was a tightness in his neck muscles and shoulders.

'Thank Christ for that,' said Moss tightly.

Den fixed his view on Taylor's back again, trying to shake off the notion that he might suddenly have another one of his turns when they were only feet from the top; that he would suddenly keel over backwards and fall on him, that they would tumble back down the concrete slope, breaking their arms and legs and finally their necks before being dumped back into the foul, poisonous sewer water below.

And then Taylor had reached the summit. The slope ended, and evened out on to a concrete platform. There was light up here, independent of Taylor's torch beam. Faint blue light was dancing on the walls and the ceiling, a reflection from the water that coursed up the culvert at their side. Reaching the top as Taylor strode away from him on the flat, Den could see that the thin culvert widened here for no apparent purpose. Now it was about three feet wide and stretched on ahead for fifty feet or so. There was nothing else to see in this bare, grey concrete chamber, apart from the dancing flecks of blue. Taylor turned back, waiting for them to join him. Moss had reached the edge now, looked back down, shining his light and shaking his head.

'Felt like Mount fucking Everest,' he said, before moving to join them.

Taylor reached into his waterproof pocket and took out Talbot's map.

'How long have we been climbing?' asked Moss, checking his watch.

'No watch,' said Den. 'Mine wasn't waterproof, or shitproof. So I didn't bring it.'

'Taylor?'

Taylor glanced at his own watch. He laughed ironically, before bringing the torch back to bear on the map. 'My watch has stopped.'

'Shit, so has mine.' Moss said no more. Had he checked his watch with Taylor's, he might have been surprised to find that they both showed exactly the same time: the moment when they had breached the defences of Draegerman's Rock and passed through the boundary wall.

'So what now?' he asked Moss.

'Let me have your flash,' said Den, holding out his hand. Moss looked at him as if he was asking the impossible. 'Pretty please, Moss. I promise I won't run away with it.' Sneering, Moss slapped it into his hand. Den shone it across the concrete chamber, following the widened culvert. There was another turning at the far end, away to the right. More flecks of blue were dancing on the wall there. Could the mysterious source of light emanate from around the corner? He began to walk towards it.

'Like I say,' continued Moss, moving closer to Taylor, 'what now?'

'We've got another problem,' replied Taylor.

'Why aren't I *incredibly* surprised by you saying that? So what's the problem?'

'According to this map, we should have reached a sub-basement of The Rock. It should begin right here, where we're standing. And there should be . . .' Taylor raised the flashlight and shone it over the bare concrete ceiling. '. . . a manhole cover up in the ceiling here that takes us right into it.'

'But there's no fucking manhole cover. Right?'

'Right.'

'And we've got nothing left to blow a hole in that roof. Right?'

'You just keep getting righter and righter.'

'Shit!'

Den had reached the corner, had turned it to see what lay beyond. For a long while, he simply stood and looked, shining his flash and not believing what he saw. When he called for Taylor and Moss, his voice was too quiet to be heard. He cleared his throat and leaned back.

'How many impossible things are you prepared to believe in one day?'

Taylor shone his flash at him. Den shaded his eyes.

'I think you'd both better come over here and have a look.'

Quickly, shoving the map into his belt and sealing the pouch, Taylor strode towards him. Moss followed, already looking unprepared to be convinced by anything that might happen, or anything that he might see. Den stood to one side, making a mock *voilà* gesture with one hand as they turned the corner to look.

They stood in silence.

Den played his beam over the impossible sight they were witnessing; then Taylor began to do the same, as if the whole thing might dissolve and vanish and simply not *be* there, if two man-made flashlights rather than one were shone on it for long enough.

The widened culvert turned the corner gradually, and then opened out into a basin, perhaps twenty feet wide. The water flowed into this man-made hollow, smoothly carved from the concrete – and ended there. But there was a great tumult of disturbance in the pool; the water churning as if massive air bubbles were constantly being released from below, keeping the surface of the pool alive with movement. Although the air remained as cold as ever, it seemed as if the water in that pool was boiling. The recess in which the basin sat and in which the water swirled and foamed was in itself barely large enough to park a medium-sized car, with blank concrete walls on three sides. But there was nothing about the recess to catch the eye. The object of their gaze was the water itself, and even as they stood and looked at it they could barely believe what was happening in the centre of the thrashing pool.

Following the mad logic of its uphill ascent, a great column of water rose foaming and twisting and thundering from the centre of the pool; spinning and glittering through the air to the ceiling. And there on the ceiling, the next impossible thing was happening.

For an area exactly the same size and circumference as the hollowed pool below, the concrete ceiling had simply ceased to be. Instead, there was a rippling, thrashing expanse of water into which the spiralling torrent of water from below was rushing.

They were looking at the surface of a pool.

But they were not looking at the surface from above.

They were looking at it from *below*.

'A fish's eye view,' said Moss in awe, summing up the feelings of the others. It was a hopelessly inadequate way of describing what they were seeing. But no one questioned it. They could only stand . . . and look. Only another shuddering in the concrete beneath their feet broke the spell. This latest tremor disturbed the surface of the water flowing down the culvert into the impossible pool with its impossible geyser, making the torch beams wobble as all three men staggered to regain their balance. Whatever was happening in The Rock, whatever it was they might have started, was still going on somewhere.

'So tell me that we're trapped here, Taylor,' said Moss. 'Tell me this is as far as we can go.'

Taylor said nothing. The water was reflecting on his face, making any emotion impossible to read, if it was there in the first place.

'So we can't go forward,' continued Moss. 'And the only thing that can move backwards in this lunatic fucking place is the water. Great!'

'Puts me in mind of an old saying,' said Den, looking down

into the churning pool. In his mind's eye, all he could see was Susan's face.

'Which is?' asked Moss, with the look of contempt he had developed since their altercation climbing the culvert slope.

Den looked at them both, almost sadly.

'If in doubt . . . go with the flow!'

And in the next moment, Den had whipped his face-mask on and jumped feet first into the pool, holding both hands over his face to keep the mask in place. The shock triggered by his action caused both men to recoil. Instantaneously, Den was swallowed by the cold-boiling frenzy of water

'Jesus, Taylor!' yelled Moss. 'He just . . . *Jesus!*'

And then he backed against the concrete wall when a blurred and dishevelled figure suddenly hurtled up from the depths of the pool, right at the centre of the twisting, geyser; a figure that could only be Den – somehow drawn to the bottom of the basin, swirled around and sucked up in the impossible vortex, and then sucked *up* through the air before their eyes to explode up and out of sight through the thrashing surface of the overhead upside-down pool surface.

A frenzied blur of motion – and Den was gone.

Taylor stood at the side of that pool, looking up.

Moss pushed himself away from the wall, hands at his side, unable to speak for the moment. When words finally began to form, he still could not adequately put them together.

'What . . . I mean . . . why . . . I mean . . . what?'

Taylor continued to stare at the geyser and the churning pool where the ceiling should be.

'He must have been . . . I mean . . . how . . . I mean . . . *shit!*'

Without looking at Moss, Taylor took the face-mask and cylinder from his satchel and began to put them on.

'Look, you're not seriously . . . I mean, come *on!*'

Taylor began to hook in his air supply. Moss saw what he was doing.

'You can't be serious. Tell me you're not serious.'

Taylor adjusted the mask.

'Fuck! You're serious.' Moss scrabbled for his mask.

Taylor looked from the geyser to the cold-boiling pool above.

'Don't you fucking dare! Don't you leave me here, you piece of . . .'

And then Taylor dived feet first into the pool, just as Den had done.

Moss scrabbled to connect his air supply, and then jerked up to look as a black blur was suddenly catapulted up from the depths of the pool through the geyser, vanishing through the erupting foam in the ceiling.

'*Shittttttt!*' yelled Moss. Then he jammed the air-piece into his mouth, hugged his chest tight, and jumped into the thrashing pool.

THIRTEEN

The corridor was suddenly filled with a great rending and grinding sound, as if massive gears were under some terrible strain. As they ran, their hands flew to their ears; the thin metallic screeching was impossible to bear.

Somewhere behind the corridor wall, something split and cracked; and then the screeching noise was gone. But the ground beneath their feet was still trembling, and a thin powder of dust was constantly falling from the ceiling. Roy had a sickening mental impression. The noise sounded as if it might come from the beams holding the ceiling up in this corridor. Perhaps something had collapsed above the beams? Perhaps there were tons of rubble above them, bearing down on the supports. And perhaps the ceiling would cave in on top of them at any moment.

The orange lights set high in the walls were constantly flickering. What would happen if the lights failed in here? Roy tried to banish the thought from his mind, tried to push away the idea that they were constantly running in this House of Horrors with no possibility of any safe place to hide.

They had reached the end of the corridor. It turned sharp right, and there was another identical stretch of one hundred yards ahead. But the lights here were green not orange, and Roy realised that they had never worked out just what in hell the change of lights was supposed to mean. He was keeping to the rear, looking back to where the corridor mouth had been blocked, anxiously scanning the ceiling above and still holding the blooded wooden railing. Ineffective though the improvised weapon might be in the long term, it felt good in his hands.

That bastard thing bled. It BLED.

Jessica and Susan leaned against the wall, struggling to regain their breath after the headlong flight from the hellish place where Bobby had died. Still clutching his attaché case, Boone staggered on past them.

'I've got to . . .' Susan almost retched with the effort of speaking. '. . . lie down, or something.'

387

'We can't stop here,' said Roy, trying to push them both on ahead after Boone. 'That ceiling could come down.'

'Face it, Roy,' said Jessica. She wiped a trembling hand across her smeared face. 'It doesn't matter where the hell we go.'

'Something's happening. This isn't planned, I'm sure of it. And anything bad happening to Draegerman and his hellhouse is fine by me. Maybe things are changing. Maybe we've got a chance.'

'You're a lousy optimist,' said Susan. Suddenly she leaned forward, grabbed him by the neck and crushed a kiss on his cheek. Roy was dumbfounded. 'Come on, then, let's move it.'

Together, they started after Boone.

The ground still shuddered beneath them, but there were no more clouds of dust from above. Roy prayed that this was a good sign.

'Look,' said Jessica, pointing to the wall on the right as they staggered onwards. Roy followed her pointing finger. It was another television screen monitor, set into the wall. Boone had already run past it without noticing, but they slowed as they approached, expecting the familiar hiss of static and the sudden reappearance of the face they hated so much. But the screen remained blank as they drew level with it. No snowstorm appeared, no taunting voice mocked them.

They moved on past it, reaching the end of the next stretch of corridor. It was a T-junction, and Boone had paused there; waiting for them to catch up before they decided on which route was best. When they reached him, they could see that it was the same corridor, the same black stone, the same orange lights.

'Left,' said Susan. 'At least that takes us further away from the street studio.'

Jessica nodded, and now they were all heading down the next stretch.

And then Boone blundered into Roy as he tried to push past and take the lead. His feet became tangled and he fell heavily against the corridor wall with a grunt of pain. Roy grabbed for him and tried to arrest his fall. But Boone had twisted in his awkward tumble and Roy's grasp on his coat sleeve was torn loose as the man sprawled full length on the corridor floor. The attaché case flew from his hands, bounced on the cold black stone and then flew open when the hasp snapped.

Boone scrabbled desperately to grab the case, as if his life depended on it.

The case spun on the ground, the lid flapping.

And Roy could see, just before Boone flung his body over the case and fumbled to shut the lid, that there was no money in it at all.

There had been a flash of light from within when the lid had opened.

Something that flashed red and green.

Boone mumbled something they could not hear properly, then began to rise, clutching the attaché case to his chest once more.

Roy lunged forward to take his shoulder, and now Boone was frantically shrugging off his grip, turning again to continue the flight down the corridor.

'Stop right there, Boone!' Roy made another lunge, this time seizing his arm when he tried to shrug him off once more. Both Jessica and Susan had seen the mysterious winking of lights where there should have been a spill of green bundled notes. 'Just what the hell have you got in that case?'

'It's mine!' snapped Boone, still struggling. Roy was having difficulty in holding him; he was clearly a lot stronger that he had assumed. 'You had your chance back there, but you all left your money behind. This is mine, and I'm keeping it . . .'

'There's no money in there, Boone. And you *know* it!'

This time, Roy was not going to argue the case. Pulling Boone around, he punched him hard on the jaw. The effect was instant. Boone keeled over to the ground, leaving his attaché case in Roy's grasp. Groaning, he rolled on the ground, dazed and holding his face. It gave all three a grim satisfaction to see that there was blood on his mouth. Roy stood back, turned the attaché case over in his hands – and then opened it.

What he saw inside left him dazed.

'What the *hell* . . . ?'

Susan and Jessica turned him around so that they could also see what the case contained.

There was no currency in there.

There was no *space* for currency in there.

Because every square inch of the case was filled with electronic equipment. There was a computer keyboard with a small screen, blank at present. The arrangement of the electronics was cramped but looked incredibly sophisticated. A red and green light was winking in the centre of the board, the source of the light Roy had first seen. There were dozens of minute but perfectly detailed function keys. It was impossible to tell just what those functions might be. In the lid of the case was another keyboard, this time with no screen but still sporting row after row of function keys.

'What the hell is *this*, Boone?' Roy's face had grown dark as he looked over the lid at the man on the ground. Groaning, Boone was trying to sit, trying to reorientate himself. There was blood from his mouth on his livid scar, making the damage look worse.

'Answer the man,' said Jessica grimly.

Boone pulled himself to the corridor wall, propping his back there and rubbing his jaws. At last he focused, and saw that they had found out.

Roy handed the attaché case to Susan and stepped slowly towards him.

'You start talking now, Boone,' he said quietly. 'Or I swear to God that I'll kill you. Here and now. Look at me, Boone.'

389

Boone stared up at him, still rubbing his face.

'You *know* I'll kill you, don't you? Things have gone too far, we've been through too much – and people are *dead*.'

Roy levelled the wooden railing, until the point was inches from Boone's face.

'So start talking – *now*!'

'I didn't have a choice!' blurted Boone, recoiling from the railing. 'He said that he would kill me!'

'Make *sense*!'

'Draegerman! I was the first to arrive, that's why he chose me. He told me that he would kill me if I didn't go along with what he wanted me to do. He gave me that attaché case, just like the others, except it had that equipment in it. He said that whatever happened, I must always have it with me. Never lose it. Never tell anyone else about it. And if I kept it . . . if I kept it . . .'

'What?'

'He said that I wouldn't die.'

'You mean you knew all the time what that mad bastard had planned for us?' shouted Susan.

'No, no, no! I didn't know about any of this. Christ, if I'd known . . .' Boone began to weep.

'What else did he say? What else did you agree to do for him?'

Boone continued to weep. Roy jerked the point of the railing in his face again.

'Nothing! That was all. I didn't know what he was going to do. I only knew that he said I'd get out of here alive if I always kept that case with me.'

'What is it?' demanded Roy.

'I don't know. Honest to God, I don't know.'

'You're lying, you cowardly bastard. We *both* know what it is, don't we?'

'He never told me, never said anything about . . .'

'It's some kind of homing device, some kind of tracking equipment.'

'Honestly, he never . . .'

'That's how Draegerman's been able to keep track of our movements in this fucking hellhole. Everywhere we've been, every time we've been manipulated or manoeuvred, he's been there – because of that attaché case. It's probably got microphones in there, hasn't it, Boone? Draegerman's been able to hear every conversation we've had.'

'No, I didn't know. I didn't . . .'

'You *bastard*!' Susan flung the attaché case to the ground. It bounced, and something seemed to spark inside it.

'*Nooo!*' Boone scrabbled like some insane wild beast across the cold stone floor, forgetting even his fear of the railing against his face. Roy stepped forward, planted a foot on his chest and slammed him back against the wall.

'If you don't know what's in there, why the hell are you so worried about the possibility of us smashing the thing to pieces?'

'You can't smash it, *mustn't* break it!'

'Susan, Jessica. Why don't we just stamp that attaché case into the ground?'

Both women moved grimly forward, their contemptuous expressions still locked on Boone's miserable face.

'Don't, for God's sake, *DON'T*!'

'Why?'

'He said ... he said that there was an explosive or something in there. Said that if it got damaged, then it would explode.'

'Hardly seems likely that he'd want any of us to be killed, Boone. Doesn't he want to feed us to his precious Daemons?'

'I swear to God that's what he said.'

'You're lying.'

Susan and Jessica bore down on the attaché case. A thin wisp of smoke escaped from the hasp. And in that moment, a sudden change came over Boone. The look of terror suddenly vanished from his scarred face.

'All right!' he said with an intensity and a new control in his voice. 'If you kill me, if you destroy what's in that attaché case ... you'll never get out of here alive.'

The sudden change stopped Jessica and Susan in their tracks. Roy moved the railing back to Boone's face, but this time Boone did not flinch. Wiping the blood from his mouth, he looked directly up into Roy's face with an expression of utter contempt.

'Yes, Draegerman told me what's in that case. Like you said, it's monitoring equipment. He told me how to use it. I had a choice. Do what he wanted me to do, just as I've told you. Or die. At least this way I had a chance of getting out of here alive.'

'You miserable ...' Roy stood back as if he meant to drive the railing into Boone's throat.

'Kill me and you'll die. Simple as that. You see, I *know* where we are.'

'And you know how to get out of here?' asked Susan, stepping towards him.

'No, otherwise I wouldn't be here with you, would I?'

'I should just kill you anyway,' said Roy grimly.

'And I know where Draegerman's control room is. At least, I think I can guess where it is.'

'How?'

'From the case. He didn't know this – but I know a little about electronics. I think I could pinpoint where the receiving signal is coming from if I had a little time.'

391

'You're lying,' said Jessica, testing him.

'Why should I? Look ...' And now it seemed that the fear was returning to his face as he looked around the corridor. The shuddering and underground thundering had continued throughout. 'Something's happening, isn't it? That collapse back there in the studio streets or whatever they were. What we can hear now. Like Roy said, I think Draegerman's lost control or something's happening that he didn't plan for. And I just want to get out of this place alive. Like you.'

Roy exchanged glances with Susan and Jessica. No one spoke.

'Give me the case,' continued Boone urgently.

Still, no one spoke.

'For God's sake, give me the case. Then I can work on that signal, we can find out where that insane fucker is and then try to get out of here.'

Susan stood back as Jessica leaned down and picked up the case. Holding it in both hands, she looked ready to dash it to the ground.

'What other chance do you have?' pleaded Boone.

Susan carefully took it from her placed it in front of Boone.

He began to reach for it, and just as his fingers made contact Roy stepped on his hand.

'Listen to this, Boone. I was ready to kill you a moment ago. I've got even *more* reason to kill you now. If I get just one hint that you're doing something other than you've said you're going to do, I'm not going to argue with you, not going to warn you – I'm just going to ram this straight through your fucking eyeball.'

'Please,' moaned Boone. 'I just need a little time to work on this, and I think I can find out where ...'

'Do we *understand* each other, Boone?'

'We understand each other,' groaned Boone.

Roy withdrew his boot.

Susan and Jessica moved forward until they were all surrounding Boone where he crouched on the ground.

Nervously, he opened the lid – and began stabbing at the facility keys, darting anxious glances up at them as he did so.

'I've switched it off. From now on, he won't know where we are.'

Their faces seemed carved from stone.

Beneath them, the ground continued to shudder.

From somewhere nearby, something seemed to crack and splinter, then collapse.

Boone continued tapping the keys, sweat beading on his scarred brow.

FOURTEEN

Taylor clung to his face-mask with both hands, feeling enormous suction on his body as he plunged into the tumultuous water.

His body twisted, and in the next instant it seemed that he was being pinned to the bottom of the crazy pool by a thundering pressure of water from above. The great roaring filled his ears, and he could feel the concrete bottom scrape him. He kicked at the bottom, tried to rise – and suddenly it was as if the terrific suction had been reversed. Instead of pressing him down to the bottom, it was suddenly plucking him up through the cold-boiling water. With another great roaring, Taylor felt himself swept into an upside-down whirlpool. His ears pinged with the pressure, and he exploded to the surface in a great foaming, glittering spray. He rolled as he plunged back into the water, kicked and was suddenly free of any pressure.

Raising his head from a now suddenly placid surface, he realised that he was in darkness. He trod water for a while, becoming accustomed to the gloom, not ready to use his flashlight until he was sure that there was no possible danger. He looked back to where he assumed he had entered. There was a low, gentle bubbling of dark water perhaps twenty feet from where he floated. Could it possibly have been there? He scanned the dark surface of the water around him, but could see no further disturbance. It did not seem credible that the gentle undulation of water could be the place where the thundering torrent from below had catapulted his body so violently. And there was something else, something that Taylor at first had trouble defining. Then he realised it was the *absence* of something in here. There was no more shuddering, no more rumbling sounds as if things somewhere within The Rock were falling apart. In this still and dark place, everything was quiet.

As he watched, a thin white mist began to creep over the water, and as it did so, Taylor was able to make out the shapes of the shore. He took off his face-mask, just as a clump of weed floated by.

Weed?

And now, when he looked around, he could see that there was a mud-bank of sorts off to his right, and that the ragged silhouettes of

393

mangrove trees were trailing their branches and leaves in the water. He turned slowly. There was a bank on the other side, too. And in the darkness he could make out a half-submerged tree-trunk on the bank, its roots trailing in the water. This did not make sense. Had they somehow come right through the sewer system to find themselves outdoors again?

There was movement, over by the half-submerged tree-trunk.

Something was clinging to the rotted bark.

'Taylor!' it hissed in the darkness, then gagged as it swallowed water.

Taylor swam forward, recognising Den's voice before he could see his face properly. Just before he reached out to steady himself on the log, there was the sound of another terrific explosion of water from behind. They turned quickly to see a figure erupt from the surface, at the spot where Taylor had seen the gently undulating water. The figure thrashed, sending out a grey foaming spray which made the slowly gathering mist fly apart in swirling, ragged eddies. The spray settled around the figure as it too began to tread water, looking around.

Taylor waved, and Moss swam over to them, pushing his face-mask back on his head and staring around him, uncomprehending.

Den seemed to be having difficulty breathing. Taylor waited for him to settle.

'Den,' he said quietly. 'You're a crazy bastard.'

Den nodded, spitting out a piece of the floating weed as all three clung to the log.

With dawning realisation and anger, Moss pulled close to Taylor and hissed: 'We're on the outside, Taylor! On the *outside!*'

Taylor did not answer. He watched the mist re-form along the edges of the furthermost bank, looked at the thick undergrowth and the branches that dangled in the water.

Moss seemed further angered by Taylor's lack of response. 'After crawling through twenty tons of shit, being a rats' appetiser and nearly fucking drowning, we're back on the *outside!*'

'No wind,' said Taylor.

'What?'

'There's no wind here.'

Taylor lifted his flashlight from the water and switched it on. The beam illuminated the ragged branches on the opposite bank. He moved the beam to the right, and stopped when it suddenly shone on a black brick wall. When he shone the beam directly above them, they could see the same concrete ceiling they had seen below in the culvert.

'We're still inside,' said Taylor.

'What the *hell* is going on?' Moss swirled around to the other side of the log, just as Den began to use the flashlight that he had taken from Moss. Seeing the other beam, Moss snatched it from his hand. 'Give

394

that back to me!' He shone it on the embankment, swung around to the other bank, and the light played through the trees, throwing gigantic shadows. Now he could see that there was a wall beyond the trees, too. 'This doesn't make sense. Any of it. Water that runs backwards. A waterfall that goes *up* instead of down. And an outdoor place that's indoors. Fucking fucked-up, that's what I say.'

Taylor shone his beam out across the black water. The mist was moving fast now, covering the surface, reflecting his beam.

'So what do *you* say, Taylor?' continued Moss.

'One thing I've learned over the years, Moss. If you spend too much time asking yourself how things are the way they are, and just hang around waiting for answers – then while you're thinking about it, someone or something just comes up behind you and bites your nuts off. Think about it. But not for too long. Let's move.' He pushed himself gently away from the log.

'Do I finally pass the test, Taylor?' gasped Den, following.

'You're an idiot,' he replied quietly.

Den laughed wryly. 'So, no brownie points, eh?'

Taylor slapped him on the back and then surged ahead through the filthy water. Quickly, Den and Moss followed.

The banks on either side narrowed, the overhanging branches forming a canopy as they swam. The fog completely covered the surface now as they swam down the bizarre inlet. And when Taylor reached up to sweep a tangled branch out of his line of vision, he seemed to judder in the water. Instantly, Den and Moss realised what had happened as they came up from behind.

Their knees had scraped bottom as they swam. There was no need to swim any further. When Taylor stood up, sweeping the clotted branch to one side, they could see that the water was waist-deep. They clambered to their feet and pushed after him. The fog was now so thick on the water that they could not see the surface. They pushed out at the entangling branches, following Taylor. And when they emerged from the rough canopy, they could see that he was standing dead still in front of them. Looking back over his shoulder, at the same time swinging his duffel-bag from the other, he whispered to them:

'Okay, open your waterproofs. It's time.'

'About *time!*' said Moss, quickly swinging his own bag from his back.

'Now we're inside The Rock, and I think we are, it's time to do business.' Taylor looked over at Den. 'Remember what I told you about these things. About magazine reload.'

'I remember,' said Den. The automatic machine pistol with its underarm stock did not feel like a weapon at all; more like one of the plastic kits that the kids used at home. And with that memory of the kids came other memories of Susan, her face swimming before his eyes. He gripped the Ingram tight and looked back at Taylor. He was still examining what lay ahead.

The inlet had broadened, the banks sweeping away to left and right. Ahead lay an expanse of fog-shrouded water. Taylor brought up his torch beam and pointed it directly ahead. There was a rough stone wall on the other side of this stretch of water, perhaps two hundred yards from where they stood. The beam played over the concrete ceiling, illuminated the spot where the ceiling met the far wall – and then moved down.

There had been some kind of jetty against the wall; a crude wooden construction by the look of it. But something had shattered the jetty. The beam played over the shattered spars which jutted from the lapping water. Parts of the wooden platform were still attached to the wall.

But more importantly, at the spot where the wooden construction had been, ten feet from the water level and probably giving access right on to the jetty's platform – there was a door.

An open door.

Moss swept his own beam from left to right. Now they could see the walls on either side, had some idea at last of the size of this bizarre chamber with its inbuilt swamp, and could be sure that there was no one else in here but themselves.

'Why the hell would anyone want to build a swamp *inside* their house?' asked Moss.

Taylor forged ahead through the water, sending rippling waves of fog on all sides. The other two followed, but now Moss was surging ahead past Den, coming up close behind Taylor.

'Would you care to share with us what we're going to do?'

'Let's get out of here first,' said Taylor, scanning all sides of the swamp-chamber as they moved. 'I don't like it.'

'What if there's two hundred armed men on the other side of that door? Did you think about that?'

'What if there's two *thousand* men on the other side of that door? Just keep your eyes open until we get to where that jetty used to be.'

Den had been looking ahead to the shattered ruins in the water and beneath the door. 'Why the hell have a jetty in here, anyway? Has Draegerman been giving his guests boat trips around the swamp?'

Something moved to Den's right. He saw the movement out of the corner of his eye, and whirled quickly, startling Moss.

'What?' Moss levelled his machine pistol but could see nothing, and looked back to Den for some kind of confirmation.

There was a small ripple of fog on the surface, about fifty feet from where they stood, on just about the spot where Den thought something had moved. But the disturbance was not enough to register with Moss, and Den supposed that it was nothing after all.

'I thought I saw something move. I was wrong.'

'Well, don't be wrong again, or I might end up shooting you by mistake.'

'Take it easy, Moss,' said Taylor.

'Yeah?' Moss turned back to look at Den. He was clearly much troubled. 'That's Mr Cool speaking, by the way.'

They had covered most of the fog-wreathed, man-made lake. The first of the shattered spars that had been the jetty's supports protruded from the water about thirty feet away from them. Clearly, they were going to have to climb the sundered wooden struts to reach the door.

'How many security men did Fisher tell you were in here?' asked Den.

'A hundred, he thought. Maybe a hundred and fifty.'

'And all the bastards are armed,' said Moss. 'We've never seen any one of Draegerman's people coming or going from The Rock without some firepower. The city authorities gave his organisation special licences for their weapons. Did you know that? Fucking city thinks that they're all fucking James Bonds. Licences to kill. Particularly if you live around The Rock and particularly if you're black.'

Taylor reached out to touch the first jutting spar. He waited there until the others were right behind him.

'What if Moss is right?' said Den. 'What if there's a hundred or a hundred and fifty of Draegerman's security men waiting for us beyond that door?'

'What the hell?' said Taylor, pushing on ahead to the next broken spar. 'That only means fifty for each of us.'

'Super-fucking-man,' said Moss, and looked up when he saw that Taylor was looking directly at him.

Could it be that Taylor was actually *smiling*?

Den looked at Moss, saw the look of puzzlement and anger suddenly begin to chance on his face. He saw the expression soften and collapse into a mock-bewildered grin, and could not help smiling himself. After their nightmare journey through the sewers and into The Rock, after the danger and horror that lay behind them and the potentially worse dangers and horrors to come, suddenly all three men were smiling – and Den could not understand why.

Taylor pushed on until he had reached the brick wall beneath the door. Handing his flashlight back to Den, he looped the belt of the Ingram around his shoulder. Bracing a leg on a spar underwater, he leaned up to grab a beam that protruded from the wall. The beam had been splintered through its centre, great jagged shreds of wood hanging from the severed end, but Taylor had a firm grip and in the next moment had heaved himself clear of the water. Fog rose with his body as he found leverage for his right foot. A three-foot section of the platform was still intact. He gripped the rim above him and tested its strength. Nodding, he pulled himself up, stood on the centre-shattered beam, and then slithered on to the remaining section of platform. Quickly, he unlooped the Ingram from his shoulder. The foot of the open door was at chest height now, and he looked quickly from right to left. Satisfied that there did not seem to be anyone lurking beyond, he leaned back out and motioned to the others. Den surged forward, and handed up both flashlights, then his machine pistol. He had greater difficulty finding the first foothold, and when he did at last locate it, Taylor lay down on the ragged platform and leaned out, offering his free hand. Den pushed out of the water and grabbed his hand. The grip seemed incredibly strong for a man who had apparently such limited time to live. Water foaming from his rubber suit, Den joined him on the platform. Taylor placed the torches on the ground just beyond the door, moving back to grip Den by the belt. Den leaned back down and offered his hand to Moss.

Moss surged out of the water, hanging on to Den's hand, his machine pistol also over his shoulder. When his left hand reached the rim of the platform, their faces were only inches apart.

'Look,' said Moss. It seemed that their shared laughter had melted something inside him. 'I've been giving you a hard time but . . .'

And then something seemed to seize his legs from below.

His face had no time to register surprise or pain or alarm. In the very next instant, he was torn from Den's grasp. Den cried out and fell back, Taylor's grip automatically tightening on his belt. A great gout of filthy water suddenly exploded from below, engulfing them – and Moss was gone.

Drenched and shocked, Den lunged back to the edge. The water directly below them was still churning and thrashing where Moss had been dragged under.

'What the *hell*?' Taylor tried to yank Den back.

'Moss has gone!'

Taylor finally dragged him back to the side, bringing his machine pistol to bear. Still too shocked to react, Den stared out across the fogged surface of the indoor swamp. Waves were surging out into the centre of the lake from the explosion of water where Moss had vanished. But there was no other movement. No sign of Moss struggling in the water, no sign of anything moving out there apart from the ever-spreading ripples of the eruption. Moss was gone, just as surely as if he had been dragged down into water ten fathoms deep.

Den braced himself to shout, but Taylor clamped an arm on his shoulder to restrain him, looking quickly back at the open door beyond.

'Let me go down there!' hissed Den. 'Maybe he's trapped under the water. Maybe he's . . .' The word that almost came to him was *fallen*, but it froze on his lips. There could be no denying that Moss had not simply fallen. The speed with which he had vanished from sight into the water almost defied logic. No, he had been seized and dragged – there was no *fallen* about it. Den looked out across the fog-wreathed expanse again, expecting to see something move out there by the hanging shadows of the mangrove trees. And was unprepared for the second explosion of water directly beneath them where Moss had originally vanished.

It was a great twisting torrent of swamp water, an eruption that flung them back against the stone wall, blinding them and engulfing them. The water roared and exploded and fell away in hissing sheets of foam and stinging spray. But what was within the exploding torrent continued to rise directly before them.

The water fell back to churn and foam and writhe at the base of the thing that reared from the surface, and although Den and Taylor were standing fifteen feet above the surface, the thing before them was at least fifteen feet taller than that as it straightened and rose, water cascading around it.

It was impossible to focus logically on the nightmare mass that looked down on them. Shocked and stunned into disbelief, Den saw it in a way that Taylor did *not* see it. To Den, the thing that had erupted from the water was a constantly shifting, amorphous thing; something that at first seemed like a serpent, its scaled and barbed neck casting a blacker-than-night shadow over them. But even as he stared open-mouthed, there was movement around the head of the thing. The yellow-slit eyes in the four-foot diamond-shaped head were larger than halloween lanterns. A forked tongue, thick as a man's arm, slithered and stabbed. But now the eyes were somehow a woman's eyes; cold and alluring and deadly in their intent. Even as the image registered, they were suddenly the eyes of some enormous, monstrous insect: multi-prismed, like the eyes of a gigantic wasp, with antennae that quivered and emitted a thin droning sound, with pincer-like mouth-parts that drooled and flexed and kneaded together horribly and greedily . . .

. . . but Taylor saw something with a huge bat-like face and small glittering red-marble eyes. He saw the hideously pointed ears of something that flew by night and fed on blood and souls and misery. He saw the furrowed, black-leather triangular snout, saw the scythe-like teeth in the glistening maw, and then, even as this registered, saw it coalesce and re-form into a mass of disgusting, twisting tentacles; like some hideous, poisonous sea anenone.

The roaring sound of the exploding torrent of water gave way to a sound like the hissing of steam or a thousand rattlesnakes preparing to strike. But there was another sound; another thin, high, shrieking sound, and even as they watched the thing rear back in the water they saw that it was clutching something in its claws. The claws were constantly re-forming and shifting and reshaping. They were reptilian, three-toed. Now covered in coarse black fur and now crescent-shaped and ebony like a bear's. Now liquid and surging like protoplasm.

399

And the thing that writhed and kicked and struggled to be free from that deadly grip ... was Moss.

He threw back his head in agony, clutched at the thing that held him – and in that moment of debilitating shock, Den saw Moss's scrabbling hands vanish into the liquid protoplasm of the thing's claws. Shaking his head in agony again, Moss kicked and screamed out loud.

The thing's head descended – much too quickly for its size and bulk.

The ragged, dark-light, shifting mass covered his head.

Moss's arms and legs spasmed and shook. His screaming ceased.

And when the ever-changing head whiplashed back, they could see that it had bitten Moss's head off in that one lunging movement. A scarlet torrent erupted from the ragged stump of his neck, flooding the front of the thing. Moss's arms and legs twitched. There was movement in the sinuous neck of the thing as it swallowed.

And then, yelling, Taylor steadied his Ingram and opened fire directly into the hideous mass.

The shock of erupting gunfire broke Den from his horrified spell. Fumbling, he grabbed his own weapon, jerked back the safety catch and began to fire. In that instant, he was suddenly aware of the secret place inside himself; the place that knew of nightmares, the place that held his secret conviction – learned in the cradle – that anything born of nightmare would not succumb to any resistance or defence from the real world. In that one moment, he knew that the bullets from his machine pistol would have no effect on the hideous monstrosity that had so suddenly erupted from the water. He knew that he would empty his clip into the thing, that it would wait until he had finished, wait until Taylor had finished, then whiplash down again upon them both. In seconds, they would be sharing the same fate as Moss.

But that secret place was immediately denied, just as the image registered in his mind. Den saw the bullets impact on the shape-changing thing, saw gouts of black-tar liquid spill out of the holes that were blown in the thing's neck and chest, saw flailing ribbons of the thing's blood. And it was as if the impact of the bullets had also somehow *solidified* the thing. The gaping wounds being torn into it were *real*, were being torn into something that had *form*.

Bellowing like a wounded elephant, the thing reared back and away from them. Den saw Moss's decapitated body cartwheel through the air as the thing discarded it, saw it fall away lifelessly into the swamp water. And in the next moment, there was another explosion of water, this time from the centre of the swamp as the thing recoiled from them so fast that their eyes could not follow its progress. They kept firing even as it vanished impossibly into what they knew to be shallow water. It sank beneath the surface, sending great waves chasing back towards them. Another exploding gout of water, and it was gone completely

400

There was only a thick black slick on the surface now. Impossibly, the fog in the indoor swamp had suddenly vanished.

Den kept his finger on the trigger, firing until the clip had emptied, his shots thrashing the water and the black slick into a frenzy. He kept his finger hard on the trigger even when the gun had emptied, and only when Taylor put his hand on his shoulder did he break from his daze and look round at him. Taylor had climbed to the threshold of the door, was leaning back down to him. Unable to speak, Den took his hand and allowed himself to be pulled up and through.

They were in some kind of black stone corridor, like a corridor in some mediaeval castle, but Den had not registered that yet. He could only stand and look back into the indoor swamp, trying to convince himself that he had seen what he had seen. Eventually, he turned to look at Taylor as if expecting some kind of explanation.

And for the first time, he saw that Taylor was also badly shaken by what he had seen. He too was standing, staring out through the doorway across the swamp. Den had been examining this man's face carefully ever since they had met, had been actively looking forward to the time when he might see some recognisable human emotion there. He had despised him for his lack of emotion.

Until that smile, just before Moss had been dragged to his death – and now.

More than anything else in the world, he wanted to see that Taylor's face was the usual mask. He wanted to see that he was in control, in command. He did not want to see that face show any sign of doubt. Not now. Not after what had happened.

But even if they had been surrounded by a hundred or a thousand armed men, they would both have been unaware as they stood there. For a moment, there was nothing but the open door, what lay beyond it, and their utter inability to comprehend what it was that had happened.

There was no time now. It had no meaning.

And then, what seemed like a hundred years later, Taylor suddenly lunged forward and seized the door edge. He swung it savagely shut, aiding its motion with the flat of his foot.

It slammed with a resolute solidity as if shutting the nightmare away for ever, all Taylor's basic instincts about keeping their presence secret either ignored or deliberately denied. Taylor breathed out. It was a quick, barking exhalation of air, as if he had just seized and raised a barbell.

Den was still mesmerised by the door.

Taylor grabbed his shoulder and spun him away.

In the next moment, Den was staggering along behind Taylor as he led the way down the bizarre corridor with its green bracket lights se high up in the ceiling.

No word was exchanged.

There was nothing to say that would make any sense.

Darkness closed around them.

FIFTEEN

The shuddering in the walls and ceilings had ceased. There were no more sounds of massive, invisible machinery tearing itself to pieces somewhere behind the scenes, but there was still a deeply unsettling atmosphere as Roy shoved Boone on before them. There was a pregnancy in the new silence; a feeling with every whisper of dust from overhead, or even in the sound of their footsteps on the bare stone floors of these corridors, that any further noise, even the echo of a voice, might split the walls or bring the ceiling crashing down on their heads.

Boone paused, rechecking the opened attaché case. Roy came up behind him again and shoved hard, unnecessarily hard, and he tried to check the deep, cold fury that had threatened to overwhelm him when Boone had finally told his story. Gloria and Bobby Pernell, both dead. And whereas it was hardly possible to mourn either Aiken or Farrow, it seemed that the weight of all the deaths was on Boone's cowardly shoulders. All Roy could think about was Boone's pathetic protestations, his desperate attempts to save his own skin, and devil take the hindmost. He remembered how Boone had almost got them killed in the revolving corridors, and again back in the Victorian street studio set. He remembered Boone's words when the thing that looked like Gloria had called her son's name and glided through the fog towards them.

Let him go to her.

And he remembered the tears of desperation that Boone had wept when Draegerman's face had taunted them from the hidden television screens. During all that time, the cowardly bastard had been carrying the very means by which Draegerman had been controlling them and monitoring their every move. Ironically, perhaps their best chance had been when Farrow had decided to go off in a different direction. He wondered why Boone had chosen to go with Farrow and Aiken, but could not swallow the rising disgust inside which made it virtually impossible to talk to this man.

It had not taken Boone long to work out how the equipment functioned in terms of its homing signal. A great deal of it was ultra-sophisticated,

403

he had said, but he felt sure that he had located the originating source of the receiver. Roy had stood by him all the time, keeping the point of the black-blooded railing clearly in his line of vision. Some of the functions had been damaged in the fall, but Boone had pressed on; stabbing at the facility keys and drawing up complex, miniature charts on the small screen inside which made no sense at all to any of them, except Boone. He had looked up anxiously every few seconds, as if desperately eager to please. The sight of his face only served to fuel the cold fury inside Roy. He struggled to contain it now as they moved along the corridor, afraid of what he might do if he was to lose control.

'Here,' said Boone at last, and the sound of his voice caused them all to feel anxious again. As if that one word might crack a supporting beam overhead. He had stopped, and closed the attaché case. Turning, he faced the corridor wall. 'I'm sure ... yes, I'm sure. Here.'

'What?' Susan stood closer to him, making him open the case again so that she could look. He pointed to the small screen. She shrugged. There was a configuration on the screen; something that looked like two coat-hangers revolving around each other. At the centre of the design, a small green blip.

Boone walked carefully towards the bare wall, fully aware that Roy had moved closer with the railing. Nervously, he began to feel the cold stone.

'I'm sure ... yes, I'm sure ...'

His fingers fumbled in the mitre between the stone blocks of the wall. When something gave a loud pneumatic hiss, he shrank back in alarm. The sound made them all start, heightening the feeling that the walls and ceiling were alive, and for an instant it seemed that their instincts were being proved right when a section of the wall turned inwards and swung smoothly from sight. There was a cabinet beyond; padded leather walls from floor to waist height where a chrome rail swept around the interior. Above the rail were glass panels, now reflecting several images of Jessica. The sight of her reflection seemed deeply shocking to her, and she stood away from it. Now they could see that the cabinet was an elevator, Roy and Jessica recognising the interior design from their arrival at The Rock a thousand years ago.

'An elevator?' said Roy.

Boone seemed genuinely pleased with himself. 'I found a symbol on one of the keyboards in here. Wasn't sure, but when I keyed in for the receiving signal I found that there was a ...'

'How long have you known how to operate the controls in this case?'

'I didn't know how ...' Boone's look of hope crumpled. 'Until I started to look properly back there. I still don't know how it all works. Like I said, it's ultra-sophisticated and ...'

'And nothing. I've seen you sneaking looks in that case since after

Draegerman's Berserker chased us out of the Banqueting Hall. I thought you were just counting your money, but I'm starting to believe that you were doing more than just carrying that case.'

'I swear to God, that's not true! Yes, I was looking in there. Trying to see if there was any way I could understand it, maybe even use it to help us. But I never had time.'

'Help *us?*' asked Susan.

'I swear! If I'd known how to operate it, surely I would have used it to get away myself. But I've been through this hell with you every step of the way. Haven't I? If I'd had the opportunity of getting away, don't you think I would have taken it?'

'That sounds nearer the mark,' said Jessica wearily.

'So now you suggest we just shut ourselves in there,' said Roy. 'What happens next? The floor falls out and drops us down a shaft to the bottom of The Rock?' He remembered how he had felt on first entering just such an elevator on the roof of the building.

'According to this . . .' Again, the pitiful wanting-to-please expression was back on Boone's face. He fumbled with the case, holding it open so that Roy could see inside. '. . . we have to travel only five levels up. I mean, I don't know how far that is, but there's a "5", see? From here to there.' His pointing finger was shaking badly. 'On that level, we travel either two or three corridor lengths – I'm not sure about that part – but it's *definitely* two or three, and that will bring us within direct range of Draegerman's receiving control. That's where his power centre is, I swear it.'

'Can't we use stairs, or something?' asked Susan. 'Roy's got a point. I don't trust anything in this place.'

'I'm sorry . . . I just don't know. I can't find anything on that. Stairs, I mean. I tried, but . . .'

'Shit!' snapped Roy, grabbing Boone by his frayed collar and propelling him into the elevator. He followed him quickly, grabbing him again and holding the point of the railing under his chin. Jessica and Susan followed apprehensively. Roy examined the interior. Just as with the rooftop elevator, there were no controls set into the wall, no floor lights to indicate which level they might be on. 'Can you control it with that thing?' he asked.

'Yes. I just key in here . . . and here. Is that all right?'

'If it gets us to where you say. If anything else happens, I'm going to kill you.'

Boone swallowed hard. 'Now?'

Jessica and Susan flattened themselves against the glass panel walls, anxiously looking back out into the corridor. Susan wondered how many of these damn things were hidden in the walls. How many had they passed in their constant wanderings down these Godforsaken stone

405

corridors? Biting her lip, she looked back as Boone stabbed at the control keys.

Again, that pneumatic hiss.

The doors slid shut. They waited for the ascent.

Nothing happened.

When Roy looked at Boone again, he could see that the man had screwed his eyes shut as if expecting something bad to happen. Opening them again, he reacted to Roy's expression and stabbed at the buttons once more.

The elevator floor bumped. Roy steadied himself with one hand on the wall, the women clinging tight now to the chrome handrails.

They were beginning to rise.

Roy wondered if the clanging sound of disintegration behind the corridor walls might have been the machinery operating the elevator. Now that they were actually moving, was it only a matter of time before the strain on the cable and their added weight shattered the weakened mechanisms? He gritted his teeth, feeling an onset of claustrophobia and vertigo. The cabin juddered. This must be the moment . . .

And then the elevator doors slid open.

Beyond, they could see the same corridor wall.

'We haven't moved!' snapped Susan. 'You idiot, we haven't moved.'

Boone anxiously surveyed the innards of the attaché case once more.

'We *have* moved. We're at level "5", according to this panel. We've definitely moved up.'

Roy seized Boone's shoulder and shoved him outside. When Jessica and Susan had stepped out of the elevator, he followed. They looked around. The same black stone, the same water drizzling on its surface. The same flagged floor, the same orange lights in their brackets near the ceilings.

'He's right,' said Jessica. 'We're on a different level.' Roy and Susan followed her pointing finger. A chunk of masonry had fallen from the ceiling and shattered on the flagged floor: significant physical evidence, unless it had happened when they were standing immobile in the cabin. They did not need to discuss the situation to realise that they would have heard something that size crashing to the ground in the new and eerie silence that seemed to have enveloped The Rock. And there had been no sounds other than the pneumatic hiss of the doors opening and closing and the bump of their ascent.

'Okay,' said Roy. 'Which way?'

Boone studied the contents of the case for a moment, then turned as if using a compass. They were at perhaps the three-quarter point of the corridor.

'That way,' he replied, indicating the shorter distance to where the corridor turned right.

'You lead.'

They followed as Boone staggered ahead, constantly checking in the opened case. At the corner, he hesitated, checking to make sure that they were still there. Roy urged him on with the point of the railing. Apprehensively, Boone looked around – then seemed to relax visibly. As he moved on and they followed once more, they could see that there was the usual stretch of corridor ahead, perhaps fifty yards. But the light had changed from orange to green. Was this a danger signal? Did it mean something? Roy was suddenly too weary to ponder yet another unknown. They walked in silence, constantly checking the way ahead, the walls at either side, the ceiling – and the way they had come. Boone kept his head down as he walked, looking at whatever viewfinder he had been able to conjure up in his damaged box of tricks.

No one spoke as they walked. Fatigue, hunger and outright shock were begining to take their toll, and they were weaving from wall to wall as they moved now. Roy kept close behind Boone, centring the point of the railing between his shoulder blades, but it was impossible to keep it in that position. Was Boone really so much more fatigued than the others that he was swaying so badly? Roy felt strange, shook his head to clear his vision and tried to tell Boone to keep still and stop swaying.

Keep still ... and stop swaying ... and stop swaying ...

But although he could think the words, nothing would come out of his mouth.

Something was wrong. There was a numbness in his side where Farrow had wounded him, and suddenly Boone was gone and the railing was pointed at the stone ceiling overhead. Was he somehow suddenly lying on the floor? There was a clatter as the railing fell from his hands, and although he wanted to speak, wanted to ask just what the hell was happening, he could not open his mouth.

Jessica and Susan's faces swam into his vision.

And then there was only darkness.

'What is it?' asked Susan anxiously. 'What's wrong with him?'

Jessica tried to turn him over, then saw the patch of red under his jacket.

'Oh God, he's been hurt.'

Between them, they struggled to remove the jacket. Roy's face was white and felt cold. There were beads of sweat on his brow and his breath seemed ragged. Now they could see that his shirt on the left side was soaked with blood from armpit to waistband.

'He's been stabbed, I think,' said Jessica. 'Probably in that fight with Farrow.'

'He never said anything, not a word.'

'Strong, silent type,' said Jessica with an ironic laugh. But her face remained a mask of concern as she pulled away the crimson-stained

407

shirt to look more closely at the wound. She knew that he had received it saving her from Farrow and the hellish monstrosity that had emerged in Draegerman's sex chamber.

'I don't know anything about first aid . . .' began Susan.

'It's okay. He's lost blood, and that's why he's passed out. But the blood's congealed over the wound. I reckon if he keeps that arm down by his side, it'll keep the gash closed and he won't lose any more. It'll have to do until we can get some help.'

'Boone!' Susan said suddenly, whirling around.

They had both forgotten about him – and now both expected him to have run off with the attaché case.

But he was still there; still standing with his back against the wall, watching what they were doing anxiously.

'Still here?' said Susan wryly.

'Where else can I go?'

'Come on,' said Jessica. 'Help me lift him. And careful we don't reopen his wound. Look, you take his other arm over your shoulder. I'll take him by the waist, and keep that arm pressed to his side.'

'Wait,' said Susan. Scooping up the railing, she tucked it under her armpit.

Carefully, awkwardly, they managed to get Roy standing between them. He moaned softly, and seemed lighter than they had both expected. Jessica seemed to read Susan's thoughts as they straightened up.

'Bet we've all lost weight since this thing started.'

'Personally,' said Susan, 'I prefer health farms.'

Jessica laughed, then looked at Boone. The smile vanished from her face.

'Get moving, Boone.'

Miserably, he stumbled onwards, looking in the case again as he moved. They followed close behind, Roy between them.

I was wrong about Roy, thought Jessica. *Wrong about a lot of things.*

Something had happened to Jessica, something that had enabled her to emerge from the deep pit of despair into which she had fallen following Gloria's death. She had been unable to function then, had been unable to comprehend her part in the hideous death. But it seemed as if the death of Bobby had taken her even deeper into that pit – and now, somehow, out of it. She had been stripped raw, had touched the bottom. And in the process there was a new clarity about what she was doing and how she felt. Her thoughts back there on Draegerman's hideous escalator, thoughts that had come into her mind as they had wandered the endless corridors, were not how she really felt at all. She was not the ghoulish passer-by, stopping to stare and enjoy the road accident. She was doing what she did because she *cared* about what she was doing. No phantom or renegade thoughts could confuse or lie to her

408

now. Gloria's death had affected her profoundly, but it seemed as if the fatigue and the hunger and the fear had hollowed her out to the extent that she could no longer be debilitated by what she had been *made* to do by fear of the Daemon in the studio swamp. She was ashamed by the memory of that fear, could never forgive herself for what the thing had made her do and could never forget Gloria's death agonies. She could never forget the way in which Gloria had looked at her just before the end. No condemnation, just a bitter-sad disappointment, after all they had been through. And when she thought of Gloria's face now, she realised that the horror and the shame were all the worse because during their ordeal in Draegerman's Rock, Gloria had come to mean a lot to her. Something about their terrifying experiences had bonded her with Gloria in profound ways that she could barely explain but could nevertheless feel – and not only with Gloria but with the others. With Susan and with Roy ... and with poor, brave, tormented Bobby. She knew what it meant to both Gloria and her son to be reunited again, to be found again, remembered now how in the bad moments they had clung to each other despite the fear and the terror and the *knowledge* of their imminent deaths. Maybe that would never have happened if they hadn't come to The Rock? What a story that might make.

Fuck the story! thought Jessica. *God, Gloria. I'm so sorry. I was so frightened. So terrified, that I let you down. I abandoned you. I should have ...*

But there was nothing you could do. The resonance of Gloria's voice in her mind was so real, so independently placed in the forefront of her conciousness, that it startled Jessica. *No way you could have stopped that thing. It killed me, then would have killed you if you'd stayed.* The voice was like a direct relay, a direct message. Could this be a symptom of the fatigue and the stress? Could it be that she was finally losing contact with reality ... ? *I don't blame you, Jessica. Conserve your strength. Get out of this place, and live your life. Please, darling. Don't give up.*

Jessica kept her face down. A searing surge of emotion flooded her, and she did not want Susan to see it lest she thought that her strength might be giving out. At first, a great burning shame at her fear, and at what she had done. Then that searing flood had wiped away the guilt, and the impossible presence of Gloria's voice was cleansing her soul with its forgiveness and its entreaties to go on.

They had reached the end of the corridor, Boone pausing at the right-hand turn until they had managed to catch up.

'Only one more stretch,' he said. And when they drew level with him, they could see that the lighting in this stretch of corridor was different from any of the others they had seen. There were no orange or green lights set in brackets high up on the stone. There were lights on either side of the flagged floor, like cat's eyes. The effect was eerie. They could not see the walls or the ceiling, only the flagged floor stretching away in front of them into utter darkness.

'You're sure?' asked Susan.

Boone looked into the attaché case, stabbed a key and waited. Then he looked up again and nodded.

'We need a plan,' said Susan. 'Put Roy down for a moment.'

They struggled to rest him carefully against the corridor wall. Susan hoisted the wooden railing, weighing it in both hands.

'You're right,' said Jessica. 'What should we do?'

Susan turned to Boone again. 'You say the source of the receiving signal is at the end of the corridor?'

'Not actually at the end, but somewhere very close afterwards.'

'And you're sure he doesn't know where we are now?'

'Positive. I found the relay and terminated it.'

Susan shrugged off an image of her kids playing with their computers at home. It was the one thing guaranteed to bring the fear crowding back in; the possibility that she would never see them again. She gritted her teeth and inverted the emotion, turning it to a cold rage against Draegerman and his sick plan.

'He won't know we're heading his way?'

'No.'

'Okay, okay.' Susan looked out across the stretch of flagged stone. 'If there's a control room or something, would you be able to understand what's in there?'

'I don't know. It depends on what computerised systems Draegerman has installed.'

'Look, is there a *possibility* that you might be able to ... work or operate whatever controls you find in there ... and be able to get us out?'

'Yes,' replied Boone, this time with something approaching optimism. 'There's a possibility.'

'What about Roy?' asked Susan, turning back to Jessica. 'Should we leave him here while we go on and try to find that place? Or take him with us?'

Jessica looked back down the corridor they had travelled.

'Take him with us. It's the safest. If any of those things are wandering around, and not just confined to one place the way Roy thinks, then we don't want to leave him here.'

'You're right. We'll find somewhere for him at the other end of this corridor.'

'Then what?' mumbled Boone.

'Then we find this place, and you go in there.'

'*Me?*'

'Look – something has happened to The Rock. I don't know what, but something's done some damage. Remember what Draegerman told us back there? Someone tried to get in. Maybe that someone is the reason that everything started to fall apart. And why haven't we seen his fucking face on television recently? Seems to me that the most enjoyable part of the whole game for him was to be able to watch what we were doing and taunt us. But where has he been recently? When we were separated back in those moving tunnels, Jessica, we got a lot of static from one of his television screen messages in the corridor. Remember, Boone? There was a hell of a lot of interference – and Draegerman looked like shit. Since then, nothing. I think he's in trouble.'

'I sincerely hope so,' said Jessica.

'So, Boone – you burst in there, into his control room. Keep him occupied, tell him we're dead. He wants the Daemons to get us, so tell him everyone else has been killed in a . . . in a rockfall, or something. That should screw him up pretty badly, if he thinks his immortality plans have been scuppered. While you're doing that, we'll get in through the door that you'll leave open . . . get that, Boone? . . . the door that you're going to leave *open*! And I'm going to ram this fucking railing right through the bastard's heart. Then you're going to get us out of here. Right?'

Boone mumbled, nodding his head.

'*Right?*' demanded Jessica.

'Right . . .'

'So get a move on,' said Susan, shoving the railing under her armpit and moving towards Roy. Moments later, Boone was walking nervously through the darkness, along the illuminated stretch of flagged stone. Jessica and Susan followed, carrying Roy between them. It was a bizarre and surreal feeling. As if the stretch of flagged stone was suspended in limbo, a narrow corridor into the night.

In silence, they walked; trying to disregard the feeling that if any one of them should step a foot beyond the cat's-eye lights on the edges of these flagged stones, they would plummet over the edge, cartwheeling and screaming into bottomless darkness. Their footsteps seemed preternaturally loud in this place, as if they were really walking through some vast cavern or cathedral. Even the sounds of their breathing seemed to hush back at them in uncomfortable susurrant echoes.

Susan looked back at the entrance leading to the corridor from which they had come. The orange light cast flickering shadows in the small square aperture. She guessed that they had walked over a hundred yards. She looked forward, struggled to see past Boone.

'How long is this corridor?'

'Longer than the others, I think,' mumbled Boone, looking into his opened case. Something beeped inside. 'Perhaps twice as long.'

'I can't see the end.'

411

Roy groaned, his feet trailing on the flags. Jessica grabbed his waist to prevent him sliding to the ground. Susan shifted her position, trying to take the additional weight. But they could not prevent him sinking to his knees. Both women knelt to hold him. Jessica began to shake his face with one hand.

'Roy, can you hear me? We can't stay here. We've got to move.'

Roy was struggling to rise to consciousness. He began to nod his head but his eyes kept rolling up into their sockets despite his attempts.

'We've got a chance,' hissed Susan. 'At the end of this corridor, we've got a chance. Come on, Roy. You can do it.'

He reached up to brace his hands on their shoulders. Jessica took the arm under which he had been wounded and kept it down as she struggled to pull him to his feet. Susan placed his other arm around her neck again and hauled. This time, Roy was able to help them a lot more than previously. His legs were weak, but were taking some of his weight.

'Good, Roy!' hissed Jessica. 'Good!'

They steadied themselves.

'Where's Boone?' asked Susan in a flat voice.

The illuminated flagstones stretched away into the darkness. But Boone was nowhere to be seen.

It was surely impossible that he could have vanished so quickly.

'*Boone!*' hissed Jessica in the darkness.

'Boone, you bastard!' demanded Susan. 'Where *are* you?'

There was no response.

'He's run for it,' said Jessica through clenched teeth.

'We've got to get to him. He's got that damned control box, knows where Draegerman is.'

'He's going to Draegerman. That bastard is going to him. He'll go crawling and whimpering and tell him we're here!'

Angrily and with renewed fear giving strength to their efforts, they hauled Roy along the bizarre corridor, straining ahead to see where it might end, or to catch a glimpse of Boone's cowardly, fleeing figure.

'Oh no,' moaned Susan as they hurried onwards.

'What?'

'Oh no . . .'

'*What?*'

'Something's happening in here, Jessica. Something's happening.'

Jessica stared hard at Susan's face, then saw how she was looking over to her left in anxiety as they struggled onwards. She looked over Susan's shoulder, trying to see what it was that had so disturbed her

There was light over there.

And the light made it completely clear that their first instinct about this corridor had been right. Because the tinge of violet was some distance away, and certainly much, much further away than the far

412

of a corridor wall. It had felt as if there were no walls in here because there *were* no walls in here. The violet tinge was creeping and spreading against a black backdrop, perhaps fifty or seventy feet from where they struggled.

Suddenly, light was flooding on all sides.

It was like the dawn coming up. And they could see that it was *supposed* to look like the dawn coming up. The light spread rapidly on all sides, streaks of orange and amber, swirling and spreading, seeming to chase them as they tried to flee this place which was so obviously *not* a corridor.

And then the studio lights went up, and they could see where they were. The awareness brought with it a great terror.

They were in another chamber, and the flagged floor ran right through the centre. It was clearly another of Draegerman's studio sets. This time, there was sand on either side of the flagged pathway. On their right the sand swept away to a painted backdrop of mountains and trees, plainly make-believe. On their left, the sand swept down to what looked like a miniature beach dotted by mounds of bristling grass. There was a studio tank beyond, perhaps a hundred yards square. Water lapped at the beach in the plainly unrealistic way that it might be expected to do in an indoor beach set, its flat blue surface stretching away to a painted skyline at the back of the tank. Back on the beach, Draegerman's set designers had constructed a cutaway section from a wrecked ship. It was a bizarre and unreal sight. The entire construction could have been no more than fifty feet in length but it had been built to scale. They could see the prow of the ship, its shattered figurehead jutting into the air, and in the side of the cross-section of hull, a ragged hole had been torn. It looked plainly unrealistic.

But this *was* one of Draegerman's studio sets.

And they had hideous experience of the things that could happen on one of those sets.

There was a ragged wooden sign sticking in the sand to their right. A sign that also looked like an old clapper board. As they ran past it, Jessica saw:

D'Man Enterprises:
'Cape Sinistre'

The title was familiar to her. Hadn't this been one of the movies Gloria had said she'd starred in? Now they were past the sign, breathing heavily, fixing their sights ahead. They could see that there was an archway about two hundred feet ahead. The flagged pathway ran straight into the darkened arch. They had to get out of this place as quickly as possible before . . .

Something started to happen.

They could feel it, even before anything had become visible. It was the feeling each one of them shared whenever the fog appeared to herald

413

the appearance of one of Draegerman's Daemons. They could feel the soul-sucking horror of a presence; again as individual and undeniable as all the others. This was something different from anything they had seen before.

'Oh *God* . . .' Jessica's voice gagged as revulsion and fear began to eat away at her faith and her hope. 'It's *coming*!'

'I know,' hissed Susan. 'But where from?'

They looked on all sides as they struggled with Roy.

The water in the tank was still and unruffled.

The fake dawn lit up the backdrops, but nothing moved on the painted skies.

No breath of wind stirred the bone-dry sand on either side of the pathway.

And there was no movement on or around the shattered hull lying on the beach. Nothing stirring within the ragged aperture torn in the ship's side.

But it was here with them – *now*.

'Roy, for God's sake!' yelled Jessica. 'Come on, you've got to *run*!' She slapped his face as they dragged him. He shook his head, tried to assist, but was still weak, needing help. The stone archway was less than fifty feet away.

'We'll make it!' gasped Susan. 'We'll make it! We'll . . .'

And then a gushing cloud of freezing fog erupted from the archway before them. It enveloped the arch in the kind of undulating, coiling twisting cloud they had seen before. The blast was like the very breath of evil, its tendrils clawing at the air. It erupted before them with a shrieking blast of noise – the voice of a thousand storms and the tormented lament of a thousand lost souls.

Susan twisted and fell, taking Roy's weight with her. Jessica tried to hang on, but in the next moment all three had fallen from the flagged pathway and were rolling down the mound of studio sand in a tangle of arms and legs.

Jessica's face slammed into the sand. Her mouth was full of it, her eyes blinded. Coughing and gagging, she clawed it from her face, twisted to rise and fell over Roy's legs. Susan's clutching hand found her elbow – and then they were rolling again, down to the beach and its fake ruined ship.

Gasping for breath, Susan was the first to pull herself out of the tangle, looking back in fear at the archway.

The shrieking cloud of fog was gone.

There was no sound. Only their own ragged breathing. Jessica got to her feet, clawing the last of the sand from her eyes, spitting out the clots from her mouth. Roy was trying to sit up, holding his side and groaning. Had the fall opened his wound?

'Where is it?' hissed Susan. 'Can you see?'

414

Jessica moved around, trying to get a better view of the arch.

'It's not in there but . . .' She whirled again, looking out across the flat blue water to the painted sky. '. . . it's still here somewhere. Can you feel it?'

'Yes. Christ, Jessica. What are we going to *do*?' Roy groaned again, and Susan moved to him, taking his arm and moving it from his side. There was fresh blood there, glinting in the studio lights. The wound had reopened.

Jessica scanned the sand up to the pathway, where they had fallen. She could see the wooden railing. Looking all around, she ran to it, expecting the fog to erupt around her at any second. Seizing the railing, she returned to Susan and Roy where they crouched in the shadow of the fake ship cross-section. Holding the railing like a spear, she scanned the studio, looking for any sign of movement or the suggestion of a wisp of fog.

'Roy hurt that other thing, remember?' she said to Susan. 'It means we *can* defend ourselves, if we have to.'

Susan rose to join her, looking around at the beach, trying to find something – even some ridiculous movie prop – that might serve as a weapon. There was nothing. Roy was on his knees now, clutching his side and desperately trying to orientate himself. The presence of the Daemon was something that he too had instinctively sensed. He knew that they were in immediate danger, and struggled to find the strength to rise from his debilitating limbo to help.

Jessica kept the railing thrust outwards, now angrily scanning the walkway from left to right and back again. Now turning again to look out over the studio tank, whirling back to face front once more. The anger was swelling and rising within her, fuelled by inner shame. She remembered Gloria's face as she had turned back and said: *After everything we've been through together.*

'Come on out!' yelled Jessica defiantly, startling Susan.

She could see Bobby's face now as the thing that looked like Gloria had called his name from out of the fog. She could see how much he needed to be with his mother, how much he loved her, how glad he was to have been found.

'You fucking bastard! Come on out, now!'

Gloria's voice again: *You didn't like me when you first met me, did you?*

'Come and get what you want. I'm here. Come on, then. Or is *his* putting you off?' Jessica waved the railing, jabbing the point in the air.

Something good has come out of this. If not for this whole fucking nightmare, I don't believe I would ever have found Bobby again.

'Death is all you know, all you want! Right? Well come and get some . . .'

415

Susan looked back at the shipwreck and at the ragged hole in its side. There was fake plastic seaweed hanging from some of the shattered boards. Perhaps she could pull one of the boards free? Maybe there was something there she could use as a weapon. Leaving Jessica standing defiantly with the railing, she hurried over the sand, past Roy to the ragged gap. Tearing the fake seaweed away, she began to yank at one of the boards. Jessica looked back to see what she was doing, nodded – and then began to pace the small beach, her feet kicking up angry flurries of sand, staring hard at their surroundings for any sign of movement.

Susan wrenched a board away. It was still attached at one end, and she began to yank hard, nails screeching in protest as she did so. The nails were fastened solid. Jessica remembered what Gloria had told her when they had travelled together in the sedan to this place; remembered her saying: *Cape Sinistre. They say it's one of his best. My best-ever death scene in that shipwreck … in that shipwreck … in that shipwreck …*

Jessica's limbs were suddenly leaden. She turned, feeling as if she was trapped in a slow-motion sequence for one of Jack Draegerman's movies, trapped in a film within a film where they must act out their parts and die, as pre-ordained by Draegerman's script. Filled with a new horror, fighting against the script, Jessica saw that Susan was looking back at her, still tearing at the wooden plank, the nails screeching and … becoming the sound of something else.

She could see movement inside the ragged gap, could see that Susan was turned away from it, looking at her, an expression of puzzlement on her face.

The screeching of nails erupted into the shrieking of a hellwind and suddenly everything snapped into real time as a gushing cloud of writhing fog erupted from the hole in the false ship's side, engulfing Susan in its freezing, coiling embrace. Roy lunged forward, grasping for her – and fell flat on the sand. The fog was taking shape as it coiled. Even as it twisted and writhed, its tentacles snaking around Susan's arms and legs and head, the gauze-like fog became solid before Jessica's eyes. Susan screamed long and loud, then her voice was cut off as one of dozens of grey-green, slime-encrusted tentacles slapped over her mouth. She fell, but the thing within the wreck was immense, swelling to fill the interior, the hideous scaled tentacles the mouth-parts of a grotesque, slavering and squid-like head. Susan's feet were no longer on the sand; the thing was holding her as the obscene voracious mouth-parts fastened around her. The thing inside the hull began to lift and drag her inside, like some hideous trap-door spider. Once inside, it could begin its feast.

Screaming, Jessica charged across the sand towards the aperture. Vaguely, she saw Roy trying to crawl forward, one hand clasped to his bleeding side, the other raised as if trying to reach Susan. Still screaming, she collided with Susan side-on, shoving her hard to one side with her hip as the tentacled mass groped and embraced and tried to keep her from falling out of its grip. Beyond, in the hull, there was a mass of dark, squirming movement. Somewhere within the obscene riot of raw flesh, something that might have been a ghastly black eye turned with one jerking and furious motion to fix on Jessica.

And with all the impetus of the fury and the shame and the terror of what had happened to Jessica in Draegerman's Rock, she rammed the railing directly into the eye, throwing all her weight behind it. The point sank deep, and Jessica threw herself behind it, ramming hard and yelling her rage and defiance and denial of the thing. The shrieking hellwind had become the screaming of some prehistoric beast in agony. Instantly, the grasping tentacles had gone from Susan's body. She collapsed headlong into the sand. There were livid red weals across her face and arms where the thing had gripped her. Weakly, she pushed herself up to see the tentacles whiplash back inside the hull and then out again to fasten on Jessica in a convulsive, agonised defence. They swarmed around her waist and legs, over her arms and face. They became tangled in her hair, tried to pull her legs away from beneath her.

Still screaming in rage, Jessica pushed deeper. Susan tried to rise and fell back, her legs too weak to hold her.

'No, Jessica! *No!*'

Black oil erupted all around Jessica, soaking her body, drenching her hair. In that moment, it seemed that the bellowing had risen several octaves to an ear-piercing shriek.

'*Noooo!*'

Susan's own scream joined with Jessica's scream of rage and defiance as the fog suddenly engulfed the ragged gap in the ship's side. Instantly, the thing inside had dissolved, losing its form and returning to the fog-cloud from which it had been formed. The gushing cloud enshrouded Jessica, billowing out to swarm over Susan and Roy. It tasted bitter and cold, made Susan retch as she struggled to rise from the sand.

And then, like steam, the fog evaporated and was gone.

The instinctive dread of the Daemon was no longer with them. Its presence was no longer registering. Susan struggled to look back at the hole in the ship's hull. Roy was trying to rise. Susan staggered towards him.

They stood in a mutual embrace, holding each other up.

And they stared into the hull.

It was empty.

The Daemon had gone.

There was nothing there but studio sand, and the edge of Draegerman's studio tank water, lapping at the edge. In the sand at their feet was the wooden railing, now entirely drenched in black oil. With Susan's help,

417

Roy leaned down and picked it up, uncaring of the disgusting mass with which it was coated.

'Jessica . . . ?' he called.

Susan began to weep then, as they stood by the ragged gap. She could no longer hold it back.

And then, after a while, Roy also began to weep.

They stood, heads bowed, flooding each other with tears.

SIXTEEN

The corridors of Draegerman's Rock were deserted.

Neither man was prepared for what they might find inside, but had formed at least a basic view that they might be dealing with a gigantic office complex from which the Draegerman empire was organised. They had been expecting ultra-modern office facilities, a hive of activity, numerous employees and at least some trace of the one hundred to one hundred and fifty security men employed by Draegerman. But they had not expected to arrive in The Rock via a swamp, most certainly not a swamp that seemed to have a drainage system which flowed backwards. And now, emerging from the place where Moss had met his end at the hands of something that defied logic, they seemed to have stepped into the labyrinthine corridors of some catacomb or mediaeval castle. When they had reached the end of the fourth identical corridor, Taylor carefully taking each corner with his machine pistol at the ready, Den hissed into his ear:

'This can't be Draegerman's Rock. It *can't be!*'

Taylor did not answer. He bent low and ran down the next corridor, leaving Den to follow. At the end he asked another question.

'Where the hell *is* everybody, Taylor?'

Finally, at the end of the sixth meandering corridor, Taylor had given up. He stopped to lean back against the stone wall, and breathed out heavily. For a man who had a tendency to collapse occasionally, Den thought that Taylor was an extremely *fit* dying man. He struggled to get his breath, wanting to ask more questions. Taylor waved his next aside before it could be uttered.

'I don't know! Right? I just don't know. What I said to Moss, I'll say to you. We don't have time to hang around asking questions. There are no answers, Den. For instance, you and I *know* that water doesn't flow uphill, and that's just for starters. That ... *thing* ... back there. We don't know what the hell it is, and we didn't just imagine it. It killed him. So we've got to apply our own logic, got to make it through the best way we can. Susan's the important thing. She's the *only* thing that matters. That, and getting her out of here.'

'Apply logic? To what we saw back there?'

'Yeah! Our *own* logic! Like, for instance – we don't know what it was, but it's no fucking good telling ourselves that something like that can't exist. Because it does, and it chewed Moss's bloody head off. It also took two full clips of nine-millimetre shells, and didn't like it. So, the logic? If there's one thing like that in here, there might be others. And if there are others, make sure your gun is primed and that you don't end up like Moss. Come on.'

Taylor walked down the corridor ahead, scanning the walls and ceiling. Den followed again. The blurring, shape-shifting nature of the thing that had killed Moss was causing problems inside his head. He was trying to get a mental fix on whatever it was that had erupted through the water, but every time he tried to do so, the image blurred and changed – just as the thing had done. Somehow, it seemed important that he be able to get the picture clear, no matter how bizarre the thing might be.

At the end of the next corridor, Taylor paused, holding out a hand behind him to stop Den. He began carefully to examine what he could see around the right-hand bend. Then, deciding that there was no threat, he waved Den on. This was a T-junction, with a corridor passing to left and right. Den quickly scanned the left-hand corridor as he turned after Taylor. It looked identical to the one down which they had come. But when he looked to the right, he could see why Taylor had paused.

Something had crashed through the corridor wall, splitting the stone apart, and spewing out into the flagged pathway. Den could see shattered machinery; could see steel rods glistening with oil, crankshafts and sundered steelwork. Something that looked at first like an enormous buzzsaw had fallen out of the demolished wall. He could see its ragged curved edge; but as they drew nearer he could see at last that this was not a buzzsaw, but some gigantic cogwheel. He had never seen anything like it before. It looked antiquated, like some relic from a museum where Victorian steam engines thundered at standstill, or spewed steam to no purpose. Taylor had reached the tangled wreck of machinery, and was looking down at it when Den drew level. At last, he could see what had taken Taylor's eye.

There was a dark pool surrounding the broken machinery. At first it looked like oil, but when he looked closer, Den could see that the pool was crimson and clotted.

'That can't be blood . . .' he said, almost to himself.

'It's blood,' answered Taylor.

'Christ, you mean that stuff came through the wall on top of somebody?'

'Look for yourself,' said Taylor. 'That stuff is all over the machinery dripping from it. But there's no one underneath this mess. Look, you can see the floor.'

Den looked and saw that Taylor was right.

So much blood, and not a body in sight.

'Someone took the bodies away,' said Den. 'Must have.'

Taylor merely grunted, looking over the top of the wreckage, down the corridor, and judging whether they could get past. He looked back in the opposite direction.

'Six and two threes,' he muttered. 'Let's head left.' He turned quickly away from the wreckage and started off down the corridor in the opposite direction.

'What's the plan?' asked Den at last. 'You said you'd tell us ... I mean me ... when we got in here.'

'Plan?' laughed Taylor ironically. 'First thing we have to do is actually *find* someone in this mausoleum.'

'And then?'

'If I'd been on my own getting in here, it would have been faster and easier – in theory. Find the air-conditioning, get into a duct. Stay there and wait. Maybe travel in the ducts and suss out the layout. Just how long that *would* have taken would be anyone's guess. Then take a hostage. If he or she was no good, kill them and stow them away somewhere. Start again, get another hostage. That way, I'd guessed I might find out where they're holding Susan.'

'And now?'

'See for yourself. No ventilation ducts to be seen. And instead of an office complex, we appear to have walked into Castle Dracula. So – first person we see is the one we take. If they know nothing, we kill him or her. Does that bother you?'

Den's face was grim. He knew that he was being tested.

'Yes, but I'll do it. I want Susan out of this place.'

'Good,' said Taylor. 'Stay close.'

They pressed on in the darkness, looking for any sign of movement.

Den looked back only once, to the shattered tangle of machinery that had crashed through the corridor wall. There was a crazy, nagging and ridiculous thought in his head. Somehow, it refused to go away.

Does machinery bleed?

SEVENTEEN

Fear and exhaustion, a debilitating combination.

Grief was a third factor as they stood in each other's arms. It was a shared channel for everything they had suffered since they had first accepted Jack Draegerman's invitation. The terrors and the exhaustion, the gnawing anxiety, the confrontations with things that could not possibly exist and whose appearance had frayed their lifelong beliefs in everything they thought they knew about the world. And it was the grief they shared which opened the inner conduits and let these ragged emotions drain from them. Time had no meaning in Draegerman's Rock, but surely they could not have known each other for more than a few days? Strangers at the outset, and now brother and sister if Draegerman was to be believed. In these few days, during the hellish kaleidoscope of nightmares that Draegerman had made them endure, they had become no longer strangers. It bound them together in a way that perhaps a lifetime together in the real world outside might never have been able to do.

And as they grieved for Jessica, the outlet of emotion began to sharpen into resolve. They had felt the anger flaring within, the outrage at that which they had been forced to endure. And the embers of that rage were being fanned as they stemmed the grief and saw in their minds' eye Jessica standing with her hopelessly inadequate weapon on Draegerman's fake beach. They heard her defiant challenge to that thing, wherever it might be. They saw the anger and the solid determination on her face as she plunged headlong into the frightful mass.

They could feel that rage. Not burning, but cold, and lodged deep inside.

Roy could feel the pain eating at his side as he gripped the blackened railing. But he did not care. He welcomed the pain because it was somehow akin to the cold rage inside. Susan braced both hands on his shoulders and stared deep into his eyes. She kissed him then, a sisterly gesture. But it was something darker and more intense than sibling love. It bound them in their unspoken resolve

The time had come. No matter what, no matter the cost – they would find Draegerman now. Nothing else mattered.

Susan turned sharply. Without speaking, Roy followed as she climbed the dry sand to the flagged pathway. The archway through which the hideous fog had erupted to throw them from the walkway was a mere fifty feet ahead. They did not discuss what they were going to do. Susan strode through the archway and he, holding the weapon tight in both hands, followed into its dark shadow. The railing felt solid and important in his hands. This was something more than a set decoration. This had blooded a Daemon once, and Jessica had empowered it now, had transformed it into something like a dark talisman. Their only weapon had become their most powerful weapon.

He would use it to finish the nightmare.

There was another corridor beyond the archway, but this stretched only thirty feet before turning right.

Susan remembered what the coward Boone had said. The power source for this House of Horrors was close. Perhaps he had run back to his master to beg forgiveness, and to hope that he would show mercy. She knew that when she found Boone, she would kill him.

They turned into the right-hand corridor.

And now they both felt, despite the dark inner resolve, that the stage had been set for them. This was too easy. They were actors, playing their parts in one of Draegerman's movies. They did not have to claw at these stone walls, or shriek Draegerman's name until one of the hundreds of hidden doors in the walls slowly swung open to admit them to his inner sanctum.

Because that door was already open.

The green-lit corridor stretched for the usual fifty-yard length. But at the midway point, a door had opened in the left-hand wall. Light was shining through the doorway on to the flagged floor. And as they stood and looked at it, they could hear noises now. The low but audible hum of machinery. A hiss of static.

They walked towards the source of the light.

They were themselves, yet not themselves. They felt like actors playing their own parts. Should there be background music? Was it something akin to battle fatigue which had given them this out-of-body feeling? How could that cold and intense anger propel them towards their last confrontation when this detachment was upon them? Was this how heroes died in battle? Was this where ordinary people, bludgeoned by the immensity and horror of conflict, found the true conviction to destroy that which was so utterly and unarguably evil?

They stood in the doorway, looking inside.

The chamber was perhaps the same size as the place where Farrow had met his death. But it was not possible here to see the carved stone blocks of the wall. Because every square inch from floor to ceiling was

423

a continuous bank of computerised equipment. They stood and looked at the winking lights and the LED displays, at the visual display units and the dozens of television screens. Some were blank, some displayed the hissing snowstorms with which they were so familiar. Others gave views of corridors and chambers and dark recessed places. Some displayed corridors filled with fallen debris and crushed machinery. But their main attention was focused on the figure who sat directly before them in a swivel chair.

The man was sitting with his back to them, but they recognised him immediately. He was wearing the same clothes as the first and last time they had seen him in the flesh. He did not acknowledge their presence, but it seemed impossible that he could not be awaiting their arrival. Motionless, he sat with both hands on a panel at waist height apparently intent on a monitor screen in front of him. They could see that screen. It was a hissing snowstorm blur. The figure stared into it, as if mesmerised. There were leather straps on his forearms, a complicated criss-cross arrangement; and as they stared at this hated figure from behind they could see that there was a multitude of coloured electrical wires in and around the leather straps. The wires completely enwrapped his forearms, and there were blue, red, yellow and green wires swarming up over his arms to his neck. The figure was wearing some kind of brass collar, and the wires that streamed from his arms all seemed to connect there. As they watched, red and green LED lights buried in the collar and in the forearms began to wink. Could it be that this man was somehow wired into the equipment before him? With the bizarre winking of lights the snowstorm on the screen suddenly blurred. Horizontal black bars span and wobbled, and then there was a picture.

It was a picture of the man and the woman standing in the doorway looking into the control chamber.

Roy watched himself walk into the room, raising the railing like a javelin. Susan saw herself walk in at his side. Their attention was riveted on the figure at the control panel. But the figure did not move, did not turn as they advanced upon him. Now they were so close to the figure that it seemed their faces filled the screen before him. Those faces were drawn, haggard and white. They looked spectral and grim, like the faces of the dead.

'Draegerman,' said Roy simply, standing directly behind the figure. It still did not move.

Was he so confident sitting here in the centre of his web?

'Draegerman, you bastard. Turn around, I want to see your face.'

The lights winked red and green within the insane criss-cross garment of wires.

Roy's face filled the screen in front of the unmoving figure.

'DRAEGERMAN!'

He grabbed the back of the figure's chair and yanked hard. The chair

424

spun around. And in that motion, wires were torn from the control panel. They sparked and hissed; spirals of smoke erupted from the console. The figure slumped sideways in its seat, its head sagging on its shoulders.

They looked on the face of Jack Draegerman.

It was the same face that had taunted them during their nightmare flight through The Rock's corridors. They recognised the hideous decomposition around the mouth which had given his face that permanent leer. The creeping shadow had spread to cover his entire visage. And it looked somehow as if the very life-force had been drained out of him by the controls to which he was connected. The eyes were sunken, but no longer gleaming with that manic, sadistic sparkle. The eyes looked like dull glass. There was no life in them.

Draegerman was dead.

Uttering a scream of rage and denial that he should be taken from them, Roy reared back, raising the blackened wooden railing high in both hands. He lunged forward, stabbing the spear into the dead figure's chest. All his weight was behind the downward lunge. The railing impaled Draegerman, bursting out between his shoulder blades and pinning him to the chair on which he was sitting. Roy staggered back, Susan taking his arm to prevent him losing his balance. The impact of the blow spun the chair around and more wires were torn from the console. Sparks leapt and danced on the control panel. The lights in the wiring around Draegerman's body popped and crackled and splintered with blue flame. A spark had begun a small fire in his hair. The hair crackled and flared. Then the flame was gone and his head was wreathed in stinking black smoke. There was no blood around the impaling spear, no blood on the chair or the floor.

Draegerman had been dead for a long, long time.

Breathless, Roy and Susan clung to each other, looking at the ghastly corpse.

Suddenly a dark figure appeared on the monitor screen, stepping over the threshold of the door behind them. They whirled to look.

'Remember me?' asked a familiar voice.

It was Boone.

They relaxed – then tensed again when Boone raised his hand to reveal that he was holding a gun.

Roy laughed. 'Crawling out of the woodwork when it's all over?'

'All over?' said Boone. 'I don't think so.'

Then he steadied the gun – and shot Roy, point blank.

The barking retort of the weapon was agonisingly loud in the chamber. Roy spun around and fell to the stone floor. Susan screamed in shock and rage, flung herself down, grabbed him and rolled him over. There was blood on her hands. She screamed in rage and shock,

425

turned with both bloodied hands like claws, ready to hurl herself across the chamber and blind Boone.

But Boone had quickly crossed the chamber and was almost standing over her.

As she turned, he pulled back a foot and kicked her hard on the side of the head.

Soundlessly, she collapsed unconscious over Roy.

Darkness . . . only darkness . . .

EIGHTEEN

Roy dreamed that he was burning alive in a pit of fire. There was agony in this dream, and he was utterly convinced that he was dead and burning in Hell. He thrashed and struggled to be free, but knew that there was no escape from this place, knew that he must suffer for an eternity.

And then he awoke.

But in this place, the pain was more dreadful than his dream and there was no escape from it.

'It's okay, it's okay ...' Susan's face filled his vision, holding his thrashing arms as he emerged from one pit into another. The red weals in her cheeks and forehead from their encounter with the thing back in the beach were livid. He could tell by her eyes as he slumped back that everything was far from okay. She turned from him, looking with concern at his left leg. Roy looked down, and at last could see where the fire that seemed to be engulfing his body was originating. From knee to groin, his jeans were stained dark red. There was a hole in them just above the knee, and Susan had tied a tourniquet there with a length of electrical wiring that had been torn from Draegerman's corpse.

'Loosen the wire,' said a familiar voice. 'Let it bleed, then tighten again.'

Roy looked across the chamber.

Boone was standing next to the corpse in the chair, still holding the gun with which he had shot Roy. Memory flooded back.

'Boone, you ...'

Susan loosened the wire. A dark bubble of blood erupted from Roy's thigh. Crying aloud, he groped for the site of the pain. Susan shoved him back with the flat of one hand, returning quickly to tighten the wire. Roy fought to catch his breath, and then saw the dark clotting of blood around her ear. A purple bruise was spreading from the base of the ear to her cheekbone.

'Keep your temper,' said Boone calmly. 'It's not good for the blood pressure to get yourself worked up. Increases the pulse rate, raises the probability of your bleeding to death. And it's not time

427

for you to die just yet. In case you'd forgotten, there's a contrac'
to keep.'

'Draegerman's dead,' said Roy. 'What the hell is wrong with you
We can get out of here now . . .'

Susan looked at him. Again, the expression contradicted what ha
been said. There was no hope there.

'What the hell is going on?' asked Roy in a flat voice. Susan looked
back at Boone.

Boone stepped forward, fingering his scar. 'I've been waiting fo
you to wake up, Roy. Been keeping this, because I didn't want t
spoil the fun.' Still holding the gun, he shrugged out of his jacke'
and perhaps there might have been a moment when Roy and Susa
could have lunged at him. But there was no strength in either of then
and the moment was gone. Boone dropped the jacket to the floor an
unbuttoned his collar.

'What the hell are you playing at, Boone?' asked Roy throug
gritted teeth.

Unbuttoning his shirt to the waist, Boone pulled out his shirt tail
There were two leather straps across his chest, and a buckle. Wit
his free hand, he unfastened the buckle, smiling all the time. Th
smile was ghastly in its confidence, highlighted by the scar on h
face. Something snicked and now Boone was fumbling at the sma
of his back. The straps fell from his chest, and something fe
from behind him to the floor; something that looked like a padde
harness.

'That's better,' said Boone – and seemed somehow to grow six inche
where he was standing. He straightened, rubbed the back of his necl
and his posture was completely different. No longer round-shoulderei
no longer timid, he stood straight and arrogant and confident. Smilin;
he waited for one of them to speak.

Both Roy and Susan looked from him to the corpse in the chair.

'Got it yet?' asked Boone.

'You're not . . .' began Susan.

'Not Boone? Correct, go to the top of the class. So that mear
. . . what?'

'Draegerman,' said Roy. '*You* are Jack Draegerman.'

'Good boy. Say hello to Daddy.'

'I can't . . . can't . . .' Susan could not find the words.

'Don't disappoint me after getting this far. Roy's right.'

'But Boone . . .'

'Doesn't exist. Has never existed. I invented him to serve n
purpose.'

Susan slumped back beside Roy, eyes glazed.

'I am Jack Draegerman,' said the man they had known as Boone.

But this time his voice was different. It was no longer Boone's tim

428

and apologetic whine, but the deeply chilling voice that had taunted them from the television monitors.

'It's a shame that I couldn't have kept the entire charade going until the end, but as you've already guessed there have been one or two unplanned setbacks and interferences. I'm afraid I have to move a lot faster than I'd originally intended.'

'Then who the fuck is that?' grimaced Roy, pointing to the figure in the chair.

'I may like this,' laughed Draegerman. 'Isn't this the bit where I spend ages explaining everything to you, then you keep me talking until you can work out a way to get the gun off me? There's a struggle, Susan screams a lot while we wrestle with the gun. It goes off, we look at each other. I stand back confidently while you fall to the floor. Except that it's *me* who's really been shot, so then I fall over clutching my stomach. Then you two walk off into the sunset, hand in hand. I've made movies like that myself. The thing is, Roy, now I get to write a *different* kind of screenplay, now I get to make a *different* movie ending from the one you might expect.' He laughed again; the taunting laugh with which they were so familiar.

'The man you see sitting there at the console is an old acquaintance of mine.'

Draegerman backed away to the chamber door, keeping the gun on them. They watched as he moved to where the battered attaché case had been propped against the chamber wall. Still speaking, he picked it up and brought it back over.

'More specifically, he was an acquaintance of one of my actors, Deborah Steele. Remember my sex chamber? Well, how could you forget? Farrow didn't forget. If anyone deserved to be fucked to death, it was that little shit. This, children, is Perry Dillman – Deborah's high-flying lover and personal pilot. Gloria was right. I knew they were having an affair, knew that Deborah would ruin the movie. So I arranged their plane crash. No bodies found, because they were here all the time – with me, in The Rock. The *fun* we had together! When I tired of Deborah, I found another use for her. But as for Perry, well – I just kept him around, knowing I'd have a use for him eventually. And there he is, all burned out and used up, serving my purpose.'

'It's not possible,' said Roy.

Draegerman laughed again. 'Okay, Roy. Here's the gun. I'm holding it right here. Now I'll explain everything to you, and you can think how you're going to disarm me and go for that happy ending. Susan, you can just lie there and look helpless, if you like.'

'You miserable fuck,' said Susan.

'Shouldn't talk to your father like that. I may have to punish you. But more of that later. Explanation time first, okay? First of all, there's never been a Boone. Only me. I set up a small independent business a few years ago, in preparation for the day. When the time came to send out the invitations, I got myself there before my own people arrived. They had already been briefed on what to expect. I went with them, back into The Rock, as a guest. You see, none of my security staff had seen me for at least three years. In that time, I arranged for *this* . . .' Draegerman fingered his scar. 'Oh yes, it's real. Not make-up. Plastic surgery. A deliberate mutilation which had time to heal the way you see it. I knew what was to come, you see. A powder puff and a Max Factor crayon just wouldn't do. There are other, more subtle effects here. Nips and tucks and skin-shaving to make me look younger. That's the purpose of the scar, you see. It wouldn't be possible for me to look exactly the same age as my children, and a scar like this hides a multitude of sins. There I go again, quoting my movie titles. The harness back there reduced my height, gave me a different shape. Perhaps it was a conceit in the movie tradition. Did you know that Lon Chaney Senior wore a fifty-pound harness for his *Hunchback of Nôtre Dame* role? Call me an old ham . . .'

'You're a fucking bastard,' said Roy. 'And a liar. You're telling us that you had massive plastic surgery and no one in your organisation knew about it?'

'Did I say no one? Of course, there were the plastic surgeons who carried out the job. Unauthorised and unethical, but paid a great deal of money. And it was a double job. Because not only had they to disguise me, they also had to work on poor old Perry there. Using my photographs to work by, until they had something that could pass for Jack Draegerman. Wish I had a before-and-after photograph to show you. I'm sure you'd be impressed. It certainly fooled Gloria – her of all people. But I'm afraid Perry's not looking his best at the moment. Anyway . . . don't forget that I'd been doing my Howard Hughes hermit thing for three years. When the job was done, I kept Perry in cold storage for a while. There were other things I required of him. Much more complex, much more difficult. It took a long, long time. Here, let me show you.'

Draegerman knelt, placing the attaché case on the floor. Flipping open the lid, he nodded to the corpse in the chair. Inside the case his fingers danced over the facility keys. Then he snapped the case shut.

Roy and Susan looked at the ravaged face.

And Susan let out an involuntary cry as the head suddenly cocked downwards to look at them.

'Gottle of geer,' said the shadowed face.

Draegerman burst into laughter.

In horror, Roy and Susan watched as the corpse's lips twitched and it seemed to clear its throat.

'You see?' said the dead body with perfect diction and in Draegerman's voice. 'The rain in Spain stays mainly on the quick brown fox jumping over the lazy dog.'

As one, they looked back at Draegerman. He was still smiling, but had not opened his mouth.

'It's much, much more than a puppet,' he said, smiling at their bewilderment. 'It's actually more difficult now, since Perry died. Rigor mortis and all that. Oh yes, he's dead now. Been dead for at least a day. I was fairly sure he would burn out, and I made plans to ensure that it didn't interrupt our ...' He struggled to find a word. '... entertainment.'

'You used him ... like a puppet?' asked Susan.

'Oh much, much *more* than that, I hope,' mocked Draegerman, cocking his head in a parody of the hideous corpse. 'Perry always fancied himself as an actor. As I recall, he had terrible trouble with his lines. Looked great, of course. Big womaniser. But also a big deficit in the attention-span department. I took care of all that while he was in my ... care. Amazing what money can do for you. A team of plastic surgeons. And a team of specialist electronics experts. Between them, they worked miracles for me. There are a *battery* of implants in Perry's brain. Surgical implants. Micro-microchips. The most amazing technology. Drugs, of course, to guarantee behaviour. I tutored Perry. Wrote his lines, developed his mannerisms. Gave him a thorough grounding in how to respond to untutored questions. Had one worrying moment back then when he made his hologram appearance in the Banqueting Hall. He didn't respond properly to someone's question, and I thought that maybe it was all over before it had started. He certainly fooled Aiken and the others. I was really very proud of that. They hadn't seen me in the flesh, you see. Always via screen or monitor. The walking hologram image was another beautiful moment, wasn't it? Perry never left the control room.

'But there was something even more important about my control of Perry. Something that went beyond technology, something that astounded even the people who were performing their wonders on him. You see, I have a psychic link with my puppet. Does it disappoint you to know that I can't throw my voice? I *think* – and Perry speaks. All of the technology that went into making him what he is, everything I've explained to you, was only a mere support to that central psychic control.'

Draegerman nudged the attaché case on the floor.

'This is how I activated everything that has happened to you in my house. What an excellent improvisation when I dropped the damned thing, and you saw the controls. I really should have acted a little more during my career. Yes, this was a monitor. But so much more than that. I was able to control everything by means of this portable equipment. And you assumed that Boone was clinging greedily to his spoils! Another big moment for method acting. I controlled the television transmissions that way. Activating Perry's appearances, keying in to where he sat waiting here. And then I could speak through him, using my mind. What, no questions about the acquisition of that psychic control?'

Roy and Susan sat and stared at him.

'Don't disappoint me, children. All right . . . I suppose you remember what I said, or rather what my hologram said, about the pursuit of knowledge. All of it was true. I was only hoping you'd let me crow about it a little longer. My occult investigation led me to explore and discover many things, including those enhanced psychic controls. Come on, Roy . . . try to be enthusiastic. Or are you building your strength for the time when you're going to make a play for this gun? Is that it? A touch of melodrama to keep things moving along nicely? No? Maybe later . . .'

'You've controlled everything through that case?' Susan's voice was still blank and exhausted.

'Most everything. Remember the escalator? Where our friends Aiken departed this vale of woe? Can you remember anything about what you were feeling then? Didn't you hear my voice in your brain? Didn't you feel me inside your head? That's because I was inside your head. At least for the duration of that escalator ride. The construction of the escalator, you see. The stones from which it was built were no ordinary stones, the design was no ordinary design. Now I *know* you must have read the newspapers over the years, children. How the nasty Draegerman Corporation was destroying important archaeological sites in its quest for oil? But those sites weren't being destroyed, at all. They were carefully being deconstructed and shipped home, to be used again in the construction of The Rock. Took a great deal of bribery, a great deal of care to transport those rocks and stones, to render them in my new design. Because that raw material was of vast importance to my plans. Those stones, that rock, has been soaked in the blood of thousands . . . of *thousands* . . . over the centuries. Those sites, you see, were impregnated with supernatural power endowed by blood sacrifice. A power that still resides in the stone. With only one small technological aid . . .' Draegerman nudged the attaché case again.' . . . I was able to key into the psychic properties of that stone, use it to talk to you all. And there are certain corridors in The Rock, constructed from the same material, where I was able to talk to you again. Fascinating, isn't it?'

'Why?' asked Roy. 'None of it makes sense. Why adopt a different disguise, why put yourself in the same danger as us? Any time since you shut this place down and brought those hideous things here, you could have been killed. Christ, when I think of everything that happened, you could have died any time. And that would have put an end to all of your crap about wanting to be immortal.'

'Good boy, Roy,' said Draegerman. 'Getting right to the point. I like that. Shows brains. Must be genetic on your father's side. And I'll tell you why I underwent the trials and the terrors and the tribulations with you.'

Draegerman paused for effect. He smiled when even his corpse-puppet seemed to be listening, its head cocked to one side.

'Fear,' said Draegerman. 'A perfect, pure, intense emotion. In all the years I've been pursuing knowledge, I've never come across something so *refined*. The driving force behind the universe.'

'I thought that was supposed to be love,' said Roy flatly.

'Don't disappoint me again, Roy. Not after having been so clever up to now. Fear, you see, is something to be engendered and savoured. I've spent a great many years in that pursuit, refining it in my guests, developing it – *savouring* it. And when I had the revelation, the sudden and utter conviction about what I must do to achieve my immortality, I knew that fear had to be part of that equation. You see, children, I had to *share* in your fear and your terror. What pleasure could there be in merely observing it through a television monitor? None! I wanted to *be* with you, experience your terror at first hand, observe and smell your own horror and despair. But much more! I wanted to feel that fear *myself*! You're right, Roy. I could have died at any time although never at the hands of one of my guests, it has to be said. There were moments when I doubted that, when I could feel that same beautifully instinctive terror in the presence of these things – when Bobby was taken, for example. But there were times when I thought I was finished. The revolving corridors. What a beautifully terrifying moment! Poor Bobby, taking out his anger on his own father, and never realising for one moment. Yes, being with you was a gamble. But such an exquisite gamble, such a wonderful experience! Haven't you been told that the best things in life are achieved only if you've gambled everything to acquire them?'

'You sick, *sick* bastard,' said Susan.

Draegerman laughed again. 'On my escalator I felt all of your fear individually, could taste it. I was so overcome with it, so overwhelmed by the naked beauty of it, that I very nearly fell headlong down those stairs. I'm starting to enjoy this. Any questions, children? Anything that you remember, anything that you'd like to ask Papa about? Come on, there must be something.'

'Someone has screwed up your plans, haven't they?' said Susan.

'Someone's tried to get in. And someone – it has to be said – has destroyed one of The Rock's Walkways. That's caused a great deal of structural damage to the west face. It seems as if everyone living in the neighbourhood around The Rock is celebrating that fact. For a moment, in my Victorian street set, I thought we were all going to die. Fear and confusion. Even outright terror when the ceiling came down. It was even more gratifying to feel these things than I can tell you.

433

So yes, there have been attempts to breach my security. First the roof. They were killed. And then someone tried to get in through the sewers. They were drowned. I wonder who that can be, wonder which one of you – living or dead – can be so *popular*?'

'The place is falling apart,' said Roy. 'It can't be long before the authorities get in here.'

'That's very true, Roy. Good thinking again. And my control systems have been damaged. You've done your own share of damage in here, but it has to be said that the front console in here and the subsidiary controls burned out a while ago. Even my attaché case has been failing me. Remember that last transmission, remember how bad the interference was?'

Draegerman started to laugh again.

'Remember how I tore that television monitor out of the wall and destroyed it? A good work-out for method acting, a good chance to show that I was on your side.'

He controlled his laughter.

'Yes, it won't be long before they come. But what do you think they'll find in here? Nothing. A vast and deserted mountain, filled with catacombs and corridors and chambers decked out in Jack Draegerman's movie obsessions. But no sign of you, I'm afraid. And no sign of Jack Draegerman. Please don't say that you've underestimated me after everything I've told you. And please don't be surprised if I tell you that I've made elaborate and solid practical plans for my future. As far as the world is concerned, Jack Draegerman will have vanished forever, missing presumed dead. But you know better. A new start somewhere else, and a long, *long* life.'

'Your contract is null and void,' said Roy, grimacing at the pain in his leg and leaning forward. Susan sat forward too, releasing the wire. Blood pumped from his leg once more and Roy threw back his head in pain. Susan tightened the wire again and Roy looked back to glare at Draegerman.

'Now what is that supposed to mean?' asked Draegerman, like a parent indulging a silly child.

'I mean that your contract with the Daemons has been broken. One Daemon for each of your children, right?'

'Right. Except that I told a white lie in the beginning. There are only – *were* only – five children. Five Daemons, for five children. Not six for six.' He smiled again, as if explaining a simple mathematical problem.

'Wrong. Jessica killed one of the fucking things back there.'

'I don't think so.'

'No?'

'No. You see, my Guests are not from this realm, not subject to the same physical laws of time and space.'

434

'But they can bleed, can't they?'

Draegerman laughed, but suddenly the heartiness of his humour seemed to trail away. 'Well, it seems you have no more questions, no more entertaining comments to make, so I'm afraid I'll have to terminate our ...'

'You were there when I wounded the thing that killed Bobby. You saw it bleed.'

'They can't be killed, Roy. They don't belong to this physical space. And they've told me ...'

'Told you shit. You weren't there when Jessica died. I'm telling you, she killed it.'

Draegerman stood back, lowering the gun.

'You're not going to kill us,' said Susan. 'That would just ruin your plans even further. Got to feed us to your Daemons, remember?'

'Right again. Can't tell you what a joy it is to have sired such intelligent kids.'

'You led us into that place with the beach and the studio tank, took us deliberately to where another of those things was waiting,' said Roy.

'I was on the verge of doing a disappearing act when you found out about the attaché case. Things needed speeding up, you see. I couldn't afford many more indulgences with all of these unexpected things happening. As it turned out, my little act did lessen the party by one.'

'And you expect us just to be led to those things?'

'I'd hardly expect you to co-operate. No, you'll need a little coaxing, I suppose.'

'You may as well just kill me here,' said Susan. 'I wouldn't give you the pleasure.'

'Now pleasure's something I know *all* about. Believe me, you'll come. If necessary, you'll beg me to take you to where they are, beg me to take away your pain. It's really easy. For Roy, well, first we'd put another bullet in him. Somewhere not vital, but, oh, so *very* painful. Then I'll ask nicely again. If he refuses, there'll be another. And believe me, children, I know what I'm doing. There would be no merciful unconsciousness, no blanking out with shock. I can keep it going for a long, long time. I've experimented on these lines before, know just how far I can take it. As for you, Susan – have you any idea what people will do if they're mutilated? I've a knife in my pocket. A surgeon's knife, taken from one of the plastic surgeons who did such sterling work for me. None of them seem to have survived to enjoy their successes, nor the electronics people I employed. Strange, isn't it? But I'm digressing. The point is, with this knife I can show you what it looks like not to have eyelids, or ears, or a nose. I can show you how ...'

On Draegerman's right, to the side of the console that had sparked and smoked, a red light began to flash. He saw it and backed

435

away from them, still with his gun levelled, until he could study it properly.

'Now, isn't that interesting.'

Still keeping a careful eye on them, Draegerman's fingers skipped over a subsidiary keyboard, moving to get a better view of a smaller VDU behind him. The light continued to flash, and now a snowstorm had appeared on the smaller screen.

'See what I mean? Systems are all screwed up, so I'll have to try a . . .' His fingers tapped a staccato burst on the keys. 'There, that's better. Here's me . . . thinking that the party's nearly over. And we seem to have some other unexpected guests.'

An image appeared on the small screen. It was too small for Roy and Susan to get a proper view, but it seemed to be one of the corridors in The Rock; a high angle looking down an entire stretch. Two small figures were making their way down the corridor, unaware of the monitor.

'Well, what do you know?' Draegerman's fingers rattled on the keyboard again. 'Let's see if we can . . .' And now the large television monitor on the main console began to flicker, horizontal bars wavering. 'Not sure about this, because of the damage.'

And then the image from the small screen suddenly appeared on the larger main screen. The figures were men, dressed in black, carrying weapons and now looming large in the screens.

Susan almost leapt to her feet in recognition.

Draegerman snapped back to look at her.

'So *you're* the reason for all this!' He looked delighted. 'I've wondered who it could be, and you're the one. Well, what about that?' Suddenly his tone changed. When he spoke again, there was menace in his voice. 'Who are they, Susan?'

Susan slumped back to the wall, eyes blazing.

'Do your worst. Take out your fucking scalpel. Use your gun. Because let me tell you, Daddy dear, those two are going to find you. And when they do, you can have all the fear and terror your heart desires before they kill you. And they *will* kill you. Don't doubt it.'

'Who *are* they, Susan?'

'Then when you're dead, you'll get that reckoning you're so afraid of,' said Roy.

This time, there seemed to be a wavering of doubt on Draegerman's face.

Nodding, he moved back to the subsidiary control panel.

'Let's have some fun,' he said, and began to stab at the keys once more.

NINETEEN

Taylor and Den kept to the shadows as they moved.

Each turning they had made seemed to lead to another corridor, identical to the one they had just covered; and Den hoped to God that Taylor could find their way back again. It was like a maze in here. There had been further signs of collapse in some of the corridors. In one, a ceiling had fallen, in another a wall had split. They had looked through the split and seen the silent, dark silhouettes of gigantic machinery beyond. But nothing had so far barred their way.

And then they had heard the gunfire; a series of gunshots, echoing down the corridors, roaring away into the depths of The Rock.

Taylor had frozen then, listening.

When Den started to say something, Taylor had silenced him, listening until the echoes had died away.

'Well, someone's alive in here,' said Den when Taylor began to move on again. 'Sounds like they're having a gun battle.'

'Not a gun battle,' said Taylor. 'That was only one shot.'

Den hurried to keep up with him. Could it be that he would be able to pinpoint the location?

Super-fucking-man. Den remembered Moss's grinning face, and then the memory of the nightmare thing that had killed him clamped down over his mind again.

Taylor had reached another T-junction at the end of the corridor. Quickly, he scanned in both directions. Den joined him.

And at that moment, they both heard the sound of a door closing on their left.

Taylor nodded again, and then they were running down the corridor, their shadows looming large. Taylor shoved Den towards the corridor wall, trying to lessen the shadow effect as they moved, trying not to let anyone up ahead know of their impending arrival. There were no doors in the walls on either side. The corridor turned right. They paused again, and this time when Den looked over Taylor's shoulder, he could see that there was a door about thirty feet down on the right. It was shut. Had that been the source of the noise? Even as Taylor turned to

437

beckon him to follow, there was another noise – this time from around the left-hand bend in the corridor. Again, the sound of a door; this time opening and closing. Den moved to pass Taylor, but Taylor stopped him. There was an expression of doubt on his face. Preventing Den from speaking by placing a finger over his own mouth, Taylor began to walk slowly down the corridor, examining the floor, the walls and the ceiling. When they reached the door with its curious three-claw handle, he paused to listen.

Taylor leaned over to touch it. It was made of thick oak. Den watched and waited for him to try the handle. Taylor paused, as if assessing the situation. Then he shook his head, beckoned – and in the next instant they were moving again. They slowed at the curve, taking it gradually.

Something scuffled ahead.

Taylor flattened himself against the wall. Den did not need to be told. He too had heard the noise and shrunk back into the shadow. They stood there, waiting to see if shadows would appear further down the corridor. The sounds had stopped, and there was no sign of movement. Taylor moved off again, slowly and carefully. Den checked back the way they had come, and in that moment remembered a story from schooldays: Theseus and the Minotaur. He wondered if they should have unreeled a giant roll of cotton before setting off. Whatever happened, he hoped to God they would not come across another Minotaur like the thing that had killed Moss.

Genetic research, he thought as he followed Taylor. *It couldn't be anything else. Some bastard's been experimenting on livestock. It was a mutation, or something.* He suppressed further speculation, remembering how he had been unable to focus properly on the thing.

The corridor straightened. This time, the lights were different. Orange, instead of green. There was another fifty-yard stretch to what seemed to be another T-junction.

Taylor stood still, looking.

'What's wrong?' whispered Den.

At first, Taylor did not answer. He merely looked ahead, then back the way they had come and ahead again.

'Taylor!' said Den wearily. 'Share it with me, for God's sake.'

Taylor shook his head. 'Something's not right. Can't put my finger on it, but something's . . .'

And then they heard another noise, from the T-junction or somewhere beyond it.

'Come on.' Taylor marched on ahead, this time almost without care, as if something was irritating him, and only when he reached the end of the corridor would it be resolved. He was still checking the ceilings and walls as they moved, but his demeanour had done nothing to soften the edges of Den's anxiety. At the T-junction, he stopped again and looked

438

both ways. On the right, nothing. But to the left, about a hundred feet away down the long stretch of corridor, they both saw an open door slowly close.

'What now?' whispered Den.

Taylor grimaced. 'If I didn't know better, I'd say we were being led by the nose.'

Den looked around at the ceilings and walls for signs of monitors.

'You won't find anything,' said Taylor, reading his mind. 'If they *are* there, they're the most professionally hidden security cameras I've ever known. But this isn't right. We hear a noise from ahead, move to it – and nothing. Another noise, get there, nothing. Now this . . .'

'So what do we do?'

'Not a lot else *to* do.' Taylor looked at Den's Ingram machine pistol. 'You primed?'

Den nodded.

'Then let's say hello.'

He moved off to the left, again striding into the centre of the corridor as if daring someone to see them. There was a big knot of fear inside Den, and for a moment he was unable to swallow. He screwed his eyes shut, drew a mental picture of Susan – and suddenly he was able to swallow again. The fear would not leave him, but he would do whatever had to be done.

When they reached the door, Taylor looked around them again, trying to spot hidden cameras. He grimaced when he could see nothing. He nodded to the side, and Den moved there, flattening himself against the wall by the door.

Taylor motioned with his hand, acted out the turning of the three-claw handle.

Den nodded, and leaned across the door. He took hold of the handle.

Taylor raised his Ingram – then gave another sharp nod.

Den yanked the door open into the corridor.

And in the next moment, Taylor was on the threshold, crouching low and with his machine pistol readied to open fire on any threat that might emerge.

But both men were unprepared for what did emerge from the opened doorway.

Taylor skipped back to the far wall as a cloud of fog gushed into the corridor. Den moved quickly from the wall by the door to join him as swirling tendrils of freezing fog billowed out over the floor and ceiling. Taylor waved at the gushing mass, now grabbing at Den and pulling him to one side. It was surely impossible that someone was using this as a manoeuvre to blind them before attacking, but Taylor was taking no chances. The initial gush had settled. The first billowing clouds were dispersing in the corridor, drifting and dissolving into the air.

439

'Stay this side!' Taylor skipped across the open threshold again, keeping his machine pistol steadied. On the other side, he stopped and waited.

It was impossible to make anything out.

A thick white blanket of fog curled and twisted, blocking off the interior from view. The fog had peculiar properties. Taylor could see that creeping tendrils seemed to be testing the very threshold itself; the thin wraith-like wisps instantly dissolving when they met the air in the corridor. The cloud that had gushed into the corridor had gone completely now.

'*Help me, please . . .*'

A woman's voice came out of the mist; plaintive and in pain.

Both men froze.

'*Den, is that you?*'

'Oh my God, it's Susan!' Den pushed himself around to face the door and the swirling fog beyond.

'*He's got me in here, Den. Oh sweet Jesus, the things he's done to me . . .*'

'Come on, Taylor! It's *her*!'

'Wait!' snapped Taylor, moving up close to the threshold and peering into the fog. 'Susan?'

'*Please help me. I can't come to you.*'

'Taylor, for God's sake! She's in pain, can't you hear her?'

'This is too bloody easy. Susan – are you alone?'

'*Alone? God, yes, I'm alone. Help me. Please . . .*'

Taylor turned back to Den. 'Are you sure it's her?'

'Don't tell me you don't know the voice of your own adopted daughter?' Den was trying to push past him now, and Taylor was standing in the doorway, blocking his way. There was a horribly deadening feeling inside him as he realised that Den was right; after all these years he did not recognise her voice. It was so much more mature, so much more like that of a woman.

'You're alone?' snapped Taylor again. 'We'll come and get you, Susan. But are you alone?'

'*I can't hear you properly. Alone, yes . . . alone. But this fog. I can't see anything but fog. Please, Den, don't leave me here.*'

'Right!' snapped Den. 'That's it!' And this time he managed to shoulder past Taylor and step into the all-engulfing fog. Taylor moved up quickly behind him.

'At least put your fucking mask on!' he snapped. 'We don't know what this stuff is!'

'Susan's in here, isn't she? It's not affecting her . . .'

'Use your head, Den. What if it's a tape, or some kind of voice imitation?'

Den pulled the mask out of his waterproof bag, angrily dragged i

440

over his head and connected up the air supply the way Taylor had showed him. By the time he had finished, Taylor was already prepared. He pushed his face-mask close to Den's own.

'Stay close,' he said in a muffled voice. 'We don't know how large this place is or what we might find.'

'*Please . . .*'

The voice was still clearly discernible even with their face-masks on. Both men strode into the fog, Taylor scanning to the left, Den to the right. The ground beneath their feet felt like stone. Taylor sincerely hoped it remained that way. There was absolutely nothing to see in here except the rolling, gushing fog.

'Susan!' Den shouted, unsure how far his muffled voice might carry.

'*Over here.*' This time her voice was coming from Taylor's left.

Den tried to push him over in that direction but Taylor resisted.

'What's the matter with you?' snapped Den. 'We've got to go to her.'

'Logic, son,' replied Taylor, scanning the fog carefully. 'How the hell can she see us if we can't see her?'

'*Draegerman's hurt me. He's hurt me in a way you won't like, Den.*'

'She's close, Taylor. Can't you hear how close she is?'

'*He made me do things. Things I didn't want to do. And I let him do things to me . . .*'

'Here! She's somewhere close!'

And then the fog seemed to grow denser. If it had been freezing cold when they had first entered, an even greater coldness seemed to descend upon them as the tendrils swirled and enveloped their bodies. Taylor suddenly felt something deep in his guts; an alarm bell was ringing, telling him that something was coming. Danger was very near, was almost upon them. Den could feel it too, could feel what Draegerman's other Guests had felt in the presence of something that was anathema to human existence. He whirled blindly as the fog enshrouded them. The chamber was a cold tomb.

Taylor's mind was blurring. He fumbled at the small oxygen cylinder to make sure that the fog was not getting through. Because surely he was feeling this numbness, this dizziness because the fog-cloud *was* some kind of gas. Like a blind, bloody fool, he had walked straight into whatever Draegerman had set up for them. The oxygen gauge showed three-quarters full. There was no fracture in the pipe or the mask, but now his hands felt leaden; he could hardly bear the weight of his machine pistol and the feeling of fear, that great enemy of his profession, was rising and swelling within him . . .

Den staggered, and saw that Taylor had moved away from him. He could see his silhouette, kneeling on the stone floor, head sagging. His arms were at his sides, the machine pistol hanging limp from one

441

hand. He looked like a condemned man, about to place his head on the executioner's block. Den felt dizzy and cold. He stepped towards Taylor, and saw something happening in the fog in front of the kneeling figure.

Something seemed to be taking shape there. Something indistinct but rapidly growing *more* distinct as the fog curled and flowed over its amorphous shape. Was it a man? No, this shape seemed more like some massive bear. Den could see broad, rounded shoulders and appendages that might be arms. And as the thing stepped towards Taylor, Den felt the fear swell inside him. It could be no more than a few feet from where Taylor knelt, head down and lost in that inner despair. The indistinct form slowly began to stand erect, a formless mass of a head wreathed by the fog.

Den had seen a similar movement before.

Back in the swamp room, when the nightmare thing that clutched Moss had thrown back its horrifying head and then lunged down to decapitate him.

The thing meant to kill Taylor, was preparing to do so now.

And in that moment, Den realised that this thing was not *hidden* in the mist. This thing *was* the mist. Even now, in that split second, the fog was coalescing and forming; solidifying and clotting in the act of making the nightmare that was about to swallow Taylor's life-force, body and soul.

'*Noooo!*' yelled Den as the thing's head swept down.

The yell misted his face-mask, but Den lunged forward regardless. The Ingram was aimed dead centre, and Den squeezed the trigger hard. The thunderous detonations seemed somehow amplified in the bizarre limbo of swirling fog. He saw the first bullets tear gaping rents in the huge, shadowy figure. He saw the fog explode and fly from its body like cobweb lacings. He saw black liquid spurt in an exploding sac, saw the shadowy head rear back again as the figure tried to retreat, staggering into the fog. He dropped to one knee and kept his weapon aimed at the mass. Over the relentless exploding chatter of his weapon, there was another noise. It was the sound of something from Hell, screeching in agony as the bullets tore into its indistinct mass.

The shape flailed and retreated.

Den rose and strode after it into the fog, keeping his weapon levelled, watching as ribbons of black liquid spouted and flew. And now, he could see with amazement what the striking bullets were doing to the retreating mass. He could see the gaping wounds torn into the fabric of the thing. They looked like spiral spider's webs surrounding a gaping black hole. And somehow the wounds were the *only* detail of the horrifying shape that Den could see properly. As he watched, the fog flowed and gushed, trying to heal the gaping wounds. But

442

the relentless barrage of 9mm shells was too much for the thing's reconstructive abilities.

Den could see that with each shot the thing was becoming somehow more *real*. And in becoming real, its wounds were steadily destroying it.

His clip emptied. He cursed, fumbling at his belt.

And another weapon detonated at his side, making him flinch.

It was Taylor, now recovered and standing beside him to empty his own weapon into the monstrosity that had first tried to mesmerise them with despair before taking their bodies and souls. Den found his second clip and started to load it.

The fog-thing bellowed and shrieked, black oil spurting and flying. Cobweb-fog tried to thicken over the wounds like some hideous candyfloss. For a brief moment, Den thought he saw something like an eye; a black, oily, hideous thing which fixed them both balefully before one of Taylor's shells blew it apart like some rotten, oversized oyster. Den's second clip was loaded, and now he joined Taylor in a grim joint assault. Now they created their own fog; a fog of cordite from their machine pistols. And with each shot, it seemed that the fog in the chamber was being blasted away by a fresh, clean wind.

Agonised and dying, the Daemon thrashed between two worlds. Hopelessly trying to find form and *reject* physical form simultaneously, it screamed and bellowed in its confusion.

Now, in this exploding hell of shredded cobweb-flesh, spouting, whirling black oil and insane screeching, Taylor and Den were executioners.

The fog gushed from all sides of the chamber, flashing over and past Taylor and Den as if they were standing in some hellish wind tunnel. The fog was streaking to the thrashing form before them, desperately trying to give it solidity to deal with the myriad, mutilating wounds it had been dealt. The shrieking became fainter, as if the thing was fading away – and sure enough, the thrashing shape began to shrink, fog pouring into it and not returning.

They stopped firing.

Now, only the cordite cloud from their weapons shrouded them, as if it was not subject to the same rushing force that was making the last of the fog sweep into the shrinking cobwebbed ball.

The fog had gone.

They were standing in an empty stone chamber, perhaps two hundred feet square.

And they watched the round cobwebbed mass, perhaps the size of a football now, spin madly six feet from the flagged stone floor. The floor was streaked and splashed with the hideous black oil that had been the Daemon's life-blood.

There was a sudden, fierce drop in air pressure.
A thin and dwindling scream.
And then the spinning cobwebbed ball was gone.
They were alone in the chamber.

TWENTY

Susan watched helplessly as Draegerman's fingers danced over the keyboard. The two figures on the main screen moved out of view, but now he had cut to another hidden monitor, this time showing Den and Taylor coming down a corridor towards the camera.

Draegerman smiled, moving aside to stab at a small button on the subsidiary board. On screen, both men suddenly froze. Draegerman laughed again, looking back at his two captives lying on the floor.

'They've heard another door open. Step by step, they're going the way I want them to go. Sorry there's no sound. Another glitch in the proceedings. But I'll be able to give you an excellent commentary – when it gets to the entertaining bits.'

'You're leading them to a Daemon,' said Roy.

'Let's say our last two guests are impatient. So this will act as a little hors d'oeuvre for one of them. Just like Gloria.'

'I've told you that it's all over. Jessica killed one of them.'

'Humour me, then. This is going to be good.'

Susan shuffled forward, and Draegerman swung the gun in her direction.

'The tourniquet,' she said.

Draegerman smiled and nodded, turning back to the screen as Taylor and Den vanished from sight. Again, his fingers skipped over the keys. This time, there was a close shot of a door in the centre of the screen. Just like all the other doors in this hellish place, with its three-claw handle. The door was open, but as they watched, Draegerman stabbed at the console and the door closed suddenly.

'A little more focus on this one,' said Draegerman, making adjustments. 'I want us all to see what happens. Could be entertaining.'

Susan turned her head so that she was looking directly into Roy's face, but Draegerman would only be able to see the back of her head. There was a glint of purpose in her eyes as she loosened the tourniquet. Roy gasped at the numbness and then the pain as she tightened it once more. Susan stared hard at Roy again, mouthing the words: *Make a noise.*

445

Roy frowned. He could not understand what she was trying to communicate.

Susan stabbed a forefinger towards his wound.

Make a noise.

'That's enough,' said Draegerman. 'Lean back where I can see what you're doing, Susan.'

Susan shuffled back until she was kneeling.

On the television screen, Den and Taylor were facing the door.

'Den!' yelled Susan. 'Get away from that door!'

Draegerman looked over at her in surprise. A smile appeared. 'What naive charm! Now we've got a name for one of our uninvited Guests.'

Roy groaned, pushing himself to a sitting position and gripping his wound with both hands. Draegerman looked at him unconcerned and then glanced back at the screen. Den had yanked the door open and the corridor was suddenly filled with fog. Draegerman laughed then, looking back to see if they were following what was going on.

'We've seen something like that before, haven't we?'

Roy groaned again, this time rolling towards Susan.

'So this is the time for your "Help, I'm wounded" set-piece, Roy? Good one! Let's see how this goes – you start to wail and moan and I'm supposed to come over there. Susan, you're supposed to say something like: "Help him, can't you see he's hurt?" Then Roy grapples with me, and you get the gun. Right?'

The two men on the television monitor plunged into the fog beyond.

Roy rolled to the other side. Susan remained on her knees, staring at Draegerman with undiluted hate.

Still watching the screen, and glancing back at them, Draegerman said: 'So it's started to hurt even more, Roy? Tell you what, I'll put a bullet in your other leg and see if we can't keep you quiet.'

'You bastard,' said Susan.

Roy rolled back and this time yanked the tourniquet from his leg. Blood began to seep through the fabric of his jeans.

'Do your worst,' he said. 'But I'm going to make sure you don't feed me to one of your fucking Daemons. I'll bleed to death here. Go on! Shoot me again, but I'll tell you this, Draegerman – you'll have to keep shooting me until I'm dead.'

'Susan,' said Draegerman gently. 'Put that tourniquet back on Roy's leg.'

'Fuck off.'

Draegerman lifted the gun and fired. The detonation made Susan flinch as a bullet tore a chunk from the damaged console not two feet from her head. But her stare of hatred was still resolute.

'I said put it on.' Draegerman moved sideways, fingers on the subsidiary board once more as he tried to readjust the viewpoint from a hidden camera inside the chamber. The screen flickered and then was filled with undulating fog. 'Pity. Might not get to see as much as we'd like in there.' Even as he spoke, two blurred figures made their way through the fog away from the screen. Draegerman turned back to Susan. 'I said put it back on. Next time I'll shoot you, Susan. Same place as Roy.'

Susan shuffled towards Roy, leaned down to pick up both ends of the electrical wiring under his leg. Roy neither assisted nor tried to prevent her. Their eyes met again as she began to knot the wiring tight around his leg. Roy clenched his teeth in pain again.

Now, mouthed Susan, eyes flaring.

'That's better,' began Draegerman. 'We've got sound now, and a much better picture on the . . .'

And then Susan lunged backwards and without looking around hurled herself at the chair in which Draegerman's corpse-puppet sat. The chair spun on impact, the corpse's wired arms flailing as both it and Susan slammed into Draegerman. Roy desperately tried to clamber to his feet, clawing at the chamber wall. Draegerman's face was a mask of rage. He swung the gun up and fired as Susan clawed at him over the chair. The bullet burned a crease in her forehead, but she had her hand in his hair now and tried to drag him down. Draegerman kicked the chair to one side and this time punched out at Susan with the gun. The blow hit her squarely on the side of the head, knocking her almost into the lap of the corpse in its seat.

Draegerman swung the gun up to bear on her.

Susan seized the railing, still impaled in the corpse's chest.

Roy was on his feet, awkwardly thrashing across the chamber towards them.

Draegerman saw him coming – an easy target – and completed his swing until the gun barrel was sighted squarely in the centre of Roy's chest as he charged towards him, bellowing.

And then Susan yanked the railing free, swung around, and brought down like an axe across Draegerman's forearm. Draegerman shrieked in pain, the gun clattering to the floor; and in the next moment Roy collided with him, smashing him back over the control panel. Draegerman writhed and thrashed beneath his weight. Roy slammed his head back on the panel, dazing him, then shifted his weight to seize him and turn him face down. Draegerman's hand scrabbled at his pocket and pulled out a scalpel – but Roy slammed him down hard again, and this time leaned on him, yanking the scalpel from his hand and pinning him there. Susan scrabbled on the floor for the gun. Her forehead burned like hell. She could smell her singed hair when she stood again, lunged forward and jammed the gun barrel against Draegerman's temple.

In her rage, she began to squeeze the trigger.

447

'No!' breathed Roy. 'We've got to get out of here.'

And then something seemed to explode on the monitor screen, a series of explosions that could only be machine-gun fire. Struggling for breath, they looked at the screen to see the fog whipping itself to a frenzy. Something was screeching and bellowing in the swirling fog, and the sound of it seemed to bring Draegerman out of his daze. Roy leaned down hard and Susan pressed the gun barrel even tighter against his temple, but Draegerman was not struggling to rise. His gaze was fixed on the television monitor, eyes wide.

Two shadowy forms were striding through the fog now, both firing their weapons. The flashes of machine-gun fire were startlingly vivid even in the clouds of fog. And the shrieking seemed to be coming from some thrashing, amorphous mass in the fog ahead of them. Black ribbons of blood spurted madly.

'See that?' said Roy grimly. 'See *that*, you bastard! They're killing your invulnerable friend. They're *killing* it!'

Draegerman stared, eyes bulging.

And Susan was full of fierce joy as she watched the man she loved advance through the fog, blasting the thing to pieces.

'Kill it, Den!' she shouted aloud. '*Kill it!*'

'No!' Draegerman was struggling now. Roy slammed him down hard on the console. 'No! It can't be happening. It can't be . . .'

The fog was dispersing, swirling from sight to clear the monitor. Roy seized Draegerman's hair, dragged his head up and forced him to watch as the fog disappeared and the firing ceased. Taylor and Den were standing with their backs to the hidden monitor, watching as something round but indistinct spun and whirled in mid-air.

'You *lied* to me!' shrieked Draegerman. 'YOU LIED TO ME!'

There was a thin, dying shriek – and then the spinning ball of cobwebs was gone. The two black-clad men stood in the chamber looking at empty space.

'Noooooooo . . .' cried Draegerman, and then he began to weep.

Roy snaked a forearm around his neck, choking off the sounds of the man's distress, dragging him from the monitor. Susan swallowed hard, looked at the gaping cavity in the corpse-puppet's chest and then moved quickly to the chair. Grabbing the body under its armpits, she heaved it to the floor. Draegerman's puppet fell with a flat slap. Susan winced. It sounded like a side of beef in a slaughter yard. Then Roy shoved Draegerman hard. He fell into the seat, head bowed, consumed with grief and hugging his forearm. Susan thrust the gun into Roy's hand as he leaned back against the console, breathing hard. She stooped quickly to pick up the wooden railing which had served them so well. It felt slick.

'So who are our friends in there?' asked Roy.

'My partner, Den,' said Susan, grim-faced. 'And the man with him is my stepfather, Taylor. He's an ex-mercenary.'

448

'Nothing "ex" about him by the look of things,' said Roy, keeping the scalpel pointed at Draegerman in the chair. Their positions were now reversed, a fact which Roy acknowledged with an ironic grunt. Draegerman began to mumble his distress.

'Look,' said Susan tensely, and Roy glanced over to see that movement on the monitor had caught her eye. 'Something's happening in there ...'

The two black-clad figures in the chamber were backing away towards the camera. On the spot where the swirling cobweb-ball had vanished there seemed to be an eruption of fractured light, like a brief blue-flash tracing of lightning. It was gone now. And here it was again; flickering, dancing in the air. There was a sound now; a low, ominous grumble of approaching thunder. Still keeping one eye on Draegerman they saw the silhouetted figures continue to back away as ...

TWENTY-ONE

A flickering pattern of splintered light suddenly appeared in the chamber directly before Taylor and Den. Just as quickly as it had appeared, the spinning whorl of blue light disappeared. And before either of them could speak, it reappeared: a crackling of fire and ice and spider's web electricity. It was the same size as the shrunken cobwebbed mass that had been the remains of the thing they had killed. There was a sound now; a grumble of approaching thunder.

It had only been moments since the shrinking ball had ceased to exist, to be replaced by this bizarre spinning sphere of energy. But the nightmare experience of the last few minutes, together with the sudden realisation that they were standing in what looked like a dungeon where a moment ago it had been a swirling mass of fog, left both Taylor and Den stunned. Even Taylor was having difficulty re-establishing his usual use of logic to determine his actions in events that made no sense. They stood, the cordite hanging heavy in the air, staring at the whirling ball of energy and hearing the distant sounds of thunder.

'Say something,' said Den at last.

'It got into my head,' said Taylor incredulously. 'That bastard thing got into my *head*!'

Den glanced quickly away from the spinning light to look at him. He saw the troubled expression on the usually impassive face and knew that they had both been stabbed to the core, had both been debilitated by the thing. This had not been just some mindless, albeit horrifying, apparition. He could still feel the residual chill, even though the thing had gone. This chaotic light was not the thing returning. He knew instinctively. But the threat was not over yet.

'Back off,' said Taylor, and Den followed him as he began to walk backwards, heading for the chamber door, still facing front and with his weapon trained on the spinning ball. No sooner had they started to move than they could feel the vibration under their feet. It seemed to be affecting the walls. Den saw a slice of hardened mortar slide to the floor from between two black slabs of stone; saw the mortar begin to shiver and rattle on the flagged floor. The blue flare of light in the

450

air shimmered again, and this time they both ducked when zags of thin lightning erupted from the ball on all sides, crackling through the air with ferocious energy. The lines of power transferred in one flashing moment to the walls, the ceiling and the floor. Neither man spoke as their exit from the chamber became an outright flight, but both knew that if any one of those fractured blue lines of energy had touched them, it would have been worse than touching a live power cable.

The walls were visibly shaking now as a great rumbling of thunder filled the chamber. Thin clouds of dust began to sift from the ceiling, and as they reached the threshold, something in the flagged floor emitted a crack like the sound of an iceberg grinding against a ship's hull.

In the next instant, Taylor and Den were in the corridor. That vibration had moved beyond the room into the corridor, and Taylor looked back to see that the flashing light was changing colour from blue to an ugly green; growing larger, somehow more ferocious in its momentum as its span. Crackling bolts, twice the size and thickness of the previous eruptions, whiplashed through the air from it. This time, one of the walls cracked and slabs of black stone began to topple inwards as . . .

TWENTY-TWO

'Speak to them!' yelled Susan, lunging from the television monitor with the wooden railing thrust forward. The point caught beneath Draegerman's chin, snapping his bowed head upwards. 'You can do it! Speak to them through that control system of yours.' His features were etched with terror; a familiar sight on the face of the one they had known as Boone, but now this man was not acting. He seemed unable to speak, unable to react. Susan jammed the point of the railing hard under his chin, drawing blood.

'You think you know about fear, Draegerman? Maybe we've learned enough ourselves to show you a few tricks. You want to live for ever? Well, why don't I just finish you here and now and send you to that judgment that terrifies you so much?'

'The handset and the board behind you . . .' he mumbled, still hugging his forearm.

Susan swung to one side, keeping the railing level with his face. 'Show me!'

Draegerman clambered from the seat and staggered to the console.

'If anything else happens,' said Roy, breathing into his face, 'I'll kill you here and now. Quickly, so you'll get where you're going – fast!'

Draegerman's hand danced on the keys of the subsidiary board. On screen, they saw the two men begin to sprint away down the corridor as another cloud gushed roaring through the doorway. This time, it was not fog; it was masonry collapsing in the chamber. The image on the screen was trembling as the hidden cameras quivered in their settings. Draegerman mumbled, as if something was not working.

'Do it, *now*!' shouted Susan, jabbing the railing between his shoulder blades.

'It's working . . .' said Draegerman, and it seemed that his voice was resonating in the thundering corridor as . . .

452

TWENTY-THREE

Taylor and Den stopped dead. A voice had suddenly boomed in the corridor; a man's voice announcing:

'It's working ...'

And in the next moment, as the ground beneath them shuddered and cracked, another familiar voice boomed: *'Den, Taylor – it's me, Susan!'*

Both men levelled their weapons, scanning the walls as they resumed running. Could it be that the thing they thought they had killed back there had returned? Was that the reason for the whirling ball of energy and the destructive eruptions of lightning that seemed to be threatening the entire structure of the building? Even now, was it trying to lure them again using Susan's voice?

'Wait ... I mean, no – keep running! Yes, keep running, until I find out ...'

There was a crackling hiss of static. Something far behind them crashed and splintered.

'I'm here with Draegerman, Den. We've got him. Listen, follow my voice. I'm getting directions from him – and if you follow what I say, it'll take you to us. We can see you on screen. Wave or something if you can hear me.'

'Is this another bloody trick?' yelled Den.

'Wave anyway!' shouted Taylor.

Behind them now, a wall suddenly collapsed into the corridor. Dust choked the corridor's throat, chasing after them.

'It's not a trick!' Susan's voice had gained new urgency as they ran, and Den began to wave. *'Listen, we can hear what you're saying down there, but it's getting more difficult because ...'* More static interference broke up her voice. They had reached a T-junction.

'What the hell are we going to do?' yelled Den as they weaved from side to side, trying to assess their position.

'Head back the way we came.'

'You mean you can remember all those twisting corridors?'

'Just follow me ...' Taylor turned back the way they had come.

But no sooner had he uttered the words than something exploded like thunder further down the corridor. Both men reeled and clutched at the wall as the ceiling suddenly came down fifty feet from where they stood. A great belching cloud of dust enveloped them. They flailed at it, coughing and choking. When it cleared, they could see that the way back was completely blocked by shattered black stone.

'*Shit!*' Taylor punched the wall in impotent rage.

'What the hell do we do now?'

'*Den, are you all right? Den! Thank God . . . thank God . . . I can see you now. I thought you were under that ceiling. Follow my voice. Please! Go back to that junction, take the other corridor. That's the way to us.*'

Den spun, looking for the speakers or the hidden monitor.

'Is it Susan?' he asked Taylor. 'Do you think it's really her, or not?'

'What do *you* think?'

'What?'

'Use your instinct, Den. We haven't got much choice. If we don't get out of here soon, I don't think we stand much of a chance.'

'*Of course it's me! For God's sake, run! Follow my voice. To the end of that corridor, then right! Do you hear, RIGHT!*'

And Den cursed then, staring desperately into Taylor's face.

'God help me, I don't know!' he said tightly as another tremor in the ground made both men stagger. 'But I think we should follow the voice . . .'

'Then move it!' snapped Taylor, and both men began to run back as . . .

TWENTY-FOUR

'*Then* where?' snapped Susan, flicking back the switch on the console.

'Left,' said Draegerman, still hugging his forearm, his face soaked with perspiration. 'There'll be another corridor, and a T-junction at the end of that one. But . . . but . . . we can't stay here.' The firm and authoritative voice was wavering with emotion now, as if watching the corridors shudder and fall was like watching his dreams and plans collapse all around him. Roy was holding the gun almost touching Dreagerman's temple, but he seemed unaware of it, as if it was now somehow the least of his worries.

Susan flicked the 'Send' switch forward and yelled, 'Left! Turn left at the end. There'll be a T-junction. Run to that!'

'But we can't *stay*!' urged Draegerman. 'I think I know what's happening. Please, those monitors over there. I need to see them, need to read the . . .'

'You don't need to do anything,' said Roy grimly. 'Except make sure that those two men get here safely.'

'No, no, no! It's not safe here, not *here* on this side of The Rock. Look, the west side has been badly damaged. When the Walkway collapsed, it weakened the structure. The building might not take further tremors – and I think we're going to get more disturbance, more damage when . . .'

'Where next?' snapped Susan.

'. . . when that feedback energy reaches its pitch. They've killed that Daemon, and if it's possible to kill them, I *know* what will happen.'

'What NEXT?' Susan jabbed the railing at Draegerman's forearm. He howled in pain, clutching his arm.

'On the right turn . . .' he gasped. 'About twenty yards in the right wall, I think. Yes . . . in the right wall . . .'

'You'd better be bloody *sure*!'

'The right wall, yes! Twenty yards down. At head height, in the gap between the fifth and the sixth stone block, there's a mechanism. It controls a hidden elevator. But I can't guarantee that it's still working, or hasn't been crushed . . .'

'Change the camera angle. They're not in sight.'

Draegerman leaned over painfully to flick a switch. Roy kept the gun close to his head all the way. The main monitor image flickered and changed. The two men rounded a corner and began running towards the screen.

'Can we operate that elevator from here?' demanded Susan.

'Yes, if it's still working, but you've got to listen, it's not safe here if we ...'

Susan began to shout instructions to the fleeing figures, and Draegerman turned frantically back to Roy when it was clear that she was no longer listening to him.

'They've come here, in the flesh – in the truest sense of the word. My Daemons. But in acquiring physical form in this plane, they've also made themselves vulnerable. Maybe *they* didn't know that would happen. But, Roy, you've got to listen to me. That reaction back there, when they killed the Daemon. It can only mean one thing. Matter and anti-matter. They *are* anti-matter, do not belong in this plane. And destroying them physically has resulted in a terrible imbalance between their world and ours. Don't you see? Jessica didn't kill my *Cape Sinistre* Daemon, or at least she may have fatally wounded it – but it had a chance to re-form, coalesce, *shrink* from its physical wounds and make its trip back to where it came from. That Daemon back there wasn't able to do it. Your men with the guns truly did kill it, didn't give it the chance to re-form and coalesce and make that journey back. Now that impossible fusion of anti-matter and matter is taking place. It's caused a rent in reality. Positive versus negative. An inversion! And the only way the fabric of reality can self-repair is by a tremendous eruption of energy. Enough to bring The Rock down in its damaged state. So, we can't stay here! *Don't you see?*'

'Good!' said Roy angrily. 'Good, because that means you're going straight to Hell where you belong.'

'Please listen to me. It's not safe any more. Not safe to be in The Rock ...'

'It's *never* been safe for *us* to be in The Rock, Mr Draegerman,' said Susan stonily, turning from the screen. 'Or had you forgotten that part?'

And Draegerman looked as if he might begin to weep as ...

TWENTY-FIVE

Taylor and Den staggered into this new T-junction, turned right as instructed by the voice, and then something exploded somewhere behind them. The detonation caused the ground beneath their feet to shift and crack again. Den glanced back. Another gushing cloud was billowing up behind them, and for a horrifying moment he seemed to see a jagged dance of lightning within the cloud. The walls juddered and shook. Taylor led the way as he dragged his fingers along the mortar between the fifth and sixth blocks of stone. From behind came the unmistakable sounds of more falling masonry.

'Shit!' Taylor had moved much further than the twenty yards instructed by the voice. Was that the intention, to give them hope and then deliver despair, just as the thing back in the chamber had made him despair? He backtracked, dragging at the mortar. Den was coming up behind, also fumbling at the mortar, ducking low when there was a rumbling crack from the ceiling and a cloud of dust hissed down over their heads.

Den's finger dragged against an indentation.

And there was another hissing from the wall. Taylor and Den shrank back and in the next moment a section of brickwork was sliding and turning in on itself in a slithering motion that strained the eye. It was impossible to believe that anything so solid, so apparently inpenetrable, could behave in such a fluid and malleable fashion. Even as their eyes attempted to focus, a doorway-sized aperture appeared in the wall – and an elevator cabin beyond.

The cloud of dust from behind gushed around the T-junction.

Part of Taylor knew that the chances of their walking willingly into some kind of trap were enormously high after everything they had experienced so far, but now it seemed there was very little choice. Pushing Den inside, he quickly followed as the dust cloud filled their vision.

Inside the cabin, Den spun looking for controls. There were none – and with that same pneumatic hissing, the door swung shut on them. They were encased in a glass and chrome coffin.

Taylor gritted his teeth and fitted a new magazine into his Ingram.

The elevator cabin shuddered as they began to move. They could still hear the grumbling roar of falling masonry.

'Are you ready?' asked Taylor, nodding at Den's weapon.

'Don't know how much is left in this clip.' Den steadied himself with one hand on the glass wall as they moved, looking around the cabin anxiously.

'You've got one clip left,' said Taylor. 'Keep it ready.'

'It *was* Susan's voice this time. I'm sure of it.'

'Let's hope so. Otherwise, we really are dead this time.'

Beyond the cabin there was another great roar, like an avalanche. The cabin began to shake. They braced themselves. If the cable on this contraption was to snap, how far would they fall before they hit bottom?

The cabin lurched again, and this time Den was convinced that the elevator was about to collapse.

The pneumatic hiss of the door opening masked Taylor's own sigh of relief.

In the next instant, they were out of the elevator cabin and into the corridor.

Someone was standing in an open door, fifty feet from then.

An apparition? Something that would turn into a living nightmare? Or was it . . . ?

Even as they saw the figure, it hurled itself out of the doorway and ran towards them with open arms.

'Susan . . . ?' Den pushed forward.

Taylor barely recognised the young woman from a distance. He tried to compare what he was seeing with the only photograph he had been allowed to keep. But the woman bore no resemblance to the little girl, and somehow that fact stabbed Taylor to the core. It was as if he had come to rescue the young girl he remembered, only to find that this was someone else. He stood and watched as the woman threw herself into Den's arms, aware now that he had unconsciously levelled the machine pistol as she had run towards him. Just in case. But there was no need for that protection because now Den was holding her so that her feet were not touching the ground, was turning slowly as they clung to each other in that tight embrace. Susan was weeping, floods of relief and perhaps even joy. Den was unable to contain his own emotion. In the next instant, he too was weeping.

Taylor walked past them to the door.

He stood on the threshold, looking into the damaged control room. He saw the grotesque corpse with its hideously blooded chest; saw the blood on the floor. There was a young man leaning back across one of the consoles – in just as battered and bloodied a state as Susan – with a rough tourniquet tied above the knee of a blood-soaked jeans leg. He turned briefly to look at Taylor, keeping his pistol jammed against the head of the other man at the console. Taylor saw the man's scar and the look of fear on his face.

'I'm hoping,' said Taylor, almost casually, 'that the man with the scar is Draegerman, and that the man with the gun is someone friendly.'

'Never friendlier,' said Roy.

Taylor looked back to see that Susan was pulling Den back to the control room. He stood aside to let them in. Den saw Roy and Draegerman and looked back at Susan for answers.

'The man who just may get his brains blown out is Jack Draegerman,' she said grimly. 'And Roy is . . .' Susan struggled, realising that they did not have the time to explain their bizarre relationship.

'A family friend,' said Roy tightly.

Den looked at them both, sensing some kind of strong bond and empathy between them which he found at once puzzling, disorientating and emotionally disturbing. He began to ask Susan to explain, but in that moment there was another grumbling tremor. The ground seemed to buckle and Taylor grabbed at the threshold, seeing the others stagger, as a whispering cloud of dust drifted down from the stone ceiling. The tremor seemed to fuel the fear inside Draegerman.

'You've wasted time!' he said plaintively. 'We have to get out . . .'

'So tell us how!' said Roy grimly. 'You must have planned some sort of escape route . . .'

'Of *course*! Now, please – will you let me use these controls? There's a way, but I have to see what's happening there.'

'All right, Draegerman. But the same rule applies,' said Roy. 'If anything unexpected happens, then you can *expect* this.' He waved the gun in his face, moving aside to let him approach the console.

Taylor looked from Roy to Susan, as everyone stood and watched Draegerman work; saw their shared look of grim determination. There was something about their expression; something with which he could identify and which he had seen before on the faces of people in places where Hell had erupted into a once-ordinary world. Perhaps they had both seen and experienced things that most people would never see or experience in a lifetime. They had been to Hell, were perhaps *still* in Hell, but would see the rest of this game through to the end. Instantly, he felt bonded with them. And instantly, something inside him – perhaps his most precious redoubt – felt crushed that Susan had not run to him the way she had run to Den. He discarded the potentially weakening notion and concentrated instead on what was happening. There were many questions to be asked, but now was not the place or the time.

Draegerman twisted away from the keyboard on which he had been working as an image filled the main monitor screen.

At first, it seemed to Taylor that they were looking at another cavern similar to the bizarre sewer chamber that had nearly been their tomb.

459

But as he looked closer he could see that the columns and towers i
this dark place were man-made. There were cars here, too; perhap
a dozen of them all parked in recesses. Draegerman turned as if t
say something, but before he could open his mouth the image on th
screen trembled. Wild-eyed, he turned to look back as the cavern bega
to collapse in upon itself.

'Nooooo . . .' Draegerman watched and seemed about to weep as th
swooping black arches cracked and crumbled, crashing from above o
to the parked sedans. A column of stone shivered and broke in a doze
places, massive carved blocks tumbling end over end. A sedan seeme
to leap into the air from one of the bays, turning end over end befor
crashing out of sight. A dust cloud erupted into vision, blocking th
scene of devastation from view – and then a blizzard of snow fille
the monitor as the hidden camera in the car port was destroyed.

'Tell us that wasn't the only way out, you bastard!' Susan pushe
forward to the console, grabbing Draegerman by the collar and whirlin
him around. Den reacted in bewilderment at her aggression, so unli
the woman he knew outside.

'There was another car port.' Draegerman struggled to speak, h
words choked with emotion. 'Beneath that one. With an undergrour
channel, out from the Rock. Never been used. Only I knew about it.'

Susan looked at the snowstorm on the screen.

'Maybe it's still there. Maybe we can still get to it . . .'

Draegerman shook his head. 'No, it's destroyed.'

'There *must* be another way out of here!' snapped Roy. 'The
must be!'

The control room shook as another tremor gripped the building.

'The roof,' said Taylor. 'Can we get to the roof from here?'

Draegerman shook his head hopelessly.

'Then is there any way we can get to the outside walls? Son
place where there's a balcony or a window or anything we can s
outside . . . ?'

Draegerman was still shaking his head.

'If we can find a place, the city authorities are bound to have suppc
services out there somewhere. If we can signal, show them we're he
they might send in a helicopter with rescue harnesses. They've got
be watching what happens, preparing to send someone in . . .'

'Can't you see what's *happening*?' Draegerman whirled around to gla
at Taylor and the others. Instantly, Roy had seized him and pulled h
back, Susan taking him by the shoulders and keeping him pinned to t
console. 'Can't you see the monitors?' continued Draegerman weak
'You killed one of my guests, and that's the consequence. That feedba
of energy, that positive versus negative, is going to bring The Ro
down. I can't be held responsible for that. It's *your* doing!'

'Can't be held *responsible*?' cried Susan, dragging Draegerman from t console and then slamming him back down again. Her face was suffused with rage. 'Do you hear that, Roy? He can't be held *RESPONSIBLE!*'

'That's it, Draegerman,' said Roy tightly, and Taylor stepped forward as Roy squeezed the gun hard against his temple. 'You're going to the last place you want to be. Right now.'

'Wait!' snapped Taylor. Somehow, the situation was out of control. 'There must be a way. What about the sewers? That's the way we came in.'

'There's no time,' said Draegerman weakly. 'The way is blocked . . . and The Rock will fall before . . .'

'Think, you bastard!' Den had been awed by Susan's rage, but after everything they had been through he was not going to stand by and let this nightmare place fall down around them now that he had found her. 'You built this place. There *must* be other ways. Christ, a man who can make water run uphill must have some other ideas about how we can get out of here!'

'Show me these monitors.' Taylor lowered his Ingram, striding across the chamber to the console. 'Show me what's still working, give me a quick layout of . . .'

'The studio swamp!' hissed Draegerman, suddenly feverishly excited. 'What you said, about the water, about the drainage there.'

'Uphill *water*?' Susan looked back at Den, finally letting Draegerman go.

'The place we got in, from the sewer. It took us into a swamp or something. There was something there, it killed . . .'

'What about it?' snapped Taylor. 'What about that place?'

'Please, the monitors! Once more, I'm begging you. Let me see, just once more!'

Something juddered and crashed close by, shaking the control room walls.

'*Please!*'

'Let him,' said Taylor, and Roy allowed Draegerman to move back to the keyboard. This time, Draegerman's fingers were trembling so badly that he seemed almost unable to perform whatever tasks he had in mind. For a moment, his fingers paused on the keys, his head bowed. He hugged his forearm to his chest and sucked in a deep breath.

The control room shuddered once more.

'Whatever you're doing,' said Den, 'make it quick.'

'There are things about this place that you still don't know.' Draegerman's voice seemed fractured as he worked. 'Things that have been happening, ever since your arrival. Since the first . . . death.'

'There had better be a good point to this,' said Roy.

'You've seen The Rock, experienced what's inside. And you must know that despite the sophisticated architectural systems there is much

461

more to its operation than can be designed and performed by a mere man. You guessed ... guessed right about the corridors here, about the mechanisms that exist behind the walls. I kept you wandering and lost by operating those mechanisms, changing your direction, making doors disappear, new ones appear.' He paused, screwing his eyes shut as he tried to recall something. Then, quickly returning to the keys, he continued: 'The Rock was designed by me – in conjunction with the Daemonic forces that you've already experienced. In return for favours – favours granted by the manner in which I've entertained guests here over the years – those forces have *added* to my designs. In a sense The Rock *is* me, a part of me. But in its own way, it's almost a living organism.'

An image flashed in Den's mind then: a remembrance of collapsed machinery that seemed to be *bleeding*.

'And there are aspects to The Rock's operation that do not conform to the earthly laws of physics. I told you about the stones used in construction, about the Escalator – but there's so much more.'

'Make your point *now*!' snapped Taylor as three more of the monitors buzzed out of existence. He had no idea what this madman was talking about, but could tell that it made some sort of sense to Susan and the man she called Roy.

Draegerman stabbed at the final key.

The main television monitor blurred and then a chaotic image appeared on the screen. Suddenly, they were looking at a swirling mass of water; a gigantic whirlpool that filled the entire monitor. That whirlpool churned and thrashed with the sound of an approaching tidal wave.

'Yes,' Draegerman was nodding vigorously. 'Yes, yes, yes.'

'Yes, *what*?' Susan looked ready to launch herself across the chamber at Draegerman again.

'I've told you that the Daemon's death is destroying The Rock. More specifically, that eruption of energy back in the place where you killed it is spreading through the brickwork and foundations of the very structure of The Rock. And in those brickplaces where daemonic energy is being used or has been used to power the internal mechanisms and structures over the years, that new inverting energy from the Daemon's demise is interacting with it, instantly changing that existing energy and power into the same destructive energy as itself. That's how the destruction is spreading; that's why The Rock is destroying itself. Now that you've caused that rent in reality, the only way it can be truly restored is for every aspect of that non-terrestrial energy to be destroyed.'

'What the *hell* are you talking about?' demanded Den angrily.

'That's the Studio Swamp you see on the monitor,' continued Draegerman. 'Daemonic energy was used to maintain and enhance its structure. You said you saw water flowing uphill. That's because it was drawn *into* the Studio Swamp by the Daemon which arrived there

That channel never existed before the Daemon arrived. The Swamp was never drained, never needed a system. But the Daemon required it – and provided it. Now, like all the other daemonic energy here, that channel is swelling and growing and expanding – before it destroys itself. My last guest must also be dead . . .'

'If you mean that nightmare fucking thing in the swamp,' said Den, 'yes, we blew the hell out of it.'

'What are you saying? We can get out of The Rock through that place?'

'That daemonic channel is drawing *clean* water out of the sewers and from beyond. Sifting out the waste products, purifying it and channelling it. The Daemon in the Studio Swamp required it, but don't ask me why. Perhaps some chemical need with which to enhance and maintain its physical existence here. Now that channel is erupting and *reversing* before it blows itself out of existence, along with everything else in The Rock.'

'You're saying we can get *out* there?'

'It's the only way.'

'Christ, look at it,' said Den. 'You mean we have to go *into* that bloody whirlpool to stand any chance of getting to the outside?'

Draegerman nodded.

'We'll never make it,' said Den again. 'We'll drown or be smashed to pieces in the sewers.'

'Den and I have two portable cylinders of oxygen and two face-masks each,' said Taylor. 'We might be able to make it. Can we get down there?'

Draegerman seemed to be hypnotised by the thrashing water on the monitor. Taylor leaned forward to seize him.

'Can we get down there?' he demanded again.

'The elevator,' replied Draegerman. 'If it's still working.' At first madly enthusiastic in his explanation, it seemed that Den's words and the very sight of the maelstrom had now caused him to doubt the veracity of his own words.

Taylor looked at the others.

'What do you want to do? Stay here and wait to be crushed to death?'

'Or drown?' asked Susan.

'Or drown,' said Taylor.

Without answering, Susan went to help Roy. Den bypassed her to swing Roy's arm over his shoulders. Taylor steadied his machine pistol on Draegerman as Susan stepped forward to drag him from the monitor by his coat sleeve. She shoved him towards the door, grabbing the attaché case on the way out.

Behind them all, the maelstrom whirled and shuddered and thundered on the television monitor.

And then the control room was empty.

TWENTY-SIX

Riots had broken out on the streets surrounding The Rock. The collapse of the Walkway had been seen as a signal, and although there was no organisation to the violence and the damage being inflicted, word spread like wildfire that the destruction wreaked upon The Rock was nevertheless part of a Great Plan. The testimonies of those who had been present at that destruction had been distorted and exagerated in the telling, until those on the street really did believe that the Time of a Great Change had arrived.

Fires had broken out all around The Rock. Abandoned warehouses had been targetted to act as beacons. A dozen premises were being consumed by raging infernos, and the fire support services were unable to get near. There had been two dozen seperate incidents reported of assaults to police or firefighters. No police car had survived unstoned or overturned in the unoffical *no-man's-land* around The Rock. Riot squads of police gathered on the periphery as politicians and officials closed down all business operations of Draegerman's other administrative headquarters, interrogating his top executives for answers to what had happened in The Rock, and why the building had been sealed to all communications or physical means of entry. People had been killed in the encounter between civilians and Draegerman's employees before the Walkway had collapsed, and this could not be ignored.

The collapsing Walkway had torn a great gouge out of the side of the building. The entire West face of The Rock seemed to be crumbling gradually into the gigantic moat that surrounded it. As decisions were awaited on military intervention to supercede any further civil attempt at controlling the area, a battery of generators on the twelfth floor of the west wing suddenly exploded, blowing out another chunk of the fascia and supports for the prestressed buttresses above. Cables erupted from the concrete face of The Rock as a huge section of the building slid away like a sheet from some enormous black iceberg. Those cables whiplashed and tore through the fascia of the building, just as they had torn from the concrete of the demolished Walkway; four parallel lines of immense force suddenly converging on the North Walkway, ripping through the support structures. The Walkway tilted and twisted like a bridge in a typhoon. There were no Draegerman employees on this stretch, most of them had been inside the building when the walls came down – all were therefore dead.

Those in buildings tall enough to see what was happening out across the way had lined the windows, ignoring the authorities' repeated attempts to clear and evacuate the area around The Rock. They cheered and yelled and got even drunker as that Walkway shook itself to pieces. This time, the supports on the Rock-side gave way with a detonating roar. The crowd were disappointed, having heard how the West Walkway smashed into the building to cause such devastating damage. This time, the Walkway disintegrated as it fell, snapping apart where it met the concrete buttresses leading to the stone gate on the neighbourhood side.

On the roof, the four inward curving towers shook and quivered. They had performed their act of Summoning, and had not returned to their original positions. One of those towers tipped further forward than the others, straining its support mechanisms. The Rock shivered again when the North Walkway collapsed into the pit around it, and with a cracking groan, the weakened tower split at the base and fell to the roof. The weight and immensity of the tower destroyed the helicopter landing pad and the platform on which it was based. It crashed through the roof itself, destroying the top two floors. Another toppling tower followed the first, and this time the shaded windows on the top four floors exploded outwards all around the summit in a great glistening, roaring spray.

Another tower shook, the support base snapped – and it fell away over the edge of the parapet, disintegrating as it fell down the face of The Rock. By the time that it reached the moat below, there was no single piece of that tower larger than a man's head. Clouds were rising from that pit on all sides, obscuring the face of the building and hiding from view the crackling traces of energy which were destroying it and the multiple fires that had broken out on all floors.

Police and civil helicopters circled the building, just as Taylor had predicted, relaying their information back to central headquarters.

It could only be a matter of minutes before this entire structure collapsed upon itself as . . .

TWENTY-SEVEN

The elevator pitched and shook as the shaft in which it travelled quivered from an unseen impact. The lights inside the cab flickered, and in the next moment they were plunged into darkness.

'It's all right!' Draegerman sounded as if he was trying to convince himself, rather than the others. 'Each elevator has an emergency override. The lights will come on in a moment . . .' And then the interior was lit again, albeit faintly by a single fluorescent strip above them. The cabin juddered again.

'You're sure there's no other way down?' snapped Susan.

'There used to be,' replied Draegerman. 'But it's gone now. I saw it destroyed on the monitors.'

And then the elevator juddered to a halt.

From somewhere above came the squealing of tortured metal.

They all tensed, clinging tight to the handrail running around the mid-section of the cabin, looking up at the roof.

The cabin shuddered and dropped again. This time, something seemed to impact and splinter on the cabin roof. They listened to rubble pattering down the sides of the cabin and dropping away into the elevator shaft.

The lights flickered – and then the elevator was moving down again.

'How much longer?' asked Den.

'Perhaps two levels.'

'We couldn't have climbed that far since we came in,' said Taylor. 'The corridors sloped upwards for the most part. But we can't have come as high as this.'

'You don't know the corridors in this place,' said Roy, gripping his tourniquet and grimacing at the pain. 'Down is up, and up is down. Right, Draegerman?'

Draegerman did not answer. His face was white and etched with fear, all his arrogant confidence drained away.

'Up I can handle,' said Den. 'Down is not so good.'

'We're there,' said Draegerman anxiously. And then the elevator shuddered to a halt. 'I think we're on the right level, but there's a way to walk. And if the corridor is blocked by falling masonry, we can never ...'

'That's enough,' said Susan as the elevator door slid open. 'Just think nice thoughts and get us out of this place.' A strong smell of burning wafted over them as they hurried out into the corridor.

The corridor looked like a passageway into Hell. In shape and design it was the same as any of the labyrinthine corridors down which Susan and Roy had wandered with the others. It stretched over a hundred feet into darkness, but the hundred feet of flagged stone was like a mass of crazy paving. The square slabs had been fractured in dozens of places, and steam was hissing through some of the cracks. The walls were juddering and cracking as if under great pressure from either side, and the heat was almost overwhelming. They looked behind them, to the next stretch of corridor, to see that not only had the ceiling come down, but one of the walls had also cracked apart. An elaborate steel structure, like some kind of skeletal scaffolding, had burst through the wall. It was impossible to go that way.

'Tell me it's not *that* way,' said Roy, looking at the blocked corridor. Taylor moved to him, slinging an arm over his shoulder.

'No,' said Draegerman, eyes wild. 'It's through there. No other way.'

'That floor looks ready to collapse,' said Den.

'So *go!*' yelled Taylor, and the shock of his voice startled them all into action. Seizing Susan's arm, Den dashed across the crazy paving. They dodged and weaved, avoiding the gushing steam. Draegerman tottered after them. In the rear, Taylor half lifted, half dragged Roy down the hellish tunnel.

Den saw the stone blocks shift in the wall to his right as they ran, saw wisps of steam erupting as if the stones were being forced inwards under high pressure. Swinging himself between the wall and Susan, he yanked her ahead – just as one of the blocks fell inwards and a scalding spray engulfed his lower body. He thanked God for the protection of his wet suit. Susan stumbled and almost fell, the attaché case falling from her hands to the fractured stone floor. She staggered to retrieve it, but Den pulled her up.

'Leave it!'

Now they were running and dodging again into darkness ahead. Did the corridor end there or ...?

Draegerman fought for breath as he ran. The sight of the collapsing roof in the parking bay had meant more horror for him than he had told the others. There had been transport waiting for him there, a single car with everything in its boot that he needed to escape from this life and begin again: planning for eternity. Pass keys, coded signatures, account numbers and a miniaturised computer containing all the other vital information he would require to disassociate himself from the *ex*-Draegerman empire to begin again under a new alias. All of it was gone, under tons of collapsing rubble. He was weeping as he ran now, trying to keep up with the others; trying to avoid the gushing steam, sure that with every step the ground would open beneath him and plunge him to that place he so dreaded. He staggered, crying out aloud as he fought to keep his balance before plunging on and . . .

Roy clung to Taylor, not knowing who this man was or what had brought him to Susan's rescue. The pain was dwindling, but in its place a cold numbness seemed to be creeping from the wound down his leg and up to his lower body. The numbness was worse than the pain. Had he lost so much blood from his two wounds that he might not have the strength to continue? Yelling aloud when his injured leg came down on a cracked slab and he skidded, Roy gripped the tourniquet and tried to keep the leg stiff and straight. The others were a blur ahead. Draegerman had slipped, but had corrected himself and was running on as . . .

Taylor felt the pains inside again. Each time they were worse, but this time, after the strain and the exertion, he could feel then *building* inside him. He gritted his teeth, fought against them and hung on tight to Roy. He had come this far, and they had a long way to go with what seemed an extremely slender chance of getting out. Susan was all that mattered. He could not allow the pain to disable him. Not now, when he could become a worse burden to them. Taylor refused to allow the pain in, forced himself on. When steam erupted to his left and scalded his face, he was *glad* of the pain. He yelled aloud, both in agony and in denial of pain. And in some incredible way, the scald combined with his anger made the spasm pass. He was sure now that the damage was much, much worse than ever before.

I don't give a fucking damn! he told himself. *Just so long as I get us out of this place. Then it can do what it wants with me* . . .

And suddenly, they were clear of the cracked floor and the hissing steam. Susan and Den were standing up ahead with Draegerman, waiting for them to catch up.

From behind came a rumbling of thunder and a sudden gout of flame from where the elevator had been. With a shattering of glass the cabin had been crushed. It was dropping away into the shaft with its cable broken. Flame gouted from the floor over which they had run and they could see that a section of the stone slabs had fallen away into the inferno that blazed below and which had turned this corridor into a pressure cooker.

Draegerman pushed on ahead, pointing.

'It's there! It should be there!'

Den and Susan overtook him.

A familiar oak door with a three-claw handle had been torn from it

468

hinges and lay shattered on the corridor floor. The door seemed to have been impacted from the chamber beyond.

Den pushed forward to the threshold and could hardly believe the sight that met his eyes. This was the room in which the studio swamp had been constructed, he was sure of that. The ruins of the shattered jetty lay just below the door frame, just as he remembered them. He could see the spars jutting from the water, could see the place where Moss had been killed by the monstrous thing that had been a second cousin to the thing they had killed in the fog room. But the swamp banks and the overhanging trees were gone. There was no inlet on the other side of the chamber where they had entered Draegerman's Rock for the first time. Instead, the chamber seemed to be suffused with a dark blue light. And what had once been still water was now a spinning vortex. The water all around the sides of the chamber was agitated, lapping at the black stone walls, but as Den's gaze moved out from the edges, he could see that the water gradually became whipped and stirred, the waves spinning and circling as they neared the centre. And in the centre of the chamber, thundering and hissing like a waterfall, was the madly spinning centre of the whirlpool; draining out of The Rock and – according to Draegerman – back to the outside world. How long could it be before there was no water left in this place? To Den, it seemed as if there was a steady level of water, as if no matter how much the mad whirlpool sucked and whirled and twisted, there was always the same amount of churning water in here. How could that be, when the water in the studio swamp had always been waist high?

Taylor and Roy had joined them to stare out across the chamber in awe.

Den almost said something, but Taylor caught his eye. He did not have to say anything.

If you spend too much time asking yourself how things are the way they are, and just hang around waiting for answers, then while you're thinking about it, someone or something just comes up behind you and bites your nuts off.

Den stepped over the threshold on to the small, shattered platform beyond. As Taylor propped Roy up against the wall, he opened his waterproof and handed his mask to Susan. Draegerman watched anxiously while Taylor fastened his spare oxygen cylinder to Susan's waist with his wet-suit belt, connected the hose and showed her the valve. Taking Taylor's cue, Den fastened his own belt around Roy's waist and jammed his spare cylinder into it. He set about connecting the air supply as Taylor had shown him, giving him his own mask.

'Den, keep the other cylinder in your waterproof bag,' said Taylor. Pass the hose from the cylinder out to your spare mask. Then fasten that bag to your back. Crude, but it should work okay.'

Draegerman continued to watch as Taylor quickly rechecked Susan's air supply connection, then flipped his own smaller spare mask on to his head and began to do as he had instructed Den. He moved to Roy then, checking his air supply and helping him to stand down next to Den on the platform.

'What about me?' said Draegerman.

'What about you?' asked Taylor.

'I need a mask.'

Taylor stepped through the door frame. 'You mean you're definitely going in there with us?'

'Yes, of course! I told you that's the only way out. Dangerous, yes. But not impossible if . . .'

'Good,' said Taylor. 'Good. You see, at first I thought that this might be a little trick. Maybe you had something else up your sleeve and that getting us in here was just your way of getting rid of us before you made your way to the *real* way out.'

'This is the way. I promise, this is the only way.'

'So you want a mask?'

'Yes, for God's sake.'

'That's good. You seem to mean what you say. Unfortunately . . .'

Taylor seized Draegerman by the shoulders and propelled him through the doorway past Roy. Yelling in surprise and shock, Draegerman hurtled through the air and plunged into the swamp water below.

'. . . we only have four masks, and you just drew the short straw.'

Seconds later, Draegerman's head bobbed to the surface. Gasping for air, he floundered at the slow-moving water directly beneath them.

'What do we do?' asked Den.

They're looking to me to be in charge, to help them, to tell them what to do – and I don't KNOW!

'Into the water slowly and gently, try to stay bunched together and hold on to each other. When I give you the word, pull your face-masks down and turn the valves you've been shown. Keep one hand on the mask. It may get torn free by the water pressure when we go in.'

'What about Draegerman?' asked Den, looking down at the feebly drifting figure in the water.

'He can hold his breath.'

Den clambered down the shattered beams to the surface. Letting himself into the softly swirling water, he braced his foot on a beam and reached up. Taylor guided Susan to the edge. Somewhere beyond, further down the corridor, something exploded and made them all duck instinctively.

Suddenly, Susan stopped – turned and looked directly into Taylor's eyes.

Her eyes were beautifully bright, shining and clear. An astonishing contrast to the multiple scrapes and weals on her cheeks and forehead.

'Taylor, you came back for me.'

Taylor looked into her eyes, tried to speak, but could not.

Suddenly, everything he had done – every risk – made sense. It made more than sense. It was the best thing he had ever done in his life. But now, finally, when they had found her – would he be able to get them out of this place alive? There was nothing in the rule book to take account of last-second desperate suggestions by madmen; nothing about how to survive descent through a whirlpool which by every physical law could *not* exist. Had they come this far only to fail?

She put a hand to his face and he clasped it there.

In the next moment, she had turned and Den was helping her down into the water. Taylor turned back for Roy.

'What about this?' Roy held up Draegerman's pistol.

'Handled one before?'

'Something like it – but not this model.'

'See this? Safety catch.' Taylor put the catch on. 'Do this to release it. Now, here. Stick it tight in your jeans pocket. Water won't hurt it, and you might need it later on.'

'I hope not.'

Taylor helped Roy to the platform, making him sit on the edge. He took his arms and helped lower him over the side. Roy's white face was contorted with pain throughout. In the water, both Den and Susan took his weight. The chamber seemed to shudder then. Something in the roof shivered and cracked. Quickly, Taylor slithered down over the platform and into the water. He surged out, grabbing Susan's hand and encouraging the others to follow suit. Draegerman floundered in the water at their side. Reluctantly, Taylor seized his collar.

And then they let the daemonic current take their drifting bodies, slowly at first, around the periphery of the pool. Then their momentum began to increase. The current swept them quickly across the chamber, away from the spiralling funnel of water. But suddenly they were all swirling back towards the centre, even more quickly than before.

'Masks!' shouted Taylor, and they fumbled in the water to pull them own over their heads.

And then Draegerman, lunging through the water, fastened on to the nearest person – Den – and tried to drag the mask from his face. Den lashed out at him, but Draegerman clawed frantically at his face. Uttering a cry of rage, Susan broke from Taylor's grip, thrashing through the water. Draegerman had one hand coiled around Den's oxygen pipe, and as Susan's lunge pushed him away he clung tight – dragging Den's cylinder from the waterproof satchel on his back. Susan screamed and swallowed a mouthful of stinking swamp water. Roy could not kick his legs, could not stop himself drifting away from the thrashing group. Flailing at the water, he tried to close the distance. Taylor saw him and lunged out for him, one hand fastening on his shoulder.

Oh Christ, he thought. *This is all turning bad and we're going to . . .*

The swirling black hurricane of water yawned to take them. None of them, not even Taylor, was prepared for the horrifying greed of the vortex as it spun them into its gaping, thundering maw.

Oh Christ, thought Taylor at the last.

And then they were swallowed in the engulfing, roaring madness.

TWENTY-EIGHT

The incredible suction pulls them all instantly apart, whirling them into the whirlpool's roaring mouth. Taylor's plan is instantly nullified; the roaring waters tear the masks from their faces, and all are in the same position as Draegerman who . . .

. . . spins and screams and in his terror does not question the fact that he CAN scream in this incredible vortex. His lungs fill with water, but he does not drown, because this is like no earthly whirlpool. It is a draining away of daemonic power, reacting with the other forces erupting in the very fabric of Draegerman's Rock. At the centre of this vortex is a limbo and as Draegerman spins and twists in this space, it is as if the darkness in his soul is stripped raw and exposed. He screams when he sees that which exists at the very core of his being. Like the proverbial drowning man, he sees his life flash before him. It is a hellish kaleidoscope of greed distorted beyond any man's limit; a horrifying quest to reach for the ultimate experience, just as he has told his Guests at length. But stripped raw in this spinning void, the tapestry of sadism, torture, rape and murder has no delights for him here. The horror and the agony of it burns like acid in his brain, and Draegerman screams, screams, screams, as . . .

. . . Susan feels her hand torn away from Den, twists and falls. Her hands surge frantically through this roaring water to her face as the mask rips from her head. Instinctively fighting for breath, she sucks in great lungsful of this embryonic fluid. Now there is no need to breathe, but like the others, the immensity of her fear eradicates any wonder at this phenomena. The wounds on her face and arms are stinging, as if this water which is somehow much more than water is also saline. In her mind's eye she sees Carl and Bennet, and in that moment it is they who are falling into this churning void. Their arms are stretched up towards her as they fall away, and Susan flings her arms down to catch them, hearing them call her name as they plummet. Something is rising from below, with arms outstretched to take them. It is Draegerman. She calls their names over and over, screams at Draegerman to leave them alone. The grotesque, swollen face of the man she hates says: 'Can't

473

keep my grandchildren from me,' and Susan is thrashing to reach
then as . . .

. . . Den pushes open the door of the control room and Susan turn
to look at him from her perch on the console. Her legs are wide apar
and the man she calls Roy is standing between them with his trouser
down around his ankles. He does not turn as Den stands there in shock
but continues thrusting into her. The corpse with the hole in its chest
sitting in the swivel chair, eye sockets black and empty, electrical wir
trailing from its forearms as it applauds the performance. Draegerma
is standing on the other side of the room, arms folded and watchin
with pride – as if the entire show has been put on for his sole benef
Susan smiles at Den. There is derision in her eyes as she sits forward
grabbing at Roy's buttocks.

'The rats,' says Draegerman casually. 'Don't forget the rats.' An
Roy looks back in slow motion to see that the corridor is swarmin
with the things that they encountered in the sewers. They see hin
begin swarming into the control room and Susan is laughing, laughin
laughing as . . .

. . . Roy looks up at the Black Suit from the bar counter of 'T
Wayside'. He has just placed an attaché case before him and given hi
Mr Draegerman's invitation.

'What's in it for me?' he asks.

'The thing you want most,' says the Black Suit, and Roy knows th
this man is wearing black sunglasses because he has no eyes and therefo
cannot see without them. Roy looks down, but the attache case has becom
something else. It is a battered photograph album; obviously somethir
that has been in someone's family for many, many years.

'Open it,' says the Black Suit, and Roy touches the cover. There
something wrong with the feel of the binding. The texture feels too mu
like skin. He flips it open anyway. And sees himself, aged seven, standin
on the porch outside the house where he used to live with his mother. S
had died the year after. Roy turns the page, and this time it is hims
aged ten years old; the same pose as a school photograph that he keeps
a battered suitcase under his bed. But this is not what fills him with su
revulsion and horror. It is the other figures who crowd this photograp
A man stands at his side, a paternal arm laid across his shoulders. It
Draegerman, in his Boone persona with the face-dragging scar. Arou
them are displayed dozens of corpses, laid out in boxes like coffins;
standing on their ends to display them to the camera. These are t
bodies of those whom Draegerman has kidnapped, tortured, mutila
and murdered in his quest for knowledge. Roy tries to look away fr
that photograph, but now Draegerman's image is smiling and sayi
'That's my boy,' as . . .

. . . Taylor reaches down to touch the face of a two year old Afric
boy. The face is blank and completely untroubled, a bizarre sight in t

474

hellish place. All around, the huts are burning; most of them already ashes. Smoke swirls and chases across this sun baked plain. Taylor kneels, and this child's face is the most beautiful face he has ever seen. The boy reaches out to touch his machine gun. Instinctively, Taylor pulls it away and tries to understand why this child is not screaming or crying for his murdered parents and family. Now, he cannot understand the emotions inside himself. Does he want this child to be shocked or stricken? Will that help him to justify his paid pursuit of the rebels who have raided this village? Will that help to make his cause just? He looks into the boy's eyes again, and suddenly he is looking at Susan. Not Susan as he knew her, but the two year old Susan he has seen in Sara's photograph album. Her face has the same untroubled expression, and then there is a screaming from behind. Taylor turns to see a dozen rebels bursting from the brush. They are screaming and whooping as they come. Taylor sees the glint of machetes and cannot move as . . .

TWENTY-NINE

Susan and Roy twisted through the air into each other's arms, flun[g] together in the last frenzy of the maelstrom. In that instant, they wer[e] both instinctively aware that they were no longer in that dream-plac[e] But there was no time to consider their sudden re-entry into reality a[s] they plummeted like stones.

This time, when their bodies plunged into water, it was not like th[e] bizarre and spiralling embryonic fluid from which they had come. Th[e] shock of the impact, the stunning cold of the water and its eruption i[n] their mouths and noses, was like some shocking kind of rebirth. Susa[n] flailed at the water, clawed to rise – and in the next moment broke th[e] surface, gagging and choking. There was substance beneath her fee[t] and she staggered upright, frantically wiping her hair from her fac[e] coughing out fetid water. Something burst above the surface next [to] her and Susan cried out in shock, but the formless mass became Ro[y] They grabbed for each other in mutual support, and in the next insta[nt] there were three more explosions of water around them. Clinging to ea[ch] other, still dazed, they watched as Taylor and Den emerged from th[e] foaming surface. Last of all, Draegerman staggered to his feet, gropi[ng] through the water to what looked like a concrete walkway. Susan a[nd] Roy looked around them, saw black stone walls running with wate[r] and began to despair. The water was still churning and foaming. The[y] were still in Draegerman's Rock.

Taylor seemed to read their minds.

'No,' he said, pushing through the water to them. 'We're out of ther[e] God knows how. But we're out of there. We're in the sewers benea[th] The Rock.'

As if in answer to his words, the ceiling overhead seemed [to] grumble.

Susan moved towards Den as he finally found his feet. Everyo[ne] continued to look at the ceiling as if the means of their escape could [be] found there. Although the water all around them seemed to be agitate[d] there was no great spinning whirlpool here, no overhead upside-do[wn] pool like that which Taylor and Den had used to enter The Rock, thundering cataract that had transported them here. They seemed to have fallen impossibly out of mid-air into the sewer canal.

'Christ,' said Roy. 'Are you sure? This could be just another place inside. Like that Studio Swamp.'

'No,' said Taylor, pointing to a sewer tunnel to their left. 'See that arch. There's a mark on the concrete walkway, at head height. I put that there on our way in.'

Den looked at Taylor in surprise. He had not seen him make any marks during their progress into the sewers. *Ever the bloody professional*, he thought, realising that his machine pistol had been torn away in the whirlpool but that Taylor had retained his own weapon.

Draegerman was floundering at the concrete platform that ran around the chamber and through the arch at which Taylor had pointed. Taylor beckoned to the others, and they began to wade through the filthy water to the platform. Above, the ceiling groaned again. Now they were aware of a distant thundering roar.

'We're not out of it yet,' said Taylor. 'And we won't be safe until we get out of these sewers. The place is still pulling itself apart, that's why the water down here is agitated.' He had reached Draegerman and gave him a shove from behind which pushed him up on to the platform. Draegerman struggled to his knees as Taylor turned back to help the others. 'Thanks to our friend here, we seem to have ...'

Draegerman suddenly swung a vicious kick that took Taylor on the side of the face. At the same time, he yanked at the strap holding the Ingram over his shoulder. Taylor grunted, arms flying back as he fell into the sewer water. Draegerman had the weapon by the strap, had pulled it from Taylor as he fell, and now feverishly clawed at the strap to prevent the weapon falling into the water after Taylor.

'You BASTARDS! You've ruined EVERYTHING!'

He clawed at the weapon, unfamiliar with it, but even now levelling it at them as ...

... Den seized Susan and pulled her under the water with him. Roy dived in the opposite direction, clawing at his jeans pocket beneath the water as ...

... Draegerman raked the surface of the sewer water with the machine pistol. Screaming hatred, eyes bulging, face a paroxysm of rage, he emptied the weapon into the water. The surface was an exploding mass of foam and twisting spirals, the echoes of the gunfire crashing and roaring through the black arches and dripping sewer tunnels all around. Tears of rage streaked his face as ...

... Roy erupted from the surface, yelling in agony as he used his injured leg for support beneath the water, dragging the pistol from his jeans pocket and thumbing off the safety catch the way Taylor had shown him. He snapped off one shot. He had no chance to aim properly and the bullet screamed ricocheting into the darkness. But the sound of the shot was enough to snap Draegerman out of his screaming rage. He whirled and ran along the platform towards the arch bearing Taylor's mark, aiming the gun back without looking and firing again as he ran. The bullets raked the chamber wall, far away from the spot where Den and Susan emerged floundering from the water in a pool of blood. Den was clutching his side. A bullet had ripped through his rubber wet suit, carving a chunk of flesh from beneath his ribs. Taylor clawed feebly at the edge of the concrete platform where Draegerman had been standing an instant before. Surging back to the edge, he had miraculously avoided any of Draegerman's manic gunfire even though he had provided an easy target. Roy floundered, tried to get a better aim, but his leg would not support him and he fell back into the water.

Draegerman was going to get away.

Taylor struggled to pull himself up on to the platform, slinging his waterproof bag ahead of him, fumbling at the bag as water surged from his back. He was still dazed.

Draegerman reached the sewer arch, almost tottered and fell as he rounded the corner – and then was gone into the darkness.

'*Noooooo!*' yelled Susan in rage.

And then the arch suddenly exploded in a gushing, churning geyser of sewage and filth. A tidal wave of water roared into the chamber, and within the roaring tumult they could see Draegerman whirling and spinning as he was catapulted back into the chamber by the thundering explosion of foam. Den and Susan were swamped once more, disappearing beneath the churning surface. Susan clawed for Den beneath the water. Then something brushed against her. She grabbed for it, and in the next instant had hauled Den back to the surface again.

Even as she rose above the surface, Susan could feel it.

Moaning in horror as she pulled Den with her, she could feel the instinctive dread inside, the same sickening feeling that she had experienced in The Rock. A fog was curling and drifting now on the churning water.

'Susan!' yelled Roy, still in the water but hanging by one hand from the concrete ledge. Taylor was still fumbling with his waterproof bag on the ledge, clearly dazed. But when Susan saw Roy's expression she knew that he could feel it too. 'Susan! For God's sake, get out of the water!'

And then the surface of the sewer water behind her erupted again in an explosion of spray. Susan whirled, dragging Den as he clutched his side and tried to rise.

Something monstrous was rising from the foam.

And the moment the serpentine neck emerged from the flying spray it was instantly and horrifically familiar to both Taylor and Den as the Daemon from the Studio Swamp – the thing that had taken Moss

478

Agonised and dying, with swarming cobweb traces on its hideous 'skin' constantly trying to fill the gaping gunshot wounds, and constantly failing, the thing threw back its swarming, ever-changing head and bellowed in fury. Caught between two worlds, its wounds anchoring it to this physical existence, Draegerman's Daemon was in its death throes. The whirlpool from the Studio Swamp had not been caused by interaction with the negative charge generated by the previous monstrosity's death, but by the multiple agonies of the Swamp Water Woman. Now, just like them, it had been swept from The Rock through the swirling vortex of its own making to the sewers beneath.

And in its death agonies, it saw a way to return.

Susan surged through the sewer water, dragging Den with her.

The Daemon sensed her as prey, knew instinctively that in consuming that which it had been promised, the sundered Pact could be made partially whole. By that act of consumption, its agonised entrapment between two worlds would be over and it could return from the physical and metaphysical death that was imminent here. The thing loomed over her.

And then Roy opened fire with Draegerman's pistol. The first shot tore a writhing chunk of the living cobweb from the thing's head. It screeched and, incredibly, a riot of confused shapes and images swarmed over the chaotic face. Roy fired again and again as Susan thrashed with Den towards him. That thing's face had become the face of the Swamp Water Woman, now Gloria, now the thing that Bobby had called the Speed Demon. Writhing appendages erupted from the thing's side like tentacles, the same tentacles that had taken Jessica. They squirmed up to the horrifying shape-shifting head as if groping at the pain. Roy kept on firing steadily, the sound of the shots echoing in the chamber as the monstrosity thrashed in the water. Now it had the face of Deborah Steele, suddenly elongating and shifting to become the face of the She Wasp, mandibles chittering and squirming, black contact-lens eyes glittering.

Roy's gun was empty. He watched in horror as Den finally found his feet and both he and Susan thrashed to get away.

Bellowing again, the thing plunged back into the water, surging beneath the surface after them.

'Christ, Susan!' yelled Roy. 'Run!'

Taylor fumbled in his waterproof, found what he had been going to use on Draegerman. It seemed to jerk in his hand, something small and metallic clattering on to the platform. Taylor struggled to rise, but fell back again, moaning in alarm when the thing fell from his hand. Frantically, he groped after it.

Susan and Den were only feet from the platform.

Roy held out his hand.

Susan reached to take it.

Their eyes met and held.

And the Daemon erupted from the water again, sweeping Den to one side in a foaming wave. Its contorting, shifting head became the face of Draegerman himself as it drew at last on the prime source of its fictional forms; knowing that its death was here, but could be avoided only in this last moment of taking its Prey. The barbed tentacles reached for Susan as she fell forward. The hideous Draegerman face stretched and contorted as the lips parted to reveal foaming jaws of barbed teeth.

'Only two ways to go,' said Roy grimly, snatching the object that Taylor was desperately trying to reach from the platform.

Ignoring the horrifying pain in his leg, Roy threw himself over the edge, over Susan, and directly into the grasp of the thing that was about to take her.

Scenting fresh Prey, another Chosen One, the Daemon's barbed tentacles coiled around his body, lifting Roy to its contorted Draegerman face. The foaming jaws widened and then . . .

Roy rammed the grenade into the thing's mouth, yelling in rage and defiance. He shoved hard as the thing reared back in the water, taking him with it and causing another explosion of foam. He kept on yelling and jamming his arm into the maw up to the shoulder.

This is for Gloria. This is for Jessica and Bobby. This is for my brothers and sisters, you fucking bastard.

The Daemon's jaws clamped shut.

And in the next instant, the phosphorous grenade exploded in the thing's throat. A great screeching filled the chamber and a blinding white light erased everything from sight. In the next instant, the killing stroke of the grenade blast triggered another detonation: ten times more powerful. It was a thundering explosion of the same concentrated negative energy that was tearing The Rock apart. The sewer water erupted where Roy and the Daemon had been.

Susan was engulfed in water, everything foaming and thrashing and howling. A great thunderous swell of spray threw her forwards and up. The same eruption of sewer water engulfed Taylor and Den.

As the thundering explosion of water swept them out of the chamber and into the tunnel arch through which Draegerman had unsuccessfully tried to escape, the full furious negative energy erupted up through the chamber ceiling, swarming to join the destructive energy that was tearing The Rock apart.

The ceiling caved in.

An avalanche of shattered stone thundered down from above into the chamber, burying the nightmare below.

THIRTY

Draegerman's Rock erupted like a volcano.

Shuddering as if some earthquake was swaying the foundations upon which it was built, the roof of The Rock finally exploded into the night sky as the daemonic forces within it could be contained no longer. The ten top floors were instantly gone, scattering tons of flying debris around the neighbourhood below. The detonation seemed to shift the very ground; lamp standards, pylons and telegraph poles swayed simultaneously; every single window within a two-mile radius was shattered completely. The debris from the explosion effectively finished the riots, sending the crowds scattering from the burning streets as rock shards rained like shrapnel and blocks bigger than automobiles crashed through roofs and shattered store fronts. Two Walkways disintegrated and fell into the pit, their destruction causing great sheets of The Rock's frontage to follow suit, sliding away to expose honeycombs of corridors and empty chambers. Smoke and steam gushed from the gigantic rents in The Rock's side.

And now a raging inferno gusted from the shattered rooftop as the daemonic force consumed everything within, bursting from the shattered windows and the tracery of fissures in the building. Floor collapsed upon floor, the very innards of The Rock falling and erupting in flame to leave only the shell of the gigantic structure, stark and blazing and surely on the verge of collapse. Black rolling storm clouds of soot and ash swirled around the dying giant, covering the city in a poisonous smog. Below, siren joined with siren as if lamenting the death of this monstrous beast. Searchlights swept the burning edifice from a dozen places, an impotent response from the civil support services still struggling to understand what had happened here. Something seemed to groan and shudder within The Rock, a tremor that was felt in the heart, rather than by the senses. It was as if the multiple atrocities committed within these shattered walls were being purged. As if those who had died in torment at Draegerman's hands had found a way to be free from the black stone and the black soul of this monstrous building.

The crowds stood in awe, surveying the damage that the Rock's dying breath had wreaked from above. Hundreds, thousands stood and watched as Draegerman's black cathedral trembled and thundered and disintegrated before their eyes. This hideous place with its roots in Hell could no longer suck the goodness out of the earth and the people around it. And although those who watched the destruction could not understand their instinctive feelings, there was a sense of great relief, a deep-seated understanding that some strange, intangible balance had been restored.

The furnace that roared within the shell was mesmerising.

There were *colours* within that inferno, swirling, chaotic patterns of red and yellow and orange and green. Could it be that those colours were somehow a hideous reflection of the *evil* that was being burned and purged within? Mesmerised by the hellish kaleidoscope, the crowd stood silently and watched as . . .

THIRTY-ONE

Coughing and gagging, Susan and Den helped each other to stagger up the mud bank of the canal.

The water level here had mysteriously dropped, leaving slime-covered banks on either side of a waterway that had, until the last few minutes, been two feet from its concrete banks.

Soaked, covered in mud, they collapsed on to the bank, Den still clutching his side in agony. They would have to get him urgent medical attention, as soon as they had recovered their breath from the last insane exist from the sewers.

Neither of them could remember anything after the tidal wave had erupted around Draegerman's last Daemon. They had both been engulfed in the whirling tumult; had both been swept away from the chamber and had both lost consciousness. Susan had recovered when Den appeared at her side, still in agony but trying to lift her from a shallow pool of sewage. They had no idea where they were, but the water level here was shallow. When Susan stood, and took Den's arm over her shoulder, he had pointed down a short stretch of tunnel behind them. There was a grating at the end of it, fifty feet from where they stood. Light was flickering through it. Staggering and splashing to the grating, Susan had kicked it out – and in seconds they were standing on a mud bank overlooking the semi-drained canal beyond. The flickering light was coming from a burning warehouse on the other side of the canal.

Now they were on the other side, looking back.

And from where they lay, they could see Draegerman's Rock. Perhaps half a mile away, crumbling and disintegrating, burning furiously and spewing ash and soot and clouds of sparks into the night sky. They could feel the tremors of the eruption beneath them, through the bank on which they lay.

Susan turned to Den.

'Roy. Where's Roy?'

Den shook his head.

'He didn't make it.'

Susan began to weep then, tears shuddering from her as the relief

483

and distress and grief burst from within. Finally, when they were so close to getting away, Draegerman's horror had erupted to take Roy. After everything they had been through, the sacrifices that had been made, it seemed so agonisingly unfair. Jessica had sacrificed herself to save Susan – and so had Roy. Could she believe that she was worth that kind of sacrifice? Grief racked her body. Den tried to reach out and touch her, but held back his hand. Despite the agony of his wound, he could not understand that sense of mourning. What had happened back there in The Rock; what had happened between Susan and the man called Roy? Uncertain now, Den watched Susan pour out her distress and could not know that the woman he loved and had risked his life for was mourning a brother, not a lover.

'And Taylor?' asked Susan, emerging from her grief.

Den shook his head.

Susan buried her face in her hands again. Den looked at her for what seemed a long time as she held her hands to her face and silently grieved.

And then they were both shocked from their inner pain as something even more dramatic happened to The Rock. There was another shattering explosion. They looked at the blazing ruin, expecting to see that it had finally blown itself apart. But there was no great difference in the flame-ridden shell which cast gigantic canyons of light and shadow and smoke across the city.

They had felt the blast deep within their own psyches. Because it had not been an ordinary explosion in any physical sense.

It had been a *psychic* explosion: the last dying burst of daemonic power within the shattered shell.

Was there some kind of movement in the flames? Some writhing shadow within the hellish riot of colour?

Susan felt the instinctive revulsion again and shuddered at the sight of the contorting darkness at the heart of the fire. She knew what the thing was, just as surely as if it had spoken its name.

Draegerman's last Daemon, the thing that Den and Taylor had mortally wounded in the fog room. The thing that had struggled to find form and shape and had been unable to claim a victim. Still trapped between two worlds, just as the thing that had killed Roy had been trapped in its agony, the hideous energy released by its impending demise destroying The Rock. Had Roy killed the other thing, cheated of claiming him as victim? Or had it been able to return to Hell, having devoured Roy's soul and essence? And what of Jessica? Had she truly killed her own Daemon, or had it too consumed her body and soul? Susan desperately needed to know. But she could feel that there was only one Daemon trapped in that hellfire, writhing in its last agonies. She pulled herself aloft. Den tried to rise, but could not.

Susan took a step forward.

Suffused with rage, she raised both hands to The Rock, fists clenched.

'Then *burn*, you bastard! Don't go to Hell, because I know you would be *happy* there, you fucker! We beat you. All of us. Gloria and Bobby and Jessica and Roy! So just DIE!'

Den looked at her as if she had gone mad.

In that moment, in her own way, she had. It was a mad *pure* rage.

'*Draegermannnnnnnnnnnn!*'

A hideous bellowing voice rumbled and echoed from the ruin of Draegerman's Rock. It was a voice of the Night, of Darkness, the very sound of it such an anathema to human existence that Susan retched. She turned back to Den. Clearly, he had not heard it. He was still looking at her as if she had lost her mind.

'*Draegerman, you still live!*'

The voice thundered in the sky, but still Den did not hear it. How could he not hear the hideous *monstrousness* of that voice? The very sound of it spoke of its love for pain and cruelty and death. Susan turned back to The Rock.

'It's not true!' she yelled into the night. 'I don't believe you. That bastard can't be alive!'

'*Hear me, Draegerman.*'

And now Susan knew that the voice was not meant for her. Could it be that only Draegerman, and perhaps his offspring, could hear what the voice wanted to say?

'*The pact is sundered. Five for five, as was agreed. But as I die unfulfilled, the pact dies with me. Hear me now . . .*'

Susan felt the terrible psychic detonation again, winced at the shock of it, but there was nothing to see on the face of the burning Rock. But after the shock came a terrible scream – the scream of the last Daemon, on the verge of death, and dying in agony.

'*Hear me!*' the voice thundered from The Rock, as the thing drew on its last reserves of daemonic energy. '*Life eternal you are granted, but not the protection from wound or pestilence. Damned in life, and damned thereafter.*' With this final curse, the voice erupted into a terrible shriek. But this time the shriek began to fade; as if the thing was being dragged away, falling into a pit of nothingness.

The flames raging in the shell of The Rock had lost their kaleidoscopic qualities. The colours had vanished; now the fire that consumed the shell was an earthly fire. At the midway section, the building began to crumble; a gigantic landslide of smoking, burning rubble that was consumed in a great gushing black cloud as it fell. The weight of the collapse bore down on the foundations of the building.

Finally, The Rock fell with the roar of a thousand avalanches into the pit. An enormous gushing black cloud erupted from below to hide the last collapse from sight.

Susan stood looking at the shuddering volcanic cloud.

She knew, deep down inside, what the Daemon's last words had don to Drageman. The horror if it overcame her rage that he should st be out there somewhere alive, that he should somehow have survive the last confrontation in the sewers beneath the Rock, after everythin he had done. Could there be anything more terrible than losing life?

Yes, there could be – and Susan knew that the Daemon had delivere that hellish curse upon him in its last moments.

Draegerman had been granted immortality, the thing he had crave above all else. But he had achieved it at a terrible price. Because Susa knew now with utter conviction that although his body would not fa prey to the normal ageing processes, he could still be damaged b accidents, or succumb to physical illness. Draegerman's Rock, his powe and his wealth had all been destroyed. There was no possibility that h could rebuild it all again. What life could there be for him now? Force to wander forever, afraid of crossing the street, afraid of contagiou disease, afraid of every shadow on every street corner. Doomed t become a derelict, doomed to an eternity of anxiety, solitude and fea – and the knowledge that if he did die, others would be waiting fo him on the Other Side to exact vengeance.

Draegerman had been consigned to a living Hell.

Nothing to live for, if he lived forever.

And no rest in death.

There was a hand on Susan's shoulder now, and she turned.

'Den,' began Susan. 'I want you to know that . . .'

But it was not Den, it was Taylor.

Dishevelled, his rubber suit ripped in a dozen places. His face badl scalded on one side. But it was Taylor nonetheless. He had made it ou of The Rock.

Susan threw her arms around his neck, and was not ashamed whe the weeping began again. She pulled back to look at his face, holdin it with both hands.

'You came back for me,' she said again, simply.

'So did Den,' said Taylor.

Den was still lying on the bank, clearly in great pain, but he wa smiling. And suddenly, Susan felt a great sense of triumph. Not fo herself, but for the others; the brothers and sisters she had lost bac in that hellish place, but who had died denying Draegerman and hi Daemons to the last.

'We've got to get Den seen to,' said Taylor, holding her tight. 'An quickly.'

'Wait until the boys find out that their father is a hero,' sai Susan.

'Father?' grinned Den. 'Don't we have to be married for that . . . ?'

'Just a matter of paperwork.'

'Susan . . .' Taylor's expression had changed. 'I have to tell you this now. It can't wait until later.'

Susan nodded, staring into his eyes.

He seemed to be struggling with what he was going to say.

'I'm going to die.'

Susan nodded again, wiping tears from her eyes and smiling.

'We've all got to die some time.'

'No, I mean I'm going to die soon.'

Susan said nothing, just continued to look deep into his eyes.

'Come home,' she said at last. And the resonance in those last words lifted a burden from Taylor so vast that he had underestimated its weight upon his heart and his soul. He pulled her close again.

Then, together, they moved to Den and helped him to stand.

Soon, they had vanished into the night.

THIRTY-TWO

The crowds who stood and watched The Rock blow itself to piece
and who had been so mesmerised by the hypnotic shifting of colou
within the ruins of the huge structure, finally shrank back on th
streets when the detonating cloud shrouded its last collapse into th
surrounding pit.

On the street down which a lost soul called Fisher had driven h
bulldozer to the Walkway gate, the crowd began to cheer. In the
minds, the driver had been the one they called Taylor, the mythic stree
god. And it had been that last sacrifice, that act of bringing down th
Walkway, which had resulted in the downfall of Draegerman's Roc
They could instinctively feel something like a rush of good clean a
on this street as the thing they hated so much vanished from sight.

Two police cars screeched to a stop on the street, sirens wailing. Th
uniformed officers inside climbed out and began to disperse the watchin
crowd. There was no resistance, no violent threats. Slowly and quietl
the watching crowd began to drift away. Even the officers themselve
now in what had once been no-man's land in the neighbourhood aroun
The Rock, could sense the change.

When the crowd had gone, only one man stood in the middle of th
street, still looking at the gigantic cloud of billowing dust and smok
that had once been Draegerman's Rock.

Wet through and round-shouldered, the man seemed rooted t
the spot.

One of the police officers walked over to touch his elbow.

The man looked back at him vacantly, hardly heard the officer
request to move on.

And then, alone forever, the figure turned and walked slowly int
the night.